Paul-Loup Sulitzer is a French financier who is as intriguing as the characters he creates. By the time he was seventeen, he was a self-made millionaire and the youngest business director in France. Today he is an expert in high finance and using his intimate knowledge of the world of money and power he is able to reveal to his readers much that is usually inaccessible behind the sealed doors of the corporate establishment.

By the same author

Money
Cash (Prix du Livre, summer 1981)
Fortune
Popoff: The Red Banker
The Green King
Hannah

PAUL-LOUP SULITZER

The Empress

Translated from the French by Christine Donougher

PARRAGON

First published in Great Britain by
Grafton Books 1989
Published in paperback by Grafton Books 1990

This edition published 1993 by
Diamond Books
77-85 Fulham Palace Road
Hammersmith, London, W6 8JB

Printed and bound in Great Britain by
BPCC Hazells Ltd
Member of BPCC Ltd

To Alejandra

To my two daughters
Olivia and Joy

'We are such stuff as dreams are made on . . .'

The Tempest

The Empress

CHAPTER 1

One and a Half Pink Sheep

Hannah's memory of those first months they spent together in America would always remain vivid. How she had dreamed of this trip, of all the new chances and changes that their emigration would bring. Filled with excitement, too, at the prospect of spending her life with Taddeuz, she tried desperately to predict every possible turn of events, rehearsing countless dos and don'ts. Of course she had had the occasional sneaking suspicion that you could not control or programme wedded bliss the way you could business, but the suspicion was quickly quashed: *You're intelligent, damned intelligent, that's an indisputable fact; and devilishly calculating – you can't help it! Are you to go against your nature? Put on an act? That would be sheer hypocrisy. You wouldn't be able to keep it up even for three months (if that!) and in any case you would never be able to fool Taddeuz: he knows you too well . . .*

That was extraordinary, Hannah, when you realized that he could read your mind almost as well as you could read his. And, having got the full measure of what a nasty piece of work you were, that he should still love you . . .

And make love to you like a dream – it makes you shiver just to think of it . . .

She would spend twelve hours a day in New York, opening her huge grey eyes impossibly wide in her eagerness to see everything, learn everything. There was the dizzying sense of elation that every minute spent with Taddeuz gave her; and the thrill of knowing that they were in America, and that it should be just the kind of

America she had hoped for: a New World fresher than all the spring-time meadows of Poland.

They were married in Vienna, and it was in Europe, on her home ground, that they had spent the first weeks of their wedded life. The marriage itself, in other words, had not greatly altered her life. It had come at the end of such a long period of waiting, of so many hopes and clever machinations on her part that it was in danger of losing its emotional power. No doubt the same was true of all triumphs so long anticipated. But while she was in Europe she had certainly had the feeling that her life was drawing to a close, and she was virtually an old woman . . .

Old? Oh, Hannah, you crazy fool, you're not yet twenty-five! Taddeuz and you are going to have seventy-five years together. Of course, it won't all be plain sailing, but to any problem there are always plenty of solutions; and if there are no solutions, there can't be any problem.

Simply crossing the Atlantic had changed her. And this was no transitory thrill. She knew this country was right for her; that she and America were ideally suited. She could see that she was completely in tune with its teeming excitement and youthful energy. For she too was young, and now felt young in every respect. And never in all her long life would she ever lose this love for America, never would she cease to feel as enchanted with the city as she first did in February 1900.

She would spend twelve hours a day in New York.

Usually, Taddeuz would accompany her (they were still at the Waldorf-Astoria: despite her initial, and in fact rather half-hearted, attempts to find an apartment, she hadn't come across one to her liking). Occasionally he would say that he wanted to write, and would entrust Zeke Singer with the task of escorting Hannah in her explorations. Zeke was the brother-in-law of the Becky she had known in Warsaw and he was with her on the day that she had a rather strange experience.

She had taken it into her head to go to Ellis Island. Zeke managed to get the necessary authorization and soon she was inside the American immigration department buildings, on the small island in New York harbour where the new arrivals were penned in – penned being the operative word. All these barriers and grilles and series of queueing areas for sorting out the immigrants were reminiscent of a cattle corral. She felt as if she were a visitor at the zoo, all dressed up as she was in her *grande-dame* finery, with her elbow-length kid gloves, her large Paquin hat and veil, her Worth dress and cloak.

On the first day she spent eight hours working with one of the Ellis Island doctors responsible for checking the immigrants' state of health, to whom she'd been given an introduction. Initially the doctor had not been very pleased to learn that he was going to have to put up with a lady from Park Avenue getting under his feet – he was of Scottish origin, with sandy-coloured hair and blue eyes, not bad-looking at all (*there was a time when perhaps you wouldn't have given up a Sunday for him, but maybe a weekday . . .*) – but Hannah raised her veil and gunned him down with the full force of her grey eyes, giving him her most bewitching smile. It was quite possible, she told him, that were it not for the sudden whim that sent her to Australia nearly seven years ago, she could well have been one of these people herself . . . 'No more or less appealing than they are. And I may as well tell you that, apart from English, I also speak French, German, Russian, Polish, Yiddish, Hebrew, Italian and some Spanish. So I'm quite well qualified to act as your interpreter – it looks to me as though you badly need one.'

That first day on the island she saw the whole of Europe pass before her eyes, from the Urals to the Irish bogs, from Sweden to Sicily. It was fascinating. They were arriving in their millions, and it made her aware of how far she had come; of the course she herself had navigated. For the first time ever, she looked back and took stock of the distance she had travelled, as this immense flux of humanity awakened vivid memories. What is more (and it was at this point that it became a strange experience), from these thousands of faces she began to pick out one, then two, then more and more . . . it was very unsettling. Because the little girl who suddenly appeared in the doctor's consulting room was the spitting image of Hannah herself at that age. She had the same enormous grey eyes that seemed to swallow up her face, the thin, almost sexless body, shrouded in the same sorry black dress; but most of all, Hannah recognized the same determined silence: a loneliness that the child had already admitted to herself and accepted. Hannah was in turmoil. While she translated the answers the little girl's parents gave to the doctor, she saw herself at the same age.

She was walking in the bright sunshine of that summer of 1882, with her hand in Taddeuz's – she was ten, he was three years older. Once again, she was filled with wonder and disbelief that he should have agreed to be her friend and include her in his games. And here were the Horsemen, harbingers of the pogrom, looming up on the limitless horizon of the Russo-Polish plains. Now came the death of Yasha, her brother, burned alive, then the death of her father. And now came the black years – absolutely unbearable. Years of waiting to grow up, to start living, to escape from the *shtetl*, the village where she was born and would certainly have died of suffocation but for the visits of Mendel Visoker, the Drayman from Mazury with a chest like a bison's and the soul of an eternal wanderer, who, when she finally turned fifteen, carried her away from that slow death, took her to Warsaw, looked after her, even killed a man on her account the day when . . .

There he was.

Oh, of course it wasn't the real Mendel. This one was younger, slimmer, and in any case he was either Hungarian, or Croatian, or Lithuanian – or something. But he had Visoker's tremendously broad shoulders, the same arrogant way of holding his head very upright, the feline litheness coupled with strength. Above all, he gave the irresistible impression of being one of those men that nothing will constrain for very long: neither the love of any woman, nor any kind of frontier; a man for whom the whole world is only just big enough.

First herself, and now Mendel . . . And in the days that followed, other doppelgängers emerged from this sea of human life – boats crowded with immigrants never ceased to arrive from Europe, and Ellis Island was always packed. One appeared in the midst of a contingent of Germans from Prussia: slow, grave people against whom he stood out, with his shifty eyes and cock-sure loutishness. He was with two women, two young girls with a bovine look in their eye: he was quite obviously a pimp, Hannah could have sworn to it. And an old hatred that she thought had died came back to her and overwhelmed her. In her mind's eye, she could see Pelte the Wolf chasing her through the streets of Warsaw, while she raced back and forth between the shops she had opened to sell her creams and the bedroom in Praga where Taddeuz was waiting for her – the running around was nearly enough to kill her. She was seventeen then, and pregnant (Taddeuz was unaware of this and still knew nothing about it). One night Pelte the Wolf had attacked her, tried to rape her and, incensed by the fight she put up, had kicked her, leaving her with broken bones . . .

. . . so that she lost the child she was expecting . . .

And Mendel, the Polish Drayman, had killed Pelte the Wolf and was sent off to Siberia.

'Zeke, I don't want that man to be allowed into

America. I'll pay whatever it costs, if I have to. But I want him thrown out. Please, Zeke, I beg you . . .'

Other doubles turned up. 'I'm hallucinating,' she thought, clinging to Taddeuz's arm – intrigued by her fascination with Ellis Island, he had eventually come with her. An Irish clan from Galway could easily have been the MacKenna family, who gave her such a warm welcome when she first arrived in Australia. She was not even eighteen at the time and had just one pound sterling to her name . . .

Except that Lizzie MacKenna, the youngest of the family, was nearly six foot tall, and she was determined to marry Maryan Kaden – though Maryan knew nothing of her plans, Taddeuz reminded Hannah.

'Talking of Maryan, I saw a man the day before yesterday – apart from his horrible teeth, he looked just like Maryan.'

She had also identified a Pinchos Klotz, a Rebecca Anielowicz, a Leib Deitch, and fifteen or twenty others that she had known in Warsaw when she was working in the grocery store belonging to Pinchos and Dobbe Klotz – the first stage after her escape from the *shtetl*. With a little bit of imagination, that very large woman trussed up in all those skirts – a veritable colossus who, when faced with the Ellis Island doctor, refused with dark fury to undress and submit to an examination – could indeed be Dobbe Klotz, the Hayrick.

You're still a mite afraid of her, Hannah, you might as well admit it . . .

But it was not only Poland that was represented. People who reminded her of other periods of her life were in evidence. She realized that there had been five quite distinct periods – it was as though she had already lived five different lives: first of all, the *shtetl*; then Warsaw; then Australia and New Zealand, where she began to grow affluent producing her own beauty creams; then

Europe, where this same affluence – *still based on the wretched creams* – had really developed into quite a sizeable fortune . . .

. . . and finally America, where she had no doubt she was going to live a new life.

'Oh Taddeuz, it's almost painful. It's as though my past was catching up with me!'

'And what's wrong with that?'

'Nothing. It's just that I'd forgotten that I'd done so many things and met so many people and travelled so many miles. I've already had a darned full life, when you come to think about it!'

He smiled broadly and she tossed her head: all right, she shouldn't have said 'darned'. She knew she talked like a New South Wales carter. She promised to mind her language.

That evening they were dinner guests of Junior – John Davison Rockefeller himself – destined to be the richest man in the world. They owed their invitation to Senator John D. Markham. Taddeuz had worked as his personal secretary for three years; it was also thanks to Senator Markham that Taddeuz had obtained his American nationality. Junior did not greatly impress Hannah. He was tormented with shyness and the fear of failure. At Number 26, Broadway, headquarters of the family business, he started out filling inkwells, and the first time he tried to spread his wings in finance he took an awful pasting, losing millions of dollars, so it was said. He was about twenty-six, of fairly small build, melancholic and withdrawn. He had recently begun conducting Bible study classes at the Baptist church on Fifth Avenue.

With two dozen guests attending this dinner, a private conversation with Junior seemed unlikely, and yet, without doing anything whatsoever to engineer it, Hannah found herself sitting next to him. Suddenly, even more extraordinarily, she was telling him how she computed her wealth: she drew sheep – very unexceptional sheep, admittedly: 'I draw with as much finesse as a stone breaker' – different coloured sheep, depending on whether they were supposed to represent her beauty parlours, her factory, her laboratory or her schools for beauticians and saleswomen. Sheep with red dots to represent the distribution network linking the factory to the chain of beauty parlours and shops; sheep with black-and-red squares for her bank accounts.

'And I give them a tail when the business they represent starts to generate profits – in other words, when I no longer need to invest money in it. They're entitled to one leg when these annual profits exceed one thousand dollars.'

'For every thousand dollars' profit net, they get another leg, is that it?'

'Exactly. Two or three of my sheep are aberrations of nature. There's one that already has seventeen legs, the poor creature . . .'

Hannah hesitated, but in the end kept to herself the fact that since her arrival in America she had created a new type of sheep. Her latest-born were pink, and each one, equipped as normal with four legs and one tail, represented one million dollars. It wasn't a big flock: for the time being, it didn't include more than one and a half sheep.

It was this half-sheep that bothered her and, compared with Rockefeller's vast fortune, made her feel at a disadvantage.

'Sheep!' said Junior.

He seemed more than interested: he was fascinated. Better still, he in turn revealed that he too had always liked to keep secret accounts. Eight years ago, when he had spent nearly a year in Forest Hill on one of his father's estates, working as a lumberjack and collecting maple syrup to be made into sugar, he had kept a daily record, in a little notebook that he always carried with him, of the quantities of syrup obtained and the money that it earned him. Similarly, when he was younger, he had kept an extremely detailed account of the minutes devoted to prayer each day by every member of his family.

'But you're going to think me ridiculous, Mrs Newman . . .'

'I'm fascinated,' said Hannah, widening her eyes, and thinking: *Heaven's alive, Hannah, you're actually talking to a Rockefeller; the family heir, no less!* Junior was telling her that when he travelled round Europe on a bicycle three years ago, not a day went past without him not only noting down his expenses, but also recording the number of miles he had covered and the state of his bicycle afterwards. Junior found the idea of the sheep very ingenious. He smiled, something he had only rarely done until that point, and it was a kindly smile, his face suddenly lighting up very pleasantly, the way that shy people's faces can do.

'I hope to have the pleasure of seeing you and Mr Newman again.'

'I hope so too, Mr Rockefeller.'

She spent twelve hours a day in New York, getting up each day at the crack of dawn. Feeling that she needed time to get used to her new surroundings, she had made an agreement with Maryan Kaden not to discuss business for a whole month. This meant cutting herself off from news of the lightning progress of her expansion in Europe – from her bases in London and Paris, she had extended her antennae and opened up beauty parlours and shops in every European capital – but the decision to do so was taken even before she set sail for New York. She had simply wanted to give herself a break. After all, she was a newly wedded wife, and living with Taddeuz was an adventure every moment of which she wanted to savour.

But now that she was treading on American soil, breathing the American air . . .

'Maryan, it's just not possible. We can't simply open up in New York the way we opened up in Rome and Vienna – they were just branches.'

It wasn't simply a question of distance, nor was it the fact that an ocean lay between them and the factory in France. How could he fail to understand that they were now in a different world, that they both had to change their approach and methods, adapt to new circumstances?

Maryan did not bat an eyelid. He was fair-haired, with a smooth face that the coldest days of winter turned a little red, and clear, almost pale eyes that gave absolutely nothing away. He simply gazed at her very calmly. He must be about twenty-three now, Hannah thought. He had been thirteen when they had first met in Warsaw, and already working like a pack-animal: sixteen to eighteen hours a day, in order to provide for his fatherless family; he had an incredible number of brothers and sisters, all of them much younger than himself. It was Hannah who had made him leave Poland. She had just returned from Australia, where she had spent three years. He had come running at her first summons, turning up to meet her at a rendezvous she had given him when there were 12,500 miles between them. After that summons, nothing could surprise him: that she should reappear after such a long time, that she should have become rich, that she was obviously counting on him to become her lieutenant and right hand. She had since asked Maryan to put himself entirely at her service (in her business affairs but also to some extent in her private life, since she had even asked him to find Taddeuz for her); to learn French, English and Spanish (he already knew Polish, German and Russian); to master finance and everything relating to banks and commerce; to learn how to determine the future site of a beauty parlour or shop, how to set them up and decorate them, how to employ people to staff them; how to dress and use a fish fork.

He learned everything, remaining unruffled whatever the task she set him.

Damn it all, Hannah, you even near enough forced him – being completely Machiavellian about it – to bed his first woman. But for you he would still be a spotty-faced greenhorn!

She looked him up and down: he was over five foot eleven inches tall.

Apart from the fact that he had his eyes open, he could have been fast asleep.

'Maryan?'

He raised his eyebrows, a sign that he was giving her his undivided attention. But to read the look in his eye – not a chance! It was as calm and devoid of expression as a mountain lake.

'Lizzie, we have no secrets from each other, we can speak freely, as one woman to another. So, tell me, what's Maryan like in bed? Does he ever – how can I put it? – become impassioned, at the point of orgasm? What do you mean, it's none of my business? Damn it, I'm interested to know, does he become impassioned, yes or no? Sometimes? And what does that mean, "sometimes"? You mean there are times when . . . No? So then it's every time, is it? And he really becomes impassioned? Amazing! You couldn't give me a few more details? No? OK, OK, forget I asked . . .'

'Maryan,' she continued, 'you don't have to answer this, but would you by any chance have earned yourself a little money, apart from what I pay you?'

And he started shifting his weight from one foot to the other, surprisingly bashful.

'A little,' he asked.

'On the London Stock Exchange?'

'Not just that.'

'You've been in New York six months now. Have you been speculating on Wall Street?'

'A little.'

'How much is a little? That is, if I'm not being indiscreet . . .'

'I've made about one hundred thousand dollars,' he said eventually, in the tone of voice that might have been appropriate had he been confessing to having strangled three old ladies.

One hundred thousand dollars, plus what he already had. In other words, if Hannah could add up (and she could), his personal fortune must amount to at least two hundred thousand dollars. *No doubt it's more than that* . . .

'Or am I mistaken, Maryan?'

'You're not far out.'

'I hear you've brought your family here.'

'Not all of them,' he said. 'There are six or seven still in Europe.'

'Can I do anything for them?'

'Thank you, Hannah. No.'

She smiled at him. *I love him like a brother*, she thought.

'Well,' she said, 'so you've found somewhere for my New York beauty parlour?'

'On Park Avenue. It's all in the file.'

'And the shop?'

'On Fifth Avenue. Next to the jewellers you told me about – Tiffany's.'

'Are you likely to find anywhere better?'

'I don't think so.' He shook his head. 'It is possible, Hannah . . .'

'What's possible?'

'That we might be able to wait a year, or even longer. The two places are occupied at the moment. We needn't arrange for them to become vacant until the day you decide to move in.'

He had given it a lot of thought and had reached the same conclusions as she had: it would be a pity – even risky – to open beauty parlours and shops on American soil as if this country were simply an extension of Europe. He didn't really know how to explain his feeling: 'It would be better to wait, to study the matter in depth and, only then, when we've weighed up all the facts about this new country, should we start from scratch and create . . .'

'You're explaining yourself very well,' said Hannah, laughing.

Maryan was no longer hopping from one foot to the other. His voice was calm, perhaps a little muted, but that was the only obvious sign of the emotion he must be feeling.

My God, how he's changed! He's a new man. Perhaps because of you and all that apprenticeship you put him through. Or else because he was always like this, with a tremendous determination to succeed. Thank goodness you spotted that ten years ago, though you didn't appreciate the full measure of it. The fact of the matter is that, beneath that calm exterior, he realized exactly what you wanted, Hannah. It's what he wants, too: to do something different in America, something bigger than anything we've achieved so far.

And one of two things was possible, as Mendel would say – which was why she asked him: 'Are you thinking of leaving me, Maryan?'

'Leaving you?'

'Not working with me any more. You're quite capable

of becoming rich on your own. And not just becoming rich: of being successful – as successful as Rockefeller. In fact, I'm convinced you will be.'

If he had replied at once, immediately protesting his loyalty, she might have had some lingering doubts. But he took his time, considered a while, a dreamy mist lightly veiling his blue eyes, with that expression of seriousness peculiar to him. Finally he said: 'You'll always be able to count on me, Hannah. As long as I live.'

He would keep his word – even after his meteoric rise – throughout the next fifty years.

Until his death, in fact.

She wanted to put the past behind her, but, inexplicably, she could not rid herself of the memory of all those faces on Ellis Island. And it was just not like her to be so obsessive; she was not much given to reminiscing. So, with typical decisiveness, she summoned private detectives to the Waldorf-Astoria. The men from Pinkerton's Agency were undoubtedly more accustomed to tackling strikers and train robbers, and were somewhat surprised by what Hannah required of them, but their efficiency was beyond reproach: it took them only three days to locate the little girl with the big grey eyes in whom Hannah had recognized herself.

Hannah went to the address they gave her, which was in a very squalid street in the Bronx area of New York. Taddeuz went with her. He insisted on accompanying her, his curiosity aroused once more – he could not see all that much resemblance between the people in Hannah's life, those he had known, and those passing through Ellis Island.

They found the little girl and her family, living in a kind of shed. There were mattresses laid out on the ground, it was bitterly cold, and the eight or ten people present were huddled round an earthenware pot hanging from an iron tripod over a fire. It looked like an encampment in the middle of the Polish plains, although they were surrounded by a teeming population of one and a half million New Yorkers. These people were Russian and came from a far-flung village south of Minsk. While Taddeuz told the father of the family some cock-and-bull story about him and his wife having had a little girl, with eyes just like his daughter, who had died, Hannah went up to the child and spoke to her. A few minutes were enough: those huge grey eyes were deceptive. What Hannah had interpreted as a cold contempt for humanity in general was simply shyness and a lack of intelligence.

She gave the family one hundred dollars to provide for their immediate needs, and at the time thought that would free her of her obsession.

But she returned the next day, and again the day after. Naturally, none of her protégés spoke a word of English, and they were all looking for work. She found them jobs, again thanks to Zeke Singer, and got the youngest children enrolled in schools, setting aside fifty dollars a week for them, nearly twice the average industrial wage.

As for the little girl with grey eyes, Hannah would continue to follow her progress for years to come and, when she got married in 1911, would give the young couple the house and the little hotel they had dreamed of – still disappointed by the girl's lack of ambition, but having long since become resigned to it.

Thirty years later, at a party in Beverly Hills, Hollywood, Hannah would be approached by a very famous actress with wonderful eyes: a worldwide celebrity. 'You are doubtless unaware of it, Mrs Newman, but all my family have a boundless admiration for you. My mother would spend whole evenings telling me about you. She was the person to whom you once gave a hotel, and your friendship.'

* * *

During the following weeks, Hannah and Taddeuz took the various doubles under their wing. Most of them were still in New York; only a few had dared venture further afield, or had any reason to do so. By a coincidence that delighted Hannah without really surprising her, the man that had reminded her of Mendel Visoker was actually the most adventurous of all. The Pinkerton agents took more than two months to find him. Not that he was hiding, but he was always on the move. When they located him, he had just arrived in Kansas City with the intention of heading out further west, to California. He was Hungarian, and taller than Taddeuz, who was himself nearly six feet two inches tall. He boomed with laughter when Hannah, on the grounds that he looked like a very dear brother of hers, offered him money – or whatever help he wanted. He would accept a dollar, just one, a silver dollar – to bring him luck – but nothing else. Hannah gave him the coin and told him about Mendel, whom he might run into on his travels. As two men filled with wanderlust, he and the Drayman were certain to hit it off. The Hungarian asked if there was a message.

'No!' said Hannah, convinced that the two men were bound to meet. She believed in these things – a little more than she believed in God.

The man who reminded her of Pinchos Klotz had already found work for himself, in a brickyard in Springfield, Connecticut. This immigrant had the same slight body, the tremendous reticence, and the gentle eyes of the late Pinchos the Silent, who died in Warsaw trying to avenge her against Pelte the Wolf. He was a Latvian, from near Riga, and about thirty years younger than the real Pinchos. It took Taddeuz half a day to drag a few words out of him – he had gazed for ages at the money being offered to him, as though the notes might have been coated with deadly poison. Eventually he revealed that he had been employed in a library, that he loved books and that his French was very good. He had probably run into problems with the Tsar's secret police. Taddeuz was convinced this was so, and it was his idea that they should set up Kaunas (that was the fellow's name) as a bookseller. Hannah wasn't sure. After all, it meant buying a business and providing him with a stock of books. And where would they find the shop?

'I have one in mind,' explained Taddeuz, who knew all the bookshops in Manhattan intimately. 'A basement in East 91st.'

'Where you'll be able to take refuge on days when I'm even more insufferable than usual, is that it?'

'The only place where I would ever be able to escape being persecuted by you is Sing Sing Prison. And even then you'd probably manage to get in, disguised as registered post.'

But it was true that he would like to see Kaunas run a bookshop; the man had some very interesting ideas about literature.

Hannah agreed, and thought that was the end of it. Not at all. The next thing was to persuade the Latvian. He could not understand what they wanted of him, nor the reasons for such generosity. He was mistrustful. And then one evening, two weeks later, he suddenly turned up in the lobby of the Waldorf-Astoria, just as Hannah and Taddeuz were leaving. Apparently he had been waiting for hours. He was holding in both hands a packet that had been religiously wrapped in Russian leather. He opened it and offered it to Taddeuz. Inside was an old fob-watch: it was gold, but badly dented.

'For you, for you,' said Kaunas, and not a word more, giving them to understand that he would only become a bookseller if Taddeuz accepted in exchange his dear old father's watch, a family heirloom.

Taddeuz took it and spent the next two days marvelling at such moral rectitude.

Not Hannah.

First of all because (just the thought of it had her and Taddeuz in fits of laughter) she was the one who had paid the six hundred and fifty dollars to buy the business, and her husband was the one to whom the Latvian had given the present!

And also because, with her usual mistrust, she had examined the watch a little more closely, had it valued at Tiffany's and discovered that it was made of copper and was not worth much more than $1.50. Furthermore, since it was manufactured in America, it would have been a sheer miracle if it had ever belonged to an old Latvian gentleman from the distant shores of the Baltic Sea.

'I thought so. And he's not even Jewish! Behind that air of innocence, that Kaunas is a bit of a villain, just like Pinchos. Except that in Pinchos's case, it was over cheeses that you couldn't trust him; everything else, yes.'

The Latvian moved into Ninety-First Street. Right up to the last, he would give Taddeuz and Hannah a three per cent discount on any books they bought from him. He was to die in 1943, never having uttered more than one hundred words a year.

She did likewise for all those doubles that, thanks to the Pinkerton men, they tracked down, dispensing varying amounts of money among them; coming to their aid or settling with them, in some bizarre way, accounts of her own from the past that she had left in abeyance.

She would spend twelve hours a day in New York, not including evenings and nights. Spring came to the city, bringing a mellowness that was very surprising – surprising to Hannah, that is, who had always thought of New York as cold and detached, even brutal (this brutality did not frighten her; on the contrary, she was convinced she could carve a niche out for herself here).

She would remember this spring as the happiest time of her life.

In the evening, whenever they went out to dinner, they would travel in a Victoria with a leather hood, drawn by two horses, which was more open than a town coupé. During the day, however, when it was not raining, they both learned to drive a horseless carriage. She had a Panhard and Levassor, with a Daimler engine sent over from France that weighed one-and-a-half tons and was capable of reaching a speed of twenty-eight miles an hour. And her friend Louis Renault promised to send her the car that he was going to enter for the Paris–Bordeaux race, a monstrous rocket that could do up to sixty-two miles an hour, apparently.

Taddeuz was better at driving than she was. And yet she spent hours trying to understand how the engine worked, what every part was supposed to do, the comparative advantages of different types of engine – petrol, steam and electric. It was no good. Between Taddeuz and these wretched mechanical things there was a very subtle, totally exasperating complicity. He only had to sit behind the wheel and the damned car would start, purring like a cat. It was enough to make you sick. Meanwhile, she had had her fourteenth breakdown.

'It's nothing to laugh about, you miserable Polack! You couldn't tell the difference between a car engine and a sewing machine.'

'Why bother? It works.'

That day, they had driven out to the country with two big picnic hampers, prepared for them by the chef at the Waldorf-Astoria, on the back seat of the car. There were just over one thousand five hundred horseless carriages in New York in that year of 1900, and three or four backfiring vehicles were at one point trailing behind the Panhard and Levassor, the speed of which made the others look ridiculous. It was a lovely April day. Their excursion was to take them to Tarrytown where, according to Junior, the Rockefellers had an absolutely magnificent estate on the banks of the Hudson and the little Pocantico River. Taddeuz was driving (they had agreed that she would drive back). He refused to put on a greatcoat or leather coat, and would not even wear goggles. He claimed to have no need of all this protective gear. Even when driving very fast. Even at twenty-eight miles an hour.

They stopped to picnic.

Taddeuz looked around and said: 'So this is where we're going to live . . .'

'In America?'

'As far as America goes, that's already settled. You decided that the day after we arrived, if not before. No, I was referring to Tarrytown. You want to buy a house here, next door to the Rockefellers, don't you? Or have one built.'

She stared at him, disconcerted. She had not anticipated this. There was no doubt about it, he was the only person in the world who could take her by surprise.

He just happens to be your husband, the only man you've ever loved or will ever love . . . but perhaps that's exactly the reason why . . .

'I agree, Hannah.'

'Agree to what?'

You know very well what, she thought.

'You want a house, don't you?'

'I swear it hadn't occurred to me.'

He smiled beneath his blond moustache.

'But now it has?'

'Now, it has. It's natural that I should want us to have our own house. On reflection, perhaps it had occurred to me.'

'I agree,' he said.

He lowered his head and then raised it, looking towards the river. 'I have another question.'

'Ask any question you like.'

And this time you know what he's going to ask you. And you know the answer, too.

'Don't make fun of me. Of course we are,' she said, before Taddeuz had time to say anything.

'When and how many?'

And still he spoke with the same courteous nonchalance, as though asking the price of a newspaper! *And the worst of it, Hannah, is that you have all the answers to his questions. And he knows it. He knows that you have everything planned.*

'Three children,' she said.

'Boys or girls?'

'Some of each.'

For heaven's sake! she thought. *What a mad conversation this is!*

'Two girls and a boy, or the other way round?'

'I'd rather have two boys and a girl.'

He nodded and Hannah was torn between the urge to giggle nervously – very unusual in her – and a desire to cry.

She went on: 'But if you'd prefer two daughters, or more children . . .'

'I shall content myself with just one daughter and two sons. And when are they to be born, these children of ours? Assuming, of course, that we're both to produce them?'

'You're being nasty.'

'You're right, I'm sorry. I withdraw that remark.'

She sat on the running board of the Panhard and Levassor: 'Taddeuz, I know I'm crazy. People can't say in advance whether or not they will have children, whether the children will be boys or girls, or when they'll be born . . .'

He finally stopped gazing at the river and came towards her. 'But you're Hannah; you're no ordinary woman.'

'In matters like these, I'm damned ordinary. Take me in your arms, please, I'm ashamed of myself.'

He put both hands round her waist (whenever he did this, and he did it often, she noted with pride that the tips of Taddeuz's long fingers met, completely encircling her) and raised her to her feet.

Which didn't really help matters: she measured four foot ten inches and he stood exactly fifteen inches taller than her.

'Take me in your arms.'

He lifted her up, but instead of holding her close he sat her on the still-warm bonnet of the car.

'You haven't answered my question, Hannah. When am I to be a father?'

'I can't . . .'

'*Hannah.*'

'I thought,' she said in a rather small voice, 'that it would be better to wait a while. Until you and I have become real Americans.'

'Until you've got your business going.'

'Yes, why not? And also until you've written your first book, and it's been extraordinarily successful, and you've become the greatest writer on this side of the Atlantic . . .'

A pause.

'On both sides, in fact. Why settle for one?'

'Five years? Ten years?'

'Two.'

And a silence fell. She felt a fool and did her best to make her eyes moisten, but to no avail – *you're really not the type to snivel, and even less to have the vapours. You should have been born a hundred years from now.* Two moustachioed oarsmen rowed past on the Hudson, and a couple in their Sunday best also went by. And they all stared curiously at this tiny little woman with such clear eyes, her Jacques Doucet dress delicately moulding her body as she sat on an automobile in the middle of a clearing beneath a frogged umbrella of the same smoky grey as her eyes.

'Hannah?'

'Yes, my love.'

'I'm going to try to write in English, as you suggested.'

Keep your mouth shut, Hannah! she told herself.

She kept her mouth shut.

He went on: 'I shall write in English. I'll have to spend six to eight months working on the language. I don't know it as well as Polish, or even French.'

'Let's say till Christmas.'

'Till Christmas. You really want to buy a house here, or have one built?'

'Here or on Long Island. We haven't yet been to Long Island. Becky says it's very pretty.'

'We'll need a place in Manhattan.'

'I'll have my offices there. I could . . . We could get an apartment. Would that suit you?'

'Very well,' he said with that gentle affable calmness that was so deceptive, that could conceal the coldest of rages.

And she looked at him avidly, as though she would gaze on him for ever. Never had he looked so handsome. He was twenty-eight and . . .

And he had not been one of the doubles on Ellis Island. They were all there, including Hannah herself, but not him. There had been no immigrant like him, not one. There was no sense in attaching any importance to such things, but the fact was that she couldn't stop thinking about it. If indeed her past had stepped off the boat with her in New York, which in a confused way was what she believed, why had Taddeuz not been there?

This absence distressed her.

'Take me in your arms, for pity's sake.'

This time, he did as she asked. And she hugged him tightly, clinging to him. *'I kept telling myself, over and over again, that it was insanely dangerous and foolish, Lizzie. I knew that the surest way of making catastrophes happen is to spend your whole time anticipating them, but I couldn't help it. I was horribly afraid of what would happen between Taddeuz and me, I could see it coming. And yet it didn't prevent that period from being the happiest time in my life.*

'Oh God, was I happy . . .'

CHAPTER 2
As Flat as a Board

As soon as spring really arrived, they set off on their grand tour of America. Taddeuz was already familiar with New York, Washington and Virginia (from the time when he was Senator Markham's secretary), as well as Boston and New England. But he knew nowhere beyond that, and it was such a huge country. They headed north, travelling by rail. Hannah had her Panhard and Levassor put on the train, and also took a mechanic by the name of Gaffouil, who was recommended by Louis Renault.

Hannah herself was accompanied by a chambermaid, having only reluctantly been persuaded to hire her. In Paris and London, as in New York, people had expressed amazement that she had no servants. Apparently it was only right and proper for a woman in her position – 'And just what is my position? All I am is someone who sells face creams!' – to have at least one. For a long time, the idea of having someone constantly under her feet, rummaging through her wardrobe, made Hannah's hair stand on end. What is more, she could not understand how anyone could spend their life waiting on other people. But Yvonne won her over. She was a twenty-year-old French girl whose aggressiveness counted in her favour – Hannah was delighted to find someone who would stand up to her.

'And I warn you, Yvonne, the day you become servile, you're out of a job!'

'You needn't worry about that,' replied the girl. 'There's no reason why we shouldn't get along together for a hundred years. I warn you, I'll give as good as I get.'

They left New York for Boston on 28 April. It was

Taddeuz's idea to go on to Montreal and Quebec. He was still a bit lost in this American environment where Hannah felt so much at ease, and perhaps he was seeking amongst the Francophones of the St Lawrence estuary a touch of the European and French atmosphere for which he doubtless felt some nostalgia. Towards the middle of May, they returned to the United States, paying the obligatory visit to the Niagara Falls, then continuing on to Buffalo, Pittsburgh, Cleveland, Detroit and Chicago. From there Hannah chose to go south, through St Louis, the Rockies, via Wichita and Dodge City, then on to Denver and Salt Lake City.

Then again they changed course and headed back north, towards Seattle and the state of Washington.

They arrived in San Francisco by boat on 16 August.

They had been there for two days when one morning, while she and Taddeuz dozed in each other's arms, she sensed there was someone else in their bedroom.

She opened her eyes and saw Mendel.

How could I have thought that Mendel Visoker could possibly have a double? That Hungarian was just a pale imitation. There's only one Mendel! She sat up in bed and studied him more carefully: he was bigger than she remembered; his chest seemed even more massive; there were a few more touches of grey in his black moustache, and perhaps his eyelids were a little heavier; but these were the only signs that he had reached forty.

He shifted his weight from one foot to the other.

'Cover yourself up, kid, you're naked.'

'You didn't have to come into our bedroom.'

'That's true,' he said.

He smiled in Taddeuz's direction.

'How's the Student?'

'Fine,' said Taddeuz, his head under his pillow. 'And you?'

And they both started chatting away in Polish – she

might as well have been in Australia. She was delighted: nothing in the world could have given her as much pleasure as this friendship between the two men in her life. Still sitting up in bed, but now modestly covered with a sheet drawn up to her shoulders, she listened to them talking. Anyone would have sworn that they had known each other for ages; there was a naturalness and familiarity between them that was almost childlike.

'I'm hungry,' she said nevertheless, a good five minutes later.

You might just as well be talking to the bedspread!

Then she yelled at the top of her voice: '*I'm hungry!*'

They turned round and looked at her, as though very surprised to see her there – by now Mendel was also sitting on the bed, as it was more comfortable. They couldn't see what the problem was: why didn't she get washed and dressed instead of screaming like a lunatic?

She got out of bed with all the dignity she could muster, naked as a worm, but neither of the two men so much as looked round.

There's no denying it: you absolutely fascinate them.

The three of them spent a week together in San Francisco. They ate bird's-nest soup in Chinatown, a village constructed entirely of wood, and visited the Bohemian Club, which looked down on the market in California Street. They went on excursions to Sausalito and Monterey, where Taddeuz wanted to see if anyone remembered Robert Louis Stevenson, who had lived there seven years earlier.

Hannah learned to swim.

If the truth be told, she didn't really have much choice. The trusty Panhard and Levassor that she'd had sent by sea deposited them one day in Stimson Bay, at the foot of Mount Tamalpaïs. Hardly had Hannah taken a few steps on the deserted beach than the two beastly men jumped on her. They removed her three-cornered hat with ostrich feathers, her veil, her skirts and underskirts, her chemises, her rustling taffeta petticoats, her suspenders and her red stockings, her long pointed American ankle-boots and, having stripped her naked, or near enough, they gleefully threw her into the waves. She thrashed about, while they laughed till they cried. Wild with anger, she deliberately tried to drown herself, but they kept fishing her out, making sure she stayed on the surface until she made up her mind to swim.

They dined one evening in Monterey, in a tavern run by the woman who had supposedly been the mistress of General Sherman.

'I think I'll leave tomorrow,' said Mendel suddenly.

From the look in Taddeuz's eyes, she could tell that this announcement came as no surprise to him. *Men always understand each other* . . .

'Where will you go to?'

Alaska. He was going to look for gold. To tell the truth, he didn't really care whether he found any or not, that wasn't the point, she ought to know that better than anyone; making a fortune had always been the least of his concerns. He wanted to stretch his legs a little, that was the truth of it. He had already covered a fair bit of ground in the thirty-odd years since he had left his village of Mazury: the whole of Russia, and part of western Europe (nearly all of it, in fact, except Ireland – not that he had anything against the Irish), and China, and crazy places like Indonesia, Japan and the Philippines, India and the deserts of Arabia . . . not to mention Australia and now America.

'Hannah, don't ask me to settle down in a city and watch these filthy horseless carriages go by: you know very well it would kill me. I need the wide open spaces.'

He was going to hike to Klondike. Then he would wander down to Mexico, or even a little further, as long as there was land to walk on; it was boats that he didn't much care for. A sailor in 'Frisco had sworn to him that the women in Brazil were very warm-hearted . . .

'I'll always know where to find you both. It didn't take me long to show up here, after all . . . Please don't look at me like that, with those barn-owl eyes of yours, you know how fond of you I am.'

He broke off and fixed his eyes on Taddeuz, who understood at once that he was to leave the table so that Mendel could be alone with her.

'Hannah, there's no need for me to ask whether you're happy with your Student. It's blindingly obvious.'

'And it'll go on like that,' she said.

'If I knew how to pray, I'd pray that it will. But I've always felt stupid talking to myself.'

'It will, Mendel.'

'Are you still determined not to interfere with his writing?'

'Yes, why? Has he said anything to you about it?'

'Don't be cheeky, kid. Your Taddeuz would sooner die than talk about you to anyone else. And you know it. What about your plans?'

'Next year.'

'Why wait?'

Tell him the real reason, Hannah You couldn't lie to Mendel even if you wanted to . . .

'I don't want to miss anything of Taddeuz,' she said. 'Nothing. Not a single second.'

His eyes met hers and she could see that he was moved.

'You really love him, huh?'

'More than that. A thousand times more.'

'I'm happy for you, little one.'

Any more of this, she thought, *and I'll be in tears . . .*

'And you're still intending to slap those creams of yours on the faces of these poor American women?'

'*Da*,' she said.

He pretended to shudder but it was just to conceal the emotion that overtook him. He reached out with his big bear-like paw and covered Hannah's hand.

'How long is it since I found you in a burning field and took you away in my *brouski*?'

'Eighteen years. I was seven.'

'I might still be in Poland if it weren't for you, do you realize?'

'Going to Australia was your idea.'

'Like hell it was. I didn't even know where it was at the time. Hannah, I love you both, you know. If either of you ever hurt the other, Mendel would give the guilty party hell. What about children – what are you waiting for?'

'Not next year, the year after. If I can.'

'Business first, is that it?'

He must have read something in Hannah's eyes at that point, because he immediately added: 'I'm sorry. Is there another explanation?'

'The same as before. I don't want to share him with anybody. Not even with any children we might have.'

After they had returned to San Francisco that evening, she made what she considered – and indeed it was – an enormous sacrifice: she pretended she was suffering from a bad migraine (when she would never have so much as a cold all her life!) and said she wanted to have an early night. Which meant that the two men were able to go off and have fun together, like two schoolboys playing truant. And in fact she spent the night waiting up for them, checking every line of the accounts that Jeanne Fougaril, who managed operations in Europe for her, forwarded to her at every stage of her trip.

Taddeuz returned to the fold just as the sun was rising over San Francisco Bay. He was as drunk as a lord. She almost had to knock him out in order to get him undressed, and then allowed herself to be ravished. At first, she didn't much relish the drunken attentions, even from him, but actually it was worth it.

As for Mendel, he had of course already left without saying goodbye and was on his way to Alaska.

Hannah and Taddeuz returned to New York towards the end of October, after another drive that took them to southern California, then across Arizona, New Mexico and Texas to New Orleans, before heading back north via North and South Carolina, Virginia, Washington and Philadelphia. The Panhard and Levassor eventually gave up the ghost within sight of Richmond. But it had covered nearly four thousand miles, almost all on rough roads.

The idea of selling the car to anyone else was anathema to Hannah and Taddeuz. They decided simply to bury it, with all solemn rites – which they did the following morning, under the thoroughly astounded gaze of some one hundred natives of Virginia, to the sound of the Last Post, played on a bugle by a survivor of Bull Run (at least, that's what he said) – a battle that took place during the Civil War.

They were back in New York by 26 October. Five days later, they made a decision: they would build their house on Long Island.

They went there twice and found a wonderful plot, of about five acres of undulating wooded terrain – Hannah wouldn't hear of anything flat – inhabited by grey squirrels like those in Washington Square, with a large lake at the centre of it. Within three days it was theirs – Hannah was amazed by their North American lawyer's extraordinary attention to detail. The building contractor undertook to have a habitable house ready for them by Christmas (for each day's delay after that, he would have to forfeit one per cent of the money due to him). The house was to be built of wood, with two storeys and a cellar. It would comprise twenty-one rooms: nine of them bedrooms, a study-library for Taddeuz's exclusive use, another study for her, and a veranda, two hundred yards square, with steps down to a lawn sloping gently to the lake. There was to be a landing stage, a boat shed, and a playroom annexe for the children.

If there were any. *It would really be the end if it turned out I couldn't have children!*

Because, after all, they had been making love for ten months now, any number of times, and nothing had happened.

You're still as flat as a board. But don't get het up about it, Hannah – outwardly, you may look like a savage shark, but you're only too inclined to worry, as it is. Of course you're not infertile. Of course not.

Lizzie MacKenna arrived by sea three weeks before Christmas. She swooped down on New York like a hurricane hitting Florida. She all but jumped over the ship's rail in her eagerness to set foot on American soil.

'Go on, you must tell me everything, every last detail,' she rattled on. 'Where have you been? Have you seen California? Did you meet any cowboys? And Buffalo Bill? And Indians – were you attacked by Indians? Can you see Australia from the coast of California? And the house on Long Island, is it finished? What, not yet? I thought Americans could build thirty storeys a day? When are we going to see it? So this is New York? It's full of foreigners! Do you still have the Panhard and Levassor? I see they have horseless carriages here as well. Where is that idiot Maryan – doesn't he even know that he's supposed to ask me to marry him so that I can say yes? Why doesn't anyone ever answer my questions?'

The young Australian – she was eighteen and a half – seemed to have grown even taller. She was blonde, not very pretty, but her smile and her whole body had an attractive, cheerful exuberance. Hannah had met her in

Sydney more than six years earlier. Their friendship was of the kind that supposedly only men are capable of. Lizzie had brought with her from Europe no fewer than twenty-four trunks of dresses and other garments – it was a wonder that Worth, Doucet and Paquin had anything left to sell.

'I had your measurements, Hannah. Of course, nearly half of what I bought is for you. I wanted them to make up the same dresses for you and me, but they refused. They know what you like, and claimed that what suited you wouldn't suit me. What can they mean by that? Is it because you're no taller than a piano stool, whereas I'm perfectly proportioned? Unless it's because I'm still a virgin? At eighteen and a half, I ask you! Especially with all those chaps who've tried to corner me on a sofa! What a fool I've been! A classic example of completely pointless heroism, just like the Charge of the Light Brigade at Balaclava. And now I'm in danger of dying a virgin! You can laugh! And where is that idiot Maryan? Where is he?'

Maryan Kaden appeared that same evening. He came to the Waldorf to introduce a friend of his to Hannah, a young financier by the name of Bernard Benda, who was more or less the same age as him. It was for all the world as though he had no other reason for coming, as though he had forgotten that Lizzie was arriving from Europe that day.

And what's more, when Lizzie came face to face with Maryan, the Australian girl was near enough struck dumb: she opened her mouth and emitted nothing but a rather incomprehensible gurgling sound. Lizzie lost for words was as unlikely a phenomenon as the Hudson ceasing to flow.

'I don't know what to do,' Hannah said to Taddeuz (they had just gone to bed; it was two o'clock in the morning). 'I thought it might have been just a passing fancy, that she believed herself to be in love with Maryan because he was the only person in my entourage wearing trousers. But no: in London, hordes of nice young officers have been chasing her to no avail; their fellow officers in Paris were equally well trounced. She saw them all off – I wonder where she learned to use that kind of language?'

'I don't wonder at all. I know,' Taddeuz replied rather indistinctly – he had his back turned to her, and was already in one of the positions he favoured when asleep: lying on his stomach with his head under the pillow.

'Don't pretend to be asleep, my dear.'

'I'm not pretending. I am asleep!'

She turned the light on again and sat up in bed. *You can be a real nuisance when you put your mind to it!* She observed the naked line of Taddeuz's shoulders, the sweep of his back, the long muscles, the soft skin. She wriggled down and pressed herself against him, placing her lips on that part of his body which she was particularly fond of, among others – and there were quite a few – on the nape of his neck where his hair curled, and from which the suntan that he had got on their trip across America had not yet faded. *I really must look like a weasel clinging to the back of a horse*, she thought.

'Taddeuz, it's absolutely imperative that we find out what that wretched Maryan is thinking of. Probably nothing at all. Outside the world of finance, he has a mental age of two. What if you were to speak to him!'

'No!' said Taddeuz with one final burst of energy.

'You're a man, so is he – luckily. You could talk man to man.'

Silence.

He's going to knock you senseless and throw your body out of the window.

Taddeuz stirred. Then, as if nothing had happened, he detached himself from her and slid down to the bottom of the bed, underneath the bedclothes, where he lay curled up in a ball.

She joined him down there and tenderly caressed him, brushing her lips against his skin, which sent an electric charge through her; and she gently brought them up to his mouth for an interminable kiss.

'I'm crazy about you,' she said. 'What were we saying?'

She breathed in the smell of his body.

'Hannah?'

'Yes, my love?'

'You wouldn't by any chance have paid a pretty young lady in Vienna to relieve Maryan of his virginity?'

'Me?'

'You.'

'That's a slanderous accusation!'

'Hannah?'

'Yes, my love?'

'*I* shan't talk to Maryan. *We*'ll talk to him. In other words, as usual, you will do the talking and I shall nod my head.' She waited until he had finished (he was blowing down the whole length of her back, in the deep furrow running almost up to her shoulder-blades, and he was blowing with his lips very close to her skin – it felt so warm, so good). Then she turned over and, by sheer coincidence, her mouth was just in front of Taddeuz's. In the semi-darkness of their little tent under the sheet, her big grey eyes seemed even brighter than usual, as though illuminated.

She knew it.

'Bitch,' said Taddeuz with a smile.

Then they stopped talking.

They spoke to Maryan Kaden. As cautiously as an apothecary measuring out potassium cyanide, they tested the ground in order to find out if, eventually, and without prejudice, Lizzie and he, Maryan . . .

Maryan the Silent, first of that name, his smooth face as expressive as Carrara marble in its natural state, let them flounder for a long time without seeming to understand the most obvious hints.

But eventually he smiled (a real miracle) and very calmly, in fact with what strongly resembled a sardonic snigger – *I'm going to tear his eyes out*, thought Hannah – he drew from his waistcoat an engagement ring with a white-blue diamond, explaining that he had had it ready for about a year and that, yes, he too was ready to get married, having just successfully completed a business deal with Bernard Benda, which meant that he thought he now had the means to provide for Lizzie and for the ten children they would have. And his task would be even easier since he believed that his Australian wife would bring a dowry of one hundred and twenty-five thousand dollars – one hundred thousand paid by Hannah and the rest by the MacKennas in Sydney – and in any case it seemed to him a good time to get married, especially as he had thought about where Lizzie and he might live after their wedding.

'On Long Island. I've just bought three acres of land there. I was told that my neighbours are people called Newman. Relations of yours, perhaps?'

The plans of the house-to-be, he said, were drawn up. All that was needed was Lizzie's approval. But from the little that Maryan knew of her, he thought that she was bound to reject the original plans, so he had already had another set done, which she would probably accept. As for children, the figure that he had mentioned could only be an approximation. His feeling was that Lizzie would want twelve or fourteen. But, in any case, he had already put his eldest son down for Harvard, leaving the first name blank. Although he thought that the boy would probably be called James.

'Any more questions?' asked Maryan, his blue eyes all innocence.

'Go to hell!' replied Hannah in a fury.

Taddeuz was doubled up with laughter.

The house on Long Island – Hannah and Taddeuz's – was almost certainly going to be finished on time. Hannah's six lawyers had promised her that it would be. She asked her favourite interior designer to come over from London – his first name was Henry but, in keeping with his amorous proclivities, he preferred to be called Beatrice. It wasn't so much the interior design of her home that she was expecting Beatrice to work on: 'What I really want you to do is to start thinking about what I could do with my future beauty salons and boutiques in this country. It's not a question of simply repeating what I've already done in Europe. I want something new and original.'

'Something American, in other words. And you're asking an English interior designer to do that for you!'

The beauty salon was on Park Avenue, the boutique on Fifth, next to Tiffany's – she had decided to go along with Maryan's choices, having returned to work as soon as she and Taddeuz got back from their trip across the United States. Letting ten months go by without devoting any time to her business, other than that spent studying the accounts sent to her by her directors, had given her pins and needles in the brain, as she put it. This was the first holiday she had taken in ten years. But for Taddeuz, she would never have lasted out so long. Latterly, she had been getting restive, consumed with the desire to get back to work.

Yet she did not close her eyes to the difficulties of setting up on this side of the Atlantic. Her honeymoon trip having taken her to more than one hundred towns, coast to coast, had persuaded her how far removed this country was from Europe. American society was made up of immigrants, more often than not first-generation immigrants, who were not familiar with the Rue de la Paix in

Paris or with the West End of London's Lucile or Redfein, the great couturiers whose creations bore the legend 'Made in England'. The rich here were like the inhabitants of a Faubourg Saint-Germain populated by parvenus: worst of all, they were proud of it. In the realm of women's fashion (the realm closest to her own, of course) the situation was significant: there were no haute couture establishments in New York, no more than in Boston or Philadelphia. At most there were a few dressmakers (usually disguised behind misleading French first names; Paris fashions remained the absolute criteria), some import agents . . .

'Hannah, you've just said it yourself, it's Paris that decides what's fashionable or not. I don't agree with you about the design: your greatest asset is that you come from Europe, why waste it by trying to be American? Assuming that were even possible.'

'I don't know, Beatrice. I'll see.'

'For myself, I visualize a very European design. Something positively Parisian, in fact.'

'I'll see. Leave your designs with me.'

The import agents would regularly cross the Atlantic and buy in Paris, in several sizes, the styles they thought would suit their American clients; these they would bring back to the shores of the Hudson so that they could be copied, and dozens, indeed hundreds, of replicas made. This was the world of the 'ready made', the *prêt-à-porter*, for the most part sold through the big stores (Maryan had cited Wanamaker, for instance, in his report) and the few specialist shops, often run by members of the same fraternity to which Beatrice belonged, who wore basque berets, hoping to pass as French.

And these are the people you're going to have to sell your creams to? You're not out of the woods yet!

Hannah could see that she was at least fifteen or twenty years ahead of the times. Even with her Australian credentials – and after all, Australia was no less a land of immigrants – even these credentials seemed to her of little consequence. In Sydney and Melbourne – leaving aside the fact that they were British territories with pretensions to, if not a tradition of, elegance – she had started from nothing, so any achievement had seemed satisfactory. This was no longer the case. She had dreamed so much of America that a merely moderate success would be infuriating.

Not to mention the fact that if you try to do things too quickly it might cost you what will soon be the biggest market in the world. And besides, she was going to have to invest a great deal, perhaps to the limit of her resources; failure would ruin her. *And it would be a great pity if you became poor again just when Taddeuz became famous as a writer; it would be a hell of a lot better if we were both rich and famous at the same time.*

Her business interests in Europe and Australia (although she had assigned a large part of the profits from the latter to Lizzie, with that rather artless generosity so typical of her) earned her between two hundred and fifty and three hundred thousand dollars per year. If she pushed a little harder, she could doubtless get more, but – she had to think of everything – there was also the danger that these stupid Europeans might start fighting amongst themselves. *And you'd look really clever with your whole organization based in Europe and you in America!* A good quarter of a million dollars a year was not an inconsiderable sum. And yet she wanted more. Because what would be ten times enough needed to open up another branch in Europe seemed derisory on the American scale.

There must be a solution – to any problem there are always loads of solutions, but . . .

Christmas came.

She had never celebrated this festival; it just didn't

figure in her calendar. Since the time when she was living with the MacKennas in Sydney, then afterwards in Melbourne, London and Paris, she had received countless invitations to join various families and abandon her solitude. She had always refused. This Christmas of 1900 was the first she had spent with Taddeuz, a pleasure she really enjoyed. Lizzie and Maryan, now officially engaged, were also there and, to add to her delight, the kindly, smiling Paul 'Polly' Twhaites and his wife Estelle arrived from England. Polly was still as plump and pink as ever – he hadn't changed since she first met him in Melbourne. And still he tried to conceal his wily intelligence beneath a show of rather faltering amateurishness; though he had brought with him a thoroughly comprehensive analysis of all Hannah's business interests in Europe.

'After all, I'm still your favourite business lawyer, aren't I? Unless you've replaced me with one of these American lawyers who, I'm told, draw up one-hundred-page contracts for the price of a cigar?'

She reassured him that he would continue to be her principal adviser, and what's more, her friend, for as long as he wished, even if she were to hire five hundred transatlantic advisers.

To tell the truth, he and Maryan were the only people she trusted absolutely.

The three couples spent a week in Vermont, where over four feet of snow lay on the ground. She would treasure the memory of Taddeuz and Maryan, rolling about in their underwear in the fresh overnight fall of snow in recollection of Poland; and playing around like children (their combined ages didn't add up to much more than fifty) while Polly Twhaites, dead drunk in his thoroughly English way – that's to say, maintaining perfect dignity before collapsing – sang 'Auld Lang Syne' by himself, wearing one of Lizzie's most extravagant hats.

* * *

Back in New York, the same Polly, completely sober now, was listening to Hannah expound her plans, his eyes growing round, shaking his head.

'You mean to attack *the* male bastion *par excellence*. You stand a much better chance of becoming a Monsignore in Rome.'

'We're not in Rome, or Paris, or London. We're in America.'

'There are about as many women on Wall Street as there are in the City in London, or at the Bourse in Paris . . . or in the monasteries of Mount Athos: none at all.'

'I've read the American Constitution and I don't recall any article prohibiting women from getting involved in financial affairs.'

'Nor does the same Constitution prohibit green-spotted horses from making their fortune in the butchering trade.'

'But you'd be surprised to see a horse celebrating its first million dollars, I suppose?'

'Exactly,' said Polly.

Silence.

She began to laugh.

'A green-spotted horse! Oh Polly!'

He laughed too.

'At least act through lawyers and specialist brokers,' he said. 'No one need know that they're working for a woman. In fact, it would be best if they didn't. I would sleep better then.'

'And I could always grow a long beard and wear an iron corset to remove the curves that I have and put them where I haven't any,' said Hannah, sarcastically.

Polly Twhaites blushed. And she thought: *I really adore him. He's the only lawyer in the world who blushes like a young girl at the mention of pants and what's inside them.*

Be that as it may, she felt well and truly cheerful. The respite she had granted herself was coming to an end; she was going back to war. And not just for more of what she had already achieved on two other continents, but with a new challenge that she had set herself. *You're going to become a financier.*

Taddeuz had begun to write. He had started as soon as they got back from their grand tour of America. At first, he worked in a room at the Waldorf, right at the top of the building, above all the floors that carried any prestige, in order not to be disturbed. But he very soon accumulated so many books that the room proved to be impractical and cramped. The house on Long Island was not yet ready, but a better solution was found: an apartment in Sullivan Street, in Greenwich Village. Four rooms, not very well lit, with windows looking out on to an inside courtyard, and with dreadful pink wallpaper that was positively nauseating. He didn't want anyone to decorate it for him, refusing to allow Hannah to send someone, and undertook to repaint it all himself, sky-blue, without bothering to strip the wallpaper. He also turned down any suggestion of acquiring new furniture: he said the table, three chairs, rocking chair, bed, and the grandfather clock that had not worked since Lincoln died would amply serve his needs.

It was supposed to be a place to work only until he could install himself in the house on Long Island. In fact, when the time came, he did not move out, saying that he was in the middle of writing and was certainly not going to interrupt his work. And then more time passed . . .

Hannah did not insist and considered herself very clever not to have insisted: it was quite natural that Taddeuz should want to be in his own place, by himself, to write, and it was just too bad about the marvellous study-library she had had built for him in the house on Long Island. After all, if, instead of being a writer, he had been an industrialist, doctor or lawyer, he would likewise have had his own place of work and she would not be interfering in his affairs.

'Lizzie, at that time, and for a long time afterwards, I don't know how much money he had. I never dared ask. I frequently offered him money. He always refused. Nicely, but he always said no. He was Markham's private secretary for about three years. I suppose he was paid for that. When we were married he gave me this gold-and-emerald bracelet, and for our first anniversary he began making up my black-pearl necklace – you know the one. From that I deduced that he wasn't a pauper . . . Oh, damn it all, what a world! If I had been a man and he a woman, no one would have found it surprising that I should give him money!'

She had not read a single line he had written. Once or twice only, she had caught a glimpse of one of his manuscripts. Once she had been alone and could certainly have read through a few pages. She didn't. *If he wanted you to read what he had written, he would say so.* She clung fiercely to the promise she had made to him (not that he had asked it of her) and, more importantly, that she had made to herself: never, never to interfere with his writing.

The house on Long Island was habitable by 24 December, but it wasn't until 2 January, after they returned from Vermont, that they really moved in. For weeks, Hannah and Lizzie, together with Becky Singer, had been more or less camping in the twenty or so rooms that smelt of paint. They chose the furnishing fabrics from the selection sent from Paris and Lyons, before deciding on where the furniture from London should go.

It was all great fun. Hannah shared fits of giggles with Lizzie that had them both rolling on the ground, under the vacant gaze of Becky, who never understood anything. Becky – Rebecca – was the young Jewish woman from Warsaw who, ten years earlier (she was three years younger than Hannah), had worked for a while in the Klotzes' grocery store. She had left after marrying a young rabbi, cheerful as the grave, who had had the good grace to leave her a widow of not even sixteen in a very short space of time. Less than six months later, in true fairy-tale fashion, an uncle in America had invited the young woman and her family to join him in Trenton, New Jersey, where one of the sons of the wealthy Singer family – one of the oldest families to settle in America, the Singers had been in the country for more than a century – came to discuss business with her uncle. He was stopped in his tracks by the young woman from Warsaw, who was exceedingly beautiful and, choosing to overlook the fact that she was a widow, he married her . . . *'Which is how that feather-brained noodle came to be one of the richest women in New York, and all she had to do for it was to flutter her eyelashes, while I was rushing hell for leather around Australia, scattering kangaroos, blazing a trail across the country. But Lizzie, of course I'm very fond of Becky! I don't much care for the way she makes eyes at Taddeuz, that's all . . . Who's jealous? Me? Don't be silly. Of course I'm not jealous. I admit she's very nice – if she weren't, that would be the last straw, stupid as she is!'*

By about 15 January – thanks to Becky, who was happy to place at Hannah's disposal the vast network of her in-laws' social connections – she found an apartment to rent, of approximately three thousand square feet, on the site where the General Motors building would later be erected. A week later, while she was deciding on the interior design with Henry-Beatrice, her English expert, she took a tremendous tumble. She was perched on a tall step-ladder, examining the mouldings on the ceiling, when she went flying through the air like a glider, came crashing down on to the decorator's trestle table below, tore through the rolls of wallpaper that the decorators were unfurling, and went sliding down fifteen marble steps, fortunately covered with dustsheets. Only a miracle, or rather an abrupt twist of her body, prevented her from falling down the lift shaft (the balustrade had not yet been installed) and hitting the marble floor twenty-six feet below. Everyone thought she was dead, but she got to her feet unaided. 'I'm fine,' she said, stunned by her lucky escape.

('Beatrice, if you say a word about this to my husband, I shall inform the whole of London society that you had an affair with a woman when you were sixteen years old!')

She thought she was completely unscathed, apart from a few aches and bruises. So that when she noticed her period had not started a few days later, she did not at first see this as a consequence of her fall: *I'm pregnant!*

She wasn't. Everything returned to normal, but she had learned her lesson: if she was to have her first child the following year, that gave her about fifteen months to get her American operation off the ground and make a success of it.

So it was time she got to work; she had already delayed long enough.

She therefore adopted the sites that Maryan Kaden had initially chosen. For the one on Fifth Avenue, next door to Tiffany's, she got a ten-year lease with the possibility of eventually buying it at a reasonable price. For the other, located about two-thirds of a mile to the south, things were almost as simple: there was a brick building on the site, but it had been virtually abandoned – only the tenth floor was occupied – and the back of it still bore traces of the great fire of 1835; it was evidently intended for demolition.

In fact, the file – compiled by Maryan with his usual thoroughness – made it quite clear: the present owners wanted to sell. Maryan had actually met the chairman of the company to which the building belonged: he was an old man, chiefly interested in a small railway company, who had little interest in property, even less in a building situated in what was now the centre of New York.

Maryan – a year ago now – had found out how much it would cost to buy: between $160,000 and $180,000. And the evaluation had been approved by Zeke Singer, Becky Singer's young brother-in-law, who consulted people even more expert than himself.

Hannah's intention was to buy the building, have it demolished, and put up a new building in its place. She would have her offices there and let the floors she didn't need.

All in all, a very unremarkable transaction . . .

There was absolutely no way of foreseeing the cataclysm she was about to unleash in the process. A cataclysm that only the last-minute intervention of nothing less than the Federal government of Washington and the highest echelons of the American, if not the international, banking world would prevent from becoming known as the Great Crash of 1901.

CHAPTER 3

The ABCD Man

It had been snowing over New York for two days now. The previous day, on Long Island, Taddeuz and Hannah had held a house-warming party in their first real home for no fewer than one hundred guests, amongst whom Hannah was extraordinarily proud to see Junior Rockefeller – to her great surprise he had accepted her invitation.

It was snowing, but not so heavily that you couldn't drive through the streets. The big Renault, capable of over one hundred miles per hour, a veritable rocket, had no trouble reaching Manhattan with Taddeuz at the wheel. The car came to a halt on Sullivan Street in Greenwich Village, and was immediately surrounded by admiring passers-by.

Hannah slipped into the driving seat her husband had just vacated. It was nearly ten o'clock in the morning.

'You won't forget our dinner engagement this evening? I'll pick you up at five.'

He nodded, distracted as he so often was before, during or after writing.

'Kiss me.'

Their lips touched. Despite the cold, he wasn't wearing a coat; over a shirt with a detachable collar he wore only a dark-red, silk waistcoat and the jacket of his English suit. He was bare-headed. With his hair, worn slightly long, and his moustache, which was also fair, he looked a bit like William Cody, otherwise known as Buffalo Bill – *except that he's a darned sight younger and more handsome!*

She drove off, turning left on to Broadway and continuing slowly southwards, escorted for a while by a gang of children who ran alongside the Renault. Passers-by looked on in amazement. It was all so new to them – both the car, with the dull vibrating roar of a big wild animal, and its driver, a very petite young woman swathed in a marvellous blue fox pelisse and matching toque hat, with a fine, triangular face like that of an Egyptian cat and bright eyes (following Taddeuz's example, she refused to put on the goggles ordinarily worn, especially in an open car).

In Nassau Street, in the heart of the Wall Street area, Maryan had rented three rooms as offices for his personal use, staffed by a single secretary – she was about as seductive as a pâté left in a cupboard for six months; Lizzie really had nothing to fear.

Four men rose to their feet when Hannah entered. She knew two of them: Maryan, of course, and also Bernard Benda, the impressively shrewd young financier. The other two were Joe Lanza and Fred Alfero. They were in their forties and had cold, killers' eyes. They were not killers. They owed to their common Lombard ancestry an exceptional aptitude for financial affairs, a taste and respect for figures, an enthusiasm for handling money. They had been working on Wall Street for about twenty-five years: one as a floor trader, the other as a dealer. They listened impassively as Hannah explained her intentions: she wanted them to act as her guides and mentors, her teachers, for one month.

Silence.

Alfero did not even consult the other Italo-American. He shook his head.

'We were told that we would meet a friend of Mr Benda. We didn't think this friend would be a woman.'

'Five hundred dollars,' said Hannah.

'Sorry, no.'

'A thousand.'

She noticed Lanza's fingers twitching and said: 'Two thousand. Each.'

'There are places you will never get into,' said Alfero.

'I know: the gents' toilets. But you can describe them to me.'

Five hours later she was walking along Wall Street with Maryan on her left and Bernard Benda on her right. Of her motorist's kit she now wore only the fur stole, but it was sufficient to make all eyes turn to look at her.

'People would pay less attention if I were a zebra.'

'Zebras have been seen before on Wall Street,' said Bernard, laughing. 'Pleased with your first day at the Stock Exchange?'

'Very. I thought it would be more complicated.'

This was not exactly what she was thinking. To tell the truth, she was filled with wonder. She adored the excitement, the activity, the quick-fire speed of transactions. What an extraordinary game! *And what a nuisance it is sometimes to be a woman!* For the first time in her life she had encountered people who thought as quickly as she did. It had given her a marvellous sense of fellowship, though it had not been reciprocated: she had been regarded as a creature from Mars.

She removed the glove from her right hand, which she then held out in front of her, with index finger and thumb extended and her other fingers folded in. 'That means: I'm buying.' Keeping her index finger out, she tucked in her thumb and extended her little finger. 'That means: there's nothing left to buy or sell.' She then extended her first three fingers only: 'I'll buy three thousand.' With her hand on its side, thumb out, only half the little finger raised, the rest of her fingers tucked in: 'I'm buying or selling at two-eighths above market price . . . Did I make any mistakes, Bernard?'

He studied the spats on his top-quality shoes, then raised his head and said: 'And you can sew too, can you?'

An hour later, after Bernard Benda had left them, she came in sight of Columbus Circle, where Broadway, Eighth Avenue and Fifty-Ninth Street intersected. At the top of Fifty-Ninth the two lawyers were already waiting for them, stamping their feet as they stood waiting alongside a ridiculous little Curved Dash Oldsmobile which, compared with the Renault, looked like a tuberculous spider.

The lawyers' names were Harvey Stevenson and Simon Marcus, both of whom had been recommended to her by Simon Guggenheim and Senator Markham.

Stevenson calmly explained that he had arranged a meeting with Dwyer, chairman of the company that owned the building she wished to buy.

'His name's Dwyer?'

'Andrew Barton Cole Dwyer. He's often referred to as ABCD.'

'I thought I read somewhere that the chairman was called MacLean?'

'MacLean died two months ago. Dwyer is his son-in-law. Mrs Newman?'

'Call me Hannah.'

'It would be best to let Simon and me handle the first interview,' said Stevenson with a certain degree of embarrassment in his voice.

She fixed her gaze on him, understanding at once what was on his mind.

'Because I'm a woman? Is that it?'

'Hannah . . .' Maryan started to speak.

Waves of anger rose up inside her, each more impassioned than the last. The decision she took then – the consequences of which it would take twenty-nine years to recover from – certainly reflected the impetuousness and even violence typical of her, but also that irritation she felt every time she was reminded of being a woman, as though it were some shameful vice – *Even Polly's guilty of it!*

And there was too, surely, an element of that intense excitement which had seized her when she visited Wall Street.

Whatever it was, she said: 'I am going to see this Mr ABCD alone. Alone.'

Maryan and the two lawyers could wait for her if they wanted to. Otherwise, they could go to hell!

She went in.

'If only he'd been ugly, Lizzie! If he had been small, fat, slimy, revolting, with lecherous eyes and damp hands with dirty nails! But no, the worst of it was that the son of a bitch was a good-looking fellow!

A. B. C. Dwyer was almost as tall as Taddeuz, with brown curly hair. He was about thirty, and his hands were perfect: big, but not too big, sensitive, supple and well cared-for. His smile was completely disarming, and there was a friendly but mocking gleam in his eye. When Hannah entered his office, he was standing in shirtsleeves (*his forearms are well muscled*), handling what seemed to be a model-sized locomotive. On seeing her, he leapt for his jacket.

'And who might you be?'

'Hannah Newman.'

'The lawyers spoke of one H. Newman.'

'That's me.'

Silence.

He studiously examined her. He nevertheless asked her to sit down and even drew up a chair for her. But instead of sitting down on the other side of the desk, or sitting next to her on another chair, he just stood there, practically touching her, leaning lightly on the desk top, which was covered with small-scale trains.

'So you're H. Newman?'

'I'm the H. Newman who wants to buy the building on Park Avenue that is part of the estate of the company that belonged to the late Mr MacLean.'

'My father-in-law, whom we were so sorry to lose.'

His eyes were smiling, vaguely ironic. He continued to examine her.

'The building is falling down,' she went on. 'Or near enough. It's of no use to you any more. But I could find a use for it. I'm prepared to pay $100,000 in cash.'

She saw one of his hands reach towards the box of cigars, hesitate, then draw back.

'You can smoke as much as you like,' she said. 'The smoke doesn't bother me.'

Nevertheless, he did not stir. He continued to watch her. *Go on, admit it*, she thought, *he's mentally undressing you*.

'One hundred thousand dollars?'

'Cash.'

'The building's worth more than that. A lot more.'

'It's worth the land it's built on. If that. Demolishing it will take time and cost money.'

He smiled.

'In other words, it would be worth more if it didn't exist,' he said with considerable sarcasm.

Don't lose your temper, Hannah! Think what a fool you would look if, when you left, you had to tell Maryan and the other two waiting for you out there in the snow that you had failed to pull off a deal that they would have settled in a few minutes!

She drew herself up – the main effect of which was to thrust out her breasts (you can never have too many trump cards up your sleeve) – and turned her most charming smile on A. B. C. Dwyer, who was now stepping backwards, with an effrontery he didn't even try to hide, in order to get a better view of the curve of her bosom and the line of her back.

'Exactly,' she said. 'I like your sense of humour, Mr Dwyer. I'm prepared to go as high as $110,000.'

He shook his head, continuing brazenly to undress her with his eyes – *you can't have much left on, inside his head.*

'To be frank,' he said eventually, 'I didn't think you were very pretty when you first came in. But I was wrong, which doesn't happen very often. You're more than pretty. The more one looks at you, the more one realizes it. Here's what we're going to do: we're going to have dinner together this evening, and we'll talk business all night, if necessary. Some of your arguments, not to say all of them, merit closer study. Then, although I never do business with women, you might perhaps stand some chance of making me change my mind. I shall expect you at six thirty at . . .'

'Go to hell,' said Hannah.

From that moment on, from that day forth, she was in a terrible rage: a rage the like of which she had never yet experienced; the like of which she would never experience again.

And which she dissembled – what else could she do? When she came down into the street, she explained to the two lawyers, with a calmness that astounded her, that the matter was progressing smoothly, that Dwyer had all but agreed; but that on reflection she was the one who was now wondering if she really wanted or needed that building.

'Otherwise, it's a deal. Thank you for your help, gentlemen.'

The lawyers drove off in their grotesque, backfiring, American horseless carriage.

She climbed into the Renault with Maryan.

She was just about to set off when, 'You've forgotten to light the headlamps,' said Maryan placidly.

'Well, do it then, what are you waiting for?'

He got out of the car and lit the two gas headlamps. The slushy snow that had been falling in the last few hours had stopped. Maryan returned but didn't get back into his seat beside her. He lowered his head and shifted his weight from one foot to the other, his pale eyes looking almost white in the encroaching darkness, while the Edison streetlights came on.

'Something happened, didn't it, Hannah?'

'Don't interfere!'

'Did he . . . fail to treat you with respect?'

She couldn't help smiling.

'This is the twentieth century, Maryan. Men don't fail to treat women with respect; they rape them. He didn't rape me.'

But this half-smile made her feel, to some extent, less tense deep down inside. It certainly didn't calm her rage, but made it turn cold, and so more dangerous. *To any problem there are always plenty of solutions* . . .

She was already working on some of these solutions. Oh, nothing very ambitious for the time being, just the tiniest embryo of an idea . . .

'Are you getting in, Maryan? I'm going back to Greenwich Village.'

No. He was going to walk down Central Park for a bit, and then he would drop into his room in Fifty-Eighth Street to change – that evening he was supposed to be taking Lizzie to Carnegie Hall, which had been opened ten years earlier by Tchaikovsky himself.

She drove off in the Renault. A few minutes before, true to habit, she would have driven down Fifth Avenue at a lethal speed, at the risk of running over three or four dozen of those New Yorkers who didn't do business with women.

Not now. An almost worrying calm possessed her.

To any problem there are always plenty of solutions, and when there are no solutions, that's because there's no problem.

Hannah, that's it! That's one solution . . .

She did a U-turn in Fifth Avenue and four minutes later Maryan's tall figure appeared on the edge of Central Park. She drew up alongside him. He listened without uttering a word.

Then he said: 'Are you sure it's a good idea?'

'Positive. Maryan? Not a word of this to Taddeuz, please. Not a word to anyone.'

'The company,' said Maryan Kaden two days later, 'is called Carrington-Fox Railway. It's not quoted on the Stock Exchange, which means that the value of the shares is determined only by the annual figures.'

'I know what it means, I'm not a complete half-wit. What are the company's assets?'

'A railway between New York and Albany. Another line near Boston. Shareholdings – none of them above five per cent – in various other companies not much bigger than itself, with one notable exception: Northern Star Pacific. It also owns some warehouses in New York and Boston, plus a few properties, the one you know and a few others besides that are very small and old. The properties are mostly in New York.'

'How did that wretched Dwyer come to be chairman?'

'By marrying the boss's daughter. MacLean himself was the son-in-law of the founder of Carrington. But Dwyer is a railways man: he worked as a railway engineer in California and Oregon.'

'He's been with the company how long?'

'Three years. Since he married Miss MacLean, who's the same age as he is: thirty-four.'

'She must have been starting to smell a bit musty if she

was over thirty when she married. Have they any children?'

'No.'

'It's obvious: he got into bed with the daughter in order to get the job. I bet he killed his father-in-law!'

'Then he must have a long arm: MacLean died while on holiday in Scotland, of a heart attack.'

'In any case, I'm sure that Dwyer has a dreadful reputation,' she said with rancour in her voice.

Maryan smiled.

'Sorry to disappoint you. According to the information I have, there's nothing in his past. He's said to be very clever and very ambitious.'

'Pity. And the Carrington shares?'

'There are 160,000 in all. At the last check, they were each worth $11.75. Dwyer himself controls approximately twenty per cent.'

'What do you mean, "approximately"?'

'He has 29,952 shares.'

Maryan could see in Hannah's eyes the next question she was going to ask.

'At $11.75 each, that makes $351,936.'

'Isn't there some discrepancy between the total value of shares and the value of the company with such a large family-holding?'

'A little, but it's quite common for the shares in a family-owned company to be undervalued, especially for tax reasons.'

'And the other shareholders, apart from Dwyer?'

'They're all over the place, and they've mostly inherited the shares. The largest shareholder after Dwyer is the daughter of the other founder of the company, and she's eighty.'

A hubbub rose from the crowd around them. Wall Street was getting more animated every minute. Hannah had met Maryan at the entrance of what was called the

Garage, where at least two hundred cars were already parked. It was 10.30 A.M., and she was getting ready, for the third day running, to take lessons on the Stock Exchange from the men she called the Lombards.

'You really want twenty per cent of Carrington, Hannah?'

'Thirty-two thousand shares.'

You could almost see the figure flashing up in Maryan Kaden's pale eyes. He said very quickly: 'At $11.75, that represents $376,000. But you'll have to allow more: there'll be expenses, and the value of the shares is bound to go up once you start buying so many.'

'I've had the equivalent of five hundred thousand dollars sent over from London.'

'That's a lot of money, Hannah.'

Joe Lanza appeared on the scene. Today, he had authorization to take Hannah to the Stock Watch Room, the control room of Stock Exchange dealings, where in a few seconds an army of employees would begin to record in huge registers the smallest transaction.

'I'm coming,' Hannah told the Italo-American.

She turned to Maryan. He had just said: 'That's a lot of money.' And he had spoken these words in a dull voice, lowering his head and shifting his weight from one foot to the other, as he invariably did whenever he disagreed with her (she was undoubtedly the only person in the world to intimidate him in this way).

'The most astonishing thing, Lizzie, is that deep down I agreed with him. It wasn't so much the half-million dollars that I was risking . . . But all that for a building! I had reached the point where I dreamed night and day of settling scores with Dwyer. And Maryan could see that: I was letting myself get carried away.'

'Thirty-two thousand shares, Maryan. You can offer up to fifteen dollars a share. Don't pay more without talking to me first.'

Maryan asked if he could let Bernard Benda into the secret of the operation.

She hesitated and then agreed.

From that moment on, the wheels started turning – inexorably.

It took Maryan and Benda twenty-one days to acquire 32,000 shares. They could certainly have worked more quickly, but at the expense of discretion. In fact, they proceeded so skilfully that their purchases passed unnoticed and, most importantly, they managed not to push up the price too much: the highest level it reached was $13.40.

They paid a total of $418,000, including expenses.

When, nearly a year before, Hannah had explained to Junior Rockefeller her bizarre accounting system based on sheep, she had been in a position to draw one and a half pink sheep. She in fact had a little more than that on paper, but in order physically to produce that one and a half million dollars, she would have to sell off virtually all her European property holdings – most of her beauty salons and shops were only rented.

She had in fact made an estimation of her assets and, with her customary circumspection, had placed a slightly less than realistic value on them – how, for instance, could she put a price on her patents?

In February 1901, despite the major expenses of buying the plot of land on Long Island, building and furnishing the house, renting the apartment on Fifth Avenue; despite the one hundred thousand dollars paid into Lizzie's account, she revised her estimate, with the same circumspection, and came up with the figure of $1,675,000, of which $110,000 were actually available.

More than you need. Fortunately!

'You see, Lizzie, I was actually prepared to use all my

reserves if necessary, just to show that wretch Dwyer that I was as good as him. Even getting the building became a secondary issue.

I was mad. I had lost something that's essential in business: a sense of where to draw the line.'

Contact with A. B. C. Dwyer was resumed through her lawyers (not Stevenson and Marcus, though, who had been retired from battle because they had already been identified by the enemy). Polly Twhaites had authorized the half-a-million-dollar transfer and she agreed to tell him all about it. For two days Polly used all his powers of diplomacy to persuade her not to go and see Dwyer in person.

'Hannah, I have never seen you so worked up. This man isn't the first misogynist you've ever encountered, and he certainly won't be the last. Calm down, for the love of God!'

'This has nothing to do with God, and I am very calm.'

'About as calm as an active volcano.'

'I want to get him, Polly!'

'In that case, hire a professional killer, it won't cost you so dear.'

Seeing the cold look in her grey eyes, he took fright: 'Good gracious, Hannah, I was only joking.'

'A professional killer,' she said with a sombre expression, 'that's not a bad idea . . .'

But then she smiled. 'I'm only joking as well, Polly.'

The new lawyers sent to the front were called Wynn and Parks. They did not reveal to Dwyer the name of the client on whose behalf they were acting. Afterwards, Hannah would learn that, without actually saying so at any point – Wynn and Parks nevertheless gave Dwyer to understand that their client couldn't possibly be the woman who had come to see him and who had made him the first offer. Who had ever heard of a woman getting involved with serious business matters? No, the person or persons who had retained their services were much more serious, and they had been instructed to point out to Dwyer that he controlled less than twenty per cent of Carrington-Fox, 'not even as much as our client or clients, Mr Dwyer; and our client or clients are anxious, for reasons of their own, that this building in Park Avenue should be acquired by Mrs Newman. Refuse this offer of $160,000 and you'll instigate a battle that stands a good chance of ruining your company, and of ruining you in particular.'

A. B. C. Dwyer betrayed no reaction and asked for three days to think about it.

When Hannah found out what arguments her own lawyers had used to persuade Dwyer, she almost choked with rage.

'Maryan, those two morons went and told Dwyer . . .'

'They did it for the best, Hannah. Besides, it might work.'

'They practically told him that I was a half-wit! And I'm paying them! I'll sack them, do you hear! Those . . .'

There followed an impressive string of insults in eight languages. For several moments she almost wished she were a man, so that she could give them all a good thrashing, starting with that wretch Dwyer. Another thought came to her, which enraged her even more:

'In other words, they made me out to be crazy, insinuating that I had a lover and that my lover was so rich he was capable of buying up Carrington just to give me the building, the way he might give me a diamond necklace! I can hardly believe what I've been hearing!'

Maryan watched her impassively. And eventually she calmed down. A little. Enough at least to ask the question that she had to ask.

'Maryan, why did those cretinous lawyers – and I'm being polite! – mention other clients apart from me, as though they were implying that Dwyer would do well to fear them? Who were they referring to?'

'To Flint and Healey.'

'And who are Flint and Healey?'

'The banker John Patrick Flint and the industrialist Roger Healey.'

'What has J. P. Flint got to do with all this?'

'He and Healey have joined forces to try and gain control of all the big railway companies in the United States. Compared with them, Dwyer is a street vendor. By suggesting that Flint and Healey were behind them, Wynn and Parks were trying to worry Dwyer, to make him think that this matter of the building was a trifle; they were trying to divert his attention.'

She thought: *Why don't you stop behaving like a fool, Hannah, and calm down a bit? Use your head for a change.*

'Was it your idea, Maryan?' she asked.

Shifting his weight from one foot to the other, he said: 'More or less. Bernard and I discussed it with Stevenson, Marcus, Wynn and Parks.'

'But not with me. Naturally! What use would a fool of a woman have been in all those male discussions?'

Incredibly, Maryan blushed.

'It's not that, Hannah. But since this whole affair started, you've been a bit . . . beside yourself.'

She stared at him fiercely and for a few seconds was on the point of saying something she might regret. *But if you hadn't been so stupid and conceited as to go on your own to see Dwyer, probably nothing would have happened. And Maryan is simply trying to make good the mistake you made. All right. Forget it, Hannah, and pocket your pride.*

'All we need is for Dwyer to think that he's up against Flint and Healey,' Maryan continued.

'Rather than anyone else. Because he'll behave more reasonably.'

Another short burst of rage flared within her – she suppressed it as she had the previous one.

'And what if Dwyer were to contact Flint and Healey direct, in order to worm some information out of them?'

'He won't do that. He knows what the situation is.'

'I don't.'

'Flint and Healey have a rival who is also trying to gain control of the railways. The battle has been going on for some time now. Dwyer knows about it, especially as he's involved in railways himself. He . . .'

'Who's the third man?'

'Louis Rosen. He and Flint hate each other. Rosen has managed to snaffle up two of the lines his rivals had their eye on. Since then, they've been on each other's tail all across America in pursuit of every company of any importance.'

'Is Carrington of any importance to them?'

'It's of as much significance to them as the first carriage they ever owned. And Dwyer knows all this. He knows too that it would be a grave mistake to contact Healey, Flint or Rosen. The battle between the three of them is a fight among Titans. Getting involved by taking either side would be very dangerous. Either of the two camps would be capable of stamping on Dwyer with no effort at all. He won't do anything.'

'And will he sell me the building?'

'We hope so, Hannah.' Maryan shook his head and said again: 'We hope so.'

Then he left. She was quite calm again now – all her hatred intact, but calm. The cold little mechanism inside her head was working again.

Their scheme isn't going to work . . . You hope it doesn't, anyway! Because, all right, perhaps you'll get your building that way, but you won't have settled any scores with that son of a bitch! Or, at least, it won't be any thanks to you that he has to concede. There must be another way.

During that period, she and Lizzie were busy with the building and furnishing of the house that the young Kaden couple-to-be (their wedding was planned for the following May) were to live in after returning from their honeymoon. There was rather a conspiracy over the house – even Taddeuz was involved. The Kadens' ancestral home was being built on the boundary of the plot bought by Hannah and the one bought by Maryan. The two homes would be almost facing each other, on either side of the lake. Four hundred and fifty yards at most would separate them.

'That doesn't seem to inspire you with much enthusiasm,' said Lizzie.

'Don't be silly.'

They were both walking around the foundations that the workmen had spent a week laying. During these last days of February, the New York winter had returned with a vengeance. It had snowed the day before and, judging by the leaden sky, it looked as if it could well snow again. One of Lizzie MacKenna's first concerns, even before she knew she was going to live here, had been to have some tiny wooden shelters made for the grey squirrels. But to the young girl's great disappointment, none of the squirrels had deigned to take advantage of the shelters, which they had turned their scornful tails on.

'You'd think the wretched creatures hated Australians . . . Hannah, have you and Maryan had an argument?'

'No.'

'In other words, yes. Don't forget that I'm engaged to the fool and I get a pretty close look at him. Though not as close as I would like – in fact I wonder what he thinks his hands are for . . . Hannah, there's something you don't want him to do which he's going to do anyway, or else it's you that wants something he doesn't approve of?'

'Mind your own business. You have really big feet, you know.'

'We can talk about my feet some other time. Although they're very handsome. Except when I'm riding: my poor horse can't turn his head round one way or the other, my feet stick out so far. If Maryan's annoying you, I'll divorce him. Before I even marry him.'

'I have nothing to reproach Maryan for.'

'Sure?'

'Positive. Let's go home. You ought to have put something over your shoulders. It's so cold, we could be in Poland.'

They returned to the Newmans' house. It was a Sunday afternoon and, as was frequently the case, there were about twenty guests, nearly all of whom had in fact come to see Taddeuz. Behind the coloured-glass windows, on the left-hand side of the veranda, figures moved nonchalantly about in a quiet hubbub of laughter and conversation. Hannah identified the profile of Taddeuz seated at a table – *Someone must have challenged him to a game of chess again, and as usual he'll beat them hollow*. Among her husband's friends were two young men: David Wark Griffith and another, barely twenty years old, who had what Hannah regarded as a woman's name: Cecil B. De Mille.

She meant what she had said to Lizzie. She was furious at having to admit Maryan was right, but she had allowed herself to get carried away, investing more than four hundred thousand dollars in a railway company she couldn't care less about – *And which is not worth a fig. No one has checked, as far as I know. Bravo, Hannah, I could kill you for being so stupid!*

Soon the guests would start back for New York, so Taddeuz and she had a quiet evening ahead of them.

We'll have a bath together and it will end up as the usual Roman orgy for two – what a delightful prospect!

And tomorrow morning, Dwyer would give his response.

And so he did.

First of all in the bizarre form of a hat box delivered by a messenger from Western Union. Hannah opened it. Inside, she found a short letter and a package wrapped in tissue paper. The note read: *My hearty congratulations to Messrs J. P. Flint and Roger Healey – should you ever make their acquaintance. As for the matter between us, my conditions have not changed: spread your thighs nicely and perhaps I shall give you the usual present. I only deal with women in bed.* This was signed *XYZ*.

The package contained the full regalia of fishnet stockings, suspenders, see-through knickers and a corset, all in a screaming red that would not have disgraced a whore in a Texan brothel.

And I want to see you in this, read the second note, pinned to the corset.

In other circumstances, perhaps, she would have laughed. Although the no doubt intended vulgarity of 'spread your thighs' would in any case have grated on her nerves.

But she did not laugh, and that genuine hatred, which Maryan Kaden's arguments had abated a little, returned to her. There was now a new element to it, which was the satisfaction of knowing that she had been proved right: it hadn't worked.

Yet she retained sufficient self-control to delay her decision for two weeks. She knew she could always call it a day. She could try to forget the ABCD man and extricate herself from that blasted railway company by selling the shares she had bought. At least then she would get back most of the money that she had invested in this crazy operation. Polly Twhaites and Maryan obviously assumed this was what she would do, seeing it all in terms of profit and loss.

It wasn't the money that bothered her most. Having decided to get mixed up in something other than her creams (in America, what's more, of which she had entertained such high expectations) and then to have been stopped dead in her tracks at the outset – that's what mattered most to her. And stopped in such a way as this! *That son of a bitch would probably have said yes to any man, but because you're a woman, he asks you to get into bed with him. And what can you do about it? Go and cry on Taddeuz's shoulder, or even Maryan's? That'll make you look clever, won't it, having always claimed to be able to look after yourself?*

Not to mention the fact that you have no idea how Taddeuz would react. You've never seen him fight anyone, or even get really angry. You never really know with him. He might well go and kill the wretch. Which would put us in a fix – do prisons in America have double beds?

That's enough, Hannah, stop being silly, you don't really feel like laughing at all. Because that son of a bitch Dwyer realized that you wouldn't say anything and that's what makes you want to scream. He knows that you would be too ashamed to tell anyone . . .

The unspeakable bastard!

At the beginning of March she went to Philadelphia with Taddeuz to see an exhibition of French Impressionist paintings organized by Mary Cassatt. Finding herself once more in this world familiar to both her and Taddeuz, Hannah suddenly realized how selfish she had been: after all, she had forced Taddeuz to settle in America without really bothering to find out if he was happy to so do.

'Would you have stayed here without me?'

'Here in Philadelphia?'

'You know very well that I'm not talking about Philadelphia. Would you like to live in Europe?'

They were in bed in a Philadelphia hotel on Chestnut Street. The day before she had bought three pastels from Mary Cassatt. He switched on one of the bedside lamps and gazed at her, resting on one elbow, his head in the palm of his hand. Once again she had the feeling that beneath that tranquil, almost indifferent manner he knew everything about her and could tell immediately what she was thinking, however dissimulated and well prepared the stratagems she might adopt.

'You've got problems, haven't you, Hannah?'

'I don't know what you mean.'

'You've got business problems. I'm not asking you to tell me about them; I probably couldn't do anything anyway. I know as much about finance as I do about engineering – I always wonder why the spark plugs in a car aren't extinguished by the wind as it speeds along. And, in any case, if I could have been useful to you in your difficulties you would have told me.'

He knows. Oh my God!

'Go on,' she said.

'And because of these problems in America, of which you had such high expectations, you're suddenly starting to think of Europe where you had such success.'

He really can read your mind, it's frightening.

'It's not that.'

He shook his head and smiled.

'Perhaps not, Hannah. But perhaps it is. And by an association of ideas which that very devious brain of yours . . .'

'Me, devious?'

(She fell back on her last line of defence – flirtatiousness – tracing with her index finger the outline of Taddeuz's mouth.)

'You're damned devious, as someone I know would

say. You haven't got to the point of admitting that you would really like to refuse this obstacle and go back to Paris or London. So . . .'

'So, I fall back on you.'

'In a way.'

'It's true that I have a strong desire to fall back on you. And I don't mean metaphorically. Do you want to go back to Europe, Tad?'

'Taddeuz.'

'Everyone here calls you Tad.'

'You're not everyone.'

She closed her eyes for a moment and, praise be to God, as the rabbis say, she didn't have to pretend to want him.

'That's true,' she said, agreeing with him again. 'But don't change the subject, please. Answer my question.'

(She had begun to edge surreptitiously closer to him in the big American bed; by wriggling as stealthily as a snake she aimed to position herself right up against him, against his chest and his naked stomach.)

'I don't know, Hannah. I really don't know.'

'You can write in English, don't try and tell me that you can't – although you've never shown me what you've written, any more than I tell you about my business affairs. I'm sure that you've already written hundreds and hundreds of pages.'

'It's not a question of quantity. And to prove it, I've a wife no bigger than this.'

(She had reached her destination and was now snuggled right up against him, with her mouth pressed to his throat, on a level with his Adam's apple, like a vampire. The round swelling of her hip was now fitted in against his stomach and from his hardness between her fingers and against her thigh she was certain that he wasn't really indifferent to her . . .)

'Lizzie, apparently you're not supposed to talk about

these things. You're supposed to keep them to yourself, not even to think them, or only with great shame. I don't give a damn, and I've never felt ashamed. I always made love to Taddeuz with passion. I treated Taddeuz to every kind of lovemaking I could think of and I don't think there was much I left out. He wasn't backward in that respect either, let me tell you. He had even more ideas than I did; there was no limit to his inventiveness. We fuelled each other . . . Once – I can tell you, it was so long ago now – once, in a lift, in a hotel in Chicago, I think it was . . . Between the ground floor and the sixth floor . . . Well, there was no lift attendant. And all the time there was that delicious danger that the door might open and someone might come in. Well, you might at least blush, you Australian ostrich! And she's laughing, the beanpole!'

'Do you miss Europe, Taddeuz?'

'A little.'

I'm sure he's realized . . .

'How good is this Henry James that you're always talking about?'

'He's a very good writer. One of the world's greatest.'

'But he lives in Europe, although he's American. What does he have against America? And what about the fellow who wrote the story about the frog and the one about the young boys?'

'Mark Twain.'

'You called him Sam.'

'He writes under the name of Mark Twain.'

'Is he a great writer too?'

'Without any doubt. Will you stop wriggling?'

'Only if you take your hand away, you cheeky fellow. No! Don't take it away, I was only joking . . . Oh Taddeuz, you beast, that isn't fair.'

There was a long pause. But the little mechanism inside her head started working again.

'You're closer to James than you are to Twain, aren't you?'

'I'd like to be.'

'I'm sure you're worth two of James. At least.'

'And why not four while you're at it?'

'I love you.'

'I know.'

At that moment she was really on the verge – she almost had to bite back the words – of telling him about A. B. C. Dwyer. Perhaps not of telling him the whole story, but of vowing that no other man would ever . . . But, in a way, she knew that would have been worse than saying nothing: she had caught the look in Taddeuz's eye when she had said, 'I love you.' It was there only half a second, not even that, but even in that brief space of time the usual dreamy veil over his eyes had dropped and the real Taddeuz had shown through: alert, analysing everything, weighing even the silences, noting every shade of intonation or the slightest hesitation. There was nothing to be done about it, that's the way he was, and she probably wouldn't have loved him so much had he been any different. *But all the same, it makes things damned awkward sometimes.*

'We can go back to Europe, Taddeuz. Whenever you like.'

But she knew what he was going to say. And he said it.

'No.'

'Do you want to stay?'

An interminable silence followed, enough to make one's ears ring.

At last he spoke: 'It's possible, just possible, no more than that, that I might in fact make a trip to Europe. But I'll go alone. Unless you have nothing better to do. Which is not the case. Hannah? Are they really serious, these problems of yours?'

'If I hold out to the bitter end, I run the risk of losing

every last cent I own. I could lose everything. Even my European assets. Even those in Australia. The lot.'

'You'll start again.'

'I wish I could be so sure.'

'You are.'

She considered this, while gently nibbling his lower lip and equally gently gyrating her stomach, with him still inside her.

'That's true,' she said.

In less than five seconds, in a lightning sequence of ideas and images, she pictured herself ruined, walking through New York in the rain – *why the devil in the rain? Why not barefoot in the snow while you're at it?* – and with no earthly possessions apart from her old dress with the thirty-nine buttons that she had always taken with her, wherever she went, for the past ten years. Walking through New York and starting again; just as she had in Sydney, in fact – dollar by dollar, pot of cream by pot of cream. It might even be fun . . .

She looked Taddeuz in the eye (she would have had difficulty doing otherwise: he was on top of her and their noses were touching).

'You know me pretty well, don't you?'

'Well enough.'

'And what am I thinking right this minute?'

He smiled.

'Not for another five minutes at least: I'm no superman.'

'Would you like to bet on that?'

Bernard Benda consisted basically of a gold-framed pince-nez perched on top of his long, thin frame. Behind the lenses were the sharpest pair of eyes a person could ever hope to see. An immigrant from Posen in Prussia, his father had served as a doctor in the Confederate Army during the Civil War before becoming Professor of Medicine and Surgery at the University of Columbia – Dr Simon Benda was the first surgeon in the world to attempt and successfully perform an appendectomy.

Three years earlier, at the time of the Spanish-American War, Bernard Benda had already shown evidence of the exceptional rapidity of his financial reflexes: during the night of 3 July 1898, a telephone call from a journalist friend of his informed him of the American victory over the Spanish at Santiago in Cuba. The next day, 4 July, being an American national holiday, Wall Street was naturally closed. But, nothing daunted, he remembered that you could buy American shares on the London market, which was open. He hired a train to take him from the depths of New Jersey – where he had been planning to spend a quiet Independence Day – and rushed back to New York, just in time to contact the City by telegraph as soon as the London Stock Exchange opened (in his haste he forgot the key to his office and had to break down the door). He spent the next few hours frantically buying. And twenty-four hours later, in a feverish American market rocked by a huge wave of rises in response to the victory, he sold, making enormous profits.

He stared at Hannah.

'Do you have any idea how much this is going to cost you?'

'I need two-thirds of the Carrington-Fox shares, plus one. According to the laws of New York State, that will give me the necessary majority to force through the sale of any part of the company's assets.'

'And then you'll sell that building to yourself.'

'Right,' said Hannah.

'So that you can knock it down straightaway and build another one in its place.'

'Right. Are you in favour, Bernard? Will you go along with me?'

Benda threw a glance in Maryan's direction.

'He's in this too, of course?'

'Of course.'

'I don't know off-hand how many Carrington shares there are.'

'Maryan?' said Hannah.

'161,727,' said Maryan.

'And you need two-thirds plus one . . .'

'In other words, 107,818, plus one, is 107,819,' said Maryan. 'We already have 32,000. We need another 75,819.'

There was a short silence. Then Benda said: 'Naturally you're aware that such extensive buying is going to force the price up?'

'That's obvious.'

'At a rough guess, it'll take one and a half million dollars. On top of what you already put into it.'

'I was reckoning on a total of $2,200,000,' said Hannah.

It had taken her nineteen days to raise the money. She began by setting aside the seven hundred thousand dollars she had left.

She still needed another $1,100,000.

Polly Twhaites managed to find them for her. Not without having begged Hannah to give up this insane project while there was still time. He finally got a London bank to come up with the money, on terms that he was ashamed to accept, but it was the best he could do in the very short space of time she had allowed him. The British bank advanced the money on condition that it was secured by the whole network of salons and shops, as well as the factory and the training schools . . . and the patents . . . and the house on Long Island.

'And then,' said Bernard Benda, 'assuming you achieve

your aim, and once the fever has died down, these same shares will probably be trading, at best, at their original price, perhaps even slightly below that. You're going to lose an awful lot of money. And you will still have to buy this building from the company of which you will simply be the majority shareholder. May I point out to you that this is the worst business deal I have ever heard of and that it will no doubt go down in the Wall Street annals?'

He smiled.

'You may,' she said. 'But I can't help wondering why you have omitted to mention one fact that is not without interest . . .'

'I really don't see what that might be,' said Benda.

'The reason for your contribution to the operation. Any good broker would have been able to do the job. Instead of which, I enlist the help of the most intelligent man on Wall Street.'

'You flatter me in the most outrageous manner,' said Bernard Benda.

But he removed his gold-rimmed pince-nez, very carefully wiped them and finally replaced them on his nose.

'It must be contagious,' he said. 'The most horribly Machiavellian notion has just occurred to me . . . Could it be that we've both had the same idea?'

Hannah explained herself.

Silence.

'God Almighty!' Benda finally exclaimed.

He smiled at Hannah again and said: 'Just as I feared, all my illusions are shattered: a woman is capable of behaving just as discreditably as a man. I hope you don't object to the word "discreditably"?'

'Not at all,' replied Hannah.

All in all, she felt *very* pleased with herself.

'And I was *very pleased with myself, Lizzie. I thought I was being fiendishly cunning and incredibly intelligent. I*

was delighted with Benda's reaction. After all, since Bernard Benda, whom everyone agreed was a veritable financial wizard, had given me his backing and thought me Machiavellian, how could I have doubted it? Lizzie, the years have gone by. Bernard is dead, like the rest of them, like all of them except you and me, who are just a couple of old ladies now. Yes, I know, you're younger than me, but nevertheless you're a great-grandmother, may I remind you . . . The years have gone by and when all is said and done, although I used to loathe her, I feel a certain affection for Hannah as she was in 1901. I find it hard to recognize myself in her: she was a pretty little monster. Very eager, passionate, selfish and generous at the same time, with thoughts only of Taddeuz as far as her love-life was concerned, and otherwise dreaming only of finance, the fool, as though it were some kind of Eldorado, not having realized yet that her destiny lay elsewhere – I've never been anything but a shopkeeper at heart . . .

'The Hannah of 1901 was unlucky, though, in running into that wretched A. B. C. Dwyer, out of thousands of others in New York at that time. She could have started with – I don't know – a Benda or a Junior Rockefeller, why not? Perhaps not with Junior himself, but with one of the countless businessmen working for him. She might have played the New York Stock Exchange, speculated a bit, and lost a little or made a little – under normal circumstances she wasn't a gambler. She would have had some fun before realizing that she had better things to do, and that this was not for her . . . But no. It had to be Dwyer. Oh, how I hated the man!'

At the very beginning of April, Taddeuz left for Europe. Including the time spent travelling, he would be away for almost two months. There was an unpleasant scene just before he embarked on the *Compagnie Générale Transatlantique* vessel, the *Lorraine*. She wanted to know whether he had enough money to cover all his expenses. He said yes. On any other occasion she would have accepted this highly laconic response. But with their separation imminent and doubtless, too, feeling jealous in advance at the thought of those hordes of European women, French and Italian especially, who were bound to pounce on him, she insisted: 'Taddeuz, I know that you haven't any money, this is ridiculous. Where are you going to sleep? Underneath the arches?'

She made every effort to slip twenty thousand dollars into his pocket. With a polite calm that was infuriating, he refused to take a cent. She lost her temper and flared up, all the more so since he kept his cool, as usual . . .

'Go to hell!'

She almost added, with all the venom she could summon up: *You're bound to find some woman who'll keep you*. The enormity of what she had thought chilled her to the marrow and reduced her to silence. She watched him get out of the Renault, in which she had driven him to the dock, and walk up the accommodation ladder of the *Lorraine*. She quite unashamedly chased after him. She ran after him, like a woman possessed, along the first-class corridors and, after trying two cabins, finally found him.

He was waiting for her, naturally having anticipated what she would do – *He'll drive me mad!* He was hiding, standing tall and straight behind the door, so that when she opened it she couldn't see him and thought he had already gone in search of a pretty young fellow passenger to brighten up his voyage. But he very calmly stretched out one of his large hands, stroked her cheek and opened his palm, revealing a wonderful black pearl.

'You see, I did have some money,' he said.

She almost burst into tears and clung to him passionately until the ship's siren called on her to return to shore.

He wrote to her that same evening, and the next day –

the first day of his crossing – and every day after that: one, sometimes two letters a day, the whole time he was away; written always with wonderful tenderness.

He stayed a while in Paris. In Germany he met someone who had been at the Sankt Pölten army officers' training school with Rilke, a certain Robert Musil, *'who has begun writing a splendid book, Hannah, although he's only twenty. He intends to call it* Die Verwirrungen des Jünglings Törless (Young Törless) *and it's going to be a masterpiece . . .'*

Then Taddeuz travelled round Spain (he liked it but not as much as Hannah, who preferred it to Italy) and also to Florence, where he did some research. He visited London before returning to Paris, where his European trip was to end.

However, at no point in any of his letters did he ever write, 'I love you.'

I suppose that goes without saying, she thought.

All the same.

By mid-April the concerted raid on Carrington-Fox shares was well under way. There were seven different buyers operating without knowledge of each other. Not one of them knew Hannah: they were all recruited by Benda.

'Let's not deceive ourselves,' said Benda. 'Not being a congenital half-wit, Dwyer cannot fail to be aware that a concerted attack is being made on the shares of his company. The important thing is that he should not guess too soon that you are the heart and soul of the operation, Hannah. It would be perfect if he found out only when it was too late, but we mustn't expect miracles.'

The share price rose steadily, despite all the precautions taken, to dangerous levels: events were making a nonsense of Hannah's calculations. As early as 7 April, when only a little more than 58,000 out of the required 107,819 shares had been acquired, the average value had risen to over $20.

In other words, the $1,100,000 I managed to get out of the British bank won't be enough, she was forced to admit.

Worse still, the price was still climbing: on 16 April the price was $21; four days later it had reached $21.50.

And she had more than reached her own limits. Having tirelessly checked and rechecked her figures, she had to face the facts: she had exhausted all her funds, and though she now had 82,000 shares in her possession, she still needed over 25,000 more in order to obtain a two-thirds majority.

Lost to shame, she called Polly Twhaites, asking for his help. All he could offer her was £50,000 of his personal fortune.

She refused it.

I'm virtually ruined.

'Don't say anything, Maryan.'

He shook his head, shifting his weight from one foot to the other as he always did when he didn't really agree with her. 'But it just isn't normal,' he said. 'No one on Wall Street has mentioned the continuous and wholesale buying of Carrington shares; no newspaper has given it so much as a line.'

'It's not a big company and it's not quoted on the Stock Exchange.'

'That ought to be the reason. But all the shareholders we've been approaching are aware of what's been happening and they're refusing to sell, except at a high price. They know.'

'So do I,' she said bitterly.

And of course she did know the explanation for this phenomenon: there was no doubt that Dwyer was working behind the scenes. *That son of a bitch hasn't got the means to confront you directly in a battle for the shares – perhaps he won't stoop to fighting openly against a woman.*

So he settles for making you have to pay a high price for them. By alerting potential sellers . . . Or perhaps, having got to these sellers before you, he bought their shares himself in order to sell them on to you now at an enormous profit. You're making him rich – that beats everything!

'Are you going to give up, Hannah?'

'What do you think?'

'You'll never give up, not even with the barrel of a gun at your temple. Hannah, I can lend you three hundred thousand dollars. Perhaps even four hundred thousand.'

This was the third time he had offered her money.

'The answer's still no, Maryan.'

'I've spoken to some bankers: they would be prepared to offer you a bigger loan than the British bank, on better terms.'

'But you'd have to stand surety for me. No. If I have to go under, I would rather go alone. Let's say no more about it, please.'

Again he shifted from one foot to the other.

'In that case I have another solution.'

'If it's as foolish as the others, forget it.'

'I would like to buy Carrington-Fox shares on my own account.'

'I was wrong. Your other suggestions were foolish; this one's different – it's crazy.'

'I think not,' he said calmly.

Silence.

She studied him. *What's he up to now?* Not for one second did she doubt – she had never doubted – the friendship and probably the affection he might have for her. But she knew that he knew that she would never agree to involve him in her folly. And she remembered what Bernard had said about Maryan: in business he was the coldest and most lucid man ever seen in New York. 'Sentimental as a guillotine,' were Benda's exact words.

'It means you wouldn't have to buy so many, Hannah.

Of course, as soon as I become a shareholder I shall vote in favour of your selling the building to yourself.'

'And you'd buy Carrington shares at $21.45?'

'Ah no. But at $20, yes.'

'In other words,' she said, 'I'm the one who's supposed to sell you these shares?'

'I don't see where else I would find them at that price,' he replied.

'In that case, I'll sell them for $18, and not a penny more.'

Because now she could see quite clearly what he was getting at. Cautious, cold Maryan was certainly coming to her aid by bringing her new funds that she was in desperate need of and without which she would have to call off her offensive the very next day . . . but he was doing it in such a way that she could hardly refuse. *He'll tell me that he's making a profit at my expense and that I don't owe him anything . . .*

'Nineteen,' said Maryan. 'Not a cent less. It's my last offer.'

'And how many do you want?'

'Fifteen per cent of the two-thirds: 16,173 shares. At $19 plus expenses, that comes to . . .' (he lowered his eyelids for a moment or two while he did a mental calculation) '. . . $307,287, plus $1,856, equals $309,143 – total.'

'Do you really have as much money as that?'

'I've made arrangements,' he said.

'Bend down, you fool.'

She kissed him on the cheek.

'You still haven't told me where you and Lizzie are going for your honeymoon.'

'The details aren't all fixed yet,' he said.

'But I'm sure that you already know which country you're going to, and how, and the date and time of your departure, to the minute, and when you're coming back and via which route, and what you'll be wearing, socks included, and what will be on the menu each day, and what the degree of humidity will be . . .'

'That much I do know. It's the rest I still have a few doubts about.'

And he takes the mickey out of you!

She immediately brought Maryan's money into play. With this sum and the little money that she still had, by late afternoon on 22 April she reached a total of 98,951 shares.

She still needed another 8,868. At $21.45 apiece, that came to the modest total of $190,218.60.

I have the 60 cents, and at a push the $218 – although I might get the electricity cut off for not paying my bills – it's just the rest that I don't have. Where the devil am I going to find $190,000? I've got nothing to sell at that price, apart from my jewellery and my paintings. I'd sooner sell myself . . .

The night of 22–3 April was a trial. She spent it alone – her maid, Yvonne, was asleep – in the apartment on Fifth Avenue, only a few rooms of which had been furnished. If for a moment she entertained the thought of forgetting the whole thing, it was not for very long: she quickly dispelled the idea, furious with herself for even envisaging this possibility. *And in any case, it's too late now . . .* Not being able to sleep, she wandered through the mostly empty and echoing rooms, in which the smell of fresh paint hung in the air. Strangely – even she was surprised – she did not feel at all despondent. In four weeks' time the loan from the British bank would fall due, which meant that if she didn't pay back the whole amount in the time agreed, she would lose possession of everything that it had taken her all those years to build up . . .

It's the patents more than anything else that upset me. I took such care to make sure that I wouldn't be robbed of them that they will act as a brake on me when I have to start all over again . . .

Pull yourself together now!

She started writing another letter to Taddeuz, but very soon abandoned it: the words just wouldn't come. *It would be quicker to send him a telegram: 'Come home. Am ruined. At last we can be happy. PS Find money to feed us.' You're making light of it, but what else can you do? Hang yourself?*

Finally, at dawn, she played her last card. She got Bernard Benda out of bed, an hour later he was with her . . .

Three times he refused her . . .

He finally gave way when, after having offered him shares at $18, then $15, then $12, she offered them to him at $10 apiece.

'Bernard, you know better than I that at $10 you're getting a good deal. Even if the shares drop once this little skirmish is over, they'll be worth more than that. But there's one condition: you give me a written undertaking not to oppose the sale of the building when you, Maryan and I control two-thirds of the company.'

He smiled.

'As a shareholder I shan't oppose your purchase. But I warn you: I shall insist on your paying a reasonable price.'

'One hundred thousand dollars is the price you yourself said was reasonable.'

Another smile. 'That was when I was on the other side, in your camp, and I was putting myself in your position. A vendor obviously sees things differently.'

'How much?'

'One hundred and eighty.'

'Merciless, aren't you?'

A third smile.

'This isn't a game of croquet we're playing on a fine summer's afternoon. I'm dealing with you exactly as I would have dealt with a man. Although on reflection, I might perhaps have forced a man down to $9.'

'I would never have agreed to that. I would have knocked on the door of every banker in New York and I would have found one to give me $10.'

He studied her.

'I think you would have done.'

'Bernard, thank you.'

'You've no reason to thank me. We have simply struck a deal, between financiers.'

Bernard Benda bought 20,000 shares at $10 a share from her. After expenses, this was the amount she needed in order to buy the 8,868 shares she was still short of – at $21.45. And then she would finally reach the critical two-thirds.

She activated the brokers and threw into battle everything at her disposal.

Someone rang the doorbell. In the absence of Yvonne, who had the evening off, Hannah answered it and found herself face to face with a tubby little woman of indeterminate age, with fat bloated cheeks, unpleasantly thin lips and hard, vaguely scornful eyes behind her glasses.

Without a word, she held out an envelope. It was addressed to 'Mrs H. Newman,' and the 'Mrs' was underlined twice. The message was signed *ABCD* and it was short: *Stay at home tonight and wait.*

'What's the meaning of this?'

The woman with the hard eyes sat down in a Duncan Phyfe armchair. She laid her fake-pearl purse on her lap: she was clearly intending to stay.

'Who are you?' asked Hannah, at that moment torn between a rising anger and the urge to laugh.

'I'm his secretary, Emily Watson.'

You remember her: she was the one who saw you into the office in Columbus Circus.

'Sorry to have made your acquaintance,' said Hannah. 'Now get out, fat face.'

Those ugly, thin lips curled into a little smile: 'He told me that you would try to throw me out. All I'm to say to you is, 8,867 shares.'

Silence.

Hannah needed only half a second to catch on: 8,867 was just one short of the number of shares that she . . . that the brokers would have to buy to attain the two-thirds majority.

Just one short.

The bastard!

'I see that you understand,' said Emily Watson. 'It's clear from the expression on your face. What made you think you could outwit him? Who do you take yourself for?'

The telephone rang. Hannah lifted the receiver. It was Maryan, explaining in his unruffled voice that a problem had arisen: the brokers had bought the shares that were needed . . .

. . . but they were just one short.

Just one.

'I've checked, Hannah, as you can imagine. We have completely exhausted the list of potential vendors, with the exception of Dwyer himself, and there's nothing else we can do. Of course I don't think it's any coincidence. According to the brokers . . .'

'I know.'

Just to get out these two words took an incredible amount of self-control. It wasn't even anger she felt but the panic of a trapped animal. *In the name of God, get a grip on yourself, Hannah!*

'I'll call you back tomorrow,' she managed to say to Maryan.

She hung up. And for the next minute it was all she could do simply to stop her hands from trembling. She started pacing round the apartment, not having the courage to face that dreadful woman who was still sitting in the armchair, no doubt continuing to smile. *If I see her, I'll kill her.*

She went into the bathroom and wet her temples and the back of her neck.

The telephone rang again. It was Maryan once more, a little worried by her earlier terseness.

'Your voice didn't sound normal. Is there something else wrong?'

'I just need to be alone. Everything's fine apart from that little hitch. Speak to you tomorrow.'

This time she managed to control the modulation of her voice. Besides, everything was beginning to return more or less to normal now. She went back to the drawing room where Emily Watson was waiting.

'You've been put in your place, haven't you?' sniggered the Watson woman. 'You've been brought down a peg or two! A woman! I ask you!'

'I'd like some explanation as soon as . . .'

'A woman and a silly Jewish peasant! Who thought she could get the better of him!'

'. . . as soon as you've finished braying. You've one of two choices, Watson: either you explain yourself clearly, or else I'll throw you out of the window. I'm not as big as you, but I'm a lot nastier.'

'Filthy Jewish whore!'

'Do you have a preference for any particular window? At any rate, they're all on the sixth floor.'

You measure all of four foot ten inches, she thought, *but even if you were twelve feet tall you would still be faced with the same insoluble problem: he's got you right where he wants you with that one blasted share. And you haven't the time to sit it out, with those nice English bankers waiting to cut your throat and two million dollars in shares that aren't even worth the paper they're printed on . . .*

'I had my back against the wall, Lizzie, as never before. I could have screamed . . . But right from the start I knew what I was going to do. With hindsight, after fifty years and more, you see things more clearly, perhaps a little too clearly for comfort. The Hannah I was in 1901 was a right little tramp . . . Well, what do you think? More or less consciously one evening in Philadelphia she had contrived to make sure that Taddeuz would be away from New York, not even in America. I've never known whether or not it was with his connivance. Perhaps. He was incredibly perceptive where I was concerned. He was away, full stop.

'And do you want to know the truth? The Hannah of 1901 had a tiny yen to get a closer look at Mr A. B. C. Dwyer. Even though she was madly in love with Taddeuz . . . I know, it is rather complicated, but that's the way it was. So much so that right up until the last, she didn't know, even deep down inside herself, which of the two solutions she had in mind she was going to opt for.'

'What now, you lump of lard?' asked Hannah.

'We wait,' crowed Emily Watson. 'He said to wait.'

Towards nine o'clock, Hannah, who was dying of hunger (all her life she would have a monstrous appetite, but would never gain so much as a pound) went into the kitchen and very calmly prepared a very good steak fillet and potatoes for herself. *You're the worst cook in America, but at least you shan't be dishonoured on an empty stomach!*

As she sat at the kitchen table, she sensed a presence and turned round to discover Watson staring at her with hatred. *Perhaps you were supposed to feed her as well?*

'Hungry, fat face?'

No reply, but there was a murderous look in her eye.

'Well, so much the better,' Hannah went on lightly, devouring the remains of a strawberry tart, 'because there's nothing left to eat. What a shame! While I think of it, has Dwyer ever laid you? Never, eh? I thought not. It must be hard being so near him day after day without his ever trying to lay you. I can see that it must be fairly intolerable for a woman, if that's what you are.'

She conscientiously licked her fingers. *You've just made yourself a friend for life here, there's no doubt about it . . .*

Nevertheless, deep down inside she was trying to suppress an increasing nervousness. *Whatever happens tonight, you're lining yourself up to do something that you will regret for the rest of your life . . .*

At eleven o'clock the doorbell rang. It was a huge Irish-looking fellow who stood there, twisting a cap in his hands. He behaved as though Hannah was transparent while his eyes searched for Emily Watson. As soon as they found her, he nodded wordlessly.

'Let's go,' said the secretary.

The town brougham, drawn by a single horse, finally came to a halt in front of a small three-storey building; only the second floor had lights on. Hannah noted that the vehicle didn't leave after she and Watson got out.

It was a small apartment, barely three rooms, and really only the bedroom was furnished, but very frugally, almost ascetically: it was a man's bedroom and a bachelor's at that. There were some books, mostly about trains, locomotives, railway networks and the fantastic future of rail travel. A few dealt with finance and banking. But in the midst of all this technical reading, as incongruous as a prostitute in an assembly of presbyterian pastors, was the Marquis de Sade's *Justine*, in one of those English editions that circulate clandestinely. A vein in Hannah's temple started throbbing urgently. *You knew there was something slightly out of the ordinary about the look in Dwyer's green eyes . . .*

'When will he come?' Hannah asked Emily Watson.

'When he wants to. Get undressed.'

Hannah's nerve was beginning to fail her.

'Get undressed,' said Watson again, noticing that Hannah hadn't stirred.

Well, here you are, Hannah. You're going to have to choose now. It's either the one solution or the other . . . The first option or the second.

'He said that you were to get undressed!'

'Help me.'

'I'm not helping any Jewish whore.'

Hannah closed her eyes. *Keep calm . . .*

'We society ladies, Jewish or otherwise, never undress ourselves. We have either a servant or a lover to do it for us.' She smiled. 'And you really don't look like a lover, Watson . . .'

And she thought: *There you are! You see, you can do it if you keep your cool . . .*

That evening she was wearing a spring coat in the shape of a cape that had three layers of flounces and a quilted wrap on the shoulders. On her head she wore a very pretty boater with lots of ribbons and a veil.

'Well, I can at least manage that,' she said.

She removed her coat and boater, and began to peel off her gloves.

'Keep your jewellery on. He said you were to keep it on.'

She put on her Sarah Bernhardt-style bracelet again (a jade-encrusted gold serpent that wound down the back of her hand).

'I can manage that much, but you'll have to help me with the rest.'

She sat on the bed and stretched out her feet, on which she wore little ankle-boots.

'Take them off yourself,' grumbled Watson.

'In that case, I shall sleep with them on.'

Watson had to admit defeat.

'Keep your stockings on.'

Hannah stood up and turned round, so that Watson was obliged to unbutton her dress for her.

It fell to the ground with a rustling of silk, followed by one, two, three, four, five petticoats, then the first of her shifts. She wore no corset, of course, she had never worn one, nor one of those new brassières that had just been invented.

'Take everything off,' said Watson fiercely.

'Nothing doing.'

They eyed each other scornfully. Hannah smiled.

'Obviously no man has ever made love to you, my dear. They adore undressing us, half the pleasure lies in stripping each other.'

'He said you were to take everything off. He wants you naked.'

'I don't care what he said. I know better than you what he wants.'

Again they confronted each other, but Watson couldn't hold her gaze. *She's almost been put out of action*, thought Hannah, who was now wearing only a very short shift with a plunging square neckline through which the points of her breasts showed, and a pair of cambric and Alençon lace bloomers tied at the knee with two red ribbons. Underneath, the garters she wore to hold up her stockings were just discernible.

'And what else did Mr Casanova Dwyer say?'

'That you were to lie down on the bed.'

'I'm lying down. What else?'

'That you were to loosen your hair.'

Lying flat on her back on the counterpane, Hannah raised her hands, reaching for the long-toothed Vever ivory comb, the top of which was carved into leaves and mistletoe berries, that, together with a few pins, held in place her heavy chignon, which formed a large soft crown on her head, leaving her neck bare.

But she withdrew her hands without doing anything to loosen her hair.

'The same holds true for my hair – you'll see, he'll love doing it himself. And now?'

'We wait.'

'Lizzie, the Hannah of 1901 had come up with two solutions. And whatever she might have thought, she had not yet chosen between them.

'The first was to let Dwyer have his way with her. No, no, you mustn't think that absurd . . .

'The second was tucked behind the garter on her right leg. It was a jolly nice razor, with a very sharp edge, nearly eight inches long – and she hadn't decided what she would do with it when the amorous Dwyer leaned over her undressed for battle: simply cut his throat or cut off a much lower part of his anatomy, one on which these gentlemen pride themselves so much . . .'

After half an hour of lying there, with her hands behind her head, Hannah got up, eyed coldly by the other woman. She went over to examine the books once more and decided on the Sade. She came back, lay down on the bed, and started to read. She was on page 100 when at last there was the sound of an automobile engine outside . . . Then the sound of a key opening a carriage entrance . . . Then footsteps on the stairs; the footsteps of a man.

Another key turned in the apartment door. Emily Watson stood up and went into the drawing room next door, closing the bedroom door behind her.

A short discussion followed, but Hannah could not make out the slightest word.

Then the Watson woman reappeared, with a savage joy burning in her eyes.

'Get dressed,' she said. 'He doesn't want you. He thinks $21.45 is still too expensive for a Jewish whore.'

She rummaged in her purse, drew out a key and a fifty-cent coin, and threw them both on the bed.

'The money's your payment and the key is to lock the door when you leave. If you feel like locking up . . . there's nothing here of any value.'

She heard the sound of departing footsteps as they both left together.

Although she ordered herself to do nothing of the sort, Hannah dragged herself over to the window. She saw A. B. C. Dwyer at the wheel of the car and his secretary getting in beside him.

Even the one-horse brougham had disappeared.

Twenty minutes later, some policemen walking their beat called out to her. They asked her what she was doing, alone, on the edge of Central Park, with a razor in her hand.

She did not reply, her big grey eyes staring into space.

But eventually, after they pressed her with questions, she gave them her address. This, and the clothes she was wearing, which were really not those of a prostitute on the prowl, together with the mask-like expression on her face, persuaded the police: they took her home and left her there, after she had given them the razor and they had watched her open the door with her own key.

The worst of it, without any doubt, was having to talk to Maryan and Bernard Benda the next day as though nothing had happened; having to suffer their curious looks – she looked like death – and to listen to them working out methods of counter-attack. Naturally she didn't tell them anything. As far as they were concerned, it was simply a matter of finding some way out of this extraordinary situation.

'Unique in the annals of the New York Stock

Exchange,' said Bernard Benda with a laugh, in the vain hope of making her smile.

That one share, just one, should be of such inordinate importance!

She hadn't slept. She hadn't even been able to swallow a crumb at breakfast. Yvonne was astounded by this. And yet, by virtue of going over and over in her mind every second of the night she had been through, something happened: her sense of humour returned. She still felt bitter, but it would only be for a matter of days, if not hours. The little mechanism inside her head began to function once more and gradually picked up speed.

All right, so you still don't have that blasted 107,819th share and you didn't cut his . . . moustache . . . off either. But on the other hand, neither did he get you. At the last minute he didn't have the guts – and I'm not saying this to console you, Hannah, I know that it's true, and so do you. All the rest of it – the insults and even that fifty-cent coin – has got Watson written all over it, I'd stake my life on it . . .

This interminable interior monologue that went on, even during Maryan and Bernard Benda's visit, calmed her down. They eventually left, anxious and surprised to have found her looking rather frantic to start with and then very abstracted.

Her tremendous level-headedness restored to her, the little mechanism was from now on going to run in top gear. Hannah was applying herself. To any problem, there are always plenty of solutions – this had always held true so far, why should it be any different now? It was only a business matter, a question of pride. Nothing anyone could die of, even if the humiliation was considerable . . .

So she refused to eat any breakfast, feeling much too tense, but in the afternoon she was prepared to respond to Yvonne's suggestion of a little tea and biscuits, after all . . .

But when the snack arrived, she stared at it as though it were a heap of poisonous snakes.

'What's this rubbish? Take it away and bring me something substantial. What do you mean, you don't understand? I'm hungry – what's so extraordinary about that? Give me a few slices of that leg of lamb, and some vegetables. Haven't you cooked some chicken vol-au-vents? I want some. And cakes. And wine – some champagne.'

Why don't you get drunk? You haven't tried that yet. Damn it all, though, it is intolerable. If you were a man, you would have been able to persuade yourself, with plenty of irrefutable arguments, that you were sacrificing yourself by sleeping with that big green-eyed brunette – that's Dwyer turned into a woman, since you would be a man – and you wouldn't be suffering the least remorse, or at least not much. How many men have fooled around like that, with less good reason? Don't even think of what Taddeuz might be doing in Europe, if you please . . .

And yet the idea that you could have been unfaithful to him makes you feel sick. Because you don't know what you would have done with your big razor. Would you really have cut off his . . . moustache? You'll never know.

Yvonne arrived with her meal, and she was just about to attack it when she froze, as though struck by a thunderbolt.

'Hannah, what's happened, what's wrong with you?'

'I've just had an idea,' replied Hannah.

The next day, nineteen days before her bank loan fell due, she went with Maryan Kaden to see Louis Rosen, the king of American railways who had so enraged J. P. Flint and Roger Healey. His last confrontation with them had been backed up with so many million dollars that anyone would have been impressed. And he won: snaffling up in one night, or near enough, two thousand miles of lines, stations, warehouses and rolling stock belonging to one of the biggest railway companies and, of course, coveted by the other two.

'And why should I be interested in this trifling Carrington-Fox company?'

'All I ask is that you should take an interest in me, a poor feeble woman lost in a man's world.'

'Unless I'm very much mistaken, you don't at all consider yourself a poor feeble woman.'

'I'm much feebler than you think, but less so than I consider myself. Or vice versa.'

He laughed. He wasn't good-looking, but his wolfish smile was not without charm.

'Simon Guggenheim asked me to see you and to help you,' he said. 'Insofar as I am able. What can I do for you?'

'Buy one thousand Carrington shares.'

'From whom?'

'From A. B. C. Dwyer. He's the chairman of the company. You will offer him $25 a share.'

'And how much are they actually worth?'

'At the moment, $21.45. But usually round about $11 or $12. Maybe $13, not more.'

'And why should I be so extravagant?'

'Because I'm the one who'll be paying the $25,000.'

'That explains everything. I understand less and less. And the expenses?'

'I shall pay the expenses too. I'm going to sell you two thousand five hundred shares in the same company for $10 a share, in other words for $25,000.'

'Plus expenses.'

'No. This time, you'll pay the expenses. There's no need to carry things to extremes. But you won't give me the $25,000; you'll keep it to buy the thousand shares from Dwyer at $25 apiece.'

'You amuse me enormously,' he said after a short silence. 'This isn't business, it's intrigue. What if we were to say $8 rather than $10? And the expenses to be borne by you?'

'You pay the expenses. But I'm prepared to go down to $9.75.'

'Nine?'

Without turning round, she asked: 'Maryan, how many shares at $9 each do you get for $25,000?'

'About 2,777,' replied Maryan, almost instantly, as though he had spent the whole of the night doing this calculation ten times over.

'And what about expenses?'

'The expenses come to $65.'

'So that's 2,777 shares altogether, plus expenses,' said Rosen, laughing. 'It's not the end of the world.'

'The $65 are yours to pay, Mr Rosen. And I shall sell you the shares at $9.25. How many shares would you get at that price, Maryan?'

'Around 2,703,' said Maryan.

'I'm really enjoying this!' said Rosen. 'It's a deal at $9.25.'

'But there's one condition,' said Hannah.

'This is turning into a real hoot. What's the condition?'

'I want a written undertaking that, once you're in possession of the 3,703 shares – Dwyer's thousand plus mine – as well as any other Carrington-Fox shares you might take into your head to buy, you promise to vote with me when it comes to authorizing the sale to Mrs Hannah Newman – that's me – of the building situated on Park Avenue that currently belongs to Carrington-Fox. On the understanding that the sale will be made at a reasonable price agreed by the two parties.'

'I can hardly contain my laughter,' said Rosen. 'You're doing all this just to buy that building?'

'I can be very obstinate. There's one question that you haven't asked me . . .'

'Your eyes are a veritable miracle of nature, Mrs Newman. I don't know what question I've forgotten, but let's assume that I've asked it.'

'Why should Dwyer sell you the one thousand shares that he's refused to sell to me?'

'I'm eaten up with curiosity: why should he?'

'Because you're Louis Rosen and because he will think, simply because you've appeared on the scene, that his two-bit company stands every chance of becoming the prize in a new battle between you on the one hand and Messrs Flint and Healey on the other. He will deduce that the shares he holds will increase tremendously in value.'

Louis Rosen leaned back in his armchair. Clearly he was thinking, and devilishly fast.

'I see,' he said. 'You have tried to obtain a two-thirds majority in order to be able to sell that building to yourself, but you have not succeeded, is that it?'

'Yes.'

'And you think that Dwyer, once he has this new information, will be careful not to tell anyone in case it turns out to be true, and that he will come and see you, and tell you that his refusal to sell you the building was nothing more than a fit of ill humour, or a practical joke; that he is now ready to say yes and to make peace with you . . . and that he will even buy back from you, at a good price, all or some of the shares you have bought needlessly?'

'Yes,' said Hannah with a smile.

Silence.

'It's intrigue all right – of extraordinary complexity!'

'Will you buy the thousand shares?'

'Only if you'll have dinner with me – I'd like some lessons in intrigue.'

'I and my friend Lizzie MacKenna, the fiancée of Mr Kaden here, will be very happy to dine with you. As it happens, we were looking for someone to pay the bill.'

She and Maryan emerged from Rosen's office, and she got behind the wheel of the Renault. Contrary to her usual practice, she did not drive off as though pursued by bandits. She moved off very slowly, with a patient smile inviting the assembled onlookers to get out of the way.

'Do you think he's swallowed the bait, Maryan?'

'He said yes. I think he'll keep his word. People usually do in business.'

'What's he going to do now?'

'Buy the shares and sign the undertaking you asked him for. But first of all he's going to make enquiries into Carrington-Fox, in case it's worth a bigger investment than those one thousand shares.'

'And he's going to find out about those Northern Star Pacific shares. There aren't very many of them, but they might put ideas into his head, mightn't they?'

'Perhaps. Usually it is Doug MacGregor who does that kind of investigation into a company for him. I've made arrangements to be notified the minute MacGregor makes a move.'

They drove on, Hannah accelerating gradually as the wild fever of battle rose within her.

'You're going too fast, Hannah.'

'Are you referring to my driving or the way I'm handling this affair?'

'Both. I'd prefer to be alive for my wedding. It made sense what Rosen said: wait until Dwyer comes to see you and tries to buy as many of your shares as he can. You'll get the building and your money back, with interest.'

'Maryan, Dwyer doesn't have the money to buy all my

shares. And I'm not so sure that he'll want to. I'm not so sure at all.'

To tell the truth, she secretly hoped he wouldn't want to. Now that she had engaged the enemy, she saw no reason why she should bring the battle to a speedy end. She was getting so much pleasure out of it.

No, she would proceed as intended, and adhere to her original plan in its entirety.

Now, having seen Rosen, she was going to pay a call on J. P. Flint, Rosen's deadly enemy.

John Patrick Flint was as tall and thin as Rosen was sturdy and squat. Without the letter of introduction from Junior Rockefeller, he would certainly not have received Hannah.

But receive her he did. He listened to what she had to say, tapping his long white banker's hands on his desk top with polite impatience; he did not interrupt at any point, and seemed not to see her, in fact, so vacant was his gaze. Before long, already rising to his feet to indicate that the meeting was at an end, he said no, that he was sorry (he didn't look at all sorry), that a man in his position could not afford to get involved in such deals, not even to be of assistance to a personal friend of John Davidson Rockefeller II (Flint was clearly wondering whether the fellow wasn't mad, cultivating such business friendships with a woman, a Jewess at that!).

She was out of the office and the double doors had closed behind her before she even realized she was leaving.

'He gave away nothing, Maryan, he didn't bat an eyelid. And he controlled his hands perfectly. I don't even know whether he heard me when I said that someone whose identity I was unaware of was buying up Carrington shares . . .'

. . . and was thereby preventing her, a poor defenceless

woman, from acquiring that building where she could manufacture her creams.

'I'm certain he heard you, Hannah. I know him slightly, I've dined at the same table as him. He's anything but a fool. Even if you didn't pull the wool over his eyes as to the real purpose of your visit – especially if you didn't – he is going to try to find out all he can about this Carrington company.'

'I'm a genius, is that what you're trying to say?'

He smiled for the second time that year.

'For a woman, yes!'

'Get out of the car so that I can run you over!'

Then she asked: 'Who is MacGregor's opposite number in Flint's outfit?'

'There are two of them: Sam Waters and Felix M. Lehmann.'

And of course he was keeping an eye on them as well.

The visit to J. P. Flint had taken place two days after MacGregor, Louis Rosen's right-hand man, had submitted to his boss a doubtless very comprehensive report on Carrington, and less than twenty-four hours after Rosen had gone ahead and bought from Dwyer five thousand shares at $20 a share: 1,250 of them with Hannah's money.

In theory, with Rosen's 5,000 shares and her own, Hannah now controlled well over the necessary two-thirds majority – but, since her capital assets were still frozen, she didn't have the money to purchase the building on Park Avenue.

Besides, what use would acquisition of the building be if it had to be forfeited to the bank in London?

But there was an even more conclusive reason why she acted as she did: the incredible cataclysm that was going to instil such panic into Wall Street was already on the way.

'The devil take me if I had any idea at the time of what was coming, Lizzie . . . Or the scale of it, anyway . . .'

There were fourteen days left before her credit with the bank expired (she had a meeting with the bankers fixed for 6 May).

And things were happening at a staggering pace.

The visit to J. P. Flint took place on 22 April. The very next day Maryan's spies reported that Waters and Lehmann, Flint's secret agents, had also made a move.

'They've been making enquiries about Carrington, Hannah, just as you predicted,' Maryan told her. 'And they've discovered that, one way or another, you weren't lying to their boss and that we – that's Bernard, you and me – are among the largest shareholders. And Dwyer of course . . . And above all they have found out that there are 2,800 Northern Pacific Star shares among the company's assets. Everything's developing as you hoped it would . . .'

When the market closed on 23 April, Carrington shares were trading at between \$20 and \$21.

Northern Star, which was quoted, was trading at \$141.6.

Forty-eight hours later, Northern Star had risen to \$152.7 and 1,026,112 shares had been traded.

In other words, the market value of Northern Star was over \$156 million – approximately seventy times the value of Carrington-Fox. *We're in a completely different category here*, thought Hannah. *This really is a game for grown-ups – people taller than me, at any rate . . .*

'Who's buying, Maryan? Rosen or Flint?'

'Rosen. Flint set sail for Europe yesterday. He has probably left instructions, but we don't know what they are. Bernard couldn't find out anything more than that.'

'What about Roger Healey, where's he?'

'Somewhere in Oregon.'

'Do you think that Rosen has deliberately launched his attack while he can take advantage of the other two clowns being out of the way?'

'More than likely. He's always very quick in making up his mind.'

Bernard Benda, on the other hand, was in New York. In the late morning of 25 April, he turned up at Hannah's; Maryan was already there. Bernard was very chipper: he had just sold Louis Rosen the 19,000 Carrington shares for which he had paid Hannah $10 each: he had more than doubled his outlay.

'And I haven't in any way hampered your own stratagem, Hannah, since Rosen has undertaken to support you in buying the building. What bothers me slightly is having made this money at your expense . . .'

'Bernard, this isn't a game of croquet we're playing on a fine summer's afternoon, as someone said to me recently.'

He smiled.

'You could sell your shares for a large profit, too, if you wait a bit.'

'Why didn't you wait?'

An even broader smile this time.

'I think I'm going to need a lot of liquidity. Hannah, there's a great opportunity to make money . . .'

'By buying Northern Star?'

'Good God, no! Certainly not! You should only buy when shares are falling, it's a golden rule. Even though I'm sure they're going to rise a lot higher. According to my information, Rosen is thought to have a buying order worth ten million dollars. Do you know what preference shares are?'

'They differ from ordinary shares in that the directors of the company concerned can at any point exercise their option over them. Satisfied with your pupil? Rosen is looking for preference shares. He aims to gain control of Northern Star. But Flint and Healey are not going to let him get away with it.'

'I very much doubt it. Northern is one of their finest jewels. We are going to witness . . .'

'What did you just say?'

'That Northern Star was one of the finest jewels in Flint and Healey's empire. Why?'

'You mean that Northern Star belongs to Flint and Healey?'

Hannah, you must be dreaming!

Now it was Bernard Benda's turn to stare in astonishment at her. 'Don't tell me you didn't know? Flint and Healey own Northern Star inasmuch as they have a majority shareholding. I thought you knew that!'

'Well, I'll be damned! And who would I have heard it from?'

Maryan made himself small. 'It must have slipped my mind, Hannah. I thought you already knew . . .'

Bernard Benda was practically weeping with laughter. 'So you unleashed this cataclysm without even knowing it? Oh Hannah, there ought to be a statue of you put up on Wall Street!'

'I noticed that there were some Northern Star shares in the Carrington portfolio, and I'd been told that this darned Northern Star was a large company: I thought that would be enough to draw them like flies – Flint, Rosen and what's-his-name . . .'

She was gradually overcome with uncontrollable laughter. Soon she was convulsed with giggles and her eyes filled with tears. And the thought went through her mind, increasing her mirth: *Good God, Hannah, you get mixed up in finance without knowing the first thing about it and you score a bull's eye!*

'In any event, my plan worked like a dream!'

And she was immediately seized with another fit of

giggles. Even Maryan almost joined in (he was smiling, which was the third time he had smiled that year). As for Benda, he had to sit down. He eventually calmed down, although he was still overtaken now and again with a little burst of renewed laughter.

'Hannah, we're going to witness a battle between these gentlemen that is going to make the previous two seem like mere skirmishes, I'd swear to it. Do you want some advice? If, as we can expect, Flint and Healey go on the attack against Rosen, Northern Star are going to become extremely scarce on the market. With one result in my opinion: other shares are going . . .'

'. . . to rise too.'

'I think they're going to drop. Thousands of brokers are going to be caught up in the turmoil. They will start shedding what they value most, the Stock Exchange's *crème de la crème*, the tried and tested shares that have never really fallen in value in living memory, the so-called blue-chip stocks. Which are going to drop. Does my reasoning appeal to you, Hannah?'

'To be perfectly honest, I think it's completely twisted, and downright apocalyptic. What do you think, Maryan?'

'I agree with Bernard.'

'I ought to buy up blue-chip stock as it's falling, is that what you're saying?'

'Exactly,' said Bernard Benda, his eyes shining with intelligence.

'I haven't any money left in any case.'

'Sell some or all of your Carrington shares to Rosen. Even at a loss. Besides, you can bull the market by paying only ten or even five per cent of the amount actually involved.'

She wavered. 'Are you going to do it, Maryan?'

'Yes.'

She wavered and then said no.

'It was all decided at that point, Lizzie. I have never

been a financier, I've always had a horror of borrowing money. Similarly, the idea of bulling, as they say, by buying and selling things I didn't really have the means to pay for, was distasteful and frightening to me. And I don't have any regrets . . .'

'Has Dwyer sold his own shares?'

According to Maryan, he was waiting, convinced that Carrington shares were going to increase in value in the wake of Northern Star. Once he had sold Rosen the original five thousand shares, Dwyer had rejected all his subsequent offers.

'I'll wait too,' said Hannah.

On 26 April, Northern Star climbed to $178.1 – as a result of the discreet offensive conducted by Louis Rosen. But, as Hannah was to find out, this was not the only reason.

Carrington-Fox was estimated at around $28.

'Why don't Flint and his friend do something? A rise like that ought to alert them . . .'

'Hannah, the market as a whole is going up, everything is rising. Northern Star perhaps a little more than average, but not spectacularly,' explained Bernard Benda. 'Both Flint and Healey would pay dearly to learn that the principal buyer of Northern Star preference shares – and such a discreet buyer at that – is in fact Louis Rosen, their sworn enemy. But no man on Wall Street, of the very few in the know, would have the nerve to tell them . . .'

On 26 April, Hannah still had 68,942 Carrington shares. She had abandoned all hope of acquiring the 'damned building' through the shares.

But her determination to get the better of Mr A. B. C. Dwyer – *the devil take him* – was in no way diminished.

And that day she did something that she would not reveal to anybody, not even, for the moment, to Maryan Kaden: partly because she was ashamed, partly because she was beginning to get fed up taking advice from everyone, from all these fine gentlemen who knew it all. Anyone would think she was completely daft . . .

Through the highly discreet intermediary of Zeke Singer, she sold all her shares to Louis Rosen.

Which, after expenses, gave her the very attractive sum of $1,918,000.

'Zeke, if you breathe a word to anyone, even in your sleep, we shall never work together again.'

Nearly two million dollars. This was an enormous sum for Hannah, who was not fabulously rich, like a Flint or a Rosen. But the main thing was that it was amply sufficient to allow her to settle her outstanding debt with the British bank. And she would end up with a profit of $200,000.

Now calm down, eat a plate or two of the sauerkraut Yvonne has prepared for you – it's as light as anything and will clear your head – and think. By yourself. Like a big girl.

Zeke Singer was a very nice young man with fair hair, who looked much younger than his age (he was the same age as Hannah). This didn't prevent him from being employed by the famous firm of Kuhn & Loeb.

It didn't prevent him either from opening his eyes very wide. 'You want me to do what?'

'You heard me the first time: I want 10,772 Northern Star shares at $178 each. If you can get them for less, I shan't grumble, and in that case you can buy more.'

'Hannah, with all that money I could buy a great deal more. Not that I could get a better price than $178, in fact it will be a miracle if I can get them for that. But by bulling the market and using your $1,900,000 as a deposit, we could . . .'

They do annoy me, the whole lot of them, the way they go on about bulling the market! Hannah thought.

'No, Zeke, no. I shall never be a financier, that's one thing I've learned over the past few months. I want those shares, and I want them to be physically mine. No conjuring tricks. When I buy something I want to be able to hold it in my hands. And likewise when I sell. Now go and do as I say, Zeke dear.'

By the morning of the 28th, Zeke Singer had finally managed to lay hands on the 10,772 shares required, and not one more. He was astonished.

'Northern Star are not only rising, they're becoming incredibly hard to find. Anyone would think there had been a raid on them. Hannah, do you know something I don't know?'

If she had been the only one involved, she would probably have told Becky's brother-in-law the whole story. But she didn't feel entitled to divulge information that Bernard Benda had given her in confidence for the sole reason that he felt he owed her something.

She was nonetheless very fond of Zeke.

'Someone gave me a tip, someone very well informed. I haven't acted upon it myself, but if you'd like to . . .'

Without revealing Benda's name she told him what to do: buy blue-chip stock on credit while prices were falling.

'Thank you, Hannah.'

'You can thank me if it's successful.'

And you would be stupid enough to reimburse him if he loses money on it.

Zeke asked her if she knew how long it would be before such a spectacular drop in blue-chip stock was likely to occur. Without a moment's thought, she replied, with the certainty that only ignorance can confer, that it would be within ten to fifteen days. It was only later, after the young man had departed, that she realized that such assurance on her part was bound to make Zeke think that she was in possession of some exclusive piece of information of the utmost importance.

And the most extraordinary thing is that it's true: your

information is so exclusive that you're the only person in the world who knows about it!

Because you know what you're going to do! Hold tight, all you fine gentlemen on Wall Street, here I come!

She played her last card in the afternoon of 27 April, nine days before her meeting with the bankers.

Polly Twhaites had once again come rushing over from London. He was very worried and made no attempt to conceal it. He was all the more worried that Hannah wasn't at all anxious, or at least she didn't show it.

'Could it be that you've taken leave of your senses?'

'It's all a bit of a laugh.'

'Not for the London bankers, it isn't. They're not laughing at all: at least two groups of financiers are prepared to buy your business from the bankers, Hannah. At a price of well over two million dollars. I can't forgive myself: if I'd negotiated better, I could have got better terms for the loan they gave you.'

'No one gave me any loan – I've a horror of that word. And considering I gave you so little time to negotiate, I'm happy with the amount you got: if you'd got more out of those hyenas, I would have even more to pay them back today.'

'Because you still hope to pay them back?'

'Naturally. By the way, Polly, you did tell me one day that your mother and Winnie Churchill's mother were very close friends, didn't you?'

He had. Mrs Churchill, mother of Winston, was American; she and Mrs Twhaites were quite fond of each other. Why?

'Because Winnie's mother and Cynthia Healey are very good friends and because I want a meeting with Cynthia.'

He stared at her and realized what she was up to. Horrified, he exclaimed: 'Hannah, you're not going to do that!'

'Why shouldn't I! According to Bernard Benda, no man on Wall Street would dare. Luckily, I'm not a man.'

She suspected that she was going to trigger off a fair old upheaval . . . '*But not on that scale, Lizzie, no, really* . . .'

'And when do you want this meeting?' asked Polly.

'Yesterday. Sooner if possible.'

The meeting with Cynthia Healey took place on 29 April.

She was a very pretty woman of about thirty-five, who was a head taller than Hannah and a good hundred million dollars better off, with all the influence of a third-generation millionaire. Hannah's very first words made her raise her eyebrows: she knew nothing of her husband's business affairs, and was not in the habit of getting involved, especially . . .

She raised her left eyebrow a little.

'Jewish?'

'Japanese,' said Hannah. 'From the Tokyo synagogue. Madame, there are two reasons why I wish to speak to you. Firstly: if I go and see this Mr Daimler you mentioned, the whole of Wall Street will know of it; and if I telephone him, he won't listen to me. Second: it gives me a certain amount of pleasure to pass on this information, woman to woman, if only to annoy these men. Now, one of two things is possible: either you inform Mr Healey as a matter of urgency that a certain Louis Rosen is in the process of relieving him of his Northern Star Pacific, or you don't. If you do, remember, I have your word of honour that you will not be surprised if Mr Flint is rather unfriendly towards you for the next six years. Goodbye, madame. You have a charming house. Except that this Cézanne here is a forgery. I know: I have the original. And another thing: you will never get rid of those little spots on your wrists – and no doubt you have them on your legs as well – with a lotion scarcely fit for horses. I have what you need, and you have my address.'

On 1 May, Northern Star Pacific were trading at nearly $161.25. They had dropped 27 points.

'What does that mean, Polly? I'm about to be ruined?'

'Probably that your Louis Rosen has completed his raid on shares, that he is now the majority shareholder, or at least he now considers himself powerful enough to oust Healey and Flint from the company. Hannah, you did tell me that Rosen had acquired mainly preference shares?'

'According to Bernard Benda, yes.'

'Good heavens!' exclaimed Polly.

'What's that supposed to mean?'

'In order to gain complete control over a company like Northern Star – its statutes allow no room for ambiguity on this – it isn't enough to hold a majority of preference shares, you also have to have at least fifteen per cent of the ordinary shares.'

'And the shares I have, what are they?'

'Ordinary shares, my dear friend. If Rosen doesn't have that fifteen per cent, he won't have a majority. It will be Flint and Healey that do. On condition that they have at least fifteen per cent. And of course, that they have some, forty per cent of the preference shares.'

'You're joking.'

'I never joke when eating Kildare smoked salmon while talking to a pretty woman worth one hundred and fifty, or two hundred million dollars: that's the approximate value of Northern Star Pacific today.'

'It's impossible that Louis Rosen should be unaware of that!'

'I hope so, for his sake,' said Polly, his mouth full of salmon.

He swallowed.

'What news does female counter-intelligence have of Mr Roger Healey?'

'None at all. When last heard of, he was still in Oregon.'

And that other fool, J. P. Flint, would probably be strolling along the Promenade des Anglais in Nice, or the Piazza Narvone in Rome – *What do these wretched millionaires think they're doing, going on jaunts around the world instead of looking after their affairs?*

'Hannah,' said Polly Twhaites, 'you really have done everything to make these men do battle with each other. If Rosen has in fact made this mistake, if Healey returns in time, if they are all in fighting spirit, if all these conditions are satisfied, you'll have your battle. It ought to be a real blood-bath, my dear, you'll be entitled to feel pleased with yourself. A little more salmon?'

'Thank you for offering. I thought you were going to finish it all by yourself . . . Oh Polly, I'm frightened!'

On 2 May, Northern Star fell to $156. Hannah made her calculations for the ten-thousandth time: the shares for which she had paid $1,918,000 six days earlier were now worth no more than $1,680,432.

She had just enough to pay back the British bank. On condition that they weren't in too much of a hurry for the interest payments – and on condition she sold the shares before the price dropped any further.

However, she refused to do that, with an obstinacy she didn't try to justify to herself any more. She was hoping for a miracle, clinging to a fierce conviction that she was lucky. That said, she just couldn't forgive herself for having called on Cynthia Healey – she might just as well have contacted Ted Daimler, Healey and Flint's main agent. She might have had more trouble convincing him, but at least, if he had been convinced, he would have got his boss back in double-quick time.

In any case, it's too late now . . .

Her credit expired in four days' time. She had learned from Polly that representatives from the British bank would arrive in New York on a Cunard liner on Saturday 4 May in order to present their account on the 6th – and of course declare her insolvent.

That evening she wrote one of her two daily letters to Taddeuz, and for the first time dared to tell him: *I miss you so much, it's killing me, day after day, hour after hour . . . I have some business worries, they're quite serious . . . Will you still be catching the boat on the 9th? In that case my letter won't reach you, or not until later. How I would like it not to reach you! That would mean you were on your way home . . .*

Late in the afternoon of 3 May, Maryan called at the apartment on Fifth Avenue. He found Hannah and her French chambermaid-cum-factotum dressed identically in grey, stain-covered smocks and French policemen's cocked hats made out of newspaper: Hannah was busy painting one of the drawing rooms white.

'I had to send the workmen away,' said Hannah. 'We had a difference of opinion over the sordid question of money. Would you like to join us? There's another paint-brush.'

She seemed calm and cheerful, but knowing her the way he did, Maryan had no doubt that she was extraordinarily tense. While he talked, Hannah got on with her painting (she slapped it on with ferocity). He reiterated Bernard Benda's reasoning regarding blue-chip stock: forced to pay a high price for virtually unobtainable shares, the brokers would have to sell the prime constituent of their portfolios, the famous blue chips . . .

Why does he keep telling me the same thing over and over again? I understood the first time. Is he drunk or something?

'Nice reasoning,' she said. 'As long as the battle over Northern Star actually takes place. But Flint is in Europe and that moron Healey is fooling about on the Pacific coast.'

'Healey is in New York,' said Maryan in that quiet voice of his. 'He's been here for five hours. He arrived on a special train – they say he had all the traffic diverted to give him a clear run and that three locomotives were coupled to his train so that it would go faster. He's here, Hannah. He must have begun to suspect that something was going on . . . or else someone must have tipped him off.

'Hannah,' he went on, 'now is the moment to decide. Very few people are in the know as yet. Northern Star are going to rise, then the blue chips will fall. You ought . . .'

'I'm not going to sell my Northern Star shares,' said Hannah.

All evening she waited, playing dominoes with Yvonne. At one point she hoped that Healey would make contact, in order to thank her for the service she had done him.

Nothing.

On Saturday 4 May, she was almost ready to go the Netherland Hotel, just a stone's throw from her apartment. With less than forty-eight hours to go before her meeting with the London bankers (they had already arrived – *No danger of their damned ship sinking!*), she had already gone beyond the stage of panic and had reached that of imbecilic resignation, and though she reproached herself for it, she could not conquer it.

Polly Twhaites, who came to see her at five o'clock, found her writing again, this time to Mendel. The only address she had was the one Visoker had given her in San Francisco, the last time she had seen him: Hotel Darling, Dawson, Yukon, Canada.

'If he's still there . . . He's probably gone to Brazil by now.'

'Or else he's found a mountain of gold and bought himself a harem,' said Polly.

'Mendel would have no use for a harem. He only likes women he meets by the roadside, if possible at hundred-yard intervals.'

It was no good, her heart wasn't in it.

Polly bowed his head.

'Not too good, hey?'

'I couldn't feel better.'

He wagged a chubby index finger at her: 'I'm taking you to Carnegie Hall this evening. They're playing Liszt. He's Polish, isn't he? Since my dear wife stayed behind in England to look after our English offspring, I shan't be able to find a lady of my size to accompany me . . . There'll be six of us. Afterwards we'll have supper and go dancing . . .' (wagging his finger once more) '. . . and tomorrow we'll go boating.'

'I'd as soon go hang myself.'

'As an Englishman, I'm ashamed to admit it, but I also have a horror of anything that floats. But we'll go all the same. There'll be some very interesting people at this boating party.'

Something in his voice made her fix her grey eyes on him. He smiled kindly.

'It occurred to me that no banker, not even a Scottish banker, would hold a charming woman with whom he had gone boating on Sunday to the expiry of a secured loan on Monday.'

And then, having examined his family tree, Polly had managed to find a cousin of his, of truly astounding imbecility ('Even my other cousins have noticed it, which just goes to prove how much of an imbecile he must be'), who by the most amazing stroke of luck – a case of mistaken identity no doubt – was something like the Governor of the Bank of England.

In short, he had got her a reprieve of four days, which was better than nothing.

Before eight, on Monday 6 May, Maryan met Bernard Benda outside the New York Stock Exchange. Together they went straight to the arbitrage room, which opened two hours before the trading floor – these two hours were intended to plug the gap between the closure of the London market and the opening of the New York Stock Exchange. Two minutes before the starting signal was given, Ted Daimler appeared, flanked by three assistants. 'If Ted comes,' Benda had said, 'that means there's going to be an enormous onslaught. He's Healey's number one man and he's also in Flint's confidence . . .'

Daimler was a fat, red-faced fellow, who wore old-fashioned bifocals with a fine gold rim, behind which his eyes glinted with suspicion.

With a great deal of nonchalance, Benda told him that he and his friend Kaden had come to buy American shares on the London market.

'Northern Star shares, Ted, to be perfectly open with you. They have dropped a bit during the last couple of days but Kaden and I think they'll go up again. A hunch we have.'

And he showed Daimler buying orders for a total of more than thirty thousand Northern Star shares.

The man in bifocals searched his face, then looked hard at Maryan. With a jerk of his chin, he sent his assistants to take up their combat positions, then led the two men aside. With obvious reluctance, he explained that 'something was up', which he wasn't at liberty to talk about but which meant that buying Northern Star shares now would set the whole of the American banking establishment against them, in particular a certain J. P. Flint, not to mention the problems they might encounter with the brokers, of whom he, Daimler, was one of the most eminent representatives.

'Obviously this isn't a question of making any threats, Bernie. I am talking to you as a friend. You're both young, it's never a good thing to make enemies when you're starting out.'

'I'm overwhelmed by your friendliness,' replied Benda. 'But there is a solution, Ted: you tell us what's going on, we swear we won't breathe a word to a living soul, and we'll sell you the shares that we were about to buy, at cost price. OK, Maryan?'

Maryan confirmed his agreement, unperturbed.

A short silence. After which Daimler, beating about the bush as if he were trying to tell them that he was suffering from some shameful disease, disclosed the reason for his being here at such an early hour of the day: Healey had instructed him to buy up all the Northern Star shares he could lay his hands on. The reason for his haste, not to say his feverishness, was that 'two-bit broker' Louis Rosen, who had been buying up preference shares in the company without realizing that he also needed ordinary shares in order to attain a majority.

'Bernie, let me give you some fatherly advice: if you cross me now I shall hate you until my dying day . . .'

'God forbid,' replied Benda.

Twenty minutes later, having handed over to Daimler the thirty thousand shares at cost price, Maryan and Bernard Benda concluded a forward deal for sixty-five million dollars' worth of blue chips in a bear market.

'You're going to be a very rich man, Maryan.'

He shifted from one foot to the other. Eventually he nodded, in the manner of someone who learns that his knowledge is his undoing.

'My main regret is that you didn't want to go along with us, Hannah.'

'We shan't discuss that again.'

This was just a statement. Without any intended mockery or, even less, scorn. She herself couldn't really explain what was going on inside her. All she could see was that in the fourteen months she had been in America she had done practically nothing – *Apart from getting mixed up in high finance and causing a terrible rumpus, which is probably not the kind of thing that's going to win me any medals*.

Perhaps it was Taddeuz's absence, and more to the point his silence – she had not received a letter from him for six days – that was wearing her down, but there was also something else: a crazy desire to spread her wings again, and go racing from one salon to the next, all over the world, the need to be creative and enterprising in an area of activity that she was meant for.

The effects of the wholesale buying conducted by the two adversaries soon made themselves felt, with the price of Northern Star rising from $180 to $195 in the course of a single day; and the blue-chip stock falling as panicked brokers began selling.

'What's your stake in the game, Maryan?'

'It's not a game.'

'You can say that again! How much?'

'About three and a half million dollars.'

'You don't have that much money!'

He didn't. He had bought on credit, by placing a deposit.

'Hannah, it's not too late, you could still . . .'

'Stop pestering me, will you?'

That same evening, no doubt in an attempt to check the panic, Louis Rosen's chief of staff announced that the battle was over and that there was nothing to prevent a return to normal: their client now had a majority holding in Northern Star.

But less than an hour later, furiously rubbing his bifocals on the inside of his jacket, the enemy's general, Ted Daimler, refuted this with a great fanfare of trumpets: 'The majority is held by my clients, Healey and Flint!'

That's not true! thought Hannah. *They're like Warsaw street urchins holding a stone to their shoulder and defying their playmates: 'Bet you can't make me drop it!'*

Nevertheless, these two completely contradictory statements mainly served to demonstrate that the gigantic battle was still in progress. The panic became ten times greater. Shares that had nothing to do with the clash were dragged into it, without anyone being able to understand why, unless it was the general panic.

'You ought to come and watch,' Polly told Hannah.

He had taken her to dinner at the Waldorf-Astoria. The atmosphere in the restaurant, the bars, the hotel lobby could well have been that marking the end of the world. As people walked past each other, those who weren't completely pale and haggard tried to make light of it: 'Are you broke?' Hannah heard herself ask the same question at least half a dozen times. At one point a couple, whose name she had forgotten but with whom she had once dined, told her their story: they had most of their money in real estate and they had been forced by the panic to sell their four buildings for a pittance, simply in order to buy Northern Star at $425. The famous millionaire Gates told her that he had lost – and he was laughing as he spoke – forty million dollars in a single day.

'Well, Hannah?'

'Well, what, Polly?'

'How does it make you feel?'

'I don't understand, my dear Polly.'

'I think you understand me very well. If it weren't for you, there would perhaps have been no battle and we would not be living through what will no doubt be called Black Wednesday in the crash of 1901.'

'All that I wanted was to . . .'

'Get the better of a certain Mr Dwyer, the man with the alphabet name. At least you're persistent. I hope that Dwyer will be able to accommodate all these millions that you've earned him.'

'Don't annoy me, Polly.'

'Very well, Hannah, my dear. Are you hungry?'

'I'm extremely hungry,' she said.

Northern Star was trading at around $485 by midday on Thursday the 9th, then at $700 at two o'clock, and $1,000 an hour later.

This time Maryan, Bernard Benda and Polly all went on the attack.

'Hannah, do you know how much 10,772 shares at $1,000 each are worth?'

'$10,772,000, of course. Minus expenses.' She smiled at them.

And when they explained, almost in tears at not being able to convince her, that with ten million dollars-plus she could buy herself twenty or thirty buildings, she replied: 'I know, but that's the one I want.'

And most of all, you want that wretched Dwyer's hide . . .

'Mrs Newman? I couldn't get here any earlier,' Louis Rosen said. 'I've had a rather busy day.' (He smiled his big wolfish smile.) 'And indeed a busy week. But you may perhaps have heard about it?'

'Vaguely,' she said.

She laid down her Waterman fountain pen – it was black and Turkey red – engraved with the double H of her first name. Then consulted the little watch that she wore on a chain round her neck, between her breasts; it was a little after 11.30 P.M.

'May I sit down?' asked Rosen.

'Forgive me. Of course. Tired?'

He had bluish rings round his eyes and looked as if he hadn't slept for months. *The very image of the financier on the night after the battle*, thought Hannah.

'A little,' he said.

'Are you married, Mr Rosen?'

He stared at her in astonishment. He said that he was and that he had two children.

'Or to be more precise, last week I was married and had two children. I don't know what's become of them since.'

'Who won?'

'The battle for Northern Star?'

'Well, I already know the outcome of Vicksburg and Waterloo.'

'I'm afraid it's not that simple,' he said.

They fell silent, while Yvonne served them – a whisky for him and a drop of sherry for her.

'Thank you for coming, all the same,' said Hannah.

He fixed her with a glance over the rim of his glass.

'How many Northern Star do you have?'

'10,772.'

'If you had sold them when the market closed this afternoon . . .'

'I didn't. Who won the battle, Mr Rosen? You or them?'

He put down his glass.

'You were the one who tipped off Healey, weren't you? No, don't answer that, it's no longer of much importance. Quite a few things happened this evening. For a start, I received a personal message from the President of the United States, then two delegations, one from the brokers on the New York Stock Exchange, the other from the whole banking establishment. They also called on Roger Healey. We were asked to stop, to lay down arms.'

He picked up his glass again and emptied it.

'The same again?' asked Hannah.

'No, thank you. That's what we've done, Mrs Newman.'

'Hannah.'

'That's what we've done. There are some requests one can hardly refuse. Besides, I got partly what I wanted: Healey, Flint and I will in future share the seats on the Northern Star Pacific board.'

'And Carrington-Fox?'

He shook his head.

'You really are the most incredibly obstinate human being I have ever met, Hannah. You realized that . . . what's his name?'

'Dwyer.'

'. . . that Dwyer would refuse to sell me the rest of his stake in Carrington, didn't you? By the way, why didn't you settle the matter of the building right after he sold me the five thousand shares?'

'I didn't have the money to pay for it then.'

'Forgive my scepticism, but I doubt that's the real reason. You surely could have found $150,000 or $200,000 somewhere.'

'Well, the fact is that I didn't.'

'If you say so. One should always believe what a lady says. The sole purpose of the visit you paid me was to get me to join battle. You reckoned on my finding out about those two thousand five hundred Northern Star shares in the Carrington portfolio . . . Just as you expected me to engage in hostilities. I can't believe what you managed to pull off: that fool Healey and I committed $150 million to this takeover battle, and almost caused a full-scale market crash for the sole reason that a little lady with big grey eyes wanted to buy some two-bit building. Who would believe such a thing were possible?'

'Will I get my building?'

'Dwyer eventually sold his shares: he is no longer chairman of Carrington. But I wasn't the one who bought them. It was Healey who won that particular bout. I offered him $42, Healey got them for $45. Carrington-Fox now belongs to Healey, Flint and me. I have fifty-one per cent, they have the rest – that's part of the overall deal we made.'

'Would you agree to sell me that building for $150,000?'

He started laughing.

'If by doing so I could be absolutely sure of getting rid of you, I would willingly give it to – I'm joking, of course.'

'Of course. But it's a shame, I love presents. Will Healey agree to it?'

Rosen stood up. Yvonne reappeared in the same instant, bringing him his hat.

'I really don't see why he should refuse. It seems to me that you did him a service.'

He was on the threshold of the drawing room, a stocky man, but not without distinction (one of his sons, after a high-flying career in finance and banking, would become a senator and later special adviser to several American Presidents, finally ending up as ambassador extraordinary). Again he nodded.

'May I ask you an impertinent question, Hannah?'

'Be as impertinent as you like.'

'Who the devil are you? Where do you come from?'

'I make creams and perfumes for women. And I sell them.'

'How much did you put into this whole affair?'

'Everything I had: over two million dollars.'

'You inherited money?'

'Not yet.'

'Are you intending to get involved in railways again?'

'Not likely!' she exclaimed, with a laugh.

'And finance?'

'No.'

'Praise be to God!'

He said this with the utmost conviction.

'Creams for women?' he said, thinking out loud.

'I'll give Mrs Rosen a good price, I promise,' said Hannah.

The tenth of May, the day when everything was to be wound up, began very early, at about 7.30. Although Hannah hadn't been able to get to sleep until 2.30 A.M., she was already up when Maryan Kaden arrived, followed shortly afterwards by Polly Twhaites. Both brought the same news: an emergency body had gathered the night before and taken steps to restore calm and halt the mad race towards catastrophe; all deliveries of Northern Star had been deferred, and Rosen and Healey had both agreed to put back on the market a reasonable number of shares, and the price of those shares had been fixed by the authorities at $260.

'I know all about it, Polly. I can sing you the details if you like.'

He stared at her, very disconcerted.

'Two hundred and sixty dollars,' said Polly. 'Do you realize what that means! They were trading at $1,000 yesterday afternoon.'

'She knows all about it,' Maryan told him calmly.

She offered them bacon and eggs and, true to habit, burned everything she put in the pan. *It's my destiny*, she thought, *until the end of my days I shall always be the worst cook in both hemispheres*.

In the end she chucked the sad product of her culinary experimentation into the rubbish bin, produced from underneath the sill of the window overlooking the courtyard a Virginia ham stuck with cloves, and extracted two bottles of Dom Ruinart from the icebox.

'Nearly eight million dollars lost in a single night,' Polly mused bitterly. 'What are we celebrating?'

'My building,' said Hannah. 'I've got it. Show him, Maryan.'

Maryan produced a document to which were appended the two signatures of Louis Daniel Rosen and Roger Gardner Healey, Chairman and Deputy Chairman respectively of Carrington-Fox Railway Company, confirming the sale to Mrs Hannah Newman of a building situated on Fifth Avenue, for the sum of $132,500.

'The price agreed was $150,000,' explained Hannah, with her mouth full, 'but they gave me a discount. One of them because he claimed I had done him a good turn – I really don't see it – the other because he was so pleased to get rid of me. Would one of you two gentlemen like to open the bottle of champagne? I'm thirsty.'

And she also told Polly that she had no more shares in Northern Star Pacific. By now Bernard Benda had no doubt already sold them; in fact he was bound to have sold them – you could rely on him in such matters . . .

'For $270 each. Ten dollars more than the official price but a certain Mrs Cynthia Healey had interceded with her husband – I wonder why? Perhaps because I sold her a cream for some spots she had . . . Anyway to cut a long story short, Mrs Cynthia Healey told her husband that he ought to pay me ten dollars more per share for the shares he was buying off me. All the same, he's not doing too badly, according to Bernard Benda. Once things return to normal, Northern Star shares will fetch more than that, but anyway it was kind of him . . . By the way, what does 10,722 shares at $270 each come to?'

'$2,908,440,' said Maryan, half a second later.

'Is everything clear to you, Polly?'

'As crystal,' said Polly, spitting out his coffee.

'Will that be enough for the English bankers?'

'I think so. You owe them $1,100,000.'

'I did some calculations last night, Polly. With all this coming and going, how the devil was I supposed to sleep? Since 20 January last, I've invested $1,665,899.70 of my own money in this affair, as well as the $1,100,000 from your banking friends in London, plus expenses, which, according to my figures, come to $26,849. Are you with me?'

'I was just about to ask myself the same question,' said Polly.

'$2,792,748.70 in all,' said Maryan, who was busy getting the cork off the champagne.

'2,792,748.70 from 2,908,440 leaves . . .'

'$115,691.30,' said Maryan.

'Added to that there's the $32,500, of course. In other words, a total of . . .'

'$148,191.30,' said Maryan. 'Less $239.75 costs, equals $147,951.55.'

'Where the devil does the $32,500 come from?' asked Polly.

The moment he asked the question, Hannah just finished making an enormous sandwich containing four slices of ham layered with butter, gherkins and mustard.

She immediately made herself small, to the point where she became almost hidden from view behind the sandwich, and invisible to the golden-eyed gaze of the lawyer from London.

'She's already sold the building,' said Maryan very calmly.

'For $165,000,' said Hannah's voice. (Hannah herself was still hidden behind the sandwich.) 'Polly, I decided some time ago that I didn't really want the wretched building. The truth of it is that I thought it too big. I'm just a shopkeeper, after all. You're going to say . . .'

Polly opened his mouth. She didn't give him time to get a word in.

'You're going to say to me: why didn't I call the whole

thing off – yesterday afternoon, for instance, when Northern Star reached that crazy price? Quite simply because I wanted to let Dwyer have what was coming to him. Because I had to have that building, at any price, in order to prove to him that I was a damned sight more obstinate and smarter than him. And because yesterday afternoon I wasn't at all sure what Healey and Rosen, especially, were going to do. After all, Rosen could very well have been annoyed with me. But no, they both came here last night, one after the other. Healey even brought me some flowers, enough to fill four rooms, and he brought his wife with him – she's going to be one of my first clients, as soon as I open my salon.'

'Good gracious!' said Polly.

She finally lowered her sandwich. If she had been clowning around a little so far, her grey eyes were now filled with a chilling fierceness.

'And I got it, the son of a bitch! I got his damned building! I sold it because I wanted to! I'll have a copy of the document that Maryan showed you taken round to him first thing this morning. Of course, that's not enough, I haven't finished with him yet. I shall wait as long as it takes, fifty years or more if need be, but I'll get him. And he won't get off any the lighter for having to wait for it!'

Two days later Taddeuz arrived.

CHAPTER 4

The Pink Brigade

Taddeuz disembarked two days later, just as though he had timed his return for the moment the battle was over. Of course, this was not the case. He could not have foreseen when it would end: during the final days of the conflict he was in the middle of the ocean.

In the end Hannah had not sent him the letter in which she told of the serious business problems she was having. However, after she had met him at the docks; after they had lunched with Lizzie, Maryan and Polly Twhaites – who was getting ready to return to London; after they had inspected both the house on Long Island and the big apartment on Fifth Avenue; and after they had made love together, then he asked her how business was.

She replied: 'Not bad at all. Why do you ask?'

'It's just an impression I had,' he replied nonchalantly.

'Someone said something to you.'

'Not at all.'

He was lying on his back, naked of course, and she, no less naked, lay curled up in his armpit, and right up against his hips with her cheek on his chest. She suddenly started to talk; she told him the whole story, or near enough; she left out quite a bit of the Dwyer episode, merely saying that he had refused to sell her the building simply because she was a woman.

'I almost lost everything, Taddeuz. I wonder what the expression on your face would have been if I had told you this morning that I no longer had a penny to my name?'

'What do you think?'

'I think that you don't give a damn whether I have any money or not.'

'Except that I know you like to have it. And I wouldn't have wanted you to be deprived of what you had created.'

'I would have started again, you told me so yourself.'

'And I still think so. That's life.'

'*You* are my life. Did you miss me, in Europe?'

'Three times a day, and twice as much on Sundays.'

'And apparently I almost caused the stock market to crash . . . A real crash, with tens of thousands of men ruined and driven to suicide. It was a close-run thing – I really went crazy. You wouldn't think I could be so fearsome, I look so small . . .'

With just one of his big hands he lifted her and slipped her on top of him, on to his abdomen and stomach, completely encircling her waist with his fingers (*You haven't got any fatter, it would seem!*).

'Were they pretty?'

'Pretty?'

'The one hundred and thirty-eight women with whom you were unfaithful to me?'

'Why not? You silly thing . . .'

She chuckled in delight. And started giving him a love bite on his neck. He protested that people would be able to see it, even if he wore a detachable collar and tie.

'That's the whole point,' she said. 'I want people to see it.'

'You could always engrave the word HANNAH on me.'

She asked him a question that had been on her mind from the moment he had disembarked. 'Are you here to stay?'

'Yes.'

'Are you going to write in English?'

'Yes.'

With a little hesitation, with that slight reticence – so slight it was hardly noticeable – that he always betrayed whenever he touched upon the subject of his work as a writer, he told her that he had actually started writing – a novel. In fact he had already written half of it. And another thing . . .

'On my return trip I was able to get better acquainted with a fellow passenger on the *Savoie*. His name is Hearst, William Randolph. He owns several newspapers. He promised to find something for me.'

She looked at him in amazement.

'You're going to be a journalist?'

'I don't see any harm in it; I even know some journalists who can read. But Hearst talked in particular about a column on the theatre and on books, on exhibitions . . .'

'Taddeuz, you won't have time to write!'

He replied that he thought, on the contrary, he would. And shut her up in the nicest possible way.

Lizzie and Maryan Kaden's wedding took place on 25 May. It gave Hannah the opportunity to realize how remarkably well Maryan the Taciturn had settled in America after barely two years in the country. She would never know exactly how much money he had made through speculating with Bernard Benda in the blue-chip saga. Three, if not four, million dollars was a reasonable guess, particularly in the light of the fact that Benda's profits on his own investment exceeded some fifty million dollars.

Hannah had expected a fairly simple ceremony, with just a few friends. At the beginning of April, although she was very taken up with her battle against Dwyer, she had offered to help Lizzie and Maryan get everything ready for 25 May. The couple, Maryan especially, had declined the offer with a rather irritating conspiratorial air – irritating for Hannah, that is, who still regarded them as her charges and her responsibility in every respect.

'I wouldn't want to interfere in any way,' she finally said, not without vexation.

And at once was angry with herself for her ill humour.

You're incorrigible, always trying to tell everyone what to do . . .

The fact remained that she was quite taken aback by the scale on which Maryan had chosen to celebrate his marriage (he had taken over all the reception rooms in the Waldorf and engaged four orchestras, a very surprising display of extravagance on his part), and also by the guest list. Apart from herself and Taddeuz, of course, who were to be witnesses, and apart from the Twhaites, the Guggenheims, the Bendas, and even Louis Rosen accompanied by his wife, as well as a large delegation of MacKennas who had come from Australia for the occasion, Maryan had contrived to invite to his wedding at least half of Wall Street and a truly impressive number of celebrities from every walk of life. Not least of whom was Thomas Alva Edison.

'You know Edison, Maryan?'

'I've met him three or four times. It's possible that we shall do something together one day.'

Maryan, who had thought of everything, planned on spending their honeymoon in Europe, France and Italy, but also in Egypt and Greece, visiting the whole of the eastern Mediterranean in a yacht hired from one of the Rothschilds.

'You and Taddeuz could join us – you must,' suggested Lizzie.

'I've a horror of the sea, as you know.'

'You're still sulking, that's the truth of it. Anyone would think you were the bride's father, being difficult with your son-in-law because he was going to rob your daughter of her virginity.'

'For God's sake, Lizzie, that's no way to talk! What if someone heard you?'

'And who taught me to talk like that, eh? Who?'

How could anyone resist Lizzie's extraordinary good humour? Hannah finally burst out laughing – imagining herself a moustachioed papa – once again rescued by her own sense of humour, which all her long life would enable her to withstand the burden of her strength of character and volcanic fits of anger.

The Kaden couple set sail, intending to be away for a little over three months. They would not get back to the United States until mid-September. There followed several unsettled weeks that would have been boring after the crazy excitement of the Dwyer affair but for Taddeuz's presence. Contrary to his expectations or, to be more accurate, to what he secretly hoped, Randolph Hearst actually kept his promise: in June, Taddeuz published his first articles. Even Hannah, who was not too good at reading and judging anything he wrote – after all, he had never entrusted her with any of his manuscripts and all that she knew of his writings were the poems that he had had published a few years earlier in Germany under a pseudonym – even she was struck by the tone of the articles: his lightness of touch was equalled only by the sardonic exhilaration he consistently displayed, and his pleasure in writing was combined with extraordinarily sound taste in art. She was astonished and at the same time amazed at her own amazement: after all, she had always known that he was talented.

'But how far have you got with your novel?'

'It's progressing.'

It would have been difficult to be more laconic. She did not press the matter, observing still the very solemn vow she had made: never to interfere in his writing.

And as the days went by, consumed more than ever with a need to be busy, she was able to keep herself occupied. She had not lied to Polly Twhaites: it was quite true that she had abandoned the ambitious plans of her first few months in America. She was no longer interested in a skyscraper on the top of which her name would be visible all over New York, or for that matter all over the world. She had fallen back on more modest tactics, more in keeping with her tastes and habits, and certainly more reliable. At the end of June she sailed for Europe – to Paris and London. At first Taddeuz had resigned himself to accompanying her, although he concealed his resignation wonderfully. But she had detected his lack of enthusiasm, if not reluctance, at having to interrupt his labours as columnist and novelist.

She left on her own, and spent three days in London and four in Paris – the time it took her to put together what she called the first detachment of her Pink Brigade. *Anyone would think I was recruiting staff for a brothel!*

She returned straightaway to New York.

'A pink brigade?' said Taddeuz in amazement. 'Anyone would think . . .'

'That I was setting up a brothel. I know. Did you miss me?'

'Why, have you been away?'

'You beast. Come here and let me straighten you out!'

She had an idea. As usual it was very definite. She had gone back to her original thoughts, those she had had before even setting foot in America: opening shops and salons like those in Europe here was out of the question. It would be stupid because, in this country, there probably weren't as many as five thousand women who regularly availed themselves of the services of a dressmaker: all the others were content to go to the large stores, and didn't care two hoots that the dress, or skirt, or blouse they were wearing had been mass-produced.

And if that was their attitude to clothes, as far as perfumes and creams were concerned . . !

'Taddeuz, I have no choice. The clientele doesn't exist. I have to create it. A woman will always need a dress, or a petticoat, and this and that to wear with it. Unless she's going to go stark naked, or worse still, wear men's trousers . . . How dreadful! Can you see me wearing trousers? Don't laugh, you wretched Polak, you're happy enough for me to wear rustling silk, with piles of lace everywhere, that you can put your big hands and all those fingers into . . . No, I'll have to start from scratch. It's not surprising: less than thirty years ago there was one woman for every three hundred inhabitants in the Wild West, so they respected her. And in order not to be taken for a prostitute, she would have died at the stake rather than put a little rouge on her cheeks. I'm simplifying things, obviously. But it's true that they're damned – sorry, very puritanical on this side of the Atlantic. Do you follow me? Because if I'm boring you, don't hesitate to let me know!'

She trailed after him round the apartment, like a poodle walking on the heels of a Great Dane, while he went to and fro, getting dressed. Now he went down on all fours in search of a collar stud. They were dining with a cousin of the Vanderbilts.

'They're puritanical, Taddeuz. And obsessed with respectability, with the fear of being taken for the immigrants that they are, or that their parents or grandparents were. A day will come perhaps when they will be proud of being a pioneering people, but for the time being what concerns them more is appearing to be more respectable than the most respectable Europeans. I'm going to have to teach them everything, and tackle the whole country town by town . . . it'll take as long as it takes – which is where my Pink Brigade comes in. There'll be six of them to start with. Jeanne Fougaril selected them. We didn't ask much of these girls: just that they should be very pretty, very polite, very elegant, very intelligent, very hard-working, always willing, capable of smiling for twelve hours at a stretch and of replying nicely to the most idiotic questions. And that they should be very well-qualified beauticians and have sufficient self-control not to crack up laughing if some fat old bag asks them how to make herself beautiful; and lastly they had to be able to speak English with a French accent even if their home town was Birmingham or Vladivostok . . .'

'And have a mining engineer's certificate and a degree in Tibetan,' said Taddeuz.

'Stop being frivolous, you're getting on my nerves. That's all I want of them. Your wretched collar stud is behind you, just under your left heel, as I've been telling you for the past hour . . . Anyway, would you believe it, in spite of these reasonable requirements, Jeanne Fougaril claims that it will take at least two months to train them. I'm very tempted to give her the sack. Kneel down, I'll fasten the damned stud for you . . . I was talking about Fougaril. I'd happily get rid of her, the trouble is she's the best director there could be, despite her damned awkwardness.'

'Wouldn't it be a good idea to get dressed?'

'Me? I've been ready for the past two hours, we can leave whenever you want. It's true that Fougaril is bloody-minded. It's lucky that I'm so accommodating.'

'Ha, ha, ha!'

'What's that silly laugh supposed to mean? I may be a bit brusque, but that's all.'

'Your dress.'

'What's wrong with my dress?'

'You're not wearing one.'

In the course of that summer, while she was preparing for her great North American campaign, they invented a game. Hannah had just taken delivery of two new cars, 26 horsepower Daimler Phoenixes. The two vehicles were identical in every respect, just as she wanted, except that one was white and the other completely black, although the black one had a turkey-red trim. Despite all her recommendations to the German manufacturer – and more especially to Emile Jellinek, a diplomat friend of

Taddeuz from Prague, who was Daimler's representative on the Côte d'Azur and whose daughter's name was Mercedes – she and Taddeuz were rather disappointed by the performance of their new racing cars: they had hardly been able to go any faster than forty or forty-five miles an hour. *We're crawling along . . .*

She decided to get the French Panhard and Levassor mechanic to come over from his native Ariège. She ordered him to increase the speed of both cars on pain of having to swim back home.

'The engines will explode,' Gaffouil, the mechanic, remarked.

'I shall explode if you don't get them to go over sixty miles an hour,' replied Hannah.

Of the two explosions, Gaffouil opted for the lesser and spent a whole month extending the wheelbase, lowering the centre of gravity, fiddling about with who-knows-what in the engines.

'But they're dangerous,' he warned.

'Not as dangerous as my wife,' replied Taddeuz on this occasion.

Finding a road on which to get up full speed in these death-machines was quite a business. Almost all American roads were mere tracks: there were only thirty miles of tarmacked road between New York and San Francisco (Los Angeles was no more than a large village). In the end, an association of amateur automobilists collected money and had a small 1,900-yard circuit built on Long Island.

Taddeuz held the lap record in the Newman family, and indeed over everyone else, at 66.8 seconds. Hannah couldn't even get close to this time; her best performance was 69.2 seconds.

This made her furious.

And that was what she . . . what they both spent their time doing, every Sunday, throughout the beginning of the summer of 1901. They took on other challengers, but the competition was slim. There were still very few people in New York whose cars could exceed 30 miles an hour. If Hannah and Taddeuz's races were almost exclusively conjugal, they were nonetheless dangerous. Some time at the beginning of July, when they were both driving at about 70 miles an hour, she tried to overtake him on the inside, on a bend. There wasn't enough room and in any case there was no sense in it, since the only correct way to take the bend was the way Taddeuz was taking it.

She hit him, sending him off the tarmac while her own car went into a spin: it was only by a miracle that she didn't overturn and have half a ton of Daimler land on her head. But Taddeuz was thrown out of his car, which did two or three somersaults. *I've killed him!* she thought, ready to die herself. She ran to him and found him lying on the ground, face down, his arms crossed, as though dead. She knelt down and leaned over him, on the verge of fainting, with only one idea in mind: *I've killed him and I didn't even manage to have a child by him!*

But it appeared that she thought this out loud, because he detached his nose from the grass, propped himself up on one elbow and said calmly: 'We can conceive the child whenever you like. Right now, even.'

He grimaced as he raised himself up to sit on the ground. He had a cut over his eyebrow, a split lip, two broken fingers on his left hand and several cracked ribs, as well as a lovely gash in his thigh, caused by the gear stick or the brake. He took her in his arms and it was he who had to console her and calm her down. She was trembling all over, with staring eyes – while Gaffouil the mechanic came running as fast as he could, beating Yvonne by yards.

The Pink Brigade finally arrived, eight women in all, accompanied by Jeanne Fougaril in person, who wanted to see the Apaches in their feathers, and by one of her assistants, Catherine Montblanc. Catherine was a tall girl whose nose was a little too long, but she had a pearly laugh and obvious charm; she was undoubtedly intelligent and wore her clothes like a society lady, or better still, a kept woman – *if there's any difference.*

'What a big horse of a woman! All she needs is a saddle!'

'You didn't see her in Paris two months ago because I'd sent her to Rome and Vienna to sort out a few problems. She's good. She speaks English with an Haute-Savoie accent, she knows more than I do about cosmetics, and most important of all, I think she's sufficiently magnanimous to put up with you, Hannah, for months if necessary. A veritable phenomenon.'

'Consider yourself out of a job, Fougaril.'

'One of these days I shall take you at your word and go. Think about it: the tours that you want to organize in America will take up a lot of time, you won't always be able to run them. You can rely on her to do it.'

'I'm giving you your job back, Fougaril, you're re-employed. Did you bring the latest figures with you?'

Jeanne replied that she would sooner have jumped into the Atlantic than arrive empty-handed. She left after a week, without having seen a single Apache in feathers, but still hiding beneath a caustic exterior her love of her work and her very sincere fondness of Hannah.

As for Catherine Montblanc, all the signs were that Jeanne had been right in her assessment of her: Big Catherine was not just anybody. She had started out at the age of fifteen as second chambermaid to an Englishwoman. She had lived in London, and then America, after her mistress married one of those Englishmen who owned huge ranches in Colorado. At nineteen, fed up with having to wait on someone, she married a poker player from San Antonio, Texas. She lost him two years later, following a disagreement over a certain ace of spades, and brought up the son that she had had by this card-sharp on a small income from a fashion shop in San Francisco. She married again in France – a shipowner from Nantes, thirty-five years older than her, who died after bringing her home down the Loire, and left her to sort things out with his children by a first marriage.

'I didn't argue about the inheritance with them – I had pike with *beurre blanc* coming out of my ears. I was happy to settle for the 5,000 francs they offered me. I wanted to work. In Paris I took classes at your school for beauticians. Madame Fougaril noticed me . . . My son is in France, I would like to bring him over, but there's no hurry. I'll do whatever you like, madame.'

'You'll call me Hannah, for a start.'

The first delivery of creams and perfumes arrived at the beginning of September. One of the most pleasant discoveries Hannah made in America was the importance and the quality of the press aimed exclusively at women. *Harper's Bazaar* had already been in existence for thirty-four years, since it was founded in 1867. *McCall's Magazine* dated from 1870, the *Ladies' Home Journal* from 1883, and *Good Housekeeping* from 1885. There was even a magazine devoted solely to children's fashions, *Buttericks' Modern Review*, launched four years earlier.

The main problem, however, remained that of retail outlets. Having decided once and for all to do without the building that would have accommodated a beauty salon and one, or indeed several, shops, as well as offices, she nonetheless kept the two sites that Maryan had initially selected, the one on Park Avenue and the other on Fifth. In July, as soon as she returned from her short trip to Europe, she unpacked from their boxes all the decorating and furnishing designs worked out by Henri-Beatrice. She saw no reason why she should not go along with her English designer in every detail: it was by playing on his

European exoticism that she stood the greatest chance of success.

She got the workmen in, with a view to having everything completed by mid-October.

'I'm going to need some girls as beauticians and sales assistants. Catherine, could you train them?'

She was now determined to do again in New York – and eventually in San Francisco, if the Wild West became a bit more civilized – what she had done in London and Paris. That meant setting up a factory in America, perhaps two. In other words, she would have to make arrangements for the gathering of plants and all the essential ingredients . . .

'I'm going to need some chemists . . .'

As for the perfumes, she doubted that she would be able to find here in America the specialists vital to production – unless she encouraged mass emigration from around Grasse?

'We'll see about that later.'

But none of her fine plans had the slightest chance of coming to anything if she did not overcome what she saw as the major obstacle: the almost total absence of a clientele. Hence the paramount importance of the veritable crusade she was going to undertake, from 10 September, and which she would continue for ten months. Her determination was all the greater because this in a way constituted for her a resumption of arms after the long break in her professional life, since February of the previous year. The first step that she had envisaged was the formation of two teams, the second of them to be entrusted to Catherine's charge.

'But not immediately. I'd rather you took charge of the staff on Park Avenue and Fifth – let's say until the end of February. That will allow me to break in the team to suit me. Then you can take my place and I shall take yours. And if among the six girls chosen by Jeanne, there are one or two who have the tiniest bit of nous, we shall create three teams and even four or six . . . Cathy? Have you been to see that apartment I found you? You like it? I'm pleased. Did you notice there was a child's room? Yvonne thinks she knows someone who could look after your son when you're not at home. Send for him – what are you waiting for? Until he's grown a moustache?'

She would remember what followed for the rest of her life. '*Damn it all, Lizzie, I wouldn't start out again for anything in the world . . .*

'*Mind you . . .*'

For five months and eleven days, apart from a very short respite for the end-of-year celebrations, she led her teams all over the eastern and central states of America. She had decided to target all the towns of more than ten thousand inhabitants (she would never have believed there could be so many). Depending on the distances, she could visit up to three towns a day. She signed up with some entertainment organizers, and hired at first one and then two scouts whose job it was to travel ahead of her and her girls, in order to book hotel rooms and lecture halls. But as the weeks went by she perfected her strategy. First of all, she drew up a rota for her models and beauticians, whom she divided into two groups of three, so that one trio was always available while the other rested. She alone maintained continuity, working eighteen to twenty hours a day. Then she employed an English woman sent to her by the institute in London, a Miss Waldringham, who was about fifty years old, dry as a stick, whose air of solemnity was intensified by her lorgnette. It was her responsibility to see off all those opera-hatted gentlemen who might threaten the moral integrity of the expedition. What's more, Eleanor Waldringham turned out to be of the utmost usefulness in contacting ladies' clubs and persuading their members to attend demonstrations. This old girl – sister of some colonel in the Indian Army, or a parson's daughter, Hannah could never remember which – was the very picture of respectability. *Short of employing Queen Victoria – but she might not have been able to get away – I couldn't have found anyone better . . .*

Hannah worked at least eighteen hours a day for more than fifty days. Even the interminable train journeys were for her an opportunity to work: as well as going over endless accounts, she collated the information she received in each town; made a record of the possible retail outlets; assessed the suitability of such and such a store as a distributor of her products; placed on a scale of one to fifty the potential importance of the clientele in every place they visited; kept a most detailed account of her expenses and income; boosted the morale of her troops, who one by one began to crack up a little, and finally made preparations for the next stopover on the basis of the information supplied by her scouts.

And that done, as soon as the train stopped and they got off, a new offensive had to be launched once again, with dreadful and wearing monotony – smiling, smiling, smiling all the time. She delivered her lectures, as many as three or four in the same day, to the most peculiar audiences. She gave demonstrations, using her models as examples; then, her models having metamorphosed into the beauticians, encouraged the women in the audience to allow themselves to be made up a little, demonstrating to them that protecting themselves from the effects of the sun or the cold by lightly colouring their lips did not lead to automatic damnation.

She readopted a cunning tactic that she had already employed in Australia – in Sydney – when first starting out. In every town she visited, and in fact before she reached a town (she had increased the strength of her scout force by taking on a female scout) she publicized through the press and with the aid of posters not only the marvellous news of her arrival, but also her intention of making a free gift of a phial of one of her perfumes to the ten most elegant women in town.

In reality, she gave away only three or four – and they were very tiny.

But it virtually never failed: she sold forty, or fifty, or more, to the women who hadn't received one and who nevertheless considered themselves as ranking right at the top of the local hierarchy of elegance.

The most important thing was to conduct the operation with the discretion required by her clients.

But selling was not her aim, at least not at this stage. She devoted herself far more to building up the best possible relations with the press. She kept a special notebook in which, town by town, and state by state, she recorded the names and addresses (and the telephone number when there was one) of future contacts. So that whenever she needed a feature article, or a story covered, she would always know whom to speak to, rather than having to ask for someone she didn't know.

She also started a file index, kept by herself and Eleanor Waldringham, that would soon have the names of over four thousand women on it. These included all the women, in all the towns she had passed through, who had impressed her by their personality, their social position or their income and, most importantly, their qualities of leadership: women who would bring other women after them. To each of these would be sent from New York a little pot of cold cream, a sovereign remedy against irritations of the skin.

Thus she took the measure of America, though she had to work like a demon to do so. The area she had managed to cover in a little over five months did not extend beyond Atlanta, although she got as far as Toronto to the north.

It would take you ten years to cover the whole country and in ten years, after running around like this, you would be on your knees, able to walk under a table without bending down.

The truth was that she was exhausted, or near enough. Even though they worked only one week out of two, the model-beauticians were beginning to look like consumptives. Even her aide-de-camp Gaffouil, used to living rough and so undemanding by nature, was grumbling. He had, however, in the course of their travels, found a pillow that suited him: Yvonne. The Breton girl had allowed herself to be seduced by the Pyrenean with the drooping moustache, whose shambling walk was strongly reminiscent of the flat-footed bears that his compatriots in the Ariège would lead by a ring through the nose in order to make them dance. Hannah fell into a fit of giggles when she discovered her chambermaid and mechanic in each other's arms one evening in Charleston.

'I thought you were supposed to be marrying a millionaire?'

'There's no hurry,' said Yvonne. 'It doesn't have to be tomorrow.'

'Nor tonight. Are you going to put a ring through his nose?'

'Mind your own business!'

Yvonne was anything but a winsome servant. When she wasn't angry she was simply in a bad mood. Taddeuz was the only human being who could silence her – *apart from Gaffouil, perhaps, but not for the same reasons*; in fact she idolized him.

'Gaffouil is a good fellow, but he's a man, a real man. Watching your girls strip naked in front of him, day after day, is bound to make his blood pressure rise.'

'And you brought it down for him?' Hannah was overcome with giggles again.

'I was glad to be of service.'

'Are you going to get married?'

'I can't see what business it is of yours. Unless you're worried whether I might leave you.'

'Are you going to leave me?'

'No. We talked about it and we've agreed, that fool from the mountains and I: as long as we can put up with you, we'll stay.'

That said, she wanted no misunderstanding: the tour was beginning to tire her, it was no life for a chambermaid. When would they be going back to New York?

Yvonne's cantankerous nature had always delighted Hannah. *You must have hired her because of it, even. But she's right . . .*

A telegram that reached her in the far depths of South Carolina gave her the excuse she needed: Lizzie was about to deliver her first child.

'We're going home, Yvonne. You can tell everyone we're calling it a day.'

CHAPTER 5

There are Two Ways of Succeeding in Business

Lizzie and Maryan's first child was a boy, as they had both hoped it would be. He was to be called James.

For Hannah, this birth was a cause of one of those fits of depression that all her life she would be able to explain in terms of cause and effect: after twenty-six months of marriage she was still not pregnant. *Don't try and kid yourself: you're worried. Why don't you go and see a doctor? But they're all charlatans! Besides, you know very well that you won't consult one, whatever you might say . . . Hannah, I'm warning you, if you aren't capable of giving Taddeuz at least two children I shall never forgive you!*

She had vowed to take things easy for a whole month after returning from her gruelling trip. She might just as well have tried to stop the rain falling. Her frenzy to get started was completely revived, more acute and urgent than ever before. As for this depression, there could be no question of her succumbing to it. First of all because the best way of improving her state of mind was to make love with Taddeuz as often as possible. Medication like that she would take again and again.

'I've always liked making love, Lizzie. Does that shock you? Like hell it does! I know jolly well that it interests you . . . Although you've never given me much detail about you and Maryan. Come to think of it, I've never seen him kiss you . . . on the mouth, I mean, not the way you kiss your nanny. What? I said that I'd never seen him, I didn't say he never kissed you! I've never seen him, that's all . . . He used to kiss you? Tell me more! What do you mean,

discretion? For God's sake, you're at least seventy-eight, surely it was long enough ago!'

Another reason not to stay at home idling was Taddeuz himself: his general attitude, as opposed to his sexual enthusiasm; the calm nonchalance – he never raised his voice – that he displayed in all circumstances (except in bed); his systematic refusal ever to take a stand on any subject whatsoever. As if he were afraid of any confrontation with her (whereas with other people, with everyone else, he was quite capable of defending his ideas). It might have been a weakness of character, but she didn't think so. It was something else, something worse. There was something he had said that she would never be able to forget: he had said it just after their wedding, during the first few minutes of their wedding night, in the house on Lake Lugano that she had rented especially. He had said that in spite of all the love he felt for her, he had almost not married her: 'Because I thought that it would be madness to live with you, almost suicide.' And they had never spoken of it again. In other words he had never revised his original opinion. And the truth of the matter was that if he withdrew in this way it was because he was acting in self-defence. *The simple fact is you frighten him.* To talk about it, to force a discussion on the subject would be pointless. She knew it. She was too clear-sighted to harbour any such illusions. He would close up even more. He would smile, apparently very calm, and invent some excuse about his writing that would be very plausible and very convincing at the time – this was not an area where she could fight against him on equal terms. *If only one of us were a little more stupid, just a little . . .*

And it was the same with his books. He had probably finished his novel by now. In all the time she had spent travelling across the continent, from one town to the next, with her band of pseudo-Parisian ladies, he must have completed his manuscript and delivered it to a publisher

– if he had managed to find one, which was by no means certain; they were all such fools, these publishers, they wouldn't recognize a Shakespeare if they saw one.

But since she wasn't supposed to interfere . . .

It's a shame. You could have . . .

She hadn't seen so much as the ghost of a manuscript. Anyone would think he swallowed the pages as he wrote them. He must surely have been hiding something in his study in the house on Long Island. He had a locked writing desk right at the back of the room. She was convinced the manuscript must be there, at least some of the time. It was jolly tempting . . . But on the very rare occasions when she had gone into his room, she had wisely kept away from that particular piece of furniture, as though afraid it might explode.

Of course, there were his newspaper articles. Those at least she could read. She found them increasingly sharp, in any event very characteristic of Taddeuz, sometimes downright malicious. This bothered her, but apparently they were enormously popular – not only was his column now given special prominence, with his by-line in a display box, but other American newspapers, in Louisiana or San Francisco, syndicated his articles. And she happened to find out that the *New York Times* had approached Taddeuz . . .

At least he was earning money, there was no doubt about that. And he spent it with his usual indifference. For the end-of-year festivities the previous year, in 1901 that is, he had given her a second black pearl, perhaps even finer than the first, which had also been bought at Tiffany's. With that dreadful pettiness she sometimes hated herself for, she almost went into the jeweller's to find out how much his present had cost. She really had to be very firm with herself to refrain from doing so at the last minute. She bought him a pair of diamond cufflinks but, fearful of appearing to be giving him an even more sumptuous gift in return, which would have emphasized their difference in wealth, she eventually gave them to Maryan.

You're damned complicated. Unless it's the situation that's complicated.

On 20 April 1902, she opened the institute on Park Avenue and the shop on Fifth.

She had ignored everyone's advice: there wasn't a single man in the whole of her New York hierarchy; only her lawyers wore trousers. *Polly in petticoats – that would be a sight for sore eyes!*

As for the beauty parlour, where the job of director required a maximum of technical competence, she had deliberately chosen a woman from Great Britain – a Scot – who happened to be a fairly distant cousin of Winnie Churchill (*Don't forget to mention that casually in front of the clients, Hannah, it's just what they want to hear*). Cecily Barton, director in London, had warmly recommended this Highland Jessie who was to run the New York operation for nearly fifty years without a break.

Becky Singer played a crucial role in the initial success of the beauty parlour, and afterwards of the shop. The Singers were extremely rich; they owned a bank, a firm of stockbrokers, a number of flour mills – half the bread eaten each day in New York came from one of their factories – not to mention all the buildings they owned. Before the salon even opened, Becky, not unskilfully, had rallied the three or four hundred important women that she knew in New York. Not all of them came, but more than half did. And two-thirds of those who paid a first visit thought it a good idea to come again. The beauty parlour was on the road to success. So much so that Sam Singer, another of Becky's brothers-in-law, requested a meeting with Hannah and volunteered his services: he was prepared to invest in her company.

'Five hundred thousand dollars, and more if necessary. When Becky told us about this project a few months ago, we didn't really believe it had a future. We were wrong.'

'And you're wrong again,' said Hannah with a smile. 'I don't want any partners.'

'We would only put money into it. Why not two million dollars, after all? Or even five? You would continue to run the company, that goes without saying. Think about it, Hannah, don't give me your answer straightaway. You've only set up in New York; we could open beauty parlours and shops all over the United States. On your own, if you had to be self-financing, it would take you years.'

'I have all the time in the world, Sam.'

'And if you don't strike hard enough right at the beginning, others will. People will copy you. And that's not all: there's Europe. We know that you already have a network there. We're prepared to buy a share in it and help you to finance other products that you'll be able to launch with our backing. When you can't avoid competition the best thing is become your own rival. That at least has the advantage of occupying the field.'

'I don't want any partners,' she insisted, even though she thought she detected behind all these flattering proposals a vague threat: by refusing this proposition, she ran the risk of seeing this 'powerful group' that Sam Singer had spoken of coming along and trampling her flowerbeds, with resources infinitely superior to hers.

Let them. She was confident of her own analysis: *You haven't travelled over six thousand miles and spoken to fifty million women without learning a thing or two!* And she didn't believe that buckets of money would make a great deal of difference: the American continent was not yet ready for a full-scale cosmetics industry. *Nor is Europe, for that matter. And if you've succeeded in Europe and Australia, it's because you've used cottage-industry methods, which all these chaps with their huge bank accounts are quite incapable of. In fifteen or twenty years perhaps things will be different, but we haven't got to that stage yet . . .*

However, Sam Singer's approach was going to be doubly useful to her.

First of all, she saw in it the sign that she was succeeding. This was encouraging, even if she hadn't had much doubt of it. She was less successful than the financiers believed: there weren't all that many women in a position to spend the astronomical sum of fifteen to twenty dollars a week – the equivalent of a secretary's weekly salary – on creams and beauty care; so her sales were soon going to level off . . .

But if she was less successful than they believed, she was also more successful than she had hoped. She had reckoned that she would already be doing very well if New York didn't cost her more than one-third – twenty-six sheep's legs – of her European profits for the first five years. But at the rate things were going, she stood a good chance of breaking more or less even towards the middle of 1903.

Especially as she had had an idea while listening to Sam Singer talk . . .

It was not a completely new idea. The basic premise of it had been apparent to her during her tour of America, when she came face to face with large numbers of buyers – tens of thousands of them. She discussed the matter with Catherine Montblanc. (As agreed, Catherine had taken charge of the teams of demonstrators, and pressed on to California; she was now shepherding four groups that worked in shifts. They were fourteen strong, ten of the model-beauticians having been trained in America.) There was no question of being able to sell luxury products to anything but a tiny percentage of American women. The day would come perhaps when this would change, but for the time being the institutes were not for the average American woman, who did not have the means to afford them and furthermore saw no need to go to them.

On the other hand, Hannah did not want to lower the quality of products that bore the double H insignia. *There are two ways of succeeding in business: either by selling in quantity and inexpensively things that everyone needs or by identifying one's clientele with the utmost care and persuading them to buy, regardless of cost, things of which they have absolutely no need.*

'This profound thought is my very own, my dear Catherine. With my institutes and shops, I've pursued the latter alternative. The time may have come to look at the other solution.'

What this amounted to was that she was going to put on the market a cream that cost no more than $1.30 a pot. She instructed her French laboratory to work on the contents of this pot: lime blossom and coltsfoot, with a drop of lavender and gentian. She tried it out on herself, and then on Lizzie and Yvonne, for a whole month without noticing any great damage. It was fresh, invigorating and it had a nice smell.

'And you're going to sell that eight or ten times cheaper than what you're selling in your shops? You've really got a nerve!' said Catherine.

'There will be three differences: the size and quality of the pot, the absence of the Hannah logo and the fact that it will be sold anywhere but in my beauty parlours or my shops. How much would you pay for a Worth dress if five thousand of the same were sold in the Bronx?'

And there was a fourth reason . . .

'Don't tell me, Hannah. It's like the Three Musketeers – there were four of them.'

And she didn't take too kindly to Lizzie's jokes regarding this fourth difference. She had worked for years, with doctors and chemists, on the composition of her creams, milks, toilet waters and perfumes. She knew better than anyone the care that had surrounded the birth of each one of them, the difference between a simple skin-care cream such as the one she was going to sell outside her normal retail network, and the infinitely more complex products that she sold under her own name. And it was in the spring of 1902 that she realized how much she missed her 'kitchen'. Whatever the qualities of those men and women working in her laboratory in Paris, rightly or wrongly she considered herself their equal. And she felt a nostalgia for handling retorts and spatulas, and for the countless decoctions she so much enjoyed creating. *You're going to have to get the American laboratory started. You never know, the French and the Germans might go to war again.*

In order to sell the $1.30 beauty cream, all she needed to do was get in contact with the big department stores. She summoned Polly Twhaites from London once more and put him in charge of a whole squadron of American lawyers who were to negotiate on her behalf, and also entrusted him with the task of filing patents. She wanted a legal arsenal that in the years to come would put a brake on any competition, even if it failed to eliminate it entirely. Her adviser on this point was someone unexpected to say the least – no less a person than Thomas Alva Edison.

She had once heard Maryan talk of how fiercely this inventor protected his rights (Maryan had been talking particularly about cinematography, but apparently Edison was no less merciless in other areas into which his astonishing genius had led him). So she went to see Edison. As soon as he had ascertained that she had not come to get anything out of him, especially not a favour –

the mere word made him tremble with rage – he was almost polite. *That's to say, he became about as cordial as a rabid dog barking on the other side of a gate.* He told her what measures he personally had taken and the names of the lawyers, dozens of them, that he used.

'I've already taken 271 cases to court and I won nearly all of them, madame. You wouldn't by any chance need a detective?'

'What for?'

'One always needs a detective. Mine is called MacCoy. He is on the look-out night and day for counterfeiters and plagiarists.'

He was obviously serious as a judge. According to Maryan, Edison was always deadly serious, and his rapaciousness in money matters was pretty incredible: 'On the grounds that he has filed a patent for the kinetoscope, he claims that anything to do with moving pictures has to be referred to him and that he's entitled to a royalty payment. If he thought there was any mileage in it, he would claim a royalty from the Lumière brothers and George Méliès. Apparently, all inventors are a bit mad, so he must be a great inventor . . .'

'I think I can do without a detective.'

'In any case,' said Edison, 'MacCoy only works for me.'

The contracts with the big stores were ready by the end of July. It took four weeks of relentless discussion to settle one final point: the stores wanted to reproduce Hannah's face on the pot-lids, or if not her face then at least the entrance to the salon on Park Avenue. She had of course refused: she certainly did not want the products that she sold through her own establishments to be in any way identified with a pot that cost $1.30. A compromise was eventually reached: the beauty cream would only be '*Recommended by HH*'. That's all.

Nevertheless it took nineteen days to agree on the

height of the letters and where they were to be placed. In order to be able to read the words you would have needed a microscope, unless you were a specially trained lynx.

'That's still too big, Polly. I didn't want my name to appear at all.'

'They wouldn't have agreed to anything less. Without your name, or in this case your initials, there would have been no contract. They take full account – and it has weighed considerably with them – of the tour you made. Women from Canada to Virginia now know you, and those that haven't seen you in the flesh have heard of you. And besides that, I think there's another reason why you should say yes: I didn't agree to it without getting something in exchange. Read clause 56, on page 85 of the contract.'

She read it and smiled. Polly had got an exclusive deal, the big stores would only be able to sell beauty products manufactured by her.

'Polly! To think that I didn't think of that myself! You're a genius!'

'It's high time you realized it, my dear. This measure blocks any future competitors you might have. Even if they made products as good as or better than yours – which of course is impossible, isn't it? – they would not be able to sell them. You control all the retail outlets. And another thing: have you worked it out? The contract is for one hundred thousand pots a year for ten years. And they are under an obligation to increase the order by twenty per cent a year for the first five years. You make twenty cents on each pot, you told me, after deducting all costs. That comes to $200,000 in the first year, $240,000 the following year . . .'

'I've worked it out. It's a darned good contract.'

'And they have to pay you even if they don't sell a single pot. However, there's nothing to prevent them selling more. In that case, on every pot over and above the one hundred thousand-pot minimum your profit margin is reduced to eighteen cents.'

'Band of robbers!' she said with a laugh.

In any event, these additional revenues would wipe out the current deficit and any further deficit on the New York establishments. And they would mean that she would hardly have to draw at all on her European and Australian income when it came to financing the laboratory, the schools and the other things she wanted to set up, if she were to continue her expansion on the American continent.

America would be completely autonomous, that was the main thing.

This final argument convinced her and overcame her final reservations. She signed the contract, but not without some regret: this was the first time she had deviated from the path she had always followed.

She might almost have felt ashamed . . .

She found the book one month later.

At the end of July they had gone away on holiday. To be more precise, Lizzie had managed to convince everyone of the absolute necessity of leaving New York and its sweltering summer heat. She was the one who persuaded Hannah to leave red-haired Jessie to look after New York by herself, and Maryan to let Wall Street survive without him. Taddeuz was the easiest to get round. In August his articles were published less frequently, only once a week, so all he needed to do was to get a little ahead with them, or use the telegraph if there were any urgency.

They headed due south towards Florida, to the little port of Miami, where the recent Spanish-American war had prompted an unexpected expansion. There they boarded a yacht that Maryan had just had built, which was equipped with a dozen cabins. Maryan had also invited other guests: the Van Guysling brothers and Cecil

B. De Mille, as well as two wonderful creatures indubitably of the female sex who must have escaped from some Broadway theatre.

'Might I ask whom these sirens are intended for?' Hannah enquired of Lizzie.

'Not your husband. Nor mine, I hope,' replied Lizzie with her usual good humour. 'No, apparently we're to be joined by another guest. My husband wouldn't tell me who it was. He'll be coming aboard at Havana and Maryan wants to give him the best possible welcome.'

'Say, you still haven't told me what happened on your wedding night.'

'How right you are!'

'What do you mean by that?'

'I haven't told you. And I'm not in any hurry to tell you. You really are obsessed with sex, you know.'

Hannah was not particularly enthusiastic about the idea of going to sea in such a tiny craft (as far as she was concerned, even a liner was tiny), but cruising round the Florida Keys had largely dispelled her apprehensions. Especially as they progressed slowly, sailing close to the shore, where they would go and eat their fill of grilled crayfish. The two crazy girls from Broadway exposed all of their charms to the sun. Their nakedness didn't bother Hannah, who had no great objection to Taddeuz's looking at them – as long as it went no further – particularly as she reckoned, from a completely impartial standpoint, that her figure was much better than that of either of these two young misses.

'Don't you agree?'

'Absolutely, absolutely,' replied Taddeuz with suspicious eagerness and a trace of sarcasm.

'You want me to strip naked too, is that it?'

'I'd rather not.'

'In any case, they're crazy: there's nothing worse for the skin than the sun.'

They reached Havana seven days after leaving Miami. There, a moustachioed gentleman with very roguish eyes came aboard, accompanied by his wife. This was George Méliès. This extraordinary fellow was on his way back from Mexico; he had had the incredible idea of going and setting up his cameras there in order to shoot what he would call his 'westerns' (it was seeing Buffalo Bill in Paris that made him want to do this). He had in his luggage his most recent movie, *Voyage to the Moon*, filmed in Paris. He was a man of fantastic imagination, really out of the ordinary. Maryan considered him a pure genius and was hoping to work with the Frenchman and the Van Guysling brothers in developing in America a cinematographic industry that would escape Edison's implacable control.

'Hannah, I would like you to come in with us. We don't need your money, the Van Guyslings and I have enough, but it's a tremendously good investment. Cinematography has an extraordinary future.'

She refused, as she would thereafter always refuse when he suggested other business deals she might take part in. She wanted to stay with her own speciality. She had no opinion one way or the other about cinematography. She thought it very probable that Maryan was right. Well, so much the better for him, and for Lizzie. As for herself, she had completed her second pink sheep, which was now merrily gambolling about, and a third was on the way. It already had its two front legs and a sweet little stub of a tail; if all went well, it would be complete in ten or fifteen months' time. Why the devil should she go and put her money into other businesses? She was not going to spend her whole life making millions. There was a fantastic difference between five and five hundred dollars, but between twenty million and two hundred million?

The charming Méliès couple disembarked after two days as they had a passage booked on a ship sailing from

New York back to France. No agreement had been reached, apparently, between him on the one hand and Maryan and his American-Dutch associates on the other. The yacht sailed along the Cuban coast for a while, in the Sabana archipelago. Then it headed north-west, in the direction of the Bahamas. They reached Nassau on 24 August and that must have been when the package arrived.

What is certain is that Hannah found it, on the evening of their second day in port, lying on the only table in their cabin.

It was entitled: *The Spiv*. The author's name: Taddeuz Nenski.

'Thank you for having told me so much about it.'

'Let's just say that I wanted it to be a surprise.'

'It's certainly that. Has it been on sale for long?'

'It will be in a few weeks' time, I think.'

'You think? You mean you're not sure?'

She had a great desire to scream.

'I'm almost sure. Edward Lucas . . .'

'Who's he?'

'The publisher. He told me that it would be available in September or October. I knew that we would be calling at Nassau. I asked him to have a few copies sent to me, if they were ready in time. For you, of course.'

'Thank you.'

'I've already read it,' he said, smiling.

She picked up the book again and flicked through it once more, torn between anger and a savage pride. *He wrote it and found a publisher to publish it! You're going to be the wife of a famous writer!*

'How many copies has this Lucas of yours printed?'

'No idea.'

'Is he à leading publisher?'

'Average.'

'And is he any good?'

'He and I have quite a few tastes in common.'

'I'd be surprised if that made him a good publisher. I would have thought the opposite. And the title! What does it mean?'

'A spiv is a profiteer who thrives on the misfortunes of others. That makes him a parasite.'

She gazed at him. He was totally inscrutable behind that smile of his. *I really will scream, but out of sorrow*, she thought in anguish.

What she said was: 'You've called yourself Nenski.'

'That's my real name, after all. Newman is just the name that appears on my American passport.'

She read the book once, the way she read the newspaper headlines, that's to say at incredible speed. She couldn't make head or tail of it. Even the story seemed obscure to her, it was almost as though there wasn't one. The characters wrote to each other, replied to each other's letters, exchanged strange confessions, there were detailed descriptions of places in Italy, or of the way a woman left her footprint on the beach.

She reread it, twice: once on board the train that took her all the way back from Miami to New York – and only at night when no one could see her; and then again in New York, when she was alone.

She had the same feeling she had already experienced three years before when Mendel brought her a copy of the poems published in Munich under the name of Nemo: that here was a world totally removed from her own, where nothing was recognizable, not even the words – *There must be 150 or 200 words here, at least, whose existence you weren't even aware of. We don't have the same vocabulary*. There was of course sensuality, and profundity, and surely intelligence, a keen sense – insofar as she could judge – of the way in which words could combine and become music. There was also, above all – how could she describe it? – a kind of delight in taking a black view of life, which really wasn't a view available to her.

'I've never been an intellectual, Lizzie. Nor have you, for that matter. For me, two and two always make four, whether it's day or night. Even when it annoys you. When I read Taddeuz's first book, I felt ashamed. Of myself, of what I thought. Because I thought that what he'd written was pointless, that it served no purpose, that it was writing for writing's sake, writing intended to prove that you know the language darned well, but that you're above ordinary people, to the point that you don't have to condescend to tell them a story, with a beginning and an end. That's what I thought about his book. I was furious: and that's what he was hoping would make him famous? Because I thought: why write at all if it's not in order to be read by as many people as possible? It's like sculpting a statue that you're only going to show to five people.

'I didn't say anything to him. He didn't ask me what I thought – I'm sure he realized, he was so good at reading my mind – and I was careful not to broach the subject.

'I went to see his publisher.'

Edward Lucas was nearly fifty. He had rather wide-set china-blue eyes, a long pointed nose, a round face, a virtually bald head, and a paunch worthy of a lawyer.

He said that *The Spiv* certainly had a number of shortcomings but that . . .

'Shortcomings? You're joking! It's unreadable!'

'Well, I like it enormously,' was all Lucas said.

If she hadn't been so het up, she would certainly have noticed the twinkle in the publisher's eye. But it was only later that this would strike her.

'How many have you printed?'

'Three thousand. Less wastage.'

'What's that?'

'That's the number of copies pulped because they're in some way defective.'

'And my husband is supposed to pay for the mistakes your printer makes? That's outrageous!'

'It's standard practice and it's justifiable. The print run . . .'

'Standard practices are designed to be altered. And how big is this wastage?'

'Twelve per cent.'

'I can't have heard you correctly.'

'Twelve per cent is usual.'

'Three hundred and sixty copies out of three thousand. That's crazy! You ought to change your printer, yours is useless. Or else he's a thief. I'm sure he must be selling the books on the sly.'

He burst out laughing, not in the least put out.

'I don't think so,' he said.

'I'm certain of it.'

'I wouldn't like to have to do business with you, Mrs . . .'

'Well, you do. My husband doesn't deign to concern himself with such mundane matters as money. But I do. How much wastage is there really?'

'In view of . . . the circumstances, we could perhaps compromise on eight per cent.'

'Four would be even better.'

'On a print run of one hundred thousand, that would be quite realistic. But not on such a small print run.'

She opened her mouth to say (with a fair degree of sharpness): *There's nothing to stop you printing one hundred thousand*. But she didn't say it, because she could see quite clearly where that kind of remark might lead. Lucas would tell her that he wasn't so crazy as to produce one hundred thousand copies of a book by an unknown author, when he expected to sell, at most, two thousand. *If only Taddeuz had put the name Newman to the wretched book he would have been able to take advantage of his reputation as a columnist! And Lucas would also tell me that if someone – me of course – were willing to guarantee his losses, he would happily print a million.*

That was the first stage of her reasoning. One-hundredth of a second later, she came to the second, having finally taken into consideration the twinkle in Lucas's eye. She bowed her head and then looked up again, and gazed at the desk on which books were piled high in incredible quantities.

'You knew that I would come, didn't you?'

'Yes, madame.'

'He warned you?'

'Yes, madame.'

'If I offered you one hundred thousand dollars in order to make him think that he had sold extremely well, would you accept?'

He smiled.

She put another question to him: 'He warned you that I would make such a proposal?'

'May I offer you a coffee?'

'No, thank you . . . actually, yes, I would like one, thank you.'

He went over to a little paraffin stove in a corner of the room and came back with a stoneware mug half filled with coffee. He sat down next to her. She drank her coffee, studying him the while.

'I feel quite foolish,' she said eventually.

'That's not really the impression you give me,' he replied gently.

He took her mug.

'A little more?'

'No, really, thank you. To be frank, it's the worst coffee I've drunk since I've been in America. Apart from the coffee I make myself. Are there any other questions that he predicted I would ask?'

He hesitated.

'Please,' she said. 'I'd prefer to drink the poison in one go.'

'According to Tad, immediately after offering me two or three hundred thousand dollars . . .'

'I didn't think I was so extravagant.'

'I may be rounding up the figures. In fact, Tad didn't think you would go above twenty or thirty thousand, fifty if you really had to, on his first book at least.'

'I see. So what happens immediately after . . .'

'You were supposed to ask me if I thought he had any talent.'

Again, she stared at him, with a fierce desire to smash his coffee pot over his head, although it wasn't really anything to do with him – *Not to mention what you would like to do to that very dearly beloved husband of yours!*

'OK,' she said, 'I'm asking you that question.'

'He has a great deal of talent,' said Lucas calmly. 'He's barely thirty, practically an adolescent still, for a writer. I've been in publishing for twenty-two years; I have never seen a writer of such great promise. And I'm being sincere.'

'You mentioned shortcomings.'

'I'm not even sure they are shortcomings. He will never write like Twain. But there's something of Henry James in his work, with a sensuality, a humour and imagination that James never had.'

'Mr Lucas?'

'Edward. Or better still, Eddy. I like your husband very much, Mrs Newman. He's an exceptional man.'

She closed her eyes and the words that came to her were exactly those that she had once thrown back at Mendel Visoker, in almost identical circumstances: 'I wouldn't have loved just anybody,' she said with extraordinary pride.

CHAPTER 6

For Heaven's Sake, I'm Crying!

She would never know whether Lucas had told Taddeuz of her visit; it seemed unlikely, but she didn't think he had. Especially as she got to know the publisher over the years.

Lucas was right about one thing at least: in the final minutes of their conversation, he had predicted that *The Spiv* would be hailed by the critics. In the weeks that followed, the book was greeted with a chorus of praise. Doubtless the fact that it was the work of a fellow critic – the identity of Nenski-Newman had very quickly become known – had something to do with this. But there was sincerity in the comparisons with Henry James. So much so that Hannah eventually became exasperated. James was an old schnook who had found nothing better to do than to leave the United States and become a naturalized Englishman, no doubt because he wasn't regarded highly enough in his native country. And what was so wonderful about being like him? She read, or rather she forced herself to read, *The Turn of the Screw*. She found it deadly boring. *Taddeuz can certainly do better than that, and at least he will have genuine readers, not drawing-room intellectuals!*

Meanwhile, she was simply enjoying the pleasure of being the wife of a writer, *even if his book has earned scarcely enough to buy a new engine for the Mercedes, but that will come. The cat grew a tail without its being pulled, as Yvonne would say.*

All in all, she was fairly cheerful.

Especially as her business interests were doing well. She had opened in Boston, following an expedition she had made there with her adjutants Jessie and Catherine, and intensive preparations masterfully conducted – she herself wrote the publicity articles announcing the opening. This was the first time she used the formula on her press releases that she would never depart from thereafter: 'I, Hannah . . .' She was told on innumerable occasions that it had an imperial – and immodest, to say the least – ring about it.

She replied that she couldn't care less.

'I may be conceited. That has yet to be proved. Deep down inside, I'm having fun, that's the important thing. But it gets me known, and I need to be known if I'm to sell my creams. If anyone can think of a better way to do it, let them write and tell me. What is of paramount importance is that my conceitedness doesn't lead me to make mistakes.'

Forty-eight other women were involved in the expedition, thirty-nine of them dyed-in-the-wool Americans. The rest of the contingent was mobilized in Europe, by Jeanne Fougaril in Paris and Cecily Barton in London. Nearly all of them were German or Scandinavian. The lessons learned from Hannah's gruelling five-month tour had not gone to waste: she invested a great deal of money in clothes – all the women who accompanied her were superbly dressed in outfits sent over from France. The result was there for all to see: under the firm rule of Eleanor Waldringham, dressed severely in black and playing the part of duenna, the Pink Brigade looked extremely smart – so how the devil could they ever pass unnoticed?

As for Hannah, she played on contrast: her own tiny self in the midst of these beauties a head taller than her; her somewhat indefinable accent (it was generally French, through choice, but she had an accent in every language she spoke); her mysteriousness. If she didn't know it already, it did not take her long to realize that her life-story fascinated journalists, especially the period between her departure from the *shtetl* and her arrival in America. She beefed it up a bit. Her adventures, particularly her Australian adventures, became more action-packed and more colourful every time she recounted them. She almost related how *she* had tried to cross the southern continent, from east to west, on foot. It seemed too much of a lie even to her. But a very attractive and romantic Aussie had made that crossing and had eventually died in the vast desert between Brisbane and Perth while in the process of writing 'Hannah' in the sand, his poor fingers already stiff as the life departed his body.

If anything's romantic, that is! And by heaven it's good for sales! But if Mendel ever got to read these articles, he would cross the globe to give you a good hiding!

At that time she still hadn't dared tell Lizzie the true fate of her brother Quentin MacKenna, the Man-eater, the hero of this story.

Lizzie wasn't even aware that Hannah had met Quentin.

On the other hand, Hannah had told Taddeuz the whole story. She had described to him the strange likeable character who was the youngest of the MacKenna sons, telling him how she had met Quentin and how he had set off one day, after she had patched his shirt, across the then unexplored desert wastes of the Australian continent, with practically no hope of returning alive.

She had seen that Taddeuz was completely fascinated by it.

But she didn't imagine for a moment the use Taddeuz would make of this story.

It happened two days before Christmas 1903. The previous day she had got back from Boston. Everything was going very well; the new beauty parlour was getting off to a creditable start. Comparing figures, which she had done one hundred times over, it was even doing slightly better than the New York salon, after the same number of weeks in operation. Of course it wasn't in the black yet, far from it, but it was up and running, a joy to behold and good for the soul.

Besides, she already had the outline of a blue sheep for Boston. (The sheep were always blue when they represented beauty salons; they were purple for the shops; black for her laboratories; orange for the schools for beauticians; yellow for the system of gathering plants and base products for her creams, milks and perfumes; red-spotted for the distribution network; and chequered black-and-white for her bank accounts.)

The Boston blue sheep didn't yet have any legs or a tail. Just a head on a very sweet curly body. If it was very good, it would be entitled to a caudal appendage when the books balanced – *next spring, if all goes well.* And it would get legs, added one by one, as soon as it could walk (how much more logical could anyone be?) – that's to say, from the moment it began to make a profit: one leg for every one thousand dollars a year. If it were a very clever sheep and nice to mummy, it would be provided with lots and lots of legs, in unlimited quantity.

The Paris blue sheep, for instance, already had thirty-three legs; the London one was scarcely less of a phenomenon with twenty-eight.

Hannah had fourteen blue sheep in her secret notebook, and thirty-nine purple ones (these were shops).

Three orange, three red, two yellow . . .

. . . only one with red spots . . .

. . . seventeen chequered sheep (she didn't really trust banks and preferred to spread the risk in case some banker made off with her money) . . .

. . . two-and-three-quarter pink sheep – the pink sheep were at the top of the hierarchy, they were the aristocrats, members of the Jockey Club, as it were. Each representative of one million dollars, they were by far the most expensive sheep in the world. They were snobs: Hannah would give them each an adorable bow round the neck.

She was the only person in the world who could understand her system of accounting. She had told Junior Rockefeller a little about it, but it was to Polly Twhaites that she had mainly tried to explain it. He had cracked at the point where chequered sheep entered the conversation; it was more than he could take. Especially as no sheep bore the name of any town or country. They sported numbers, which were conferred on them in accordance with some secret code that she kept to herself:

'But it's very simple, Polly.'

'No! It isn't at all simple . . .'

And in any case, he didn't like sheep unless they came with beans.

It was two days before Christmas. Having got up as usual at 4.30 A.M., she had gone out for a short walk, and then spent two hours studying her balance sheets. After breakfast with Taddeuz – she invariably ate like a horse: at least three boiled eggs and as often as not a steak – she met the architects who had come to show her the plans of the laboratory she wanted to set up, though she didn't yet know where. Taddeuz closeted himself in his own study – which she practically never went into, or if she did she knocked before entering – while she took the Mercedes and drove to Manhattan (they had retired to the house on Long Island for the festive season). She spent the rest of the morning at the salon, getting very angry because someone had forgotten to turn the lights out when leaving the building the night before. She lunched with Lizzie and Catherine Montblanc, who was as ever aghast at her appetite: 'How do you manage not to put on weight, Hannah?'

'I haven't the faintest idea. Aren't you going to finish that rum baba?'

She spent the afternoon interviewing four young women graduates of the beauticians' school in Thirty-Fourth Street, and selected one for the future beauty parlour in San Francisco. Then she called in at the shop, where the six sales assistants became petrified with terror at the mere sight of her (*What ninnies, you've never so much as laid a finger on them!*). At four o'clock she had a meeting with two of her lawyers: she wasn't at all satisfied with the way her beauty cream was being sold in a number of department stores in Chicago (she had received a secret report on the matter from three of her spies): her name was being made too much of, when the contract stated quite specifically that she was only supposed to appear to be endorsing the product, nothing more. No, she didn't much like court cases, better to come to an amicable agreement, but tell those people in Illinois to watch it: the next time, she would shoot. Seated behind the wheel of her Mercedes (Gaffouil, seated on her right, was responsible for parking the car), driving at a crazy speed, she went and put in an appearance at an exhibition, did two or three errands, bought herself a new hat – it was adorable – and a pair of gloves, called in at the salon again to get the day's figures, telephoned Boston to find out what had been going on there, sent a cable to Jeanne Fougaril in Paris, in case she forgot (*as if she were in the habit of forgetting anything! You're going to drive her mad with this! Well, so much the better, it's good for the circulation and it puts some colour in your thighs . . .*) to authorize the French consignment destined for America. She just had time to drop into the apartment to welcome the eight guests that Taddeuz had invited that evening . . .

And at two o'clock in the morning, she returned to Long Island, bringing home Yvonne and Gaffouil.

She began writing a letter to Mendel but didn't finish it: Taddeuz was tickling her. A week earlier Eddy Lucas had given him the figures for nearly three months' sales of *The Spiv*: 1,432 copies. Lucas thought the figures were good, he was expecting them to be worse. 'Hannah, it's a first novel, I'm sure we'll sell more twenty years from now . . .' She did not comment on these results, which she considered catastrophic: *It's as if I had sold fifty pots of cream – we would have long since died of hunger!*

She had made enquiries about Lucas – and not just about him, in fact. She had asked her spies to make enquiries about every publisher of any importance on the East Coast. Lucas was not one of the leading publishers, but he had an excellent reputation; there was no reason to suppose that if Taddeuz had been with another company, he would have fared any better. *The Spiv* was turned down by six editorial directors, three others offered to publish it. Taddeuz had chosen Lucas – *He told you so himself.*

'What about going to bed? It's late.'

He picked her up and put her to bed.

The next day was a Saturday. She . . .

'Hannah, are you asleep?'

She had actually woken up at her usual time, but she hadn't got out of bed. An hour at least had gone by, if not more, but she hadn't been able to get back to sleep. The first light of dawn, on that 24 December, broke through the gap between the curtains.

'Hannah, are you asleep?'

He was whispering. She lay curled up with her back to him, her eyes wide open, staring.

'You aren't asleep,' said Taddeuz.

He slipped one hand under her hip.

'Down in the dumps?'

If only I was capable of crying a little! she thought. *What on earth's the matter with me? I must be a real monster!* When she had lunch at the restaurant in the Waldorf-Astoria the previous day, she, Lizzie and Catherine had joked together. The former Australian, less than ten months after the birth of her first child, was already expecting a second, who in all probability would be born at the end of April, beginning of May.

'Or else you must be ill,' said Taddeuz. 'It's quite difficult to believe that, though . . . What's the matter, Hannah?'

'I'd like some coffee if you don't mind. You make it so much better than I do.'

'OK.'

She felt him move away from her, heard him get out of bed, put on a dressing gown, open the doors. She remembered the letter to Mendel that she hadn't finished writing; it was simply tucked under the blotter. But Taddeuz wasn't in the habit of rummaging through her things, thank God.

He returned a few minutes later. She still hadn't stirred. He sat down on the bed next to her, having placed the tray on the bedside table piled high with books.

'I'd rather you didn't look at me,' she said quietly.

Ten seconds went by.

'All right,' he said, just as calm as ever.

Then she said: 'I know an incredibly stupid writer who didn't say a word to anyone when he published his first book, and contented himself with just laying it on the corner of a table one day. I'd like to have done the same. Impossible. Even stupid writers have eyes.'

'Oh my God!' exclaimed Taddeuz.

'I couldn't very well get through the remaining two hundred-odd days and then leave it lying on the corner of the dining-room table for you.'

'Hannah, my love . . . .'

'I'm pregnant,' she said. 'It'll be a limited edition. Probably just one copy. Happy Christmas!'

She opened her eyes a little wider.

For heaven's sake! she thought in wonderment, *I'm crying!*

CHAPTER 7

That Dreadful Year of 1913

Their first son, Adam, was born on 21 June 1903.

Hannah made a slight mistake in her calculations – human error: she had wanted the birth to be in August, or July if need be.

'Because July–August is a slack season for business.'

'You fell a bit short of target, Hannah,' said Taddeuz, laughing, but also kissing her stomach with tears in his eyes.

'It's not my fault, though, that he was born sooner than expected. According to Dr What's-his-name and his pals, he wasn't due to arrive for another two or three weeks . . . Now don't tell me he isn't wonderful! A little pink and wrinkled perhaps, just like you when you've stayed under the shower too long. He weighs eleven pounds four ounces and measures twenty inches. A real giant. I can't imagine how I had room for him. If I'd had more time, he would have been your height and weighed 12 stone, and he would have been able to start at Harvard at the beginning of the September term. Now please don't tell me you're happy, you lousy Pole!'

Her first labour pains came while she was in a meeting with her directors from all over the world – even Maggie MacGregor from Sydney was there. She was about to open in San Francisco and was already working on plans for Philadelphia and New Orleans.

She was back at work nine days after the birth, having told the doctors they were fools.

And Adam would grow up to look so much like Taddeuz, it was just like seeing an hallucination.

* * *

Jonathan, the second, was born three years later, on 2 September 1906, at Mount Sinai Hospital, New York. His first name was a happy combination of the names of Taddeuz's father, Jan Nėnski, and Hannah's father, Nathan.

Naturally, he had blue eyes when he was born, but by about the third month the truth became dazzlingly obvious: the blue was very clearly turning to grey, exactly the same as Hannah's grey eyes. The younger son's eyes were identical to those of his mother, they swallowed up his face in the same way, and as soon as they met another gaze they had that piercing, almost harrowing intensity that Mendel Visoker would be able to identify among millions of others.

'He's even got my wretched character!'

Hannah was jubilant, although not very maternal in fact – she never would be, and it would take her years, almost a whole lifetime, to make good this deficiency.

But everything did indeed turn out as though the relentless schedule she had settled on had been scrupulously observed.

'And this time was even better than the last: I was just two days short of giving birth bang in the middle of August. If I had six children, I'm sure I could eventually deliver on 15 August, at midday exactly.'

'Are you going to have six?'

'I'd be surprised. You may think it's enjoyable! I don't mean conceiving them – I like that. I like it a lot. It's getting them out afterwards!'

'You almost make me blush, kid. You certainly weren't brought up to be a lady, you know . . .'

'The only person in the world who can boast of having brought me up at all is you.'

'That explains it,' said Mendel Visoker.

He had come from Peru, or Bolivia: he wasn't very sure himself. Anyway, there were mountains and llamas there, of that he was more or less sure. He was forty-eight and, apart from a little greying at the temples and in his moustache, he would have passed for a young man. Three years earlier, when Adam was born, he had turned up in New York, having been told of the event by heaven knows whom; with all his furs, a trapper from the far north, he caused one hell of a sensation when he appeared in the main reception of the salon. Jessie, the director, had him thrown out, thinking he was some kind of outlandish freak. He didn't protest or say who he was. He waited four hours for Hannah to emerge, chatting in Polish or Italian with the policemen doing their rounds. That same evening, after he had managed to calm her down (she wanted to give Jessie the sack for her lack of discernment), he found himself seated at the same table as Junior Rockefeller and eleven other almost equally prestigious guests. She expected some caustic comment, or awkwardness, and was ready to cut the throat of anyone who might speak ill of her Mendel. But not a bit of it. He had everyone enthralled with his stories of being a gold-digger in the Klondike; of his time spent in Siberian penal colonies, and his trek across the Gobi Desert and then the whole of China; of his rovings across the seven seas and his wanderings the world over; and they were all fascinated by the fact that he knew fifteen or twenty languages.

'How many countries have you visited, Mendel?'

'How should I know?'

'All you have to do is count them.'

He shrugged his enormous shoulders and replied that he didn't give a damn.

And it was three years ago too, after the dinner in question, that he and Taddeuz had gone out together for a drink. They came back three days later, in a terrible state.

'You were carrying my husband on your shoulders . . .'

'These young people, they can't stand the pace. How are things between you, kid?'

'I can't see what that has to do with you,' she said, with a guffaw.

'How long is it that I've known you?'

'It must be about twenty-four years.'

'Well, it must be twenty-four years that I've been wanting to tan your hide. How are things between you?'

'I've given him children.'

'You took your time about it. Apart from that?'

'Things are fine.'

'Are you making him happy?'

'Shouldn't you be asking me whether he makes me happy? I'm the feeble woman, you know.'

He smiled at her, showing a mouthful of white teeth.

'You're all right, anyone can see that by looking at you. You can't tell with him, though. How are his books doing?'

'He's published three.'

'I read *The Spiv*.'

'Did you like it.'

He fixed his hunter's eye on her – a hunter of sable and women.

'Yes.'

Silence.

Then: 'What else has he done?'

'A big book about a fellow called Giovanni delle Bande Neri, set in fifteenth- and sixteenth-century Italy. Do you know the Medicis?'

'Not personally,' replied Mendel sardonically. 'I went through Italy without seeing them. Was the book successful?'

It had sold some four thousand copies, and had it been slightly different – if the style had been a little less opulent, and the book less heavily researched, with less psychological probing and more action – it might have enjoyed the triumph of *Quo Vadis?* by Sienkiewicz, Nobel Prize-winner the year before.

'And the third?'

'Why don't you ask him?'

'Because he wouldn't tell me. Or else he would give me any old reply, with a smile.'

She thought: *So I'm not the only one who has that feeling with Taddeuz. It isn't just me . . .*

'The third didn't sell at all,' she said. 'Not even a thousand copies. It was even more unreadable than the first.'

He shook his head. 'And you'd really like to stick your sharp little nose in there, eh?'

'I promised I wouldn't.'

'Best not. For his sake and yours.'

'I know.'

And a little later he said that under no circumstances would he stay in New York. He was going to go walking again for a while, here and there: he would like to take a look around Patagonia. He didn't really know where it was – somewhere down near the Argentine pampas – but the name of the place made him laugh. And there was Africa, which he hardly knew at all, apart from Cape Town and Dakar. The countries of Arabia didn't interest him: he'd been told that in terms of alluring women, it was a damned desert.

'Money?'

He laughed. Down Santa Fe way, in New Mexico, he had set up a little transport business, as well as a hotel and bar. It was all ticking over very nicely without him. He had invested his money without really knowing why. Perhaps because the blonde who was taking care of everything in his stead knew how to count. And then he had to do something with all that gold from Alaska.

Why yes, he'd found gold. A huge pile of it. Quite by chance, without even looking for it. There was nothing more inane than the job of gold-digger: 'You kick a mountain and the ingots hit you in the face.' Why hadn't he mentioned it earlier? Oh, well, it didn't seem that important.

And this time too, just as they had three years before, he and Taddeuz went out on a memorable binge.

Taddeuz came home alone, of course.

'You know what he's like, Hannah, he doesn't like saying goodbye.'

In the end she opened her laboratory in the state of New York, almost in New York itself. Just north of Yonkers, in fact, in a deserted spot called New Rochelle, right in the middle of the countryside. It wasn't rented – she had it built: 1,200 square yards, tucked away under the trees. It was more like a hotel than a place devoted to research.

On one of her trips to Europe she paid another visit to the scientist Marie Curie, who was Polish by birth; it was she who found Juliette Mann for Hannah, who was now in charge of the laboratory in Paris. But she was unable to think of another woman who would fulfil the same function in America.

In the end, it was quite by chance, and in New York itself, that Hannah found what she was looking for: an Irish woman who was also wanted by Her Majesty's police: Kathleen O'Shea (her father was a chemist and she had followed in his footsteps) was a remarkable specialist in bombs of all kinds. Kate had not been jumping in the air with enthusiasm at their first meeting. Her first response was unequivocal: 'I've better things to do than waste time on your wretched creams!'

'Wretched' sounded delightful to Hannah's ears. *She speaks as badly as you do; you were destined to get on together!*

'Quite a few people can make bombs, Kate . . .'

'You don't know what you're talking about, you half-wit!' (The Irish woman was quick to flare up.)

'. . . whilst the work that I'm offering you will have to be given to a man if you don't accept it. And all the money that you'd earn could go to the Cause . . .'

Physically, Kate was about as alluring as a barrel of gunpowder, which she somewhat resembled. She finally said yes, on condition that she could take a holiday once a year – presumably to go and cause some explosions among the cursed English. But after all, everyone was free to do what they liked in their own time.

As well as opening in San Francisco, Hannah opened salons in Philadelphia and Chicago, New Orleans, Toronto and Montreal, bringing to a total of eight the number of beauty parlours she had on North American soil. She had also expanded the number of shops, which required less investment and the formula for which was simpler: there were now eighteen in all. Fully trained young women were now graduating every six months from her schools for sales assistants and for beauticians run by Catherine Montblanc (who was also responsible for general co-ordination and liaison with Europe). This was too many for her own real needs.

But she followed up a suggestion made by the intelligent Catherine and started negotiating with the big stores, through a pretty staggering number of lawyers. The ten-year contract she had previously signed was about to expire, and the shops now wouldn't hear of an exclusive deal of the kind they had granted her before, when she more or less had the market to herself.

After four months of discussions, Polly Twhaites' team finally managed to extract an agreement: Hannah's schools would supply the department stores with qualified personnel to staff the so-called ladies' counters.

'But we got what you wanted in exchange for something

else: for the first five years they keep twenty per cent of the profits made on the counters they operate; only ten per cent after that.'

'My schools are making money!' Catherine proclaimed joyfully. 'And another advantage of this scheme is that the girls we train will mostly remain loyal: in a choice between your products and anyone else's, they'll opt for yours . . . and give intelligent advice.'

'Have I given you a pay rise recently, Montblanc?'

'Well, it was over a year ago now.'

'Well then, it can wait. After all, I don't want to be too generous.'

She had now drawn five pink sheep and the hind quarters of a sixth.

She went to Europe six times and in 1908, thirteen years after having left, she went all the way to Australia and New Zealand. This time, though, Taddeuz went with her and that made all the difference.

But before that came the six-month stretch that she and Taddeuz spent in the private mansion she had rented on the Rue d'Assas, opposite the Jardin du Luxembourg.

They bought at least twenty paintings, four of them by Derain and five by Vlaminck. Hannah lured the two artists into a guzzling competition – there was no other word for it – for fun. It took place at the restaurant Les Vigourelles, on the Boulevard Raspail, after she made a bet with Derain and Vlaminck: it involved ordering and, more to the point, eating everything on the menu, beginning with the hors-d'oeuvre and progressing to the desserts – and then starting all over again. The first to give up had to pay for the meal. She lost, of course. (Vlaminck got through three-quarters of the menu, the most disgusting sequence of dishes he ordered being chocolate profiteroles followed by marinated herrings.)

She paid up, but had to go and lie down afterwards, after consuming nineteen hors-d'oeuvres, three fish and four meat dishes, plus vegetables.

'I wasn't going to give up without a fight, after all.'

'Try to vomit,' Taddeuz advised her, himself a teeny bit bloated.

During that same period there was a day when she wanted to go to Bagatelle, to see Santos-Dumont fly.

'Can you imagine, Taddeuz, if one day it became possible to take an aeroplane from Ireland to America! When I have such a horror of those wretched boats!'

At Bagatelle, Santos-Dumont attempted to set a world record for flying distance. A few weeks earlier he had managed sixty-nine yards in the air. That day he did infinitely better: 240 yards. He remained off the ground for 21.2 seconds (this was very accurately timed: a serviceman broke plates by throwing them on the ground at the rate of one plate per second throughout the flight). His plane reached a speed of more than twenty-five miles an hour, according to the calculations Hannah made.

'I think it would be better, though, to get the boat back to New York,' said Taddeuz.

'Clever puss!'

Taddeuz had stopped writing. At least, he had stopped writing novels: he continued with his newspaper columns, notably for the *New York Times*, and his highly sarcastic commentary on Parisian life, which he filed by telegraph, delighted his American readers. But as far as she knew – and to tell the truth, she didn't know much about it – he wasn't working on anything that might satisfy Eddy Lucas, who despaired of the situation. He too had come to Paris (as had Lizzie and Maryan, for that matter) and spent two weeks in the mansion on the Rue d'Assas. But he failed to extract from his author a single word of any use to him.

'You know him better than I do, Hannah. He smiles at

you and at the same time with all the politeness in the world he's actually telling you to go to the devil. He's unapproachable. However, I think that eventually he'll get down to it again. He's a born novelist, he'll never be able to go long without writing. He'll write. What and when remains to be seen. And anything we might do to force him would be a cure worse than the illness.'

'How could I talk to anyone about it, Lizzie? People would have thought me mad. Even you, and in any case you were pretty busy having children at the same frenetic rate as a good laying-hen. How many did you have at that time, between 1901 and 1908? Eight? Only six . . . That wasn't doing too badly, for seven years of marriage. I couldn't talk to anyone about it. Mendel was the only one, but he knew, we said everything to each other in a glance. It was only with other people that Taddeuz was calm, friendly, attentive, courteous and to all appearances wonderfully normal. Anyone who had never met him might well think that he was a kind of prince consort; a gigolo, even, living off his wife's fortune – despite the fact that he earned quite enough from his journalism to support himself. But when these same damned fools made his acquaintance, they had to bow to the evidence: he had charm, and not just in my eyes, he was devilishly intelligent; he knew a thousand million things that most people didn't know, and I would be the first to count myself one of them; he had a sense of humour. People liked him – it was impossible not to. People liked him a lot more than they've ever liked me, the greedy little Jewess. People all but came to pity him for having married me. I'm sure that people must have often said: 'She's not a patch on him.' Of course I don't mean you, or Maryan, or Polly, or various others, but there were quite a few . . .

'And with me, Lizzie . . . When we were alone together . . . Oh God! No man could have been the way he was

with me. He was everything I had ever dreamed of from the day I first opened my eyes on the world. Don't cry, Lizzie, please don't cry. Why do you think I turned out the light? I wouldn't really like you to see my face right now . . . But I have to tell someone after all these years, I'm not going to die without having spoken at all. He was gentle and cheerful, he would get round my terrible rages and embrace them, and I would always end up laughing without being able to understand how he'd managed it. And his constant tenderness . . . We had a lot of fun together over the years . . . I would begin a sentence and he would finish it: he could read my thoughts, with that amused look – so kind and amused – in his eye, as though apologizing for having been so perspicacious. And as a lover . . .

'I'm not telling you this just for the pleasure of shocking you. Not this evening . . . These things are very important . . .

'I could have been satisfied with all this, Lizzie, and not seen, not tried to see, what lay beneath the surface; pretended to ignore the fact that inside him raged an inferno. Because he was born like that, with a need for self-destruction and a need to hate himself, to turn himself into an object of derision. And perhaps I wouldn't have loved him if he'd been otherwise, I'm pretty complicated myself . . .

'But I had seen, I knew. Not all the time. There were periods when I told myself that I had too much imagination, that I was worrying unnecessarily, that it was all in my mind, as they say. Except that I wasn't the only person to see it: when Eddy Lucas told me that Taddeuz was unapproachable, he was basically saying what I thought. And Mendel had always known, he must have known before me, I could read it in his eyes . . .

'And what could I do, what could I possibly have done? In the name of heaven, what more could I have done than

what I did? Apart from leaving him, but I would sooner have died.

'Oh, that dreadful year of 1913!'

So, 1908 was the year they went to Australia together.

She revisited Melbourne, Sydney and Brisbane, retracing her steps thirteen years on, and found dozens of people who had known her during her first visit: the MacKennas naturally, but also Dinah Watts, and the two Rutge brothers, who were miraculously still alive, unlike her dear Mr Soames, the botanist; and then there were of course her directors, and Régis and Anne Fournac, and many others.

They went as far as the mining town of Cobar, and even further along the banks of the River Darling. Then on another excursion, from Perth this time, they found roughly the place where Mendel and Simon Clancy had discovered the skeleton of a man – Quentin MacKenna, they thought – who must have crossed the whole southern continent on foot, alone, unless you counted a few aboriginal companions, now also vanished for ever.

'Quentin MacKenna, the Man-Eater . . . Did you love him, Hannah?'

'Like an elder brother. After you and Mendel, he was one of the most important men in my life.'

'Thank you for putting me top of the list.'

'You always have been, and you know it. You were in a class of your own, Taddeuz. You still are and you always will be.'

He took her face in his huge hands.

'Hannah, oh Hannah!'

She had done her utmost to give him the most thorough appreciation of Australia at its most attractive – *Anyone would think you owned the place and were trying to sell it!*

'It's amazing when you think about it. If it hadn't been

for you, Taddeuz, I might have stayed here for the rest of my life. I only went back to Europe to find you.'

She began singing 'Waltzing Matilda' to show him how Australian she could have been, but he laughingly made her stop: she sang horribly out of tune.

They spent eight days on the boundless deserted beaches of the Great Barrier Reef, and sailed home via New Zealand, the Tuamotu Islands, Yokohama and Honolulu.

She gave up all hope of having a third child. This caused her enormous frustration and even distress. She had intended to have three children, not two. *Well, it's certainly not for want of trying! You will end up bringing charges against yourself and claiming damages plus interest! But this is no laughing matter. You wanted a daughter, though God only knows why. If she turned out looking like you and was even half as much of a nuisance as you are, better that she never saw the light of day. But it would have been preferable to have the choice. Even if you ended up having to drown her.*

Especially as Lizzie was doing absolutely everything to annoy her: with a certain nonchalance, she had just got her seventh child under way.

'Are you doing this deliberately, or what? You get on my nerves, you big ostrich. How does it make me look, with only two notched up?'

'You keep giving birth to beauty salons, that makes up for it.'

She now had twenty-five blue sheep and forty-nine purple ones. She was beginning to eye up the colonies and Latin America – and Asia. She was wavering between Mexico and Bombay, not to mention Saint Petersburg, which she felt she ought to visit some time. But the idea of going to Russia did not fill her with much enthusiasm, despite the insistence of Jeanne Fougaril, who knew a whole lot of archdukes. Hannah had an extremely unpleasant memory of her own stay in the Tsar's palace, when she went to plead tearfully on behalf of a certain Mendel Visoker, who had been sentenced to a Siberian penal colony and who in the meantime had been clever enough to escape all by himself, covering an incredible distance – thousands of miles – on foot.

No, she could wait a while longer before worrying about those Popov ladies.

She counted her money. Her wealth was increasing. Oh, not in any spectacular fashion – by about seven or eight hundred thousand dollars a year on average. She couldn't complain.

She now had six and a half pink sheep.

Taddeuz started writing again at the beginning of 1909. She didn't know why or how. He didn't say anything to her, of course, but she knew him a little too well not to notice at once – as she noticed his buoyant cheeriness on emerging from his study, where he remained closeted eight or ten hours at a time, breaking off only to eat, his mind elsewhere, or on returning from his own apartment in Sullivan Street in Greenwich Village. When he was in such a good mood, there could be no doubt but that he was reasonably happy with what he had written.

And what's more, he makes love to you! You get laid! Even though he's never really needed any extraneous encouragement along those lines, it helps.

But he was writing and she knew that it appeased him, perhaps even made him happy. In *The Spiv*, one of his characters had said: 'When I write I feel almost alive again, and not too distressed to be alive . . .'

Maryan went more and more frequently to California – not to San Francisco, but to the south where scarcely anyone ever went. On two or three occasions Lizzie went with him, although she didn't like being separated from her brood.

'Don't ask me what he does there, Hannah. He combs the hills with some kind of instrument for measuring the area. You know what he's like: when it's a matter of business, he is about as communicative as a tin-opener. That said, the countryside is not at all bad, it's nice down there. It's a place called Los Angeles. Pretty name, don't you think?'

Hannah had her own ideas on the subject: not on Los Angeles, which was almost unknown to her, but on what it could be that attracted Maryan to such a remote place. The year before – or was it two years ago? – she had asked him what state he had reached with his old plan of going into business with Thomas Edison. Maryan had shifted from one foot to the other.

'I've broken off all negotiations with Edison, Hannah.'

'You wanted to make films, didn't you?'

'Not make them. Get other people to make them.'

'And Edison is too greedy?'

'He's not greedy: he wants it all.'

She burst out laughing, remembering her own encounter with the inventor.

'But you're going to go ahead anyway, aren't you, Maryan?'

'I don't know. It depends.'

It was impossible to get any more details at all.

As a father and head of the family, as a husband, he was perfect. But for Lizzie's restraining influence, he and his seven children (at the latest count) would have put the house on Long Island to fire and sword. Once, in imitation of his elder sons, he had painted himself red in order to turn himself into a Sioux: for a week he had to go to Wall Street with his skin the colour of boiled lobster.

It left him completely unperturbed – a strange

transformation in a man who was otherwise a very hard worker and deadly serious in business.

'I adore the fool,' said Lizzie.

Mendel made two passing visits, in 1908 and 1910. He had been to Africa, for a change.

'A very interesting continent. African women have extraordinary buttocks, sturdy and streamlined, like . . .'

'Mendel! You're talking to a lady!'

'Where? I don't see any lady. If you're a lady, then I'm Oscar Wilde. How are you, kid?'

In 1911, thinking they would surprise him, Taddeuz and she made a detour to Santa Fe, New Mexico. They might just as well not have bothered. The bar-restaurant certainly belonged to him, as did a ranch with five hundred head of cattle on the banks of the Rio Grande, about twenty miles to the north-west . . .

'But he won't be there either,' the very voluptuous blonde who ruled in Mendel's absence warned them. 'He's either in Tibet or with Earp.'

'Earp who?'

'Wyatt Earp, the former marshal. You know, the one involved in the settling of scores at the OK Corral at Tombstone.'

Apparently, if the blonde was to be believed, Mendel and Earp were friends, despite their difference in age. Two months ago, apparently, a letter had arrived from Los Angeles. From Earp. Mendel had left at once.

'Any excuse is good enough for him, in any case . . .'

'Would you be his wife?' asked Taddeuz.

The voluptuous blonde laughed, or rather whinnied with rage: she was as much married to Mendel as the fifteen hundred other fools like herself.

'That guy is a real public danger to the women of this continent.'

'And of other continents too,' Hannah corrected her –

she thought it killingly funny but was also convulsed with pride.

They drove to Santa Fe in their latest acquisition, a Rolls-Royce Silver Ghost, a bewitching beauty. To get back to New York, they put it on a train. Gaffouil and Yvonne were travelling with them, as ever. They were now married.

Hannah felt her life was over; not over in the sense that she was going to stop living – *The day I want to die, I shall inform the appropriate authority. For the time being, it can wait another century* – but over in the sense that she had achieved all her objectives – *Short of one child! I've only had two.*

By the beginning of 1913 she had succeeded professionally: all that remained to be done was to apply the finishing touches and to sweep out the corners. She had been married to Taddeuz for thirteen years, and it had been wonderful; not a day, not a minute gone by, nor a word spoken did she regret. *And he's writing. His last book obviously wasn't a triumph but once again the critics raved about it – perhaps you have to choose between being appreciated by the critics and having real readers. It pains him though, but – how can I put it? – he suffers no more than usual. Besides, sooner or later it will be common knowledge that he's a genius. No doubt about it.*

'I love you.'

He took her in his arms.

That spring, having returned once more from Europe, they set off together for California.

It was the spring of 1913, the first of the black years.

CHAPTER 8

Kiss Me, Kid

The telegram arrived on 19 May 1913, at about 6.30 A.M. It came to the house on Long Island, which was near enough deserted. There was only a caretaker couple looking after the garden and the dogs; six days earlier, having entrusted Adam, nearly ten, and Jonathan, aged six, to the care of the Kadens and their governess, Charlotte O'Malley, Hannah and Taddeuz had gone to California.

The caretakers were Poles and recent immigrants to the United States; they had been in the country barely four months. Their knowledge of English was pretty sketchy, they didn't like to disturb anyone so early in the day, and they weren't used to the telephone. They wasted an hour at least before deciding to do something, which was to go over to the Kadens on the other side of the lake.

Lizzie was still asleep at such an early hour, but Maryan had already been at work for an hour in his office on the ground floor (it was a Sunday).

Unfortunately, the Polish caretaker hadn't thought to bring the telegram with him. He had thought it would be safer with his wife, whom he had left in charge of the house. Maryan decided to take his car, without being in any particular hurry. From her bed on the first floor, Lizzie heard him leave and wondered where on earth he could be going. She heard him return and the unusual screech of tyres as the car turned into the drive made her realize that something was wrong. She put on a dressing gown and went downstairs. Maryan appeared, his face as white as chalk. All he said was: 'Mendel.'

* * *

It was a place called Keota, in Oklahoma, in the eastern part of the state near the border with Arkansas, at the far end of one of the many creeks that fed Robert Kerr Lake. It was hardly a town, with no more than a thousand inhabitants.

Hannah and Taddeuz didn't get there until Tuesday 22nd, a little after eight o'clock in the morning, after a mad dash from Los Angeles. Hannah had to hire a special train, since there wasn't a sufficiently quick regular service, and Taddeuz had driven like a maniac from the little town of Oklahoma City at the wheel of the fastest car they could find.

Maryan was waiting for them.

'Don't tell me he's dead,' said Hannah with genuine savageness in her voice.

'He isn't. By rights he should be. But he isn't.'

'Why hasn't he been taken to hospital?'

'He can't be moved. And he doesn't want to be moved.'

There were a dozen people there, three of them doctors that Maryan had summoned: one from New York (Maryan had brought him along; he was a surgeon at Mount Sinai Hospital). The others were local: great, raw-boned giants, who looked pretty dirty; they had come down from the Ozark Mountains, and wore chequered shirts and trousers with braces and straw hats, and stood there chewing. The heat of an early spring was already considerable. The group parted at the approach of Hannah, Taddeuz and Maryan. *And the three of us advance, led by one Pole, towards another Pole who is going to die in a remote part of America*, thought Hannah with dreadful, chilling sadness.

The car had had to stop when the road became completely unsuitable for any vehicle, and they had continued on foot through the oak trees, walnuts and elms. They reached the cabin, which stood on a strip of land on the edge of a wood, in the midst of a fabulous riot of flowers, the pink magenta flowers of the Judas tree.

'He lived here?'

'If he could be said to have lived anywhere, Hannah.'

She entered the cabin where there were two women: Lizzie, and a very beautiful young Indian, who must have been about fifteen or sixteen.

'Take her out, please, Lizzie. Leave me alone with him.'

'Don't touch the boy, Hannah. He'd just had too much to drink.'

'I'll see him hang, twice over,' she said through clenched teeth, with incredible, hate-filled fury. 'If I have to hang him myself . . .'

'That's just what I don't want you to do.'

He had been stripped naked in the hope of cleaning him up, or doing something to that horrible wound in his abdomen, where the two bullets filled with buckshot had been fired into him at point-blank range. And then, despairing of being able to treat it, the doctors had simply covered it with bandages. The lower part of his body lay under a garishly coloured Indian blanket, the upper part of his torso was bare, revealing the astounding broadness of his shoulders and his impressive muscularity.

'Hannah? I want you to promise.'

'No!'

'How old are you?'

'Thirty-eight.'

'I'm fifty-five, so we've known each other for exactly thirty-one years. One of two things is possible, kid: either you promise not to go after that child or I shall hold it against you for the rest of eternity. If there is such a thing. I hope not: life is already long enough, if they add on any more time, especially if it's eternal, there'll be no end to it.'

'Don't talk so much.'

'And·why not? I waited for you to come before I went to sleep but I'm beginning to get damned sleepy. I'd tell you that you were the only woman I've ever loved, but that would probably make you snivel, so I'd better keep my big mouth shut.'

'I'm not going to snivel.'

'OK. You're by far and away the only woman I've ever loved.'

'You see, I'm not snivelling.'

The tears were streaming down her face, but soundlessly.

He managed to raise his head and smiled: 'Very good,' he said. 'I could see your owl-like eyes when I was walking in Siberia. They lit my way.'

He closed his eyes but immediately opened them again, with a very slight start, fighting against the sleepiness that was overtaking him. He was right: it was indeed thirty-one years, give or take a month or two. It had been very sunny then, and similarly hot, when he had appeared out of nowhere with his *brouski. He came into your life – and he's leaving it – in the heat of summer; and yet how he loved the cold*. It was all very well trying to fight against it, she couldn't rid herself of the feeling that he was betraying and abandoning her by dying.

'Hannah, I'm quite content with my life, overall. I've wandered as much as I wanted. Recently I've been feeling a bit tired; I'd started to drag my feet a bit. That brat with his gun did the necessary, so you're going to leave him alone. I've never asked anything of you before, but this time, I am.'

'I'll make sure he gets a medal for it.'

'Don't try to be sarcastic with me, you dreadful child. You do as I say, and that's that. For once in your life, you follow orders. Agreed?'

'Agreed.'

'And another thing: the Cherokee girl who was here just now. She can read and write and she's sweet at making love.'

'I'll look after her.'

'Thank you. What else? Ah yes, the flower market in Nice. That day or the next, when we had a man-to-man talk, he told me that he loved you more than anything. I told him that if he was lying to me I would break his neck, but I don't think he was: he was sincere, you could see it a mile off. Does he still make love to you well, Hannah?'

'Better than in my dreams. But he told you something else.'

'And you've stuck together for thirteen years . . . I wouldn't have laid a kopeck on it – which just goes to show how mistaken you can be, even if you're Mendel . . .'

'He told you something else.'

'Which is his own concern. He'll tell you if he wants to. I'm feeling sleepy, Hannah.'

He closed his eyes again, his right hand releasing the long-barrelled Colt Peacemaker he had been using to prevent anyone from trying to move him. She thought he was already dead . . .

'Kiss me, kid. As though you loved me.'

Full on the mouth, like that one time in Vienna, before he left Europe: 'Oh Mendel! Mendel! Mendel! Mendel!'

He smiled.

He smiled, his eyelids irrevocably closed.

'If I'm not here when I wake up, don't be angry with me, Hannah . . .'

And after that nothing, apart from the regular cries of two or three mocking birds perched in the Judas trees. The moment came when all movement in the gigantic breast ceased. Only then did she collapse, and it was Taddeuz who carried her out, having caught her as she fell.

* * *

Through the bars of the prison she saw a little runt with straw-coloured hair, looking scared, his face bruised from the blows he had received after firing the gun.

'And *he* killed Mendel?'

'There was trouble in town,' explained the sheriff. 'These oil fellows became unruly, they were beginning to smash the place up. I took on one lot and Visoker took care of the others. He always refused to carry a gun, although I gave him one when I gave him his star. But he had power enough to calm the worst hotheads. I don't know how well you knew him: just the way he smiled could make your blood run cold.'

'Come here,' said Hannah to the prisoner.

'Keep calm, now,' said Taddeuz behind her.

'I'm very calm.'

Without even turning her head, she asked the sheriff: 'Can I go into the cell?'

The lawman finally opened up for her. She went in.

'How old are you?'

The boy stammered. Far from approaching her, as she had asked him to, he drew back when she came in, flattening himself against the back wall, completely terrified now that he tried to meet the look in those grey eyes. He repeated, more distinctly, that he was seventeen and a half. Yes, he had been drinking on Saturday evening; he had been with his two older brothers. He saw Visoker bang their heads together and knock them senseless. He thought Visoker was going to do the same to him. The guns were in the wagon; he picked one up with no intention of using it at first, he couldn't remember exactly . . . He was frightened of the man who came towards him, smiling beneath that moustache of his; everyone said that he could kill you with a single punch. Yes, he'd seen the star on his chest, and after he'd pulled the trigger the first time he was terrified to see the man still coming towards him as though nothing had happened, and so he'd picked up the other gun . . .

He was hardly any taller than Hannah. And puny, sickly, stinking of filth and urine. Pathetic.

She came out of the cell and said to Maryan: 'Get him a lawyer, the best there is.'

He stared at her impassively, as though with eyes turned inward on himself, and she remembered that there had been something more than mere friendship – although that in itself would have made it bad enough – between Maryan and Mendel.

'I know, Maryan. But that's what he wanted. And we shall do what he wanted.'

Personally you would happily kill the pathetic little runt twenty times over . . . Or you would have done before coming here. Not any more. Because it really wouldn't be worthy of Mendel to take vengeance on such a snivelling, tearful little creature . . .

CHAPTER 9
Sunset Boulevard

She and Taddeuz had gone to California together because, for once, their professional paths had crossed. She had decided to open a salon in Los Angeles. The town as it was now didn't warrant it. But she had learned something of interest. She had found out about make-up when first starting out by talking to actors. A dinner in New York had brought her into contact with a young actress called Gladys Smith, who was beginning to make a career for herself under the name of Mary Pickford, and worked for a film company called Biograph. The actress was fascinated by Hannah's work, and enthusiastically agreed to wear mascara and a blue kohl, which emphasized her eyes on the screen. In March 1910 Mary Pickford came to tell her that Biograph had decided to leave New York in order to build studios on the West Coast. Hannah's curiosity was aroused.

'Maryan, that's why you're always going off there, isn't it?'

'It's America there too.'

'What about these studios?'

They did not amount to very much, according to Maryan: Biograph's studios basically consisted of a fenced-off plot of land, a wooden platform and a few so-called sets made of cotton canvas blowing in the wind. The actors (Mary Pickford, Mack Sennett, Harry Carey, Lionel Barrymore and the like) changed behind screens – they were shooting several films a day; rehearsals took place in a barn; and there were only three chairs for all the people working there.

'But you believe all the same that cinema has a future?'

He nodded. And told her that if Pickford, or Mae Marsh, or Priscilla Dean were to become very famous, if they were made up by one of the beauticians trained by Cathy Montblanc, and if this were publicized, it could have a big effect on the sales of products that bore the double H trademark.

This had already occurred to her.

'Are there any other companies moving out to California?'

'There have been quite a few for some time.'

'Because of Edison getting everybody here annoyed, is that it?'

'That's one of the reasons. His detective is everywhere, but California is a long way off. And because it's sunny there the whole year round, you can film almost without a break.'

Yes, there was a list, constantly subject to revision, of the companies like Biograph who were migrating. Biograph in fact had followed in the footsteps of a producer called William Selig, who in November 1908 filmed a version of *The Count of Monte Cristo* in Los Angeles. Since then, they had been followed by Bison Life Motion Pictures; then Essany of Chicago; Kalem; the Horsley brothers' company, Nestor; Vitagraph from Brooklyn; Pathé Exchange; Pilgrim; Zukor's Famous Player; and Jesse L. Lasky's Lasky Feature Play Company, whose artistic director was Cecil B. De Mille . . .

'Hannah, it's beginning to get very important.'

'But I'm not going to get much business out of a place populated by farmers and oil prospectors. Not even with three dozen unfortunate actors lost in the wilderness.'

'The population has grown from one hundred thousand to three hundred thousand in ten years. It won't be long before it reaches a million.'

Maryan, to the best of her knowledge, had never been wrong in his forecasts before now.

She asked him: 'And you've found a place for a shop?'

He's perhaps two or three times richer than you – even someone like Bernard Benda is full of admiration for him – and you still treat him like an errand boy!

'You'll need more than one shop,' he said. 'I can negotiate deals with the companies, I know quite a few people. Maybe they won't all agree but I can get an exclusive make-up contract with eight or ten of them.'

'I'm going to ask Polly to come over from London.'

'You ought to come along as well.'

'I shall. You haven't told me where you were thinking of setting up the salon . . .'

'It's got a pretty name,' he said. 'Sunset Boulevard.'

(All this took place when she and Taddeuz had just returned from Europe, before Mendel died.)

'I would have preferred Sunrise to Sunset,' said Hannah with a laugh. 'You couldn't ask them to change the name, could you?'

And then, by a combination of circumstances that Hannah had nothing to do with, Cecil B. De Mille, whom they had known for several years, came to see Taddeuz and asked him to write some film scripts.

'Tired?'

'No.'

From Oklahoma, they drove down to California, taking turns at the wheel, although Taddeuz did most of the driving. She preferred going by road, when there was one, to the train. She still felt empty, as though maimed. Taddeuz had been overwhelmingly gentle with her, comforting her with the right words, saying what needed to be said. He even realized that she didn't want to make love for a while. He talked of Mendel better than she could have done . . .

In New Mexico, they spent a few days in Taos, a little town three centuries old, withdrawing into a state of solitude that was scarcely breached by the inexorable and daily reports of Jessie in New York, of Cathy Montblanc, of Jeanne Fougaril in Europe and two calls from Maryan and Lizzie, who were worried by their silence.

Only once did they have to change cars, having picked up the Rolls that Gaffouil had brought down for them on the other side of the Rockies.

They reached Los Angeles on 15 June. The Lasky studio was a barn on Hollywood's Western Avenue, the scrub land around it representing the Wild West. De Mille was busy shooting *The Squaw Man*, with the stage actor Dustin Farnum playing the title role. He seemed surprised, and a bit put out, to see Taddeuz so many thousands of miles from New York. It very quickly became apparent to the young couple that the enthusiastic promises he had made on the banks of the Hudson had melted away under the California sun.

'It doesn't matter at all, Hannah. And it's not Cecil's fault either. He's right: I'm not a screenwriter, and doubtless not a playwright either.'

In 1913 he published his fifth novel. He had abandoned the historical novel: he had grown tired of this, and of what his publisher, Lucas, called the popular novel. In his last two books, Taddeuz had returned to his former style. *The Red Key*, published in 1908, and particularly *The Mendicant*, which appeared in 1911, met with the same fate as his first work: the critics praised them but only a few hundred people read them. Eddy Lucas argued with him over the titles, but to no avail. *The Red Key* was all right, but how many people knew what a mendicant was? ('A mendicant is someone who is dependent on alms for sustenance,' Taddeuz had explained with very calm but very unyielding stubbornness.)

'Hannah, try and convince him, for pity's sake! About the titles, but especially about the text. He is extraordinarily talented, he could be a Melville or a Poe, if he only put his mind to it. Those short stories that he wrote are a sheer marvel. If he would only fill two hundred pages with them, I'd sell fifty thousand . . . Hannah, he'll listen to you – I give up. It's not a question of money, although at the rate things are going I won't be able to carry on publishing for much longer . . . No, please, I won't accept anything from you, ever, I'm not launching an appeal for funds. I simply find it lamentable and sad that he should be so stubborn . . .'

'Taddeuz is Taddeuz,' was all Hannah had said in reply, without any further comment.

She read the famous short stories that Lucas had made such a fuss about. She was horrified by the harrowing morbidity they gave expression to. Worse still, she thought she recognized herself, described in clinical detail, in one of the characters, and was sickened by the very idea that Taddeuz could have depicted her as the abusive, despotic, smothering, monstrous mother that he had inflicted on the hero of one of his stories – in which the hero, what's more, ended up committing suicide in the most appalling manner.

That wasn't all he wrote: he had produced two plays, both of them totally bleak. One of them had been done on Broadway. There was a full house for the dress rehearsal and the opening night (with all the friends they had in New York, this was easy to explain), but then empty, or near enough, by the third performance. It was taken off after four days. And those unbearable moments in the foyer, when people came up, adding insult to injury, to congratulate the author with an embarrassment they could not quite conceal . . .

'It doesn't matter, Hannah . . .'

And he wore that half-smile she hated for the self-mockery it expressed!

In the end, the only area in which he was successful was as a critic, at the moment a literary critic. He now had a weekly article in *The New Yorker* – he had got this on his own, she had had nothing to do with it. Hannah was told by people on all sides – in those very limited circles that took an interest in such things – that in his comments on books and the theatre he was remarkable, caustic, very funny.

But the fact is he's paid only a little more than your beauticians, and there are six hundred of them!

So it didn't matter? Still suffering from the terrible blow of Mendel's death, she found herself trembling with rage. It didn't matter! But in that case, what did? My wretched beauty parlours?

She could almost have killed poor De Mille, although she couldn't really hold it against him. She was too much of a professional herself not to be able to understand the film director's reactions.

'Lizzie, the times I've turned away a girl or a woman because I thought her incapable of doing the job she was hoping to get from me . . . It never gives you any pleasure, it sometimes makes you feel a bit sick, especially when you know the person really needs a job. I have occasionally helped those I've had to turn down, and it was never very successful. And I can't look after the whole world . . . Who ever did me any favours? Do you have any idea of the number of men who've tried to destroy me, to take my place, because or although I was a woman?

'I never held it against Cecil. In his place, knowing only what he knew about Taddeuz, having read nothing else by him but The Spiv *or* The Mendicant, *I'd probably have done the same.*

'But, coming on top of Mendel's death, it was all too much. I'd kept my promise for thirteen years . . . It's a damned long time, thirteen years, when someone close to you is drowning.'

* * *

They took a suite at the Hollywood Hotel, the usual meeting place of the actors. One of their windows was set in the middle of a bizarre façade in the style of a Mexican church. Down below, wild parties were thrown nearly every evening. Mary Pickford was one of the queens of these parties.

Hannah rarely went down during the weeks that she and Taddeuz spent in Los Angeles. As usual she got up at about four thirty and after her daily walk went through the accounts – American, European and the rest. However, four o'clock was the time Taddeuz went to bed: he preferred to write at night – and two months previously he had started on his new novel.

The first miracle was that he had told her what it was about: the second miracle was that she understood everything he said. He was taking as a starting point the crazy desert odyssey of Quentin MacKenna. But of course, with that distorting prism he had for a brain, Taddeuz had greatly modified the narrative line that Hannah had given him. Quentin had chosen self-imposed exile, because he had eaten human flesh when shipwrecked and because he had been emasculated. Taddeuz's character had no physical or social handicap, and a large part of the book consisted of a dazzling description of his inner life, written in wonderful language – it was these aspects of her husband's novels that most perplexed, not to say terrified, Hannah: she had a horror of explanations and psychological probing. '*People who want to explain things have always bored the pants off me, Lizzie . . . All right, I'm sorry, I didn't mean to be so crude . . .*'

Nonetheless, the second half of the novel was very romantic – Eddy Lucas almost wept with joy, even though the desert that the hero had to cross was phantasmagorical, to say the least, and rife with symbolism.

Of paramount importance in Hannah's eyes, this novel would allow her to shed the inertia of the past thirteen years. Every time it surfaced she pushed the idea to the back of her mind, but it was as though Mendel's death had removed the final check on her. Had he been alive, she would probably not have risked it. But she did, her decision was made, she was going to take a hand in his career and sort things out.

You're going to help him succeed. You ought to have done it a long time ago. Would he have hesitated to give you his support if you'd been in difficulty in your business affairs? Why should this be any different?

Of course, he mustn't know anything about it, that went without saying.

She had already chosen the men she would deal with.

There was Eddy Lucas, of course, but the New York publisher would know nothing of what she was plotting and would be only one of her instruments. Mary Pickford, who would not be taken into Hannah's confidence either, had a part to play as well: she supplied Hannah with the names she needed. Mary thought that the best possible team, in terms of producing a film in Hollywood, was the one that had gathered around the Biograph renegade, David Wark Griffith, who had an assistant called Raoul Walsh.

'I know Griffith. He's been a guest at our house on Long Island two or three times.'

'David is the most brilliant director, Hannah; the most intellectual, if you like. For him, cinema is bound to become an art form. He has some fantastic projects. This Walsh fellow is remarkable too, and they have people like Allan Dwan and Jack Conway, who are really very talented . . .'

Two other major film-makers, apart from Griffith, were beginning to rank high on Sunset Boulevard: Thomas Harper Ince and Mack Sennett. But the former was specializing more and more in westerns – thanks to his own Inceville studios in Santa Monica – while Sennett was a frenetically creative man who had set himself up in Ellendale, where his Keystone company was turning out comic shorts full of gags and bathing beauties.

Griffith seemed to Hannah the best possible choice.

His employer at that time was a certain Harry E. Aitken, head of Reliance Majestic.

The first time Hannah met Aitken, he was accompanied by a big illiterate Mexican, with a moustache and a booming voice, whom he had the nerve to employ as an actor in one of his films: his name was Pancho Villa.

CHAPTER 10

Old and Ugly, Eh?

Aitken shook his head.

'This really is a very strange proposition you're making . . .'

'You can say no.'

He burst out laughing: who would ever turn down so much money? And this Karen . . .

'Kaden,' Hannah corrected him.

'This Kaden is the most fierce negotiator I've ever encountered. Does he never smile? And for all his politeness he actually went so far as to threaten me, though you wouldn't think it to look at him . . .'

'If anyone gets to hear about my project through any fault of yours,' said Hannah, 'anyone at all, I shall set aside one million dollars, and even five if necessary, for the sole purpose of utterly ruining you. And that won't be the end of it. I can supply you with proof that I do actually have five million dollars. More, in fact.'

He studied her. Their meeting took place to the north-west of Hollywood, in an area that was still virtually desert, called Glendale, which lay between the hills of Verdugo and San Rafael. There were no witnesses. Acting on instructions given him by Maryan, Aitken had come to the meeting place alone in his car; he had found Hannah, also alone, standing by her Rolls.

'You inherited the money?' he asked.

'Of course. After all, you don't imagine that I earned it all by myself, do you?'

He nodded his head, narrowing his eyes. 'Upon my word, you might be capable of it . . .'

'OK, I earned it myself.'

He nodded.

'I admit, I'm interested,' he said. 'Extremely interested. There's always a need for injections of cash in the cinema. Especially when the money's . . . clean. Which is the case, is it not?'

'The Rockefeller Bank will confirm that for you, Mr Aitken. Satisfied?'

'Completely. And you've already made your choice?'

'Yes. The director: David Wark Griffith. If it can't be him: his assistant Raoul Walsh. The actor: that man Ullmann who calls himself Douglas Fairbanks, and as his co-star, Lillian Gish.'

'Who slightly resembles you, apart from the eyes. About as much as a Persian cat resembles a starving panther.'

'Sheer coincidence,' she said as coldly as she knew how. 'Aitken? I want total secrecy. Don't ever forget that.'

'And how am I to proceed?'

She told him.

She agreed with Maryan about setting up a beauty parlour in Los Angeles. In her opinion he was right in predicting an ultra-rapid development of the town and of this new industry, the cinema. Especially as Maryan was planning to have a house built locally . . .

'Here, in Los Angeles, Maryan?'

'I happen to own a little plot of land hereabouts,' he said.

'Maryan, we can come to some arrangement between ourselves about the extra cost, but in addition to the rooms for Lizzie and you and the children, I would like you to allow some room . . . for us. And especially for him. Somewhere he can work, as he usually does . . .'

'With pleasure, but don't you think a separate house would be better for him? My kids are going to disturb him . . .'

'You're usually so smart: if I have a house built or buy one here, he might realize what I'm up to. Do you have any idea which area you're going to live in?'

He nodded, almost reluctantly. And then revealed that for the past four or five years he had been buying 'a few small plots, here and there, in the locality' . . . A few hundred acres in small lots in the mountains of Santa Monica, south of Bel Air and Westwood . . . And a bit elsewhere, as well . . .

'Are you sure it comes to only a few hundred acres?'

It was possible that it might be more extensive, yes. He couldn't say off the top of his head what the total area was (*Like hell you can't*, she thought) but there might be more. True, he had already sold some of the land, over near Vine Street, for instance, to some studios that wanted to set up there. And then there were those plots on which there were plans to expand the university . . .

'Roughly speaking, Maryan, just how much land do you own for this house you're going to build?'

'Roughly? Let's say, virtually everything that lies between Washington Boulevard and Santa Monica.'

'Roughly, eh? Oh Maryan!'

And, would you believe, he had a very attractive plot that would be perfect for a house of some thirty rooms.

'To tell the truth, ever since Lizzie first came here, she's been dreaming of California, and of the sun. She's always refused to leave New York, because of you, but if I tell her . . .'

He broke off short and shifted from one foot to the other.

'Sorry, I won't tell her anything, of course.'

'Even Lizzie mustn't know, Maryan. There'll be only three of us who do: Aitken, you, and me.'

'I'll find some way of persuading Lizzie.'

She gazed at him, overwhelmed by an immense feeling of fraternal tenderness. Mendel's death had affected him almost as much as her and this impassive man had held her in his arms and wept with her at the burial. Images from the past surfaced in her mind: a thirteen- or fourteen-year-old urchin slaving away, doing the work of two men at Vistula Station in Warsaw, sleeping two or three hours a night and doing everything possible to feed his mother and his eight or nine brothers and sisters; shouldering with a quiet courage the responsibility of being head of the family: as soon as he was able, he had sent to Poland for his mother (she had died, exhausted, in 1901) and every single one of his brothers and sisters; and he had taken care of all of them, and was today head of a clan of nearly a hundred, including the new generations.

In Hannah's eyes, though, despite his breathtaking wealth, he was still exactly the same as ever. 'I owe everything to you, Hannah,' he had said to her one day, 'absolutely everything. Including Lizzie.' He was not her employee, she hadn't been paying him a salary for more than twelve years; he had told her it was pointless. He was nothing, he had no title. But she only had to ask him to go and take a look around Toronto or Rome and he acted on it instantly, or sent one of his fiendish spies.

His marriage to Lizzie was a complete success, she could no longer doubt it, despite being so ready to anticipate catastrophe. The sight of Maryan the Taciturn playing with his children melted her heart, kindling a fierce joy within her.

'The place where I'm going to build is called Beverly Hills,' he said, almost loquaciously, or at least with untypical forthcomingness. 'It's more or less on the corner of Coldwater Canyon Drive and Sunset Boulevard. It's only natural I should live there, virtually the whole place belongs to me. Lizzie is going to spend a fortune on gardeners again – she'll be the ruin of me, but never mind.'

A fond gleam came into his blue eyes. But then it faded. He fell silent. He began shifting from one foot to the other again, even more than before.

She lowered her head, then looked up.

'I know, Maryan. But I have to help him. However dangerous it might be . . . Maryan, do you think this is a mistake?'

He shook his head. He didn't know.

The salon on Sunset Boulevard would be a stone's throw from Fairfax Avenue; there would be one shop in Pershing Square, another in Bunker Hill. And there would be flying squads of beauticians and make-up specialists whose services would be utilized by film production companies – Universal in particular.

Taddeuz was the first to leave Los Angeles. After a good period during which he was able to write fairly quickly he had once again ground to a halt. The Hollywood Hotel environment was intolerable to him: there was too much noise, and he needed the books in his library. De Mille had suggested – in all seriousness – that he became a film actor.

'I'm forty-three,' replied Taddeuz.

'You look thirty, not even that. On screen, people would take you for twenty-five. Tad, I'm not joking and I'm not just talking about a walk-on part. I've got a wonderful part for you, with Fanny Ward and Sessue Hayakawa.'

Taddeuz wasn't interested. He took the train back to New York.

'I shan't be long in joining you, my love. I'm going to miss you.'

The night before, they had made love for the first time since Mendel's death.

She got into the compartment with him now and, but for the imminent departure of the train, she would gladly have made the beast with two backs again, on the padded seat. It was true that he didn't look his age. *People will end up taking you for his mother!* He was one of those tall blond men with a smooth face on whom the years seem to have no hold. The Californian sun had given him a tan. She had never seen him so handsome – and all the damned whores in Hollywood had not been able to stop devouring him with their eyes.

She was frightened.

She knew what intelligence – constantly lying in wait, terrifyingly astute, capable of seizing on the slightest inflection in her voice, on the least word too many, on the merest twitch of her finger – was hidden behind those somewhat dreamy eyes, that famous half-smile. She did not underestimate him. There had been many previous separations; but this one was different. *It's the first time you've ever lied to him.*

'Kiss me, for pity's sake.'

In the end he picked her up in his arms and put her down on the platform. Hours later she could still feel the touch of his fingers around her waist.

The next day, through the highly anonymous medium of a bank, Hannah placed the sum of $250,000, as agreed, at Aitken's disposal. The money was to finance a big film to be made by D. W. Griffith, called *Birth of a Nation*. Aitken would keep ten per cent as an agency fee, as it were. The rest would go into the film. If the film made any profits, they would be divided ten per cent to Aitken and ninety per cent to Hannah. Her share was to be paid into the accounts of the three hospitals on the list she had given him. The division of the spoils had been the topic of fierce discussion: Aitken had asked for a fifty-fifty deal (without much conviction), hoping to get twenty-five per cent. She had proved all the more intransigent because she wasn't acting on her own behalf. *It would really be the end if you actually made money out of this.*

'Harry, if the film doesn't do at all well, you will have made twenty-five thousand dollars, which, if my information is correct – and it is – is near enough three years' income for you. Otherwise, you can work it out for yourself. Let's not waste any time, please. Now, let's look at the other part of the deal. I shall pay you seventy-five thousand dollars as agreed for the second film that you will produce, based on a scenario by my husband. Fifty thousand of that is to pay the director and the scriptwriter, or writers. You'll pay the rest. Since you're going to get the profits, it is right that you should invest in it. Or else I'll finance it, but then I take everything.'

'I don't even know what the film is supposed to be about!'

'You can read, can't you? You know what you have to do. Do it. If not, I take back everything, starting with the $250,000. Harry, look into my eyes, and look carefully: if this secret ever gets out, I give you my word I'm capable of having you killed. Do you believe me?'

He was ten or eleven inches taller than her, and certainly double her weight. He shifted from one foot to the other, like Maryan.

'No problem, Hannah. I'll take the secret with me to my grave. Would you have dinner with me? We can be discreet about it.'

'And I won't sleep with you either,' she said.

Taking advantage of being in California, she went upstate as soon as she had finished with the architects who had come to present their plans for her salon (she had a good reason for staying on in Los Angeles, she made sure of that).

She spent five days in San Francisco. She hadn't been there since 1906, the day after the earthquake in April, when she had come to see the damage. Happily, not a single member of her staff had lost their life. The San Francisco establishment was run by a man, Emmet Wayne.

'I'm giving you the OK to open in Sacramento, Emmet. Send me some photos of the premises and the projected decor. However, you can get rid of that fat, bored-looking blonde in California Street. Three weeks' pay and out. I don't like sales assistants who don't know how to smile . . . What do you mean, she didn't recognize me? Don't say things like that or you're the one I'll kick out. It doesn't make any difference. I might have been an ordinary client. Show me your books, please . . .'

She returned to New York.

'I'm not beautiful, Taddeuz. I'm old and ugly.'

'Absolutely.'

'I was horrible to that poor Emmet Wayne. If only I could hold my wretched tongue . . . I'm old and cantankerous.'

'Absolutely.'

'But you're not ageing. What's worse: you're getting more handsome. Mary and Lillian and the other girls were drooling over you.'

'Absolutely.'

He caught her round the waist, picked her up and took her upstairs, carrying her like a bolster under his arm. She hung limply on either side, deliberately, like a broken doll.

'No one wants me any more. Everyone hates me.'

'Absolutely,' he said.

'Stop saying absolutely!'

'*Ya*.'

A shadowy light filled the room in the house on Long Island, the shadowy vibrant light of summer, when it's too hot for a rattlesnake outside. Taddeuz dropped her on the bed with ebony bedposts and a sumptuous white lace counterpane that smelt slightly of vanilla. Hannah had taken three days' holiday and, apart from the two hours at dawn that she devoted to going over the figures, she had broken off all contact with her business affairs. From California she had brought back half a wagonload of presents for Adam and Jonathan. The elder of her two sons had smiled in ecstasy; his younger brother had retained his usual impenetrable expression. It was almost disturbing how much the two children resembled the two adults, one a replica of Taddeuz, the other another Hannah, at least in terms of eyes and personality. On these three mornings when for once they had both parents together, the children had come rushing into the couple's bedroom as soon as they woke up. The four of them shared the bed together, while files and documents lay forgotten in the study next door. Joining in the laughter, the cleaning ladies brought them all breakfast in bed, a treat that degenerated into a battle with boiled eggs. Hannah lost, her three men smearing four on her face and the others on any part of her that wasn't covered by the sheets. All the bedding had to be changed and then they sat down to breakfast all over again in the dining room downstairs. They went boating on the lake, where they had another battle, which they won – a naval battle this time – against the Kaden crew which put out from the opposite bank, but was short of their captain, Maryan, who was still in California. True, the enemy were superior in number – Lizzie already had eleven children. However, the Newman clan won, even though Hannah, as a result of a cunning manoeuvre involving combatants on both sides, was thrown into the water in her beautiful white dress, her wide-brimmed hat, her Irish lace gloves and the provocative chiffon ribbon that fell from the crown of her hat on to the nape of her neck.

'This really isn't my day. First it was the eggs, and now a ducking.'

'And the day's not over yet,' said Taddeuz.

It was about four in the afternoon. After lunch, Lizzie had taken the whole horde of children riding. Hannah and Taddeuz were left on their own. The servants had made themselves scarce. There was no wind, just the full heat of summer and the silence broken only by the buzzing of bees.

She was lying with legs straight and arms outstretched while he peeled off her clothes.

She watched him, on the brink of tears, while he stripped her naked, without even bothering to undo buttons or untie laces, calmly, almost nonchalantly, ripping her silk and lace clothing. He stood up and gazed at her in such a way that she would almost have blushed had she known how; her nipples were erect and she felt the familiar burning sensation in her stomach.

'Old and ugly, eh?'

'I feel old and ugly.'

'Hannah?'

She looked into his eyes.

'Hannah,' he said tenderly, 'I love your white milky skin. I love your breasts like little apples, and the line of your shoulders, the curve of your back, the smoothness of your stomach as it rises below your navel, the roundness of your hips, the contours of your thighs, and your dainty hands and feet . . . What else? I love your mouth and that greedy lower lip of yours, and your nose when it starts to look pinched – the way it does now. And your eyes that widen, and the way your breath quickens. And the smell of your body, which I would recognize among a thousand others, even when you've just stepped out of a bath. And the smell of our lovemaking, which reminds me of the sea. It's like a drug, Hannah, exquisite to the senses. In other words, I have an extraordinary desire for you right now, but also day in, day out, year in, year out. And I love to look into a fire with you, to laugh with you, to meet your gaze, to sense your presence in the room next door, even if you are huddled over account books. I love to hear your footsteps, I love your rages and even your absences, because I can look forward to your return. Have I made myself clear enough, Hannah?'

He didn't smile, and his green eyes were luminous in the shade. He was utterly serious. This was the one human being whose heart and mind she would never fathom.

'Yes,' she said. 'I think I get the message.'

CHAPTER 11

The Desert of the Tartars

In September 1913, they made another trip to Europe. They travelled on the *France*, a four-funnel steamship of the Transatlantic line. Taddeuz as usual had chosen this French company over Cunard's *Mauretania* (although Cunard held the blue riband for the fastest crossing: four days, seventeen hours, twenty-one minutes) and the 52,000-ton *Imperator*, belonging to the Hamburg Amerikan line.

They stayed at 10 Rue d'Anjou. Marcel Proust was still living at that address, and another tenant had moved into the building: Jean Cocteau. They soon became friends. If 'Little John' appreciated Hannah's quick-fire conversation, he found Taddeuz very handsome and wonderfully intelligent, and he told him so. *This is really too much*, thought Hannah, feeling almost jealous. But she choked with laughter at the sight of Taddeuz being pursued like a young girl – although he didn't find it so funny. They attended the tumultuous première of *The Rite of Spring* and witnessed the no less tumultuous arguments between Sergei de Diaghilev and his star dancer, who not only wanted to get married, but to a woman, what's more!

They went to Monte Carlo, where the Ballet Russe had been based for two years. There they split up, Taddeuz going on to Switzerland and then Lugano and the mansion at Morcote. He had almost finished his novel, the one inspired by Quentin MacKenna, and he even had a title for it: *The Desert of the Tartars*.

'Where the devil do the Tartars come into it? They didn't figure in your story before.'

'There still isn't so much as a shadow of one.'

'Then what the hell are they doing in the title?'

'It's precisely because there aren't any that their presence needs emphasizing. There aren't any, but my character imagines them, riding on the horizon, and with every step he takes he believes he will reach them.'

'I see! But there are no Tartars in Australia.'

'My novel isn't set in Australia. Or America. Or anywhere . . . Hannah? I love you.'

She laughed: words, words.

But it wasn't all words, as he proved in their hotel suite in Paris. *My God, how is it that a man you have loved, as lover and friend, for so many years, can still give you so much pleasure?*

Meanwhile, Hannah went her way, turning up unannounced in all her beauty parlours and shops, her laboratory and her factory, arousing terror every time she appeared, tiny though she was.

She went to Milan, Rome, Venice, Zurich, Vienna, Prague. In Prague, which she didn't know well, she lingered longer than necessary. Hugo von Hofmannsthal had given her some addresses there: that of the wife of a pharmacist who had a literary salon, and those of several men with whom Hugo felt she ought to become acquainted. The woman's name was Bertha Fanta. Hugo's introduction was unnecessary: in fact, Bertha was delighted to meet another woman who wasn't solely preoccupied with frills and bows. She introduced Hannah to a lawyer, who was acting vice-secretary of the Workers' Insurance Office for the Kingdom of Bohemia: Franz Kafka. He gave her a lecture – all the more unbelievably comic in that he delivered it completely straight-faced – on how cylindrical trees were put through surface-planing machines, on which he claimed to be the world expert, having been obliged to write reports on the subject for the past seven years. Yes, he wrote other things too (he had just published *The Verdict* in the magazine *Arcadia* and, with the publishers Kurt Wolff, *The Driver*). She managed to get him to talk about himself a bit, and was oddly struck, and very troubled, by a certain resemblance – not a physical one – between Taddeuz and him. Particularly when he said at some point: 'I'm not happy outside literature except when I am incapable of writing, so that doesn't last long . . .' And this was said with a mocking look in his eyes that begged you not to take him seriously.

That's exactly like Taddeuz . . .

She completed her tour in London, where she met up with Taddeuz again.

He had more than one reason to be delighted: first of all, she was back with him, after an absence of forty-three days, and also because he had finished his *Desert of the Tartars*. He had sent off the manuscript, along with a batch of articles, and had even sketched an outline for another little something and also . . .

'I've got some news for you, too, Taddeuz.'

. . . and also, on top of all that, he had received a telegram from Eddy Lucas, who with his usual absurd excitement – only publishers got more excited than writers – informed him of what he considered a major event . . .

'What's your news, Hannah?'

'I'm pregnant.'

'Oh Lord!' he said finally, with tears in his eyes.

He took off the Tyrolese hat he had put on to make her laugh – he was otherwise completely naked.

'Are you sure?'

'I saw some doctors in Paris.'

'Girl or a boy?'

'You've always hoped for a girl, haven't you?'

'Mmm.'

'Well then, it's bound to be a girl.'

'We should have had a girl after Adam. Her name's Jonathan and she'll soon have a moustache.'

'Everyone makes mistakes.'

In fact, you wanted two boys to start with, Hannah. But as you have no control over these things, there was no need to tell Taddeuz . . .

'It'll be a girl this time, I promise.'

He laid his cheek against her belly, inhaling the sea-smell of her body. He closed his eyes.

'It makes me incredibly happy, Hannah . . .'

She curled up around him.

'And what did Eddy Lucas have to say?'

'Nothing important in comparison with your news.'

'Fine. You don't have to tell me . . .'

'He's sold one of my books to a film company. Or the rights to it. For twenty-five thousand dollars.'

Control yourself, Hannah, even your breathing!

She curled up tighter, wanting to take him inside her belly, or her mouth, big as he was, and keep him there. She weighed every word she spoke, measuring her every intonation.

'That makes me incredibly happy.'

'It's not important.'

'My eye! It jolly well is important. Which book?'

'He didn't say.'

'And you didn't ask? That's typical. When did you receive his telegram?'

'Eight, ten days ago. It's really of no importance.'

'But you replied, didn't you?'

Yes, he had, believe it or not. He had simply cabled that he didn't give a damn.

On 8 November of the same year, Eddy Lucas was in New York. He was horribly put out. That transatlantic cable in which Taddeuz had been so brief had stuck in Eddy's throat. It was one thing knowing that every author was a paranoid mental defective, but this was going too far.

'Perhaps you think it's easy to sell your wretched books!'

'Huh!' said Taddeuz sarcastically.

'We count ourselves lucky if five per cent of our authors make us any money – that brings us within sight of El Dorado . . .'

'Olé!' said Taddeuz.

'He's annoying me, Hannah. Tell him he's annoying me.'

'Don't annoy Edward, darling,' said Hannah. 'He's already quite red in the face.'

'Yes, darling,' said Taddeuz.

She was seated at the far end of the room, in front of a huge pile of mail, having refused the help of her two secretaries to get through it. As usual after a long absence, she wanted to check the pulse of her affairs, get back in touch with what was going on. And this was also the best way of witnessing Taddeuz's meeting with Eddy Lucas, a way of being there while pretending not to be, of not trembling too much with anxiety, or at least of being able to hide her trembling.

'Taddeuz,' said Lucas, 'this is your big chance. And, let it be said in passing, mine too – try and remember that; a publisher has to eat as well, from time to time.'

'What's this fellow's name?'

'Aitken. Harry Aitken. I made enquiries: he's a very important film producer, he has a lot of money and he's got some talented people working for him. He has checked out all the publishers looking for material. I told him about your Giovanni delle Bande Neri and he expressed interest in it. And then I thought of showing him what I had of *The Desert of the Tartars*, the first two hundred pages. He called me back the next day. The idea of the book appealed to him. I wasted no time in getting him to sign a contract, as you can imagine. It took me ten days to get him to agree to twenty-five thousand dollars;

he didn't want to pay more than ten thousand. But his readers were a great help. They adored your manuscript. Anyway, it's settled. Of course, there'll have to be a change of title. Tartars – I ask you! Especially as not a single Tartar appears, or did I misread it?'

'There are none.'

'That's reassuring, I was beginning to see Tartars hidden everywhere, setting devious traps.'

'Are they going to change my story, Eddy?'

'Tad, forgive me for saying this, but I haven't exactly made a fortune publishing your work . . .'

'Are they going to change it, Eddy?'

'If there's a film of your book, I'll be able to sell ten or twenty times more copies than usual.'

'Eddy?'

Silence.

Without looking round to see, she knew that Taddeuz was smiling. She told herself fiercely not to move, not to say anything.

'A little, maybe, yes,' Lucas said finally.

'A lot,' said Taddeuz.

'Tad, it took me another three days but I managed to persuade Aitken to take you on as co-scriptwriter. You'll be working with people like Gardner Sullivan and Larry Noltman, who aren't just nobodies. And of course you'll be paid for the work, your expenses will be covered and your name will appear on the title credits.'

Again he smiled.

Hannah thought: *He's going to say, 'It's not important, Eddy'* . . .

Silence.

'And another thing I got them to agree to,' Lucas went on, 'was that you have a say in the choice of director. I called up Mary Pickford, in Los Angeles, and she says that the best choice would be David Griffith, but he's working on a big project. She suggested a certain Raoul Walsh. You trust Mary's judgement, don't you?'

'Of course,' said Taddeuz, with worrying quietness. 'What sort of book are you going to publish, Eddy? The one I've already written or the one that will have to be written after my Tartars have been turned into Apaches?'

Oh my God! Hannah could feel Lucas's pleading eyes on her, begging her to come to his aid. Behaving as though completely oblivious to what was happening on the other side of the room, she continued opening her mail.

In a very calm voice Taddeuz said: 'And once my desert has been turned into the back lot of a Hollywood studio, and my main character into a poor lonesome cowboy?'

'Oh goddammit!' exclaimed Lucas.

'It's not important, Eddy,' said Taddeuz. 'Don't worry, I'll sign your contract for you. What am I going to do with all this money? Will you help me to invest it, Hannah?'

She dared at last to look round but, thank God, he didn't have his eyes on her. She stood up.

'Will you have lunch with us, Eddy?'

The publisher said he couldn't. Another day, he'd love to.

'I'm sorry,' said Taddeuz, 'I shouldn't have made those last two remarks. Eddy's right, it's a chance I can't afford to turn down. He's gone to such a lot of trouble. And I can always publish *The Desert* at my own expense, with all the money I'm going to earn from Hollywood. Do you know this Walsh character?'

Hannah said she didn't, which was true. She dared not say a great deal else, and was very pleased that she had refrained over the past thirteen years from commenting on her husband's career as a writer. At least she could continue to do the same now, at a time when Taddeuz's eye had perhaps never been so sharp.

'When will you be going to California?'

In January. He wanted to spend the festive season with her and the children.

And that is what he did. As for Hannah, she began to put on weight. For a while it seemed that this was going to be a more difficult pregnancy than the previous two, perhaps because of her age – she was now thirty-nine – or because of the crazy hours she continued to work. It reached the point where, for once, Taddeuz made her go a whole Sunday without doing anything, not even allowing her to write any letters . . .

But miraculously, as though she didn't want anything to prevent him from going to California, she recovered all her vivacity and that transparency of complexion which, together with that extraordinary fire in her gaze, was one of the few attractive features of her triangular face. She really had the most resilient constitution. Lizzie, who had so casually brought her own children into the world, couldn't get over it. The friendship between the two women was unfailing. They still shared fits of giggles and, to tell the truth, as far as Jonathan and Adam were concerned, Lizzie rather took the place of Hannah, who didn't have time to look after them: 'Hannah, I don't like to worry you with this, but there's a problem with one of your sons. It's not Adam, he's doing very well.'

'So, it's Jonathan?'

'Yes. It's not that he doesn't work – he does, though it depends on the subject. But it's a question of discipline. He hit one of his teachers and broke a soup tureen over a schoolmate's head.'

'I've always had a horror of soup, too.'

'And I've never been very keen on soup tureens. But Jonathan is pretty difficult.'

'He's a male version of me. I was expecting the worst.'

She laughed, dismissing the problem, if problem there was.

* * *

Taddeuz left at the beginning of January.

'I'll be back in two months at the outside, Hannah.'

'No, you won't, I'll come and see you. Without any warning. To catch you in bed with those Hollywood ladies. I'll come by aeroplane.'

This idea of flying was really beginning to become an obsession with her. She had been to the aviation meeting at Sheepshead, on the south-west tip of Brooklyn, and had again managed to go up, tucked in behind the pilot, whose name was Ovington.

'What if I were to fly to California?'

Ovington had run off, panic-stricken. Maryan and Taddeuz had taken one arm each and carried her away from the aeroplane; her feet didn't even touch the ground.

She saw Taddeuz off once more.

'Don't be unfaithful to me, please.'

This was said in a tiny, not very brave voice. She didn't feel very brave. *Old and ugly, with a huge stomach. If it turns out to be a boy, I'll drown him.*

The trip she made at the beginning of March was dreadful, despite having Lizzie with her. (Maryan and Lizzie had been living at their house in Beverly Hills since January.) Lizzie had insisted on coming to New York to accompany her back on the train – 'In your condition, there's no way you should be left to travel on your own.'

Although 'on your own' was only a manner of speaking: Hannah was in any case accompanied by Yvonne and Gaffouil, plus two secretaries and a messenger, who had to make sure the three typewriters – two Remingtons and a portable Blick – and the Rectigraph photocopier got to California all right; and it was also his job at every station *en route* to collect the mail, which Joshua Wynn, her new office manager, made sure was there waiting for her.

'If I had an aeroplane we'd already be there by now. Oh what a waste of time this is!'

'If you had what?'

Lizzie was horrified. She just couldn't see herself in any flying machine.

'Nor you with that big tummy of yours.'

'Let's talk about something else, shall we?'

The child inside her was beginning to move about: *It must be a girl, giving you so much trouble*. She was quite sure it was a girl.

They talked and talked as the dismal plains that lay between the Appalachians and the Rockies went by, whenever Hannah gave her secretaries some time off. As night fell over Kansas, Lizzie asked: 'You've never told me, Hannah, whether or not Taddeuz ever knew that you were pregnant when Pelte the Wolf beat you up in Warsaw . . .'

Only Lizzie would have dared broach this subject. And even she suddenly realized how dangerously close this brought her to the blazing heart of the love affair between Taddeuz and Hannah.

'I'm sorry, I should never have . . .'

But Hannah said: 'I've often asked myself that question, Lizzie. And I don't know the answer. I didn't tell Taddeuz before our wedding – naturally, I would have been ashamed to get him to marry me on account of that. In fact, I've never mentioned it.'

But it was possible that Taddeuz had found out from Mendel, on that famous occasion when they met in the flower market in Nice in 1899, and had a man-to-man talk – 'I don't know what they talked about: even on his deathbed Mendel wouldn't tell me.' Or he might even have heard about it from Dobbe Klotz.

'But I don't think so, Lizzie. In any case, it's all in the past now. It happened such a long time ago . . .'

There was a veritable horde waiting for them at Los Angeles Station, with Taddeuz and Maryan to the fore and a lot of children bringing up the rear. In the hours prior to their arrival, Hannah had experienced moments of real panic. *With this bulging stomach, he's going to think you look like a Zeppelin. He'll see you as an old woman crazy enough to get herself pregnant who looks more and more like her husband's mother as the days go by . . . Whilst in Hollywood, he's surrounded by hundreds of pretty young girls only too willing to open their arms to him, and everything else, because he's handsome enough to make you weep and because he works in the film industry. You don't give a damn whether he's been unfaithful. All you want is for him to stay with you . . . Although you'd be terribly hurt if you knew he was with another woman . . .*

She and Lizzie travelled in a special coach coupled on to the regular train. The coach had a real bathroom, with a proper bath, and when the train stopped at Barstow, it was filled with clean water, so that as they came within sight of Los Angeles, Hannah was splashing about in a cold bath, in the hope that it would make her look more presentable.

'You look wonderful,' he said. 'Radiant even. How are the children?'

He looked so good – suntanned and even more youthful – it took her breath away.

The Kadens' house in Beverly Hills was completed; it was a Spanish-style villa, with the benefit of an English-style garden. Taddeuz had moved in there; he had a wing all to himself. Yes, he was working. David Griffith had asked him to work on *Birth of a Nation*, and he had struck up a friendship with Thomas Ince, who had built some stunning sets in the Santa Ynes Canyon, including a New York street. He had also made the acquaintance of Scott Sidney, a former stage director, who liked his play, and a remarkable Englishman by the name of Charles Spenser

Chaplin . . . And of course he was working on the screenplay of *The Desert*.

He laughed, to all appearances greatly at peace with himself. What Raoul Walsh and the other two screenwriters were doing with his novel was of course quite astonishing. She would be hard pressed to recognize the story, but then why not?

To all appearances . . . She scrutinized him. It was difficult, if not impossible, to read the expression on his face and tell whether he was horribly unhappy or, on the contrary, whether he was adapting willingly, with pleasure, to the constraints of his new career as a writer for the cinema. Particularly as he was more loving and tender towards her than ever before.

He took her almost before the trunks were open, and though the little mechanism inside Hannah's head whirred away furiously, there was nothing to fuel her anxieties. *You worry too much, Hannah. He's happy with the fate you've arranged for him. He's only forty-three and, as he told you himself, for a writer that's the beginning of maturity. His experience of the cinema with De Mille was a failure but this isn't. All these people are discovering how talented he is – and so is he, which is even better. And however intelligent and astute he might be, he hasn't an inkling of your part in all this. In a year's time, his name will be on everyone's lips, he'll be famous and earning lots of money, everything you've always wished for him . . . You'll have saved him from himself, you scheming witch.*

Shooting of the film by Raoul Walsh was due to start at the beginning of May. Hannah read the latest version of the screenplay, disconcerted at first by the way that cinema people have of chopping up a story like a leg of lamb . . . And even more disconcerted when she discovered what had become of the real-life adventure of Quentin MacKenna: the hero of the film (Douglas Fairbanks) gets married at the beginning; a crafty, cruel and jealous cousin abducts his wife (Lillian Gish) seventy-two minutes (approximately) after the consummation of the marriage and, aided – God knows why – by sneering Apaches tanned as dark as African negroes, he carries the poor woman off to an inaccessible cabin in the heart of a totally hostile desert (they had kept the desert) with no watering holes. Nevertheless, the Lone Hero sets off in pursuit of his Beloved and the Traitor; crosses the desert on foot – the tanned and sneering Apaches kill his White Horse – and eventually reaches the cabin, exhausted but still with enough strength to fight the Wicked Cousin and lay him out cold just when the Villain is about to inflict upon the Beloved the Ultimate Dishonour; finally re-united, the couple ride off on the White Horse, whose reappearance is never explained.

Hannah was appalled by the idiocy of it all.

But Taddeuz smiled, unruffled. 'That's cinema, my love . . .' Besides, Harry Aitken and Eddy Lucas were delighted. They thought it was wonderful.

'Eddy wants me to write a novel telling exactly the same story. He's had an original idea: he wants to have the book ready when the film comes out, and put a striking cover on it; it'll be on sale to the audience as they come out of the cinemas. He says that he'll sell a couple of hundred thousand copies that way . . . Hannah, don't look at me like a sad owl, please. I tell you, I'm having a lot of fun.'

It would be called *The Lone Rider*, he said.

12

Now I'm the One in the Wrong – That's Terrific

The film and the book came out in the middle of June, four or five weeks before she was due to deliver, so it was out of the question that she should travel across America to attend the première. Taddeuz's telegram reached her just as she was about to sit down at her desk in the house on Long Island, at about four thirty in the morning: *A triumph, though I say it myself. I love you.*

Taddeuz himself arrived a week later, looking every bit the successful author. Thanks to the contracts so skilfully negotiated by Polly Twhaites and his American team, Taddeuz would receive twelve per cent of the profits made on the film, which he would share with Eddy Lucas. This amounted to thirty or forty thousand dollars at the very least. And that wasn't all: he was contracted to do two more screenplays – *The Return of the Lone Rider* and *The Lone Rider's Revenge.*

'I also suggested *The Lone Rider Versus the Antmen* and *The Lone Rider Meets Frankenstein*, but they weren't in a hurry to sign those up. They're still undecided. Later perhaps. As for Eddy, he's completely delirious: he's offered me a five-year contract, guaranteeing me fifty thousand dollars a year, on the sole condition that I write him a Lone Rider every three months. As you can imagine, I'm going to accept. And while I think of it . . .'

He held out a red and black jewellery box. Inside was a diamond necklace.

'Taddeuz, it must have cost a fortune!'

'Well, I'm rich . . .'

'You know, I almost preferred the black pearls.'

'I'll go on giving you black pearls, one a year, for as long as I live. This is something else . . .'

This time she succumbed to pettiness. She went and found out how much the necklace cost: more than $150,000. Overwhelmed, she thought: *He can't have kept a cent of all that money he made out of the film for himself. I'd even swear to it that he must have put himself in debt . . .*

He just smiled, with not the slightest hint, either in his face, in his voice, or his hands, as to whether his apparent good spirits concealed any other feelings.

'When's Eddy going to publish *The Desert of the Tartars*?'

'Think about it, Hannah: what publisher would agree to publish simultaneously two books written under the same name that differ so wildly? Hannah, I don't know anything about your business, but would you put on the market at the same time and under the same trademark your luxury products and a soap for washing underwear? You see what I mean.'

Intuition told her – she was sure of it – that he was going through hell.

'Lizzie, it's always easy to rewrite history. And to understand it, with hindsight. The problem between Tad-deuz and me wasn't just that awful thing about money – the fact that I found it so easy to make whilst he never managed to make any, except when I took matters in hand. From the time when we were first married, I came up with all kinds of solutions, including giving him a capital sum to do with as he pleased, even if it meant inventing some uncle from whom he could inherit it and making the money over to him without anyone ever finding out where it came from. Niet. *I offered him a job – any job – in my organization; the one Jos Wynn later took up, for instance.* Niet. *I proposed making him chairman, the official head*

of the company, the person with all the ideas; I would have been no more than a colleague. Niet . . .

'But he had to live, though, he had to buy himself suits and underpants and cigars, he had to pay for his trips somehow. Whenever we ate in a restaurant or a hotel, I tried to get him to take the money so that, in public, he should be the one to pay. Things like that counted for an awful lot in 1900, and I'm not so sure they don't still count, even today, seventy years later. Niet. *I would pay and he would just sit there. People took him for a gigolo – and treated him like one. Two or three times he punched the bastards, but in fact he would be smiling: "It's of no importance, Hannah . . ."*

'He never asked me for anything, not once, not even for a book. For the first three years I bought him his clothes, his shoes, everything, in secret. I felt ashamed, you can't imagine how ashamed, and I was unhappy, Lizzie . . . No, I've never spoken of this, not even to you, before now. It seemed so pathetic, everyone would have laughed. "It's of no importance, Hannah . . ." God, how I hated those words!

'But it wasn't just a matter of money. The one thing in the world that I've wanted all my life, more than anything else, a thousand times more than money or my own success, was that he should be a success as a writer, since that's what he was cut out for. Because he couldn't do anything else, didn't want to do anything else. And it was dreadful that the years passed and nothing happened. Materially, he appeared to be ideally situated, he didn't have to worry about anything else but his writing. But he wrote his books and nobody ever wanted to read them. Except when he betrayed himself, and wrote stupid things. People say the Jews are tormented, but he was much more tormented than me. This bitch of a life is a real mess, I don't know how I've managed to put up with it for so long . . .

'He made no money and he didn't achieve any real success. And he expected such a lot of himself: he was too sensitive, immoderately so – it just wasn't normal.

'And then there was me, of course, giving him such a hard time for years, always ready to sound off. I still can't hold my tongue, I know. I wasn't an easy person to live with, to say the least. It wasn't enough that I loved him to distraction.

'What use would it have been if I'd been able to understand these things at the time? What could I have done that would have made any difference?'

She gave birth to Abigail on 4 July. It was a difficult birth, extremely difficult. She was in labour for hours. The baby wasn't in the standard presentation position and the five obstetricians attending her, having failed with the forceps, began to think a Caesarean delivery might be necessary. She had just about managed not to scream until then. At that point she let rip: 'You stupid fools, try again. Come on, let's count together: one, two, three . . .'

Then, white-faced, her eyes closed, she asked: 'Boy or a girl?'

A girl.

She laughed.

'Doesn't surprise me. Almost as bloody-minded as her mother.'

Forty-eight hours later she had already summoned her chiefs of staff to her bedside. Joshua Wynn was formerly a lawyer whom she had met on first arriving in America. He was starting out then. For a long time, he worked for her as a legal adviser. After Polly Twhaites', it was his opinion she valued most highly with regard to contracts and rights. She eventually offered him the job of general manager; for a man, he was doing all right.

'Jos, I want to separate my European and American interests. I want them to be completely independent of each other, with only three things in common: you, me and the fact that both companies produce cosmetics and perfumes.'

She was now fully engaged in her business once more. A newspaper headline (she never read more than the headlines) had alerted her to the situation in Europe.

'Check the details with Polly, Jos. I've already written to him about it, he knows what to do. Let me be quite clear about this: I want three separate companies – the third being the Australian and New Zealand operation. And each of these three companies must undertake not to encroach on the others' territory. Just as though they were led by three different people who had made an agreement among themselves not to compete against each other.'

It was annoying, but lawyers would always take their time. It wasn't until several weeks later that Wynn set sail for London and Paris, in order to settle the final details with Polly. And he was in the middle of the Atlantic when war broke out. *That's men for you*, thought Hannah, *you just can't rely on them!*

Never having opened a newspaper except to check the placing of her ads, Hannah had paid hardly any attention to what might be happening in places as obscure as Bosnia-Hercegovina and Sarajevo – *I don't even know where that is! And yet I've done some travelling in my time!* This was her only reaction to the outbreak of the First World War: these cretins were scuppering most of her projects, fooling about like this, just when she had decided to resume expansion in Europe after neglecting the area for some time. *This certainly makes you look pretty stupid! The morons!*

It took her several days, listening to people talking around her, to get the full measure of what had happened. She was appalled, could hardly believe it. From an American viewpoint, these European countries looked alike – even to her, and she knew and loved them all. That they should take up arms against each other and send their citizens to make mincemeat of each other seemed insane. Taddeuz could see beyond this: he thought that a certain kind of Europe – the world into which they had been born and in which they had grown up – would vanish for ever.

'You aren't proposing to go and fight, are you? You're an American!'

'And proud of it. But I'm just as much a European.'

'In any case, you're too old to fight.'

'That's true. Except in your bed.'

And Adam and Jonathan were too young. So why should she worry?

What of her friends in France, Germany and England? She was sure they would not be affected – especially as she employed mostly women. And the idea of Cocteau and Marcel Proust in uniform was quite amusing . . .

How about her family in Poland? Nine years ago, in 1905, she had received a letter, forwarded by her salon in Berlin, from her brother Simon: *I have just learned, quite by accident, that you are still alive, which, alas, is not true of our poor mother, God bless her* . . . This was followed by extremely bitter reproaches, a veritable Talmudic litany of rebuke: how could anyone be so lacking in family feeling, take so little interest in her own flesh and blood, fail in all her duties, and especially her religious duty? These reproaches left Hannah completely unmoved. What did she owe Simon, who had never taken any notice of her when they were living together in the *shtetl* and paid even less attention to her when she left for Warsaw? She nonetheless replied to his letter, offering to send him any money that he might need and even asking what had become of him. In return she received twenty-eight pages of even more vehement censure . . . culminating, all the same, in a request for five thousand roubles. She sent twenty thousand, hoping that would be the end of it.

Two months later she was informed by her director in Paris of the presence, in the luxurious salon in the Faubourg Saint-Honoré, of a bearded rabbi with a wife and nine children in tow, each one as cantankerous as the next.

'*Throw them out*,' cabled Hannah. In the end Taddeuz intervened, advocating a more kindly approach. And he took it upon himself to provide the family of the man who was, after all, his brother-in-law, with the means to move to France. This was not enough: the brother-in-law decided there was too much competition for the many Jews and rabbis there. A move to Algiers – why Algiers, only Allah knows why – had to be paid for. Hannah paid for it, and more besides, and in the end was persuaded to go and see them. A fatal error: the rabbi and his two eldest sons refused to open the door to her and would not let her see her other nephews and nieces, on account of her meanness. She returned home, beside herself with rage. Again Taddeuz calmed her down, and persuaded her to provide them with a generous pension.

Heavens alive, it would cost you less to support the whole corps de ballet *at the Paris Opera!* (She was already paying them ten times more than she paid one of her directors.)

And then the Warsaw Four (father, mother and the two eldest sons) demanded more: Simon wanted a synagogue built for him, of which he would have been the spiritual leader.

'Send your lazy sons to work,' was Hannah's reply.

Simon poured opprobrium on her: his sons, like himself, would devote their lives to the study of holy Scripture, and they would pray for her, who had sinned so greatly . . .

'Shit!'

And with that decisive expletive, relations between brother and sister were severed. Simon certainly continued to write to her, disguising his handwriting and getting his letters posted from the most surprising places. She threw the whole lot in the dustbin and never wrote back again.

She read *The Revenge of the Lone Rider*, which was due to come out at the end of September. Eddy Lucas sent her a set of proofs at her request. She found the book dismayingly idiotic, even more so than the first. The cover was aggressively vulgar: a half-naked woman being carried away on a horse, pursued by Apaches in feather headdresses – *how bizarre!* – brandishing Iroquois tomahawks – *curiouser and curiouser*. Even Lucas was a bit embarrassed about it. But not much: after years of restraint, he had just discovered the virtues of big print runs.

'And Taddeuz wrote this?'

'In eight days. He can write very fast when he wants to.'

'Eddy, are you going to publish *The Desert of the Tartars*?'

Not in the immediate future, he admitted. And in any case Taddeuz had taken back his manuscript. It would be his decision.

'Hannah? What is this? You've never shown any interest in what he writes, except on one occasion. Apart from that once, I don't remember your ever passing any comment. I'm not criticizing you for your indifference, I can understand it. May I be frank with you? Taddeuz is now extremely successful, even if it's not the kind of literature that he first set out to write. I think that you're too European in your attitude, in the way you distinguish between a writer and a popular author, and . . .'

'Are you trying to suggest that I'm jealous of Taddeuz's success?'

'I never said that.'

'Lucky for you. I'd have broken something over your head if you had. Now, please go away. Don't expect to get the proofs back, I've burned them.'

In September a certain Marshal Joffre defeated a certain General Moltke somewhere along the Marne. Recalling the time she spent with René the Painter, this distant incident put Hannah in mind of a confrontation between the Apache gangsters from one side of Paris and the painters of Montparnasse under the bovine gaze of Casque d'Or. This stupid war didn't interest her in the least.

Taddeuz was in Los Angeles. She hadn't seen him for three months. Of course he wrote to her, three letters a week, and telephoned her every Sunday. She could always get news of him from his articles in the *New Yorker*; he wrote a lot about what was happening in California, the way one might write about the Kalahari Bushmen or the Zulus – it was very funny. *He must be very well acquainted with all these young actresses whose adventures he relates* . . .

Lizzie and Maryan had returned from their house in Beverly Hills at the end of October, to spend the winter in New York. They brought back with them only the children who were too young to go to school; the others they left in the sun. Lizzie felt guilty, but Maryan had something else on his mind: one of his brothers was French; he had been called up and the last Maryan had heard, he was fighting somewhere in Artois or Flanders. Hannah looked at him in astonishment.

'You mean to say that he gave up organizing supplies for the factory in order to go and shoot at Rainer Maria Rilke? And why not Apollinaire and Rilke shooting at each other from opposite sides of the Rhine? It's incredible. But what can you expect of men?'

'Hannah, I'm afraid you don't appreciate the importance of what is happening over there . . .'

In more than twenty years this was the first time Maryan openly suggested she was wrong. It annoyed her. This came on top of a certain degree of hesitation that Lizzie and Maryan had shown in response to her questions about Taddeuz. She took Lizzie aside.

'He's being unfaithful, isn't he?'

'You're crazy.'

'Lizzie!'

A few affairs with no future, said Lizzie. Passing fancies. There were so many pretty girls there dreaming of a future in the cinema. And when you were a famous author like him . . .

'Hannah, I very nearly didn't come back to New York because I knew that I couldn't lie to you. What are you going to do? Go down there with a gun?'

The temptation to do just that was considerable, but she did nothing of the sort. *You wanted him to be famous? Well, now he is. But in a way that he's ashamed of, which must be a torment to him – might even make him want to hang himself. It's all your fault. You can be proud of yourself . . .*

She continued to write very loving, very cheerful letters that were as funny as she could make them. She told him the latest exploits of Kate O'Shea, for instance, the director of her laboratory at New Rochelle. Seized with a frenetic bout of feminism, Kate had insisted that in future even the horses that brought the base products to the laboratory should be mares, and that the vehicles they pulled should be driven by women: *And what's more, she lights candles every day at the Catholic Church for a German victory – not that she's enamoured of the Crown Prince, but because she wants the Cursed English to take a beating. I had to get her to take down the German flags she had raised and the portrait of William II. To tell the truth, she annoys me slightly . . .*

She avoided anything that might be taken as a sign of distress, or self-pity, or any kind of reproach for his long absence.

She went even further in a letter written at the end of November: *It's ages since I was last in Europe. What with this ridiculous war, I'm worried about the people working for me. Because of my business interests here, the best time to go would be during the holidays. I've been assured that there's no danger. I'll be travelling on an American ship, and of course we're neutral. I'll go to London . . .*

She knew only too well that he would read between the lines. It meant that it was up to him whether this first real separation went ahead or not. She would send Adam and Jonathan to him, so that they wouldn't be left alone, whilst she . . .

His response came back at once: *Will sink your ship if necessary. Am coming home.*

He arrived with Charles Spenser Chaplin. *Like a husband who, having played around with another woman, thinks he has to bring home some flowers*, thought Hannah, to whom the little Englishman with a moustache and the eyes of a Warsaw Jew seemed like a kind of cushion that was supposed to protect Taddeuz from attack. She was quite prepared to hate him. But – as she was loath to admit – Charlie was hard to resist. His antics made even Jonathan laugh – the boy's cold aggressiveness and withdrawn nature were becoming increasingly marked (Lizzie was right: he really was a very difficult child).

But Charlie was much more than just a clown, albeit a brilliant one; there was a very unusual ardour about him: a touch of the sex maniac. Having left Mack Sennett and signed up with another film producer, Essany, he went to Chicago in order to make his first film (in fact he would only make a start on it there; he was to return to California, to San Francisco, to finish it). At the breakfast table he improvised a fantastic dance using forks and rolls. He was very sharp-eyed. He took advantage of a moment alone with Hannah to say to her: 'Taddeuz is too good for what he is doing at the moment, you know?'

'Yes.'

He benignly kissed the palm of her hand.

'I'll do everything I can to help him, Hannah. Is he Jewish?'

'No, not even Jewish.'

'I've been unfaithful to you.'

Silence.

She was lying naked on her stomach, her face buried in the pillow. She had turned down all the lights in their bedroom, contrary to their usual habit, such a short while ago, of making love with all the lights on. She knew it was a fairly pitiful thing to do, but she didn't want him to see her face looking like that of an old woman. . .

'You knew it, Hannah. You must have known about it even before I thought of touching another woman. I'm sure that you knew it was going to happen.'

'But of course. I always know what's going to happen.'

'You mostly do. It's fairly terrifying.'

'I'm a monster.'

'With the most beautiful back in the world. Don't try and fool me, Hannah: I know that it pains you, but I also know that you don't attach any more importance to these women than I did.'

His voice was soft and gentle in the dark. And the little mechanism inside Hannah's head implacably noted every inflection: *Watch out, Hannah, he's about to tell you that he knows perfectly well what you've done for him and how he came to be in Los Angeles earning heaps of money, and that it's your fault we've ended up in this situation . . .*

That once again you've taken over his life, in spite of all the promises you made . . .

'May I touch you, Hannah?'

She really was on the point of saying no, and of launching into a diatribe about how women in Los Angeles made love. But she said nothing. *Where would it get you if you did what your pride dictated and played the part of the aggrieved spouse, you silly fool? You shouldn't have taken all your clothes off when you got into bed. Or better still, you should have slept in a different bedroom – there's certainly no shortage of spare rooms. Sulking and giving him the come-hither at the same time really isn't a very sensible solution. You want a divorce? No? All right then, shut up and don't let me hear another word!*

Taddeuz's fingers crept all the way down her back, stroking first her shoulders, with the most exquisite and lightest of touches, without ever pausing, then the deep furrow in her back that ran from her shoulder-blades to down below her waist, where her body filled out.

'There were three women, Hannah. Three altogether. The last time was in October – I only slept with her once. There hasn't been anyone since then. And there won't be any others. Would you please turn over?'

She clung desperately to the pillow in which she had buried her face. And continued to keep her eyes closed in the vague hope of hiding from him the effect his caresses were having on her; nor would she open her mouth. Especially as she could feel him against her hip and her thigh, and he was teasing her flesh with the tip of his tongue. That he should know her so well, and know her weaknesses, could have been – ought to have been – thoroughly exasperating, as should his apparent certainty of being able to manipulate her, literally and metaphorically, as easily as one might toss a pancake. *But you want him, and that's that . . . And if it turns out that he doesn't suspect anything about Aitken and all your scheming, you'll have got into a panic for nothing . . .*

'Turn over, Hannah. It's stupid to hide your face from me, I don't like it.'

Unless you're using your fear in order to force yourself to surrender that part of yourself to him that didn't want to surrender. Do you follow me, Hannah? . . . Here we go, now you start to giggle, you fool!

'Let go of that pillow, damn it!'

A pancake. *You love him and you don't give a damn whether he slept with every woman in Hollywood.*

She turned to face him, but found it was too dark to see. She lit the bedside lamp, ready to laugh with him.

But he wasn't laughing, far from it. In fact it was the first time she had ever seen him on the verge of being truly angry.

'Where did you get the ridiculous idea that you were old? Don't ever think that again, do you hear? Never.'

And I'm the one in the wrong, she thought, *that's terrific*.

'You were there, Lizzie, that last Christmas we spent all together in the house on Long Island. Everyone was there, including Maryan's brothers and sisters, and my dear Paderewski, all talking about Poland, except you – you couldn't understand a word. You thought everything had been sorted out between Taddeuz and me, you told me so yourself, do you remember? While Jan was playing Chopin for us.

'The worst of it is that I thought so too . . .'

Taddeuz did not go back until the end of February. Hannah and he had agreed on new arrangements. There was to be no question any more of their being separated for months on end, he in California, she on the East Coast, three thousand miles away. They would never go more than three or four weeks without seeing each other, never mind their work. Either he would come to New

York, or she would go to Los Angeles. Moreover, Taddeuz had lent a very willing ear to the pianist Paderewski's proposals: he would play an important part in the campaign the world-famous pianist had undertaken in America. Paderewski had set up a committee to help victims of the war in Poland, and was now seeking to go beyond this humanitarian gesture and pursue a purely political objective: the independence of Poland.

There were four million Americans of Polish origin. Nothing could be achieved without money: funds were needed. Taddeuz was responsible for raising a large proportion of these funds. He produced ten Lone Rider stories in eight months and paid the $120,000–$130,000 earned in author's royalties straight into the committee's account. He took great pleasure in extracting twice that amount from his wife and from the Kadens. Paderewski later told Hannah that Taddeuz alone had raised more than three million dollars for the Cause.

He travelled the length and breadth of the continent, giving lectures on Poland, organizing charity sales, balls, dinners at one hundred or five hundred dollars a head. Hannah went to California three times that year, 1915. When she was there in July, Taddeuz took her to a dinner, and she found herself sitting next to Harry Aitken. She officially made his acquaintance there. Aitken played his part magnificently, pretending never to have seen her before. He even had the nerve to suggest she invest her money with him: he said he needed the capital to start a new production company, to be called Triangle, which would bring together Mack Sennett's Keystone, D. W. Griffith's Fine Arts studios, and Thomas Ince's Kay-Bee (Kessel and Bauman). The conversation became rather unreal: Aitken needed no less than four to five million dollars; he had already raised most of that, thanks to the petrol company Standard Oil, but he would like to have more at his disposal.

'There's a lot of money to be made in the cinema, Mrs Newman. The people who helped to finance *Birth of a Nation* have already made an enormous profit, less than five months after the film's release . . .'

I'm going to kill this guy, thought Hannah, who was well placed to know how well Griffith's film was doing: her own stake of a quarter of a million dollars had more than doubled in five months. But she did not at all appreciate the performance Aitken was putting on, with Taddeuz sitting there listening to them, smiling.

The next day, unable to see how she could avoid it, she asked Taddeuz about it. He shook his head.

'It's your money, Hannah, it's up to you how you invest it.'

'But he's the guy who is producing your Lone Rider films, isn't he?'

'Another reason for me not to get involved,' he replied with his usual calmness and that gently mocking – almost ironic – look in his eye that she knew might conceal anything.

In September they went to the Knickerbocker Cinema on Broadway, in New York, with the Kadens, Mary Pickford and Douglas Fairbanks, who was starring in another film (*The Lamb*, a comedy) on the same bill. They were attending the first full programme – three films in a row – presented by Triangle.

In the end Hannah had not put any money into the company, although, had it not been for Taddeuz, she probably would have followed Standard Oil's lead, because she was actually tempted to invest in the cinema, having developed a passion for it herself. To her surprise, and almost to her shame, she had become fascinated by these silent moving images. Even more astounding was the fact that, although she had found the screenplay completely inane, the film of *The Lone Rider* had pinned her to her seat. And watching Cecil B. De Mille's melodrama *The Cheat*, she had wept buckets, though Lizzie had cried even more, which was a consolation.

She was in a paradoxical situation: having paid the film-makers to give Taddeuz work, she dared not put her money into the cinema now for fear that he might think she was trying to meddle with his career as a writer . . .

Or vice versa – I don't know where I am any more, she thought.

Taddeuz knew precisely what she expected him to say – it was enough to make her scream. How could she possibly hope for any advice on how to invest her money from him?

But though she knew him so well, she still felt annoyed: it was silly, the cinema could give them the chance to work together for the first time . . .

And besides, she was beginning to have had quite enough of that half-smile that was constantly on his lips, his knack of always underestimating himself when he had more talent in his little finger than all those dozens of hacks often better known than he was!

As the minutes went by, exasperated by his calm, she became even more annoyed, and succumbed to one of those ice-cold but furious rages that she had so far reserved for Jos Wynn, or Polly, or Maryan – indeed everyone except Lizzie and Taddeuz. But enough was enough, they had been married for sixteen years. God knows, she had done her level best to try to understand him and to apologize – as if she needed to apologize! – for being rich and for getting richer every year . . .

'Damn, damn, damn, Taddeuz.'

The worst of it was that he was the one to calm her down, with all his gentleness and tenderness, and at no point did she break through his shell. And she was all the more susceptible to being calmed down because she was ashamed of this row in which she had been the only one to lose her temper. *Although you kept your head sufficiently not to give away your secret . . .*

When he went away in mid-October she almost begged him to give up writing 'these silly stories'; of course he could go on writing screenplays, but why didn't he tackle a book worthy of him? Or else, if he was determined to stay in the film business, he could work with Dave Griffith.

He told her that there were no two ways about it, she was meddling in his career as a writer.

But he said it with a smile.

'It's of no importance, Hannah.'

After all, she was probably right to, he said.

'I had no idea of what was coming, Lizzie. For once in my life, I just wasn't prepared. Not in the least.'

CHAPTER 13

It's Not a Great Tragedy

In the end she did invest money in the film business. At the time, Maryan was there, reaping the profits of his real estate investment – and the profits were enormous. The long legal battle between Thomas Edison's Motion Pictures Patent Company and the independent producers came to an end with the judgement passed in the Supreme Court, on 15 October 1915, whereby all the patents Edison laid claim to were annulled. Overnight, Hollywood, still at an embryonic stage of development, became the Mecca of the cinema industry. People were fighting over the plots that Maryan owned . . .

Nevertheless, he had taken the time to carry out the investigation Hannah had asked of him. According to him, there were at least three production companies destined for a brilliant future: Carl Laemmle's Universal, Zukor and Lasky's Paramount, and Fox, run by William Fox, a Hungarian Jew who had started out as part of a comic act called the Schmaltz Brothers.

'And there are other very clever men: Marcus Loew, who set up Metro, Samuel Goldwyn – he was born in Warsaw, by the way, his real name is Goldfish – or the Mayer brothers – they are also from Poland. And Selznick, who is Ukrainian.'

She burst out laughing.

'You didn't find a Smith or a Dupont, by any chance?'

'No, but I can always try and find one,' he replied imperturbably.

She chose Paramount, where Cecil B. De Mille was artistic director and principal director; he was working on *Joan of Arc* and preparing to make *The Conquerors*, which would establish his reputation. Hannah had known him for years and had a high regard for him. Not that she would confuse business with pleasure and simply indulge her personal preferences. Furthermore, she pursued her policy of keeping her companies quite separate from each other – there would be no question of any disastrous investment in the cinema affecting her other enterprises. Besides, yet again, being a woman seemed to be a handicap; this was a man's world. She created an independent company, with one of Maryan's brothers, Joseph Kaden, as chairman.

Joseph Kaden and the lawyers worked with Zukor to negotiate a share in Paramount. The documents were signed on 25 November. Hannah was not in the States: ten days earlier a telegram from London had brought her devastating news: kind, gentle, wonderful Polly Twhaites had died of a heart attack at the age of fifty-six. He had been a support to her for twenty years, and it was not just a bond of loyalty that united them: they shared a genuine affection for each other that dated back to her time in Australia. After Mendel, this was the loss of another witness to her adolescence, the first of a sombre and heart-rending litany of loss that was to keep ringing in her ears for the rest of her life.

She cabled the news to Taddeuz straightaway, but the valet sent back a reply saying that the Master was away for two or three days. So she travelled alone, sailing on the *Touraine*, one of the few liners that ventured to carry civilian passengers across the Atlantic. (Six months earlier the German Imperial Embassy had published a sinister warning in the *New York Times*, which was followed a few days later by the tragic torpedoing of the *Lusitania*.)

She was so absorbed in her memories of Polly that she hardly noticed how her travelling companions spent the whole time anxiously scouring the ocean for signs of U-boat torpedoes. In London she fell into the arms of Estelle Twhaites and Winnie Churchill, who was in uniform, having rejoined the forces despite being forty-one, and whom she had first met at the Twhaites's wedding.

She stayed ten or twelve days in London, where she confirmed what Cecily Barton's weekly accounts had already suggested: far from damaging her turnover, the war was increasing it. It was as though women, her clients at least, found some consolation in her beauty preparations for the absence of their husbands, sons or fathers who were fighting on the various fronts. She crossed the Channel and reached Paris. It was the same there: the salons had never been so full; production at the factory at Evreux was uninterrupted and the staff, almost exclusively female, had been unaffected by mobilization.

She had planned to be back in the United States by 15 or 18 December, in time for Christmas. Maryan's telegram reached her at 10 Rue d'Anjou (Cocteau was no longer living there; believe it or not, he had gone off to be a soldier).

Suggest you return soonest, was all it said.

She met his gaze and knew at once: 'Taddeuz?'

'Yes. It's not a great tragedy, though.'

'What is it that you know, in the name of God? Do you know where he is? No? Well?'

He had come to meet her off the Cunard liner. It had taken her nine days to cross the Atlantic as the ship was constantly changing course: it even put in at Galway, in Ireland, after receiving warning of a German submarine.

'I may have worried you needlessly. I really didn't know what to do.'

He had come to fetch her from the New York dock in his new Pierce Arrow, which he drove with the same slow calm that he seemed to bring to everything he did.

'Don't rush, take your time,' said Hannah.

'First of all, he has disappeared, and we haven't had news of him for three weeks.'

'And that didn't worry you?'

'You'd just left for Europe. Lizzie and I thought that he might have joined you. You know what Lizzie's like.'

I was made to be happy: Lizzie's optimism was such that even while falling from the top of a fifty-storey building she would never say die; she would still be planning the menu for dinner the next day.

'Go on, Maryan.'

'We received a letter from him on the twenty-second day. From Mexico: Oaxaca to be precise. It's about two hundred miles south of the Mexican border. He said in the letter that everything was fine, that we needn't worry, that he had started writing again, and that we weren't to alarm you.'

'When was the letter dated?'

'The ninth of November. Hannah, he had started writing again some time ago – I don't mean things like *The Lone Rider*, but books like the ones he used to write before he started working for the cinema.'

'He didn't say anything about it to me.'

'Lizzie knew but she didn't tell me either. She only told me recently. In any case, he wasn't able to write, so Lizzie says. She's not even sure about that, it's so hard to tell with him . . . Hannah, I really didn't know what to do. I made enquiries and found out that there's an English consul in Oaxaca. I sent him a telegram. The reply was: *We have Mr Newman's car but not Mr Newman himself*. I went down there. It's miles from anywhere. Taddeuz had rented a little house there for a year, but he had been gone for three weeks.'

'Leaving his car behind?'

'That worried me as well. I organized a search for him throughout the whole area. There's a war going on there, with Pancho Villa and Emiliano Zapata. It even occurred to me that he might have become a war correspondent.'

'Why not a revolutionary for that matter?'

'It took me ten days to pick up his trail. He had taken a train to Veracruz and from there he had embarked on a ship bound for the United States.'

'What date? I mean when did you learn that?'

'The seventeenth of November.'

'I was still in London. You ought to have let me know straightaway.'

'What was I supposed to tell you? That he had just returned to America? That was when we received a second letter. From Veracruz, with reassuring news: he was travelling in search of inspiration, he was thinking of sailing round the Caribbean and everything was fine. And we weren't to say anything to you because he wanted to give you a surprise.'

'But all the same you had someone look for him in New Orleans. Even though he had asked to be left in peace.'

'It was you who taught me what to do, Hannah. In fact he stayed in New Orleans only a few days. Hannah, when he left Oaxaca he had a manuscript of about two hundred pages, which he carried in a leather bag. The consul remembered it. We found the bag: he had sold it in Bourbon Street for five dollars. And he burned the manuscript in his hotel bedroom, in Vieux Carré, before sailing. It was then that I sent you a telegram.'

No writer in the world would burn a manuscript that had cost him months of work, unless there was a very serious reason for it.

'Before sailing where?' asked Hannah.

'San Juan de Porto Rico. He was there a few days ago. But the two detectives . . .'

She closed her eyes.

'You had him *followed*, Maryan?'

'You would have reproached me if I hadn't. Was I wrong to?'

Don't be angry with Maryan, Hannah. It's true, you taught him to react like this. You had him trail Taddeuz for months, if not years. You turned him into a tracker dog, and he reacted like one. You're the one who's responsible, not him . . .

And you can imagine what went through Taddeuz's mind – and he must have been in a dreadful state if he couldn't write – when he found himself being followed again, hunted down. He was bound to think that it was you having him followed and hunted down, as you did before, as you always do . . .

'Where is he, Maryan?'

'We don't know, Hannah. I'm sorry. We scoured San Juan, but we couldn't find him. He's vanished.'

The Pierce Arrow miraculously forged a path for itself through the horde of Ford Ts on the road. New York was beginning to be decked out with Christmas lights.

There were four long months of dreadful silence. Then Taddeuz's letter arrived. It was posted in Paris on 11 April.

CHAPTER 14

The Incident at Quatre-Cheminées

Jean Cocteau wore combat uniform designed by the couturier Paul Poiret: pearl-grey knickerbockers marvellously set off by a ravishing lilac tunic in Armentières twill, a reddish-purple fatigue coat with deep pockets and charming epaulettes, and plum-coloured boots; he also wore a blue Russian-leather belt with silver studs, designed to put a more military stamp on the outfit.

On his left arm he wore a hand-embroidered armband that indicated he was a volunteer nurse.

'Hannah dearest, what in heaven's name are you doing here? This is a man's world.'

And he smiled cheerfully and affectionately at her. He was sitting in the rear of an Opel 10/18 double phaeton with black leather cushions and white bodywork, driven by a strange creature whose outfit was reminiscent of Captain Nemo's diving suit – this was the set designer Paul Iribe, the future great love of Coco Chanel. Cocteau gave Hannah a kiss.

'My poor darling! And the monster brought you running all the way over here? We'll find him for you. Come and see Etienne.'

The Etienne in question was a Comte de Beaumont, also a very cheerful fellow, who had organized the ambulance service for the armed forces. He was therefore Little Jean's boss. They met in a Flemish-style inn not very far from Dixmude where the marines had been fighting – they might still be fighting there, Little Jean was not very well informed about the war – and not far either from where there were British and Canadian troops.

'Not more than three hours ago, I met a charming little

English lord who used to go hunting little boys in his woods before the war. These hostilities are insufferably snobbish. Here's Etienne, my dear. We're going to have a charming little cocktail party. You have nowhere to sleep? How dreadful! I'll see to that. I know an adorable Algerian sergeant who . . . Ah, at least I've made you smile! Hannah, this war is crazy, all you can do is be even more crazy, and I don't have to try very hard. You can sleep here. We'll go down later. Have you anything to change into or would you like me to lend you something? Now that was a proper laugh! Come along, my dear, I love you, and you'll find your fair-haired adventurer . . .'

She had arrived in Paris on 4 June 1916, after another perilous crossing; she had a passage on the American ship *Mount Vernon* (which would be hit by a torpedo and sunk at a later date).

In the French capital she enlisted the help of Gertrude Stein, amongst others, who had been separated from her brother Léo for the past three years and was living happily with Alice Toklas, another woman writer, who was from San Francisco but a descendant of Silesian Jews. The two women gave Hannah the warmest of welcomes.

And they cast covetous glances on the superb creature with black hair and a dark complexion who accompanied Hannah: Eulalia Jones was about twenty-one years old. She had been working for about eight months as Hannah's personal secretary, sometimes filling in for Yvonne as chief chambermaid, having trained in New York, London, Paris and Zurich.

Eulalia was the young Cherokee who had been at Mendel's bedside when he died. Hannah had kept her word and looked after her, and took all the more pleasure in doing so because the young girl was worth the trouble: she was beautiful and intelligent.

Gertrude Stein was not personally acquainted with any

minister in the French government of the day; in any case, Alice and she had just got back from a trip to Majorca, where they had gone to get away from the German Zeppelin raids. On the other hand, she was a friend of a friend of a journalist on *Le Figaro*, Joseph Reinach, a specialist in military affairs who therefore had good connections among senior military staff.

'He will do everything within his power to help, Hannah.'

Hannah herself remembered her old friend Georges Clemenceau – whose wife was American – who had been Minister of the Interior ten years earlier and even President of the Cabinet, and who was now working as a journalist and champing at the bit.

And so it was that a whole network was established in Paris, a city that Hannah had expected to find febrile and frightened, but which she found to be calm and cheerful, even if people were talking about a certain Vaux Fort that was completely unknown to her, of a big battle at Verdun (equally unfamiliar to her), of a British naval victory in Jutland (she thought this must be somewhere near her salon in Copenhagen). Yet the efforts of all these friends proved ineffectual: there was no trace of anyone called Newman or Nenski having signed up. The two or three American organizations who had set up ambulance and hospital services for the injured did not have any name like it on their lists. Nor had the American Fund for French War Casualties seen anyone answering to Taddeuz's description sign up as a volunteer.

She haunted the ministries and eventually came upon a man who paled at the sight of her. She recognized him as André Labadie, now close on sixty and a very highly placed banker, and therefore an important participant in the war effort. He was also a personal friend of Raymond Poincaré, the President of the French Republic, and advised him on certain issues.

André took Hannah to dinner at Maxim's, in memory of their past affair. This was the only condition – a tactful handsome gesture – that he made before agreeing to help her: that for one evening at least she should consent to make believe that they had once been married, that they were married still, and still loved each other.

'We'll even try and argue the way old couples do: in lowered voices and veiled terms . . .'

Of course they didn't. He addressed her formally as '*vous*', although eighteen years ago they had been intimate with each other. He made her smile, and even got her to laugh once or twice. At the next table was René Fonck, one of France's ace fighter-pilots, together with other pilots on leave between flying missions. André was married, with two daughters, but his family lived in Biarritz. After they had dined, he took her back to Rue d'Anjou but would not go up to her apartment.

She gave him Taddeuz's letter to read.

He asked who Lermontov was. 'I vaguely recall a Russian writer by that name.'

'That's the one.'

'It's a beautiful quotation. And you think your husband has left the ball to go and call his carriage himself?'

'I'm afraid so.'

She told him the little that she knew and gave him a photograph of Taddeuz. In his short letter Taddeuz had given no indication of his plans – in addition to the line from Lermontov, he spoke only of his extreme despair and his shame for all the harm he had done her, and he begged her to forgive him.

The letter had been posted on 11 April at the Gare Montparnasse. Enquiries were made in all the nearby hotels, but it was near the Closerie des Lilas, at the Hôtel de Nice, that a Russian finally admitted having given a room to someone called Nenski. The Russian's name was Ilya Ehrenbourg. No, he had no precise information. All he knew was that Nenski had tried unsuccessfully to join the First Foreign Regiment, and on the 21st of the month he had vanished, without any explanation.

'I'll do my best,' André Labadie had said. Hannah was amazed at the workings of fate: Mendel had once found Taddeuz; how strange that she should now be depending on another man who had loved her to help her find him again.

She endured two terrible weeks of waiting, refusing at first to leave the apartment where she could listen out for the sound of a messenger's footstep, or the telephone, then allowing herself to be persuaded by Gertrude to go out a little. She went once or twice to Rue Schoelcher, near the cemetery at Montparnasse, where the Spaniard Pablo Picasso had his studio at the time. She bought four of his canvases – and felt terrible about it: *He could be dying somewhere, and here I am buying paintings!*

Labadie kept her regularly informed of the progress of his search – for which he seemed to have mobilized the French and British military command, and probably military intelligence as well.

At last, on 23 June, he came in person to bring her a pass signed by Foch himself; he also had some information: 'Hannah, there's absolutely nothing to prove that he's one of the three, but we have three foreigners on our lists who match his physical description and who presented themselves as Russians or Poles. Your Ehrenbourg was right: he did in fact try to enlist in the Foreign Legion, but he was turned down because of a weak heart. You didn't know? I'm terribly sorry: I wouldn't have told you if I'd known. But at least there's some comfort in that: he was turned down once, he was probably turned down elsewhere, especially as he's not a young man of twenty any more, so he isn't necessarily at the front. Of the three men who could be him, one is in Flanders, the other two at Verdun.'

She tried Flanders first. Leaving Eulalia in Paris, she took the best car she could find, which she bought from a Brazilian businessman who still believed in the Belle Epoque: a 1911 Rolls-Royce Silver Ghost – which she drove herself. She took with her as guide and adviser a young infantry captain of twenty-six, recommended to her by André. His name was Pinsun, and he'd lost his right arm and three fingers on his left hand in an attack in the Argonne.

She had a little over one hundred thousand gold francs with her.

It was quite by chance that she came across Jean Cocteau, on 27 June.

The first of the three foreigners – 'very tall, very blond, aged between thirty and forty, describing themselves as Slavonic or American' – turned out to be a Russian, from the Ukraine. He was taller than Taddeuz and hardly spoke any French; he was a nurse, working in a country hospital.

Jean Cocteau laughed kindly.

'Hannah, my dear, you have always been an astonishing woman, to say the least. As soon as this bloody interlude is over, you and your husband must come and see me more often.'

He started telling her what he would do once he got back to Paris, citing names: Max Jacob and André Breton, Erik Satie, Braque and Derain . . .

'You know Picasso too, do you? That's good.'

She was lying on the bed, virtually exhausted after four days' crazy driving; constantly obliged to show the pass issued to her by Foch, she had somehow made her way through convoys of troops marching to and fro. She couldn't think of anything she felt less like doing than discussing painting or music, she thought with bitterness and sorrow.

And yet she wasn't fooled by Jean's cheerfulness; he was simply trying to get her to relax. She was fond of him, and appreciated the exceptional liveliness of his intelligence; contrary to most of the friends they had in common, she even thought him profound and almost desperately clear-sighted beneath that crazy exterior.

'I don't feel much like talking, Jean, I'm sorry.'

He stood up and moved away from the bed. He had sat down there without making an issue of it, and had even helped her to undo some of the buttons on her dress. As a joke, in order to make her laugh, he and Beaumont, behaving like a couple of lunatics, got dressed up for dinner: they both put on silk pyjamas, black for the count and pink for Jean, and wore jingling gold bangles round their ankles, drawing a lot of attention when they walked into the dining room of the inn – where Field Marshal Haig and his general staff happened to be eating.

She left the next day with Pinsun, her little one-armed captain.

Nine days later, having had to return via Paris to bypass the front, she arrived in Saint-Dizier. She was kept there for more than twenty hours by the police, who could not be persuaded to let her continue her journey, even on the authority of Foch's pass. On Pétain's express orders, they would not let her go one step further. Pinsun went to put a call through to Paris, leaving her with the Rolls on the banks of the canal linking the Marne to the Saône, in the midst of a huge tide of men and vehicles. She was stared at by tens of thousands of haggard and exhausted men, amazed to see her there in her white car.

'I was wearing a very straight grey-blue suit that day, Lizzie, a Jeanne Lanvin creation, the most masculine outfit I've ever possessed in my life and probably the least

feminine that Jeanne made in her whole career. I had a kind of three-cornered hat on my head, a style that became fashionable the following year, and I sat there like a fool, clutching my handbag in one hand, with a Derringer in the other. But there was no need for it, those poor devils had no strength left in them. A lot of them smiled at me, just because I was a woman, and no doubt for many of them I was the last woman they would see before they died. Those poor boys, I wanted to kiss every one of them, although, God knows, they were filthy . . .'

Pinsun finally returned, six hours later: it was impossible to get through to Foch's office, or even André Labadie, the exchange at Saint-Dizier refused to allow any private calls. He shook his head.

'We'll never get through, Mrs Newman.'

'Offer them money.'

He met her gaze and replied with an embarrassed air of reproach: 'They'll throw it back in my face if I do that.'

'I'm very sorry,' said Hannah, 'please forgive me.'

He looked around, then shook his head.

'I'll try again.'

Eventually she fell asleep, with her arms crossed on the steering wheel, succumbing to the exhaustion of sixty-four hours' driving without a break, as though lulled by the freakish undertow of armies on the march. It was five o'clock in the morning when the one-armed captain, himself reeling with fatigue, woke her and handed her papers authorizing them to continue. They left at daybreak – the date was 9 July – after breakfasting on a piece of bread and the little coffee remaining in the Thermos flask.

The police directed them to the small town of Badonvilliers, to the south, explaining that the direct route via Bar-le-Duc was completely blocked, and that their only hope was to try and join the endless procession, which had been on the move twenty-four hours a day for months now.

The scene rapidly became Dantesque. At Gondrecourt-le-Château a sub-lieutenant in the infantry, who was probably not even twenty, came up to their car and asked whether they were 'by any chance' going to Verdun. His name was Forissier, he had been in this sector for eleven months, and was returning from leave spent in a hospital in Dijon. His unit, 'if there's anything left of it', was the Third Company of the Seventh Infantry . . . Yes, of course he knew the American Medical Corps; they were based at the Saint-Paul barracks in Verdun. No, he had never noticed a tall blond fellow among the ambulance drivers, or rather none in particular of the several he had seen.

The Rolls managed to join the astounding tide of trucks filled with groundsheets and bandages, engineer vans and mail vans, motorcycles, self-propelled guns and searchlights. Two streams of traffic, some six thousand vehicles, explained Forissier, flowed daily up and down what Barrès would call the Sacred Way, only six or seven yards wide, at most. And he also pointed out the emblems painted by the likes of Kisling, Foujita and Soutine on the sides of some of the three and a half thousand lorries that were constantly driving backwards and forwards along this route.

They were stopped when they came to the River Aire, a tributary of the Aisne. From the heights of Saint-Mihiel, the enemy batteries were trying to cut the umbilical cord that kept Verdun provided with men and supplies, and occasionally a mortar shell or two would come down on the road. This is what had just occurred here, but teams of territorials wearing uniform dating back to the war of 1870 were already at work repairing the damage.

'Sixteen battalions, more than eight thousand men, are employed to work on the road day and night,' the ever-talkative Forissier told them. 'General Pétain has had the quarries opened especially. What were those names you mentioned?'

'Newman, or Nenski. Or Nemo, or Nunnally – any name beginning with an N.'

'Never heard of any of those.'

The Rolls entered Verdun by the Faubourg de Glorieux, having picked up five infantrymen in sky-blue uniform *en route*. Despite the presence of two officers in the car, they were openly critical of the police. Gaunt beneath their helmets, with rather awful black humour they imitated the bleating of sheep being led to the abattoir. They had been on a lorry that broke down and which was ruthlessly cleared off the road. They were from the Vendée, and had never crossed the Loire before now, but if they had to die, the idea of going to their death in a Rolls-Royce driven by a woman dressed by Jeanne Lanvin was one that filled them with wonder.

The American commander of the Medical Corps answered to the name of Lovering Hill. He managed to raise his drooping eyelids, heavy with lack of sleep, and stared at Hannah as he might have looked at a ghost.

'Nunnally?'

'His first name probably begins with a T.'

'This Nunnally's name is Jim.'

Sub-lieutenant Forissier and the five soldiers had got out of the Rolls about twenty minutes ago. Before disappearing, the sub-lieutenant had smiled at Hannah and called out, 'Good luck,' crossing his fingers for her.

'The man I'm looking for,' said Hannah, 'is very handsome. He's six foot two, fair-haired, with green eyes. He's over forty, although he looks ten years younger. He speaks English, French, German, Russian, Polish, Italian and Spanish. But he doesn't say very much, and he always has a self-mocking half-smile on his face.'

There were two dozen ambulances lined up in the yard of the Saint-Paul barracks at Verdun. The men were about to draw lots to decide who would have the dubious honour of being the first to go to the little village of Bras, four miles to the north – in other words, on the front line. It meant driving almost continuously under German fire with the enemy positioned less than a mile away, at Vacherauville, Douaumont, on the slopes of Le Poivre and Froideterre. A Nieuport sailed slowly through the air in the direction of an enemy observation airship, with the calm assurance of a killer.

'I would rather be told the truth straightaway, Mr Hill.'

She had noticed the gleam in her compatriot's eyes.

'We know him under the name of Mendel,' said Hill. 'I can assure you, to my knowledge he's alive.'

'Wounded?'

'He's not in any danger of dying.'

'Where is he?'

He had been evacuated nearly three weeks ago. He was returning from the forward position of Quatre-Cheminées, where he had been working for several weeks as a stretcher-bearer. 'He was always volunteering for duty. It's a miracle that he was never hit.' The accident had happened between Bras and Verdun, in fact on the outskirts of Belleville, less than a mile from Verdun.

'The accident?'

Hill looked ill at ease. And then he asked her: 'Who the devil are you, coming here like this?'

'His wife. What accident?'

The stupidest and most ludicrous imaginable. And, according to Hill, the most dramatically upsetting that could have happened to a man who had until then constantly risked his life in the midst of this hell.

'The ambulance that he was driving broke down. A supplies truck, driving up in the dark to the brigade command post at Quatre-Cheminées, hit his stationary vehicle, which he was trying to get started again. The lorry's load came down on top of him . . .'

He was hurt by potatoes.

CHAPTER 15

Don't Let Me Stop You, Becky

'It's of no importance.'

She drew the Derringer from her bag and laid it on the bed.

'Try it. It'll speed things up.'

'And stop me feeling sorry for myself.'

'Among other idiotic things, yes.'

She saw his large hand move and seize the weapon. Despite herself, she closed her eyes.

A shot rang out.

'Extraordinary,' said Taddeuz. 'I would have sworn that you hadn't left it loaded.'

The one-armed captain appeared at the bedroom door.

'Everything's OK,' said Hannah. 'It's just a kind of game.'

Pinsun went away.

'Yet another of your completely devoted servants, Hannah.'

She ignored his comment and asked: 'Can you walk?'

'A double fracture of the left femur,' the surgeon at Saint-Dizier had said, confirming the diagnosis of his colleague at Verdun. 'The strained ligaments in the shoulder are nothing. It's your husband's morale that worries me most . . . and yet he's the most charming man I've ever met. You both speak French extremely well for Americans.'

Taddeuz's only response was to sit up, swing his legs over the side of the bed, and take a few steps, pretending not to see the hand that she held out to him.

'We can go wherever we like,' he said.

'I could have spent months trying to explain to him that

I hadn't had him followed and tracked down, first to Mexico, then to New Orleans, and San Juan de Porto Rico – I would have been completely wasting my breath, Lizzie. You tried yourself to tell him, and so did Maryan – he spent hours doing everything he could to convince Taddeuz that he had acted on his own initiative. Taddeuz wouldn't believe any of us any more. After all, I went right up to the front line to find him, the way one would go looking for a child that had run away. The story of the potatoes would have made anyone else laugh, it really was extremely comic, enough to make you die laughing. And some of them did laugh . . . I shall never forgive them for that, I hope they die in agony, the bastards.'

'We could go back to Morcote,' she suggested. 'It's not very safe to cross the Atlantic right now.'

And at least in Switzerland, where there's no war, you'll be alone with him, Hannah. And you can try and cure him of these crazy ideas he's got fixed in his mind.

She used his leg as an excuse for taking things slowly. She had thought of driving down to Florence, which he loved so much, and which was associated almost as much as Morcote with so many memories of their honeymoon. But Italy, which was already fighting against Austria, declared war on Germany at the end of August.

So it had to be Morcote.

Pinsun accompanied them. Apart from losing a limb, he had also been gassed and some days it took him an incredible amount of guts just to walk two hundred yards. He and Taddeuz became friends – just as she had hoped. Of course she could see that there was in Taddeuz's acceptance of the Frenchman's presence a deliberate ploy to avoid direct confrontation with her. But as well as gaining time, she hoped that by spending time with Pinsun, who had such a fierce will to live (he was training himself to write with his remaining two fingers, a thumb and third finger, on his left hand), Taddeuz would eventually realize how light his own misfortunes were in comparison . . .

'And I was wrong again, Lizzie, I was still making the same mistake: I was gauging what he must be feeling in terms of how I would react. And I thought that it was just a matter of time before he got better, as I would have done had it been me . . .'

She too saw many qualities in Pinsun. They had talked a great deal while driving together in the Rolls along the front from Flanders to the Ardennes. Before being called up, Pinsun, who was coming up for his twenty-seventh birthday, was destined for journalism; he had studied literature and law. The first time she told him of the idea that had occurred to her, he refused with a laugh: he knew absolutely nothing about perfumes, he had barely heard of Guerlain, Caron, Coty or Roger et Gallet. And in any case, while the war lasted, he couldn't really see himself devoting his energies to such frivolities when others were fighting. She thought his mind was made up, but one morning he told her that he had decided to accept her offer.

'Your husband persuaded me.'

She was surprised to hear this, not to say astounded. In sixteen years Taddeuz had never intervened, in any way, in her affairs. This was a new development.

She thought it signalled some change in him.

They got back to Paris on 10 October. A doctor in Lugano had removed the plaster cast that had been on Taddeuz's leg for two months. Taddeuz was walking normally now. Only his shoulder still gave him some pain. But there was no outward sign of his injuries when they returned to the United States in November.

They didn't make love; he hadn't touched her for more than a year. She had never said anything about it and didn't now. Either he didn't want her any more because she was too old, or he wanted to punish her for having pursued him to Verdun. As she saw it, it was not up to her to make the first approach – that was all she needed: for him to rebuff her advances, with a smile, of course, and with all the kindness in the world, which would be a million times worse, in Hannah's view, than a slap across the face. All the same, there were moments, and nights, when it was almost unbearable; as it was throughout their Atlantic crossing, when their hips touched as they lay in the narrow berths – not a patch on the wide beds of the French line or Cunard ships – of the Spanish-flagged ship.

She deliberately allowed herself to be 'surprised' naked, on three or four occasions, but to no avail. She ended up feeling ashamed and almost as though she were 'touting for custom', to use her own expression.

They slept in separate bedrooms once they got back to the house on Long Island. It was true their time-tables had never tallied very well, and it was even worse during this peculiar period: she always started work more or less when he was going to bed. As for Taddeuz, if there was any chance of his being able to sleep, he would go to bed early whenever he could, knowing that she would in any case be up before daybreak. He began leading a completely independent life (there had already been some precursory signs of this in Morcote, but having his leg in plaster limited him in his movements). He would go to bed at all hours, showing no concern for her any more, and spending more and more of his nights away from home. As he was no longer using his apartment in Sullivan Street, he lost the lease on it; but this didn't worry him since he managed, through the intermediary of the inevitable Becky Singer, who was always ready to meddle in what was none of her business, to get the loan of a little place in Minetta Lane, which was still in the heart of what might be considered the New York equivalent of Montparnasse: Greenwich Village. It became a venue for writers and artists. Hannah went to a party there once (Taddeuz had invited her) when all the guests (of both sexes, indeed of all three) were friends of his. She spent four dreadful hours there, which were dominated by the very strong feeling of being excluded, or at least of being an outsider.

She thought, she hoped, that he had started writing again. This would be a sign, she believed, that he was himself again. Eddy Lucas, whom she questioned on the subject, could only confess his ignorance of what Taddeuz was up to.

'The only time I've seen him since your return from Europe he told me that he was going to rewrite *The Desert*, that's all I know. Hannah, I'm sure I'm not telling you anything you don't already know, but he's not at all well . . .'

'What do you mean, not at all well? Is he ill? Has he said anything to you?'

But what did she think Eddy Lucas could tell her? Taddeuz wasn't himself, that was obvious, but it was all happening inside his head.

When he condescended to visit the house on Long Island, he shut himself up in the huge study-library she had specially provided for him. One evening, taking advantage of one of his absences, she went in, racked by remorse, and actually found something resembling a manuscript, of some one hundred pages, except that all the pages were blank, apart from the top one, on which he had written in his broad hand: *Don't look any further, Hannah.*

She emerged from the study feeling torn between rage and shame.

And there was another thing, another new development: he had asked her for money. Very calmly, very naturally, with his eternal half-smile. As though it were an everyday occurrence, he explained that the Chalmers (a car) was decidedly too small to drive his friends around in, and he would like something more spacious and more comfortable, the big Packard, for instance. And he would also need twenty to twenty-five thousand dollars – he didn't bother to say what for.

She gave it to him.

He had always been a loving and affectionate father. Even when he was working in California he would write individual letters to his sons, as well as those he wrote to Hannah. He was always greeted with an enthusiastic welcome on his return: the boys both adored him, including Jonathan, who was usually so cold and reserved; and little Abigail, at the age of three, would screech with joy as soon as she set eyes on him. For a long time Hannah had taken pleasure and pride in the close relationship between father and sons. To tell the truth, she had often served them as Aunt Sally, when they ganged up to make fun of her. One of their favourite tricks was acting out a parody of 'Madame Hannah': bursting into one of her beauty parlours or shops without warning. Jonathan would play the part of his mother – he could do a perfect imitation of her way of walking very fast, taking little steps, and shouting at people much bigger than herself, while Taddeuz and Adam pretended to be the terrorized staff, either cringingly loyal or downright grovelling.

And when she brought Taddeuz home from Europe, after so many months during which he sent the children no word at all, he was welcomed by his sons as though he had only been gone since the day before. Adam was more demonstrative, his younger brother more reserved, but they both greeted him with immense love and affection. *Whereas they scarcely glanced at you, and gave you only an absent-minded kiss . . .*

But his behaviour in public had not changed. The constant stream of visitors to Long Island, whether friends or business acquaintances, encountered the couple they had always known; a close, loving couple, who had obviously managed to reconcile the demands of her life as head of a business empire with his as a writer. These were actually the only times when he would touch her, putting his arm round her shoulders, or even kissing her – as long as there were witnesses; it was a performance which took her hours, sometimes days, to recover from.

Even someone like Charles Chaplin, who stayed with them for a whole week, was taken in by it. (He was under contract to Freuler's Mutual Film Corporation, but wanted to produce films himself, and was thinking of building his own studio in Los Angeles, in the vicinity of Sunset Boulevard.) Eddy Lucas was fooled, and the Singers, and Cecil B. De Mille, whose *Joan of Arc* was a recent triumph (he was unaware that Hannah was partly responsible for financing it); and so too were Mary Pickford and Douglas Fairbanks.

Only Lizzie (and Maryan, but he said nothing) could see through what she called 'an idiotic and ghastly game'. Acting with her usual generous impetuosity and great common sense, she even went against Hannah's wishes, not to say orders, and tried to talk to Taddeuz about it.

'I would have had more chance of breaking into the Rockefellers' bank by banging my head against it. It was like talking to a brick wall, Hannah.'

'I told you it was pointless.'

'I'm almost as fond of him as I am of you, so how could you expect me just to sit by and not try to do anything about this nonsense? And it's no use giving me dirty looks with those big eyes of yours. I'm probably the only person in the world whom you'll never succeed in intimidating, old girl, it's time you realized that. I explained again to that fool of a husband of yours that it was my fool of a husband who had him tailed by his best men, in Porto Rico and everywhere else. And that Maryan acted entirely on his own initiative, without consulting you since you were at Polly's funeral in England at the time, and even that you were furious and worried when you found out. And I also told him that had it been me, if I'd had the courage, or the idea had even occurred to me, I would have gone looking in hell to find the man of my life. Then I lost my temper a bit, and I don't remember very much after that. What I do know is that I spelt it all out very clearly to him, you can be sure of that.'

'And the result?'

'As they say in Australia, it was like peeing into the sea in Brisbane to raise the level of the water in San Francisco. Completely pointless.'

'"It's of no importance, Lizzie."'

'Exactly.'

Then they wept in each other's arms.

Actually, it was mostly Lizzie who cried, while Hannah, her grey eyes wide and staring, consoled her.

'He'll get over it, Lizzie. It's just a matter of time.'

She believed this – most of the time – with the same fierce conviction that she had always applied to the pursuit of her objectives. If you really want something, you always end up by getting it, as long as you want it long enough.

Even the scene that took place on 4 December would not in any way undermine this conviction.

That was the day she came home from an eleven-day trip to several towns on the East Coast – Boston, Philadelphia, Baltimore and Washington. She had just got rid of Kate O'Shea (with some regret, but the situation was becoming intolerable) who ran the laboratory at New Rochelle. They had had a terrible row, not for the first time; whilst men would have come to blows, they had confined themselves to words. Leaving aside Kate's political ideas (although even these were beginning to get beyond a joke

– *I'm sick of hearing about her wretched William II!*), the Irishwoman's rampant feminism was too much. Kate wanted to stop doing any research on the grounds that she was making herself party to the exploitation of the women to whom the beauty products were sold. Hannah gave Kate six weeks' salary, the money for a passage from New York to Galway, and five minutes to get off the premises, with a request to take her bombs with her, if possible. For want of anyone better, she appointed Maud Goulding, previously Kate's assistant, as temporary head of the laboratory. But she was not very happy with this arrangement. Maud lacked dynamism, and she was another feminist, scarcely less virulent than Kate.

Hannah's trip had otherwise gone very well. Business had never been so good. The figures bore this out, and so did the immense coverage that the press gave to each of her presentations – she had sometimes given lectures to audiences of thousands of women. Why should she pay for advertisements in newspapers and magazines if she didn't have to – it would cost her a fortune! By luck or design, and doubtless a bit of both, she had managed to reconcile the irreconcilable: the genuine revolution in beauty care for which she was responsible (she had been working on it for more than twenty years now!) with the demands of the American feminist movement, which had just given birth to an organization called the Social and Political Union for Women. The presence of Maud Goulding at her side gave her credibility with the feminists, if such were needed. She had also organized a formidable line-up of talent: her three secretaries, including Eulalia Jones – and the Cherokee, dressed by Poiret, with her dark, fascinating beauty, did her proud – and five models. Each one had no less than fifteen dresses, all from Paul Poiret's ateliers, as well as outfits designed by Worth, Jeanne Lanvin, Nicole Groult (Poiret's sister) and Marco Fortuny, the Spaniard from Venice. As well as the curiosity aroused by what she dared to do with make-up, Hannah awakened in her audiences an avid desire for the clothes worn by her personal retinue. There were countless questions about the smallest details of their outfits. The fact that they wore no corset; the appearance of the strange garment invented by Poiret (under the influence of Isadora Duncan) called a brassière; the short lace slips; the simplicity of their underwear generally; the way they left the natural shape of the body unrestricted, free from any artificial constraint – all this raised a great sigh among these women, caused them to shiver with excitement . . . with tangible results, reflected in the sales of the 160 creams, lotions, eaux de toilette, and perfumes available under her double H trademark.

She left the others at the central station and went with Eulalia to Forty-Ninth Street, where she had an office at that time. She spent an hour there. Then she telephoned the apartment in Fifth Avenue: Yvonne, the governess and Abigail had gone out; only the cook and one of her chambermaids were there.

She drew a blank, too, at Long Island. The caretakers were there, as well as the five servants. There were letters from Adam and Jonathan, written from their college in Connecticut. And Mr Taddeuz? No, Mr Taddeuz wasn't in. It was four days since they had last seen him.

She quickly dealt with those things that required the most urgent attention. In the enormous pile of mail was a letter that she opened for pleasure, having recognized the still-clumsy handwriting: it was from young Pinsun, telling her that he had carried out to the letter the instructions he had received from her, and that he was busy learning all about the perfume business. He listed some of the new words he had learned: bouvardia, ylang-ylang, oil of mirbane, musk, ambrette and piperonal.

He wrote: *I owe a lot to you, Hannah. I hope one day*

to be able to return some of the strength that you so generously gave me.

'Eulalia? I'm going out for an hour, perhaps longer. Don't wait for me to get back before you leave.'

She took the little Rolls-Royce torpedo that she used in town and which she had ordered in black and turkey-red. Although she drove, she took the chauffeur with her, a Polish-American with the fairly classic name of Kowalski.

It was midday when she stopped the car a little beyond the south-west corner of Washington Square.

'Wait for me here,' she told Kowalski. 'Don't come up unless I call you.'

Minetta Lane was a little road leading into Sixth Avenue, known as Avenue of the Americas. The red-brick building, like several others in this formerly elegant residential quarter, belonged to various members of the Singer family. Taddeuz's apartment was on the second floor. She simply had to turn the handle to get in; the door was not locked. The place had been decorated since her last visit: someone had put in carpets and furnished it with Turkish divans; there were paintings on the walls and a few very fine photographs taken by Man Ray. *Now you know what happened to the twenty-five thousand dollars he needed . . .*

The first room was empty; an almost inaudible sound came from the bedroom. Hannah's footsteps were muffled by the Persian carpet; she advanced several yards.

Taddeuz was sitting in a rattan armchair, she could see his face in three-quarters' profile. His head was resting on the back of the chair, he looked as though he was asleep; his eyes were closed, and there was no expression on his face. She registered too his extraordinary, constant youthfulness. There was a naked woman kneeling in front of him, between his legs. She had taken him in her mouth: her long black hair cascaded down her back, contrasting with the milky whiteness of her skin.

After a few seconds, as though sensing the presence of someone behind her, she tensed.

Hannah said very calmly: 'Carry on, Becky. Don't let me stop you.'

She raised the Derringer.

'Carry on with what you were doing or I'll kill you. I'm not a very good shot but I can hardly miss from this distance. Rebecca,' (she started speaking Yiddish instead of English), 'it's not that I don't want to kill you. I'll try not to, I'll settle for crippling you. I rather fancy shattering your spine, so that you remain an invalid for the rest of your life. Carry on. Finish the job.'

Hannah sat down less than six feet away from them.

'Go on!'

She kept her eyes fixed on Taddeuz's face, which betrayed nothing whatsoever. One minute went by. Becky Singer fell back, still on her knees. And naturally, she was crying.

'Hannah . . .'

'Get dressed and get out of here.'

Over the sobbing of her one-time companion at Dobbe Klotz's in Warsaw she heard the sound of rustling silk as Becky put on her dress. Hannah didn't even turn round, the little Derringer still lying in her lap.

'Hannah, at least let me . . .'

'Get out,' she said, without raising her voice.

She heard the door gently close. She continued to watch Taddeuz, who remained oddly impassive – he still had not opened his eyes. She stood up and walked over to him, hesitant and now worried by his abnormal torpor. She raised one of his eyelids: his eye was glassy and dull, although his pupil was enormously dilated.

'Can you hear me, Taddeuz?'

After a long pause, he nodded, almost imperceptibly, having tried unsuccessfully to open his eyes. And she began to be afraid. She thought he was drunk at first, but there was no smell of alcohol on his breath. It must be something else.

'Don't fall asleep! What have you taken, Taddeuz?'

He mumbled incoherently. First she tried to lift him, but couldn't manage it; he weighed twice as much as she did. By bracing herself, she was able to push the rattan armchair over to the bed and then managed to pull his large body, inch by inch, out of the chair and on to the bed. She worked very fast.

She rushed out of the apartment, then tore down the stairs and signalled to Kowalski from the entrance to the building.

'Take the car and go and find Maud Goulding for me, and make sure you bring her father. You know where she lives. Her father's surgery is in Thirty-Third Street. Hurry, and don't come back without them, or bring another doctor if you have to. Quickly!'

She went upstairs.

'Don't fall asleep, Taddeuz, I beg you. Don't fall asleep, my love . . .'

She tried to get him dressed and one way or another managed to get him into a pair of trousers and a shirt.

'Can you hear, Taddeuz? Can you hear me? Do you know who I am?'

'Hannah.'

She almost jumped, he said her name so distinctly. She thought he had woken up, but no, on the contrary he seemed to have sunk deeper into his lethargy, although he was seized with short convulsions.

'Don't fall asleep!'

Why do you keep saying that? You must be crazy. And it was true that she was in an almost complete state of panic. She fought against it by walking round the room, constantly returning to him, shaking him, caressing him, holding him close – she had never been able to do quite as well with any of her children. She eventually decided to search the room, keeping an eye on him (he was still having fits, with shivers going through his whole body; he was sweating profusely and his breathing was irregular). *I must have been mad*, Hannah thought. *Why didn't I get Kowalski to take him to hospital straightaway? If he doesn't find George Goulding, I'll kill him!*

The two wardrobes contained nothing but clothes, underwear and shoes. She turned her attention to a roll-top desk. She was about to break into it when it occurred to her that the keys must be somewhere – in his jacket or waistcoat. She found them.

'Taddeuz, don't fall asleep.'

It had become a kind of incantation. She thought of Mendel who had also fallen asleep on her. *For pity's sake, not that!*

She opened the desk, again with the sense of committing an act of desecration, even more so than when she had hunted for his manuscript on Long Island. She found a dark wooden box, with its own lock – to which she also had the key . . .

Inside was a very thick pile of handwritten pages – at least seven or eight hundred pages – written, unusually for him, in a very neat hand, and an album bulging with photos.

Don't look at it, Hannah!

She read the first few lines and her eyes at once filled with tears. It was all about her, how could anyone doubt it? He had taken the trouble to give the date and location of all the events described, the earliest of which went back sixteen years at least, to the time when he came to her beneath the shadow of the Prater in Vienna, and then in Morcote, on Lake Lugano, and the whole of their life together over all these years, translated into a fabulous, riotous torrent of words and images. Everything was there – the whole time they had lived together, the shared silences and laughter, their sexual passion for each other

– all recounted with extraordinary lack of inhibition. It was a personal diary, but also a literary achievement, the unimaginable, overwhelming proof of his almost obsessional love for her, then and now. *And that's what makes you cry so, Hannah, you wanted him to write, and so he has, and what he has written is a record of the love he bears you, a work that he denied himself in advance the right to publish. So you've killed him twice over, firstly by smothering him as a man, and then by monopolizing his existence as a writer. Because you can tell, as he must have known it too, surely better than you, that this is without any doubt the best thing he's ever written. This is his masterpiece . . .*

And the album contained nothing but photos of her, chosen from among the thousands and thousands he had taken and always developed himself; photos that often showed her naked and shameless in the extreme.

The Gouldings, father and daughter, were as much chemists as doctors. They identified a white powder resembling cocaine.

'Cocaine chlorhydrate, but he seems to have taken something else as well . . .'

As for Taddeuz's condition, he was in a state of semi-coma, no less. Yes, he might die, he might well have died already.

'But getting him into hospital wouldn't have helped: it would have been a miracle to find an intern trained to deal with drug addiction. You did well to call me. I know that you are not a woman who's easily panicked.'

George Goulding was one of the foremost American drug specialists. She was thankful she had thought of him. However, he advised her to call one of his colleagues.

'Louis Macke. Before the war he worked with Fourneau in Paris. You won't find anyone better . . . if he's in New York.'

He was. Kowalski brought him back an hour and a half later. In the meantime Taddeuz had still not regained consciousness, although he seemed to react to the sound of Hannah's voice. He had passed through several worrying stages: a state of semi-coma, in which his breathing was slow and very irregular, had succeeded his initial torpor; his eyes eventually opened after a second injection administered by Goulding. His pupils were contracted, his eyelids puffy, and his eyes couldn't take the light – they had to close the curtains, plunging the room into semi-darkness. Then he vomited twice and started shivering, like a person suffering from the cold, but when they tried to cover him he threw off the blankets violently, irritated by the mere contact of them.

All of which were symptoms that Louis Macke was very much inclined to attribute to morphine . . .

'Perhaps taken with a barbiturate, such as Gardenal, which has recently come on to the market.'

'In other words, you don't know,' said Hannah in an icy voice.

'Mrs Newman, your husband is obviously a chronic drug addict, and in my view he has been for a long time. I do not believe that I am mistaken in this. No more than I am mistaken in thinking that he has not confined himself to one drug in particular. I would say that he has tried several. Has he been anywhere recently?'

'He was in Verdun, where he was an ambulance driver and . . . [an idea occurred to her] . . . he also spent time in Mexico.'

'They have some hallucinogenics there that we know nothing about. Anything is possible. If he comes through this . . .'

'He will,' she said furiously.

Louis Macke was a portly little bald-headed man, with sharp eyes behind his spectacles.

'Perhaps he will survive this crisis. But there have been

others and there will be more, so it won't solve the problem. Let's not mince words, Mrs Newman: he tried to kill himself today.'

'You're a damned fool!'

'That's very possible. He has at least entertained the idea of dying.'

'He won't do it again.'

'I can't see inside his head, madame. Nor can you. Your husband has become psychologically dependent on drugs. He's addicted to them. He's a writer? Doubtless he started with opium, like Baudelaire, in the hope that it would make things easier for him . . .'

And then he must have taken larger doses, tried different drugs, in search of more powerful stimulants. Macke was obviously on his favourite theme and he talked on and on. *I hate this fellow – he's so sure of himself*, thought Hannah with rage. And it wouldn't have taken very much for her to have Kowalski throw him out.

She remained at his bedside all that afternoon and through the following night, not for one moment moving more than a few yards away from him. She even threw Eulalia out of the room when she brought Hannah some documents that needed urgent attention. Left alone, she read through Taddeuz's journal, her cheeks aflame, and when she reached the end she started again. At about five o'clock in the morning, on the 5th, the first signs of an improvement in his condition appeared, as Macke had said they would: his breathing gradually returned to normal, he stopped sweating, and the colour of his skin changed – the bluishness that worried doctors and made them talk of cyanosis disappeared.

An hour later he smiled at her. Feebly, but there was no mistaking his invariable smile, expressive of all the derision in the world.

'Yet again you've come and found me, Hannah.'

CHAPTER 16

I Think You're Lying to Me

It was Macke's idea to send him to Vermont.

And it was Macke who chose where in Vermont – one of his sons ran a sanatorium there. At first Hannah refused point blank: no one else was going to look after . . .

'I don't want to meddle in your married life. And I'm only going to meddle because it seems obvious to me that it has an important bearing on all this,' said the little professor. 'We have two problems to deal with, madame. The first is his dependence on drugs, whatever drugs they might be. It will no doubt take months to cure him of this dependency. If he can be cured at all. That alone would be plenty to occupy us. But I mentioned two problems: the second is the problem that you pose . . . forgive me, that you pose for him. Need I say more?'

'No,' said Hannah eventually.

'I don't know to what extent the two things are related. Of course, you don't have to tell me about it.'

She took off her gloves without even being aware of doing so, then put them back on, with staring eyes.

'All right, I will,' she said.

'You're a very intelligent woman. And I don't say that to flatter you.'

'And the proof of it,' she said with great bitterness, 'is that I can see how it is with us, with Taddeuz and me.'

In the course of several successive meetings she told him everything, from the summer of 1882 right up to Verdun, leaving out nothing, and with more impartiality and detachment than she had thought herself capable of.

Macke made no comment.

How was he going to treat Taddeuz?

Breaking the habit was the only treatment available at the time. Taddeuz would be given progressively smaller doses, and kept under strict supervision to make sure he didn't find his own supplies. An added attraction of Vermont was its distance from New York.

It was a place called Smugglers Notch, in the Green Mountains. When the weather was fine, as it was the day they arrived, you could see the jagged outline of Lake Champlain and as far as the Canadian border. The sanatorium was a large building erected barely two years ago. The private coach that Hannah had had coupled to the train from New York was uncoupled at Essex Junction, and they continued the journey in the big Rolls, driven by Kowalski, climbing a winding road through the heart of a marvellous forest of firs, beeches and maples.

The whole third floor of one wing had been reserved for Taddeuz, eight rooms in all, one of them a study-library which had been enlarged by the removal of several partition walls. He would be attended to by seven people, as well as a doctor especially assigned to him.

She intercepted his glance and said, 'You're not obliged to stay here, Taddeuz. You're here because you agreed to come. You can leave whenever you like, it's up to you to decide.'

His only response was to nod. They had not exchanged a single word more than strictly necessary since he had come out of his coma six days earlier.

Once in the apartment in Minetta Lane and then a second time on the train, he had suffered a kind of epileptic fit. It had taken no less than the combined strength of two huge male nurses and an injection given by the doctor accompanying them to quieten him down.

And he had tried to throw himself out of the window.

He was calm now and incredibly normal as he wandered

through the third-floor apartment, stroking the spines of books and the paintings by Klimt, Mondrian, Klee and others.

There was no portrait of her, nothing to remind him of her in any way. At first she had hung up the picture that Gustav Klimt had done of her in 1899, in which she was painted with bare breasts – Taddeuz had always wanted it in their bedroom – then she had it taken down, with Louis Macke's approval.

He finally halted in front of the padlocked casket in which his secret journal and the album of photos was locked, and which he himself had taken from the roll-top desk.

'Did you touch any of my things, Hannah?'

'No.'

He smiled.

'I think you're lying to me . . .'

'You wouldn't believe me even if I told you the sun existed. I haven't touched anything,' she said with all the more conviction for not being so certain that it was in her interest, in the interest of both of them, to deny it.

The windows in all the rooms were sash windows, but the panes of glass were too thick to break, and the latches had been padlocked. Two nurses watched Taddeuz all the time. He pretended not to see them.

Outside, as the daylight faded, the soft-edged rounded mass of Mount Mansfield, made even softer-edged by its snow-covered vegetation, turned a curious pink, while the narrow, hemmed-in valleys below slowly darkened. There wasn't a building in sight; they hadn't seen another living soul all the way up to Smugglers Notch. The sense of isolation and silence was very oppressive. *How have we come to this?* thought Hannah, prey to a great feeling of sadness. During the previous days, in which she had had to confront and resolve the problem of what she called – and would always call – Taddeuz's illness, she had drawn on her usual energy. She had no doubt of having acted for the best, but now she took the full measure of what those decisions entailed: she had had him confined to a prison – had she ever done otherwise?

Their dinner that evening was almost ordinary, as long as they pretended to ignore the constant presence of nurses who replaced each other in shifts. After dark, once they had eaten, the doctor injected Taddeuz with his daily dose of drugs. He immediately became talkative.

'*We talked about our children, Lizzie, it was the only subject we could pretend to agree about . . .*'

They continued to pretend the next day at dawn, when she left with Kowalski. She had slept two or three hours at most, alone. He hadn't come to bed at all, spending the night pacing the study-library, reading or perhaps writing.

He saw her to the Rolls.

'And what shall we do for Christmas?'

He replied that he would rather spend Christmas alone.

And also the coming months, for as long as he was here. Unless his sons agreed to come and see him, during the school holidays, for instance. In which case (he smiled) he would do his best not to give them too pitiful an impression of their father.

She was about to move away in order to get into the car when he took her in his arms. The next moment their lips met, very briefly. Already he was stepping back and holding out two letters, one addressed to Adam and Jonathan, and the other to her.

She waited until she was in her private coach travelling back to New York before she opened hers: in it he described in a few sentences what future each of them could look forward to. He would pull through on his own or not at all; she had done everything possible but it was up to him now to take charge of his life. He agreed in advance to any form of separation she might envisage;

and in the event that he succeeded in curing himself completely, and that she was still willing to have him, they might be able to rediscover some way of living together, as long as it proved possible. But she must give him time, and above all she must leave him alone.

Not a word of love or tenderness.

The last image of him that she took away with her, as the Rolls began the descent, was of his silhouette against the snow and bare trees, against a background of cold solitude – his silhouette for once dwarfed by the presence of those two giant nurses.

CHAPTER 17

He Told Me that You Would Never Give Up

The brother of Maryan's who was fighting in the French Army was killed at the beginning of February 1917. March brought news of the abdication of Nicholas II, the Tsar whom Hannah had once met in the gardens of Tsarskoie Selo. In April the United States joined the war. It seemed as though the world was trying hard to pack with events this period in Hannah's life, which was otherwise desperately empty. It wasn't that her companies were doing any less well, or that business was sluggish; quite the contrary, they had never been more flourishing. The same phenomenon that she had noticed in Europe repeated itself in the States. Far from checking women's spending in her salons and shops, the war increased it. A new clientele appeared, made up of all those women whom the great wind of war, and perhaps also the twentieth century, at last under way, liberated from tradition and customs.

But these were incidental matters. There were days when, in some hotel in one of those American towns that were all so much alike, she felt not tiredness but lassitude, a weariness of the mind more than of the body. She was forty-two and, after all, for more than a quarter of a century now she had maintained the frenetic pace of her life. She was rich beyond any dreams of wealth that she might once have entertained. She had received at least ten offers to buy her little empire – the most recent to date an offer of ten million dollars, which she had rejected as she had rejected all previous offers, not for one moment tempted to accept, and amazed that anyone should think she would be willing to part with what she had created.

She lived through those first months of 1917 to the rhythm of the weekly reports sent to her from Vermont, a poor substitute for the letters that Taddeuz didn't write to her, and the visits that she wasn't allowed to make.

'I feel sad and empty, Lizzie, and all I can do is wait.'

But not for one moment did she despair.

And yet the reports were bleak. He had made two further attempts at suicide, and very nearly succeeded the second time. He displayed all the symptoms of paranoia and even more obviously suffered a persecution mania. His attacks came without warning – they could happen at any moment, sometimes at the end of several weeks' apparent remission, or indeed complete cure, which turned out to be highly deceptive ('I myself was taken in,' admitted Louis Macke).

The worst of these attacks was the one he had in April, when his sons came to see him during the school holidays. It happened while they were out walking. First he was seized with a fit of trembling, with spasms and convulsions that threw him to the ground; the nurses immediately intervened, the terrified children looking on – Adam was fourteen, Jonathan eleven. They thought they had calmed him down, but turned back just in case. It was then that he started to shout at Jonathan – 'Calling him by your name, madame, and it's true that of the two boys he's the one who resembles you most closely' – then he rushed at the youngster and tried to strangle him.

They tried substitution drugs but nothing worked, cocaine was the only thing that more or less quietened him down, destroying him at the same time.

'You insisted on having complete reports, madame, and it has to be said that we are not making any progress. We have so far proved tragically ineffectual. He complains about his legs and some days has difficulty walking, his nasal passages are beginning to be eaten away by the cocaine. The only hope now is a brutal therapy that carries risks for a patient whose main problems no doubt lie elsewhere.'

'He could go mad, is that it?'

'His mental equilibrium at present is extremely precarious, I have never tried to hide that from you.'

Right at the outset Louis Macke had spoken to her about this last resort – the total withdrawal, from one day to the next, of any drugs at all, even if it meant locking Taddeuz in a padded cell. And it was Louis Macke who had confirmed, had she still doubted it, that at the heart of the complex feelings Taddeuz had for her, there was almost as much hatred as love: the worst thing she could do would be to go and see him. He was fighting this battle alone. Besides, he had no choice. He would save himself through his own will power or die. Macke knew that she understood: Taddeuz had taken refuge in drugs the way other people seek solace in alcohol; it was his way of escaping the problem that she, Hannah, posed for him . . .

Gozlin! A Yiddish word, meaning charlatan, it sprang to Hannah's lips, but did not pass them. This discussion by a third party, albeit a doctor, of the innermost secrets of her relationship with Taddeuz enraged her. Only afterwards did the sorrow come: the little professor was probably right; that's what she found hardest to forgive him.

She had laid down her conditions: they would first of all try the gentle therapy for six months, twelve if necessary, and only then . . .

'You seem to disregard a cardinal factor,' said Macke. 'Your husband is fully responsible for himself. If the treatment he's following has the slightest chance of succeeding it is precisely because we can count on his total co-operation. We have no legal means of constraining him. Unless you wish to start proceedings to have him declared incapable of taking responsibility for himself?'

Her grey eyes bored into him.

'I was only asking,' the doctor had continued. 'Your husband is an exceptionally intelligent man, he is working with us in the most remarkable fashion. So he will make up his own mind.'

She discovered her own children: not so much Abigail, who was coming up to four, as her sons. She had never really known them, having always been caught up in the whirlwind of her own life. Even when they weren't at school, or afterwards at college, or weren't permanently resident with the Kadens, she hardly ever saw them, being frequently kept late at the office in the evenings, working even on Sundays.

'A father who had behaved in the same way would probably not have been greatly reproached for it, he would have been forgiven. But I was a woman, and apparently that changes everything. It's true that I made a disastrous mother. Not a bad one, just non-existent. But I tried, from the summer of 1917 I tried.'

On 31 July the two boys, accompanied by Yvonne and Gaffouil, came home after spending two weeks in Vermont – Macke and his colleagues had decided that their presence presented virtually no danger; Taddeuz's attacks were becoming more infrequent and according to the reports there seemed to be signs of a slight improvement: they had managed to reduce the doses of cocaine he was taking by seventy per cent.

Adam and Jonathan came back apparently delighted with their stay in the Green Mountains. Although they were very uncommunicative about what they had done there; the most they would say was that they had been out for walks together, gone horse-riding, and taken photographs. 'Father taught us how to develop films. He has a laboratory all to himself.' And they had actually brought home lots of pictures taken by Taddeuz or one of the nurses. It was only because of this that she was able to see how her husband looked after eight months' treatment – he seemed to have grown very thin, but was otherwise unchanged; his eyes staring into the camera were still dreamy, and there was that famous half-smile.

As for the dramatic scene that took place during the Easter holidays, when Taddeuz had rushed at Jonathan and tried to strangle him, neither of the boys had ever made the slightest allusion to it; it was as though they had wiped it completely from their memories. It was with the utmost naturalness that in answer to the question, 'How is he?' they replied, almost surprised: 'Very well, mother, very well indeed.'

They were both going to be tall. Adam, at fourteen, was already almost a foot taller than her. And Jonathan, three years younger than his brother, was already the same height. Of the two he was the one most like Hannah – there was a resemblance in the eyes, of course, and in his smile (when he smiled!) but also in his evident predisposition to a caustic aggressiveness, not to say a great inner violence.

And not always so inner: he had twice been suspended from college and, but for the generous donations made to the establishment by his mother, he would probably never have been allowed back. Especially after his second escapade: furious at having been left out of some sport's team – she never did learn which – on account of his age, he had vandalized the cloakrooms, ripped apart the team's kit, and given the coach's son a thrashing; then (Hannah couldn't help laughing at this) he had managed to get a donkey – wearing a pair of trousers, shirt and cap belonging to the same coach – into the headmaster's office on the second floor. Then he ran away and got as far as Kansas City, no one knew how. He was finally picked up after he had already landed himself a job as a messenger for an auctioneer in livestock.

She realized with amazement that neither of her sons knew anything about her business interests (whereas they seemed to know all about their father's every published line; indeed every line he had ever written). They had only a very vague idea, strongly coloured with indifference, of the nature and scope of her enterprise. The money she spent on them? They had never asked themselves where it might come from – 'You sell things to women, don't you?'

She felt jealous and genuinely annoyed. But whose fault was it, if not her own?

Their eyes opened wide in astonishment when she suggested they might like to accompany her on one of the long trips she was about to make, which would take her as far as California. They would not be alone: she was travelling with one of her usual teams. Of course they would be with a crowd of women, if that didn't bother them too much.

Not at all. They thought it rather fun. She was not long in finding out how much fun: they would persistently plant themselves wherever the models were changing, the younger boy dragging his elder brother after him through the midst of all these naked and very pretty ladies. Within a few hours they had made themselves at home – Yvonne protesting indignantly that it was no spectacle for young children, while Hannah found the whole thing extremely comic.

She must have devoted more time to them during those six weeks than she had since they were born. Driven by a sudden need, she told them about herself, about the early days in Poland, then in Australia. She knew she wanted a closer relationship with them. She especially wanted to change the image that they had so far had of her – though she was well aware that she wasn't being very subtle about it. What kind of woman was she to be so adept in business and so ridiculously, so sadly clumsy when it came to showing a simple love for two boys who were her sons? Or even having an ordinary conversation with them?

'And yet I do love them, Lizzie! Not in the same way that I love Taddeuz, of course, but differently, the way I love you.'

'You always make everything so complicated, Hannah. Just tell them that you love them, and try to spend some time with them.'

'Everything's simple for you.'

'I was made to be happy . . . Hannah, I'm not being serious and I want to be. Adam adores you, even if he dares not show it very much. Abigail is adorable. Jonathan's obviously a bit of a problem but that will sort itself out in the years to come . . .'

At that time Lizzie Kaden was more than ever a picture of fulfilment, the wife and mother who had everything she could hope for from life. The house in Beverly Hills might seem like a zoo, constantly overrun by dozens of children of all ages, but the impression of happiness there was striking, in painful comparison with the Newman family house.

Maryan continued to make money in his own sweet way, although two more of his brothers had now gone to fight in France: one of them was seriously wounded; he wore the American uniform, unlike the brother who had first gone to fight. Maryan was too old to join up.

The Kadens never said a word about Taddeuz in all the time that Hannah and her sons spent with them in Los Angeles.

On the way back she took Adam and Jonathan to visit Mendel's grave, and told them all about him.

For once she got it right: presenting her past to her children in this way, and introducing them to those she had loved, was the best way of telling them about herself. *Yet again you're using Mendel . . .*

Adam was fascinated and moved: he took Hannah in his arms and wiped away the tears she wept.

Not Jonathan though, whose big cold eyes kept looking from his mother to this simple grave.

And Hannah had the feeling that he was another version of herself, watching and judging her.

Having completed their tour they returned to New York; the boys went back to college, in New Hampshire now, after the official start of term.

A few weeks later she heard from Louis Macke in Vermont that the decision had been taken by both Taddeuz and his doctors: the brutal therapy was to be tried, a complete withdrawal of drugs from one day to the next.

'It's what he wants, Mrs Newman. He has said so and he has put it in writing. If you want to intervene, there is one possible course of action open to you, and only one: you can have him examined by any expert you care to choose and get a judge to rule that he is not in his right mind.'

'Go to hell.'

The little professor was not in the least disconcerted by her remark. He shook his head.

'And for the love of God, don't go and see him.'

The Kadens came back from California for Christmas – they didn't want her to be left on her own. It was no small undertaking; apart from Maryan and Lizzie and their twelve children, there were dozens of other people who had to be accommodated in the two houses that faced each other across the small lake on Long Island. At Maryan's instigation, the whole Kaden clan had gathered once more, its members arriving from all over America, but mostly from California and Chicago. Clearly they were now fully integrated into this country that they had made their own; Maryan had made sure of it. There wasn't a single brother, brother-in-law or cousin of his who had not achieved a position of importance, in every domain from automobiles to real estate.

But after the first few days of January 1918, silence and solitude returned. Hannah hadn't even told Lizzie exactly what was happening in Vermont; she was too ashamed to speak of drugs, and had referred only to nervous problems. It was true that the degree to which they understood each other made any sharing of confidences unnecessary. When Hannah said no to Lizzie's offer to stay on at Long Island, Lizzie realized she meant it and didn't insist.

Hannah wanted to be alone. Louis Macke's weekly reports had become daily reports, and through familiarity the horror was robbed of its impact.

'*Tuesday 17 January. He continues to refuse any medication, and no longer recognizes anybody. Pulse taken at six o'clock: 130–180. In a coma for almost a hundred minutes this morning. No further suicide attempt since 4th of this month. Short period of lucidness, lasting about one hour, during the afternoon, then another, twice as long, at dinner time. Confirmed his refusal of any medication. Tried to write but couldn't hold the pen.*'

As she had insisted, the reports kept nothing from her. Relations between Louis Macke and herself were most peculiar. She entertained a deep hatred for the fellow – he was so sure of himself and of his analysis – and yet at the same time she had the utmost confidence in him, or close to it, if only for the skill and patience with which he had gradually made her understand and acknowledge what he called Taddeüz's schizophrenia.

'It's a term that was first used in Germany several years ago by my colleague Bleuler. It so happens that when I was in Europe I worked for a few years with the psychiatric team in Zurich. Have you met Freud? I've also met him. As well as Emil Kraepelin and Jung. Do you think I'm trying to impress you with the people I've known?

You're right. But I am hoping to convince you that I have tried to ensure that I am equipped with every asset that the latest scientific knowledge has to offer, neither more nor less.'

Hannah would never have believed it possible that anyone would one day talk to her about Taddeuz's insanity without having his eyes scratched out. Louis Macke did though, and what's more, he managed to convince her that his diagnosis was correct.

He waited until mid-February before telling her that the treatment was 'now giving cause for some hope'.

'What does that mean?'

She read and reread the latest health bulletins from Vermont, and was unable to find any reason to hope.

'We can expect a full recovery,' said Macke.

It would no doubt be a matter of several months. He started telling her a little more than he had before, smiling at her . . .

And it suddenly came to her. Without explanation. By some instinct. *He's lying*, she thought. *The son of a bitch is lying to me!*

She returned his smile.

'You're already done so much,' she said. 'I can wait a while longer.'

Two days later she was in Vermont, within sight of the sanatorium. It was 18 February and she was alone at the wheel of the Rolls (she hadn't even wanted to let Kowalski into the secret), having driven all the way from New York without a break – twenty-five hours' uninterrupted driving.

Although more undulating, there was something of Poland in this snow-covered, deserted landscape that extended thousands of miles to the west. After Montpelier the landscape changed (in Montpelier she had got a mechanic out of bed and asked him to check the Enots pump of the Silver Ghost 40/50). She started the climb up to Smugglers Notch. Twice the engine stalled, and with the brakes not strong enough to hold the thirteen hundredweight vehicle, the car started slipping backwards. On each occasion it was only by deliberately reversing it into the bank that she managed to stop the car. The narrow tyres just couldn't get a grip on the dirt track that was covered with a sheet of frozen snow. She was frozen to the marrow herself: only the passenger seats enjoyed the protection of being enclosed. The third time the engine stalled she couldn't restart it.

She decided to abandon the Rolls and set off on foot, sinking up to her knees in the freshly fallen snow, with a feeling that she knew the answer to the question she had come to ask.

It took her an hour to walk the last, exhausting mile and a quarter uphill in the grey light of a leaden sky and the bitter cold.

The caretaker who opened the door to her couldn't believe his eyes. He caught her as she collapsed and carried her to a bed, calling for his wife, who undressed Hannah, heaped a pile of blankets on top of her and gave her two hot-water bottles and plenty of scalding-hot tea with rum.

The couple confirmed what she had suspected: they had been alone here for forty-four days. The doctors, the nurses and all the other employees had left: the sanatorium was completely deserted.

'Newman left too, of course. That must have been about three months ago . . .'

He was accompanied only by one of his nurses, Adamson, with whom he got on very well. Yes, Mr Newman seemed to be in good health, in fact he was the one driving the car that he and his friend had left in.

No, the caretaker couple had no idea which direction they had taken. They hadn't said where they were going.

And in any case, there was only one road you could take from here.

The only instructions the caretakers had been given concerned the mail, which was to be forwarded to Professor Macke, no matter whom it was addressed to.

'I'd do the same again,' said Louis Macke. 'You entrusted me with the task of curing your husband and, more to the point – forgive me for thinking this had priority – your husband placed himself in my hands. I've never concealed my views from you: the only person in the world who can cure him is himself. I certainly haven't enjoyed this play-acting we've been treating you to since last December. It was his idea, not mine. I did all I could to dissuade him, but I was unsuccessful.'

'Where is he?'

'Don't expect me to tell you. I can swear to you that he is as safe as he can be. Mrs Newman, as far as I'm concerned, he's cured. He hasn't had an attack for seven months, his treatment is over, he's a normal man. With just one qualification: he refuses to see you again. It's a small thing, and at the same time it's a huge thing. These things are still a mystery to us. Let's say that he still hasn't sorted out his problems with regard to you.'

Silence.

She stood up and paced about the room for a while, then drew back the curtain to look outside, amazed by her own calm.

'What else did he say?'

'That he came close to killing you. Killing you for real. Especially after the business with Aitken and the film. Which he told me about in some detail.'

'I see,' she said. She turned her back on Macke.

'Make no mistake, Mrs Newman, he far from blames you for everything. In fact he's convinced it's all his own fault. He also told me about a trip he made to Mexico, to Oaxaca. Did you send someone after him then?'

'Yes and no.'

'You don't have to answer my questions.'

'I didn't send anyone after him. But a friend did, without telling me, thinking he was doing the right thing.'

'Did you tell your husband that?'

'He wouldn't even believe the opposite of what I said was true any more.'

Silence.

She turned round. Macke was nodding his head.

'I have a young niece,' he said, 'whose dream is to work in one of your salons.'

She didn't turn a hair, and eventually took out of her purse one of the tiny calling cards she often used to communicate her instructions to her directors.

'What's her name?'

'Shirley Storch.'

She wrote the name on the card and initialled it with a double H.

'Tell her to go and see Catherine Montblanc in New Rochelle.'

'Thank you. But I confess I was really trying out an experiment.'

'To see how I would react to your request?'

'Yes.'

'Your experiment was no good,' she said with indifference. 'I guessed it was an experiment. Will it tell me whether my husband is cured or not?'

'I think you know the answer to that. Are you going to give up on him?'

'No.'

'He told me that you would never give up on him.'

She looked him in the eye. 'In reply to the other question you would like to ask me: I'm not going to go after him, in any way. I'll wait for him to come back to me, if he wants to. And now I would like to settle my bill with you.'

Her attempt to keep the children with her for the Easter vacation proved to be an appalling fiasco. One morning she found her account books ripped to pieces, partially burned and covered with urine stains. Another time, it was her dresses that she found in shreds. Or again, the Pissarro she so adored was torn. The wonderful toys she had given them the previous Christmas had not been touched. They hadn't even bothered to break them as a sign of their utter contempt.

Yvonne was the only person who knew; Hannah had asked her not to breathe a word about it to anyone, least of all to Lizzie and Maryan. Especially as the contrast in the boys' behaviour when they were present was so startling. Adam and Jonathan would immediately join the Kaden horde of their own generation, and Jonathan would be all smiles, addressing Hannah politely and respectfully as 'mother' (he never called her Mom, except when he was very small). A natural leader, he was always the one to organize games for the rest of the pack, and on the very rare occasions when his eyes met Hannah's he would stare at her with a hard ironic gaze, as though throwing down some kind of challenge.

They had to be sent to different schools. Not that Jonathan was a bad student; he was sometimes quite capable of coming top of the class, but at other times he would come bottom. He had already had to change schools five times: physically stronger and taller than average, he was able to hold his own against boys much older than himself, and he never let an opportunity for a fight go by. He almost killed a student at yet another school where Hannah had just enrolled him (in the previous place he had broken a teacher's nose by hitting him with a heavy inkwell). He had already run away three times, on the last occasion getting as far as Quebec (like Adam, he spoke fluent French, having learned it mainly from Yvonne and Gaffouil, and he could get by pretty well in German and Polish).

Hannah tried to teach her sons Yiddish, but Jonathan didn't see why he and his brother should learn the language of the Jews – 'Our father is a Catholic.'

There were far fewer problems with Adam. There probably wouldn't have been any at all if he hadn't been so susceptible to the influence of his younger brother. Adam worked hard in class, he was a year ahead of his age. It was not unknown to him to repeat the gesture that he had made at Mendel's grave, when he took his mother in his arms (vice versa would be laughable – he measured six foot at the age of sixteen). But Jonathan had only to appear and he would immediately move away from Hannah.

Neither of the boys ever spoke of their father.

She took them to Los Angeles for the summer holidays.

'Lizzie, I don't know how to put this to you . . .'

'Don't bother. Maryan and I have already discussed it. Adam is the same age as Doug; there's only a year's difference between Jonathan and Owie and Mark, and they all get on very well together. As for Abigail, she'll have Sandy and even Melanie to play with. In other words, your children are welcome to make this their home for as long as you want to leave them with me. And it's no problem at all – on the contrary, as you well know. Let's say no more about it, please, and stop tormenting yourself: you're not the type to stay at home and be a mother, but there's nothing wrong with that. When term starts they can go to college and Abie will go to school. After all, California's no desert, people do learn to read and write here.'

James (born in 1902), Dougal (1903), Elizabeth, known

as Colleen (1904), Owen, known as Owie (1905), Mark (1907), Suzan (1908), the twins Patrick and Melanie (1911), Sandra (1912), Rodney (1914), Jeremy (1916) and Marion (1917): these were Lizzie and Maryan's twelve children – they lost one in 1909. In some vague way Hannah hoped that permanent contact with this joyful band would restore to her children, the youngest especially, some of their former balance.

She did not stay long in Los Angeles. She headed back up north, to San Francisco, where she spent two weeks, going off on long solitary drives in one of the cars she owned at the time – she had nine in all – a Rolls-Royce Alpine Eagle with six cylinders, nearly 7,500 cc.

She then went to Europe, having once again booked a passage for the transatlantic crossing with a Spanish ship. The main visits she intended to make were to Madrid, Lisbon, Barcelona, Paris, Monaco, Milan, Rome and Zurich.

In Paris, Jeanne Fougaril had just lost her second son: the first had been killed at Ypres, the other met his death at Le Chemin des Dames. Hannah suggested she take a break: 'I'll find someone to replace you.' But Jeanne clung on courageously: she was now left with just one daughter, who was herself married and whose husband was also at the front.

'Hannah, either I carry on working or I'll go mad. My work is virtually all I have left.'

Hannah lingered in Paris until November.

She celebrated the winning of the war in Père-Lachaise Cemetery, at Apollinaire's funeral. She was so sad that day, lost in the crowd, that she didn't understand when she heard someone shout out, as the funeral cortège went by: 'Death to Guillaume!' It took her a moment to realize that the 'Guillaume' in question was not the poet but Emperor Wilhelm of Germany.

* * *

The last days of 1918 found Hannah in Vienna. To be more exact, she arrived in the city on 20 December and three days later, apparently acting on a whim, she took a train to Warsaw.

There she wandered along Krochmalna Street, Smocha Street, Goyna and others, to which she had not returned in twenty-six years. Nothing, or very little, had changed, except that it was a little more crowded, a little more cramped. Dobbe Klotz had died six years earlier, of something pretty horrible that had been tearing away at her stomach for months, making her suffer atrociously – *At least I'm avenged*, thought Hannah, her old hatred still intact.

Although if the Hayrick had still been alive, she would no doubt have spoken to her and perhaps even forgiven her.

Through the porter at her hotel she found a car to hire, a 25 horsepower Renault with four cylinders, a sports model, which had belonged to a count, and which his widow was anxious to sell. Hannah drove round Warsaw, with that feeling one always gets on returning to the scenes of one's childhood and adolescence: a sense that everything is reduced in size and proportion, to the point that one is amazed to have thought it all so big in the past.

You should never have come back. You're killing your memories and making them seem pathetic, more effectively than if you were dying.

The Saxe Gardens were still there, the Potocki Palace, the University and the whole of Stare Miasto, the old city huddled round Rynek Square, the market-place. She crossed the Vistula into the Praga district. There was the street, on the right, but today it was paved . . .

And there, too, was the house, unchanged. She knocked on the door and waited, almost open-mouthed. The person who answered was the same Marta Glovacki of long ago, more than a quarter of a century in fact: a little heavier now, her hair a yellowish grey, and completely toothless, the skin on her face very wrinkled and pitted with smallpox scars, but otherwise still looking like a barrel of brine, and smelling just the same as before.

'Do you recognize me?' asked Hannah, suddenly seized – she didn't really know why – with a sudden rather bitter cheeriness.

The Glovacki woman said no.

'It was in 1890, in September and the following months. You had a tenant by the name of Taddeuz Nenski.'

'Perhaps,' said the landlady.

'He was very tall and very handsome. He had your biggest room, the one with the terrace and a view of the Vistula and Stare Miasto. He was a student, the kindest student in Poland.'

Silence.

Money changed hands.

'I remember very well,' said the Barrel of Brine. 'You wanted to see him. You were his sister.'

'No. I loved him and he loved me. I was never his sister. That was a lie.'

'All men are scum.'

'He wasn't.'

More banknotes appeared.

'No, that's true, he wasn't,' said the landlady. 'He really was an exception: kind and gentle, and very polite. I remember him very well. A very tall fair-haired boy with lovely blue eyes . . .'

'Green,' said Hannah.

'That's what I meant. Green. And impossibly good-looking. Wait, I remember very well: the secret police came looking for him.'

'They never found him. May I see the room again?'

'There's someone living there.'

'A student?'

'Yes. At least, the room is full of books.'

'He's my son,' said Hannah, getting carried away.

More money changed hands. They looked each other in the eye.

'Fine,' said the landlady, 'he's your son. And he doesn't live alone.'

'I know,' said Hannah carelessly, wondering what she was getting herself into.

'His wife's here too. Did you know he was married?'

'Of course. Since I'm his mother. May I go up and see them?'

'They're out. But you can go up. For this price, you can buy the house.'

When she entered the room in Praga for the very first time, all those years ago, she had never seen a terrace before. Or french windows. She didn't even know such things existed: *I had come straight from my* shtetl, *loosed upon the world like an anarchist bomb, all puffed up with pride and ambition . . . I really don't like the Hannah I was twenty-eight years ago very much at all. Perhaps when I grow very old, I might eventually end up with a little affection for her, but at the moment I can't bear her.*

She sat down on the only chair in the room, in front of a little table covered with books. She looked to see what books they were: history books mainly, but also some literature, mostly French, although some were in Polish and Russian, and she wasn't really surprised to discover Mikhail Lermontov among these authors. This was in the order of things.

As for the rest of the furniture and decor, there was the same four-poster bed, the same geraniums in a pot (or at least their direct descendants), the same book-shelves. However, the engraving of the Ponte Vecchio in Florence was no longer hanging on the wall.

She did not stir, although she felt a great desire to go and lie down on the bed. From there she would have seen the view through the windows that she remembered so well – a view of the centre of Warsaw, of the bell-towers on the baroque churches and the faded ochre-coloured ramparts. *And you would be able to feel Taddeuz's hands on you again, hands that made you melt beneath their caresses, although they weren't particularly adept at that time. Oh God, Hannah, what's the point of torturing yourself like this?*

They turned up a good two hours later; it was beginning to get dark. They were both fair-haired, and you could tell a mile off that they were Polish and in love with each other. He wasn't as tall as Taddeuz, and she was much prettier than Hannah had ever been.

'I'm not your mother of course.'

He smiled.

'There's a very good reason for that: she's been dead for ten years. Would you mind telling me . . .'

She didn't lie to them, she told them exactly what had happened – without getting to the very end of the story: she told them that Taddeuz and she had eventually found each other again, after being on opposite sides of the globe, that they were married, had children and lived in America, and that they were happy. *You couldn't help lying, after all.*

The young woman's name was Maria, and she believed she had an uncle in Chicago. It was quite dark now, and the lights of Warsaw glistened on the other side of the Vistula.

'Maybe you'll come to America,' said Hannah. 'In the event that you decide to stay in Poland these five thousand dollars are for you to spend as you wish. You can have the rest in Paris, London or New York, or even here; all you have to do is write to this lawyer, at this address in Geneva, and tell him where you want it: the same sum will be paid to you every year on the same date. No, I don't think we shall ever see each other again, but you never know. Jan? Would you repeat that line of Lermontov's that you said you liked?'

He did so, quoting again from memory.

'Thank you,' said Hannah. 'And may life be kind to you both.'

Gaffouil and Yvonne joined her in Berlin, where she reopened the salon and the two shops. Gaffouil, who was by now forty-seven or forty-eight, was still in charge of Hannah's fleet of cars: on his way through London he took delivery of a new Silver Ghost, which he then drove over to the German capital. He told Hannah that he had been able to make the whole trip without changing gears. He was fully satisfied with the Rolls, although he felt that it would not be long before the other car manufacturers launched some interesting new models.

'I've been told about a Hispano-Suiza that will soon be on the market. The engine is modelled on a V 12-cylinder used in aeroplanes, so it must be pretty powerful. And I heard something even more surprising: the Americans are also beginning to make big cars now. Duesenberg, for instance. They've got an 8-cylinder lined up. Shall I make enquiries?'

He knew Hannah's passion for cars, and more often than not it was he who tried out the vehicles before she bought them.

Yes, he could make enquiries. It was now the end of January. She set out for Rome in the Silver Ghost, with Gaffouil following on with the luggage in the Polish Renault – she had ended up buying it, partly so that Gaffouil and Yvonne could travel on their own, and partly because the owner of the vehicle, the countess, lived in one of those fine houses overlooking the Saxe Gardens that Hannah had thought the height of refinement when she was young.

They stopped over in Zurich, at the Hotel Baur-au-Lac, where twenty years earlier, although he hadn't noticed her, she had seen Lothar Hutwell, her ex-lover from Australia, who had one day suggested murdering his wife so that together he and Hannah might enjoy her fortune – and who, she was quite sure of it, had eventually committed the crime with a different accomplice. *It's all so long ago now . . .*

Amongst the rest of the mail awaiting her in Zurich was a letter from Lizzie. And the first line said it all: I've seen him, Hannah, I've seen Taddeuz. It happened one morning at about nine o'clock, three days before Christmas. Maryan had just left and suddenly I saw him in the garden. He seemed very well indeed, as far as I could judge. He was very tanned, and there was another man with him, a big burly chap called Adamson, who didn't say a word. You know what Taddeuz is like: he gave me a kiss as though he had just come back from a short trip and asked me if his children, your children, were with me. I said yes, and went to wake up Adam and Jonathan and Abigail. It all went very well. Taddeuz took them all out for the day in a little car that he had. The other man didn't go with them. I was a bit worried about it, but the three kids came back in the evening in time for dinner. The boys wouldn't talk to me about it, except to say that they had had 'an excellent day'. Abie was a bit more talkative. Taddeuz took them to the seaside, where they walked along the beach, then they went to a restaurant and ate oysters and crayfish. Your daughter couldn't think of anything else to tell me, other than that her father was 'very kind'. I didn't see Taddeuz again in the evening. Maryan wanted to go off and look for him but I wouldn't let him, and he didn't insist. I hope we did the right thing . . . Oh Hannah, I'm only writing to tell you this because I love you, knowing there's a risk it may be giving you groundless cause for hope. I saw Taddeuz for about four or five minutes in all, and we didn't speak of you. To be honest, I dared not mention your name and he didn't raise the subject either. If you really want to know, I hesitated to write to you.

That evening she replied to Lizzie's letter, reassuring her: what she had done was perfectly all right.

And then she caught herself writing a letter to Mendel; she had written four or five lines before she realized . . .

How extraordinary it would be if Mendel were still alive! All her life she had depended on him, even when his travels took him to the other side of the planet, even when a year or even two went by without seeing him. Now that she looked back, she realized that he had always turned up when she needed him. For a start there was that morning in 1882, the day she lost both her father and her elder brother, the only other human beings in the world with whom she could have found such a safe refuge as she did in Mendel. Then again, Mendel was the person who rescued her from the *shtetl*; it was thanks to him that she had gone to Australia; and it was Mendel who had found Taddeuz. And had Mendel been alive, Taddeuz would surely still be with her; he would have known what needed to be said, or done, better than all the damned doctors in the universe. He and Taddeuz would have gone off, just the two of them, and got very drunk; and once again Mendel would have carried him home on his shoulder. Everything would have been sorted out for another two or three years, and he would have been able to set off on his travels again in search of wide horizons and women who would offer him a warm welcome.

And he would probably have known how to talk to Jonathan. Because that was another problem Lizzie had mentioned in her letter: Hannah's younger son had been getting up to more mischief; he was becoming a real terror. He had even given Lizzie trouble (she didn't say what exactly, she simply referred to 'a few instances of insolence', but Hannah suspected that it must have been a lot more serious for Lizzie to have felt obliged to mention it at all).

Oh Mendel, why have you abandoned me?

She liked Rome. Her salon in the Via Veneto was so successful that the blue sheep representing it now had twenty-three legs. And the two shops, in Via del Tritone and Piazza Navone, were always full of customers, so much so that she was thinking of opening a third on the Via Sixtina. She liked the city and she liked Italy. She thought Italian men the most handsome in the world, and as a result of trying to understand Taddeuz's reasons for liking this country so much (she herself preferred Spain), she had found reasons of her own.

Her director in Italy was a man – although she did not make a habit of appointing men – whose name was Bruno Metaponte. He amused her greatly with his ambition of sleeping with her (an ambition evident in his burning eyes). He was a Lombardian, fairly small in stature, with sandy-coloured hair; one of his uncles was a cardinal and by virtue of this highly placed ecclesiastical connection he had managed to persuade the ladies of Rome that daubing their faces with Hannah's creams was not a mortal sin.

As far as premises in the Via Sixtina was concerned, he said that he had not been able to find anything suitable, apart from a building that needed completely doing up.

'And?'

'The owner doesn't want to sell or let.'

'To any problem there are always plenty of solutions. Who is this imbecile owner?'

A family who were direct descendants, apparently, of no less a person than Lucretia Borgia. Hannah called on the Principessa d'Arcangheli and found herself face to face, eye to lorgnette, with a dowager who looked as antique as the catacombs, enthroned on red velvet in a drawing room little smaller than the New York Stock Exchange.

The princess confirmed her refusal with icy courtesy.

'I don't consider myself defeated, Bruno. It's a question of principle, if not of "*principessa*" . . .'

It wasn't that she was obsessed with the idea of a third shop, especially as she could have found another location, but what else was she to cling to during that dreadful period of waiting?

She had the Arcangheli investigated. There wasn't much to find out: the dowager had only one grandson, who was thirty-six years of age, a widower with two children. They weren't fabulously wealthy, but nevertheless, in addition to several buildings like the one in Via Sixtina, they owned a palace in Rome, a large summer estate of farming land in Lombardy, a few paintings and a number of other antiques, and a villa on Anacapri.

Then events took an unexpected turn. While she was actually reading the report she had asked for, a man turned up at the Grand Hotel and asked to see her. By coincidence, he happened to be the very person whom she was trying to have tracked down. She agreed to see him, of course, and found herself confronted with an utterly charming man, short of stature but wonderfully well groomed, with attractively greying hair at the temples. She noticed his hands were very beautiful. He spoke French perfectly.

'But I can get by in English,' he said with a smile.

'French will do very well.'

And thereupon, still smiling roguishly, he presented her with a thick wad of papers, documents, photographs.

She stared at him in amazement.

An explanation was forthcoming: 'These are the exact plans of our palace in Rome, as well as those of the buildings we own and of the farm in Lombardy. I'm expecting the plans of the villa in Anacapri to arrive within the next hour or so. I've had an inventory drawn up of every item of furniture bigger than a stool. You will notice the excessive number of prie-dieu. This is a list of paintings – some of them frightful horrors, I'm afraid – and you will also find my complete genealogy, which explains why my second name is Hercules, in memory of the Duke d'Este. Of course these antecedents that I ought to be so proud of are completely fictitious. If we have any connection with Lucretia, it must be through one of her chambermaids, in my opinion. The truth is that one of my charming ancestors was the mistress of a pope, which means that we got our title by what you might call a papal bull. These are photographs of my children, and a reproduction of a portrait painted of me when I was one – I hope you'll forgive the clothes I was wearing at the time. I am of course perfectly well aware that a considerable amount of information is missing from my file, but I shall be delighted to answer any questions you might wish to ask me.'

Initially dumbfounded by his speech, she then burst out laughing.

'It seems I owe you an apology,' she said.

'My mother has asked me to invite you to dine with us one evening at your convenience. Accept and the matter is settled.'

During the remaining three weeks she spent in Rome, their friendship took root and developed. Though he knew little about her, never having asked any questions, he was aware that she was married. Actually, she had no need to take refuge behind her marital status: Pier-Nicola d'Arcangheli was tactful in never extending any invitations to her that did not include other friends, invited for her benefit.

On the eve of her departure, he asked if he could write to her. She said no.

'I'm sorry, Nicki. I'd rather you didn't.'

She had cabled Louis Macke, knowing that it was a total waste of time. The reply had come that morning: *I don't even know where he is any more. Contact lost thirty-five days ago.*

'I would like you and Gaffouil to return to Paris,' Hannah told Yvonne.

'I'm not very keen. In fact, I really don't want to.'

'Too bad. Take the Renault, it's yours. Go now. Good God, Yvonne, do as I say!'

Their eyes met.

'And leave you on your own? Who do you take me for?'

'Do what I tell you. Please.'

'If anything should happen to you, I would never forgive myself,' said Yvonne. 'Are you sure there are servants there?'

'Nothing's going to happen to me. And you know as well as I do there are servants there: someone answered when I telephoned. Take her away, Gaffouil.'

She waited until they had transferred her personal luggage from one car to the other, then drove off. After two miles she turned into what seemed no more than a very steep little street, up which she drove. She passed the terrace of the church of Santa Maria del Sasso, which was perched on top of a cliff. The car rounded several more bends and emerged on to a drive in front of a gate. This stood wide open, and the snow had been cleared to allow cars to get through. The garden looked very different under snow: strange forms were sculpted in the shrubbery, and hedges had appeared where there used not to be any.

The house was on the right, to the left lay the lake, which was beginning to be shrouded in the evening mist. Having heard the sound of the car engine, the couple looking after the place came out. Hannah had never seen them before. As far as she could remember, it was Polly Twhaites who had hired them, acting on her instructions. They were both close to sixty, and spoke a language that must have been Romansh: they understood German and a little Italian, but no French or English. They stared with slightly anxious curiosity at the proprietor, whom they had never met and whom – after all this time – they must have come to think of as mythical.

She went inside, having exchanged a few inconsequential words with them. She recognized the vaulted ceiling on the ground floor, and there was even the table where she and Taddeuz had dined that first evening, in front of the monumental fireplace.

The Pommier divan had disappeared.

'Mr Twhaites told us . . .'

'Mr Twhaites has died. Put that piece of furniture back where it belongs. Immediately.'

Why are you being so unpleasant to these people?

She managed to force a smile. 'I was once very happy in this house, and I would like to keep things just as they were, you see.'

They nodded, reassured, at once ready to do anything for her. She went straight up to the second floor. The thirty-foot-long master bedroom, with its four windows and huge four-poster bed, was just as it used to be.

'You needn't keep the fire going, I will be sleeping in the little room on the first floor with red-and-white wallpaper. Please close the shutters and lock the door. No one is to come in here without my consent.'

Nevertheless, she lingered. This was the room with the best view of Lake Lugano. And if she leaned out of the window on the left she would be able to see the roofs of the Swiss village of Morcote. There wasn't any kind of boat on the water, but that was as it should be: neither had there been any eighteen years ago, the day they left this house, having spent a whole month here after their wedding in Strauss's Vienna. The end of an era.

Don't cry. You vowed you wouldn't cry.

She spent the next six days, eighteen hours a day, going over her accounts, completely indifferent to the fact that the best accountants had already checked all the figures. Her solitude was completely undisturbed, nothing troubled her, not a sound, and certainly not the two servants who respected her wishes and made themselves invisible.

It wasn't mistrust that made her want to check everything for herself, down to the very last cent, or centime, or penny, or kopeck. These figures had always provided a kind of refuge for her.

She filled in cards for each country.

There were eighteen cards. In chronological order of the opening of her establishments in each country, these represented Australia, New Zealand, the United Kingdom, France, Belgium, the Netherlands, Germany, Sweden, Denmark, Switzerland, Austria, Italy, Spain, Portugal, Hungary, Czechoslovakia, the United States and Canada.

And Monaco. That counts as another.

Forty-six blue sheep (representing beauty parlours) with a total of 324 legs, each one symbolizing onc thousand dollars a year – with a few one-legged sheep among them.

Seventy-nine purple sheep (shops) with a total of 206 legs.

Three orange sheep, one of which was in the happy position of possessing four legs: this was the school at New Rochelle for beauticians and sales assistants run – in addition to her other activities – by Catherine Montblanc. By encouraging the big department stores to participate in her students' training, Catherine had made the school profitable for the past two years.

As for the red sheep (schools located in Europe), the yellow sheep (the gathering and dispatch of plants), the red-dotted sheep (the supply network for the salons and shops), none of these had any legs at all, since none of them was making a profit.

One of her black-and-white chequered sheep (it filled a whole page) had 411 legs: this was the one that represented her bank accounts, for she had finally given way to Maryan's vehement entreaties (at least insofar as Maryan was capable of being vehement) and consented to invest her unused capital. Maryan had suggested every form of investment available: the Stock Exchange, for instance, in which case either he himself could advise her or she could go through a broker, one whose scrupulous honesty he could vouch for (apparently there was such a thing as an honest broker). She wouldn't hear of it: speculating on the Stock Exchange didn't appeal to her in the slightest. She saw it as a game for people who wanted to rob each other, and she wasn't interested in robbing anybody or in being robbed. The very most she was prepared to do – and with what reluctance! – was to buy some Treasury bonds at five per cent. She had little enough confidence in bankers, let alone politicians . . .

And finally there was the cow, the most stupid animal she could have come up with (she had tried to draw a chicken but without success, and had eventually settled for the cow). She put horns on it so that her feeble, shapeless sketch could be identified as a ruminant (whether or not ruminants actually had horns was not her problem).

The cow represented her profits from the sale in departmental stores of beauty creams 'recommended by HH'. Just for a change, she had used udders instead of legs, each udder symbolizing ten thousand dollars.

Now, in early 1919, the cow had sixty-three udders.

In other words, if she added together all the legs plus the udders, she came up with a total of $1,574,000 as her annual income, and total assets – not including any real estate, her jewellery, paintings and cars – of fourteen and a quarter pink sheep.

It was then that she made up her mind, assuming that it hadn't already been made up weeks, or even months, before.

That same day, 9 February, she sent twenty-six telegrams from Lugano post office.

CHAPTER 18

Don't Argue, Jeanne, Please

She wrote to Taddeuz, with whom she had had no communication whatsoever for fourteen months: *I don't know if the news will be of any importance to you. I'll give it to you straight. I'm preparing to sell everything: my beauty parlours, my shops, and my patents.*

Nothing more. She rewrote the letter ten times, without being able to improve on this laconic message.

There had been an immediate response to the first of her telegrams: Stahlman and Javitts of New York had, as instructed, contacted Hannah's team of American lawyers led by the Englishman Henry Christie. Hiram Javitts would be arriving in Lugano on 23 February, ready to finalize negotiations.

The other replies had varied very little. To be honest, the text that she had sent had been too brief, too full of menace for the recipients to have the slightest doubt of the telegram's urgency. *Please be at Hôtel Excelsior, Lugano midday 8 March for sale: Hannah.* She had considered delaying the meeting until 22 March to allow her people in Australia and New Zealand to attend, but even then there would be little hope of them making it in time.

Jeanne Fougaril was on the phone the very next day, being one of the very few people who knew where she was.

'Hannah, I want to see you.'

'We're meeting on 8 March.'

'I want to see you and I'm on my way.'

She had called from Lugano. An hour later her chauffeur-driven car appeared in front of the gate.

'Hannah, what's come over you? Are you crazy?'

'You don't even know what I plan to do.'

'Everyone knows, there's talk of nothing else. You haven't been yourself for months. Your reasons are none of my business, of course. Although I find it hard to believe that you could let any problems with your love-life get you down; anyone else maybe, but not you. And if you think that Hannah can kill herself off from one day to the next and the thousands of people who work for her fail to realize it, you're very much mistaken.'

'You haven't got any wiser with age.'

'Then there's nothing to choose between us. You want to sell? OK. Sell up in America, Australia, New Zealand, but not in Europe.'

'I'll make sure your interests are safeguarded. I'm not forgetting that you have a stake in the profits.'

'It's not a question of money. It's more than that. I'm sure you're acting on impulse.'

'Absolutely not.'

'Then it's worse! But I don't believe you. We've worked together for more than twenty-five years. If I'd ever called you a fool before now, you would have instantly leapt at my throat. Who are your buyers? American?'

'Probably. If they agree to my conditions.'

'I thought as much. I can just see myself having to answer to a bunch of cowboys.'

They argued for two hours, at the end of which Jeanne Fougaril got the biggest surprise of her life: Hannah gave in, having been won round to the Frenchwoman's way of thinking. Jeanne had argued her case strongly: she had suggested that splitting the empire into three and selling the sections off to three different buyers would ensure that Hannah got the best possible price for them, and if the contracts were worded correctly it would allow her to buy them back again if ever . . . or would allow Jeanne . . .

'So that's what you wanted?'

'I wanted you to change your mind. I failed. So I tried to make the best of it. You didn't keep me on as director of your European operation because you thought I was a fool . . .'

. . . would allow Jeanne to find a buyer in whom she could have reasonable confidence, since she would have to work for them. The buyer would have to guarantee her job and authority.

'Hannah, it's not just ridiculous egotism that's driving me to do this. Nor is it the money: I have more than I need. But unlike you, I believe that you will come back to it one day. I want you to find it the way you left it.'

Jeanne became a little emotional and Hannah moved away to defuse the situation.

'I assume you've already found a buyer for the European outfit?'

'There's a French perfumer called Auriol, and there are those English people who have already contacted Henry Christie on several occasions. There's even that German group. And the Australians would be . . .'

'You're thinking of a Franco-British consortium?'

'Preferably, yes.'

'All right.'

'I can talk to Christie about it?'

'Yes, go ahead.'

Jeanne left. Henry Christie was Polly Twhaites' successor, and had been warmly recommended by him. One of his young assistants was Nigel Twhaites, Polly's nephew. Christie would not do anything except on Hannah's express instructions, not even if Jeanne communicated them to him. In fact, he had already received instructions, at least a week ago, to sell the empire in three separate parts. *But it gave Jeanne so much pleasure to let her think it was her idea . . .*

* * *

An initial meeting of forty-one directors of her beauty parlours took place on 8 March at the Hotel Excelsior in Lugano. All the American branches were represented. The seven directors from Australia and New Zealand were unable to attend, and Hannah sent each one of them a personal letter. There was only one representative from Europe absent: the Dutch director was expecting a baby and had sent her deputy instead, a tall fair-haired Batavian fellow with a curiously high-pitched voice.

All the laboratory chiefs were present, as well as the senior staff of the supplies and distribution networks. Cecily Barton from London, Jessie from New York and Jeanne Fougaril sat in the front row with Joshua Wynn.

The Fournac brothers had sent word from Melbourne that they would be arriving on the 22nd.

Hannah spoke for only a few moments before handing over to Wynn. There was a deafening silence as she spoke. She announced her decision to retire completely, definitively and irrevocably; she thanked all those who had been good enough to work with her, and made it clear that nothing could make her change her mind and that, once the sale was completed, she would have no involvement in the company whatsoever, there should be no mistake about that. She would endeavour to make sure that her departure was in no way detrimental to her former colleagues. Whoever the new owners might be and whatever their ambitions, she did not believe that any jobs were threatened. However . . .

'If any of you should wish to retire at the same time as me, I personally undertake to pay you five years' salary in addition to any compensation your new employers may offer. Thank you.'

She practically ran away, to avoid any unwanted display of emotion.

* * *

On four occasions during the days that followed, she agreed to attend the meetings of her own team of lawyers, headed by Henry Christie and Jos Wynn, which now included one of her best advisers, the Genevan Pierre Poncetti. But contrary to past performance, she said very little, and was aware of a feeling almost of relief at her silence and her decision not to intervene in future discussions with buyers. She simply wanted the contracts to be drawn up and ready for her to sign as soon as agreement had been reached.

More now than ever before, she shut herself away in the house at Morcote.

The only person she allowed to visit her, throughout almost the whole of March, was Maryan Kaden. He came over from Los Angeles especially to see her.

'Is it really over, Hannah?'

'Yes, really.'

He lowered his head and contemplated the toes of his shoes.

'Lizzie and I talked about it. She thinks I shouldn't try and do anything to make you change your decision.'

'Lizzie's right. And in any case there wouldn't be any point.'

'I know.'

'Thank you, Maryan.'

Silence.

Then he said: 'He wrote to me, Hannah. Just a few words to tell me that he would drop by now and again to see the children, but that he would prefer not to see me. He asked me to forgive him.'

Silence.

'Naturally, he can see the children as often he likes.'

'Naturally,' said Hannah.

Another silence.

Maryan's face was impassive as ever, his pale eyes expressionless. But she knew that he was terribly upset.

'It breaks my heart, you know,' he said suddenly.

'I know, Maryan.'

He opened his mouth and breathed heavily, turned round and stood looking at the lake for a few moments.

'Can Lizzie and I come and see you?'

'I'd rather you didn't, not for a while. I'm sorry.'

He nodded.

'How's business?' she asked, to give him a chance to regain his composure.

Good, very good, he said. He had helped to finance Cecil B. De Mille's *The Admirable Crichton*, and it was now making a fortune. He had also put money into Rex Ingram's *The Four Horsemen of the Apocalypse*, which was to make a star of Rudolph Valentino; and he still owned a lot of land in Hollywood, which he was selling off acre by acre, in exchange for cash or shares in the studios. Lizzie was fine, and so were the twelve children. He thought they would probably stay there, for the sake of the children.

'Adam and Jonathan are no problem any more, Hannah. Abie's adorable. Jonathan was a bit of a worry for a while, but since Christmas he's changed, calmed down.'

That was just after he saw his father, thought Hannah.

'He's doing well at school. He wants to be a sailor. He's very bright, Hannah.'

'I know.'

It was Hiram Javitts himself who led the delegation for the New York buyers. He had been informed by Wynn more than a month ago that he was being offered the chance to buy the North American section of the empire. Although it was offered on a take-it-or-leave-it basis, he wasn't too worried: it turned out that he wasn't much interested in the Europe operation, still less in the Australian outfit.

'We would have bought the lot had it proved absolutely necessary, but we would have laid down other conditions.'

In fact, he proved to be an extremely tough negotiator. Wynn and Christie had started out by asking fourteen million for the business. Javitts didn't want to pay more than ten. After several days of meetings, with each side either raising or lowering the stakes, they had reached a figure of $11,625,000.

'Hannah, give us another two weeks and we stand some chance of getting it up to twelve,' said Henry Christie on the telephone, on the evening of 16 March.

'I want things settled. Accept the offer.'

The European zone found a taker for the equivalent of twelve and a half million dollars, with half payable over a period of five years. The buyer was the Franco-British consortium that Jeanne Fougaril had favoured.

An interest rate of seven per cent was agreed on the six and a quarter million dollars to be paid in later instalments.

And again Hannah would not allow Christie and Poncetti to let things drag on for weeks in order to get a better deal.

'I want things settled.'

This had become her refrain.

She likewise granted the Australians more time in which to pay at reduced rates of interest – the Fournac brothers had reached Lugano on the morning of the 23rd after a frantic dash from the other side of the Pacific. The price agreed for Hannah's interests in the southern hemisphere was two and a quarter million. The Fournacs had been able to raise only one and a half; they believed they could pay off the rest in eighteen months. The deal was made easier by the fact that both she and the Australians had the same advisers, the lawyers Melbourne, Wittaker and Wittaker, the practice where she had first encountered Polly Twhaites twenty-four years earlier.

The three sales went through on the afternoon of the 23rd. She was not present when the contracts were signed. It was Jos Wynn who made the return trip from Lugano to Morcote three times that day.

'All three agreed fairly readily to clause 14,' he said.

This was the clause binding each buyer not to attempt any kind of expansion into the clearly defined territory of each of the other two. This arrangement was made easier by the fact that a quarter of a century earlier, with his usual foresight, Polly had persuaded her to register her patents in each country – he had even included in the list, which was regularly updated, territories that were liable to become independent. She had thereby made herself her own competitor. At the time Polly had thought that compartmentalizing her affairs in this way would safeguard her against a general collapse in the event of any local disaster.

'Nor did we have much trouble with clause 23,' Jos Wynn went on. 'Javitts argued a bit as usual – that guy must argue with his alarm clock in the morning. For a long time he maintained that giving you a priority option to buy back the company was a limitation on their rights of ownership if they ever wanted to sell.'

'I don't care, Jos.'

'I have to talk to you about it. He was wrong and he knew it: if you ever wanted to buy back the company, you would obviously have to match the highest offer they could get elsewhere. Priority option or no.'

'I don't want to buy it back, and you know it.'

'I have to take that precaution, Hannah. That's my job. Javitts gave way on it.'

She could see that he expected her to ask a question. So she asked it, although she was completely indifferent to whatever the answer might be.

'All right, Jos, why did he give way?'

'Because you're a woman, because he thinks you're

incapable of going back and doing it all again, and most of all because he has great plans: he's convinced that under a different management he'll be able to double or even triple profits.'

'I'll make a note of that,' she said wearily. 'In my next visit to earth I shall take my revenge against wicked Mr Javitts. Is that what you wanted me to say?'

'Hannah, it's going to be jolly sad without you.'

'Is everything done?'

'Yes. None of us can really believe that . . .'

She closed her big grey eyes. On his third visit that day Wynn had found her seated in a fantail rattan armchair, with black and turkey-red cushions, on the corbelled terrace looking out over the marvellous view. He had never been inside the house, although once he had been in the conservatory where exotic plants abounded.

'What are you trying to get at, Jos? You want me to throw myself a challenge?'

'I'd like to see you do that,' replied Wynn with a passion that surprised himself.

'Don't count on it.'

She reached out for copies of the third and final contract, the one with the Australians, and initialled and signed them without even reading them.

'Goodbye, Joshua, and thanks for everything.'

One of the clauses that appeared in all the contracts related exclusively to her: it barred her from having anything to do with beauty-care and perfumes, whether acting on her own behalf or through intermediaries. Great care had been taken to itemize all the products that the ban extended to, for the purpose of business and commerce. She could neither create them, nor manufacture them, nor distribute them, nor sell them, nor promote them in any way whatsoever. The famous double H logo was no longer hers: it could still be used, but not by her.

And this applied to every country in the world that presently existed or might come into existence.

Javitts' lawyers had thought of everything.

'I shouldn't be surprised if they feared you greatly,' Pierre Poncetti had commented; the Swiss lawyer had to a small extent replaced Polly for her – a very small extent.

That same night, in the big vaulted room on the ground floor, she burned page after page of the three hundred-odd notebooks that she had for years taken everywhere with her. She had carried them in a metal box that she was never without and which she alone had the key to.

The earliest notebook dated back to the autumn of 1890 and the winter of 1891. She had arrived in Warsaw – she was fifteen and a half – and was already supervising the running of her three shops, for which she kept the accounts. It wasn't until she got to Australia that she had thought of using sheep. *In Canada, you would probably have used bears.*

Very carefully folded inside this particular notebook were some loose sheets of paper. She had no need to read them to remember what they were: the first poems that Taddeuz had written especially for her. She even knew what else was written on each sheet in her handwriting, already tiny then – it had become even more so over the years – in such contrast with his large and ample hand. She read it all the same: 'The sixth of September 1891 – Taddeuz made love to me for the first time.' Further on, on the back of another poem: 'The eleventh of December 1891 – I'm a bit scared.' (She had just realized that she was pregnant and that Pelte the Wolf was relentlessly pursuing her.)

She burned the lot with a wooden expression on her face, and with staring but tearless eyes – in any case the burning heat from the hearth would have dried any tear before it could fall. She had stoked up a fire fit for hell in order to destroy completely all these notebooks, especially those of recent years with their superb leather bindings.

On 19 April the couple from Engadine left very early in the morning. They had asked for three days' holiday and she had agreed to let them go: they had to attend a wedding in their village. They had suggested a young girl from Morcote to replace them. She didn't want anyone. She had risen at dawn, at about five, as always. She heard them leave.

For the past twenty-seven days she hadn't received any more of the accounts that had until then been sent to her, without fail, wherever in the world she might be, and the steady arrival of which had set the rhythm of her days. She had spent thousands of hours poring over them, and they had often been a refuge to her.

The first days were the worst. She was thrown into a gnawing, hate-filled rage against herself; it made her want to scream. Then came despondency. But even at night she had never been able to bring herself to resort to the Gardenal that Louis Macke had given her.

And then finally that fierce will to live, which had always carried her through, returned. *You'll end up even crazier than you were before if you don't pull yourself together*. Like a real statistician, she had systematically considered all the possibilities for keeping herself occupied. This did not amount to very much. She couldn't knit or sew; painting and sculpture were not for her – she didn't have an ounce of talent and what's more she was cruelly aware of it.

Music was equally out of the question – she knew that being quite so tone deaf as herself was tantamount to a miracle. Her one attempt at writing – albeit at Marcel Proust's suggestion – had been quite enough. Proust was astonished: 'Why are you so cold on paper, when that's so far from the case in the flesh?'

That left needlepoint, gardening and charitable works.

She was able to laugh at herself again, so she must be on the mend; more or less recovered from the sale of her empire, which had seemed like a veritable amputation. Feeling the need for movement again, she set off on forced marches in the mountains, despite her unsuitable shoes and clothing. Once she came very close to killing herself by trying to climb an extremely steep and rocky slope (in her high-heeled boots, wearing a hat and carrying a handbag and an umbrella to protect her skin from the sun) which she could quite easily have skirted but which she went at head on, out of defiance. Having reached the top, relishing her victory with a pride that took her back to childhood, she had carved the double H of her first name in the rock, like the Alpinists of Zermatt.

She had started reading again, avidly, exploring the library she had provided for Taddeuz, then having books sent from Geneva, as many as two or three hundred at a time.

She was reading on 19 April. About ten hours had passed since the servants had left. As soon as the sun came up, she had gone out for another of her solitary walks, and must have twisted her left ankle slightly, landing badly after a jump. Having limped back to the extraordinarily deserted and silent house, she had taken a bath, staying in it so long the water had eventually grown cold (she had a horror of cold baths, but could not rid herself of the idea that they were good for you) and her teeth had started to chatter. She had tried to bandage her ankle and had more or less succeeded, though she felt very frustrated by her clumsiness, and not only as a nurse: she had also burned her finger while heating the water for her bath, and gashed her elbow four days earlier while trying to fix something or other (she didn't know the name for it) in the Rolls's engine – not to mention the aches in her legs, now that her muscles had seized up.

What a wreck you are! You will end up in tatters.

She was reading in an alcove, nibbling on biscuits that she dipped in half a glass of tokay, surrounded by a supernatural silence. The lake lay before her. It was not her favourite time of day, she preferred the evening. At sunset the water turned silver, the sides of the mountains became dark green, then blue, and finally dissolved into the sky. For a few miraculous moments only the phosphorescent lake seemed still alive.

She was seated, or rather sunk in her chair, with her chin on her chest, which was slightly puffed out, making her lower lip protrude. The book was resting on her breasts, for which purpose they proved useful. Huddled up in the fantail armchair, which was slightly too big for her, she looked slightly sulky, and it quite suited her, with a rebel curl covering her ear very fetchingly. She had drawn up another chair in front of her, with a big cushion to rest her ankle on and relieve her aches and pains. That day she was wearing a Jeanne Lanvin dress, which was white with a braid round the hem in her favourite colour: turkey red. The dress was mid-calf in length and the V-shaped neckline revealed the base of her throat thanks to the undone button – the skin of her neck was milky-white, creamy even, she had never exposed it to the sun. Around her neck she wore the fine gold chain with seventeen black pearls that Taddeuz had given her.

She was reading Walter Scott in eighty-four volumes. She had just started volume seventy-one, the first part of *The Chronicles of the Canongate*, and she was feeling pretty bored. She had reached the passage where Crystal Croftangry comes to see Miss Nelly . . .

She stiffened.

It was a very slight sound, hardly perceptible at all, and

nothing had preceded it, not even the squeaking of the gate.

'You ought not to have sold up,' he said.

She dropped the book over her face and with a movement she would never be able to account for, she literally shrank back into the fantail armchair, as though she wanted to disappear. She couldn't have opened her eyes any wider.

CHAPTER 19

It's as Simple as That . . .

'Hurt yourself?'

'Nothing serious.'

She was still huddled in the fantail armchair. But Taddeuz was now standing close by, scarcely two yards away from her, leaning against one of the alcove's white wooden posts. He wasn't wearing a jacket, just a shirt with the sleeves rolled up underneath a waistcoat, and no tie. He hadn't shaved for at least three days and his hair was longer than usual. His face was very tanned and so too were what she could see of his chest, his forearms and the backs of his hands. He was extraordinarily handsome, which came as no surprise to her; he would pass for thirty.

For someone who's not looking, you certainly do notice things.

'How long have you been in Europe?' she asked.

'About four weeks. Are you alone?'

'Yes.'

'No servants?'

'Just a couple. They've gone to a wedding in Engadine.'

Now calm down, Hannah . . . For God's sake, try to think. You're virtually on the edge of panic.

'I'm very hungry,' he said.

Only then did she move. She put her book down on the ground and sat up properly, taking it very slowly, resting her weight on the palms of her hands. She stood up. For a moment she felt like exaggerating her limp, but she rejected the idea. On the contrary, she tried to walk normally. *He'd think you were trying to make him feel sorry for you – and he'd be right.*

'There's not much to eat. I wasn't expecting anyone.'

(Damned liar! As though one second had passed since you wrote that letter to him, and even before that, when you had not been expecting him!) 'There's some ham and cheese in the kitchen.'

'Perfect.'

He had followed her into the kitchen. He sat down at the long table, but she remained standing, with her arms crossed in front of her, waist-high, in the classic stance – it took her a moment to realize it – adopted by women when their man has just got home.

'Sit down, Hannah.'

'I'm OK the way I am.'

He had just cut a long slice off the big country loaf; he laid a piece of smoked ham on it, then some gruyère. He watched her as he ate it, while she tried desperately, but in vain, to think of something to say to break this dreadful silence.

'Some wine?'

'Yes, please. If there is any. Otherwise, water will do.'

'There's wine.'

She noticed that he followed her everywhere with his eyes, whilst she went off to find the bottle of tokay that she had opened. *Thank God you put this dress on, rather than any other, and that your hair is more or less tidy . . .*

'You still don't want to sit down?'

'Not yet.'

She hadn't even seen him rise, but suddenly he was there in front of her, had seized her by the waist and lifted her up on to the dresser. That was not all: he ran his giant hands the length of her body, for a moment covering and caressing her breasts, and then . . . they circled her neck.

She did not move. For once she was able to look down on him.

'Scared, Hannah?'

'No.'

'Louis Macke didn't tell you that I wanted to kill you?'

'Twice, apparently.'

'And now we're alone. No one saw me come in.'

'I'm not afraid since you're with me,' she said very calmly.

And the crazy thing is – although on reflection I'm not so sure it is that crazy – you're not a bit scared, not in the least. Fear is not exactly the feeling he arouses in you . . .

She almost expected to see him smile. But he moved away.

'Let me see your ankle.'

'It's nothing.'

He undid the clumsy bandage, and the mere touch of his fingers on her skin set her stomach afire.

'It doesn't even hurt,' she said.

'In that case, why aren't you wearing shoes? I've never seen you go around barefoot before.'

He gently turned her ankle, and she couldn't help wincing with pain.

'All right, it hurts just a little.'

'You've sprained it. Where do you keep the bandages?'

All the time he was away, she considered the possibility of jumping down from the piece of furniture she was perched on. She gave up the idea. Firstly because she stood a very good chance of injuring her other ankle, and also because he put her up here, so it was up to him to lift her down. *That way he'll have to touch you again . . .*

He came back with enough bandages to wrap up an Egyptian mummy, selected one and then bound her ankle with impressive skill; it all looked very geometrical when completed.

'That's not too tight?'

'No.'

She stared at his mouth, feeling an insane desire to nibble his lower lip.

But she suppressed that desire. He moved away from her and went and sat down again.

'And how long am I supposed to stay up here?'

'You're fine where you are.'

He ate.

She smiled, and already there was wickedness in her smile.

'You're afraid to take me in your arms, aren't you?'

No reply.

Don't rush it, Hannah, you'll spoil everything.

'How long is it since you last ate?'

'Yesterday morning.'

He finally consented to raise his head and meet her gaze:

'I disembarked at Marseilles on the evening of 23 March.'

'That was the day I sold everything.'

'I know. You shouldn't have.'

She was on the point of replying: I did well to sell since you've come back to me. But she remained silent. Nothing was straightforward with Taddeuz. If he had really wanted to prevent her from selling, he could have cabled her from America. She had always been the easiest woman in the world to contact, once Queen Victoria was dead and buried. All anyone had to do, until a few weeks ago that is, was to go into any one of her salons and ask them to get a message to Mrs Hannah. On one occasion she had received a letter from Ontario that was addressed simply to 'Hannah, New York'. *Or else he could have caught a boat that got him to Europe well before the deal went through.*

A suspicion suddenly occurred to her.

'When did you leave Vermont?'

'In December.'

'Where did you go?'

'To Oaxaca, in Mexico. A consul there put me up for a while. Then . . .'

'What about my letter?'

'I never received any letter from you.'

'I wrote telling you that I intended to sell out.'

'Never received it.'

'So Macke didn't forward your mail? I sent it to him . . .'

'I left Oaxaca with Adamson – he was one of my nurses – at the beginning of the second week in January. From that point on, Louis didn't know where to contact me.'

'Well, I'll be damned!' said Hannah. 'So when did you find out I was selling?'

'I read it in the newspapers in Athens. It was as simple as that.'

'How long ago was that?'

'A fortnight. And it wasn't the latest edition of *The Times*.'

She was quite dumbfounded.

He shook his head.

'I'm not here because you sold your company, Hannah. I didn't know about it when I boarded the ship for Europe. I'm sorry you did it, and that's the truth. But it had nothing to do with my decision.'

Eventually he lifted her down from where she was perched, then announced that he could really do with a bath. He had indeed touched her, but almost casually, the set expression on his face not for a moment altering – not that it was an expression of impassive coldness, but rather of distant reverie, and somehow sad.

'I'm going to heat up some water for you,' she said.

'There's no need, sit still.'

She heard him go upstairs (he had gone straight up to the second floor, where they had slept during their honeymoon eighteen years ago) and, hobbling because her wretched ankle did actually hurt, she went to see what luggage he had left in the garden, since he had taken nothing but a small case upstairs with him. She found nothing but a rucksack – she had seen people in the mountains of Austria and Germany carrying them; you wore it on your back, with the aid of straps. This one seemed very full – of books probably.

Don't touch it! Don't touch anything, you silly fool!

She moved away and, still limping, went and sat in the fantail armchair again. She tried hard to read, but it was no good. She gazed at the lake. The light was gently fading, shadows crept up and insinuated themselves with contemplative slowness.

She didn't hear him approach.

'Don't turn round, Hannah.'

Again she felt a desire to curl up in her armchair and make herself small.

'I've come to stay, Hannah. If you'll have me . . . No, don't say anything, I'm not finding it easy to talk. When I left Vermont, I had no idea what I was going to do. After you've been locked up like that, even at your own request, you lose the habit of being responsible for yourself. If indeed I ever was. Do you understand what I'm trying to say?'

'Not very well.'

'All right. I'll try to explain it differently: I was insane, Hannah. I may still be, whatever Louis Macke may think. It was one thing to feel almost sane as long as those people were around me, it's quite another when you're on your own. Do you understand now?'

'Yes. I think so.'

'I had to be more or less sure of myself.'

'You knew that I was waiting for you?'

'Of course. I knew that you were waiting for me every minute of every day. Or at least I hoped so . . . Don't say anything. Besides, you would never have come back to Morcote except to wait for me. From Marseilles I went to Germany and then to Greece . . .'

'Anywhere but Italy.'

'Anywhere but Italy. I was planning to write to you from Greece, and to give you the choice . . . of taking me back or not.'

'Don't say things like that!'

'I don't see how else I can say it.'

To hell with all this talk, she thought. *To hell with his need to explain everything, analyse everything! He's come home to me, I've got him back, what else matters?*

'I love you,' she said.

What's keeping him from taking you in his arms, for God's sake!

'Except that I didn't have the courage to wait for your reply,' he said. 'I thought I could better plead my cause if I were in front of you.'

'I love you and I don't care a damn about anything else. You wouldn't believe how little I care.'

Silence.

Taddeuz still made no move. However, seconds later – seconds that seemed to last weeks – she heard him laugh very softly.

'I have to hand it to you, Hannah, one of your many virtues is your single-mindedness.'

'Life is complicated enough, without adding to the confusion.'

'You love me, I love you, it's quite simple, there's no more to be said.'

'Exactly. That's how things ought to be. Except that you haven't really said that you love me. You have never said it very often, you've always been rather unforthcoming from that point of view.'

The sun decided to go in; it suddenly disappeared behind them, to their left. But the lake did not darken; on the contrary, it looked milky, with furtive shadows here and there, and strange reflections. *The lake is being very good and really trying its best to prove equal to what's happening . . . Oh my God, Hannah, this was well worth waiting for . . .*

'I went to Warsaw, to the bedroom in Praga,' she said. 'There was a very sweet young couple there. His name was Jan. He too had loads of books. She was pretty as a picture. Taddeuz, I don't know anyone more idiotic than us. Life was meant for living, I really don't see what else it was meant for. You love me and I love you, it's as simple as that. And we're going to make sure it stays that way for a very long time. I want to live for a hundred years. After that, I'll see. And you had better do the same if you don't want any trouble.'

'I love you, Hannah.'

'I didn't catch that.'

'I love you, Hannah.'

'It's terribly noisy, I can't hear anything.'

'I love you, Hannah.'

He placed his hands on her shoulders. She removed one of them and licked his palm with her hot little tongue.

She closed her eyes and said in a low voice: 'Do you want me? Just a little?'

'To be honest, I want you so much it's killing me.'

'That's as it should be,' she said. 'Now, isn't that lucky?'

CHAPTER 20

Do I Really Have a Dimple There?

He started writing again three days later. He wrote fast, contrary to past performance. Ten, twelve and sometimes fifteen pages a day. He gave them to her to read every evening, and this too was an extraordinary change. The first time he emerged from his study to hand her a bundle of papers, she felt almost intimidated, not to say panicked. To the point that he tired of holding out his arm and eventually put the manuscript down in front of her, on the table where she was playing patience.

'It's only a first draft, but these are the first two chapters. I want you to read them and tell me what you think.'

'But I couldn't do that.'

'You're just as capable as all the London and New York critics put together, if not more so.'

'Because I'm stupid, is that it? If I can understand, it's because everyone else can too.'

'Exactly.'

'Don't put your hand inside your critic's knickers. It counts as bribery and corruption.'

She read what he had written. Four times, and then once more in case she had missed something. *Anyone would think you were going over a contract, you nutcase!* The story he told – a story that she was able to read at the astonishingly regular rate of one chapter every other day – was a strange one, and very disturbing. It was set in Mexico, in a village lost in the middle of nowhere, crushed by the heat, blighted by dust, whose inhabitants were no more than shadows, silent and afraid; here lived a young defrocked priest. Then . . .

'The way you describe him, your priest is even more seductive than Rudolph Valentino and Douglas Fairbanks put together. Can a priest be handsome?'

'I almost became one.'

'You've convinced me. Lucky for me you didn't, by the way. Can you see us cuddling in a confessional?'

Then the two other main characters turn up in the village (they don't arrive together; they don't know each other – at least they appear not to, Hannah hadn't read the end yet): a woman and a bandit. *His bandit's even more handsome than the priest!* It is not long before the woman has brought the two men together. And all three set off on a bizarre expedition into the mountains in search of treasure which the woman claims to know about. Along the way, one of the two men dies.

'It's nothing to cry about, Hannah.'

'It's so sad. I liked that bandit. And the other fellow as well – does that make me depraved? I don't really know what to tell you about your book.'

'You've already told me.'

'By crying over Kensing's death?'

'And also by the expression on your face while you were reading. Especially that. I adore your eyes, Hannah.'

In May they returned to America on the Cunard liner *Berengaria*, formerly the German *Imperator*, which had been handed over to the British as part of the war damages they were able to recover. Taddeuz had finished the second draft of his novel, and had provisionally entitled it *The Rattlesnake*.

'But Eddy Lucas will change it.'

She had never seen him so relaxed. At first she was pleased, but then she worried about such a remarkable transformation.

But to tell the truth, her anxiety was quickly dispelled

once they had disembarked. Adam and Jonathan had come to meet them. And there was such a contrast between the intense love they clearly had for their father and the near indifference they showed for her that she was chilled by it. Of course, it was what she expected. *You did everything to make them hate you – perhaps not Adam, but certainly Jonathan. How could they love you? Did you ever spare so much as a single thought for them while you were hiding away in Europe? You can't complain now . . .*

'Where's Abigail?'

'In Los Angeles, with Lizzie.'

'I think we should go to California,' said Taddeuz.

'Whenever you like. I'm free now.'

She had of course noticed the look that Taddeuz had given Jonathan, telling him what to do. And the boy had eventually come over to her and kissed her.

'I'm happy to see you again, mother.'

There was no doubt he spoke in English deliberately, to avoid the intimacy of using '*tu*' that French would have allowed.

She felt almost relieved to see her sons go back to their respective colleges at the end of the special exeat they had been granted.

Less than forty-eight hours after Taddeuz had given it to him to read, Eddy Lucas came back with the manuscript. He found Hannah on her own, busy redecorating one of the guest rooms in the apartment – she was incapable of just sitting there doing nothing – under the critical eye of Yvonne, who was knitting something for little Chinese babies.

'Hannah, have you read this?'

'I warn you, I loved it,' she said fiercely, quite prepared to paint him too if he dared to voice the slightest reservation.

'Well, so did I,' said Lucas.

She put down her paintbrush and stared him in the eye: 'You wouldn't be trying to pull my leg, would you, Eddy?'

'God help me! Hannah, he's done it, he's finally found the right voice. And what a story! You can't put it down. For the first two pages, I was a bit worried, I won't try and hide that from you. But after that . . . You did read it, didn't you?'

'I skimmed through it.'

(She had read it nine times. Or ten, she couldn't remember. In addition to the passages that Taddeuz had read out to her, when he felt the need to see the reactions on her face. *You wouldn't know it any better if you had written it yourself!*)

'Well then, when she – I say she because he doesn't give her a name – when she appears on the scene,' said Lucas. 'As a female character, she's the hottest . . .'

Lucas suddenly broke off. Hannah threw Yvonne a threatening look. *If she laughs, I'll kill her!*

Silence.

'You didn't finish what you were saying, Eddy,' she said.

He rubbed his neck.

'The last time I felt such a fool,' he said finally, 'I was twelve years old and Reverend Partridge had just found some dirty pictures in my Bible.'

Hannah smiled graciously.

'And now you've found some dirty pictures in Taddeuz's novel. Is that what you're trying to say?'

That's what's called turning the knife in the wound, Hannah.

Lucas immediately reddened; turned quite scarlet, in fact.

'Hannah, for pity's sake . . .'

Her smile broadened and she opened her eyes wide: 'I don't see any reason why the whole world shouldn't know that my husband is in love with his wife. It doesn't bother me. To tell you the truth, I'd be delighted. And if . . .'

'Hannah, people are going to be scandalized by the book!'

'. . . and if he paints such a detailed picture of my body in his book, it must be that either he has no imagination – which would surprise me enormously – or there was no one else he could lay his hands on, so to speak – which I would find even more amazing, knowing all too well the way that other women look at him – or because he wanted to. And I'm very proud to be in his book, Eddy Lucas. It's no mean achievement being depicted nude, even by a writer, at the age of forty-two.'

'Eddy Lucas came by.'

Taddeuz had just got home from taking his sons ice-skating.

He looked at her.

'He loved it,' she said. 'He loved it, but he's afraid you'll both end up in prison for obscenity. Do I really have a dimple there?'

'Who's going to check?'

'Good question,' she said.

Edward Lucas was genuinely worried. The first time he read the book, he read it straight through. His second and subsequent readings were more considered.

'Tad, I'll never be able to publish it as it stands. We'll have all the morality leagues and churches against us. It'll be banned.'

'Too bad,' said Taddeuz, looking as though he really didn't care one way or the other.

'So what's to be done about it?' asked Hannah.

'Cut it. Tone it down. Both probably. And that won't be easy, given the way that it's written. It makes me sick to think of it, but I don't see any other solution. Particularly that scene where the rattlesnake . . .'

He broke off again, and started staring at his hands, in which he held the lid to the fish dish, as though he had just noticed their existence.

'Oh, my God!' he exclaimed.

Silence.

Taddeuz smiled.

'Hannah?' He didn't even turn his head towards her.

'Not a single comma,' said Hannah.

'Not a single comma,' Taddeuz said to Lucas.

Another silence.

'Of course,' said Lucas with considerable bitterness, 'writers don't mind going to prison. At least they can write in peace while they're inside. But can you see me running my company from Sing Sing?'

'Poor little Eddy,' said Hannah.

'You just have to feel sorry for him,' said Taddeuz.

'What about Baudelaire?' said Hannah.

'I know all about *Les Fleurs du Mal*,' said Lucas looking very gloomy.

'Baudelaire had quite a success with it,' said Hannah.

'It has to be said that Baudelaire did have a certain talent,' said Taddeuz.

'Yes, you're right,' said Hannah.

'I hate you both,' said Lucas.

Taddeuz stood up.

'The answer's no, Eddy. You either publish it or you don't. But if you do, you don't change a single word.'

They were in Los Angeles at the end of June. Lizzie and Maryan's house, big though it was, was nevertheless not big enough to accommodate the Kaden couple, their twelve children, and the servants, plus Adam, Jonathan, Abigail and her governess, as well as Hannah, Taddeuz, Yvonne and Gaffouil.

Especially as it wasn't a short stay that they were planning.

'Lizzie, we don't know how long we'll stay. And no, thank you, I don't want to sleep in a tent in your garden.'

'Hannah, I'm delirious with joy.'

'I can't think why. Nothing happened between Taddeuz and me. Nothing.'

They finally decided to rent a villa in Coldwater Canyon Drive, just round the corner from Sunset Boulevard, a villa where Charlie Chaplin had once lived. It was not as huge as the Kadens' place, but all the same there were twelve rooms, as well as a separate apartment for Yvonne and Gaffouil, and three rooms over the garages for the servants. The delightful Erich von Stroheim soon became a frequent visitor – the year before, in the film *The Hearts of Humanity*, which was intended to support the war against Wilhelm II, he had played the part of a totally evil German officer who threw poor little French babies out of windows.

As ever, Lizzie and Maryan had been perfect friends. The whole Kaden clan had turned up at the railway station to welcome them. The family brass band had played, bursting eardrums for miles around (the band was Lizzie's idea: she had issued each of her offspring with drums, trumpets and even two sets of bagpipes, with the sole purpose of making as much noise as possible, never mind the tune; Lizzie herself played the cymbals with uncommon exuberance, and after a relentless campaign conducted day and especially night, apparently, she had persuaded Maryan to bring the big bass drum and strike it for all he was worth – which he did, with a lugubrious air).

Behind this eccentric performance – Lizzie was never one to be at a loss for ideas – lay a great deal of tact and thoughtfulness: this was Lizzie's attempt to defuse the situation, to play down the importance of Hannah and

Taddeuz's reconciliation, of their reappearance after such a long absence. This thoughtfulness was evident in the days and weeks that followed. The Kadens' house in Beverly Hills was a haven for all, and a meeting place for the whole of Hollywood. The evening that Hannah and Taddeuz arrived, Mary Pickford and Douglas Fairbanks came to dinner. Subsequent guests included Cecil B. De Mille and Gloria Swanson, Lewis Selznick and Sam Goldwyn, Louis B. Mayer, Sam Warner, Harry and Jack Cohn.

'Thank you, Lizzie.'

'What are you thanking me for?'

'You and Maryan have been wonderful.'

'I'm always wonderful, it comes naturally.'

Who in Hollywood and the whole of California did not adore Lizzie? She had put on a bit of weight. Quite a bit. Her numerous pregnancies had given her a bosom on which you could rest a plate and a glass – Hannah knew, she had tried. Her enjoyment of life had increased over the years, her sense of humour was boundless, she held sway over her seven boys and five girls with almost terrifying good temper. Even her fits of anger – she had a ready tongue and was impressed by no one – were part of her charm. Because Lizzie was captivating, even though she wasn't very pretty. Maryan idolized her and he wasn't the only one: a certain Franklin Roosevelt, who had become Assistant Secretary of the Navy, having been a frequent guest of the Kadens, was seriously considering naming a destroyer *Lizzie*. She had once told Hannah: 'I was made to be happy.' If this was a programme for happiness, she carried it out to the letter.

'We can talk whenever you like, Hannah. If you want to talk.'

'About Taddeuz?'

'Who else? There isn't much to say about my husband:

he makes money and gives me children and makes me happy. I can't think why I ever married him.'

'Everything's fine.'

'Oh yes!'

'Actually, everything isn't quite as it should be.'

'Perhaps you're imagining things.'

'That's why you brought up the subject, I suppose? We're talking about it because there's nothing wrong?'

'I think you may be imagining things.'

'Perhaps.'

They were both in the swimming pool, where they could touch the bottom since Hannah was still a bit wary about swimming. Fifty yards away, in the second pool – 'for kids only' – six or seven dozen children were throwing cream cakes in one another's faces: one of the Kaden children was celebrating a birthday.

Hannah moved a few inches: the parasol that had been set up on a float especially for her had moved, exposing one of her ankles to the sun.

'I really think you're imagining things, Hannah. Maryan thinks so too. Taddeuz has never looked as well as he does now. He was exceptionally witty the other night, we were all captivated by his charm, even that producer who can't read. He's cured, Hannah, and not just of his recent problems. And he loves you.'

He had his first relapse – the first she knew about during this period of their life together – at the beginning of September.

Adam and Jonathan, together with the four eldest Kaden children, had just caught the train that was to take them back to their universities and colleges under the watchful eye of one of Maryan's brothers, Stan. On his return from the station after seeing off his sons, Taddeuz had gone to a meeting with the directors of a company set up two years earlier, called First National Exhibition, which had just signed up Chaplin, giving him free reign in the choice and direction of his films, as well as full ownership of them.

As for Hannah, she was playing mother, a fairly rare occurrence. She piled eight or ten kids into her Rolls, including her daughter Abigail, and took them all to play on the beach at Malibu. At about twelve thirty, she registered the absence of her husband, who was supposed to join them, but saw no cause for worry; the people at First National must have invited him to lunch – men love discussing business over food – and he wouldn't have been able to let her know because these wretched kids were right now trying to bury her up to her neck in sand.

She telephoned the villa in Coldwater Canyon Drive just before one, but only Yvonne replied. No, she hadn't seen a soul.

At about two o'clock, having fed her squealing horde with as much as they could eat, she drove back to Beverly Hills to return the children to their respective parents.

Lizzie wasn't at home, but Hannah didn't expect her to be: she had a meeting that day with one of the charitable organizations of which she was president in her free moments – *How she manages to find any spare time, I just don't know . . .*

She dropped off the last remaining kids and headed for home, with Abigail who prattled on.

The first alarm signal went off, very quietly, when Gaffouil did not emerge to park her car as he usually did.

The second rang out when Yvonne did not come to the door to take charge of Abigail. *Something's going on.*

But she was still calm, not panicked, more intrigued than anxious.

'Yvonne?'

Assuming Gaffouil and Taddeuz were out, and had taken Yvonne with them, which was already odd enough, there still ought to be three or four people in the house:

the governess, the cook and the two Filipino maids, who had been taken on a couple of months before.

No, not the governess, it's her day off. But what about the others?

'Abie, you're to go to your room, please, like a big girl.'

'You promised I could have some ice cream.'

'Just give me time to milk the cow and I'll bring it up to you. And just for once, you can lie down on your bed. Find a good book to read, darling.'

She went out, still hesitant to disturb Taddeuz, whose study was on the second floor and who must be working, if he was home. She heard the noise the moment her hand touched the banister. It was a dull noise, it sounded like something very heavy suddenly falling.

She ran up the stairs.

'Taddeuz?'

No reply.

'Taddeuz!' she shouted.

The heavy oak door was locked from the inside. Pressing her ear against it, she thought she heard a groan from the other side, despite the double thickness of the padded door panel. Then she remembered that from their bedroom you could get to the other rooms over the balconies. He had done it once or twice for fun, to take her by surprise.

She was running now.

A man like Taddeuz, and no doubt a woman like Lizzie, could easily climb from one balcony to the next; if they stretched their long legs they could reach. Not Hannah. In the end she hoisted herself up on to the wrought-iron railing and jumped. She almost fell, catching herself full in the stomach on the handrail. But she regained her balance and clambered on to the balcony.

The french windows were half open.

She found Taddeuz lying face down on the floor, with

one hand trapped under him where he had caught it when he fell. His eyelids fluttered, but his face was extraordinarily pale; chalk-white, in fact. He had a vacant look in his eyes – as though drugged; there were bubbles of yellowish foam in the corners of his mouth, which was wide open.

Oh no, not again!

She turned him over on to his back.

'Taddeuz, what's happened?'

She checked him for any sign of injury – for a moment she even imagined that he might have put a bullet to his head – but found none.

His hand moved, and caught her by the wrist; he squeezed three times.

'You've taken something, is that it?'

He nodded.

'You tried to kill yourself? You took some poison?'

A few seconds went by. Then he shook his head. He mumbled two or three words she could not distinguish. She leaned forward, kissed him, and as she did so she licked a little of the foam from his mouth with the tip of her tongue: it tasted horribly bitter.

'Let go of me, my love,' she said.

She had to prise his fingers open one by one to free her wrist. As soon as she got to her feet, she ran to the door, opened it and rushed out on to the landing

Then tried to calm herself.

Think.

She counted to five. And then again to five. She went downstairs.

'There's nothing to worry about, Abie. Nothing at all. It's just father getting annoyed because he's finding it hard to write. Can you give me another minute?' (She smiled at her daughter.) 'Thank you, darling. Wait for me in your bedroom. That's a good girl.'

She found the telephone number and dialled it. It was

the number of a young doctor of whom Adolf Zukor had spoken. He was tending to the young Paramount leading actor, Wallace Reid, who had been seriously injured in an accident with the scenery while filming *Valley of the Giants*. So that he could continue filming, he had been given morphine and, after further doses in hospital, was now an addict.

The doctor answered the second time she rang – he was in the swimming pool – and said he would be there in no time.

'Alone,' said Hannah. 'Come alone and as though you're not in any hurry. You're calling on us, that's all. And if you breathe a word to anyone . . .'

'I'm on my way.'

'He sent all the servants away,' said Hannah.

The doctor was about thirty-five and his name was Darrell Price. Yes, of course he knew Louis Macke. He would get in touch with him.

'As for your husband, everything should be back to normal by tomorrow. He doesn't actually need a doctor. In a few hours from now he would in any case have recovered most of his faculties. He might still have shown a few signs, a slightly dreaminess, an air of distraction, but if you hadn't found him you would probably not have suspected anything. Has he been anywhere recently?'

'Why?'

'I've already seen cases like this. Where did he go?'

'We were in Europe at the beginning of the year, Italy, France, and then . . .'

And then Hannah suddenly remembered: between leaving Vermont and arriving in Morcote, Taddeuz had gone to Oaxaca again, in Mexico; he had even talked of a consul who had put him up.

Price nodded.

'They have some strange drugs in Mexico. Have you ever heard of mescaline?'

'No, of course I haven't.'

'It's an alkaloid derived from the peyote cactus. According to recent studies, it's supposed to be rather like adrenaline. But it has different effects. Has he vomited?'

'Seven or eight times between the time that I called you and your arrival. What effects?'

'Hallucinations, impairment of the senses, particularly vision. He . . .'

'He answered when I spoke to him, by moving his head.'

'All right, Mrs Newman. He's a writer, I believe?'

'Yes.'

'He's playing with fire.'

'He's quite capable of writing without drugging himself,' said Hannah with a cold but intense rage.

'All writers are. Drugs don't make them better, whatever they might think. And he's the person who needs convincing.'

He then noticed the diamond brooch in the shape of a double H that she wore on her left breast.

'My wife uses beauty creams that carry the same symbol. Would you by any chance be Hannah? I ought to have recognized you. My wife attended one of your lectures. You made a great impression on her.'

'I'm not concerned with creams any more. Nor with anyone else apart from my husband.'

The Rattlesnake came out the following April. There was no publisher's name on the book: the only thing that appeared on the black cover with a fine turkey-red border was the author's name: T. Nemo.

'Why Nemo rather than Nosferatu, Nicodemus, Nibelungen, Nicephorus or Newfoundland?'

'It's Latin for "nobody" – that's "*nadie*" in Spanish, "*nixnix*" in Chinese, and in Serbo-Croat . . .'

'I don't care! Why the hell didn't that damned fool Lucas put your name on it?'

'I would rather you didn't swear. Unless you really need to.'

'I don't really need to. Answer my question.'

'The lawyers didn't want to see us thrown in prison. They were afraid they wouldn't be paid.'

'Why should you be thrown in prison for writing the best book of the past twenty years? What do you mean?'

'I'm not so sure that it is the best book of the past twenty years.'

'You're right. It's the best book of the century. Or longer. What has anyone ever written before that's so extraordinary? Can you name even one book?'

'The Bible,' said Taddeuz with a laugh.

'You must be joking! The person who wrote that didn't overtax himself – it's full of proverbs.'

Hannah's anger, which in fact she played up a little, died down over the following weeks: for all that it was circulating clandestinely, it seemed that everyone had read *The Rattlesnake*, or was reading it.

And everyone, in Los Angeles and New York at least, seemed to know who had written it.

And what about the person who inspired it?

The way all these men are looking at you, they must know. And they're obviously wondering if you're as good as your husband makes you out to be. Be honest, Hannah: the attention you're getting is not at all unpleasant.

'Lucas might just as well have put my photograph on the cover. Or better still, two pictures of me, naked of course, one frontal, the other a rear view. That would have sold thousands of copies. What do you think?'

He said that he didn't think much of it. He would prefer exclusive rights, if possible.

'Well, we could have included a sign saying "Private Property",' she said. 'Where are we going?'

'To choose a site for the sign. That idea appeals to me.'

Her anger died down all the more quickly because all kinds of people kept approaching Taddeuz, who would smilingly deny being the author of the book, with proposals for a film adaptation. And this time, they all swore, they would remain faithful to the original text, it wouldn't be turned into a western – besides, someone like Lubitsch or Murnau would direct it, and with a director like that, it was bound to be treated seriously. Taddeuz didn't say no, but nor did he say yes. Eddy Lucas had come rushing down from New York. He denied any part in the publication of *The Rattlesnake*, but he happened to know the lawyers who knew the agent of a friend of the brother of the author: what a coincidence!

Armed with this precise information, he felt able to assert that the Unknown Publisher would go along with the decision of the Unknown Author.

'Hannah, what do you think?'

'It's Taddeuz's decision, Eddy. It's his book.'

In the end Taddeuz said no.

Nonetheless, all these rumours brought him once again to the attention of the producers. First National Exhibition asked him to write an adaptation of Conan Doyle's superb novel *The Lost World*; an agreement was signed. A little later he was hired to work on a version of *Ben Hur*, in which George Walsh was supposed to star, but he was eventually replaced by Ramon Novarro. Taddeuz also worked on *The Mysterious Island*, based on the novel by Jules Verne. The two films, made on gigantic budgets, would not be made until after the birth of Metro-Goldwyn-Mayer, when Carl Laemmle's Metro Pictures Corporation joined forces with Sam Goldwyn's company and Louis B. Mayer.

Taddeuz became one of the best paid and most highly respected screenwriters in Hollywood.

Hannah had already searched his study six times during his absence, looking for anything that might resemble drugs.

She found nothing.

When all is said and done, you're happy.

CHAPTER 21

All the Love in the World, and More

On 25 July 1921, she received a very long letter from Jeanne Fougaril and Cecily Barton. They had written it together. They had both retained their jobs as directors, Jeanne in Paris, and Cecily in London, in accordance with the terms of the contract of sale signed by Hannah twenty-eight months earlier. The new owners were certainly entitled to sack them if they wanted to, but the price they would have to pay in compensation was so high that it would deter any businessman. Nor had they been sacked, that wasn't the reason for their letter. In a sense, it was worse than that, they said; they were being squeezed out, more and more every day, to the point where they didn't even have honorary duties to fulfil, they no longer had any say in any of the important decisions, they were kept out of things, while new directors, male directors, had been appointed. *It's not the fact that they are men, Hannah. It's a question of major upheavals going on, after a period of research. All investment has been reduced if not cancelled altogether. The owners have systematically refused to renovate any salon or shop, even when there's a glaring need for it. The number of beauticians and sales assistants has been reduced by thirty per cent, the training schools have been closed because they weren't making an instant profit. In all, there have been over three hundred employees sacked, and the replacements we've been sent by the employment agencies are girls whose only merit is that they have a recommendation from one or other member of the board of directors, for reasons all too easy to understand once you have seen them. These girls know nothing, and they don't care. You always taught us that to build up a clientele it was sometimes necessary to treat some clients without charge, on the grounds that they would bring in their wake a clientele prepared to pay. Now we have been officially instructed not to extend any credit or allow anyone preferential treatment . . . except to the wives and mistresses of the bosses. The membership cards have been scrapped. Now every treatment has to be invoiced and prices have been raised by between ten and forty per cent, which makes us more expensive than our competitors. A number of our best clients immediately voiced their discontent; many have simply gone elsewhere. Admittedly, turnover has increased, because of the increase in prices and the reduction in expenditure, but we fear that trouble is brewing. The salon in Berlin had to be closed. There's no longer any turnover from Vienna, Prague, Budapest or Stockholm, where the staff you took on have all been dismissed. The laboratory in France has been closed and the budget for the laboratory in Wembley has been halved; for all the work they do there it might just as well be scrapped altogether. We're being overtaken by what our competitors are offering.*

Hannah, we know that you're no longer responsible for what you created. But having known you for so many years and worked with you for such a long time, we are certain that you won't remain indifferent to all this. We no longer entertain any hope of seeing you come back to sort things out. Besides, at the rate things are going, there won't be anything left to sort out. We hesitated for weeks before writing to you. We have only done so because we wanted to tell someone who would understand our sadness. And we also hope that you will get in touch with the people running our company and tell them what mistakes they're making, to the detriment of your life's work.

She was more or less expecting an approach of this kind. The Australians Régis and Anne Fournac, whom she had met somewhere between Melbourne and Adelaide, and who had started out with her (they had since made their own way, having bought out her stake in the southern hemisphere, together with Régis' brother, Jean-François) had also written to her. It predated the letter from Jeanne and Cecily by quite some time, since she received it in April. Régis Fournac didn't ask her to do anything, he simply informed her of what was happening, as though thereby assuring himself a clear conscience, but in sufficient detail to give a very clear picture. The Melbourne head office had broken off nearly all links with Europe. Not on account of any fanatical desire for independence but because of the initial negligence shown by the new European proprietors, and then their greed. Consignments of products were not received sufficiently regularly either in Australia or New Zealand; the quality of the products was dropping, or at best not improving; prices had gone up to unacceptable levels. The Fournacs had turned to other suppliers – American – with regret, wrote Régis, but they had little choice. The agencies in Melbourne, Sydney, Brisbane, Bathurst, Adelaide, Perth, Hobart, Auckland and Wellington, unlike their counterparts in Europe or America, were not completely bound by the double H emblem. (This was due to the fact that Hannah, who was then starting out and had not yet fully developed her own ideas, had entered into a partnership with the Fournacs. This partnership had not been solely concerned with cosmetics and perfumes, the group also had considerable interests in women's fashion and even tea rooms.)

These agencies were no longer selling HH products exclusively. They had now had a range of suppliers and sold what was currently available.

In other words, wrote Régis Fournac, *the creams, lotions, toilet waters and perfumes that you created now represent an ever-diminishing proportion of our turnover.*

It's the end of a whole era, I fear. Anne and I think that obviously your departure – I daren't say retirement – has ruined this marvellous enterprise that was your creation. But no doubt you took all this into account when you made your decision. We hope that you will in any case come and visit us again and bring your charming husband. We ourselves are planning a trip to America, but not for two or three years. Do you remember Bates – you broke a tobacco jar over his head because he didn't like Polish women, whether Catholic or Jewish? He's dead. Not as a result of his injuries, I assure you. After twenty-eight years, that would be surprising. He was hanged yesterday for murdering his partner. And while we're on the subject, perhaps you recall the name of Lothar Hutwill, that Australian of Swiss origin who was more or less suspected of having played a part in the death of his wife in order to inherit from her? He too has died: he was rather brutally assassinated by his very young wife and a male secretary, who wanted to lay their hands on his wealth. Life is curious, isn't it.

'Well, you got what you wanted,' said Cathy.

Cathy, formerly Catherine Montblanc, had just remarried – her husband was a certain Charles Roadhouse; he was in oil and would tell anyone prepared to listen that he had ten times more assets than he had teeth. Being a Canadian, he had been a Trench Cut-throat during the Great War, his mission being to carve up as many Germans as he could with a knife as big as a halberd (he loved explaining how he went about it). 'He's a complete fool, but I'm very fond of him. We both have our little weaknesses,' Cathy would say of him.

'I don't understand,' said Hannah. 'What do you mean?'

'You sold what it took you a quarter of a century to build up. Although I'm not complaining. When Javitts closed the school for beauticians and sales assistants, he offered me a choice of becoming assistant director at Poughkeepsie, or of taking early retirement and leaving. I didn't hesitate, I already had Chas eating out of my hand.' (She imitated the sound a farmer's wife makes while feeding the chickens.)

'Who the hell is Chas?' asked Hannah.

'Charles, my husband. The Cut-throat. If he comes up behind you and asks you to play the German whose throat he's going to slit, lie down on the floor. It throws him into confusion, and it's the only way of getting rid of him. I can't think why the Germans didn't think of it. They probably would have won the war if they had.'

'The schools have been closed?'

'Sold. And the laboratory. Duval of Nemours bought the laboratory, from the walls to the cleaning staff.'

'Dupont of Nemours, not Duval. Was anyone fired?'

'Not all that many. Fewer than in Europe. But it wasn't too bad. Yes, I know what's been going on in Europe. Chas and I went over there for our honeymoon. All he knew of France were the trenches, three brothels and the song "*Auprès de ma blonde*". The rest of the time he was too drunk to notice anything. I saw Jeanne in Paris. She was pretty miserable, poor thing.'

'I know.'

'Did she write?'

'Yes.'

Silence.

'I'm not going to do anything,' said Hannah. 'I'm not going to see those people in Europe and tell them that they are the biggest fools on earth. Can you imagine it, coming from a woman! To hell with them.'

Cathy was passing through Los Angeles with her husband on the way to Venezuela. She picked up her bag and her gloves.

'They won't be the only ones to suffer, Hannah. God knows, I have a horror of big words, but you were the only person who ever gave us a chance – Jeanne, me, Cecily, Jessie and hundreds of others. You were a symbol. How long will it be before anyone gives us another chance?'

Another silence.

And Hannah had what felt like a lump in her throat.

'I can't do anything,' she said finally. 'Nothing at all.'

That night she couldn't sleep. As she stared into the darkness an endless series of faces that had been stored in her memory passed before her eyes: from the little girls in Sydney – she wasn't much older than them at the time – recruited from an orphanage to become her first lab assistants and her first shop assistants – to the hundreds of young girls and women, perhaps even as many as a thousand – whom she had hired, some to become directors. Some she had paid as much as a cabinet minister might earn because had she been in their place she would have expected the same, if not more. What was so extraordinary about that?

Cathy's remark disturbed her. At no stage in her life before now had she ever looked at herself in this light. And now she realized how naïve she had been not to have done so earlier. *You, naïve, that's a good one!* She couldn't have said why she had nearly always employed women in preference to men. No doubt because with women she felt she could assert herself more easily than with men and get them to do what she wanted. It surely wasn't in the name of any kind of female solidarity – despite the Kate O'Shea episode – with which she was now apparently being credited; female solidarity had always been about as important to her as her milk teeth.

The same was true of the salaries she paid. It was all very simple. Yes, of course she had always known that it was common practice to pay a woman just over half what a man would receive for the same work. She had almost never conformed to common practice. In 1910, if she remembered correctly, she had even worked out, to the nearest decimal point, how much what others called her 'dangerous generosity' was costing her. In all (the abstraction of it was sheer poetry), she found she had given away the price of a building on Park Avenue or the Avenue Foch, plus the amount she paid on postage in eleven years seven months. The postage worried her, but not the building – what the devil would she have done with another eight apartments? 'As far as savings are concerned, you're a hopeless romantic,' Polly had told her with a laugh.

But she couldn't see herself telling Jeanne, Jessie, Cecily or Cathy that she was going to reduce their salaries by forty-five per cent, solely for the sake of conformity with the age she lived in, when they worked almost as hard as she did – about sixty to seventy hours a week.

They would have stabbed you to death with their umbrellas!

You're dreadfully depressed, Hannah. Not on account of these ridiculous stories about salaries and the condition of women. But because of all the rest of it – the really important issue, which you daren't examine too closely. It makes you sick to your stomach not to have your work any more, it's eating you up, you're like a panther pacing round its cage day after day, you've nothing left to do with your life. You knew that it was going to be like losing a limb, but not to this extent . . . it's much harder than you expected. Thank God 'he' is with you; he'll stay until the end of time, until you die together. You gave him what you valued most, apart from him, and you would do the same again given another chance. For, whatever he might say, if your marriage survives it's undoubtedly because of the sacrifice you made – and you had better believe it, because it would be damned awful to have done it for nothing. So don't go feeling sorry for yourself and shedding any tears over it. You had to make a choice, and you made it. It just hurts a bit, that's all.

'I'm not asleep either,' Taddeuz said softly in the silence of the bedroom.

She lay still, not really feeling up to it. But he did. His arm reached out across the bed and lightly touched her shoulder. She turned her head and buried her face in the palm of his large hand. They didn't speak. They could hear the faint whimpering of the two Groenendael puppies, which Jonathan had brought them a few days earlier, coming from the ground floor of the house on Long Island.

'Catherine ought never to have spoken to you. Jeanne and Cecily should never have written.'

'These things pass.'

Nothing stirred. Even the two pups fell silent. Again, Taddeuz moved his hand, slowly, stroking her shoulder, then her throat, then dropping his hand to cover one of her breasts, caressing it.

'I don't really feel like it, Taddeuz,' she said.

His hand immediately stopped moving and began to withdraw. She caught it, the fingers of both hands encircling his wrist.

'Unless we take it very slowly. With lots of love.'

'With all the love in the world, and more,' he said.

CHAPTER 22

And You Expect Me to be Passionate about Finance?

On 28 March they boarded Maryan Kaden's yacht. They had Jonathan and Abigail with them. Not Adam, who had gone to Wyoming with Lizzie's two eldest sons – whom he called his cousins although they were not actually related in any way – where a distant relative of the MacKennas' had a ranch.

Had Adam been there things might not have happened the way they did.

The yacht sailed down to Baja California, hugging the coastline, only straying further out to sea when it became too dangerous to sail so close to the shore. Apart from the six-man crew, there were nineteen people aboard, ten of them children or adolescents. Their first port of call was Rosario, then San Andres, from where they made an excursion to the edge of the Vizcaino desert. But their destination was the Gulf of Cortez, or the Gulf of California, into which the Colorado debouched, and which extended for nearly five hundred miles. The yacht rounded Cape San Lucas on 9 August and entered the biggest aquarium in the world. The clearness of the water was fabulous; through the glass-bottomed prow of the ship they were able to observe the teeming multitude of fish; manta rays leapt astonishingly high out of the water; a pack of blue finback whales swam past, cutting through the flat surface of the sea at a speed of about thirty miles an hour. There were sea-lions on the desert coastline, beyond which rose the peaks of the Sierra Madre and the Sierra de la Giganta. Birds in their hundreds of thousands, millions, thousands of millions – terns or Herman's gulls – at times crowded the skies.

When the party landed and the younger passengers were given a chance to stretch their legs, they came back with enormous crabs with blood-red claws, and were struck with wonder to learn that these crustaceans, capable of disappearing in an instant, should be called phantom crabs.

To her own surprise, Hannah had grown fond of the two puppies. They were adorable bundles of black fur – you couldn't really tell head from tail. Beneath their still-floppy little ears glistened their tiny, crafty, elephant-like eyes.

'What names have you given them?'

Jonathan pretended not to have heard. He stood up, abandoning his pets, and rejoined his playmates round the ship's swimming pool. Hannah had never had a pet, none figured in her childhood memories, apart from a dreadful yellow dog with a nasty temperament that had terrorized her as a child. Not even a cat; she had always cherished the belief that her father would have given her one had he not been killed when she was seven. The Groenendael puppies melted her heart. They were only five or six weeks old when Jonathan brought them home. He was allowed to let them sleep on the terrace outside his bedroom in Coldwater Canyon Drive, or in the kitchen in the house on Long Island – though his father had to intervene before Yvonne could be persuaded to agree to this. As housekeeper and a good Frenchwoman, she had at first energetically objected; as far as she was concerned, dogs didn't sleep in the house; they had fleas and they pissed everywhere. Then, when they were about to set off on their cruise, it was Lizzie who spoke up for him: with ten children and two parrots already coming along, why not take the dogs as well? (She might have drawn the line at bears.) In any case, they could always eat them if they were shipwrecked on a desert island.

And it seemed to mean such a lot to Jonathan, who had

always been rather too self-contained. Usually nothing interested him, or at least he feigned not to take an interest in anything. But, by some miracle, he was mad keen on the Groenendaels, to the point that he would not let his brother or sister, or his Kaden cousins, near them.

As the days and nights went by, the combined effects of an endlessly flat sea, of the constant sweltering heat, and the solitude of a ship that progressed almost soundlessly, instilled everyone with languor. It wasn't at all disagreeable. It was as though time was suspended and they were living in a cocoon that no outside event could penetrate.

For a long time they sailed slowly up the Gulf of Cortez. On the morning of 19 August, they saw the volcano of the Three Virgins, with the no less Mexican town of Guaymas lying to starboard. And still they sailed on up the Gulf. Large islands appeared, arid and mountainous, dry as a hot oven. In places, they took soundings of only a few fathoms beneath the keel. Taddeuz had locked himself in his cabin. His holidays were over; he had a screenplay to finish, which had to be ready to deliver on their return to Hollywood, and what's more, he had confided to Hannah with a very strange hint of reticence, he had just embarked on a new novel.

The Sierra San Pedro Martir extended to their left. They were nearing the end of their voyage. Soon they would reach the Colorado estuary, and shortly afterwards they would be back on dry land. (There would be cars waiting for them there, then a train was to take everyone to Mexicali, and from there to San Diego and Los Angeles.)

So Hannah had grown accustomed to playing with the dogs, partly because she had developed a genuine fondness for them, and also because she saw them as a means of at last making peace with her younger son.

However, she was making no progress in this respect.

'You still haven't told me what names you have given them . . .'

'Aramis and Porthos.'

Names of the musketeers. He had read Dumas' novel in French; he read voraciously – that was something else he had in common with her. He spoke in a rather expressionless voice, and the words seemed to be forced out of him. Jonathan didn't start talking until quite late, when he was about three, whereas Adam and Abigail had been advanced for their age, but as soon as he had made up his mind to talk, he had adopted the language of an adult, or near enough, disdaining the baby talk that the very young are thought to need to learn first. He had always objected to anyone shortening his name – simply refusing to answer if anyone tried to call him Jon or Johnnie; only Abigail, for just a little while, was allowed to call him Atan, but it was made clear to her that permission to do so would be withdrawn as soon as she could express herself like an adult. Among other young children, he was always the leader, always the one to decide what games they would play; but he would never speak first. He would wait until chaos reigned before making up his mind to speak, and everyone would do as he said. He would be found reading in the most unlikely places: on a roof, or lying flat on his stomach under a car, in the garage.

He stole a quick sidelong, almost furtive, look at Hannah, and she felt the impact of those grey eyes of his that were so similar to her own, except that they gave nothing away.

'I would very much like to help you bath them,' she said, choosing her words carefully. 'You can be in charge and I'll carry out your instructions. They certainly need a bath. When we put in to land yesterday, they got themselves covered with dust. Which of them is Aramis?'

No reply.

He was now staring at his mother, his gaze as impenetrable as ever . . .

Don't panic, Hannah. You're not going to give up yet again. He's your son, and if he's got a filthy character you know jolly well who's to blame.

'You decide, Jonathan. They're your dogs. It's not so much the dust as the guano that they rolled in. Frankly, they don't smell like a bouquet of roses.'

She smiled at him, though overwhelmed by a sudden feeling of despair. *Jonathan, I love you with all my heart. I . . .*

He rose and, as on previous occasions, with the same icy impassiveness, he walked off.

The next day the dogs were not in the pen that the sailors had set up for them on the foredeck. Maryan had the ship searched, to no avail (Jonathan locked himself in his cabin to read; he wouldn't answer any questions, not even from his father). The screams of one of Lizzie's daughters finally alerted everyone to what had happened: the two little creatures hung dangling from ropes in the wake of the yacht, their bodies cut to pieces by the propellers.

She didn't believe in psychiatrists. And the memory of her meeting with Freud in Vienna did nothing to make her change her mind. She refused to go with Taddeuz the day he went to see Dr Weiss, who was supposed to explain Jonathan's action, and everything going on inside the young boy's head. *As if you didn't know already. Your son hates you, but adores his father. You are the destroyer. It's perfectly obvious. And what can anyone do about it? Drugs aren't going to teach him to love his mother, especially when that mother doesn't behave like one. Did you love your mother, Hannah?*

She became withdrawn, for the first time in her life.

Weiss, the psychiatrist, damn him, had nothing unexpected to say; it would take time and a great deal of patience, it was something that had to be worked at day by day. The doctor didn't think that Jonathan was particularly abnormal. Translating his professional gobbledygook into plain English, what he said was that the boy was exceptionally intelligent, that at fourteen he was at that critical age, poised between childhood and adulthood, and that he was bound to feel things with particular intensity – this was because of, indeed proof of, his unusual sensitivity and depth of character. Jonathan was supposed to have killed his dogs because of the attention and affection his mother was showing them, and because he felt unsettled by his own feelings. He had acted, in a way, in self-defence; Hannah's attempt to get close to him was a threat, in that she was beginning to succeed; he had pulled down the bridge that she had thrown between herself and her son.

Stuff and nonsense. *Oh my God, Hannah, never would you have believed you could be so unhappy.*

Especially as she lived in daily dread of Taddeuz's suffering another crisis. What she called a crisis. The word comforted her a little, insofar as it suggested an illness that was only intermittent rather than recurrent. Over these last few months she had been following the advice of Darrell Price, the doctor who specialized in the treatment of drug addicts, and remained vigilant, searching through his belongings for the drug she was afraid Taddeuz might still be obtaining supplies of, and even more afraid he might be using. Only once did she find a packet containing some white powder, which she burned, just in case. She didn't have the nerve to mention it to Taddeuz. And he didn't say anything, any more than he seemed to notice this implacable surveillance she was subjecting him to.

But he must have been aware of it, there was no doubt of that.

After the 'dog incident', to which no one made any reference after they returned to Los Angeles, she feared another crisis was imminent. She watched him, filled with shame and remorse, not daring to confide in anyone. But no, belying her fears, Taddeuz did not crack up. As the days went by, she came to the conclusion that she was once more a victim of her own anxiety, and that her fears were groundless.

'In the end, you only believe what you want to, Lizzie.'

Maryan returned to the fray round about 10 September. He considered it completely unreasonable that she should have so many millions of dollars lying idle, not even bringing in the smallest amount of interest. It was more than a crime, it was a sin in money terms.

Perhaps he was also trying, in his own tactful way, to get her out of the depression he could see she was in, by encouraging her to do something, anything, to occupy her mind.

His initiatives met with weary indifference.

'Maryan, I don't want to hear of playing the stock market. You know I don't.'

'Have you read the file I put together for you?'

'Vaguely. I'm not interested.'

He had drawn up a very comprehensive list of stock market investments she could make. Even from the quick glance she had given this remarkable piece of work she could tell that Maryan's suggestions did not involve any risk. He had selected only blue-chip stock for her.

'Hannah, you ought to give it some thought . . .'

'I've thought about it.'

'You're losing out on a fantastic amount of money.'

'I'm not going to start entrusting my money to people I don't know, when I don't even know which of them is actually making all the decisions. No.'

Besides, the few investments she had made three or

four years ago, under insistent pressure from Maryan, were earning her an average annual income of hundreds of thousands of dollars.

'After tax. I have more than enough to live on. I could survive on my savings until the year 2250, what more do you want? And I know all about money markets. I've had my fingers burned. Remember ABCD?'

Yes, he remembered the ABCD man. And it was true that there was no inflation, so money wasn't losing any of its value from one year to the next, as Maryan had no choice but to acknowledge. But he was so insistent, and she was so indifferent to these things, that she agreed to accompany him to New York, where he wanted to introduce her to a few brokers and bankers, and financiers too.

'You think that I'm going to develop a passion for finance, Maryan?'

'No. But it's better than sitting around doing nothing,' he said with an untypical dryness.

(And this was one of the rare occasions when he allowed himself to criticize her openly. But she could see that he wasn't very happy doing it, and that he felt bad about it.)

'All right.'

She had a strong desire to make the trip by aeroplane this time. She was sick of all those interminable train journeys, she could think of nothing more mindless than watching cows watching you. She had flown on numerous occasions, and in her frenzied determination to keep herself occupied and to find something to offset the dreadful loss of her business career, she had taken her pilot's licence, flying a Farman with a Salmson engine, which held the record for the longest distance covered – nearly 1,250 miles. Louis Blériot had written out a very pretty licence for her, covered with festoons, but apparently it wasn't valid.

Why not fly from Los Angeles to New York, stopping

to rest on the way, if need be, in some Kansas wheatfield or other? Two years earlier (in 1919), after all, some American Navy sea-planes had flown from the United States to England in three laps.

'We're not quite ready for it yet,' said Taddeuz. 'In fifty years' time maybe, or longer.'

'In fifty years there'll be flights to the moon and to Mars. At least. What do you bet me?'

'Not another night of love. I doubt that I'll be up to it half a century from now.'

'I'm ready to bet on that too. You'll come with me, won't you?'

How could he, with all the work he had then? And in any case he wasn't terribly keen (much as he adored driving a car, aeroplanes left him completely indifferent). He had nothing to do in New York, where she would be rushing from one banker to another, unless she went window-shopping, which didn't really appeal to him either.

And of course she must go by train. Aeroplanes might come later, but he didn't want her taking any risks.

'If you won't come, I shan't go either.'

'That would be silly. Maryan's right: you need something to keep yourself occupied. You've been rather on edge recently.'

Their eyes met and they held each other's gaze. He was very calm. And words were not necessary. She could have sworn that he had just alluded to the watch she had been keeping on him. And what another person would have said in so many words, he expressed by silence: that she was taking things too far, that she was very wrong not to trust him, that she would end up by making their lives impossible if she continued to spy on him.

Then he resumed the conversation. He said that he had nearly finished his screenwriting. The company that had hired him to work on the adaptation of Conan Doyle's

Lost World were very satisfied with what he had done, his collaboration with the other screenwriters working on it was considered very positive, and a schedule had been fixed for shooting. He had one other script to finish and also the final three chapters of his novel. She knew how impossible it was for him to interrupt his work and get started again. It would cost him weeks of concentration, which he might never be able to recover.

He was very persuasive, despite her suspicions. He had been wonderful about the whole business of Jonathan and the dogs (except that she would have liked to have talked it over with him, heart to heart, but he had avoided any direct confrontation, perhaps rightly). He had had two very long sessions with his son, doing everything he could to break through the child's sullen taciturnity and quell his unreasonable hostility towards his mother, and he had to some extent succeeded: when Adam and his brother went back to college, Jonathan even kissed Hannah goodbye.

But what had Taddeuz himself made of the incident? It was so difficult to know what he thought behind that infernal politeness and kindness! She was reduced to trying to interpret small signs: one evening at Sam Goldwyn's, he had suddenly wanted to leave, for no particular reason; there was also the way he drove his 8-cylinder Duesenberg – Gaffouil had fixed it so that it could reach incredible speeds, even outclassing Hannah's remarkable Hispano-Suiza H6B; he often retreated into silences that lasted the whole day and were all the more exasperating because he would practically jump if you called him, as though emerging from a dream, and at once offer the most polite apologies. And though at first he had talked about the new novel he was in the process of writing – it was vaguely inspired by the life of a certain Johnston, or Johnson, she wasn't quite sure of the name, who was a trapper during the last century and had the distinction of eating the livers of his Indian enemies raw – he hadn't said a word about it for weeks now; long before the trip to the Gulf of Cortez, he had stopped reading passages aloud to Hannah or getting her to read them. It wasn't a return to his former ways, when he used to keep her out of his writing activities, because now he would remark on how his manuscript was progressing, and mention the number of pages he had written, or how much he had still to write, and sometimes confessed, with that half-smile she so disliked, that, 'It didn't go too well today.'

By 10 September he must have written about three hundred pages; in other words, a little under two-thirds of the total, so he said.

'Just the three final chapters to do, in fact. Quite long chapters, but I have the whole story in my head, including the last hundred lines. It won't take long.'

She could see, from a distance, the sheaves of paper lying as usual in the oak box she had had made for him especially.

'I would rather you read it straight through, Hannah, after the second draft – which I'll write when I get back.'

'So you will come with me?'

'I'll follow you. You go on ahead and I'll join you there.'

'I'll delay my departure.'

'That's absurd, Maryan has arranged all kinds of appointments for you, it would make him look silly, you can't do that to him. I'll join you as soon as I can.'

He was still holding her gaze, just as oddly, and she sensed that he was now on the verge of referring to the surveillance he was under.

'Just a few days?'

'I swear it.'

He smiled, but she had the feeling that if she had insisted any further they would have had what could have been a violent argument, the like of which they had not had for ages. *You're giving him too hard a time – why do you always have to boss people around?*

She left with Maryan on the 11th, as planned.

No sooner had she arrived in New York, having barely got settled into the flat on Fifth Avenue, than she telephoned. But it was Gaffouil who picked up the receiver.

'Mr Taddeuz is out.'

She called back six times and finally, in the evening, Taddeuz answered.

'Gaffouil was mistaken, Hannah. I went out for a short walk, but the rest of the time I was in my office. You know that when I'm working I don't hear anything.'

Without the slightest reason, a wave of fear washed over her.

'Are you all right, Taddeuz?'

'But of course. A little tired. My eyes especially. I'm going to go to bed early tonight, without a book to read for once.'

She heard him laugh softly. He was capable of reading in bed until dawn, and it annoyed her because she couldn't sleep with the wretched light on.

'When are you leaving?'

'The day after tomorrow or Friday. I've booked a seat for both days.'

His voice sounded normal, a little dull, and just as serious as ever. Yet she had the vague impression that the way he articulated his words, almost as though he had trouble in finding them, was more strained than usual. But their conversation, by sheer chance – they would normally have spoken French or English to each other – was conducted in Polish. Because they didn't speak it enough, they were beginning to lose the habit. And in any case, telephone conversations were never the best means of communication.

'I'll be expecting you, my love.'

'I've booked a seat,' was all he said, just before hanging up.

And this repetition of his earlier words threw her briefly into a total panic even more irrational than that previous moment of fear. She very nearly called him back. She wrestled with herself and managed to calm down. *You're becoming hysterical. He has always had a horror of passionate declarations, especially on the telephone, you ought to know that after all this time!*

Nevertheless, she did dial the number of the railway company. An hour later she received confirmation that two places had been booked, both in the name of Mr Taddeuz J. Newman (J for Jan, his father's name) for the dates she had given.

You see, you're getting all worked up over nothing.

But the next morning she rang Lizzie, who burst out laughing, with her usual tremendous good humour.

'What do you imagine, old girl? I'm keeping a closer eye on your husband that I would on my own!'

'Have you see him today?'

'Not two hours ago. He's still alive. Dazed but alive – you know how intelligent he looks when he's been writing for too long. Listen, Hannah, do stop worrying. Relax a bit.'

'All right.'

'Don't say all right as though you don't mean it, please. If I look hard at the receiver I can see very clearly those big grey eyes of yours staring at me reproachfully.'

'All right,' said Hannah again, smiling against her will. 'And how is your husband?'

'Fine. Every evening he comes home with two or three Broadway dancers. At least he's not showing any signs of wear,' Lizzie replied cheerfully.

'Promise you'll ring me if anything happens, however unimportant.'

'Honestly!'

'Promise me.'

Early in the afternoon the next day, she was at Merrill Lynch and Co., one of the most powerful and most famous brokerages in the business. They had prepared an investment programme for twelve million dollars for her. For three hours she listened while the best brokers explained the marvellous advantages of such and such a share. She was promised a return of fifteen, or twenty, or even twenty-five per cent.

'We'll start with six,' she said. 'After that, I'll see. Six million, I mean.'

The phone rang and it was for her. It was Yvonne ringing from the apartment on Fifth Avenue to say that she had just received a call from Lizzie: 'Mrs Kaden wanted to let you know that Mr Taddeuz caught the train to New York an hour ago.'

'Why didn't my husband ring?'

'Mrs Kaden said that he didn't have time, that he had been working until the last minute.'

She was about to ask some even more stupid questions – for instance, whether Lizzie herself had actually seen Taddeuz board the train. But apart from her awareness of how paranoid she was becoming, there were also the five men sitting there watching her, pretending not to hear, while she was on the phone.

'Thank you, Yvonne. I shan't be home for dinner. You can have the evening off.'

She hung up, then apologized for the interruption.

'Six million only, to start with.'

She told them she was happy with the composition of the portfolio they had suggested.

That evening Maryan took her out to dinner with two of his friends. One was a great entertainer with a crazy sense of humour and eyes like lotto counters, who had appeared on several occasions with the Ziegfield Follies – his name was Eddie Cantor. The other was a young Romanian actor born in Bucharest, who had not yet changed his name from Emmanuel Goldenberg to Edward G. Robinson. He was twenty-five years old at most, but surprised Hannah by his knowledge and love of painting, especially of the French Impressionists. She had attended this dinner on Maryan's insistence, almost against her will, and ended up laughing at Cantor's stories, and then fervently discussing Claude Monet with Goldenberg-Robinson – he was amazed that she knew the painter personally.

'I knew you would like them,' said Maryan when he took her home.

'Thank you, Maryan. You and Lizzie . . .'

'Don't ever thank me, Hannah. Ever. I'll never be able to repay what you've done for me.'

And suddenly she was almost on the verge of tears. *What's the matter with you? You've never been this tense and nervous in your life before.* Even she, who had always viewed herself with the most implacable lucidity, couldn't determine the reasons for the anxiety she felt. She had reached the point of counting the days and the hours that separated her from Taddeuz's arrival.

On Monday 22nd, she was at the station a long time before the Pullman from California came in. She was so tense that Yvonne eventually lost patience with her and threatened to hand in her notice if she went on like this. She'd had more than enough of it; her three children by Gaffouil spoke American better than they did French, which was a crying shame – what was to prevent them all going back to France and living out their days in peace, far away from a grey-eyed grasshopper who was making their lives impossible.

Silence.

'You don't even have an answer, and that's not funny.

There was a time when you would have put me in my place and given me the sharp edge of your tongue. Things are definitely not as they should be. I wonder why . . . And you ought to go and put some more of those filthy creams on your face: you haven't been getting any sleep and you look like death. When he comes, he'll think you're ill – and you're never ill. Besides, this is his train coming in now. Try and smile, here he is.'

But he wasn't.

Taddeuz wasn't on the train.

CHAPTER 23

I am Like a Man Who Yawns at a Ball . . .

With that mixture of disbelief and certainty attendant upon disaster, she ran up and down the train, checking every compartment, attracting looks of surprise from the teams of cleaners already at work.

She found the guard on the platform.

Yes, he remembered very clearly a single-berth compartment reserved in the name of Newman, from Los Angeles, but as far as he knew, the passenger had not turned up. She would have to talk to old Sam, who did the service in that carriage.

By the time they caught up with the black waiter, he was already on the subway platform. He had indeed seen a Mr Newman, a tall blond fellow with green eyes, about thirty, thirty-five years old, who had seemed a bit drowsy.

'But he got off the train just before it left LA.'

She telephoned Lizzie eight times in the next two hours, but it was always the Filipino servant who answered, saying that Mrs Kaden wasn't back yet.

Finally: 'He wasn't on the train, Lizzie. He boarded it all right, but he got off a few seconds before it departed. He gave the waiter a hundred dollars and told him that he had changed his mind, and asked to have his luggage sent on to New York. I have it here. What was he wearing when he left?'

Lizzie thought she remembered him in a light suit and a hat.

'The suit is in the case,' said Hannah. 'Rolled up into a ball. He changed in the compartment and left.'

In a way she felt more self-possessed now than she had

for many days. At least she knew that her foreboding was justified, that her worst fears – *no, not your worst fears, not yet* – had been confirmed.

And at least she had something to do. Maryan had mobilized his Californian assistants by telegram and by phone. Less than an hour and a half after the express from Los Angeles had arrived, one of them got back to him: the Duesenberg had disappeared from the villa in Coldwater Canyon Drive. The doors of the garage had not been forced, they had even been locked after the car had been taken out. Neither of the two Rolls-Royces had been touched, nor the Hispano-Suiza, nor the Mercedes, still less Gaffouil's Ford T (Gaffouil had gone to France three weeks ago). No one had entered the house from the garage, which could have been done easily, and the servants in the house had heard nothing.

'Maryan, he's taken the car. Can you get a checkpoint set up on all roads that cross the Mexican border?'

'Hannah, he may have wanted to drive the Duesenberg to New York.'

'Knowing that I would be waiting for him at the station? Don't be stupid! Can you get that damned border control or not?'

'The Governor will certainly do it as a favour. If you really think I should ask him.'

He didn't say any more, but it was enough to remind her of the last time Taddeuz had disappeared. The very fact that they had pursued him then had not exactly improved matters. And seeking the Governor of California's help would make it all public, however discreet they tried to be.

'I think you ought to ask him, Maryan. This time, it's worse. Please do it, I beg you.'

Where did her conviction that 'this time, it's worse' spring from? She had no idea. The fact that Taddeuz had returned to the house to pick up his car alarmed her even more than his disappearance. On the morning of the 23rd, after a sleepless night waiting by the phone, she flew down to Los Angeles.

Literally flew down, in an old Vickers Vimy bomber that cost a fortune to hire, and even then it was only thanks to Brendan Benda's intervention with the Vice-Secretary of State for Defense in Washington that it could be arranged.

She was at Coldwater Canyon thirty hours later, after touching down only once, on a stretch of tarmac road outside Dallas.

'No sign of any Duesenberg crossing between Tijuana and Nogales.'

The man who gave her this information was a very gentle giant by the name of Dale Fitzpatrick. She took him for one of Maryan's assistants.

'We could extend the roadblock to El Paso,' he suggested.

'Do it.'

Fitzpatrick spread out a map in front of her: extending border control to El Paso would mean mounting surveillance along seven hundred and fifty miles of the border between America and Mexico.

'What details have been given out to identify him?' she asked.

'We have issued every checkpoint with a description of your husband, and the number and make of his car. He is to be intercepted and held on the pretext of a search for stolen cars, but he will not of course be imprisoned. And we shall be informed the moment he is sighted. We also have men in Mexico.'

'Is there a reward for finding him?'

Fitzpatrick shook his head, clearly embarrassed: he had not dared go so far.

'Twenty-five thousand dollars,' said Hannah. 'To anyone who provides correct information.'

Calm down and think. His life is in danger and you know it, whatever all these people around you may say, even Maryan and Lizzie. If you panic, you'll be responsible for his death.

She said: 'The Duesenberg has a fuel capacity that will take it approximately ninety miles. Assuming he filled up before leaving Coldwater Canyon Drive, I want a list of all the petrol stations in Los Angeles itself and within a radius of a hundred miles of the city. Usually we get our petrol at the station in Santa Monica Boulevard. Check that out, please.'

The pump attendant had to be got out of bed, but she had the information forty minutes later: Taddeuz had filled up the Duesenberg an hour after the train left. He had also filled the reserve can.

She made a rapid calculation.

'With the reserve, he could have gone an extra twenty miles. Extend the search area to within a 125-mile radius of Los Angeles. Is that list of petrol pumps coming or not? Dale, put everyone you can on to it. Five thousand dollars' reward for finding the station.'

From New York, she had asked the telephone company to install thirty extra telephone lines for her, as a matter of urgency. They were now installed, and some fifty men and women – friends, employees, sales assistants and beauticians from the salons and shops, off-duty policemen, neighbours – desperately tried to contact every telephone subscriber in the zone they were looking in.

Hannah couldn't take any more. She hadn't slept for nearly sixty hours. But she refused to take any of the tranquillizers the doctor Lizzie had called wanted to give her.

'Leave me alone!'

The calls kept coming: friends who didn't know anything about what was going on; friends who had heard the rumours the whole of Hollywood was buzzing with and who wanted to help; practical jokers; newspaper reporters and radio reporters, harassing her and persecuting her remorselessly. Even Lizzie was finally driven into a rage by it:

'What if Taddeuz were to ring and the line was engaged!'

'He won't ring,' said Hannah with terrifying certainty.

On the third day of the hunt, 27 September, she extended the search zone to a 300-mile radius. If Taddeuz had planned his flight, he could very well have taken not just one reserve can but several. She hated herself for not having thought of this sooner.

Finally, on the 28th – eleven days and thirteen hours since Taddeuz had got off the train for New York – one of the trackers struck lucky: one of the waitresses in a little restaurant remembered having served a tall, fair-haired man with green eyes, 'handsome as a film star'. She had been struck by the fact that, although he spoke English without the slightest accent, the man had been reading a book printed in strange characters.

Russian written in Cyrillic script!

It must have been Lermontov. She rushed to the library, searched the shelves and found that the original, leather-bound edition of *A Hero of Our Time* by Mikhail Lermontov was missing. A wave of self-hatred washed over her: *You should have thought of that too, you damned fool!*

And the quotation from the book came back to her, with all the monotonous and painful repetition of a refrain that she now discovered had marked the secret rhythm of the last twenty-one years of her life: *If I am to die, I'll die! The loss to the world will not be large and, anyway, I myself am like a man who yawns at a ball and does not drive home to sleep, only because his carriage is not yet there . . .**

And Taddeuz has a Duesenberg for a carriage . . .

* * *

* From Vladimir Nabokov's translation, p.130, Oxford University Press, 1984.

The restaurant where Taddeuz had stopped nine days earlier was on the north side of Wickenburg, in the state of Arizona, a little over sixty miles to the north-west of Phoenix.

'The waitress doesn't remember which direction he was travelling in, Hannah,' said Maryan, who had come down by train from New York.

It's as though he planned it that way. See for yourself: from Wickenburg, he could just as well have headed for Phoenix to the south, or Flagstaff to the north-east, Las Vegas to the north-west, or even returned to Los Angeles.

Where he would be by now, had he intended to come back.

Three hundred men, plus all the municipal and county police, were now taking part in the search. The area they were detailed to cover extended one hundred miles around Wickenburg. Early in the afternoon of the 28th, Hannah left for Phoenix on a special train that had a private car for her. She had barely slept ten hours in the whole of the last two weeks, and even then her sleep had been plagued with dreadful nightmares in which she had had visions of Taddeuz lying as though dead, his body burned.

The police in Phoenix considered it virtually impossible that a car as big and unwieldy as a Duesenberg could have gone very far off what was hardly a road, more a dirt track.

She froze them with a single glance – exhaustion had dilated her pupils so much they were just about all you could see in that narrow triangular face with the high cheekbones.

'He left the road.'

Air searches revealed nothing.

At dawn on 3 October, the news came through. She was on the spot three hours later. The special train set her and

Maryan down within sight of a small town by the name of Wenden, in the heart of the Sonora desert. The Mercedes-Benz was taken off the train and they drove along the dried-up bed of the Centennial, a small tributary of the Gila, with an Indian on horseback acting as their guide; from time to time he pointed out to them the tracks of the Duesenberg's tyres. A gruelling heat that seemed to increase with every passing moment bore down on them; the air was suffocatingly dry and completely still. Erosion had sculpted every rock, whether of brown sandstone, or yellow limestone, or green or red clay; giant cactuses towered over them, and in the sides of these bizarre, candelabra-like plants with the silhouette of a crucifix, you could see the damage inflicted by the Duesenberg's fenders fourteen days ago. An hour later – they had to drive some twelve miles – the invisible track suddenly turned south-west. The view broadened, and the gorge opened on to a relatively passable undulating landscape. They crossed the Gila Bend Mountains, then the Kofa Mountains loomed up, barring the horizon. Often the tyre tracks disappeared for several hundred yards – it seemed impossible that a car could have got through – but the Apache on horseback always found them again. They crossed the bed of another tributary of the Gila, even more dry than the previous one, if such a thing were possible. It grew hotter . . .

The Indian rider came to a standstill, his hands clasped on the pummel of his saddle, staring ahead, impassively.

The Duesenberg was the first thing you saw, stopped halfway up a slight incline no more or less steep than any other – so it could have climbed it. There were ten or so men there, standing by their horses. Only one of them glanced up at the Mercedes-Benz as it approached, but immediately lowered his head. Most of them were squatting on their haunches, staring at the ground.

'Let me go and look, please,' said Maryan in a low voice.

She barely heard him. She stepped out of the car and started walking in a daze, in which only her eyes seemed alive, and all she could see was his blond hair and his head resting on the back of the seat.

'Lady, you shouldn't go any closer . . .'

It was one of the policemen who addressed her. She saw him only as a shadow to her right, and his voice sounded incredibly distant. She heard herself ask: 'Why did he stop here?'

'He didn't have a drop of petrol left.'

'Does it lead anywhere in this direction?'

'Nowhere. If he had continued following the river-bed he would eventually have reached the railway line. He chose a different route.'

She continued walking, vaguely sensing that Maryan was following her. Another six steps brought her alongside the driver's door.

He was sitting behind the steering wheel of the convertible, his big hands, white as chalk, stretched out on his knees. His neck was resting on the back of the red leather seat. He was wearing a white shirt with the sleeves rolled up, as he often had them.

His face had been covered with a scarf.

She stepped on to the running-board and raised her hand . . .

'No, Hannah! For the love of God!'

She carried on regardless and gently drew back the scarf.

His eye-sockets were empty, not even bloody, just empty. His eyeballs were gone and the wrinkled skin all round what had been his eyes was marked with countless little round, very deep wounds inflicted by the beaks of scavenger birds.

She leaned over and gave those sunburned lips a

lingering kiss. The lower lip, the one she had tenderly nibbled a thousand times, was torn and cut, and roughened with scabs of dried blood.

She stepped down from the running-board and everyone moved back as though afraid of her. She walked round the car and went and sat in the passenger seat, gently slipping her fingers into his petrified hand, and rested her cheek on Taddeuz's shoulder.

Only then did she close her eyes.

I'm dead. It's all over now.

CHAPTER 24

I Want to Bury Myself Alive

He was buried in the Franciscan cemetery in Santa Barbara. Twenty-one years earlier, when they had together made their first grand tour of America, they had stopped in this place for two whole days, entranced by the charm of Spanish California and the wonderful coastal landscape.

She went to the funeral knowing what to expect.

And it was just as she had anticipated: but for Lizzie and especially Maryan, for once in his life prey to the blackest of rages, the mad hatred that Adam and Jonathan felt for her, the younger boy encouraging the elder, would perhaps have found expression in more than mere looks and a complete refusal to go near her.

The ceremony was an intimate one, and yet people came in their hundreds, from Hollywood and New York, some even from Europe, as a mark of their affection for Taddeuz.

For the next three weeks, she cloistered herself in a little hotel very close to the monastery that had been founded some one hundred and thirty years earlier.

She went to his grave every day, and failed to reply to Lizzie's incessant and importunate calls.

On 6 November 1921, she left for New York, where she stayed less than two days – the time it took to settle all her financial affairs.

She set sail for Europe, and from Le Havre made her way directly to Lugano, then Morcote.

She was not alone: Yvonne and her husband refused to

leave her, despite her orders and despite any offers she might have made them.

'I want to bury myself alive, Yvonne. You and your husband have better things to do.'

'You'll have to throw me out if you want to get rid of me,' said Yvonne, in tears.

She did not leave Morcote for the next eight years, except once a year in the autumn when, without stopping anywhere, she would travel through France, cross the Atlantic and the United States to go and spend three weeks in Santa Barbara.

Her daughter Abigail came with Lizzie to visit her in 1921, 1923, 1924, 1926, 1927 and 1928. On each occasion she would stay at the house for two to four weeks. But the silence of the place upset the young girl.

Neither Adam nor Jonathan ever visited. Nor did they write.

In 1929 Adam was twenty-six, Jonathan twenty-three, Abigail sixteen.

Hannah was fifty-four.

CHAPTER 25

A Crash is not to be Ruled Out

'We're arriving,' said Yvonne.

Hannah looked up from her book – *The Sound and the Fury* by Faulkner – and cast a quick, indifferent glance through the window on which the Frenchwoman had just raised the blind. They had reached Manhattan. It was 23 October 1929, nine thirty in the morning. The train started to slow down.

'Do you want your fur coat?' asked Yvonne.

'You must be joking!'

'We aren't in California any more. I can't get this wretched trunk closed!'

She struggled with the locks, but she had no sooner got one closed than the other sprang open again. Hannah had returned to her book and, still reading, she moved to sit on the recalcitrant trunk, which finally consented to remain closed.

'Six and a half stone of muscle!' said Yvonne. 'What a weight! I bet you haven't put on an ounce since you were fifteen.'

'Well, the same certainly can't be said of you, you great whale.'

'But I do stand a little higher than a chair. Are you going to keep that handbag or would you like a different one?'

'I don't care either way.'

The train slowed down again and eventually stopped. A whole group of sporty-looking youngsters went by, dressed in red-and-white striped Norfolk jackets, wearing round caps with the colours of some university or other.

Yvonne got the last case closed and tried to catch the eye of a porter.

Hannah was still reading – and continued to do so as she walked along the platform, a path skilfully cleared ahead of her by the Frenchwoman, who advanced with arms akimbo as though to herald the approach of a special convoy, herself preceded by a luggage trolley and two porters.

'Mrs Newman?'

It took her a few seconds to recognize Dale Fitzpatrick.

'Maryan sends his apologies, he was detained at the last minute. May I be of service?'

The two women installed themselves in the 12-cylinder Packard, while their luggage was loaded into a Chevrolet.

'I have a suite reserved for you at the Waldorf and one at the Plaza,' said Fitzpatrick. 'We didn't know which hotel you would prefer.'

'The Plaza.'

She did eventually close her book, but kept it on her lap, with a finger marking the page. She thanked Fitzpatrick with a smile and looked out at New York, without really taking any of it in, her eyes wide open.

Suddenly she said: 'I'd like to go via Wall Street.'

'The street or the area?'

'No place in particular.'

The two cars turned down Broadway.

'It's absolutely incredible,' said Fitzpatrick, 'you haven't changed at all.'

'Thank you.'

Only then did she really remember who he was: it was he who had led the search eight years ago.

'How long have you been working for Maryan?'

She was mistaken in assuming he was a mere assistant of Maryan's, but he was far too polite to tell her. All he said was: 'About fifteen years. He's a very fine person.'

'I know.'

The Packard drove slowly past the six Corinthian-style columns of the New York Stock Exchange. Hannah tilted her head slightly. It was a little after eleven and dealing had started. There was an atmosphere of calm, insofar as Wall Street can ever be calm.

She said: 'About a month and a half ago, I read an article in the *New York Herald* by someone called Babson. According to him, a crash is likely.'

'A crash?' said Fitzpatrick with a laugh. 'I haven't been told about it myself. That Babson fellow is a notorious joker. He lives in the middle of a forest in Connecticut and talks finance with the squirrels, who are his source of secret information. I did go to a seminar he organized. He has a curious theory, a theory of cycles. According to him, prosperity and depression return at regular intervals, every thirty years or so. He couldn't tell us whether it would be morning or afternoon . . . You know what they say, Mrs Newman: if you keep talking nonsense, sooner or later your predictions will turn out to be true.'

'But there's no sign of a crash?'

'Good God, no . . . Forgive my language.'

The Packard had stopped at the junction with Broadway, in order to let a fire engine pass, all sirens wailing. She suddenly recognized Junior Rockefeller, with the *Wall Street Journal* in his hand, standing on the pavement opposite; he was about to get into his Cadillac. Hannah thought of getting out and greeting him. But it was a good seventeen or eighteen years since she had last seen him. He had aged a lot and his bearing was much more confident than she remembered.

'To the Plaza now, please,' she said to Fitzpatrick.

Maryan bent down and kissed her on both cheeks. For a few seconds she rested her face against his chest. *He's the only man you have left now . . .*

'You haven't changed,' he said.

'I'll end up believing it.'

'But it's true, Hannah, I promise you.'

She returned his smile. He had just returned from South America, where he had gone to keep an eye on his interests there – she didn't know exactly what those interests were, although he had told her the year before, or the one before that, when she had also been returning from her annual pilgrimage to Santa Barbara: she hadn't paid much attention.

She examined him. His hair had started to turn white five years ago and was receding slightly at the temples, but his suntanned face set off his blue eyes. He had never been truly handsome but getting older suited him, enhancing that ability to listen attentively (or at least give the impression of doing so) which he had developed over the years. He was fifty-two.

'And we've known each other now for thirty-nine years,' she said.

He looked at her in surprise.

'I was thinking out loud, Maryan. I read somewhere that you were worth close on sixty million dollars.'

'Not as much as that.'

'Fifty-nine million nine hundred thousand?'

And there he was shifting his weight from one foot to the other, just as he used to, for all that he was a millionaire. But eventually he smiled: 'Perhaps a little more than that,' he said.

'I adore you.'

His only reply was to kiss the back of her hand. Then he asked: 'When are you leaving?'

'I'm sailing tomorrow on the *Ile de France*.'

She knew what his next question would be: couldn't she stay a while longer in New York?

'No, Maryan, no more than I have before.'

'You're only just going to miss Lizzie, and I'm the one who will be blamed for it.'

'I'll write to her. And I'll send you some bandages to dress your wounds.'

There was a knock at the door of the suite in the Hotel Plaza; it was the *maître d'hôtel* and a waiter with the luncheon she had asked to have sent up to her rooms. It was twelve thirty, Wednesday 23 October.

The two men departed.

'Do you remember Eddie Cantor?' asked Maryan. 'He dined with us ten years ago. He's become a star. I've invited him out this evening.'

Once again, she shook her head in refusal – this had become a rule, almost a rite with her for the past eight years. She always spent the little time she had in New York, on her way back from Santa Barbara to Morcote, cloistered in her hotel bedroom.

But this time she hesitated and he sensed it.

He insisted.

She accepted.

'We'll go to Delmonico's. I've booked a table. There'll be twelve of us, including Jack Benny, Al Jolson, and someone you don't know – I want it to be a surprise.'

'Will I be the only woman?'

'Lizzie was supposed to come but . . .'

'In other words, I'm standing in for her.'

'She's not arriving until tomorrow, just in time to drive you to the boat with any luck. We thought that you wouldn't be in New York until Friday. No, you won't be the only woman. Fanny Brice, Sophie Tucker and one or two others are also coming.'

'I don't know them.'

For eight years she had cut herself off from the world.

'They'll probably all end up throwing food at each other, like the last time, but never mind,' said Maryan with unexpected levity.

He invited her to have lunch with him, rather than eat alone, but she refused, sure that as usual he must have a lot of work to do, with meetings and appointments to keep.

It was just as he picked up his hat and was preparing to leave that she mentioned Roger W. Babson's name, as she had done two hours earlier to Dale Fitzpatrick. He was on the very threshold of the double doors opening on to the landing, when her words caused him to pause, turn round and meet her gaze.

It certainly wasn't Babson's name that was responsible for this; he knew Hannah too well, well enough at least for her question to set him thinking. *And, intelligent as he is, he's probably cottoned on . . .*

What he said was: 'It's not just Babson, Hannah. The President of the Manhattan Trust, Paul Warburg, also believes there will be a crash some time during the next few weeks or months. And in Europe – in London and Paris – American shares, even government bonds, have been selling heavily. At the beginning of the month the American Association of Bankers recommended its members to be cautious; it thinks that credit is too readily made available by the banks. The Federal Reserve Bank has expressed concern on several occasions. Do you know Clarence Barron?'

'By name.'

'He's the proprietor of several magazines and newspapers, including the *Wall Street Journal*. Yesterday he spoke of an overheating of the market and the risk of a general collapse. I could cite other examples.'

'Lots of others?'

'Not hundreds, admittedly.'

She lifted the silver dish cover on the table and bit into one of the chips that accompanied the lamb chops.

'And what do you think?'

His blue eyes became veiled, as always when he was about to weigh his words particularly carefully.

'A crash is not to be ruled out,' said Maryan.

'You've taken precautions in case it happens?'

'You taught me to be prudent. I'll come by and collect you at seven, OK?'

'OK.'

She spent the rest of the day in her suite in the Plaza, while Yvonne, tired by such a long train journey, slept in her room. Hannah knitted, with her usual clumsiness at this kind of thing, a clumsiness partly compensated for by the fierce determination with which she applied herself to everything. She had begun this particular piece of knitting six years ago, and according to the extremely precise calculations she had made, she had worked 12,623,800 stitches. Yvonne had threatened to hand in her notice if she was given any more of Hannah's horrible scarves done in moss stitch for her grandchildren.

'If only you tried to do something other than those scarves, at least!'

'You're always grumbling. I don't know how to do anything else.'

'You're really hopeless – you're not even capable of doing a simple jersey stitch!'

Once, wielding her needles for no other reason but to combat the appalling sense of death that oppressed her, she knitted a scarf twenty yards long.

'Hannah, something happened on Wall Street this afternoon.'

She and Maryan were in the Packard, sitting behind the black-liveried chauffeur. They were on their way to Delmonico's.

She looked at him.

'For no good reason,' Maryan went on, 'there was a general slump in the market. A drop of thirty-one points on all stock, with more than two and a half million shares changing hands in fifty minutes. Instructions to sell were coming in from all over the country, and are still coming in. Some deals went through only just before five, after an hour and a quarter's delay, because the dealers were so overworked.'

'How unusual is that?'

'It's quite exceptional. It's never happened before in the one and a half centuries of Wall Street's existence. How much is invested in your portfolio?'

'Six and a half or seven million dollars. Perhaps more. I don't pay much attention to these things.'

'You're not with Merrill Lynch any more, are you?'

'MacHill, Drexel and something or other. Am I going to lose money, Maryan?'

'Things would have to get considerably worse before that happens. And even then, you won't lose anything if you don't have to sell for a while; all you have to do is wait until the market returns to normal, which will take a few days, or a few weeks at most, assuming there is a crash.'

'So the crash hasn't happened yet.'

'No. Wall Street and America are solid . . . This is Julius Marx, Hannah. But he prefers to be called Groucho.'

The next day was a Thursday. She got up at dawn and went for an hour-long walk through Central Park before breakfast. New York was enjoying an Indian summer, the air was warm, nearly sixty-five degrees Fahrenheit already. The sky was still a bit hazy – it was obviously going to be a nice day.

She was eating her three boiled eggs, while reading the sports pages of the *New York Times*, when Bernard Benda arrived.

He told her again that she hadn't changed, and how truly incredible it was. He had already said this the day before, as he too had happened to be dining at Delmonico's – at another table in fact, but he had eventually joined Maryan's party, attracted by their laughter. He offered to take Hannah to Wall Street.

He told her the latest joke:

'A broker is on his way back from the doctor, who has just told him that he has developed diabetes at the age of thirty-seven. He meets one of his stockbroking friends and tells him the bad news: "Can you imagine, I've got diabetes at thirty-seven?" "What are you complaining about?" his friend replies morosely, "I've got Chrysler at one thirty."'

Wall Street seemed calm again.

'Although there are a few more people around than usual,' Bernard Benda observed.

(Ten years earlier, when called upon by President Woodrow Wilson to represent the United States at various international post-war conferences, Benda had sold out of his stockbroking firm and financial consultancy.)

They entered the New York Stock Exchange a few minutes before ten, and went straight up to the gallery overlooking the floor.

Hannah took a seat. From this vantage point, she looked right down on to the trans-lux, a huge illuminated screen on which blinking yellow lights indicated the transactions being made, both sales and purchases, and the type of shares being traded.

'Coffee?'

'No, thank you.'

She leaned forward, fascinated by the peculiar silence that had suddenly descended. On the floor below her, there were about three or four thousand men – brokers, pages, telephone operators and people working on the trading board.

They all stood immobile, looking up.

They were staring at the wall clock which would give

the starting signal at ten o'clock precisely. She suddenly shivered; Bernard had just pointed out to her the enormous bundles of orders the brokers held in their hands.

Suddenly all hell was let loose.

CHAPTER 26

I Hope This isn't Happening Because of Me . . .

More than one and a half million shares were sold in the first thirty minutes alone. Hannah could see the counters almost overturned by frenzied hordes, with some of the brokers on their hands and knees, clutching desperately at their papers. Others were trampled underfoot – they were screaming but their cries were drowned in the tremendous tumult. The floor was beginning to disappear under the heaps of orders that the pages were no longer able to deliver. *They've all gone mad!*

She had caught some names that floated to the surface like bits of wreckage in this ocean of clamouring voices, and recognized one or two as companies she thought were in her portfolio, although she wasn't very sure.

As time went by, even the gallery where she was sitting had been invaded by a dense crowd of drawn faces. Two people at least had fainted right next to her; one man fell to his knees and, with his forehead pressed to the balustrade, started crying, racked by sobs. A little way off, without realizing what she was doing, a woman had torn the string of pearls from her neck, and didn't even bend down to pick up the pearls from the ground.

'Let's go, Bernard, please.'

Benda complied, though obviously with regret. He too was extraordinarily fascinated. He shook his head in disbelief.

It took them twenty minutes to cover the fifteen yards to the only door leading out of the gallery. *If a fire started, not one of us would get out alive . . .* Hannah was finally pulled out of the human maelstrom by two security men who recognized Bernard Benda, and for the whole length of a corridor her feet didn't touch the ground.

Benda and Hannah met up again by the reception rooms, only because there was slightly less of a crush in this area. People were now crowded into these rooms where the brokers usually received their best clients; they stood packed like sardines trying to follow what was happening on illuminated boards linked up to the board on the floor.

'It's getting worse,' said Benda.

And he too looked very pale, his intelligent eyes reduced to two slits behind his pince-nez.

'Do you want to see any more, Hannah?'

He wants you to say yes; he has no desire to leave. This madness must be contagious . . .

But she felt suffocated. In any case, she couldn't really see anything in this throng of people all taller than she.

Shouting in his ear in order to make herself heard over the din, she told him: 'I'm going back to the hotel, Bernard. Get me a taxi and I'll leave you to it.'

A broker went by, his tie torn, his sleeves rolled up, clutching to his chest a pile of papers gathered up haphazardly. Distraught, he called on Hannah to witness the chaos: 'There are some two thousand telephone operators, they've just doubled the number, and I still can't get through to my office!'

He ran off, evidently in a total state of panic. A little way off a young page had cracked up completely. He was shouting: 'The bears! The bears are devouring the market!'

Hannah and Benda finally managed to get outside into the fresh air.

'The bears are the brokers who systematically trade on a falling market,' explained Bernard.

'Yes, I remember. The opposite of bulls,' said Hannah.

They were standing on the pavement.

'I've never seen anything like it,' said Bernard Benda. 'Never.'

His hands were trembling.

'You were talking of a crash, Hannah? This is it. Oh my God!'

He eventually found her a taxi. At that point she was still intending to sail on the *Ile de France*. She saw no reason to postpone her departure; the thought didn't even occur to her, not consciously at least. '*I don't know when the idea came to me, Lizzie. It had probably been inside me for a long time. When I read that article by Babson in the* New York Herald *on the train, it wasn't even recent news then, and when I put those questions to Dale Fitzpatrick and then afterwards to Maryan . . . I don't know when I thought of it, but once it was inside my head . . .*

'Could you stop here, please.'

The taxi that Bernard Benda had hailed for her had barely driven a hundred yards down Nassau Street. The driver turned round and looked at her; he virtually had to shout to make himself heard:

'What exactly do you want, lady?'

'I just want to get out. I've changed my mind.'

There was an incredible amount of traffic, a lot of taxis but also an unusual number of chauffeur-driven luxury limousines. Later she would learn that many stockbrokers' clients, panicked by radio reports of the drop in the market, had first of all tried to contact their brokers by phone, then in desperation decided to go to the Stock Exchange in person, with a single purpose in mind: Sell. Get out of the market.

This was the main reason for what was gradually turning into a rout as all the roads leading north–south to the tip of the Manhattan peninsula became blocked. There was another, even more dramatic reason. Tens of thousands of New Yorkers, and indeed millions of Americans, spellbound by a market that had been continuously rising for such a long time, had been seized in a frenzy of speculation. With the excessive indulgence of banks and brokers, the large majority had been dealing speculatively on unsecured credit, actually paying out only ten, fifteen, or twenty per cent – or less, and sometimes nothing – in cash. The tidal wave which was now breaking on Wall Street had forced brokers to make margin calls, that is, to ask their clients to settle urgently, within the hour, the total or partial sums outstanding.

Some of their clients reacted to this by giving orders to sell other shares in their portfolio that were less under attack, and to use the money raised in this way to settle their other pledges . . .

As a result the fall extended, at lightning speed, to all stock on the market, even affecting, as in 1901, the famous blue chips. But this time nothing and no one could stop the infernal machine.

And among all those people virtually fighting to get to Wall Street, to their brokers' offices, were some who had nothing but cash to fall back on in response to the margin call. And in order to raise money, many of them sold their jewellery and real estate in the panic and, having done so, joined the rush to Wall Street. For most of them it was too late. Bernard Benda would later meet a man who lived right on the other side of New York State, near the Canadian border. Having listened to all the reports on the radio, and unable to contact his broker by telephone, he had set off in his Cadillac on a mad dash that took him forty hours, including punctures and breakdowns, only to learn on his arrival that his position had collapsed the day before and he was ruined.

It was eleven fifty. Hannah was trying to return to the Stock Exchange. She couldn't get near it, and dared not persist for fear of being trampled. At one point she caught sight of the characteristic lower lip of her old friend Winnie Churchill standing some sixty yards away from her (by the sheerest fluke he just happened to be in New York giving lectures, as she was to find out later). She tried to attract his attention but she was too small; she saw him enter the New York Exchange and then lost sight of him.

She managed to slip into New Street just as a squadron of police arrived, in search of the Communist riot – completely imaginary – that had been reported to them.

She finally heard someone calling her name: it was a breathless Dale Fitzpatrick. He had seen her get out of her taxi and had been fighting against a human tide to reach her. He picked her up and deposited her in the safety of a doorway, away from the crowd of people rushing to avoid more police officers on horseback . . .

'Forgive me for calling you Hannah.'

'This is no time to stand on ceremony. Could you get me out of here?'

'All the way to Florida, if you wish, madame. Where are we going?'

'Call me Hannah, everyone else does. I'm going to MacHill, Drexel and What's-his-name – they are on Broadway. Would you mind putting me down, please?'

'Forgive me, I'm terribly sorry,' he said as though he meant it.

He set her down on the ground.

He had nice blue eyes and what's more, he was about six foot five inches tall and must have weighed around eighteen stone, which was jolly useful in the circumstances. She stood behind him, with her hands on his hips, while he forged a passage through the successive walls of stunned onlookers and brokers; all she had to do was follow in his wake.

They emerged on Broadway, where the crowd was less dense on the pavements.

'Thank you, Dale. You must have an awful lot to do on a day like today.'

He shook his head energetically.

'Maryan would fill me with holes if I left you on your own. Or worse still, he would fire me. I'm not letting you out of my sight.'

She thought: *God, but it's good to have a man around!*

They crossed Broadway. In the offices of MacHill, Drexel and Smith, even the corridors were full of people, but there were no more than thirty people in each room. Dozens of telephones were ringing continuously and she found employees working three to a desk, frantically recording in their books the transactions reported to them by the brokers and the telephone operators.

Vance MacHill's office was by comparison fabulously quiet. He was a little bald man, whose pince-nez was attached to his waistcoat by a fine gold chain.

'Get out!' he said unceremoniously to Dale Fitzpatrick.

Then he saw Hannah and leapt hastily to his feet.

'Mrs Newman! I didn't know you were in New York.'

She smiled at him.

'I hope all this isn't happening because of me.'

She sat down and straightened her Elsa Schiaparelli hat, which had been knocked about during the last few minutes.

'I have of course come for the Hannah Incorporated shares.'

This was the company name – the correct name in full was Hannah Cosmetics and Perfumes Incorporated – under which the American part of her former empire had been operating since it was purchased ten years earlier by Stahlman and Javitts.

MacHill closed his mouth, which had been open in amazement. He removed his pince-nez, finally replaced the receiver without paying any further attention to the person on the other end of the line, and pushed the telephone away from him.

'Thank God you haven't come to sell,' he said.

'I've come to buy. Whatever shares are in my portfolio can remain where they are. I'm not in the least bit interested in them. I've come to buy but not straightaway. Have shares in Hannah Incorporated been affected by the general fall in the market?'

How should he know? He said that he had no particular reason for taking any interest in those shares.

She nodded, as though this was exactly the reply she had expected to hear.

'According to my latest information,' she said, 'which dates back to this morning before the market opened, those shares were worth $158.25 each. I believe – which is another way of saying that I know perfectly well – that to date 226,211 shares have been issued by the company for a total of what would be $35,797,890. Those are the shares I would like to buy. Perhaps not all of them, but at least eighty or ninety per cent of the total.'

She smiled at Dale Fitzpatrick.

'Of course I can't count as quickly as Maryan Kaden, but I manage. Your tie is crooked, Dale.

'Mr MacHill, I would like to buy back my company. Not at that price of course: $158.25 is absolutely absurd and that alone would explain why your Stock Exchange is exploding the way it is – if the shares of other companies are as overvalued, there's no need to look any further for the reason for a crash . . . Please let me finish . . . Thank you, Mr MacHill.' She smiled at him. 'I will buy back my company if the shares fall by at least half, let's say to $80. I am not hoping for a crash, nor for the collapse of the entire American or world economy, but if it has to happen, I shan't be to blame, for once, and I don't see why I shouldn't take advantage of it. Eighty dollars, Mr MacHill. I authorize you to buy them cheaper if you can.

I will pay cash, naturally. No messing about with delayed settlement, deposits or any other tomfoolery. I want the shares in my hands. As I have always wanted my shares.'

'I swear to you, Lizzie, I hadn't the least idea of what I was going to say to MacHill when I went into his office. Stop sniggering like an idiot, will you? I'm not lying, I really didn't know, it was all done off the top of my head. On my left, there was Dale with his eyes as big as saucers, making me laugh . . . All right, it's true that for the previous four years . . . let's say five, I had followed the progress of my company day by day. I had sold out at a bad time, too early, it didn't matter that it was 1919 – 23 March 1919, to be exact – we were still in the nineteenth century. No, I'm not crazy. What's really important when times change is not the way people dress, the fact that they drive around in petrol-fuelled automobiles rather than having to gee up a horse; and it isn't a matter of flying in aeroplanes, of having radio or television. What's important is the way people think. It's less obvious, but that's what counts. In the months after I sold my business, the world changed. Millions of men had gone off to war, the women had to take their place. It taught them a thing or two. That was the beginning of the twentieth century. Before 1914, I had terrible trouble trying to persuade women to plaster their faces with my creams. After 1919 they needed no persuading, or very little; they were crying out for emancipation. I sold out too soon . . .

'When I went into MacHill's, I knew more or less why I was there, but not how I was going to handle it, and even if I was going to do anything at all. That price of eighty dollars a share, for instance: I arrived at it by counting discreetly on my fingers while I told Dale that his tie was crooked – which wasn't actually true. I quickly divided twenty million dollars by the number of shares. Roughly, that came out at ninety. I knocked off ten per cent on principle, and ended up with eighty dollars. I felt very silly

when I came out with it. I didn't think I stood the remotest chance of being able to buy them at such a price . . .

'I didn't even think I would be able to buy them at all. You want to know the truth? I still thought I was going to sail on the Ile de France *that evening. So you see . . .*

'On the other hand, as far as that wretched son of a bitch Mr A. B. C. Dwyer was concerned, I'd had a little idea in mind for some time. I had been waiting to get my own back on him for twenty-eight years, four months, and thirteen days!'

'Dale, I'd like you to do me a favour . . .'

'Consider it done.'

He gave her a broad cheerful smile. *He's like some big, sweet-tempered dog waiting for you to throw him a stick to run after.*

'I would like you to find out everything you can about a certain Andrew Cole Barton Dwyer.'

'His initials are ABCD.'

'I had already noticed. I want to know if he's still alive, if he's still in business, what kind of business and with whom, whether he's married and to whom, how much he is worth and a breakdown of his wealth, and whether there are any skeletons in his cupboard.'

'And he is not to know that enquiries are being made about him . . .'

'He is not to know.'

'I'm not a policeman, Hannah.'

'I'm not asking you to do it yourself. Hire people to do it. Money is no object.'

'I'll need a starting point.'

'The most recent information I have about him dates back to June 1921. At that time he had just got married – I assume he divorced his first wife – and was living at Number 73 on Eighty-Eighth Street. He was running something called Crane Railway Consolidated. He was a member of the Railway Club – you ought to be able to find out their address – and he had a house in Maine, in a place called Wiscasset.'

'I've got that. Hannah? Does Maryan know about this . . . favour you're asking me?'

'He does. You can discuss it with him. But no one else.'

'That's good. I wouldn't like to keep anything about you a secret from Maryan. Is this A. B. C. Dwyer a friend of yours?'

'Not exactly.' She shook her head, amazed by the intensity of her hatred after all these years, and said again: 'No, not exactly.'

They had just emerged from the offices of MacHill, Drexel and Smith, and found Wall Street worse than when they had left it. The traffic was now at a complete standstill, a bluish haze was beginning to rise over the din of hooting and shouting. There were thousands of people spilling from the pavements on to the road, ranting and raving, reviling the banks and the moneymen. In front of the bronze doors of the Church of the Trinity, a very emaciated-looking man, in shirtsleeves, wearing a black waistcoat, was perched on a soapbox. Thrashing the air with his strong bony hands, his terrible black eyes sunk in their sockets, he was preaching in a thundering voice, proclaiming the end of Babylon-on-the-Hudson, and the imminent unleashing of God's anger on the satanic Golden Calf.

'Sweet Jesus,' sad Dale Fitzpatrick, 'the end of the world is going to seem pale in comparison . . . Forgive my swearing, Hannah.'

'It's dreadfully bad-mannered to swear,' she said.

Two ambulances went by, one after the other. They had to drive right up against the façades of the buildings. Hannah and Fitzpatrick heard a passer-by speak of seventeen suicides. At least three film crews, wearing their caps back to front, their peaks covering the back of their necks, had their cameras rolling.

'Look,' said Dale.

He pointed his finger and by tipping her head right back Hannah could see high up in the sky, perhaps thirty storeys above the ground, a man leaning out.

'He's going to jump!' shouted a woman.

At once the crowd moved back, obligingly forming a circle directly below, in order to give him all the room he needed to dash himself on to the pavement, while the workman busy repairing some part of the roof, more than three hundred feet above the ground, tapped his forehead with his index finger and carried on with his work.

It was about one o'clock when Fitzpatrick led her to the foot of the glass and steel skyscraper housing US Steel.

'We could go in here and get out the back way,' he suggested. 'We would stand more chance of finding a taxi.'

'OK.'

He laughed.

'After all, I'm a shareholder in this outfit, aren't I?'

They had not gone ten yards inside the building when Bernard Benda caught up with them. He had just that moment left the Stock Exchange, having seen Richard Whitney who, as everyone knew, or assumed, or hoped, was very closely connected with John Pierpont Morgan, the very incarnation of financial banking power (was he not said to have more or less direct control of seventy-five billion dollars?).

'Hannah, Whitney has just started buying. He paid fifty million for US Steel shares at $205 a share; he's also been buying Westinghouse, American Can, and General Electric. The effect on the market has been galvanizing. The fall in prices has stopped for the moment.'

'For the moment?' said Hannah, thinking, *These fools aren't going to stop halfway, are they?*

'If Morgan really is buying, it must mean that things aren't as black as they seemed, that's what everyone has started saying to themselves. Things have more or less quietened down.'

Newspaper vendors went past the front of the building, shouting out the printed headlines announcing the crash loud enough to burst their lungs.

'For the moment, Bernard?' Hannah said again.

'I personally believe that Morgan is buying because the share prices have reached as low as they'll get, and that now is the best time to increase his portfolio. To be perfectly honest with you, I thought of doing the same. Isn't that shameful?'

'For the moment?'

'For the moment, Hannah. For nearly two hours the floor was swept by a wind of madness. Those people were completely insane. I would never have thought it possible. Given the state of frenzy they were in today, the brokers would have been quite capable of selling Manhattan to the Indians for eighty dollars or less, if the Indians had wanted it.'

'But the fall has stopped for the moment?' Hannah insisted.

'It has. This is a real crash. Everything is going to collapse. We haven't seen anything yet. At least, that's my opinion . . .'

Other newspaper vendors went past, some of them waving single-sheet special editions, on which were printed, apart from a vague editorial describing the apocalypse, share prices that had been filed by reporters actually working on the floor (it was all the more remarkable that the figures published would turn out to be for the most part accurate, although published eight hours ahead of the official figures).

Hannah eventually found Hannah Incorporated.

The share price had fallen from $158.25 to $112.5.

For heaven's sake! Keep your fingers crossed, Hannah!

'You know, you really annoy me,' said Lizzie. 'You haven't changed a bit. How do you do it?'

'I eat carrots. How's Abie?'

'Wonderful. I think she'll be able to spend Christmas with you.'

'We can talk about that later. What about your children, and the grandchildren?'

Lizzie took a deep breath.

'James and his wife have just increased their score to four. They're still in Rio and haven't yet been eaten by cannibals. Doug is in Australia with his wife, Shirley – they were married in April last year and she's due to give birth in February or March. Colleen has just had her third daughter and is still living in Boston. Owie and Mattie had their first child in May. Mark got engaged the following month to a girl called Lisa Kinkaird, from Philadelphia, another banker's daughter – what with the crash, I'll never live it down. Kate is at university at the moment, and intends to go off to Italy on her own; Maryan is furious but as usual he's going to say yes and I'll be worried sick about my daughter's virginity. The twins, Patrick and Melanie, are in Europe and enjoying orgies of *foie gras*. Sandy wants to get engaged, but we think that at sixteen and a half she would be better off applying herself to her French and History lessons at college. Rod has just smashed up my brand-new Cadillac by driving it straight into the florist's. Jeremy and Marion are both in bed – Jeremy with mumps, and Marion with German measles. That's it. Latest report from the front. Are those your breasts sticking out like that or have you got them encased in aluminium?'

'I can undress if you like.'

'And they still haven't got droopy?'

'They were holding up all right this morning.'

'You make me sick. Where does that suit come from?'

'Schiaparelli.'

'If I wore that, with my behind and big boobs, I'd look like a Graf Zeppelin. Are you going to marry Dale Fitzpatrick?'

'Are you crazy? He's young enough to be my son.'

'He is not, he's forty-seven. You would have had to be extremely precocious to have a son that age. He's a widower. And you made a blunder taking him for Maryan's assistant; in fact they're partners in several businesses, don't ask me which. He isn't wildly rich, but he has one or two million dollars to his name. I saw you arrive together – he looked like a grizzly bear from the Rockies who had found a pot of honey and was carefully bringing it home, wondering how on earth he was going to get the damned lid off. He's in love with you. Yet another one. I wonder what all these men see in you?'

'Lizzie?'

Silence.

'Tell me more about Abigail,' said Hannah.

'I told you, she's doing fine.'

'Thank you for being so laconic.'

'You saw her in August when I brought her to Morcote, what more can I tell you? She's still as calm as ever; she's really no problem at all, that child. She's working hard at college, as ever. She hasn't grown much, she takes after you as far as height goes. We got a little worried about three weeks ago, she was going out with a young chap who seemed a little too clever by half. But she's stopped seeing him. She's got her head screwed on properly. And when she got back from . . .'

Lizzie broke off.

Hannah put down her tea-cup.

'Go on.'

'Oh all right! She went to stay with her brother in Montreal.'

'Which one?'

'Adam.'

'I didn't know he was in Canada,' said Hannah in a calm but lifeless voice.

'He builds apartments there. I don't really know much about what he does, you know.'

'Don't lie to me, Lizzie.'

'You really want me to tell you about him?'

Don't, Hannah, you'll be in a state over this for weeks!

'Yes,' said Hannah.

'He and his wife came and spent a few days with us in Los Angeles.'

'Was that the first time?'

'No.'

'It's no fun having to drag every word out of you, Lizzie.'

'All right. They came once before, two years ago. And Maryan has visited them several times in Montreal.'

'What about Adam's children?'

'He and Jacqueline have three children. They had a second son two years ago . . . Hannah, I don't know what to say to you!'

'Tell me about my son, that's all.'

'I don't know what you know about him.'

'It's quite simple, I don't know anything.'

Don't you dare start feeling sorry for yourself!

'Adam finished studying to be an architect, then spent a year in Europe. He came back three years ago. He got married to a French girl called Jacqueline while he was there and they already had little Marianne.'

'He was very young to get married and have children.'

'Jacqueline is very nice. Really she is. After returning to the States, Adam found a job with a Chicago firm. And for the past eighteen months he's been earning enough not to have any more need of . . . the money Maryan was giving him.'

'He never knew it had anything to do with me?'

'The money? I don't know. In any case, he never asked us any questions about it.'

But Jonathan did, thought Hannah, overcome with a familiar despair. *He must have done, just as surely as he must have refused any money from Maryan or Lizzie, in case it actually came from me . . .*

Hannah said, almost angrily: 'Tell me about Jonathan.'

'We haven't seen him for three years, ever since he went to Poland. He wrote to us last January. Just a few words to wish us a Happy New Year and to let us know that everything was all right. His letter was posted in Rome. We don't know where he is right now. Hannah, I warn you, I feel a bit like crying . . .'

'Blow your nose.'

At that point Maryan appeared, in the midst of the crowded Plaza restaurant that was buzzing with conversations about only one thing: what was happening on Wall Street. He looked from one woman to the other. He kissed Hannah on the cheek, and Lizzie on her fingers.

'Everything's falling apart,' he said.

'Are we going to be ruined, as all the rest of these crackpots around us pride themselves on being?'

'Not for the next two or three centuries.'

But the quiet depths of his blue eyes rested on Hannah: 'Are you still sailing to Europe tonight?'

'Lizzie, I sensed it from the moment I saw that the shares of Hannah Incorporated had fallen in two hours from $158.25 to $112.5 . . . but it was really then, when I was sitting with you and Maryan, that my decision became a conscious one . . .'

'No,' she said. 'I think I'm going to stay a while. I have the impression that I am beginning to like disasters.'

CHAPTER 27

May I Use Your Kitchen?

Two men, who were partners in the same company, asked at the reception desk of the Ritz Hotel for a room on the top floor. They gave a thousand-dollar tip to the lift attendant, then jumped into space, hand in hand.

Another victim of the crash doused himself in petrol and set fire to himself in the garage of his luxury estate in New Jersey. A few took a more traditional way out and put a bullet to their heads. '*Men are such fragile little things, Lizzie. As in fact is the male of any species. Women will be completely equal with men the day they become as stupid. I don't think it's something that's going to happen overnight.*'

Nineteen million shares changed hands within five hours, and fifty to sixty per cent of smaller speculators, all over the United States, were thought to have been ruined. It was estimated that between eight thousand million and ten thousand million dollars were lost in the upheaval. For the first time in one hundred and fifty years, the cleaners who arrived when the markets closed at three o'clock, had to leave without having put their brooms and mops to use. Nearly a thousand brokers and clerks, some of them on all fours, were desperately searching through a sea of paper eighteen inches deep in places, which was composed of selling orders and buying orders that had not yet been processed and wouldn't be until dawn on Friday. Not that all the orders were ever found: some documents torn, or stuck to the soles of shoes, or thrown away in error, would never turn up, and it would take months and an army of lawyers to restore a semblance of order.

The volume of transactions was fifty times greater than usual.

'And it's not over yet,' said Maryan. 'I share Bernard Benda's opinion, even if there are only a few of us who think the same: the fall is going to continue. Were you thinking of selling your shares, Hannah?'

'You told me it was best not to.'

'Don't. Under any circumstances. Not until the market returns to normal. And that won't be for months yet.'

'Never mind. So it's going to drop even further?'

'I'm afraid so. That's why you stayed, isn't it?'

'Yes.'

'Can I do anything to help?'

'I don't see how you could help. Thank you, but no. Dale told you what I asked him to do?'

'Yes. He's a good man, Hannah.'

'He said the same of you – are you promoting each other or something? Is the government going to intervene?'

He thought not. Under no circumstances, according to information he and Bernard Benda possessed – information that came directly from the White House. Neither President Hoover nor the Secretary of State for the Treasury, Andrew Mellon, was in favour of intervention; both of them were convinced – with the unshakeable self-confidence of those who have made their own considerable fortune or inherited several million – that everything would return to normal, and that there was no remedy but individual initiative and free enterprise. Besides, on Wall Street itself, the biggest brokerages remained imperturbably optimistic. As early as the morning of Friday 24 October, the day after Black Thursday, one of them had a display advertisement published in some one hundred newspapers all over the country, saying: 'We think the present conditions favour investment in . . .' Then followed a list of recommended shares. For their part,

Merrill Lynch and Co. urged people to buy with the statement that, 'Two of the biggest New York banks inform us that they have never received as many buying orders as they are receiving now.'

'These people are either mad, or they're bluffing in an attempt to restore calm. But perhaps I'm the one who is mistaken. Be careful, Hannah.'

She smiled at him, the wild gleam back in her eye after eight long years.

'Yes, yes, of course I will!'

On Friday 24th and Saturday 25th (Wall Street traded for two hours on Saturday mornings), she didn't leave the Plaza while the market was open.

The news that Bernard Benda reported to her was both good and bad.

It was good insofar as Wall Street seemed to have quietened down after the tremendous upheaval – but perhaps that was just the numbing effect of the shock – and bad as far as she personally was concerned: Hannah Incorporated had not only failed to drop any further, but they were trading at $114 at midday on Saturday, having regained one and a half points.

'It's not over yet,' said Bernard, echoing exactly the words Maryan had spoken twenty-four hours earlier.

Thereupon he burst out laughing.

'This is unbelievable. Here I am trying to console you by telling you that the biggest crash of the century has only just got started!'

Monday began quietly. Hundreds of thousands of investors, in response to the margin calls they had received, had settled their accounts by instructing their brokers to sell shares that had remained more or less unscathed to make the payments owing on shares that had fallen heavily. It wasn't realized straightaway what was going on. And when it did dawn on the brokers, who were still dazed by what had hit them four days earlier, they adopted the reasonable tactic of breaking up the parcels of shares that they were selling – and reducing their own commission – in order to avert another tidal wave.

A pathetic barrage, which burst one hour before the market closed.

In sixty minutes nearly four million shares were thrown to the bears. The Dow-Jones Index dropped by thirty-eight points.

But nevertheless the newspaper headlines the next morning, Tuesday 28th, read: 'Relative calm yesterday as selling continued . . .'

But as soon as the market opened on that same Tuesday morning, a million shares were sold in six minutes, three million in half an hour, eight million by midday, sixteen and a half million by the close.

Added to the seven and a half million sold through the annexe called the Curb, this brought the total number of shares traded to twenty-three and a half million.

The Dow-Jones Index fell to 200, having lost 125 points in seven weeks.

On Monday and Tuesday alone, losses totalled between fourteen and twenty-five thousand million dollars. Of the eighty thousand million that the Wall Street market represented a few days earlier (more than the combined budgets of every country in the world at that time), thirty-five thousand million had disappeared in the space of just one week.

The share price of Hannah Incorporated stood at $69.75. Vince MacHill came to see Hannah on Tuesday at about seven o'clock in the evening.

'I can't believe it's going to fall any lower, Mrs Newman.'

'Who has the majority holding?'

'Hiram Javitts himself.'

'Would he be prepared to sell any?'

'He has no choice; he is in a difficult situation. He's a man who has always taken risks, and he's heavily committed elsewhere. He's desperately in need of ready cash. Mrs Newman, if you wait any longer, you run the risk of seeing the share price rise, or of Javitts finding another buyer. It's now below seventy. And you yourself said you would buy at eighty.'

She hesitated. Two-thirds of 226,221, the majority she would need to run the company without actually having to defer to anyone, worked out at 150,814 shares. At $69.75 each the total cost would be $10,519,276.

She went over her calculations again and again: she had twenty-five million dollars at her disposal, or just a little under. But from this amount she would in fact have to deduct about thirteen million dollars, which represented her own share investments, and which she couldn't touch – if she did, as matters stood at the moment, she would only recover half of it, and that's if she were lucky . . .

'I'll wait,' she said.

But she did ask: 'How many shares is it possible to buy now?'

'Javitts' and Stahlman's for sure. As far as the rest goes, it's difficult to say: they're in many hands.'

'How many does Javitts have?'

'About 140,000.'

Javitts. She hadn't forgotten him either! He had been pretty contemptuous ten years ago in Lugano!

And two-thirds won't satisfy you, Hannah. You want the lot, every last share. If you pay Javitts $69.75 a share, you won't have much left to buy the rest.

Especially if you want to buy back the European and Australian companies as well. After all, that is what you have in mind to do, isn't it?

'I'll wait,' she repeated.

* * *

During the night of Tuesday 28th to Wednesday 29th, the legendary John Davison Rockefeller, the first of that name, father of Junior, broke his silence. At the age of ninety, he issued a statement on the national airwaves that was intentionally sensational: he announced that he and his family were going to buy two hundred thousand shares in the steel industry.

Because of this placatory initiative by the richest man in the world, and also because the bears of Wall Street needed time to catch their breath, trading on Wednesday was comparatively normal after the dreadful tornado of the previous day.

The market closed. For three days. All the troops were exhausted and it was hoped that this closure would restore people to their senses. It was a quite extraordinary measure.

The market opened again on Monday 4 November, but only for four hours. And so it continued for the rest of the week. 'It's like turning out the light and closing the curtains in a room where a man is having an attack of appendicitis,' Eddie Cantor commented sarcastically on the radio. 'It doesn't do him any good, but at least you can't see him.'

On Wednesday 13th the third tidal wave hit an already weak market head-on. Even the Rockefellers' Standard Oil collapsed, changing hands at fifty dollars. Virtually all shares had continued to fall even during those first two weeks of November when the market had just been ticking over.

This was true of Hannah Incorporated. '$39.75,' announced MacHill, who was paying his eleventh visit to the Plaza and had finally despaired of ever hearing Hannah say yes.

'Exactly how many shares?'

'138,640.'

That works out at . . . $5,510,940, plus expenses.

'I'll take them,' she said.

She was at the wheel of her Bugatti T41 Royal. It was a two-door coupé. A marvel, according to Gaffouil. She had had the steering wheel and driver's seat adapted to her size, otherwise she would have had to stretch to reach the steering wheel and would only just have been able to see the road over the dashboard.

On this dashboard Gaffouil had installed a petrol-level gauge, an oil-pressure gauge, and a rev counter – although the monstrous engine never went over 2,000 revs. There were only three gears, two plus an overdrive, but the second gear was good for five to seventy-five miles per hour. After Gaffouil had made the usual few adjustments, Hannah managed to clock up 124 miles an hour.

On the straight. This marvel did not like corners.

She drove into Charlotte, in the state of North Carolina, on 16 April 1930. Her daughter, Abigail, was at her side. They had been living together since Christmas and the New Year. It all came about very simply, very quietly. On Christmas Eve, Hannah had taken Abie to one side: 'Don't interrupt me, please. I have been the worst possible mother, I shan't give you any explanation, I shan't try and excuse myself. You may find this hard to believe, but I love you. More than even I realized. You have his eyes . . . Give me three months, it's not a lot, three short months. If after those three months you decide that I'm completely unbearable, you can leave. I shan't hold it against you, and I shall still be prepared to give you everything. I'm not very good at expressing my feelings. All I can say is that I love you.'

There was a heart-stoppingly long silence, while Abigail looked at her with Taddeuz's eyes, and a serene tranquillity that was rather surprising in a sixteen-year-old girl. Then she said, in French (and her choice of language was clearly deliberate): 'I should be able to get through my exams in June all right. Except in maths. Could you help me with my maths, mother?'

The Bugatti turned into a superb drive lined with oak trees that must have been at least one hundred years old. She stopped the car in front of a big white house with a colonnaded porch.

A black maid appeared.

'I have an appointment with Mrs Lettice Holme,' said Hannah.

With Abigail still at her side, she entered the house. They were shown into a drawing room where, in the midst of all the family portraits, was a framed letter from General Lee, expressing his sincere sorrow at the death of one Horatius Holme, killed at the battle of . . .

'Mrs Newman?'

The voice was that of a little old lady with very white hair, dressed in black and wearing a satin ribbon round her neck. Hannah introduced Abigail, who curtsied very satisfactorily.

'And why should I sell you these shares?'

'They have dropped considerably in value, with the crisis.'

'I checked after having read your charming letter: they used to be worth $160, or near enough; today they're worth no more than $34. At least that's what Harvey Whyte, my lawyer, told me.'

'He's right.'

'It's quite possible. He can count, more or less, although he's a lot older than I am. Don't tell him I told you, but his first name isn't Harvey; in fact his name is Polonius.'

'I shall carry the secret to my grave,' said Hannah.

'But I don't see that this fall is sufficient reason to sell. I remember Mr Holme, my late husband, always used to say that you should never sell shares when prices were dropping.'

Hannah gave her a smile.

'May I ask you a question?'

'Please do,' said the old lady very courteously.

'How do these 1,853 shares come to belong to you?'

'Because we bought them, I suppose.'

'You bought them yourself?'

'Oh no! I don't think I've ever bought so much as a bar of chocolate in my life. No, Mr Holme must have bought them.'

'Did he say why?'

The old lady thought a bit.

'Because I use the creams made by this company. Mr Holme was a very attentive husband. Would you believe, he once had a whole street in Paris painted pink, when we went back there on the twentieth anniversary of our honeymoon?'

'He must have been a very exceptional man,' said Hannah, thinking, *I've done it!*

She smiled at her daughter and said: 'My first name is Hannah, Mrs Holme. I myself created the company you're talking about. And before that, I created every one of those creams and toilet waters, every one of the lotions and perfumes that company distributes. It all began thirty-six years ago. I could tell you the whole story, if you would like to hear it. But first of all, I would like to show you something . . .'

She pointed to the black and turkey-red leather bag that the black maid had taken out of the boot of the Bugatti, at her request, and brought into the drawing room.

'I believe that the beautician you called must have recommended either the 183 or else the 211.'

'The creams have such pretty names.'

'For me, who created them, they are identified by numbers. May I use your kitchen?'

The old lady looked at the two creams, each spread on wooden spatulas.

'They both have the same perfume. And the same colour.'

'The composition is the same as well, I assure you. Unless the recent proprietors of the company have let things slide, which is a possibility. Mrs Holme, eleven years ago I sold the company I created for personal reasons. Today I would like to buy it back and restore to it the quality it has since lost. It's . . . it's as though it were a child of mine, from whom I was crazy enough to allow myself to be parted, and all the years I have yet to live will never suffice to prove to that child all the love I bear it. I am prepared to buy those 1,853 shares from you for $40 a share. I'll even go higher if necessary. For once in my life, I have no desire to count the cost.'

Silence.

Hannah felt Abigail's eyes upon her and her heart flipped, turning crazy somersaults: *You said it, Hannah, and it wasn't shares you were talking about – you couldn't care a hoot about them – any more than it's the company you want to get back. It wasn't easy, but you said it, and she understood all right what you were talking about* . . .

Eventually she looked round to meet her daughter's gaze, and held it.

'You are a very unusual woman,' said the old lady finally. 'Would you and your charming daughter care to have lunch with me? And if I'm not being too indiscreet, I would very much like to hear more of your story.'

Abigail smiled at Hannah.

'Abie?' asked Hannah.

The young girl nodded, with what might be mistaken for shyness, but which was in fact only her reserve.

'We'd love to,' said Hannah. 'It would be a pleasure, Mrs Holme, both for me and my daughter.'

By 10 May 1930, she had managed to acquire another 71,096 shares, in addition to the 138,640 she had bought from Javitts, making a total of 209,736.

This gave her an ample majority. However, she still had not relinquished the idea of gaining total possession, but she didn't have time to devote herself personally to this quest, and MacHill, Drexel and Smith didn't seem capable of this kind of activity.

She thought of Catherine Montblanc.

'All you have to do – it's child's play – is get hold of the 16,845 shares still missing. You approach the shareholders – quite a few of them are women – one by one, and you persuade them to sell their shares to you. It's so easy I'm wondering whether I should pay you for doing so little.'

Catherine was now a widow. Her oilman, the former Cut-throat in the trenches, had gone to join the victims of his knife. She had absolutely no need to work; with the money her husband had left her, she would not want for anything for a hundred years.

'But you're afraid I might get bored doing nothing.'

'Precisely,' said Hannah, with a laugh. 'Taking care of one's staff is the secret of any success.'

'One's staff, my eye! But you're right, as virtually always – I did say virtually. I am a bit bored. And where are all these shareholders?'

'Everywhere but in or near New York. I've already approached all the ones who live in this area . . . I've also approached all those who had one thousand shares or more. The rest are yours. There are about 956 of them . . . Here are their addresses – the list is in alphabetical order. You would be well advised to sort them out geographically, otherwise it will take you the next twenty-five years. You can offer them $39, not a cent more. You know what to say to them.'

'Vaguely,' said Catherine. 'You've only told me forty-three times. I'm beginning to get the idea.'

She examined the list and exclaimed: 'For heaven's sake! You expect me to go to Honolulu for just sixty-six shares?'

'What are you complaining about! Honolulu's a lovely place. While you're there, see if it's worth opening a salon.'

'You know that Jessie has been replaced as overall director of the salons?'

'Yes. By someone called Dennis LaSalle. Who paints his toenails pink. I've been told all about it.'

'Well, I'll be blowed, does he really paint his toenails pink?'

'Only on his left foot. And just the big toe. I got him to take his shoes off to see. I'm going to keep him on: women adore homosexuals – they're like cream cakes that don't make them get fat. As for Jessie, the silly fool had already retired to Scotland on grounds of her age. At forty-eight. I ask you! She'll be here the day after tomorrow.'

Silence.

'It really is Napoleon returning from Elba, isn't it?'

'Except that it's for a damn sight longer than one hundred days!'

'Jessie, you're going to do a complete tour for me: New York, Philadelphia, Baltimore, Washington, Atlanta, Miami, New Orleans, Saint Louis, Chicago, Detroit, Los Angeles, Toronto and Montreal. I want as full a report as possible on each salon, right down to the number of doorknobs.'

'How much time do I have?'

'From now until 25 August. We'll meet again on that date, at seven fifteen in the morning. I would also like you to compile a list of other cities, maybe eight or ten, where we might open up. You ought to take Mary Lindsay with you, she has just lost her husband and the trip would do her good. And that young girl as well . . . the German one, Alicia Testerman. She's no use at all as a beautician but she remembers everything. I don't have to impose anyone on you, though. If you can think of anyone better . . .'

'I'm the one who hired Alicia.'

'Another thing: I asked for a report on the company's products. I'll be getting it in July, along with a comparative study of what we are selling and what our competitors are selling. Practically nothing new has been developed in my absence. That is going to change . . . I'm going to shake up those chemists and start working with them. I've bought another laboratory. On your travels, ask women what they think about the products and announce the arrival of a great wave of new products. They won't be disappointed, believe me.'

'I shall tell them that Hannah has returned. That's all I'll need to say.'

The Scotswoman's eyes were filled with tears.

'Oh Hannah, thank you for having asked me back . . .'

In June 1921, just before withdrawing to Morcote, she had sold or, to be more precise, had arranged for the sale of the house on Long Island and the apartment on Fifth Avenue.

She found another apartment, also on Fifth: the top two floors of an eight-storey building with a roof terrace, and total floor space of 1,480 square yards.

She was about to sign the deeds when the lawyers, with considerable embarrassment, had to explain that the sale could not go through: the owner had succumbed to pressure from the other occupants, who did not wish to live in the same building as a Jewess.

She bought the whole building.

And gave it a name: Jerusalem Building. With a cross of David over her front door.

Her intention was to turn the roof into a garden.

But for the time being, working sixteen hours a day, she hardly had time to spend on furnishing and decorating the apartment. The laboratory she had bought was located only a few hundred yards from the other one, in New Rochelle. Within a few weeks she had managed to get together a team of ten experienced chemists (she poached them from Dupont de Nemours) headed by a Czech émigré, Ladislas Storer, who had been strongly recommended to her by Juliette Mann (Juliette was still working at the laboratory in London – Hannah had not dared ask her to come to the States; until she had regained possession of her former European empire she would not allow herself to headhunt staff).

Storer was a big strapping fellow, quite handsome, with a gypsy look about him; it was easier to imagine him looking after horses than test-tubes. He was thirty-three or so, and had done all his studies in Germany. Dermatology was his specialism, and he loved doing research. Not without some reluctance, Hannah had to admit that she was outclassed. On the other hand, Storer told her that he could develop any cream she cared to imagine. And he was to keep his word. All the many years that followed, she would bless Juliette for having sent her such a treasure. Storer, together with Paul Travers, who was to join them a year later, was largely responsible for completely updating the whole range of HH products.

She had reassembled her former senior management, with Joshua Wynn as overall supervisor, but she had strengthened it by adding some new faces, two of them men; one was Dennis LaSalle of the pink toenail who had replaced Jessie.

Everyone called him LaSalle Darling. Including the

clients, who adored him, and liked nothing better than to summon him while they lay naked, being massaged. He came from New Orleans, where, if his story were to be believed, his ancestors arrived before the plans for the *Mayflower* had even been drawn. He must have been close on forty, even though he swore to having recently celebrated his twenty-eighth birthday. He had a rather disturbingly androgynous beauty and a rare elegance. But he never forgot a face, nor the name that went with it, and even less the husband's bank account. With clients, he could gauge to perfection how far to go in spicing politeness with insolence.

And there was no denying he knew more about cosmetics than any beautician.

'Where did you learn it all?'

'I shall tell you this evening, my dear, if you invite me to dinner.'

Hannah invited him (to eat in the kitchen; she didn't have time to prepare anything grander) and he turned up dressed as a woman – and a very convincing woman too – in a pretty Madeleine Vionnet dress, with a squirrel-fur stole and plunging neckline. He explained that the clothes belonged to him, that he had some two or three dozen dresses, and that he had attended the courses at the beauticians' school run by Catherine Montblanc.

'I enrolled under the name of Denise Coquelet, which was my poor late mother's name, and for six months not one of the ladies there noticed a thing. They just thought I was a bit tall. I even graduated top of the class in 1918, you can check that, *ma très chère*.'

He actually addressed Hannah as *ma très chère*, speaking French with a very strong Cajun accent. He reminded her a lot of Henry-Beatrice, the English designer, who was now dead; the poor thing had committed suicide after the death of the great love of his life, a handsome lieutenant in the Coldstream Guards, who was killed leading his men on to the battlefields of France.

'Dennis' – *You can't very well call him darling . . . but then why not?* – 'Dennis, I'm going to replace you with Jessie. Please, don't sulk. She is without equal as an administrator, and you have other talents. I'm offering you two options: you can either be responsible for everything concerning the way clients are received, the training of staff in that respect, and for increasing the clientele, in which case you would be directly answerable to Joshua; or you can work for me, as . . . let's say, minister of foreign affairs. It would mean a lot of travel, I warn you . . .'

To Hannah's surprise – she thought him incapable of leaving all his admirers – he chose the second job, and she discovered that the fellow had ambition! For the first few weeks, she worried a bit, afraid that she had allowed herself to get carried away, if only because of her friendship with Henry-Beatrice. *You like cream cakes that don't make you get fat, too. Even though you've never had any problems with your weight . . .*

But no. It was not long before she realized that he was in many respects much like herself, in particular when it came to sensing what clients wanted, before they even knew they wanted it. He never failed: the turnover of a salon or a shop had only to take a downturn and he was off; he would go there and give his diagnosis and in practically every case would turn out to be correct.

Very often, for pleasure or because he had a real need of it, he would dress as a woman, which led to police raids.

She ended up calling him Mata-Hari. He replaced the Furets, who were no longer with her – but he had even greater qualities; he was at the same time capable of giving an intelligent opinion on a new cream, of soothing an important client who, rightly or wrongly, thought she had cause to complain, and also of organizing any event that seemed to them both likely to promote the chain of establishments and recruit new clients.

In a word, he perfectly complemented the unseen and thankless work of someone like Wynn, who dealt mostly wth administrative and legal problems.

But all this happened over a period of months, if not years. The time of triumph had not yet arrived, it was simply a question of surviving a difficult period. The whole of America was now in the grip of the Depression, which the crash of October '29 had so spectacularly heralded. An entire section of the new clientele acquired in the '20s seemed to have vanished. *You sold too early eleven years ago, and now you've managed to buy the company back again just when everything is collapsing. You're really in a league of your own as a businesswoman! It's true that but for the Depression you would never have been able to buy it back, or else it would have taken you ten years . . .*

She postponed her plans for expansion, circumstances being so unfavourable.

But she was ready at last to close the file on Mr A. B. C. Dwyer . . .

CHAPTER 28

Now I Know How a Pig Feels in Front of a Delicatessen

In March of that same year, 1930, Dale Fitzpatrick reported back to her his extensive findings:

'Hannah, if he's a friend of yours, now is the time to go and comfort him. If he's your enemy, you can open the champagne.'

'Is he really so badly off?'

'Couldn't be worse.'

It appeared that Mr ABCD had not had much luck. The way things had turned out it was as though fate had willed that the most prosperous period of his life should coincide with his meeting with Hannah. The first high point of his career was the three years following the battle over Carrington-Fox.

'It was bound to be,' said Hannah, gritting her teeth. 'He made a fortune thanks to me, the bastard!'

Fitzpatrick, who had not the least idea of what might have passed between Hannah and Dwyer, gazed at her searchingly.

'Go on, Dale,' she said.

'He bought two companies, one after the other, one that manufactured railway carriages, the other specializing in railway equipment.'

'He didn't have enough money for that.'

'He didn't. He borrowed money from the banks, and things were more or less OK for three years. He's a bluffer, very smart, a little too smart, the kind of man . . .'

'Or woman. Don't be misogynistic, please.'

'The kind of human being who thinks that things will always work out for them and that the world is populated with fools who are there entirely for their benefit. Eventually, after many ups and downs, he went under, despite his trickery. One of the companies, for instance, was in his wife's name . . .'

'Is that important?'

'How the hell should I know? Forgive me for swearing, Hannah. I don't know. I don't know what it is you're looking for.'

'Right. Tell me about his wife. We must have a lot in common, she and I.'

She could picture herself reading Sade – *it would have to be Sade!* – stretched out like an odalisque, with hardly anything on, if truth be told, just enough to conceal the keenest of razors . . . and not very sure of what she would do with it when Mr ABCD came in: lie back and close her eyes, or cut off his . . . let's say, nose. *And keep it as a souvenir? Like hell!*

She met Fitzpatrick's appalled gaze and said:

'You needn't look so horrified, Dale; I was never his mistress – that is the idea that has just occurred to you, I know.'

'I swear to you . . .'

'That's all right, I forgive you for swearing. Go on.'

'Dwyer managed to salvage enough money from the collapse of the two companies to buy a small bank.'

'What an eclectic bastard!'

'If you keep interrupting me . . .'

'OK. I won't say any more.'

'Then he got divorced, having taken the money that had been in his wife's name, naturally. He was remarried in 1911, to the daughter of a Baltimore industrialist. A year later his father-in-law died . . . No, no, there's no reason to believe that our man had anything to do with his death. But it certainly suited him: he found himself chairman of the steel company, which went bankrupt shortly afterwards.'

'But not Dwyer? I forgot: I'll keep quiet.'

'Not Dwyer, who disappeared for two years. We eventually picked up his trail in Seattle. He had married for the third time and his third wife was still unaware of the two who had preceded her. But she met the same fate as the others; she ended up penniless after five years of marriage. Her families' footstuffs factories had passed into different hands . . .'

'The hands of A. B. C. Dwyer under a different name.'

'Exactly. Until he sold them. It seems that Dwyer isn't really a swindler. Whatever the nature of the business that he acquires by marriage, he always does his best to run it properly, but he wants things to happen too quickly and aims too high; he can't wait. With the result that the business gets into difficulties and instead of sticking with it, or trying to salvage something, he prefers to run out on it, taking everything he can. And he does it very cleverly, thanks to a whole battery of front companies.'

She raised her finger to speak, the way schoolchildren do – although she had never been to school:

'Is anyone after him?'

'The FBI opened a file on him in about 1912, in response to charges brought against him by his victims in Baltimore, but the case was closed when a senator intervened and the charges were dropped. The children played a part in that, as was his intention.'

'The children? What children?'

'I'm afraid I haven't had time to mention them so far. There are nineteen children.'

She was flabbergasted.

'You must be joking, Dale.'

'Six by his first wife. Three by the second. Four by his third. Four by the fourth. Two by the fifth. But he still lives with the fifth, so he may yet improve his score there. According to my chief investigator, Dwyer has children for the same reasons other people take out insurance policies: if his current wife, or her family, start giving him trouble, the fact that he is the father of her brood affords him some protection. At worst, thanks to his charm, he is regarded as having been inept or ill inspired, or unlucky in business, but not dishonest. They can't believe that he could have tried to ruin his children. Of course, they never know that he has other families elsewhere.'

'Nineteen children! Heavens alive!' said Hannah. 'You mentioned two other marriages . . .'

'Which are no more legitimate than the one in Seattle, since he never divorced his wife in Baltimore. In 1920 he married a rich Toronto heiress, in Canada.'

'Whom he also left penniless, right?'

'Right. And five years ago he married – dare I say it – a widow from Chicago. Which explains how he comes to be the majority shareholder of a brokerage dealing on the Chicago Mercantile Exchange, the second largest exchange in the world for primary products.'

'But you told me he was in desperate straits, you said so at the beginning.'

'Desperate for anyone else but him, certainly. Hannah, he must have made twenty or twenty-five million dollars in his life. He has lost it all – and the only explanation for his having made such a mess of things is his incredible self-confidence, even arrogance: he takes everyone else for fools. I have details of all the bad speculations he has made: there are more than six dozen. If he had devoted one-tenth of his intelligence and imagination to a single one of the businesses he was involved in, he couldn't have failed to make a fortune.'

Silence.

Hannah was walking on the roof terrace of her apartment on Fifth Avenue.

'In what way is his present situation desperate? You still haven't answered my question.'

'In Chicago he speculated with his clients' money. The

crash and the Depression hit him like the wrath of God. He may not be the only one in such circumstances, but he seems to have exhausted his possibilities.'

'Dale, that man has offended me, I've had a score to settle with him for years. I want to corner him and get him into a trap he can't escape from, however smart he might be. In all that information you gathered, is there anything I could use as a lever against him?'

'To send him to prison?'

'I am neither the police, nor a judge. I just want his hide. Figuratively speaking. And I'll get it. Do you have any suggestions?'

He thought he did. He was even sure of it.

All this happened in March. Two months later she was in Chicago, calling herself Sarah H. Kirby, an Australian widow, with a very tidy fortune of some ten million dollars to her name, plus another twelve or thirteen million temporarily (on account of the American Depression) tied up in stock.

On 24 May she was taking high tea, chatting with her companion, a buxom Frenchwoman of fifty plus, answering to the name of Adelaide Mounicot ('Why Adelaide, for heaven's sake?' asked Hannah. 'You're changing your name, why shouldn't I? In any case, I've always wanted to be called Adelaide,' replied Yvonne).

'Mrs Kirby? Mrs Sarah Kirby?'

There he was, looking very elegant, his boater held in his hand, his hair fashionably plastered down with hair cream. With an engaging look in his eye, and that charming smile of his, he didn't look at all his age (he was fifty-seven and looked at least fifteen years younger).

'I'm Andrew Dwyer,' he said in his wonderfully deep melodious voice. 'I'm the senior partner in the firm you honoured with your visit three days ago, in order to discuss your little problems of investment. I was unfortunately absent, and so did not have the pleasure of seeing you. But by a miraculous stroke of luck, I happened to catch your name just now, when you were talking to the *maître d'hôtel*.'

Three-quarters of an hour later, having sat down at their table and first had them in gales of laughter with his anecdotes about the Mercantile Exchange, and then moved to tears when he told them the appalling tragedy that had almost wrecked his life (his poor wife and their four little children had perished in the sinking of the *Titanic*), he invited them to dine with him.

'Not here. To be honest, I'm surprised to find you at the Hotel Lexington. Did you not know that it serves as Al Capone's headquarters?'

Sarah Kirby then confessed that Mr Capone's fame had not yet reached Sydney or Brisbane, where she lived.

And at that point who should walk in but Al Capone himself? He crossed the lobby, flanked by four or five genuinely terrifying characters. At least, Sarah Kirby was terrified; her big grey eyes widened in the most touching manner . . .

'How fortunate that you should be with us, Mr Dwyer . . .'

'I'm beginning to hate Chicago,' said Dwyer. 'How can I continue to live in a town that frightens a pretty woman so? And where you might meet any Tom, Dick or Harry?'

'It's fortunate that you should be with us, Mr Dwyer,' Yvonne said again. 'Mrs Sarah and I were so alone . . .'

The next day they lunched together. Then in the evening they went to a concert in the Orchestra Hall. The day after that, and those that followed, he took them to see the Art Institute and the Natural History Museum, and the two million pieces of furniture in the Merchandise Mart, and the Water Tower on Michigan Avenue, and the new *Chicago Tribune* tower.

And he took them on a cruise on Lake Michigan . . . ('Hannah, the yacht he claims to own actually belongs to one of his biggest clients, to whom he owes a good half-million dollars . . . Hannah, our man's situation is getting more critical every day. He's got his back to the wall.')

'A little boat I bought three years ago,' said Dwyer. 'But I'm not going to keep it. I'm planning to get rid of it – I may give it to some youth organization – just as I got rid of my private mansion on Woodlawn Avenue. Too soon, alas, since I can't even invite you to my house. What a pity! But you know what a poor bachelor is like. And there's another reason: I've tried as hard as I can, but the burden of my memories is more than I can bear, my dear lost ones haunt me in this place where I was happy with them . . . No, I must go away, and leave this town where I have known such grief. I don't know where to go. To Europe perhaps, or South America. What can I expect of life? Money? Yet more money? Is that all? I'm already rich, what use is money to me?'

Sarah Kirby cried her eyes out, deeply distressed. (She had finally got rid of her chaperone, Adelaide Mounicot, by dispatching her to New York, supposedly to finish packing their trunks. Yvonne had turned green with rage at being summarily dismissed from the front line.)

She wept and, overcome by the violence of her emotions, allowed him to steal a kiss from her.

'My God, what are you doing, Andrew? Have you gone crazy?'

He said that this was indeed the case. That he was crazy about her and her big eyes, her marvellously neat body, her little mouth with its slightly rectangular lower lip, and her hands . . .

(*I know now how a pig feels in front of a delicatessen*, thought Hannah.)

. . . and her hands were so deliciously tiny, and her delightful Australian accent.

He kissed her a second time.

And the bastard knows what he's doing! Don't try and kid yourself, Hannah: you were expecting this to happen when you sent Yvonne away. You were expecting it and looking forward to it, you might as well admit it. Ever since I've known you, you've always liked men. And after nearly thirty years, this one still has the same effect on you . . . At your age! You really are wicked. When a woman is as old as you are, she does needlepoint. But what is the monster getting up to now, rummaging under my skirts? Holy mackerel! It's not unpleasant either!

'Have some respect for me, Andrew,' she said in a dying voice. 'Have some respect for me, I beg you . . .'

His hand was still against her thigh (the very top of her thigh): *He's doing as he's told, the fool!*

He withdrew his hand.

'I love you, Sarah. I've struggled for eighteen years. But I can't go on . . .'

What's he on about? Eighteen years? Ah yes, the wreck of the Titanic, *when he supposedly lost his wife and four children! What a liar! What a pair of liars we are!*

'But I can't go on, Sarah. Seeing you here, in my arms, with your eyes looking at me beneath your half-closed eyelids, and seeing your little nose and your breast rising, I went crazy. Forgive me, say that you forgive me . . .'

Now he's going too far! Although it was no fluke that he married those five silly fools. He really does have considerable charm . . .

'You can't be more than thirty-five,' he went on. 'You don't even look that. I'm forty-six. These things don't mean very much to me, but my financial situation . . . What I mean is that I have more than enough to be able to offer you a life worthy of you. Even if you were poor . . .'

She closed her eyes. *Now is not the time to laugh, you idiot!*

Then she opened them again and found that he was closer to her than he had been a moment before. In fact their faces were almost touching. *My word, he's like a cloud when he moves. I didn't even hear him!*

She pressed down on her buttocks – he had slipped his arm beneath them – so that he should fully appreciate the roundness and firmness of them, and note the delicious curve in her back . . . And she kissed him – with all the shyness and confusion that circumstances required.

But even so, darting out her tongue to prove that she was no innocent, and in promise of the pleasures she would give him the day when . . .

'That's in celebration of our engagement, my darling. And to give you the courage to wait until we're married.'

'He's made his move,' said Dale Fitzpatrick in a pretty morose tone of voice, the following 1 July.

Four days earlier Hannah had received a telegram from Australia telling her that enquiries had been made in Sydney and Brisbane about a Mrs Sarah Helena Kirby. The information acquired by Mr A. B. C. Dwyer, via an intermediary, must have been like a river of honey to a grizzly bear: Mrs Sarah Helena Kirby actually existed, she was actually a millionairess, and actually widowed. She was sixty-one and presently travelling overseas. She was also the niece of Clayton Pike, the great Australian multi-millionaire, who – until his death; he had been dead for years – happened to be (though no one told Dwyer's emissary) a personal friend of Hannah.

Hannah was quite happy with the way things were going: she had foreseen that Dwyer might check her credentials and chosen her pseudonym with that in mind. *It was a good thing you did, he's a smart one. Although it's a bit annoying that he should think you're sixty-one . . .*

Dale Fitzpatrick was undoubtedly sulking on that first

day of July, though he made a great effort not to appear to be. Obviously, the way the Dwyer affair was developing did not suit him at all. *It wouldn't surprise me if he were jealous. Poor Dale . . .*

Hannah was busy studying the plans for the new laboratory with Jessie, Dennis LaSalle and Joshua Wynn. Storer had eventually convinced her that the building she had initially intended to use would not be big enough. The decision had been taken to enlarge it, as soon as the profits from the beauty parlours could finance the work, which was not the case at the moment. *You're not losing money, but only just.* The Great Depression was taking its toll, thousands of businesses were closing and beauty-care products were not among the basic necessities. Hannah ought certainly to have closed some of her establishments already. She hadn't and she wasn't going to. Because it would give Javitts too much pleasure if she did, and because it would only put in an impossible situation all those employees who were counting on her now more than ever for their survival.

'Jessie and Dennis, leave me now, please. You too, Joe.'

The door closed on the three of them.

'Yes, Dale.'

'He's made his move. He's packed up and left Chicago. This very afternoon he withdrew everything from the three bank accounts at the First National – his own, his office's and his wife's. He had power of attorney over his wife's. You women are really crazy.'

After a moment he said: 'I'm sorry, Hannah.'

'In that area, as in every other, you men surpass us. How much does he have?'

'One million two hundred thousand dollars. As you predicted, he arrived at the bank barely quarter of an hour before the counters closed. He said that he was going to San Francisco to conclude a big business deal for which he needed the cash. He had a letter from his partner. A forgery . . . I told you he had his back to the wall. Today is Friday and Monday is a public holiday, so he has four days before anyone starts asking questions. And his partner is on holiday in Florida.'

'Has he bought anything?'

'My investigators haven't let him out of their sight for a moment. According to them, he didn't realize he was being followed. He bought a very handsome gold and diamond bracelet for eighty thousand dollars.'

'The exact price, Dale.'

'$83,678.43, including tax. He went to a florist and ordered two hundred and one red roses to be delivered to Mrs Sarah Kirby at the Hotel Netherland here in New York, and then he spent twelve thousand dollars on tropical clothes for himself, toiletries and suitcases. Shortly before eight, he telephoned the shipping line to make sure that you had kept your promise and that first-class cabins had been booked for Mrs Sarah Kirby, Miss Adelaide Mounicot and himself on the steamer sailing for Sydney on Sunday, the day after tomorrow. In the meantime the information on Australia that he had asked for was delivered to his room. Hannah, may I say something?'

'No, Dale. Please, don't.'

Silence.

'The day after tomorrow, at the very latest, it will all be over,' said Hannah.

On Saturday 2nd, a little before nine in the morning, Lizzie's eldest daughter, Colleen, called at the apartment on Fifth Avenue with her husband, Norman Lincoln, and their three children. They were taking Abigail away with them for the weekend, to Great Kills on Staten Island. The Lincolns had a very pretty place by the sea there, and a yacht. And most important, one of Norman's younger brothers, Craig, would be there; he was two years older than Abigail and in her eyes was as seductive as John Gilbert when he held Greta Garbo in his arms (with Abigail playing Greta Garbo's part, of course).

'Craig is really extraordinary, mother.'

'That's exactly the impression he had on me, my dear,' replied Hannah, although she hadn't the least idea what Craig looked like.

Then Yvonne left, fussing impatiently: 'Try not to be late . . .'

'I'm never late and you know it. Why did you get them to put "Miss" on your boat ticket?'

'I've always dreamed of being a virgin.'

The servants went too – she told them they were on holiday until Monday evening.

Left on her own, she went over the figures once more. They gave no cause for rejoicing: several salons were operating at a loss, and profits from the others were hardly sufficient to cover the deficit.

'For heaven's sake, I only asked the Saints of Wall Street for a little shower and the fools sent a downpour!'

The phone rang at about eleven fifty. It was Yvonne.

'I simply want to make sure you haven't forgotten. In thirty-nine minutes thirty-five seconds you're going to be late.'

'Go jump in the lake.'

She was just getting out of the bath when the telephone rang again.

Fitzpatrick was on the line.

'He arrived from Chicago this morning on the nine o'clock train. He travelled under the name of George Barrett of New York City. He has a lot of luggage, but he kept with him – in his sleeping compartment and in the taxi – a fawn-coloured leather suitcase, the one in which he put the twelve hundred thousand dollars yesterday. The taxi drove him to the docks, where he once more checked the cabin reservations for tomorrow morning and entrusted nearly all his baggage to the shipping company; he kept only two cases, including the fawn-coloured leather one, and arrived with them at the Netherland half an hour ago. As predicted, he asked at the reception desk whether there was a Mrs Kirby staying at the hotel, and when told there was, he asked to speak to her on the phone, but the French lady's companion answered, and told him that Mrs Kirby was still asleep. He is now in his own room. Hannah?'

'I have to go now, Dale, I'm sorry,' she said quickly, in order to cut short the comments that Fitzpatrick was preparing to make.

The Hotel Netherland was only three blocks away from her apartment. Normally, she would have walked, but not wanting to take any chances, she had Gaffouil drive her there in a very nondescript Chevrolet. He dropped her outside the staff entrance on Fifty-Ninth Street, rather than at the front entrance on Fifth Avenue. There was a bellboy waiting for her inside who, without a word, led her to the suite reserved in the name of Sarah H. Kirby.

She entered the rooms a few seconds before twelve thirty, punctual as ever.

'Your bath is ready,' announced Yvonne, full of mirth.

'When you laugh as stupidly as you're laughing now, you look like a horse with toothache.'

She undressed and actually got into the bath made bubbly by salts she herself had made up: a combination of wild camomile, St John's wort, cucumber, and a dash of erythraea to give the mixture body.

She heard Yvonne on the telephone in one of the suite's two drawing rooms.

The Frenchwoman returned.

'He'll be here in three or four minutes, at most.'

'Did you tell Dale Fitzpatrick?'

'Of course, what do you take me for?'

Hannah was immersed in the bathtub, with only her head above the water, to keep her hair dry. The rise of her creamy-white breasts could be discerned just below the blue-green surface: *It's true they stay up all by themselves – what fantastic good luck to have a body that's hard and firm. If you weren't so old inside your head, you could almost believe you were still thirty . . .*

'It's just that I'm not really decent. In fact I'm not at all decent,' she said.

'We're engaged, my love.'

She counted slowly to five, which seemed quite long enough a pause to convey her modesty. (She even tried to blush, but just couldn't manage it; if she had wanted to turn herself into a Chinawoman she couldn't have found it more difficult.) Finally she told him he could come into the bathroom.

He came in.

'What have you talked me into!' she said simpering. 'I must be crazy about you . . .'

He came in and leaned against the door-frame, the way men do, with both hands behind his back. He stared at her, a little disconcerted, and in fact taken by surprise; for a few seconds he betrayed himself by the sharp gleam that came into his eyes when he saw that she was naked and still in her bath.

Hannah thought: *I want him to desire me, really desire me. I don't want him simply to feel that by marrying Sarah Kirby of Brisbane, Australia, he is marrying twenty or twenty-five million dollars, which will all become his. It's absolutely imperative that he should think of me as a woman . . . Oh, of course I don't expect him to be in love with me, there's no point in expecting the impossible. And as I can't really hope to set any passions alight with a face like mine, at least my body can be of some use to me, since it's not too decrepit.*

She stared at him too, delighted not to meet his gaze: there was no question, he was actually ogling her breasts. *It's working,* she thought, *he was expecting to find a wizened and wrinkled little old lady, a bit past it in fact, and now he finds that getting into bed with me might not be such a bad way of spending time. And that's not all, my friend, Hannah has plenty more surprises in store for you yet, you'll see . . .*

'Sarah?'

'Yes, Andrew, my dear?'

A strange expression passed across Dwyer's face. And again it occurred to her that if he was putting on an act, he deserved one of those Oscars they had just started to award in Hollywood.

'Sarah,' he said, 'I won't touch you, I give you my word. But when you get out of the water, don't ask me to leave the room or to turn round.'

Silence.

Damn it, why can't you blush? This would certainly be the ideal moment for it!

But since she couldn't, she contented herself with closing her eyes and then opening them very wide; the steam in the room made them clearer than ever. It was guaranteed to produce the right effect.

'No other man but my dear departed Mortimer has ever seen me naked,' she said eventually.

'I shan't touch you.'

She counted to five again, and with no great surprise noted that her own body was starting to send out the usual signals (not as usual as all that, she had been dead to the world from that point of view for the past nine years!). Ah well, so much the better! She wouldn't have to pretend. She stood up and stepped out of the water.

Slowly. Now fixing her grey eyes on him; now chastely lowering her gaze – which made her bow her head to just the right angle – very conscious of the effect produced by this movement, which gracefully emphasized the line of her neck and shoulders, and the narrowness of her waist, and the curve of her back, and the fullness of her rump.

She wiped herself with one towel, unhurriedly, rubbing her hardened nipples a little more than strictly necessary, so that every time the towel passed over them they quivered. Then she wrapped herself in another bathtowel – it was turkey red, the shade that most suited her complexion and the colour of her eyes, not to mention the pleasing contrast that the dark fabric made with the milky whiteness of her ivory skin.

'I'm ashamed, Andrew,' she had the unbelievable nerve to say.

He did not reply and, after the final furtive glance that she threw in his direction from behind the screen of her loosened hair, she realized why: he was dumbfounded. *He wasn't expecting this, that's obvious. Not in a woman of your age, and even less so in a woman of Sarah Kirby's age. You've found your mark, all right. He desires you, he really does, and the twenty-five million dollars have nothing to do with it* . . .

Yvonne's footsteps could be heard outside the bathroom.

'Quickly, get out,' she whispered. 'I don't want Adelaide to know how far you have driven me to distraction . . .'

They lunched in her suite, in the company of Adelaide Mounicot herself, who did not leave them alone for one second – Yvonne took great pleasure in carrying out these orders – and bored them to death with her account of her quarrels with the nuns at her boarding school, at Lourdes in France, in the days – almost ancient now – of her adolescence.

This was a deliberate ploy intended to deflect any

emotional demonstration, given the likelihood that, stimulated by the scene in the bath and by the communicative warmth of their banquet, Mr ABCD might show too much initiative.

As he obviously would like to. If you were alone with him, he would have pounced on you by now! And the worst of it is that you would probably have let him have his way with you . . . Well, maybe. You shall never know. And you would prefer not to. But there's no denying he's attractive, the bastard . . .

After lunch they played gin rummy. Hannah lost $7.91. Although she was used to losing – she was hopeless at any card game – she did not have to make much of an effort to appear disgruntled.

'I hate losing. And Adelaide was cheating, I'm sure of it!'

ABCD consoled her.

It was now four o'clock in the afternoon, on Saturday 2 July, only nineteen hours before they were due to board ship.

Now was the moment.

'Leave us, Adelaide.'

The door had no sooner closed behind the Frenchwoman than Sarah Kirby adopted a solemn manner and sat in an armchair where she could at least be sure that Andrew Dwyer would not try to take her by force.

'I need to talk to you, darling. It's a serious matter.'

And he must understand, she begged him to understand – she knew better than anyone else in the world that he was not a fortune-hunter, still less one of those vile adventurers who take advantage of the credulity of poor defenceless and lonely widows; she would sooner die than believe for one second such awful things of him . . .

But . . .

'But I have friends and family at home, in Brisbane and Sydney especially, as well as in Melbourne, where my dear Mortimer and also my uncle Clayton Pike bought up a few streets.'

And they were bound to ask questions about this second marriage of hers. After all, she was the richest widow in the southern hemisphere, with the exception of Glynis Caledon-Jones, although . . . *That old trout is three and a half years older than you are. She may have three or four hundred miserable pounds more than you do, but she has bad breath. Where were you now? Oh yes!*

'But I'm digressing, my dearest Andrew. It's because I'm a little embarrassed, a little ashamed. But Clarence Campbell was so insistent . . . Now, let me explain: Clarence Campbell – he's my lawyer and I trust him – thinks that it would be better for all concerned if, before we board ship, we . . . how can I put it, I don't remember exactly what his words were . . . we put down on paper what each of us owns, what we will be bringing to the marriage . . . My God, darling, I'm expressing myself so badly, can you understand what I'm saying?'

'I think so,' said Dwyer.

And Sarah-Hannah, without herself giving anything away, noticed the sudden clenching of his hands. *He's on his guard*, she thought. *He knew from the moment I spoke what was coming. I was right to be so careful: he's no fool . . .*

Dwyer stood up and started pacing the room. He looked impassive, but his lips were tightly pursed, and she noticed an expression of complete devastation come into his eyes. *He's certainly not at all happy, he's enraged even. With only a little under twenty hours to go before getting away from America where he's beginning to be a little too well known, and three days before people discover that he has vanished from Chicago after raiding the coffers, this little upset is going to unnerve him . . . But he'll keep calm. He has no choice.*

He recovered himself. Shook his head and said: 'Today's Saturday, Sarah. The banks are closed now.'

'It's true, I should have spoken to you sooner about this, my darling. I should have written to you. But as you know, I spent the last few weeks in Europe, with my dear departed Mortimer's family in the wilds of Scotland, where they didn't even have a telephone – can you believe it? – and the days just went by . . . My dearest Andrew, is there really nothing you can do?'

Dwyer's eyes were fixed on her. They were very cold and searching. He was weighing her up, all his suspicion aroused.

'I can't really see what I could possibly do,' he said. 'I've realized all the assets that I had in America and I've instructed my bank to transfer everything to Sydney, to the bank you yourself suggested to me.'

'Oh, how stupid this is! And of course you can't prove it!'

'Not today. I wasn't expecting anything like this, just a few hours before our departure.'

At that point he betrayed his annoyance, though she could see it was partly feigned – but only partly.

'Perhaps I should have thought of getting an affidavit from my caretaker and another from the milkman to prove that I've paid what I owed them!'

'My poor darling, now you're angry! And was it . . . was it a lot that you had transferred?'

'Nine or ten million dollars,' he said, shrugging his shoulders with admirably affected indifference.

Silence.

'That's good,' she said. 'Nine million dollars is not an enormous amount, but it's good. It'll stop tongues wagging, at least. And I shall only be one and a half times richer than you, that's not such a big difference . . .'

Don't overdo it, Hannah, he's watching you!

'Of course one solution,' she went on, 'would be to

leave together tomorrow, hoping that your money will be in Sydney by the time we arrive . . . But I refuse to let you run that risk, my love. Imagine if the nine million weren't there, it would be dreadful!'

She decided to take the risk of looking him right in the eye as she said this. In fact, she was playing her last card: he may well have believed until that point that he was dealing with a widow who was very nearly over the hill, a widow who could ask for nothing better than to have a man in her bed again at last, but she saw no harm in his now discovering another facet to Sarah Kirby (of Brisbane, Australia): a millionairess who was indeed amorous, and indeed hungry for the satisfactions of the flesh, but not to the point of completely losing her head, which was firmly fixed on her shoulders; a woman who, before committing herself, insisted – it was not too strong a word – on knowing whether the suitor to her attractive little white body, and more importantly to her bank account, was not a fortune-hunter and whether he had any money behind him.

Silence.

'All right,' Dwyer said finally. 'All right.'

He moved away from her again.

'That was when the die was cast, Lizzie. It was then that it was all decided . . .'

With his back turned to her, he asked: 'You would even go so far as to leave alone tomorrow, Sarah?'

'What else can I do, my treasure? I was so looking forward to taking your arm . . . perhaps even . . .' (she gave a husky little laugh that was supposed to convey her scandalized modesty) '. . . perhaps even lying in your arms, during that long voyage to Sydney . . .'

Twenty, maybe thirty, seconds of total silence went by.

He said with obvious reluctance: 'Just before catching the train to New York I sold a few buildings I owned in Chicago . . .'

But the deal went through so late in the day that he hadn't had time to pay the money into a bank so that it could be transferred to Australia along with the rest. And in any case, it was always good to have a little loose change on you when you were travelling.

'And how much does the change come to?' asked Sarah Kirby.

'Twelve hundred thousand dollars.'

'That's a bit more than just loose change, my dearest. I know that you're not the kind of man who has to worry about money, but it seems to me that you talk rather lightly of it.'

'Have you ever noticed, Lizzie, that millionaires are always the most hard-headed when it comes to money; they're always the least generous, especially with tips. Sarah Kirby was no exception to the rule, and that's why I had her make that remark . . .'

'That said, Andrew dearest,' said Sarah Kirby, 'one million two hundred thousand dollars is not a great deal . . .'

Further silence.

Oh what fun I'm having! thought Hannah, who nevertheless had her heart in her mouth.

'There's something else, isn't there, darling?' she said.

He finally nodded. There was something else. A little over three million dollars, in fact. He had almost forgotten about it . . . These were the assets of a company of which the sole official proprietor was a certain Mary Meagher. Hannah recognized the name, having read it in the file Fitzpatrick had compiled for her: she was one of Dwyer's wives, the first, the one who had had six children by him . . . *You had almost forgotten that Mr ABCD is a lady-killer, a real son of a bitch . . .*

'For various reasons,' said Dwyer, 'I preferred not to have my name publicly associated with this company. Please don't be jealous, Sarah darling; this Mary Meagher is a simple soul whom I felt sorry for, although there was never anything between us. She worked for me a long time, and I use her name . . . you know how it is in business. But in actual fact the company belongs to me. I have a trust deed to prove it.'

Sarah Kirby clapped her hands joyfully.

'Ah, I can breathe easily now! Four million two hundred thousand dollars, that's quite a substantial sum. After all, no one will be able to say that I married a fortune-hunter. Glynis Caledon-Jones will die of envy . . . Because of course you can produce the trust deed, can't you? As well as the twelve hundred thousand dollars in cash?'

'It's all in a case that I put in the hotel safe. Sarah, who the devil am I going to have to show them to?'

'Don't swear, my angel, I detest swearing . . .'

'Forgive me . . . Sarah, I only told you about it because we're engaged and have no secrets from each other. But giving a complete stranger all these details is quite another matter . . .'

'Clarence Campbell is no stranger, my darling. And in any case he's as silent as the grave. Oh Andrew, my beloved, what a wonderful trip we're going to have, I'm delirious with joy. You'll see, you're going to love Australia. Of course, these little details were not very pleasant but everything is settled now, thank God. In any case, what difference does money make when two people love each other . . . ?'

Hannah, you've really got a cheek, to put it mildly! But that little grating noise that you hear is the sound of the trap closing on Mr A. B. C. Dwyer.

'Clarence Campbell' came and went, having scrupulously examined the contents of the fawn-coloured leather suitcase – he even counted the twelve hundred thousand dollars, bill by bill. He behaved like a lawyer – anyone would have been taken in. He was as miserable as sin and examined every document with considerable suspicion, as though convinced in advance that everything was fake.

However, he didn't find anything untoward, either in Mrs Sarah Kirby's documents, in particular a document from the Manhattan Bank certifying that the aforesaid Mrs Kirby had a fortune of $25,654,000, or in the famous trust deed produced by Andrew Barton Cole Dwyer.

Campbell left. Yvonne had not yet returned.

The case was still there, locked.

And Sarah Kirby again clapped her hands and went into raptures, simpering – rather winsomely in fact – and becoming radiant when Dwyer decided at last to present her with the gold and diamond bracelet.

That was close, thought Hannah, *he almost gave me the slip. There was a moment when he was very tempted to tell wretched Sarah Kirby to go to hell, and when he would have been prepared to try to find some other means of extricating himself from the mess that he's in. But the twenty-five million dollars turned up just in time to restore his spirits, even though he's still wondering whether it was worth it, after the Australian woman turned out to be so money-grabbing. Although he must have come across others like her, running after women the way he has since his earliest youth. And besides, he has just revealed that he has given in and that he's going to go through with it: he gave me the bracelet, that's a sure sign of what his intentions are – and a very pretty one too, by the way, this wicked fellow has good taste. He's given in because he's confident of himself, and he's told himself that he'll find some way of getting the Australian woman's money off her once he's with her in the land of the kangaroos . . . I believe I even know how he intends to do it, and what he's going to play on: bed, and the games you can get up to in bed. That scene in the bathroom convinced him that Sarah is crazy about his body and that in a little while she'll be eating out of his hand. I would bet three kopecks that he is a wonderful lover: he has the look . . . and the rest of it . . .*

Her eyes widened at the sight of the bracelet.

'Oh Andrew, my precious jewel, what madness! How you spoil me! I wasn't expecting this at all!'

She threw her arms round his neck and kissed him – a good long kiss that was for real. *After all, this is the last time. You may as well make the most of it!*

Having finally parted from Dwyer, whose hands were beginning to wander, she put the bracelet on her left wrist and went and stood in front of the big mirror in her bedroom, leaving all the doors open behind her.

'You must have paid an enormous amount for this little thing!'

'Nothing is too good for you.'

His tone of voice was still a bit cold. Despite the genuine emotion he had felt a moment earlier when she came into his arms, he was still nursing his resentment over the lawyer.

It's time to get this over with, Hannah . . .

'How much, Andrew?'

'What difference does it make, my love?'

'How much?'

A pause.

'One hundred and forty thousand,' he said.

She smiled at her own reflection in the mirror.

'Eighty-three thousand, six hundred and seventy-eight dollars, including tax, would be more accurate,' she said.

She came back to the drawing room. He stood there with his hands in the pockets of his superbly cut jacket, staring at her, and a kind of veil began to descend over his eyes.

'Don't bother trying to work it out,' she said. 'Twenty-nine, nearly thirty, years have gone by, but I would have thought you might have recognized me sooner. Admittedly, so many women have crossed your path . . . to their great misfortune. My real name is Hannah, of course.'

She watched his hands.

And saw him slowly draw them out of his pockets.

Careful, Hannah . . .

'Before trying anything stupid, Dwyer, you ought to go and see what's behind the door to the landing.'

He finally stirred, and went to open the door. And even though she was standing several yards behind him, she could not fail to see the three men waiting outside, including Dale Fitzpatrick, who had managed to find two others even taller and bigger than himself.

'You can close the door, Dwyer. They won't come in unless I call.'

He closed the door, and walked back to the middle of the drawing room, where he lit a cigar. His hands did not tremble at all.

Good self-control. Dale was absolutely right: if he had devoted the energy, imagination, boldness and intelligence that he has demonstrated in his swindles to any one of his businesses, he would be one of the wealthiest and most respected men in America. The folly of men is boundless and equalled only by that of women . . .

'I remember now,' he said. 'The Carrington-Fox affair. How could I have forgotten those eyes?'

He smiled, already playing on his charm again.

'The money first,' she said. 'According to my investigations, the twelve hundred thousand dollars you have in that case divides up as follows: $418,000 belongs to your so-called wife in Chicago; $764,158 belong to your stockbroking partner – they belong officially to your office but you owe quite a lot of money . . . I will undertake to return these sums in full. You can keep the difference, which comes to $17,842 . . . Less my expenses, naturally. That leaves you with $906.'

He didn't bat an eyelid.

His brain must be working overtime!

'Next, the $3,238,000 belonging to the company. I knew of the company's existence, but had no idea that it had anything like these assets. It was another matter establishing any connection with you. That was achieved through the trust deed . . . By the way, don't bother looking for it in the suitcase, it isn't there any more. That Clarence Campbell was no more a lawyer than you or I. He's a fairground conjurer. He made the substitution when I kissed you, remember?'

'Mary Meagher is my wife. We have some children.'

'You divorced her on 23 April 1906. I have a copy of the document. But as far as Mary's six children are concerned, you're right. I only regret that you should have neglected your responsibilities as a father with regard to the other thirteen . . .

'Now, this is what we're going to do. I will take care of the investment of this capital. Mary Meagher and her children will receive fifteen thousand dollars a year from the interest, for the rest of their lives. As far as you're concerned, you won't receive anything, and if you go anywhere near your wife, if I even suspect that you're with her, the payments to her will immediately cease and will not resume until after you've left. You will, however, be entitled to visit your family four times a year. The rest of the interest will be divided into fifteen and shared between your thirteen other children, with the additional two parts going to your creditors. Who won't get back everything they're owed, but we can't do everything. Besides, it's their own fault, they shouldn't have lent money to someone like you.'

She removed the bracelet from her left wrist.

'As for this, Dwyer, this is your present to Mary

Meagher. Your farewell present. You have the choice, Dwyer: you can wait until Tuesday, in the company of Police Captain Fitzpatrick and his men – they're the ones on the other side of the door to the landing – when people in Chicago will start looking for you, and suffer the consequences after they've read a number of documents supplied by an anonymous informer . . . And I'm sure that the people in New York, Baltimore, Seattle and Toronto will soon follow the example of those in Michigan . . .'

'Or?'

'I actually knew an Australian called Clayton Pike. He was a very dear friend. He's dead now, but he had a niece who was a little older than I am, called Sarah Kirby – as a matter of fact, I know that you made enquiries about her. He also had a son who, among other things, owns several million acres and a railway line. I've written to Terry Pike. He has a job for you, as station master. It's a place called Alice Springs. If you look for the exact centre of Australia, you'll find a tiny dot on the map: that's it. It's only a small town, but he's counting on you to liven things up a bit. He will inform me of your arrival – he will also tell me if you should happen to leave, especially if you should take it into your head to return to America.'

He suddenly looked up, seemingly upset – either it was a very clever performance or his emotion was genuine.

'I'm very fond of the children I had by Mary,' he said.

'That's a possibility I took into account,' she said. 'So I'm offering you a variation on the second solution. I spoke to Mary Meagher yesterday evening. She'll agree to live with you again if you really do settle down. In that case, and only then, my arrangements for the payment of the fifteen-thousand-dollar pension will be cancelled, or to be more accurate, revised. Mary will get the money, but you will also be able to benefit by it, on condition that you don't leave her and that you're not unfaithful to her.'

'You're a real bitch!' he said.

She smiled at him.

'It depends. Mary is also prepared to go to Australia. With your two youngest children, Thomas and Lisbeth – the others are old enough to look after themselves, and I have to admit that, oddly enough, you have taken care of them. That's what made me a little less uncompromising with you. Dwyer, I'm four foot ten inches tall and I weigh six and a half stone, but I've waited twenty-nine years to get even with you. And I would wait just as long again if necessary to settle the score with you once and for all, without showing any pity the next time, if you hurt that woman any more. She's a fool to be so much in love with you, but there's no reasoning with these things.'

'She would go with me?'

'By a happy coincidence, the first-class cabin reserved for a Mrs Sarah Kirby and the cabin in the name of Adelaide Mounicot are free on a boat sailing for Australia tomorrow. The two ladies in question have decided not to travel. And there's also the cabin in your name. You won't be short of space for your family.'

Silence.

He stared at her, shook his head in disbelief, and then stared at her again.

'Hannah – may I call you Hannah?'

'Why not? Since you're about to leave.'

'Hannah, you have a wonderful body. And I mean that, I see absolutely no point in lying. I was completely stunned by it earlier. I envy the man who can take you in his arms and keep you there. And I shall never forgive myself for having been able to forget those eyes. When do I have to give an answer to your ultimatum?'

'There's no hurry,' she said. 'As long as you say yes within the next ten seconds.'

CHAPTER 29

But You are a Good Sport

'This is supposed to be a very good wine,' said Dale Fitzpatrick.

'I can believe it. It's a Saint-Emilion Balestard-les-Tourelles. Where did you buy it, Dale?'

'It was given to me two years ago in Paris. But it isn't very fresh any more. According to the date on the label, it's at least three years old. Do you think it will still be drinkable?'

'As long as you stop shaking it about. Anyone would think you were trying to attract the attention of a ship at sea. Take the cork out gently, please. The way you might help a lady to remove her petticoats. Abie, will you help me lay the table?'

It was exceptionally sunny this 4 July. The beach lay just below them, behind a cluster of black rocks over which towered a huge pine tree. Hannah had consented to put on a bathing suit and take a dip in the Atlantic, for the sole reason that Abigail wanted someone to go with her. *Being a mother calls for some sacrifices*. But she had not ventured much deeper than her ankles, and watched with genuine anxiety while her daughter, who swam like a fish, frolicked in the water.

This brief exposure to the sun was enough for her. She had come crawling back into the shade of the trees, where the Bugatti was parked.

'Mother?' Abigail spoke in a whisper.

'Yes, darling?'

'You look very good in a bathing suit. Dale couldn't take his eyes off you.'

'Shut up, child. He might hear you.'

'We're speaking French, he won't understand.'

'Another reason not to, it isn't polite.'

'Hannah Newman teaching me manners – that'll be the day!'

'I'm quite capable of being well mannered when I want to be.'

'Well, it doesn't happen very often.'

'I'm a very polite old lady.'

'But you're a good sport.'

Their hands touched while they were laying the black and turkey-red chequered picnic tablecloth. They were at Oyster Bay, on Long Island, not very far from where Dale Fitzpatrick had a country house. Dale himself had walked off, carrying the bottle of Saint-Emilion as though it were nitroglycerine. He was rummaging in the boot of the Bugatti, looking for something he could use as a corkscrew.

Hannah's eyes met Abigail's.

A moment passed.

'Oh Abie!' exclaimed Hannah, suddenly overcome with tenderness.

She took her daughter in her arms – they were both kneeling.

'Thank you for coming with us, darling, especially against competition from Craig . . .'

'Craig? That's ancient history. It's Les now.'

'Les?'

'Les Forbes. He's at Yale.'

'I'm sure he's wonderful.'

'He was last week. He's beginning to lose ground though. If you knew Jimmie!'

'My daughter is a man-eater!'

And you didn't know how marvellous it could be, Hannah, to be with a child you loved, who loved you . . .

'Jimmie is absolutely fantastic,' said Abigail, 'a real miracle of nature. But you're not to appear in front of him in a bathing suit, please. I wouldn't stand a chance if you did.'

Dale came back, looking vexed. He hadn't been able to find anything, he was going to try with his son's scout knife . . .

'There's a perfectly good corkscrew in the basket by your feet,' Hannah told him.

And she and Abigail burst into fits of laughter.

'Hannah!'

'I know what you're going to say, Dale.'

'You're quite capable of it. I'm going to say it anyway. I don't know anything about wines . . .'

'Nor do I,' said Hannah, laughing. 'I was thinking of something completely different.'

'. . . about wines, or painting. Or about art in general, or about the things that you sell to women. I have never really been able to understand why you had such a grudge against the fellow who sailed for Australia yesterday, with his wife and two children. I'm not even sure that I know what I was doing behind the door with those two footballers. I imagined all kinds of things happening . . .'

'He didn't touch me, Dale.'

'I would have killed him if he had . . . If he'd forced you, I mean. I wouldn't prevent you from . . . What I mean is . . . Oh, good God, I'm out of my depth here. I'm sorry for swearing . . . And don't look at me like that.'

'Who was the chap who played the part of the lawyer?' she asked in the hope of changing the subject. 'Dale, he could have been a genuine lawyer! I couldn't believe my eyes . . .'

'He was a genuine lawyer. He's my lawyer. I asked him to pay attention only to Dwyer's documents and to pretend to examine the others.'

She burst out laughing.

'For heaven's sake! And I told Dwyer he was a fairground conjurer who was capable of spiriting away a trust deed without being seen!'

'But I don't understand: the trust deed was in the suitcase, before and afterwards,' said Dale, completely lost.

'Of course it was! Since your lawyer was a real one and Dwyer himself put the trust deed back in the case after the genuine fake lawyer had left . . . or was he a fake genuine lawyer, I wonder? Anyway, I bluffed with Dwyer and he fell for it, there's nothing easier than deceiving a fox, especially when he's very proud of being foxy with others. Dale? I would rather you didn't ask me the question you have in mind . . .'

He asked it.

She slowed down. It was dark now. Abigail was asleep, lying on the back seat, with one hand under her cheek, looking very pink and very vulnerable – it was enough to make you melt with tenderness. Hannah was driving, pleading the way the seat in the Bugatti was specially fixed for her as an excuse to sit behind the wheel. They were driving back to New York.

'The answer's no, Dale. I'm very sorry to have to say this. But I did warn you.'

'I shall never give up hope of marrying you.'

The car was going no faster than a walking pace. They had just come within sight of Manhattan. Ahead of the Bugatti, and to the rear, a huge stream of vehicles stretched away as far as the eye could see, a winding line of twinkling lights. Hannah was reminded of New York thirty years ago – when she and Taddeuz drove through in the Panhard and Levassor; at that time encountering another horseless vehicle inevitably led to cheerful greetings, such as the members of a very exclusive club might have exchanged.

'I'm old, Dale, I feel very old.'

And now one memory led to another. They came flooding back to her, as they had done for the past nine years. Beside her, Dale Fitzpatrick was talking but she wasn't listening; in fact she didn't even hear him.

'I am like a man who yawns at a ball and does not drive home to sleep, only because his carriage is not there . . .'

What's come over you, Hannah? You're dying again . . . And going back to the worst moments at Morcote . . .

Almost without meaning to, she slammed her foot down on the accelerator and the Bugatti's twelve cylinders and 300 horsepower reacted immediately. A whole column of Ford Ts flashed past. Woken by the sudden change of speed, Abigail sat up and rested her two hands on her mother's shoulders.

She smiled at Hannah in the rear-view mirror.

CHAPTER 30

I'll Go to Prison . . .

Groucho Marx wanted to enrol his children in a swimming club. His application was rejected because he was Jewish and so consequently were his children. Groucho sent a very polite letter to the chairman in which he argued that since his wife was Christian, his children by her were only half Jewish; could they be allowed to join the club and get wet up to their navels?

Hannah laughed. She adored the Marx Brothers' crazy humour. She went to watch them shooting *Duck Soup* and found this experience even funnier than the film that eventually came out of it. Every morning the devilish brothers would turn up with a new scenario – when they didn't decide to change it in front of the cameras – so that their colleagues, and of course the director, were all on the edge of a nervous breakdown.

It took her no less than two years to restructure completely her American organization; it wasn't until the last few weeks of 1932 that she felt she had finished – at least as far as point-of-contact with the clients was concerned. By that date she had increased to nineteen the number of North American beauty parlours. Cathy Montblanc – who had resumed her maiden name for the purposes of working with Hannah – was examining the possibilities of opening a twentieth establishment, in Mexico, in 1931.

As for the shops, there were now seventy-four of them.

And months of frantic discussion had led to renegotiation of the contracts with the department stores. Javitts had considerably extended this part of her former empire, concentrating on making an instant profit. Hannah had a completely different approach.

'Jos, I want to put an immediate stop to this business of putting what I sell in my own shops and salons in the same category as the products sold under my name – "Recommended by Hannah" – in the department stores.'

'Those contracts haven't expired yet, Hannah.'

'That's of no importance.'

'We don't really have any weapons to use against them . . .'

'What do you mean? We have an enormous weapon: if they don't agree to renegotiate the contracts, the department stores won't receive another pot of cream out of us, or else just enough for the chairman's wife. If that.'

'You wouldn't really do that, would you?'

'I wouldn't hesitate!'

'You would lose a lot of turnover – and turnover is already down with the Depression.'

'I'm prepared to lose that money, Jos. In the long term, fifty years from now, you'll see that I was right. You can't sell the same wretched creams in a luxury store full of charming beauticians specially trained by me as you find amongst the pots and pans in a drug-store in North Dakota.'

'In fifty years' time I'll be dead.'

'Not me. Unless I've changed in the meantime. Now go to it, Joshua Wynn, and be quick about it.'

Scarcely seven months later Wynn had met her demands. As he realized, his task was made easier – otherwise it would probably have taken him fifteen years – by the omnipresent Depression. The department stores were also affected by the crisis and couldn't afford to lose one of the most profitable lines on their shelves.

'They turned to our competitors but it would have been a year at the earliest before they could get supplies. It won't always be like that, of course; the next time our competitors will be prepared. This time they were taken by surprise.'

'The next time we'll find some other cannon to shoot at them.'

In the presidential elections she voted for Roosevelt. Firstly because she didn't support Hoover's position, and also, most importantly, because she remembered the charming deputy minister at the Kadens' house in Beverly Hills, who made a better Martini than anyone else she knew.

'It is the same Franklin Roosevelt, isn't it, Maryan? I'm not mistaken?'

'It is.'

'His wife is dreadful.'

'But she isn't the one who will be President.'

She found out that Maryan was vigorously championing the Democratic candidate's campaign . . . and that he had even largely financed it.

'Heavens alive, Maryan, do you mean to say that you paid for that fellow to be elected?'

'Exactly.'

'And who's going to pay you back the money?'

He went so far as to smile. Things didn't work like that, he explained. It wasn't a question of a loan, and even less of corruption. He simply thought that Roosevelt was the most capable of restoring order to a country sorely in need of it. Otherwise, he hoped that once Roosevelt got to the White House, he would leave him in peace.

'Hannah, I and a few others in this country only expect one thing of government: that it should let us get on with our work.'

This was quite a speech, something of a surprise coming from Maryan, who didn't usually have so much to say for himself. She looked at him in some confusion, she didn't know that he was so interested in politics . . .

Nevertheless, because she had really taken against

Hoover, and because Roosevelt had a nice smile, she found herself one fine day responding to an appeal for funds for the Democratic campaign's support committee. She contributed ten thousand dollars, convinced that she was mad to do so. Money was something you invested or gave away, so what was this bizarre transaction that fell somewhere in between? But after all, a fairly sophisticated President who liked cocktails and French Dom Perignon champagne – what could be better than that?

She re-opened the school for beauticians and sales assistants – a little reluctantly. It didn't seem reasonable to her to invest too much too quickly, as long as the situation remained the same. According to Maryan and others, even Roosevelt (he was elected in the end, and she felt that, one way or another, he owed her ten thousand dollars) couldn't get things going again before the following year, that's to say, 1934.

You can wait until then, but if things don't improve after that, you'll be writing a letter to that drinker of Dom Perignon that he won't forget in a hurry!

She re-opened the schools because she could not bear denying work to hundreds, indeed thousands, of young girls all begging for it – and this despite her horror of charity (not through meanness but because she was convinced that you were not doing people any favours by giving them money). Providing work, or the chance to find work, yes, but not handing out coins in order to buy yourself a clear conscience for a couple of dollars. *Or even a thousand, since a thousand dollars to you is worth the equivalent of two dollars to the caretaker . . .*

'Cathy, we're going to re-open those wretched schools. See to it.'

'We need beauticians and sales assistants like we need yellow fever.'

'You'll open those schools and keep your big mouth shut, please. Take the best, as usual.'

'We won't be able to give them work afterwards.'

'We'll see about that when the time comes. At least they'll stand some chance of finding a job. Even if they have to find it for themselves.'

'Practically none of them can afford to pay for the courses.'

'They'll pay us back when they start working. So much a month. Have you quite finished arguing? Do I need to spell it out for you in words of one syllable?'

'I'm warning you: Rome will never canonize you, you're Jewish.'

'Well, I'll worry about that when I'm dead.'

She herself taught the first classes, and noticed that almost all her students had rather hollow cheeks and looked pale.

'Cathy, you're to open a canteen. Get something sorted out.'

'And the girls will pay when they've found work, I suppose?'

'Don't try to annoy me, Montblanc. And I'm warning you: if a single one of them comes up and thanks me, or takes part in a demonstration in honour of Hannah, I shall throw her out. And I'm not joking.'

With a timidity fairly untypical of her, she went and worked from time to time with the chemists at the laboratory, which was situated next to the schools in New Rochelle. Storer had just taken on a fair-haired boy with glasses – he was very good-looking – who answered to the name of Paul Travers. He came from Cleveland, had a genuine passion for research, and a great deal of imagination. Storer and he made an exceptional team, complementing each other's skills. At first she was content to watch them work . . .

But it did not take her long to realize – with enormous pleasure! – that she knew more than they did about plants, even if their terminology and hers did not always coincide. (Through speaking half a dozen languages or more, she had ended up evolving her own personal jargon, a strange mixture of English words, French, Polish, Yiddish, German, Russian, Spanish or Italian . . . not to mention the words she borrowed from the Engadine dialect, or from the language spoken by the Australian Aborigines!)

So when (very cautiously – Ladislas Storer could be a bit difficult) she suggested adding some 'dibo-watou', he stared at her, rather taken aback, as was Paul Travers. She explained that 'dibo-watou' (pronounced as written) was a plant only to be found in New South Wales, in Australia, on the banks of the River Darling, and maybe elsewhere but she had never seen it anywhere else, and that it looked a bit like a mushroom, or – not that it was the same, but just to give them an idea of what it was like – what was called in Savoy *'l'herbe à Eustache'*.

Storer did not seem very convinced by these explanations, lucid though they were. It was Paul Travers who tried the hardest to understand. He made her head spin with Latin names (she could make more sense of Hebrew) and then, two or three hours later, in a flash of inspiration Paul asked her if by any chance it could be a kind of *Sapona caryophillaceae*?

They tried some saponine extract and it did indeed produce the result they had been trying to get, without success, for the past three weeks: the cream became light and almost foamy.

'Do you really know all the plants in the world, mother?'

'Just as I'm personally acquainted with every single person living in New York – don't be silly, darling.'

Abigail had turned eighteen the previous 4 July. *If*

there's a prettier girl between here and Mongolia, I would be curious to meet such a marvel. It's not just because she's my daughter – or only a little – but Abigail is lovely enough to make you weep. She doesn't get that from me, Hannah thought.

Abigail was calm, even serene. She was taller than her mother. (This was no surprise: apart from the dwarfs at Barnum's circus, everyone was taller than Hannah.) What did come as a surprise though was that the young girl should have chosen to study botany, plant biology and chemistry at university, without any prompting from Hannah.

'If you wanted to give me pleasure, Abie, you've succeeded. It makes me very happy. But I wouldn't want you to . . .'

'I'm not studying these subjects just because you did, mother. But because I like them. Is that what you wanted to know?'

It took Hannah well over a year to persuade herself that her daughter loved her, really loved her, independently of the pride or admiration she might feel as the daughter of the person talked about in all the papers. It was one of the paradoxes of Hannah's character – she herself was well aware of it – that she could be so confident and resolute when it came to running her business and at the same time so singularly lacking in any confidence in the love she might inspire in those whom she herself loved . . .

Abigail followed every stage of the building and setting up of the laboratory in New Rochelle. During the summer of '32 she even worked for three weeks as a laboratory assistant, earning 62.5 cents an hour, which came to $30.62 for a forty-nine-hour week. She didn't work a whole month because Hannah told her that it wasn't right that she should take a job she didn't need when so many people were out of work.

For her nineteenth birthday, Hannah bought Abie her first car, a modest little Ford – not without some reservation: *If your driving's anything like mine, it would be better if you took a train or a bus . . .* But no, the young girl drove the same way she did everything else: serenely, without any excitability.

When all was said and done, Hannah was more worried about her daughter's love-life: she collected boyfriends with disturbing regularity. *Some of them weren't bad at all . . . Oh Lord, what can you be thinking of – you're supposed to be a grandmother.*

Rather annoyingly, Lizzie burst out laughing when Hannah confided her worries: 'You told me that when you were fifteen you used to wander around Warsaw, at night, on your own, with wolves on your heels.'

'Not wolves plural, just one. And that was a nickname. And in any case, things were different then . . .'

'In a hundred years' time, mothers and fathers will still be saying, "in my day, things were different." And wasn't it you who travelled the world at Abie's age?'

'That was a different continent.'

'You make me laugh. I'm sure your daughter is much more sensible than you've ever been – which is not saying very much.'

Lizzie's right, thought Hannah. *It's a bit rich my jealously guarding my daughter's virginity.*

It was spring 1933. A month earlier, in March, as was still customary at that time, Franklyn Delano Roosevelt took up office as President. As far as Hannah knew, he wasn't doing too badly: on 12 March, in the first of his fireside chats that were to become famous, he launched an appeal for greater confidence in the banks. It was not long before this had the desired effect: for the first time in ages, more money was deposited than withdrawn . . .

'That's well worth twenty-five dollars. He only owes me $9,975 now.'

'Who are you talking about?'

'Roosevelt.'

'Roosevelt owes you money?'

'In a manner of speaking.'

Hannah only rarely used her Bugatti any more. (She had decided not to sell it, she was too fond of it.) That day she had left it in the garage at Yonkers, parked alongside a Rolls-Royce Phantom I made in Springfield, Massachusetts, a Pierce-Arrow, an Aston-Martin, a Napier that she didn't much care for and had bought on the spur of the moment just to please Gaffouil, and lastly a Hispano-Suiza with a huge capacity of 9.5 cc, which she had almost taken out this morning. Gaffouil had dissuaded her, though; he said there was a strange noise in the steering mechanism.

'It would have been better if you hadn't driven over that three-yard-wide pothole at more than 110 miles an hour.'

She had taken the Duesenberg SJ.

She was very pleased with it. Despite the weight of the vehicle (over two tons) the 320 horsepower engine took no more than seventeen seconds to get from nought to sixty and it could reach a speed of 130 miles an hour.

At last you'll be able to leave Groucho standing!

(Groucho Marx, a fervent advocate of the Mercedes, had beaten her hollow two months ago, when she was driving the Aston-Martin. But she wanted her revenge: *I'm going to make him eat that damned cigar of his!*)

'Mother?' said Abigail very calmly. 'There's a . . .'

Three seconds later: 'A what, darling?' asked Hannah.

'A horse and cart. The one that's now a mile back. We drove past that horse so close I could feel its breath. Don't you think you're driving a bit fast?'

'I lose my concentration if I drive too slowly.'

The speedometer registered exactly 125 miles an hour.

And of course the inevitable happened. Over the past three hours they had streaked through a number of towns in this part of Connecticut, to the north-east of Hartford, on the road to Boston. Fortunately, Hannah noticed the roadblock, consisting of a police car and a charabanc, and brought her monstrous vehicle to a halt just a few yards short of it.

The policemen who came up to the car were very blond, very pink and very sweet.

'What's going on?' said Hannah. 'It's dangerous playing with barriers across the road. If I had been driving any faster, I would have flattened you.'

The policemen explained that their colleagues in the county, and in a few others besides, had reported a black car driving at . . .

'My car is red and black,' said Hannah. 'Turkey red, to be precise. It isn't black.'

Apparently this was a very unimportant detail and the judge would be very happy to see the two ladies. They were both asked to get out of the car and taken to a house in which the drawing room had been turned into a courtroom. There was a little man with glasses, who quite obviously abhorred the automobile and anything to do with it.

'Five hundred dollars' fine or five days in prison.'

'I'll go to prison,' said Hannah spiritedly.

There was a heavy silence.

The judge and policemen looked at each other, while Hannah laughed to herself: *Really, what do they think? That they can frighten me? After all, I haven't killed anyone. And besides, I'm sure they don't have a prison for single women . . .*

'Four hundred dollars,' said the judge reluctantly.

'Or four days in prison? Is that it? I'll go to prison.'

This little man is losing his nerve. But she decided to help him along a bit.

'Come outside and see for yourself, Judge.'

She went out, followed by the two policemen and the judge, as well as Abigail and four or five curious bystanders, and went and stood beside the Duesenberg, its chrome exhaust-pipe on the right, gleaming in the late-April sunshine.

'Is it reasonable,' she said, opening her eyes wide, 'is it reasonable to think that a harmless little old lady like me could ever have driven this thing at – how fast did you say?'

'A hundred miles an hour at least. Probably more.'

'A hundred miles an hour? I give you my word that I have never driven at a hundred miles an hour in that car. Or if I have, just for a second or two, but no more than that.'

She glared at Abigail, who was on the verge of giggles.

It's mostly for her benefit that you're putting on this performance, Hannah. You want her to see her mother clowning about . . .

'All right,' said the judge. 'Couldn't we compromise on $250?'

'Two and a half days in prison. Where is the prison?'

Three minutes later mother and daughter found themselves in the company of a very skinny scarecrow who unfortunately had not had his guitar taken away from him, and a snoring drunkard.

'Don't you think you should have agreed to pay that $250?' Abigail asked her in French.

'You don't think you can teach me to bargain, do you? He'll settle for half the price.'

'Oh mother!'

And that very nearly set them both off laughing again. But they heard some movement in the sheriff's office.

And in due course the sheriff reappeared, looking like the decent fellow that he was.

'I can't keep you here all night, it wouldn't be right. Won't you come over to the Hotel Abbott? The judge says it's OK for you to do your time in a hotel bedroom.'

'I know my rights,' said Hannah. 'And I don't want my daughter and me getting carried off into any white slave trade. I shan't leave this prison under any circumstances. Right, darling?'

'Absolutely,' said Abigail.

The sheriff went off, looking very despondent.

'Will your friends in Boston mind if you turn up late?' said Abigail, speaking in French again.

'They won't mind. What about your friends?'

A strange gleam came into Abigail's eyes, which Hannah noticed. *Just like in New York, when she was so insistent about coming with me. I could swear that she had a lover in Boston. And yet, I think it's something else . . .*

'I don't suppose they'll mind either,' said the young girl.

The guitarist gave them a smile, exposing all his rotten teeth, and started to play them a song that could have been one of either Roy Rogers' or Beethoven's – it was hard to identify the tune.

Ten minutes later the sheriff was back.

He opened the bars to their cell.

'Would you come out, ladies?'

He took them back to the judge.

'Well now,' said the judge, 'I've managed to contact New York and it seems that you haven't stolen the car. However . . .'

'The game's up, Franck James,' Hannah said jokingly to her daughter. 'Mount your horse and let's get out of here.'

'However,' said the judge, 'the police in New York

know you, Mrs Newman. I would even go so far as to say that you're extremely popular with them.'

(With good reason: they got ten to fifteen thousand dollars out of her every year for their various charity functions . . .)

'And with good reason,' said the judge. 'Apparently you have been fined for speeding twenty-three times. That said, they asked me to let you go. They would miss you, in some way, if I had you incarcerated. One hundred and fifty dollars' fine and you and your daughter are free to leave right now.'

'One hundred and I'm your man,' said Hannah. 'Plus five hundred for the school in this very pretty little village of yours.'

Twenty minutes and eighteen miles later, she asked: 'And is there anyone special amongst these friends that you're going to see in Boston?'

'Yes, mother.'

'Handsome?'

'Very.'

'And is it serious between you two?'

'I think so.'

'If I'm bothering you with my questions don't hesitate to tell me.'

'No.'

'What does that mean?'

'You're not bothering me with your questions.'

They smiled at each other. Hannah started singing at the top of her voice, and off-key, as usual. Abigail joined in the chorus, and sang even more tunelessly than Hannah, if that were possible.

They reached Boston on 23 April 1933. Hannah spent the next four hours at the salon in School Street, settling an annoying matter of competition and commercial leases, then at lunchtime returned to Louisburg Square, where she had arranged to meet Abigail.

She saw her from a distance, through the restaurant window, and noticed that she wasn't alone, that there was a man with her. As she went into the restaurant, a couple of Boston clients crossed her in the doorway and engaged her in an endless conversation. Sitting at the table opposite her daughter was a man who seemed vaguely familiar, but he was impossible to identify from behind.

Finally able to escape, she walked over towards them and suddenly noticed the extraordinary solemnity and tension in Abigail's face.

'What's going on?'

She had now reached the table. The man stood up, enormously tall, and turned round. In the next tenth of a second Hannah got a shock that almost stopped her heart beating. She closed her eyes, thinking that for the first time in her life she was going to faint.

She finally opened her eyes.

It wasn't him of course.

It was Adam, her eldest son.

'I've brought you some photos,' he said.

And he spread the snapshots out on the seat between them.

'This is Jacqueline, my wife. She's from Nice, I met her in Paris twelve years ago. And these are the children, Marianne, who's the eldest, then Tadd, Ewan, Beth and Debbie, the twins, and finally Tim . . .'

'How old are they?'

She knew this from Lizzie, but was still at the stage of cleaving to banal questions.

'Marianne is eleven, Tadd is ten, Ewan eight, the twins are three, and Tim will be one in September.'

Throughout the meal in the restaurant, he and Abigail talked a lot. Hannah said very little. Adam's resemblance to his father made her tremble every time she looked at him, but the more she reproached herself for her silence, afraid that it would be interpreted as a sign of anger at having been confronted with a *fait accompli*, the less she could think of what to say. She felt at a complete loss for words. *Why are you so dreadfully awkward and tongue-tied, when all you need to say is that you're overwhelmed with happiness and emotion at seeing your son again?*

After the meal, during which he explained in great detail his work as an architect (he and two of his partners were about to finish work on a forty-storey building, in Griswold Street in Detroit; and he was probably going to be commissioned to do another skyscraper on Michigan Avenue, Detroit), they all got into the Duesenberg, the three of them squeezing up together on the front seat.

With no particular destination in mind, Hannah drove very slowly, immured in silence. Only Abigail tried to keep the conversation going.

Eventually Hannah stopped the car at the edge of a pond, called Jamaica.

They all got out.

'Mother, I'd like you to come and see us in Detroit. Whenever you like.'

Abigail had wandered off, no doubt deliberately. She was walking by herself, about fifty yards away, looking graceful and slender in her Nina Ricci outfit.

'I'll come, Adam. God knows how I've dreamed of seeing my grandchildren . . .'

She had the photos on her lap and was unconsciously tapping them, as though they were playing cards. *And what can I do?* she thought. *Take my son in my arms – he must be six foot four or five! Oh God, it's so stupid being so small!*

'They know you,' said Adam. 'Marianne collects all the advertisements from the newspapers and also any articles about you. She has that picture of you with Charlie Chaplin and Groucho Marx in her bedroom. She and her brothers are very proud of their grandmother.'

'And you, Adam?'

At last you've managed to ask an intelligent question!

'I'm here, mother. And I should have come back to you years ago: Abie was right. Forgive me.'

She leaned forward, clutching the pack of photographs to her chest, fighting back the tears the only way she knew how: with her mouth half open, as though on the verge of suffocation, she widened her eyes.

Oh my God, he even has 'his' voice. And yet it's not him. It's his son and yours, and all that you have left of him . . .

She hardly felt Adam's large hand encircle her wrist until it travelled up her arm, and took her by the shoulder and very tenderly drew her to him in a gesture that 'he' might have made, a gesture that he actually had made thousands of times . . .

For the first time in an eternity she let herself go: she rested her cheek against Adam's shoulder and slipped her hand into her son's.

'Oh mother,' Adam said again in a low voice. 'Oh mother, forgive me, please forgive me . . .'

CHAPTER 31

You Know, He's Crazy About You

She went to Detroit the following month, in May, and stayed five weeks. The first two days were very difficult, not to say painful. Certainly not because of Jacqueline, her daughter-in-law, who was perfectly adorable; nor on account of the children, who gave her a welcome fit for a living legend . . . It was her own fault . . . she wasn't used to this kind of family reunion, not any more, and continued to feel a timidity that really wasn't like her at all.

Everything became much easier from the moment when, at Adam's request, she started relating episodes from her past – not that this was like her either, usually she refused to share her memories of Poland, Australia and Europe of the last century with anyone apart from Lizzie. The one and only time that she had risked doing so was on that day when she had taken her two sons to visit Mendel's grave.

Naturally she toned things down a bit, and did not dwell too much for instance on what Pelte the Wolf tried to do one dark night on the streets of Warsaw. But for someone who thought she couldn't tell stories, in telling her own she found words that sang: *Pelte the Wolf had eyes like a gypsy and a silver-sequined jacket. He had a dancing sardonic kind of walk, he had worked in a circus as a knife-thrower . . . And Mendel the Drayman killed him one winter's night, to the sound of beating drums, by squeezing his neck very hard . . .*

Marianne and Tadd and Ewan, and even the twins who couldn't have understood a word of what she said, listened spellbound . . . and no doubt Adam and his wife too, seated side by side and hand in hand on the sofa in front of her, occasionally exchanging glances full of pride while she spoke.

Jacqueline was a ravishing brunette with black eyes; she was very cheerful and lively. Her family grew flowers, which were even sold to the English Royal court. The two women took less than three days to feel at ease with each other, especially after Hannah had become herself once more. They both went to the salon in Detroit (where Hannah's arrival, as usual, unleashed the most feverish excitement), went window-shopping together and talked about Monte Carlo and the flower market in Nice.

'You speak remarkable French,' the young woman said to her one day. 'Where did you learn it?'

'In Poland, from reading *Les Liaisons Dangereuses*, just as I learned English from reading Dickens.'

Her stay in Detroit gave her such pleasure and happiness that she had already twice postponed her departure for Europe. But she finally got Adam to agree that they should all go together. Hannah and Jacqueline and the children would sail on the Italian ship *Rex* – it held the blue riband for having made the crossing from the American coast to Gibraltar in a little under four days and fourteen hours. Adam was to follow on after, at the beginning of August, and sail back home with his family, who would by then have spent a month and a half in Nice.

Only once was Jonathan mentioned in Detroit. Truth to tell, Adam didn't know much more about his brother than the Kadens – in other words, he hadn't seen him for more than four years.

'At that time he had just returned from travelling round the Pacific. He told me he had stayed on one of the Solomon Islands, but he didn't say anything about what he had been doing there; I understood that he had been working on a plantation.'

Since then, Jonathan had written twice – only twice. First in 1930, a few words to say that everything was all right, nothing more, and then another letter, hardly any longer, in which he said that he was planning to go to China.

'He vaguely mentioned some articles he wanted to write about the war between Chiang Kai-shek and the Communists, but he didn't say what newspaper he was working for, if he was working for anyone. I made a few enquiries, but without turning up anything. None of the more important editors know him.'

She then asked the question that she was so ashamed of having to ask, coming from a mother.

'What does he look like, Adam?'

'He's not quite so tall as me, about six foot two inches maybe. But he's thinner, more sinewy.'

And of course he had Hannah's eyes.

From Genoa, where they left the liner belonging to the Italia Flotte Riunite recently created by Mussolini, Hannah, Jacqueline, plus the six children and the two nannies, travelled to Nice by train, escorted by an Italo-American that Uncle Maryan had assigned to them as a precaution.

Three years earlier, as well as investing in 'a bit of land here and there' in the area, Maryan had bought a big property at Saint-Jean-Cap-Ferrat, nearly on the tip of the peninsula, beyond the signal station. The house consisted of twelve rooms, a big swimming pool, a tennis court and a very attractive private funicular down to the beach. It occurred to Hannah that she too should buy something in the vicinity. The day was bound to come when she would be old and decrepit, and would start seeing sheep everywhere, and someone would have to look after her, she would be so doddering. Why not choose this place since it was so pretty?

And it was time her grandchildren had their own house.

Holy mackerel, it's true, you're a grandmother, six times over all at once, which doesn't happen to everyone . . .

She made a telephone call and a lawyer came down from Paris, one of the team she had asked the Genevan Pierre Poncetti to set up four months earlier. The lawyer arrived by train the next day. His name was Jean-Claude Brana. She had him trailing after her, on foot, for two hours, all over the peninsula, through strawberry trees and laburnums, with the sun beating down on them. While she gaily twirled her parasol and remained cool and fresh, he, poor devil, looked as though he had just emerged fully clothed from a steam bath.

'And there's also this plot, young Jean-Claude. As with the others I've shown you, I want you to find out the price, what the likelihood is of getting a deal through quickly, and the possibilities for building on it and getting it connected to all the main services. If any of the owners you come across should happen to be someone called Kaden, let me know, but don't on any account tell him who you're representing – that crook would be quite capable of selling it to me for a special price or even giving me the plot for nothing . . . No, don't try to understand, it's a story that dates back forty years. This plot here is only four acres. It's not very big but it would be big enough for me. It's the one I prefer, especially as it overlooks all the others, and in particular that huge place down there. I would build my house here, so that from my bedroom window I could finally discover how Maryan and Lizzie make love . . . No, don't try to understand that either. It's what's called in English a private joke.'

'I speak English,' Brana managed to get out. 'And Spanish.'

'Excellent, young Jean-Claude, excellent. And you have a lovely moustache as well . . .' *How sweet – he's blushing!*

The 'huge place down there' was of course Maryan and Lizzie's villa – and the idea of getting the better of them was not at all unappealing. With a strong pair of binoculars she was sure she would be able to catch Maryan and his wife making love, since that stubborn mule wouldn't tell her anything . . .

'Young Jean-Claude, don't waste any time, please. As soon as I've bought it, I want to start building, so that my house will be ready for next summer.'

Three days later she left for Paris.

All ready for the second phase of her reconquest.

The team of lawyers she had put Pierre Poncetti in charge of had taken 130 days to compile their report. Hannah received it just a week before she set sail for Europe.

'Now is the time to act,' Poncetti had concluded in a hand-written note attached. He was of course referring to the repurchase of the whole European part of her former empire.

Once that was done, the only other thing left to do was to come to some agreement with the Fournacs, even if it meant her having to return to Melbourne in order to regain control of Australia and New Zealand.

The enormous, dramatic interval would then be no more than a memory.

And you'll really be able to expand . . . As to how those conquests were to be made, she had some very specific ideas.

Lulled by the movement of the Blue Train as it travelled through the night, she fell asleep.

She had always loved trains.

'And high time too!' said Jeanne Fougaril tartly. 'I was wondering when you were going to make up your mind to act.'

'I had to tighten the screws in America before turning my attention to the rest of the world.'

'You certainly took your time. Five years' tightening screws is carrying things a bit too far.'

'That's enough, Fougaril. You're just as cantankerous as ever, I see, if not more so. It must be the menopause. It's always worse when it comes late. Well?'

They were lunching together in Avenue Montaigne, in Paris. Jeanne's meal consisted of a boiled egg and tea, plus an apple. Hannah had two portions of *foie gras* in pastry, turbot, saddle of lamb, a peach melba and a soufflé. Jeanne was well covered. Hannah was as thin as a rake – she was wearing a dress designed by Roger Piguet, a former pupil of Paul Poiret, who had just opened a salon in Rue du Cirque.

'I hate you,' said Jeanne.

'Have you found a new reason or is that still for the same reasons as before?'

'You haven't aged at all. And it makes me sick to sit here watching you eat . . . Oh Hannah, I'm so wildly happy to see you again, I'm almost in tears. I've counted the days since you sent that letter telling me you were coming back.'

'Hannah rides again, alleluia!' said Hannah before sipping the Corton-Charlemagne that she had ordered with her *foie gras*. 'How far have the lawyers got, Fougaril?'

'They'll tell you themselves.'

'But I'm asking you. I'll see them later.'

In 1919, in March 1919, when Hannah had sold out in Europe, Jeanne had bought a twelve per cent interest in the company.

'That leaves eighty-eight per cent. The French group, Auriol, took forty, the English consortium headed by Bishop took the rest. Auriol's son agreed to sell fairly readily, on the express condition that you and you alone bought back his share – he's a personal friend of mine, what's more. He'll let you have twenty-five per cent and keep fifteen, but he undertakes to back you in all circumstances. I had no difficulty in persuading him that with you back in control he would make three times as much money as he would on his own with the English.'

'He doesn't get on with them?'

'They have an *entente cordiale*: they hate each other. And it's been that way for years. I don't like to boast, but if it hadn't been for me with my twelve per cent bringing a little order to the proceedings by supporting now one and then the other, they would have long since reached the stage of hurling pots of cream at each other across the Channel.'

'Does that explain the present difficulties the company is in?'

'Yes and no. Yes, insofar as it slowed down or made impossible any plans for reorganization – they never agreed about the smallest investment – and no, insofar as there are other reasons. The crisis which hit America four years ago is apparently – I'm no economist – now affecting Europe, Great Britain especially, France a little less. Hannah, business is terribly bad at the moment . . .'

'Are you losing money?'

'It's not as bad as that. But nearly. Haven't you seen the figures?'

'Bishop is taking his time in sending them to me.'

'I can give you what I have, which is almost everything apart from the United Kingdom, the Netherlands, Denmark and Spain, which London has always insisted on managing directly, and Portugal as well. But I have some estimates. Nearly all the women and girls working in the salons are graduates of the schools you founded, thank God. They have the family spirit and never hesitate to give me information when I ask for it. Hannah, Bishop will never agree to sell. He's offered to buy me out hundreds of times.'

'To any problem there are always plenty of solutions.'

Hannah started attacking her lamb, which was accompanied by mixed vegetables and a spinach salad.

Two days later she took an Imperial Airways flight to London.

Arthur E. Bishop was a corpulent, red-faced man of about forty-five. According to the file she had had compiled on him, he was married with two daughters; he was the son of a Leeds ironmonger and had been in the RAF for four years during the war, rising from the rank of corporal to that of pilot captain. He had made his fortune selling saucepans throughout the British empire. He was said to be very intelligent and very stubborn.

'You asked us to tell you his weaknesses,' said one of Hannah's London lawyers, who was none other than Nigel Twhaites, dear Polly's nephew. 'The only thing we could find was his rather naïve ambition to be introduced into the poshest circles. He has made several applications to various clubs but has always been rejected.'

'And are you a member, Nigel, of the clubs he wants to join?'

'Some of them, yes. But things . . .' He broke off and smiled. 'Perhaps I'm a bit of a snob, is that what you mean?'

'You happen to have been born into the right circles. Not that I'm blaming you for anything.'

'Uncle Polly often said that you were more of an anarchist than Bakunin.'

'I never knew Bakunin. And Mr Arthur Bishop doesn't want to sell?'

'He agreed to see us on two occasions, when we put your offers to him. It was on the second occasion that he was most categorical.'

To any problem there are always plenty of solutions . . .

She was with Bishop the day after her arrival in London. The previous day she had called in at the beauty parlour in St James's Place, the first to open in Europe. *That was thirty-seven years ago, how time flies!* She was expecting the worst, but what she found there came as a relatively pleasant surprise: there wasn't too much devastation, in fact little had changed. She eventually came round to thinking that it was all a bit too conservative. *But this is England!*

No one recognized her at first, which annoyed her but at least gave her a chance to examine everything – the staff and the facilities – without everyone panicking. She had even checked the conveniences, which she thought needed attention.

'It's important, Lizzie . . . You may laugh, but I tell you, it's important. Firstly, as a place to pee – that's obvious. You're going to pee in your pants if you carry on laughing so stupidly . . . And for another reason. What do you think a woman does when she's had her face done in a beauty parlour? She goes to the ladies. Absolutely right, madame. That is indeed where she goes. Not to have a pee. To look at herself. No matter how many mirrors the beauticians may have held up for her to admire herself in. She wants to look at herself alone, without anyone watching, with the kind of critical ruthless eye you can only have when you're on your own. And that's where you win or lose a client, Lizzie: in that solitary scrutiny in the privacy of the ladies. This is the kind of thing you have to know, my dear . . . It's what the job's all about.'

Cecily Barton was no longer running the salon in St James's. She had retired at the age of seventy-five, six years ago, and when last heard of was living with one of her sons in Canada. She had been replaced by another woman, called Harriet Morris.

'She's not too bad,' Hannah told Bishop. 'Except that

she doesn't know a single word of French, or German, or Spanish, or Italian, or any other foreign language. Furthermore, her hair looks a mess, and she should never have put her office on the second floor: one of her staff could slit a client's throat downstairs and she would never know.'

Bishop smiled.

'Fortunately, that kind of accident doesn't happen very often. So, you want to buy me out? I thought I made myself clear when I spoke to your lawyers.'

'I have a completely different proposition to put to you.'

And she explained in what way this one was different: she was no longer offering to buy back the whole forty-eight per cent. Only fifteen. She saw no objection to Bishop's retaining thirty-three per cent. (It was a simple calculation: with the twenty-five per cent Auriol's son had sold her, plus Jeanne Fougaril's twelve per cent, and the fifteen per cent Auriol's son still held . . . but he had formally undertaken to give her his backing in every instance – and the extra fifteen from Bishop, she would either own or control sixty-seven per cent: in other words, a two-thirds majority.)

'For the time being, I don't want any more than that,' she said.

'But I still don't want to sell them to you, Mrs Newman. In fact, I'm offering to buy out your shares.'

She gave him a smile.

'You don't want to sell because there are some things you don't know. I'm not blaming you for anything; I suggest you reread the contract I signed in Lugano just over fourteen years and four months ago. I undertook then never to compete in any way at all with the businesses I was handing over. I shall keep to that agreement, naturally. I shan't start anything new. However, I have just been taken on as European director by the shareholders in the company in which you yourself hold forty-eight per cent of the shares. These people own fifty-two per cent, a majority which – under clause 39, paragraph 6 of the contract dated 23 March 1919 – authorizes them to open any beauty parlour they consider necessary to the expansion of the company. I am quoting from memory, I'm not a lawyer.'

Bishop gave her a penetrating look. She thought: *He's looking at me the same way that he must have looked at that German pilot whose name I have forgotten, the one with the face of an angel who shot down so many British and French planes. Von something or other . . . He's no fool when it comes down to it . . .*

He asked: 'And you would open another salon in London?'

Careful, Hannah, now's the time to knock him out cold, as Dempsey would say. You must get this off pat, without making a mistake. Good luck, my girl!

She took a deep breath.

'In London, Lisbon, Madrid, Barcelona, Copenhagen, Rotterdam, Amsterdam, and The Hague. And elsewhere if necessary. Would you like to make a bet that they will all be open by the end of this year? No, don't answer that, I haven't finished yet. Clause 66, paragraph 3, anticipates the possibility of your company entering into partnership with another company, as long as the partnership is approved by a simple majority of the shareholders – fifty per cent of the votes plus one – if such a partnership is liable to be of help in the setting up of one or more beauty parlours in one or more countries. There again, I'm quoting from memory, I haven't become a lawyer in the meantime. There is a restriction on this possible partnership: the newcomer cannot hold more than one-third of the shares – clause 67, paragraph 1 – and any company created under these terms is subject to paragraph 3 of clause 61. Do you follow me, Mr Bishop?

'I was told that you were a war hero. I personally consider it a scandal that you should be refused membership of that club in Jermyn Street when so many little fools are admitted who aren't worth one-hundredth of you. I believe we have something in common, sir: we both hate people who inherit, because we are our own ancestors. As for that club, it just so happens that one of my dearest and oldest friends, Winnie Churchill, whom you may know, holds some important position in the club. But that's for you men to settle, it's not something I should interfere in. Now, let's get back to the matter in hand . . .

'As European director of your company – I was appointed to that position the day before yesterday by fifty-two per cent of the shareholders – I plan to open these new institutes. Clause 61, paragraphs 1, 2 and 3 are relevant here: in order to set up these new establishments, a new partner comes on to the scene. An American company that has its head office in the State of Delaware; I shall not try to conceal from you the fact that I am associated with this company, which will own a thirty-three per cent stake in all the new salons. And let me tell you what will happen, Mr Bishop: in a year's time, the existing salons in London, Lisbon, Madrid, Barcelona, Copenhagen, Rotterdam, Amsterdam and The Hague will be seriously in deficit. I anticipate that within eighteen months they will have closed their doors. The majority shareholders who selected me as director won't lose out because they will own sixty-six per cent of the new establishments, whereas they had only fifty-two per cent of the old ones. You of course won't be so lucky: your share of the new salons will be only thirty-three per cent, as opposed to your present forty-eight per cent, just when the losses of the old salons start to hit you.'

Silence.

'These things can be argued in court,' said Bishop finally.

She joyfully clapped her hands.

'Marvellous! When do we begin? I adore trials! Especially trials like this one, which will drag on for three or four years. Or more. The new salons will be at least three years old by the time the final judgement is delivered.'

She smiled more broadly than ever, making eyes at him.

And one of two things is possible, as my wonderful Mendel would say: either he'll smile at you and offer you some tea, or he'll throw you out . . .

He did neither. He rose to his feet and paced round the office. She sensed his eyes on her neck, on the curve of her back, which she thought very charming and which her fashionably revealing dress showed off to good effect. While she studied the framed photographs that showed Bishop, fifteen years younger, at the controls of an RAF Sopwith Camel. *If Winnie doesn't do you this little favour, you can tell everyone that he tried to rape you in the rosebushes at Marlborough. It's not true, but since he was too drunk to remember what he did . . .*

Bishop came and sat down again. He studied her pensively.

'When you came in,' he said, 'I thought you were your daughter. I was told there was an old lady to see me.'

'That's one of the kindest compliments anyone has ever paid me,' she said with her most dazzling smile.

Bishop, this is not a fight that you should get involved in. I'm not Manfred von Richthofen, and we are not fighting in aeroplanes. The jury who will adjudicate on our fight will consist solely of women, think about it. And I happen to be a woman.

Silence.

'Would you care for a cup of tea?' asked Bishop.

'I thought that you were never going to go into partnership with anyone?' said Jeanne. 'Bishop sold you only fifteen per cent . . .'

'Seventeen. He was perfectly charming, these lawyers are really hopeless. And fifteen didn't make a round number. Auriol *fils* sold me twenty-five . . . plus seventeen, makes forty-two. Plus your twelve, that's fifty-four . . .'

'I haven't yet sold you my twelve per cent. I just might not sell them to you.'

'Don't annoy me, Fougaril. You'll sell them to me – do you want to bet on that?'

'To any problem there are always . . . I know. No, I'm not betting. I know you too well. You're capable of anything.'

'And Bishop will let me have the rest of his shares. Ditto Auriol *fils*. It's just a matter of time.'

She was absolutely sure of it. And as it turned out, Auriol sold out three years later and Bishop let her have his shares in April '39, a few days before he was ennobled by George VI. (Bishop marked the occasion by sending Hannah a very fine nude by Whistler and a photograph of Von Richthofen with a note attached: 'He was less formidable than you . . .')

That said, Jeanne was right: apart from Australia and New Zealand – and her partnership with the Fournacs related solely to the cosmetic side of her business – she had always refused to entertain even the idea of having a partner, let alone several partners. It was as abhorrent to her as borrowing money from banks.

But she had no choice: she didn't have enough capital . . . And – a fact that annoyed her, but she had to admit it – she was a little less intransigent than in the past.

She bought Jeanne's shares. This was all the more easy

to do since Jeanne hadn't paid the full price in 1919 for the twelve per cent that she controlled. She had in fact only acquired ten per cent of the twelve per cent, in other words, 1.2 per cent. The rest of the money had been invested by a Swiss consortium led by Pierre Poncetti. And the sale of the shares in 1919 had been accompanied by a clause giving Hannah, and Hannah alone (who had been unaware of this and only now found out about it), the chance to buy back the shares when she felt like it: 'Like me, Pierre was convinced that you would buy back the company one day.'

'In other words, everyone but me knew. Jeanne, it's your choice: you can either keep the 1.2 per cent stake that you paid for out of your own pocket, or I'll buy it back from you.'

'Whatever suits you.'

'I don't have a lot of money at the moment.'

'I'll give you an undertaking to sell and you can buy them back whenever you like.'

'Fougaril, I love you.'

'It's time you realized it. I would prefer to sell – I may as well tell you this now – because I'm going to retire.'

'You what? You must be crazy.'

'I don't have your stamina. And I'm a bit older than you. Yesterday, seeing you dancing with that handsome Italian made me feel like your old aunt. Who was he?'

'A friend I met in Rome. We happened to run into each other.'

'Happened to, my eye. He's crazy about you, you know?'

'We were talking about your wretched retirement.'

'There's no more to be said, my dear. I'm stopping work at the end of next year. I think he's very handsome, very distinguished. I adore his silvery temples. And what a lovely smile!'

'Who are you talking about?'

'You know very well who I'm talking about.'

CHAPTER 32

A Certain Niccolo Machiavelli

'I met him in Rome, Lizzie. He invited me to dine with his mother, in their palazzo. I thought I had forgotten about him, but he must have been waiting for me all that time. He wasn't in Genoa, though, when we docked there on the Rex *. . .*

'But he was in Nice. It happened the day after our arrival. I was walking with Jacqueline along the Promenade des Anglais, and suddenly he was there, in front of us, with that charming little smile of his, his ivory-handled walking stick, his panama hat, his white spats, and his cute moustache. We talked for – what? – perhaps five or six minutes, and we had no sooner walked away from each other than my fool of a daughter-in-law burst out laughing: "That gentleman is completely crazy about you, mother," she said, or something to that effect. And then in the days that followed, wherever I went, there he was, holding his panama in his hand, with that kindly and slightly mischievous little gleam in his eye that you know, as though he were saying: "Yes, it's me again . . ."

'I went to Paris and he was sitting in the restaurant where I had lunch with Fougaril. Try as I might to look reprovingly at him, nothing doing, he was always there . . .

'And naturally he turned up in London. He checked in at the Dorchester, just like me, and spent most of his time – when I was asleep, or arguing with Bishop – going to florists, sending me peonies upon peonies. At one time I had as many as 160 bouquets of peonies in my hotel suite . . .

'I returned to Paris and he was still there. I went to that

fancy-dress ball – having forged a path through my apartment in the Ritz which had been overrun by a jungle of peonies – and who should I find there, disguised as a peony?

'I almost forgot to tell you that he had booked the four seats nearest to mine on the flight from London to Paris, not for himself – I wonder how he managed to cross the Channel so quickly – but in order to surround me with peonies, even in the sky . . .

'To cut a long story short, he invited me to dinner and because I was beginning to find it hard to control my laughter – you're well placed to know how susceptible I am on that score – I accepted. I asked him the reason for the peonies, and he said: "Because they're cheaper than roses . . ."'

'I regret to say that my mother is no longer with me,' he said in reply to Hannah's question. 'She died five years ago, very peacefully in her sleep. Ours is not a family that favours the spectacular or likes to call attention to itself. As for my children, thank you very much for remembering them – my daughter has just got married to a Frenchman and my son has gone to Argentina, where we still own some property; he's going to look after it.'

As usual Hannah had risen at dawn that morning. She had left the Ritz at about six o'clock and had found him waiting for her, next to his Alfa Romeo 1750, on the Place Vendôme, on the corner of Rue de Castiglione. Not really surprised to see him, she had passed within a yard of him, and he had immediately started walking alongside her, on her left, at the same rapid pace. They crossed the Rue de Rivoli and the Tuileries Gardens, and the Seine via the Pont Royal. Then they followed the *quais* on the Left Bank as far as the massive feet of the Eiffel Tower, where they recrossed the Seine . . .

She had always loved walking through cities like this, in the early morning, while sleep and silence still reigned.

They returned to the Place Vendôme.

'I'm very hungry,' she said.

He studied her, his hands in cream leather gloves crossed on the handle of his cane, as neat as if he had just been created and put into the world. He was really quite small in stature for a man – barely five foot five inches. She had only ever seen him wonderfully turned out – so refined that in others it would have seemed forced, but not in him; it was impossible to imagine him otherwise.

They got into the Alfa Romeo. He took her to one of the avenues on the Bois de Boulogne. The apartment was superbly furnished, with some of Robert Adam's work, in lemon wood, providing the basis, to which some marvellous pieces of Chinese porcelain added a touch of exoticism.

'I simply happen to have been Ambassador to Peking,' he said.

The manservant who served them tea – every tea imaginable – and a delightful breakfast, was also Chinese. She ate hungrily, watching the horsemen ride past along the avenues through the woods.

'I love a woman who eats,' he said.

He watched her constantly and gradually a strange shyness – almost a sense of confusion – came over her, the like of which she had not experienced for years, if indeed she ever had.

He asked her to marry him in the same tone of voice as he had asked her a few seconds earlier if she would like some more chocolate mousse.

It was her turn to stare at him, incomprehensibly thrown into a state of panic. He smiled and, without waiting for her to reply, he at once started talking about André Malraux, who had just published his book *La Condition Humaine* a month ago.

'If you would like to meet him, Hannah . . .'

He took her back to the Ritz and at the hotel entrance kissed her fingers.

'I've been waiting fourteen years for you, Hannah. I can wait longer.'

You're too old and your life is over. And besides, you don't love him. You will never love him, or any other man, even if you live to be a thousand.

This is what she told him a few days later. She had just concluded her negotiations with Auriol, Bishop, with the Swiss and Jeanne Fougaril. She now held fifty-four per cent of the company she had set up in Europe, and had control of some of the remaining shares. She was preparing to make an extended tour of Europe, from Lisbon to Stockholm, from one salon to the next, which would allow her to see how each of the shops was doing, and to review the whole network, before taking matters very firmly in hand again . . .

'I know,' he said. 'But I've never hoped that you could love me. Hannah, please, don't try to use your age as an excuse.'

She was a few years older than him, why pretend to be unaware of it?

His only reply was to look at her with that calm, imperturbable gentleness, with such intense feeling in his eyes that she would almost have blushed had she been capable of it. As it was, without her really understanding how it happened, her anger against herself gave way to that strange confusion she had already experienced in his presence and which had so exasperated her. It has to be said that his great desire for her was quite apparent beneath that well-mannered exterior he presented.

Here you are behaving like a shy young virgin again . . . Oh Hannah, what's happening to you? You can't possibly be in love with him . . . You're fifty-eight years old. It would be perfectly grotesque to feel anything of the sort at your age. It would have people laughing as far away as Australia. So quickly, please, do something, take a lover, or even four, if that's what you want.

Except that it's not a lover that you want. Although I wonder? So what is it then, you fool? A companion? Someone you could employ the way you might hire a cook?

She set off on her tour of Europe without having said yes or no. She was annoyed at herself for her indecision. Especially when she realized how disappointed she was not to find him in Lisbon, or Madrid, or Barcelona, or even Rome, in the rain in September.

There she heard that kindly, gruff Gaffouil, who had worked for her for thirty-three years, had died of a heart attack. From Italy she returned to south-west France, to Pau, where Yvonne had chosen to bury her husband. Hannah insisted on attending the funeral and was surprised that anyone else should be surprised at her presence. All her life she had shown and would always show a fierce loyalty to those whom she loved – and to those whom she detested: she had waited a quarter of a century to get her revenge against Dwyer, but conversely she demonstrated the same determination and patience in consoling Yvonne and helping the children Yvonne had borne Gaffouil.

She resumed her tour on her own, having refused to allow Yvonne to accompany her: 'I want you to take care of that cough of yours.'

Yet now, for the first time in forty-five years, her solitude weighed heavily on her. She was even looking out for the letters signed by Niki – Pier-Paolo d'Arcangheli – that reached her regularly at each of the places on her itinerary. Similarly, in every hotel where she stayed, there were flowers waiting for her, peonies, naturally, but now in reasonable quantities – as though he had abandoned his initial extravagance.

In November she arrived in Berlin, under freezing cold rain. She knew very little about Nazism at that time – but enough to have formed an opinion: she was already thinking of closing the salon in the German capital, as well as those in Hamburg and Munich. But her decision was actually made on 19 November. Less than three hours after her plane landed from Zurich.

The director of the German salon was a certain Fred Hauptmann, a distant relative of the dramatist of the same name. He told Hannah that he had in fact been visited by three government representatives. 'But nothing came of it.'

'Something did come of it: we're closing. Within the hour, please, Fred.'

'We have at least forty clients here.'

'You've got thirty minutes to get them out.'

She sat down in the entrance hall to make sure her instructions were carried out. She settled herself on one of those two-seated sofas called a love seat and watched the first of the clients depart. It was from this vantage point that she saw a tall, handsome young woman with a haughty expression approach her, accompanied by a very uncomfortable-looking Fred Hauptmann.

'I'm Magda Goebbels and my husband . . .'

'I'm Jewish, and to you I'm a damned nuisance,' replied Hannah with her chin resting on her fingertips, her hands clasped together.

She took a plane to Amsterdam that same afternoon. Only later would she learn that the police, having searched for her in all the hotels in Berlin, had forced Hauptmann to re-open the three salons – to no avail. Hauptmann himself was arrested for having carried out Hannah's orders: he had dismissed the beauticians and sent them all away (three of them were transferred to the salon in Vienna, two agreed to go to Prague, others were re-employed in Zurich and Amsterdam – those at least who were able or wanted to leave Germany).

Hannah spent eight months getting her director out of prison and then out of Germany – through the intermediary of her lawyer Pierre Poncetti, she got the director of the Reichsbank, Dr Schacht, to intervene on Hauptmann's behalf.

She completed her tour at the end of February. On the 21st of the month, she returned to Paris (Abigail had joined her in Stockholm for Christmas and the New Year).

There were peonies waiting for her in the Ritz. There had been peonies too in the Rolls-Royce that had come to pick her up at the Gare du Nord – the car was driven by Laurent Gaffouil, Yvonne's nephew.

And there were not only flowers for her in the suite overlooking the Place Vendôme, there was also a painting by Chirico, with a dedication from the artist, which had been delivered an hour earlier.

'Whenever you want to, if you want to,' read Niki's laconic message.

'Even my own daughter has taken to meddling in my affairs,' she said. 'I suppose that you deliberately set out to meet her and seduce her.'

'A certain Niccolo Machiavelli was one of my ancestors, on my mother's side.'

He said that his meeting with Abigail had been a sheer coincidence. He just happened to be there, with his car and his chauffeur, when Abie arrived in Paris (she was on her way to Stockholm at the time). It was a stroke of luck that allowed him to oblige the young lady, who otherwise would have had problems with her luggage, since some practical joker had rung up and cancelled the reception committee that Jeanne Fougaril had arranged to meet her.

'Machiavelli, eh?' said Hannah.

'No one can be blamed for his family.'

'But you didn't have to invite Abie out the next day, or bewitch her with your irresistible Latin lover's charm. A poor innocent young girl fresh off the boat from her native America . . .'

'That's true,' he said.

He bowed his head, looking contrite, asking to be forgiven. She couldn't be angry with him, and placed her hand on his, where it lay on the table.

'Niki, things aren't too good. There's a cancer growing in Europe.'

Despite the time she had spent in Sweden, when Abigail hadn't stopped talking about how marvellous Niki was, Hannah was still thinking of what she had seen, read and heard in Berlin, and even in Amsterdam, Brussels and Anvers, and indeed Paris.

'I'm here,' said Niki. 'Don't laugh, but I think I was created for you alone.'

'I'm not laughing.'

'I love you.'

She closed her eyes, once again seized with that bittersweet pang. That evening after dining at the Tour d'Argent, where he was a regular patron, Niki took her to a literary gathering at Adrienne Monnier's place in the Rue de l'Odéon. Paul Valéry, Cocteau, Gide, Valéry Larbaud and André Breton were among those present. Hannah was surprised to find all these people whom she knew; Niki was an even closer friend of many of them than she was.

It was Niki who introduced her to an Irishman in his fifties, called O'Driscoll. He had been one of Lenin's companions, before and after the Revolution, and retained from his anti-British terrorist past the manner and behaviour of a spy, which Hannah was much taken with. He would never sit down at a table, not even at La Coupole or La Closerie, without checking to see whether there was a bomb under the seats.

One evening O'Driscoll asked her why she had never opened any salons in Soviet Russia, or even before, when the country was still tsarist.

'One, because I'm Polish and I don't much care for the Russians, and two, because I don't really see how my creams could do anything to improve their mujik faces.'

'She's joking,' said Niki.

'I'm not joking at all,' said Hannah. 'And I doubt very much whether your precious Mr Stalin would be very interested in beauty lotions.'

It was true that she had no interest in opening an establishment in Joseph Stalin's Russia. She couldn't imagine how it could ever be viable, or even allowed. But on the other hand, she saw that it would attract a lot of publicity . . . as long as she made sure that Western newspapers picked up the story of her Moscow campaign, which shouldn't be too difficult to arrange – journalists could be very nice to her when she took the trouble to show an interest in them.

Dealing with the Reds wouldn't make her a Communist; after all, a few months earlier, on 16 November 1933, President Roosevelt and Litvinov had signed an agreement at the White House, re-establishing diplomatic relations between the two countries.

But even so, it took a considerable leap of the imagination to visualize herself representing the glories of American capitalism among the Soviets.

So she looked on O'Driscoll as a likeable lunatic.

She was wrong: a little over a month later, the same O'Driscoll reappeared. Would she by any chance know of Gorky? She said that she knew of a writer called Maxim

Gorky, whose novel, *Mother*, and whose play, *The Lower Depths*, she had read.

'That's the one,' said the Irishman. 'Would you go to Moscow if Gorky invited you?'

'Why not? But I thought he was dead.'

'He was still alive ten days ago when we had dinner together. You speak Russian, don't you?'

'Certainly, better than you.'

Spring 1934 arrived. Within a few months Hannah had resumed control of her whole European operation. There wasn't a beauty parlour or shop that she hadn't visited, or whose accounts she had not gone over with a fine-tooth comb. She now knew names, faces, strengths and weaknesses, and how long all her employees had been working for her.

Every month, either Jessie or Dennis LaSalle, or more rarely Wynn, who suffered the handicap of not speaking any other language but English, came over from New York. Besides the accounts – she received the figures daily in any case – they also brought her very welcome news: America under Roosevelt seemed to be getting back on its feet nearly five years after the crash of 1929. *Franklin owes you only $7,500 now, and if he carries on the way he's going, you can consider his debt paid in, let's say, three years' time . . .*

Everywhere business was booming; she calculated that at the rate things were going, she would make a net profit this year of one and a half million dollars out of the American network alone.

And according to Maryan, the Wall Street Stock Exchange was also much healthier.

'Hannah, if you want to withdraw your investments you'll soon be able to do so. It looks as though share prices will reach a reasonable level . . .'

She eventually bought the apartment on the Ile de la

Cité that she had wanted to buy in 1913. At that time the owner had categorically refused to sell: only death got the better of his stubbornness. It was a two-storey apartment, three counting the attic. The place was indescribably dirty (the deceased proprietor had apparently lived with 103 cats), the seventeenth-century wall hangings were mostly in tatters, the parquet floors were on the point of collapse, so too was the wood-panelling, and the furniture was so full of woodworm it would have been unwise to sit on any of the chairs.

'It all needs completely redoing,' declared Adam, whom she had asked to come especially from Detroit. 'Apart from the walls, and even then . . .'

She and her son climbed out on to the roof. Though the view was breathtakingly magnificent, the little building next door slightly obscured it. And in any case it was too close, scarcely five or six yards away.

'Mother, while you're about it, you ought to buy the top floor of that house. And I'll design a glass bridge so that you can go from one to the other . . .'

He also thought of a garden that would take up the whole roof of both buildings. With a fountain, or better still a little waterfall, and some Japanese bonsai trees. And in the midst of all the flowers and greenery would be one or two, or even three rooms, that would form a kind of retreat; almost entirely glazed so as to preserve the wonderful panoramic view over the whole of Paris.

Adam stayed a week in Paris. He was thirty-three and almost regretfully she had to admit that with each passing year he became a little less the image of his father. Even though the physical resemblance, in his hands and face especially, was striking, Adam was taller than 'him', and more athletic, and most of all he was calmly and quietly self-assured. His Jacqueline had a lot to do with this. And he was always ready to talk about his wife, his children, his work as an architect, the life he had made for himself in America – was he not already a captain in the National Guard, in other words a reserve officer? And had he not been asked to stand for the Democratic party in the municipal elections in Detroit?

'But I can't accept, mother. Your chances of seeing your son in the White House one day are practically nil.'

She knew what he was going to say before he had even opened his mouth.

'Mother, are you going to marry Niki?'

'I don't know.'

'Abie thinks he's absolutely marvellous. I don't know whether he's marvellous, but I think he's more than likeable.'

Here we go again: you're all in a panic!

'Would you agree to it, Adam?'

'It's not for me to agree to it. But I would be happy if you did. I think you need him . . .'

She stared at him in amazement: *need Niki?* The idea had never even occurred to her. All her life she had lived independently, expecting nothing of others except what she could give them. That she could possibly need anyone . . .

It took her all night to persuade herself that Adam might be right, and then only after her initial annoyance, and indeed anger, had subsided – what right had Adam to interfere in her life? But by the morning she could stand back and laugh at herself – proof that she had recovered her usual clear-headedness.

You really have the most insufferable character anyone could imagine, Hannah! If you were my daughter, I would give you a good hiding. It's not inconceivable that you might be crazy, the way you talk to yourself as though you were two people – when one of you is quite enough to make everyone's life a misery! Why keep poor Niki dangling like this?

Now, don't tell me you don't know. You know very well

why. Remarrying and day after day finding yourself in the arms of another man would seem like a horrible betrayal to you . . .

And you would continue to think about 'him' even in moments of passion.

Or so you believe . . . Unless it's the opposite that you're afraid of – finding out that 'he' is no more with you now than he was in the past. That's what really scares you, Hannah . . .

Adam returned to the United States. Niki was not in Paris but in Saint-Tropez (a little village no one had heard of), where his daughter was about to give birth to her second child.

She was therefore on her own when the letter arrived – a very official letter, brought to her by an employee of the Soviet Embassy: she was invited to Moscow, and if possible, she was asked to bring six of her model beauticians. When could she leave?

The following Monday.

That gave her no more than four days to make all the arrangements: choose the young women who were to accompany her, make sure their passports were in order and that they had visas, and also dress them, get their hair done, buy gloves for them, tell them two hundred times a day what they were to do and say ('Never say *niet*, always say *da*, that's simple enough, isn't it?'); assemble a truckload of stock, all the products she wanted to take with her, as well as a few essential pieces of furniture and equipment that they might not be able to find there; inform the press – not just the French press but also the press in the rest of Europe and America – in order to turn this expedition to the steppes into a colossal event, so that there would be some fifty photographers and twelve radio reporters crowding round when she boarded the train for Moscow, wrapped up in her sable coat, replying in French, English, Italian, Spanish, Polish and Russian to all the questions fired at her, looking delighted and very vivacious, drawing attention to the exceptional beauty of the six young women travelling with her, the smallest of whom was a head taller than Hannah . . . (all the while trying to think whether she could have forgotten anything in the excitement, convinced that she must have forgotten something, something important that she should have done or said – *What the hell could it be!*) . . . checking the stock, even though Jeanne Fougaril swore on her own head that there wasn't so much as a knicker button missing, making sure that she had with her the first-edition copies of Balzac's *Le Père Goriot* and Gustav Flaubert's *Sentimental Education* that she intended to give as a present to Maxim Gorky . . .

And even when the train was leaving, long after it had already left, when it was travelling across Europe and across the boundless plain where she had been born, while giving her beauticians a further briefing, to the point where she almost drove them wild, she still kept wondering what it was that had escaped her attention in all this rush.

She kept checking and rechecking, but couldn't think of anything.

How damned annoying!

His head shaven, his moustache like that of a mujik, his eyes blazing with intelligence, Gorky greeted her as though they had always known each other. He wouldn't confide in her, of course, but he would say enough, through his eloquent silences, to give her to understand that he was no longer the enthusiastic eulogist of Stalinism that O'Driscoll had portrayed him to be. He displayed reserve and nostalgia. With all his questions he made her talk more about Paris and Montparnasse, London and New York than he spoke about Russia – or else the Russia he described and took pride in was his own Russia, with its fragrant samovars and vast expanses, not the Russia of the Reds. During the whole of her stay in Moscow, he did not leave her side. His face wreathed in smiles, he would attend the daily demonstrations that, contrary to their usual submissiveness, people fought to get into (Hannah organized three demonstrations a day instead of the single one originally planned, but she nevertheless failed to satisfy the enormous thirst felt by the women of Moscow for the knowledge she brought them). He introduced her to painters, many of them very talented, and also writers and musicians, and made a point of taking her back to her hotel on the Prospekt Marksa every evening. One evening, just after he had left her – it was nine thirty and she had decided to retire early in order to go over her notes – he called after her and asked her if she would agree to go out again to meet someone. She hesitated and then said yes, only because the writer's voice sounded so strange.

Half an hour later she was at the Kremlin, feeling rather dazed. If it hadn't been for the friendly smile of old Gorky, she might almost have been worried. But there he was, smiling, and saying: 'He wanted to see you, Hannah,' sounding even more surprised than she was.

They were escorted by one guard after another to the heart of an incredible surveillance network. They finally reached the Saint George Room in the Grand Palace, where she and Maxim Gorky sat down, each as lost as the other in this huge resonant space measuring two hundred feet by seventy. The parquet floor was a sheer marvel, the wood blocks from twenty different types of tree. An hour at least ticked by. Had she been on her own, Hannah would have left: *I don't give a damn about this fellow who not only gets me out of bed but then keeps me waiting!* Eventually someone came for them and led them through a maze of corridors and staircases. At last, scarcely able to credit it after such a long wait, Hannah found herself in a small salon filled with rather heavy furniture. There was a man in the room, writing at a little table. He was scarcely of average height, and had a thick moustache. He finally laid down his pen and stood up. Gorky made the introductions and Joseph Stalin was seen to frown slightly, as though searching his memory. Gorky again intervened, diplomatically – Stalin and he were evidently on familiar terms. A conversation then ensued that, but for the place and the person involved, would have been very ordinary.

Stalin said to Hannah that she must have actually been born a Russian. She agreed, but replied that she was now American, and had been for thirty-four years.

He questioned her about her fortune, how she had made it, being a woman, and how much she was worth.

'I made some cream, one pot and then another, and then a few more,' she replied. 'Today I sell them in twenty-one countries, and I now have twenty-nine million dollars to my name. It's not a very complicated story.'

A kind of smile lit up the Georgian's rather slit-like eyes. Suddenly, having sat down next to her, he told her he had been to London in 1907, the only time he had ever been abroad, when he had also stayed briefly in Vienna. Then without any logical progression, he started quoting Walt Whitman, his favourite poet – along with Gorky, of course. And finally he asked Hannah whether she was going to open one of her beauty parlours here in Moscow.

'If the government grants me permission,' she said, 'I will.'

He was openly smiling now. He believed that the government would give her permission. And he had even heard talk of beauty salons throughout the whole of the Soviet Union. Could she set up a school for beauticians, like those in France and the United States?

Good God, Hannah, you must be dreaming! This peasant with dreadful strangler's hands taking an interest in beauty – who would have believed it possible!

The interview rapidly came to a close. Her stupefaction had still not worn off when she found herself back in Red Square.

'Did he really authorize me to open an institute? Did he really ask me to open a school for beauticians? I didn't dream it, did I, Alexei Maximovich?'

'You didn't dream it,' said Gorky.

From the door of the Tower of the Saviour emerged a non-commissioned officer and two soldiers, who walked off in the direction of Lenin's mausoleum, completed four years earlier. It was two minutes to midnight: *I shan't be satisfied with Moscow, I shall have to go to Leningrad and to other towns* . . . Already she was making plans for this unexpected opportunity for expansion . . . *And after that, China and Japan. And the Indies too, of course. And Istanbul, Cairo . . . And Bucharest, where I should have opened already. After that I might go and take a look at the southern tip of Africa, in the Cape, to see whether there's anything to be done there. That would only leave Latin America, starting with Mexico. Argentina, for instance, where Niki's son* . . . 'Oh my God!'

She had sworn out loud. She stopped dead just as she was about to enter the hotel.

'Is something wrong?' asked Gorky.

'For several days now I've had the impression that I had forgotten something when I left Paris. I've just realized what it was: I forgot to get married!'

CHAPTER 33

I'm Happy and I'll Never Grow Old

They were married in Rome on 6 June 1934. This made her Princess of Archangheli, but she would always remain the same Hannah.

Among those who attended the ceremony were Maryan and Lizzie Kaden, together with eight of their children, accompanied by their respective spouses and offspring; Adam and Jacqueline with their six children; and Abigail, escorted by Paul Travers, the chemist from the laboratory in New Rochelle, to whom she had just become engaged.

'Don't you think you could have told me, Abie?'

'I wanted it to be a surprise, mother. Don't be angry with me, and don't be angry with Paul. I had terrible trouble trying to persuade him to come.'

Hannah had always thought very highly of Paul Travers, she would never have employed him otherwise, but it seemed to her quite a different matter having him as a son-in-law. *Could it be that Mr Four-Eyes imagines that marrying your daughter is the best way to get on in the company?*

Her anger evaporated as quickly as it had flared up: young Paul was evidently terror-stricken in the presence of his future mother-in-law and present employer, but he and Abigail were extremely determined and no less clear-headed: 'Mother, Paul and I want to set up our own laboratory. He has a bit of money and I have some savings of my own and. . .'

'I don't think I've ever heard you say anything so stupid,' said Hannah. 'Not only would I lose my best chemist, but on top of that my own daughter would be working for my competitors! Tell me I'm dreaming!'

And she burst out laughing. Then she asked Paul exactly how much money he had. He told her. She nodded. She didn't think he was that rich. He said that he had been saving up for six years.

'With a bank loan. . .'

She started. Borrow money from those thieving bankers? (This scene took place fifteen hours before her wedding.)

'Paul, there's to be no more discussion about this. Here is what we're going to do: in exchange for your money I'll sell you a half-share in the laboratory at New Rochelle. You haven't enough money for it, but you can pay me the rest in grandchildren. Ten per cent per grandchild. Fifteen per cent if they're really sweet and don't look like me. But of course you can arrange for them not to look like me – you only have to want something badly enough in life. . .'

Jeanne Fougaril also came to Rome, and Estelle Twhaites, Polly's widow, and Jessie from New York, and Cathy Montblanc, and many others. Winnie Churchill, whom Hannah had not dared to invite, sent two presents: one was a superb Pissarro, the other a lady's corset from the 1890s which ten Hannahs could have fitted into with ease.

Originally planned as a quiet affair for only close friends and relatives, the wedding turned out to be a gathering of more than three hundred people, many of whom came without an invitation, hoping at least to attend the ceremony.

As well as the palazzo in Rome and the country estate in Lombardy, Niki also owned a country house in Tuscany and the Villa Anacapri in Santa Maria Cetrella. It was here that the couple spent four days. Four days only. Niki made no protest when on the morning of the fifth day she announced that they would not be making their planned trip to South America just yet. She first wanted to devote herself to getting established in Moscow, and also opening up in Istanbul and Bucharest, and even Sofia . . .

'It'll only take two or three months. Would you be very angry with me?'

He shook his head, smiling with the same incredible sweet gentleness that he would always show towards her; demonstrating the patience and understanding which he would never cease to display until the day he died.

'Not if I can come with you, Hannah.'

'You'll be bored.'

'I don't think so.'

He went with her, and they would always travel together ever after.

As a lover, he reminded her in many ways of André Labadie. *Except that when you knew André you weren't free, and no man could have been more than a last resort to you then. Whereas now, and at your age . . .*

In all honesty she believed that she felt great tenderness and affection for Niki, and no less fervent feelings of friendship. As the months went by, she realized that she had grown so used to him, to his often silent presence and to the attentions he paid her, that even the idea of being separated from him was no longer tolerable.

Niki even put up with her rages with disconcerting composure. It was enough to discourage a person from getting into a rage. When she became too exasperating – and she could be unbelievably exasperating – he would merely take himself off into a different room; or he would pick up a book and become immersed in reading it, as though nothing was happening. She could scream, he just didn't hear her, or pretended not to – which amounted to the same thing. When the storm was at its worst, he would actually go out for a walk, without uttering a word, and by the time he got back she would be whispering almost, instead of shouting, feeling subdued and amused. This little man who was always so impeccably groomed and invariably polite knew just how to deal with her. 'I think I was made to look after you,' he told her one day.

And he proved it to her.

He never interfered in her affairs, except when she asked for his opinion, which she would do increasingly often, but never in front of anyone else. It was really he who suggested Maud Derry, a young woman, scarcely more than thirty, as a replacement for Jeanne Fougaril (Jeanne could not be persuaded to change her mind about retiring). Maud had a French mother and an American father, she had been a director for Paul Poiret, then ran the salon in Monte Carlo before taking over the running of the Spanish operation and finally acting as co-ordinator for Europe, once Hannah had regained control of the company, and of the American network.

Hannah couldn't decide between her and a Milanese with lots of qualities, who had been partly trained in New York at Mainbocher.

'Why not Luigi, Niki? He's Italian like you, after all.'

'You asked me my opinion, and I've given it to you. I think Maud would be better for the job.'

'And she's lovely-looking, you satyr.'

'And she's lovely-looking. I don't see the harm in that.'

Niki had started painting, rather nonchalantly. *Like a woman working at her crochet, waiting for her husband's business meetings to be over,* she thought for a second or two, before reproving herself for this gratuitously wicked notion. And feeling very contrite, she enthused about her husband's paintings.

'There's no need to flatter me, Hannah, I'm only a dauber, like your friend Churchill. And it doesn't bother me.'

They were in New York for the end-of-year festivities. (The American magazines featured Hannah on their covers: she was often photographed in Red Square, having been the first to raise the capitalist flag in the

Stalinist world; and the women's press never tired of devoting pages to her; she was recognized in the street with increasing frequency.)

She started looking for a country house outside New York either to buy or to rent; she was even prepared to go quite far out, but couldn't find anything suitable.

They returned to Europe in January.

For months, Pierre Poncetti from Geneva, Nigel Twhaites and Henry Christie from London, Joachim Hueberschmidt from Zurich, and Jos Wynn from New York had been preparing the ground for her, even travelling across the globe: now she could buy back Australia and New Zealand.

It was in London that she met the Australian delegation, consisting of Régis Fournac and two of his nephews, sons of Jean-François, who had died two years earlier. Despite their French names, they were dyed-in-the-wool Aussies, and their French was hesitant, especially the younger man's.

She had never lost her love for Australia, and her friendship with Régis Fournac was rock-solid. An agreement was reached and signed at the end of March, whereby Hannah took back seventy per cent of the cosmetic part of the business, and only fifteen per cent of the huge chain of restaurants, hotels, tea rooms, and shops of all kinds that had been set up over a period of forty years by the former French immigrants and herself. ('Can we go back there, Niki? I feel a little nostalgic for it.' 'Whenever you like, my dear.')

It was on Niki's highly discreet insistence that she bought the fifteen per cent, departing from her cardinal rule of never going outside her own area of beauty products. But after a year of marriage, and having known him for several years before that, she had discovered with some surprise that for fifteen years Niki had been a financial and legal adviser to the Vatican.

'Good God, you mean you almost became a cardinal?'

'I could have been a cardinal.'

'What is this you're telling me? You're not even a priest!'

'You don't have to be a priest to be a cardinal.'

So she could have been the wife of a cardinal! The idea made her fall about laughing.

She was extremely cheerful and full of energy. When, at about that time, she totted up all her money and earthly possessions, she was thrilled to learn that she had close on one hundred beauty salons and nearly three hundred and fifty shops. . .

'A veritable empire,' said Niki.

She was continually improving her operation, running around from one establishment to the other. For a while, in the interests of surprise, she would disguise herself . . . until the day in Barcelona when, as she left the Rambla de Canaletas wearing the most outrageous camouflage, she heard the beautician – who had dealt with her without turning a hair even at her most idiotic demands – say: 'By the way, Madame Hannah, we are all very pleased to have you with us. We thought that these few flowers . . .' It turned out that despite her blonde wig, big thick-lensed glasses, Valkyrie-like false breasts, and six-inch high heels, she had been recognized the moment she crossed the threshold.

Talk about looking stupid! she thought, deeply mortified.

And this time it was Niki who fell about laughing.

Abigail married Paul Travers with the same quiet determination that she brought to everything. The first of her five children was born in September 1935. It was a boy, and Hannah's seventh grandchild. Abie wanted to call him Nicholas, but Niki opposed this, almost curtly, which was very rare with him. Hannah was happy. She had to go back twenty-five years to remember a time when she had known such a sense of well-being and fulfilment. (No further, though, that would have been sacrilege, and would have called into question that period of her life when she felt choked with happiness.) Her life now, with Niki by her side, was in no way comparable; this was a different kind of happiness, a calmer, less fraught happiness, and less susceptible to dramatic reversals; safe from disruption in fact. She had now developed the conviction that she had nothing to fear from Niki; he played the part of prince consort with such even-temperedness and such unparalleled equanimity. Sometimes, she knew, people would mutter that he was her secret adviser, to whom she owed all her success . . .

In any case, it was Niki who, with infinite circumspection, one day announced the news to her: he had found Jonathan and spoken to him.

'We had a long talk, Hannah. But for the difference in size, he looks disturbingly like you . . .'

Suddenly, having felt so light-hearted the moment before, she was overwhelmed with an immeasurable sadness of the kind she had almost forgotten existed, and the fullness of which she was only now discovering.

They had been in San Francisco, at the Hotel Fairmount on Nob Hill, for the past three days.

Niki drew her to him and she did what she would never have believed herself capable of: clinging to a man, seeking comfort and consolation from him. Niki started talking in a low voice in the silence of their bedroom. He hadn't run into Jonathan by chance. Like everyone else, he knew that Adam's younger brother was probably in the Far East. So he had written to friends of his in Hong Kong and Singapore, and also Shanghai.

'They eventually managed to track down a Jonathan Nenski, owner of a tramp steamer that was plying the South China Sea.'

'You. . .'

'Let me finish, Hannah. I wrote to him about five months ago . . .'

'Without telling me.'

'Without telling you. I very much doubted I would get any reply. But I did.'

'Which you didn't tell me about.'

'No, I didn't. All it said was: "Who the devil are you?" I sent back a long letter in which I tried to be . . . as convincing as possible.'

'I don't understand.'

'Hannah, I tried as best as I could to explain that whilst I had had the unbelievable joy of marrying you, I had had to fight against the incurable love my wife felt for her first husband; the only one who mattered to her; infinitely more than I ever shall. And I tried to explain as well to Jonathan that his mother was an utterly marvellous human being, whatever he might think of her, that I had never been able to take the place that you, Hannah, still reserved for the only man in your life and, despite all that, I was extraordinarily happy with what you were prepared to give me.'

She started to cry, unable to hold back her sobs.

'Oh Niki! Niki!'

'It was a very easy letter to write, Hannah. It was all very clear in my mind; the whole story is basically very simple.'

He rocked her gently.

'And after that,' he said, 'there were three months of silence, to the point where I thought I hadn't been as . . . convincing as I should have been. But, no. He wrote to me again, hardly less succinctly than the first time: he offered to meet me here in San Francisco.'

'I see now why you were so insistent that we should come here.'

'I was hoping to be able to surprise you. Don't be angry with me.'

'I'm not angry with you.'

'We were to meet in a bar on the Embarcadero. I waited more than three hours and eventually decided he wasn't going to turn up. I left a message for him and walked out. He was waiting for me outside.'

'How is he?'

'Fine, as far as I could judge.'

'Describe him to me.'

'He's very tall and very thin. Very handsome too, in a way.'

'What are his hands like?'

'A bit like Adam's, but much stronger. He looks like the kind of man who could crush your arm between his fingers. He was dressed like a seaman, with a peaked cap, he . . .'

Niki gave a very detailed description. And of course she eventually asked in a whisper: 'Is he going to come back to me, Niki?'

'He's already left. He sailed that same day – it was yesterday – on a cargo ship to Japan. He told me that he had sold his own boat, but that he was probably going to buy another. I didn't dare offer him any money. He is not the kind of man who would accept . . . Or even need it.'

'You didn't say anything yesterday evening.'

'I was hoping to be able to find him this morning and talk to him again, in the hope that, having slept on it, he would have reconsidered. He told me that he didn't want to re-establish any kind of contact with his family.'

'But he turned up to meet you.'

'He made sure I was alone; I think that it was because of that that he waited for me outside the bar . . . Yes,

Hannah, yes, of course I told him you were in San Francisco.'

Silence.

'I want the truth, Niki.'

'Word for word, what he said was: "I've agreed to meet you because you're a complete stranger to me . . . and also because I was curious to meet the man who . . . who was fool enough to marry my mother."'

'Niki, are you sure he said "my mother"?'

'No. He said, "to marry her," without specifying who he was talking about. I'm dreadfully sorry, Hannah. I'm so sad. I would so much like to have reconciled you . . .'

'You're the best thing that could have happened to me, Niki.'

They went to South America. Niki's son, Pier-Francesco, had a huge estate in Argentina, part of which had been left to him by his mother, and part of which had come to him through his marriage to the daughter of another *facendero*, also of Italian origin. It was near Bahia Blanca, to the south of Buenos Aires. Hannah and Niki spent about two months there. On the way, they had stopped over in San Salvador de Bahia and in Rio, where she selected two sites for her salons, one on the seafront on the Avenida Atlantica, in Copacabana, the other in the centre of the city, next to the Opera.

She also planned to open a beauty parlour in Sao Paolo – a friend of the Arcangheli who was in charge of several factories there managed to convince her of the *paulista* dynamism and, with a little exaggeration, of the fact that this city was to Rio what New York was to Washington – in Montevideo, apparently another capital city, and of course in Buenos Aires; at the same time she opened shops in Rosario and Mar del Plata – according to Pier-Francesco, this was the future Cannes of Argentina. And why not?

She summoned Xesca Vidal from Barcelona and entrusted him with the new branches, teaming him up with the Milanese Luigi Cabrini, who spoke Spanish and Portuguese fluently, and whom she intended to appoint director for the whole of Latin America.

They went straight from Bahia Blanca, by sea, to Santiago in Chile (the salon here was to be run by Philippe Zaval), then on to Lima (another salon), also by sea. They arrived in Panama (another salon) on 26 October. The salon in Caracas was opened nine days later, with Jamie Aguiló as director, who had just arrived from Madrid at Hannah's request. Aguiló was accompanied by his wife, Carmen, and a small team of four Spanish beauticians whom he had persuaded to emigrate (Carmen would be in charge of the beauticians' school on the Latin American continent).

This interminable trip, and especially the gruelling heat, rather tired Niki, who also suffered a bout of malaria. Not Hannah, though, who would have liked to end the trip with a visit to Mexico City. But despite protests from Niki, who declared himself fit enough to continue travelling after two weeks' rest in Jamaica, she decided to postpone the visit to the Mexican capital, and they returned to New York.

That was the year she decided on her American country house: she settled on Virginia, in the Shenandoah Valley. It was of course quite far from New York, but that didn't matter – very soon she expected to be able to travel between her office and her Virginian residence by plane. Adam chose the site, on the edge of an area that had just been designated a National Park; he drew plans for a house that she thought wonderful: the building blended in perfectly with the landscape, hardly disturbing its harmony, and stood next to a waterfall that supplied two swimming pools with water (one of these was completely covered, with picture windows all around). Most important of all was the spectacular view from two big terraces, one above the other, of the winding Shenandoah River, across the Blue Mountains and the Appalachians, over forests stretching to infinity, where bears and lynxes and birds lived in their millions – and all this only a little more than an hour's drive from Washington.

This was her fifth home (there was also the Parisian apartment on the Ile de la Cité, the apartment on Fifth Avenue in New York, the house in Saint-Tropez on Pampelonne Beach, and the one at Saint-Jean-Cap-Ferrat), the fifth, that is, not counting the house at Morcote, over which the Swiss servants continued to mount guard, although Hannah hadn't been there for six years (she would probably never go back; but she would sooner be burned alive than sell it).

She also wanted to buy something in London, perhaps too in Switzerland, in the mountains, and – her stay in Jamaica had given her the idea – she was thinking of buying a little *pied-à-terre* in the Caribbean. Nigel Twhaites had suggested the Virgin Islands or, if she wanted to be closer to the United States, why not the Bahamas?

'Hannah,' said Niki, 'that would give you eight or nine different homes, and if you were short of a place to stay – I can't really see how you ever would be – you could always go and stay in Anacapri, or the palazzo in Rome, or the house in Tuscany, or even the farm in Lombardy. Not to mention the *fazenda* in Argentina.'

'Those are yours. Or your children's. And anyway I need somewhere to hang up my paintings. Besides, I'm beginning to get fed up staying in hotels!'

While on the subject of paintings, having started to build up a collection forty years earlier, she now had some thirty dozen canvases, including seven Renoirs, nine

Monets, five Modiglianis, two Cézannes, four Gauguins. . . as well as paintings by Pissarro, Manet, Whistler, Mary Cassatt, Kandinsky, Klee, Klimt, Kokoschka, Matisse, Degas, Chirico, Stael and Picasso (seven canvases by her friend Pablo, including a portrait of herself), Van Gogh (eight), Derain, Miró, Juan Gris, and many others.

The end-of-year celebrations found them in California, where Maryan had bought a second house, up on the heights of Palm Springs. It was huge (there had been plans to turn it into a hotel before he bought it). Big though the house in Beverly Hills was, it could no longer contain the whole Kaden family. Maryan and Lizzie, together with their twelve children – all married – and their grandchildren, formed a contingent of some seventy individuals that was constantly increasing in number. In addition, there were the Kaden brothers and sisters, with their own spouses and two generations of their offspring, and a few MacKennas who had wandered into this Polish-American sea of humanity – they could have been mistaken for an army on the march in a film by Cecil B. De Mille.

'Abigail and Paul with their two children, Adam and Jacqueline with only six, plus Niki, Yvonne and myself are really pathetic in comparison, like Liechtenstein's army next to Mr Hitler's.'

'The more of us lunatics there are, the more fun we have. In any case, there are forty-nine bedrooms, not to mention the stables and the dog kennels.'

At fifty-three, Lizzie had grown a little portly, and now looked very stately. She said that she and Maryan had been invited to the White House, where she had been a great hit with her dirty jokes.

Even Hannah was a bit worried by this. Not Lizzie though: 'You're the one who first told them to me,

Hannah! By the way, did you get your revenge on Groucho?'

Yes, she did. The Duesenberg SSJ (there were only two models in existence and Gary Cooper owned the other) beat Groucho's Mercedes by half a length.

'We also raced each other up the stairs of the new Empire State Building and I beat him again, but more easily: I won by five storeys.'

(What she didn't say was that she had needed smelling salts to revive her once she had got to the top. But it was true that Groucho was fifteen years younger than she was.)

'Does Roosevelt still owe you money, Hannah?'

'Not much. Only $1,725, according to my calculations. I don't think I shall be sending the bailiffs round to collect it. I've pretty well had my money's worth.'

This was true, or at least Hannah was convinced of it. Every time she came back to the United States during the 1930s she was struck by her country's opulence and zest for life. The contrast with Europe was enormous. Adolf Hitler's Germany made her want to weep, nor was there anything in Mussolini's Italy to inspire Niki and herself with enthusiasm. America, which she never ceased to explore, usually by car (she would take the wheel; Niki was not very keen on driving), touched her heart anew, and the love she had conceived for the country in February 1900 was once again awakened.

During the next ten years she hardly ever left its shores – except in 1937, when she and Niki made that long trip to the Indies, Burma, Siam, Cochin-China and Tonkin, Malaysia, Hong Kong, Canton, Shanghai and Peking, Korea, Manila and finally Japan. Maryan found her an Austrian couple who had settled in Singapore, while Niki recommended an English couple, who were born in Shanghai and still lived there, whom he remembered from his days as Ambassador to China. She divided the whole of the Asian network that she was then setting up between them. It was to be supplied by both the American factory and the one in Melbourne.

With her company now operating in the East, she had well and truly encircled the globe, with 141 beauty salons, 512 shops, and nearly 6,000 employees, the names and faces of nine-tenths of whom she was familiar with, working directly under her orders.

Among the other reckonings she made was the extent of her fortune:

Nearly thirty-eight million. Forty-three years ago to this day you were wandering the streets of Melbourne without a penny in your handbag. . . In fact, you didn't even have a handbag.

Plus a son and daughter, both married.

Plus ten grandchildren, with an eleventh on the way.

Plus Niki.

Heavens alive, you're going to end up thinking you're happy!

One thing amazed her, and gave her satisfaction, confirming the opinion she had always had of herself: though years had gone by, the enthusiasm that had carried her through the past fifty years had never waned, and there was no sign of its weakening. The rhythm of her life remained unchanged: every day that dawned found her already up and about, wherever she might be (more often than not at the house in Virginia, which she and Niki had filled with books). Her early-morning routine was always the same: she would slip out as it grew light, and walk for an hour along the mountain paths in the Appalachians, come wind, rain, snow, or the droning heat of summer. Then she would return home, by which time Niki would be up too. They would breakfast together – he would have a little tea and toast, while she ate her three eggs, or an even more hearty meal – exchanging smiles across the table. And all the while it would be getting lighter, with the sun reaching the depths of the valleys, dispersing the shadows of the night and revealing the eight or ten winding loops of the Shenandoah.

I'm happy and I shall never grow old.

CHAPTER 34

There's Nothing Wrong with Getting Old, Lizzie . . .

At about eight o'clock, the mist began to lift. The Rhine appeared first, then in the following minutes the Appenzel and Vorarlberg Mountains emerged like ghostly apparitions. It was freezing cold and Niki, seated next to her, adjusted the big red-and-black chequered blanket so that it covered her legs more snugly.

He gave her a questioning look, but she shook her head.

'I'm still not cold.'

And yet, for maybe half an hour she had not stirred. Her gloved hands were resting on the leather-covered steering wheel of the 1939 Bentley Streamline that registered a mileage of only 1,600-odd miles on the clock – not much for six years, but she had hardly used the car, which had been left in a garage on Gotthardstrasse in Zurich: she drove it only in Switzerland, on the eight or ten occasions she had been in the country between 1939 and 1945.

On this 8 February 1945, she and Niki had left the Hotel Baur-au-Lau in Zurich at five-thirty in the morning. It took them a little over an hour to reach Saint-Gall, then a further ten minutes to Rorschach, and about as long again before they reached their destination: Sankt-Margarethen, where the Bentley had now been stationary for an interminable length of time. To the right was a vineyard on the now sunlit hillside, to the left lay Lake Constance, and beyond the rounded bonnet of the car was the Rhine, the frontier with Austria, the road to Bregenz. The frontier post was two hundred yards away. Through the windscreen they could see not only the Swiss guards, but also the helmeted soldiers of Hitler's army on the other side of the bridge.

'A little more coffee?'

Niki unscrewed a Thermos flask.

'Yes, please.'

She also bit into a biscuit. At the same time, two cars drove up behind them, their headlights still on, although it was growing lighter all the time. They came and parked next to the Bentley. The Genevan lawyer Pierre Poncetti got out of one, his white hair set off by his suntanned face, a tan acquired while skiing. He was with one of his colleagues, Peter Erlenbach. Both lawyers carried thick leather briefcases bursting with documents.

'Everything is in order, Hannah,' said Poncetti in German.

She nodded, her face in the Thermos cup. The second car was a big luxurious Horch 853. There were four men in it, including a chauffeur. The three passengers got out and bowed stiffly. Still sitting behind the wheel of her car, Hannah stared at them; but the only acknowledgement she gave them was a frosty movement of the head. One of the men in the Horch was Jean-Pierre Mary, former President of the Swiss Confederation, former head of the finance and customs department. He was decidedly bald, with a moustache, and his face quickly turned red with the cold. He had never ceased to declare his sympathy for Nazism, but it was precisely because of his personal friendship with Reichsführer Heinrich Himmler, Chief of the SS, that he had been able to act as mediator.

His two companions were German. One of them was a diplomat posted to Berne, the other, although dressed as a civilian, was an SS Gruppenführer – a major-general – who, thanks to Mary, had been granted a visa to enter the country by the Swiss authorities.

'Hannah, it's horribly cold and nothing's going to

happen for thirty minutes. You ought to go into the warm.'

'I'll wait here.'

She stared at the SS officer with a hatred that made her tremble.

She had been working on the Sankt-Margarethen affair, and had instructed Pierre Poncetti and Peter Erlenbach to work on it too, for nearly eight months. It had taken all Poncetti's and Niki's patience combined to ensure that she did not become personally involved in the diabolical negotiations. 'Hannah, the only way to achieve anything is to conduct these discussions as though it were an ordinary transaction, such as the purchase of building materials or pharmaceutical products. Forgive me for being so brutal, but your presence would represent an additional risk of failure when the risks are already enormous.'

Just a few days before Christmas 1944, a price was agreed: ten million Swiss francs, a little under seven hundred thousand dollars; and the number to be involved: two thousand. When she heard the figure, Hannah was thrown into a desperate fury. She had travelled to Geneva via Lisbon and Madrid on a Spanish aircraft, flying over war-torn France (her last visit to that country had been three years ago, under the protection of her American passport). In Poncetti's office she had given vent to her rage and distress: 'Two thousand? It was supposed to be ten thousand! And the price, my God! Didn't you tell them I was prepared to pay ten times more than that! Pierre, I made thirty million dollars available to you!'

Two thousand, and not a single refugee more. Poncetti eventually managed to convince her that he and Erlenbach had done their best: 'Hannah, it's a miracle that Himmler should have agreed at all.'

* * *

'Here they are,' said Pierre Poncetti.

There had indeed been some movement on the other side of the bridge, in Nazi territory. A grey car had appeared. It advanced some thirty yards and then halted.

On the road behind the car, the bonnet of the first truck came into view.

Hannah opened the door of the Bentley and stepped out. Less than thirty seconds later, she heard a rumbling of engines on her right: the enormous convoy of buses, ambulances and lorries that she had hired was arriving dead on time. In the leading vehicle she recognized Suzanne Dubois, her director in Geneva, who waved to her.

That too put her in a bitter rage: despite all their efforts neither Poncetti nor Erlenbach had been able to obtain the slightest help from the Swiss Federal Government. Nor had they been able to get permission for those rescued – if they managed to get so far – to remain in Switzerland. There was just the possibility that an exception might be made for those who had family already settled on Swiss soil, but as it had obviously been impossible to find out anything at all about these miraculously freed people, this effectively did not apply.

She had spent days sitting outside offices. Even the International Committee of the Red Cross had shirked the issue, giving her the same response as one of her compatriots – who was a representative of the Joint Distribution Committee – had given her six months earlier: 'Under no circumstances can we join forces with anyone resorting to illegal means to help Jews.'

At the United States Embassy in Berne she was warned that it was impossible for Washington to agree to participate in any plan to buy Jews from the Nazis, which would enable the enemy to prolong the war.

Finally she herself hired the twenty-eight buses, thirty-four trucks and only nine ambulances – she had not been able to find any more, and as it was she had had to buy three of them outright at a high price. She had also obtained warm clothes, shoes and blankets for two thousand two hundred people, in case more got out than expected. With Niki's help she had organized all the necessary supplies, hospital facilities in six private clinics, and transport through Switzerland to Annecy in French Savoy (France having recently been liberated), where she had booked whole floors in the hotels.

'You're going to catch cold, my dear.'

Niki had also got out of the Bentley. She felt him put his arm round her shoulders, and though his gesture was one of affection, she found it almost unbearable, so tense and nervous was she. She kept her eyes on the grey car four or five hundred yards away that hadn't moved for such a deadly long time.

Twenty minutes.

Mary's two companions and Mary himself went and huddled in their Horch. Even Poncetti and Erlenbach were blue with cold. Still she would not budge, taking a fierce and bitter pleasure in defying the elements, when these men were unable to withstand the cold.

She kept her eyes fixed on the grey car, slowly succumbing to despair.

It's going to fall through at the last minute! It's going to fall through!

But no. Pierre Poncetti, who had a pair of binoculars despite the ban on them, was the first to anounce the news: 'They're moving, Hannah. And my God, I think they're coming this way. . .'

Half an hour later the sun had gone in and, with amazing rapidity, the sky once more became overcast. A large formation of fat grey clouds had come from the north-east, darkening the sky, and a little while afterwards the first snowflakes started to fall. And all their faces, already grey and horribly wasted, took on a frightful, deathly pallor.

They were already coming across the bridge. The most able-bodied came first: they clambered down from the trucks unaided and staggered the whole distance they had to cover from one frontier to the other. Then they came more slowly, until the worst of these living corpses appeared, and slowly the no-man's-land between the Swiss and German border-guards was filled with nurses walking to meet their patients.

Hannah finally stirred. Less than thirty yards away from her a bus was now filled, mostly with women, but there were also five or six children, one of them a little girl, maybe seven years old. Hannah walked over to her.

'What's your name?'

She asked the question in German. She repeated it in Polish, Russian, and Yiddish but got no reply.

'Filthy whore!'

The abuse came from her left. Hannah turned and was struck in the face. Then someone spat at her. Niki and Erlenbach came rushing up and dragged her away, rescuing her from the derisory blows – so feeble were they – of two of the survivors, both shaven and haggard, their features distorted with hatred.

'Come away, Hannah, for the love of God . . .'

But she calmly disengaged herself and, with a wave of her hand, called Suzanne to her. She wanted the names, nationality and all the information that could be obtained from these women; women who were on the threshold of death, but who were still capable of standing up and fighting.

'What do you have in mind?' asked Niki.

She returned to the car without a word, and resumed her place at the wheel. What did she have in mind? Sorrow, pity, anger and hatred. And shame too, for having paraded herself in her mink coat and Bentley in front of these survivors of hell. And also admiration for the two women who had just attacked her.

Three minutes later, something in Poncetti and Erlenbach's bearing caught her attention. She went over to them. Poncetti was shaking his head, and in reply to her question said: 'It's enough to make you sick with anger, Hannah. They freed the first thousand, and then after the second half of the payment had been made, they sent the second batch. We've just counted them: there are only 186 instead of one thousand. And the last ones to arrive say that there are no more coming after them. Oh God, the rotten bastards!'

On 10 February, the convoy she had organized crossed the French border and dispersed. Winnie Churchill, busy though he was, intervened personally with de Gaulle so that she and her protégés should be allowed free passage. For the next three days, snatching only an hour or two's sleep in the Bentley, she went tirelessly from one group of refugees to another, as they now scattered over an area stretching from Evian to Annecy and Saint-Julien-en-Genevois. Nineteen people had not been able to travel: their state of health would not allow it. She had them admitted to a clinic, but after a few days two-thirds of them were flown in a hospital plane to a hospital in Lyons. Three others died. Only three. Perhaps because of the speed with which they were treated, but perhaps too because the Nazis only put up for sale the least feeble.

'Put up for sale, Hannah? That sounds terrible,' said Niki.

'I can't see any other way to put it. And it doesn't just *sound* terrible.'

As well as appealing to the French authorities, she also turned to two men who did their utmost to help her. One was Douglas Kaden, Maryan and Lizzie's second son; he was forty-two and, after being wounded in the landing on

Omaha Beach in Normandy, was appointed to General Hodges' staff as lieutenant-colonel (Hodges was in charge of the Twelfth American Army Corps in the Ardennes). The other man was General Shelby, a relative of the MacKennas. He had just come from Italy to take charge of the military communications centre in the French capital. Both men did all they could; Shelby even managed to send two C47s filled with supplies to Lyons.

There were some children among the 1,186 Sankt-Margarethen refugees. By 8 March Hannah had managed to track down some surviving family for thirty-nine of them. That left nineteen, including the little seven-year-old Hannah had noticed at the border. The little girl turned out to be Hungarian and one of her fellow prisoners thought she remembered the child being in Theresienstadt concentration camp for the past two years.

'Her mother's dead, Niki. Her name's Charlotte.'

'No family name?'

'No. Either she's actually forgotten it, or she never knew it. Niki?'

Eight months earlier Niki had fallen from the extending ladder in the library in the house on the Shenandoah, and had fractured his femur rather badly. He still had a slight limp. The accident had aged him, even though he wasn't as old as her. However, he had done more than his share in the rescue operation throughout the past weeks.

And he understood at once. *Even if he thinks we are both a bit too old to take care of a little girl when we don't even speak her language. Especially you; you'll be seventy next month, and you've never been very maternally inclined anyway.*

'Do whatever you think right, Hannah. Charlotte's a pretty name.'

Charlotte became Charlotte Travers – Paul and Abigail adopted her instead of Hannah – and seventeen years later married Pier-Paolo Archangheli, Niki's eldest grandchild. It was never discovered who her family were.

Hannah and Niki arrived in Paris at the beginning of March. Hannah had appointed Suzanne Dubois and Pierre Poncetti to look after the interests of the other 1,182 who had escaped from Theresienstadt. Poncetti was to devote two years of his life to the task, working with one of his colleagues, Thierry Masselon, a Frenchman living in Geneva.

In Paris her wonderful apartment on the Ile de la Cité had been devastated: soldiers had been billeted there for weeks on end, and before the Liberation they had smashed everything, including the glass walkway designed by Adam. The marble fountains on the roof, the marquetry and mouldings on the ceilings had been blasted with machine-gun fire, just for the pleasure of causing destruction, it seemed. However, with new furniture and bedding, the twenty-two rooms would be just about habitable.

Once again she turned to Shelby, who managed to have sent to her from England enough to equip three bedrooms and two sitting rooms. Through one of his former classmates at West Point, Douglas Kaden managed to obtain enough bedding to transform the large drawing room, designed by Paul Iribe, into a dormitory for fifteen of the concentration camp survivors. And what had been the library five years ago, Hannah turned into a canteen serving 120 meals a day.

She wrote to Jeanne Fougaril, not having heard from her for three years, asking her to come and join her. One morning in March, Maud Derry turned up, the person who had succeeded Jeanne as director general for Europe. Maud had heard of Hannah's return by chance, having bumped into one of her beauticians, who told her that all those who had worked at the Rue de Rivoli and the various other HH establishments in Paris were welcome at the canteen on the Ile de la Cité. Maud was terribly thin and pale, and had scarcely recovered from the nightmare she had endured: she was arrested in November 1943 for belonging to the Resistance, and incarcerated in Fresnes Prison, then at Breendonk Fort in Belgium; only through a combination of circumstances (the train she was travelling in had been bombed) did she escape being deported to Ravensbrück. Her own sister was less fortunate; she was decapitated. But this tall, thin young woman with violet-blue eyes, a slightly husky voice and plenty of charm, had a will of iron. She lowered her head.

'You won't be getting a reply to your letter to Jeanne, Hannah. She died in '43. Two of her grandsons were shot, and she lost the will to live. She wrote a letter for me to give to you, but they took everything from me.'

'Getting old is nothing, Lizzie, the worst thing is surviving . . .'

'Hannah,' said Maud, 'you must open the salons again. The sooner, the better.'

Acting on the orders she had been given, in June 1940 Maud had closed all the salons and shops in France, Belgium and Holland, and then, in September of the same year, all the other establishments in Europe, except those in Spain, Portugal, Switzerland, Sweden, Britain and Russia – as far as Hannah knew, not only did the institute in Moscow stay open, but so did the one in Leningrad, even when the city was under siege.

'As we agreed, I made a file of the names and addresses of all the people working for us and gave it to Harriet Morris in London; I suppose she still has it,' said Maud.

Yes, she would try and track down as many of these hundreds of people – in fact there were two thousand five hundred – as she could. She had already made contact with two or three members of her former management team, including the Brussels-born Nicole de Wulf, the Dane Willy Clausen, and Jacques de Pinsun and Pascale

Dufresne, who were both French. And she had also heard from the Italian team, which had not suffered so badly: Rome, Milan, Turin, Florence, Venice and Naples had been able to keep their doors open throughout the war.

'Not to mention, of course, the British and the others who were able to continue functioning without interruption. Hannah, give me forty-five days and I'll be in a position to tell you when I can get started again.'

No, she didn't think she needed any reinforcements from across the Atlantic.

That evening, 6 March 1945, Yvonne managed to improvise a meal that was just about equal to the occasion. They sat down to eat in one of the rooms on the top floor under the eaves, where Hannah had her office before the war. There were eight of them at the table. As well as Hannah and Niki, there was Maud and Pascale Dufresne, and Biff MacKenna, who had come all the way from Australia to fight in the RAF, General Shelby, the journalist and writer Ernest Hemingway, and a young nurse he had brought with him.

The telephone rang just before ten o'clock. 'It's for General Shelby,' announced Yvonne. Shelby went down to the floor below – most of the telephone lines had been pulled up and the system had not been entirely restored.

Two minutes later Shelby reappeared. 'Would you come down, Hannah, please.'

She followed him down. A few moments later Niki, aware that something must be wrong, joined her. The receiver was back on the hook and he found her sitting on a folded mattress in one of the bedrooms, with her back against what remained of the Jouy canvas that served as a wall hanging.

She was pale but she wasn't crying, and she had an expression on her face that Niki had never seen before, one that reflected unspeakable anguish: her grey eyes stretched open impossibly wide and her mouth gaping in a desperate attempt to breathe.

'It's Adam, Niki,' she said. 'They've killed him.'

He had died two days ago. On a silly little island no more than six miles long in some remote part of the Pacific. The place was called Iwo-Jima.

The day after Pearl Harbor, Adam had at his own request been taken on by the regular army and given the rank of captain – he was a major in the National Guard. Hannah had begged him to take a post in Washington, which she could easily have arranged for him. At first he agreed. But a few months later, after the fall of Corregidor in the Philippines, he got himself transferred to a fighting unit. It wasn't until October 1943 that he was assigned to the Marines. In November he was involved in action in the Gilbert Islands, on Tarawa Atoll, then in the recapture of the Marshall and Mariana Islands. In the last letter he wrote to Hannah, dated 26 February, four days before his death, he told her of his pride and anxiety: he had just learned that Ewan, his second son, had now enlisted at the age of eighteen, following the example of his elder brother, Tadd. Both had joined the Marines. *The last thing I heard, he was a lieutenant on the* Indianapolis*, *while Tadd was a lieutenant on the* Cecil-Doyle, *a destroyer. But I assure you, mother, they're both safe: there is not a Japanese ship still sailing the seas, and this war is nearly over . . .*

Adam had just turned forty-two.

* On 30 July 1945, the cruiser USS *Indianapolis* was sunk by a Japanese submarine in the Pacific. There were 316 survivors out of a crew of 1,196. Ewan Nenski was among the survivors. By sheer coincidence, the *Cecil-Doyle*, with his brother on board, was one of the first ships to come to the rescue.

CHAPTER 35

Lizzie, I Wonder if It's Quite Right at Our Age . . .

Niki had a heart attack, which might have passed unnoticed, as on previous occasions – Hannah was sure there had been others before now. But it was two days before Christmas and the cars kept arriving at the huge house on the Shenandoah: a full complement of the Kaden horde; Jacqueline, her children and her two little grandchildren; Abigail and her husband, Paul, together with their five offspring; and a dozen more guests besides. Adam's son Ewan was there: he had finally stopped telling the story of how he had clung to a raft in the middle of the Pacific, been attacked several times by sharks and, for four days, floated in an oil slick; and then had the astounding surprise of being rescued by his own brother. It was now 1947 and he had just come from Paris, where he had learned to speak French and had doubtless too discovered what French women were like . . .

It was he who gave the alert. He had gone to the studio Niki had fixed up for himself right next to the 35,000-volume library, in order to say hello to him.

Niki had collapsed before his very eyes, just as he was reaching out for a book on Mantegna. Hannah had come running, and immediately arranged for him to be transferred to a hospital in Washington, refusing to pay any attention to the protests of her husband, who was already recovering. But all the doctors could find wrong with him was a slight arrhythmia and, having kept him for thirty hours under observation, they eventually bowed to his calm determination.

'I want to go home, Hannah.'

He was sixty-nine.

'You've already been through this before, haven't you?'

'Every time I see you,' he replied with his kindly smile.

For her, he had given up everything, or nearly everything, that had been his life before their marriage. The war certainly, and political circumstances to some extent, had forced the decision on him: no friend of Mussolini's dictatorship, he had refused to set foot in Italy until the war was over. The German Occupation meant that he couldn't go to Paris, and for a long time before that, he had decided he didn't want to go to Germany any more, a country he had once loved. He found it difficult to get used to life in America, and yet he had never been heard to voice even the mildest complaint. He had always accompanied her on all her trips, waiting around for hours on numerous occasions while she inspected one of her domains, or discussed business. Together they had been round the world maybe seven or eight times. As soon as the war ended – May in Europe, September in the Pacific – she had resumed her tours. He had never complained; on the contrary, he had always been the most agreeable, the most soothing of companions; sometimes he would go half a day without so much as opening his mouth – true, she talked enough for two . . . *And yet he knows, almost to the second, when he ought to speak and what to say . . . just as he did when Adam died.*

And when his own daughter died in a car accident, he almost begged Hannah to forgive him for the grief he was making her share.

She and Niki had been on the first flight inaugurating a commercial air link between America and Europe at the beginning of December 1945. They left Washington on a Constellation, called Paris Big Chief, in the company of a personal friend of Maryan's, who was secretary of state responsible for the postal service, and twenty-seven other passengers. It took them sixteen hours to reach Orly Airport, near Paris, with a stopover in Ireland. Since then, they had made the same journey roughly every two months, except in the spring of 1946, when they went to Australia, New Zealand and Japan.

From the end of '47 and throughout '48, she completed the rebuilding of her empire – what Niki called her empire; she talked simply of 'my shops'. The salons in Berlin, Munich and Hamburg were re-opened, and she greatly extended her German operation under the management of Fred Hauptman, who had returned to his native country after ten years' exile; it was he who introduced her to Konrad Adenauer, the future Chancellor of Germany. Adenauer was amazed to learn that she was able to keep her Berlin salon open during the blockades. She was happy to explain: for some reason that she couldn't understand, she had obtained permission to supply her Berlin establishment via her Soviet subsidiaries; there was no point in asking her why such consideration should have been shown to her, ever since 1934 in fact.

'I suppose that Stalin gave an order at that time that I was to be left alone, and as he must have forgotten to rescind the order and no one dared ask him about it . . .'

In 1949 she applied for a visa, just to see what would happen. The answer was *da*. And the same went for Niki. But the redoubtable Soviet administration's benevolence did not extend very far where her husband was concerned: he was simply authorized to wait for her. On the other hand she was allowed to go to Leningrad. She found it very difficult to reconcile the place with memories of her youth, a good half-century ago. The hotel where she stayed was on the banks of the Neva, with the museum ship *Aurora* on the right. Every day she would walk to her salon, near the Nevski Prospekt, on the Quai Griboyedov, followed at a distance by two or three policemen who pretended not to know her. Twice she took malicious pleasure in losing those tailing her: once by slipping into the ladies at the Maly Theatre, and the second time in the Hermitage Museum, from which she emerged wearing a scarf on her head and a blouse she had bought for one hundred roubles from an astounded cleaning lady. On both occasions she passed within a few feet of the secret police agents, and to her delight they didn't even give her a second look. The experience positively enchanted her; she ought to have been a spy. She was even more amused when, on returning to her hotel, where she was immediately surrounded by a mob of her frustrated minders' colleagues, she simply opened her eyes wide in disingenuous innocence and asked them (she had discarded her disguise) if it seemed plausible that trained policemen could lose the trail of a little old lady of nearly seventy-five who had merely gone out for a walk.

'In any case, Niki, I don't care whether those uncivilized wretches close my salons; I can't get the money I make out of the country, and this certainly isn't the place I would choose for us to spend our holidays!'

She did, however, come home with nearly a ton of caviar and six wonderful sables. That was all she could find to buy.

And yet it was strange that she should enjoy such special immunity there. 'If Maxim Gorky weren't dead, I could understand it . . .'

'Perhaps Joseph Stalin goes to your beauty parlour disguised as a granny, to get a facemask?'

'You may be right!'

She changed her habits. She continued to get up early, at dawn or even earlier, depending on the seasons, and whether she was in Virginia, New York, London, Paris, Saint-Tropez, or in the new house she had just had built at Fex, in Switzerland, near Saint-Moritz, she always began her day with an hour's walk – a little less if it were very steep terrain, but she always walked quickly. (She had forbidden Niki to go with her, because of his heart. 'Mine's fine, thank you . . .')

And she continued to spend an hour or two going over her accounts, after she got back from her walk.

'I can't understand why you do all those calculations. You have enough accountants around the world to staff three companies.'

'My calculations are like my walk, they help me to keep you fascinated, with my ravishing body and the phenomenal liveliness of my mind – that's enough applause! And in any case, the accountant I could trust has yet to be born. Niki, will you stop fooling around on that ladder, you're going to break your leg.'

And once she had done her accounts, she would eat. The big change in her life was that she had discovered how 'jolly nice' it was to have breakfast in bed. Niki, of course, did not share this view. ('You would put on a suit and tie if you got up to pee during the night, my darling.')

It was so jolly nice that she made a habit of it. Once she had taken her physical exercise, been over her accounts, and had a foam bath, she would get back into bed – and not just any bed. She had decreed – 'by imperial command', as Niki would say – what the dimensions of her bed should be in all her homes: eight foot by six foot six inches – the latter being the length, contrary to expectation. The sheets had to be black silk, with a turkey-red trim, the pillows (it was imperative there should be eight) were turkey red with black lace. And in this huge bed, against which her grey eyes and pale complexion looked most striking, she would receive her senior staff in imperial style, eating her three boiled eggs, seasoned either with a little basil or Mexican chilli, depending on her mood, followed by two apples and a pretzel (a croissant if she was in France), drinking tea without sugar.

Sometimes there would be fifteen or twenty seated in a

circle around her bed, some of whom had come from the other side of the world just to ask her advice, or to be told that they had not done exactly what she had expected of them. And woe betide the man or woman whose memory was not as good as Hannah's and who made the slightest mistake about the salon, shops, or group of establishments that he or she ran. Biting into her apple or pretzel, Hannah would fix them with her glinting grey eyes: 'Are you absolutely sure of the figures you're so confidently quoting?'

Often she would choke with laughter after her field marshals had departed.

'Niki, did you see the expression on Ota Schinichi's face? I thought he was going to commit hara-kiri! And he was right, his figures were right, I just said it as a joke. I would be sorry if he committed suicide, he's rather nice. . .'

By the 1950s, the value of her jewellery exceeded four million dollars, and her total wealth now came to more than one hundred million dollars.

Where she kept her jewellery was a big problem: by an incomprehensible paradox she appeared to be incapable of remembering the combination for the safe in which it was locked away.

'It's no good, I just can't remember those damned numbers!'

And thereupon she would lose her temper and start shouting.

'Niki, I'm sick of this. This time I'm sure of it: I dialled the right numbers and it won't open. I want this rubbishy thing changed! It doesn't work!'

And Niki would arrive, completely unruffled, and calmly form the right sequence of numbers – 12345 or 67890 – and of course the thing would open without the slightest problem.

She even tried to keep a note of the wretched numbers on a piece of paper that she stuck to the door of the safe, so as not to lose it.

'Excellent idea!' said Niki. 'You ought to write the numbers in red so that burglars will be able to see them better. And have signposts pointing the way to your room from the lift on the ground floor.'

In the end it was Lizzie who found the solution: she turned up with the most ordinary filing cabinet, which she had bought at Macy's. It had some twenty drawers and on each of these drawers Lizzie had stuck labels that just had letters on them: A, D, E, G, PE, PL, R, S . . .

'And what are those stupid letters for?' asked Hannah suspiciously.

'A for Amethysts, D for Diamonds, E for Emeralds, G for Gold, PE for Pearls, PL for Platinum, R for Rubies, S for Sapphires. Et cetera. There's nothing to stop you adding more letters.'

Lizzie had to sit down, she was laughing so much.

Three seconds later Hannah joined her, and the two of them were seized with a fit of hysterics that left them both panting for breath.

'Lizzie, I can't help wondering whether it is a good thing to be seized with such uncontrollable fits of laughter, at our age . . .'

They were both in London. Lizzie had come to visit Sandy, one of her daughters, the ninth of her twelve children. Sandy had married a film director, an Englishman who lived mostly in Ireland. As for Hannah. . .

'What's come over you, Hannah? We've been laughing like this for fifty years.'

Hannah was there, with Niki of course, to supervise work on the house she had just bought – her seventh home, since she had also bought her very own island, in the Virgin Islands, near Puerto Rico, with not much more than a cabin on it and the ruins of a small fort built by French buccaneers. Perhaps it was actually the eighth. . . She was forgetting the apartment in Paris on Rue de la Varenne, which she had bought because it overlooked the Prime Minister's garden.

The house in London was a three-storey building on the edge of St James's Park. Each floor was in fact quite small, the whole house consisting of only ten rooms, four of them bedrooms, and the means of access to each floor was via an outside staircase, so she had a very charming little lift installed that played the tune of '*Le Temps des Cerises*' as it went up and 'Waltzing Matilda' on the way down. It was the lift that had provoked their hilarity; Lizzie and Hannah were trying to think of some other music that could eventually replace these two old songs, while they went up and down in the lift, seated on two Louis XV chairs, having a whale of a time. Lizzie set them both off by saying that, sitting in this lift with no door, they must look like two old ladies with their knickers down on their way to seventh heaven. They collapsed into hysterics, under the bemused gaze of the English workmen (in fact they could have been Scottish or Welsh).

Their mirth redoubled when they thought of their difference in height, one of them measuring four foot ten inches, the other five foot nine.

'Lizzie, I'm very worried about Niki.'

'His heart? It's nothing.'

'I don't know. He's aged a lot.'

'But not you.'

'Not me and it's not fair. Has he said anything to you?'

'Niki? Not a word.'

'You wouldn't by any chance be fibbing, would you?'

The Rolls-Royce was driving very slowly down Regent Street. Hannah, who still adored driving, had no interest in doing so in urban traffic. So she had let Laurent, Yvonne's nephew, take the wheel.

'Of course not,' said Lizzie. 'Why ever should you think that?'

'He's spoken to you. I'm sure there's something wrong with him, some illness that he's hiding from me.'

'You're imagining things.'

'Lizzie, that was the second time you used that phrase. The first time was in 1921, some time before "his" death. And I wasn't imagining things. That's what I thought, that day in London, but I didn't dare mention it to you.'

'He's grown terribly thin,' said Hannah.

She watched Lizzie's hands and noticed how they tensed slightly. All her suspicions were confirmed. Her first intimation that something was wrong had come in the autumn of 1948, on their return from yet another world tour, starting from New York, then heading west via San Francisco, Honolulu, Tokyo, Manila, Hong Kong, Hanoi, Bangkok, Calcutta, Katmandu, Kabul, Tehran, Cairo, Rome and Paris. Her consuming passion for travel, which nothing, neither repetition, nor her advancing years, seemed capable of diminishing, had made her almost blind to the obvious; it was months before she noticed that Niki must have been suffering agonies trailing round after her. Sometimes he took advantage of her being kept late in a meeting to stay and rest in his hotel bedroom, waiting for her, when ordinarily he was so interested in everything and everyone.

It's true that he has friends everywhere but you've been terribly selfish. You should have been able to see that he was worn out . . . She felt guilty and almost hated herself: *If you were in love with him, really in love, loving him as much as he deserved, you would have noticed the very first signs of his exhaustion. But you've never paid very much attention to him, he was just someone to keep you company so that you didn't have to be alone. Oh Hannah, what a swine you are!*

'Lizzie, his heart's all right, the doctors told me so. There's something else wrong with him. I'm sure that he went to see someone in Paris, I don't know who it was. He was lying when he said that he had stopped to chat with a bookseller. Niki lying to me – it's so unlike him. I almost had him followed, or followed him myself. I was ashamed.'

'Laurent, would you please turn round and take us back to Kensington,' Lizzie told their chauffeur through the intercom.

'It's something serious that he refuses to tell me about,' said Hannah, her eyes suddenly filled with tears. 'I've been incredibly hard on him. I've never once told him I loved him. Not once . . .'

'He wouldn't want you to lie to him, and you know it.'

'I should at least have tried.'

The Rolls turned on to Piccadilly and drove along Green Park, passing within a few hundred yards of St James's Park.

'I should have tried. I've let him love me without giving him anything in exchange but a little affection and friendship. I really am a swine.'

'Absolutely,' said Lizzie very calmly. 'You're the worst swine I've ever known, and that's why we all hate you – Niki, Maryan and I, and Abigail and Jacqueline and your grandchildren and a few hundred others scattered around the world. You've descended to such depths of ignominy that the only thing left to do is to throw you in the Thames with a stone round your neck.'

She spoke into the internal telephone again.

'Laurent, will you drive very slowly, please.'

She replaced the receiver.

'I think you've talked quite enough nonsense for today, Hannah.'

'What did Niki tell you, Lizzie? That he was going to die?'

The Rolls advanced along Rotten Row, Hyde Park, in extraordinary silence, going no faster than an unhurried stroller lost in thought. On their right lay the Serpentine and ahead, among the trees with their spring foliage, was the Albert Memorial and Kensington Gardens.

'We're all going to die, Hannah. Even you. It isn't what I would call news. Let Niki live his life the way he wants to. I believe he has made you happy these past fifteen years, as far as he was able, and you, for your part, have given him all the happiness he could have hoped for – he told me so himself. Don't try and complicate things, life is simpler than it seems. Stupid but simple.'

Niki died on 29 June 1949, having managed to conceal from her until the last three weeks that he had cancer. Right to the very end, taxing his strength to the limit, he refused to impose the burden of his suffering on anyone, least of all Hannah.

The twenty days before his death were nonetheless dreadful. Despite his extraordinary courage – as long as he could still speak, he asked to be shaved and to have his hair combed – sometimes a muffled groan would escape him, which he would immediately try to stifle.

But he would then manage a smile, and every time he saw her face bent over him, he would whisper: 'The sight of you has always made my heart skip a beat, Hannah.'

She was at his bedside day and night, in the white room in the villa on Anacapri where, very timidly, as though embarrassed to be such a bother, he had asked to be taken.

An incredible number of friends from all over the world called up; the phone never stopped ringing. Many – dozens of them – came all the way to see him just to tell him how fond of him they were.

She wondered whether, when she was dying, she would receive even one-tenth of the demonstrations of affection shown to this man who had always cultivated his discretion.

'I love you, Hannah, you've given me all the happiness I ever expected and more. Forgive me for leaving you . . .'

After she had closed his eyes, Hannah wept bitterly in Lizzie's arms.

'This is the first time he's ever caused me pain. Oh my God! I would never have believed that I loved him so much. And I wasn't able to tell him . . .'

CHAPTER 36

I'm Immortal, Maryan

Maryan followed shortly afterwards.

In January 1950, on the advice of Averell Harriman, one of his oldest friends, he turned down Harry Truman's offer of the post of United States Ambassador to Moscow. It was a worrying time for him. Though not in the least tempted by the job and the prestige attached to it, he was not sure it was right to refuse his country anything. But in the end he said no: at seventy-three he considered himself too old; he had begun to retire from his own business concerns three years earlier, either selling out or handing over – to those of his sons who were interested – his shares in the property business, in banking, and in aeronautic engineering. He had kept only his stake in the film industry, in radio and, most important, in the commercial exploitation of the 1923 invention of the Russian Vladimir Kosma Zworykin, a naturalized American, father of television.

Maryan firmly believed in the future of this new means of communication.

'Hannah, the day will come when it will be possible to transmit images between any two points on the globe. From your armchair, you will be able to see what's happening, live, in the Antipodes.'

He had come to see Hannah in Anacapri, taking advantage of a business trip he had to make to Paris, Zurich and Milan. Even when excited, as he was when talking about television, though his blue eyes would become slightly dilated, he remained calm. He was a cool dreamer, his passions contained, though none the less ardent. His fair hair had turned white as snow and, over the years, the Californian sun had given his smooth face a golden tan; he stood very straight. His discretion had become legendary in America and in financial circles everywhere; he had never been seen to open up, to smile, even less to laugh, except, first, with his children and then his grandchildren.

And Hannah was still the only person in the world before whom he would display a strange timidity, shifting his weight from one foot to the other.

'It's incredible, Hannah, the years go by and you remain unchanged.'

'I work at it, you know.'

'It's not just that.'

He had found her in the conservatory whose big bay windows gave a clear view over the gulf, the sea, the green plateau of Anacapri and Monte Solaro, and even Axel Munthe's Villa San Michele, just visible between the cypress trees. She was writing a long letter to Abigail, but close to hand, in one of the famous black-and-red leather files, were her accounts, which she had just spent two hours going over.

'I'm immortal, Maryan.'

When he came in, she practically ran to meet him and fell into his arms. A servant brought him the coffee he had asked for. They spoke of this and that, of their children and grandchildren, of friends and everyday life. Then a silence fell upon them. And she knew then that there was a reason other than the fraternal love they bore each other for this visit.

'What did you want to talk to me about, Maryan?'

He simply looked at her and she understood in a flash.

'Jonathan?'

'I was in Hong Kong last week. I saw him. I didn't speak to him. He was crossing a road and by the time I had stopped the car he had disappeared into the crowd.'

'But you found him again.'

'The next day, through a Chinese friend. Hannah, it's possible that this friend was expecting my enquiry.'

'You mean that Jonathan had seen you?'

'And he may have deliberately allowed himself to be seen by me. It's only an impression I have. Hannah, Jonathan has a house on Hong Kong island. Not in Victoria, on the other side, in an area called Stanley. He wasn't there when I called. But there was a very beautiful young woman . . .'

'His wife?'

'His daughter. She's of mixed race.'

'So her mother's Chinese.'

'Yes. But she's very beautiful. More than beautiful. I told her my name, and she said that she recognized it. Her father had spoken to her about me and warned her that I might pay him a visit one day.'

She was thinking, rather doubtfully: *So I have a granddaughter with slit eyes!*

'And where was Jonathan?'

'I asked her that. She smiled and shook her head. That was her only reply.'

'Did she tell you whether she had a mother, or brothers and sisters?'

'No reply.'

He started talking about the house in Stanley, which was a simple building.

She asked: 'What's my granddaughter's name?'

Out of habit, she looked at Maryan's hands. There was a tiny movement, but real enough.

'Hannah,' he said. 'Her first name's Hannah.'

Maryan had lunch with her and then, in the afternoon of 11 February, he returned to Naples and the Italian mainland. His private plane was to take him back to London, but he would only stay a few days in the British capital – long enough to complete the sale of his remaining interests in Europe. Then he was to return to the States. Lizzie and he were planning to go to Australia, where they would stay six or eight months. ('Now that all the children have left home, the house seems very empty, Hannah; even the house in Palm Springs, with only Melanie and her little family. Perhaps we'll go back for the school holidays, if only to see the grandchildren. We'll see. Lizzie will decide, as usual . . .')

She drove him to the pier in the brand-new Alfa Romeo she had just bought – in September the previous year, she had almost killed herself when a cart suddenly pulled out in front of her on a road in Umbria; her Ferrari had ended up amongst the vines and burst into flames, but she had escaped with a slightly sprained wrist.

'Why don't you come and join us in Australia?'

'I may well do that. Give Lizzie my love.'

He's the only surviving witness of my youth, she thought, watching the *vaporetto* sail away across a cobalt-blue sea. But she fiercely repressed this painful nostalgia that would lead her nowhere. Slowly – she couldn't go very fast on the roads on Anacapri – she drove back to the villa. Yvonne was in France, staying with her children. *She's getting quite old now too, poor thing . . .*

Hannah spent the rest of the afternoon in Niki's library, leafing through the wonderful collection of art books he had accumulated. She came upon various letters among the pages – a few lines from Pablo Picasso, Malraux's tormented handwriting, or a drawing on a page from an exercise-book by Giorgio Morandi, done one evening when they had dinner with the artist at a restaurant in Trastevere, in Rome. *So many cities and so many faces, Hannah . . .*

By about six, the sky was overcast and the wind was getting up. Soon a real storm broke, coming from the north-east and bringing angry purple clouds. She went out on to the windswept terrace and rested her elbows on the bougainvillaea-entwined balustrade. *With a bit of luck, this damned wind will carry you away – you're small enough* . . .

At one point the telephone rang. One of the servants answered it, but there was no one on the other end of the line.

'It must be the wind, *signora*.'

She never slept more than four or five hours a night. Lying in her huge bed, she would sometimes play chess by herself, though she would often have to break off and put the game aside when memories came flooding back. Some evenings it was almost hallucinatory: as she moved a piece she would see 'his' huge hand slowly reach across the board, and she would all but feel the touch of his hand on hers, and smell the scent of his body – though she had not uttered his name in twenty-four years, even in the course of the bizarre monologues she conducted with herself.

At dawn she went out to walk around the island, wearing a large straw hat that kept her face in the shade. All night the storm had raged, making the weather-vane creak.

She went down to Damecuta, where the ruins of the Emperor Tiberius' villa were to be found.

The telegram arrived while she was out. And as soon as she got the news, the two deaths – Niki's death and this one, eight months later . . . but what were eight months in a lifetime? – seemed to blend into each other, becoming one and yet multiplying into infinity.

Maryan collapsed with a stroke after leaving the aeroplane at London Airport. He did not survive two minutes and, Hannah was told later, he entered the next world with the same impassive expression on his face, his blue Polish eyes fixed for ever in dreamy stillness.

* * *

They were alone now, the two survivors, Lizzie and Hannah: *'Getting old is nothing, Lizzie, the worst thing is surviving – surviving a world of change, time passing, all those we loved . . . The problem with feeling immortal is not so much the weariness that comes over you, but the self-hatred for still being in this world when your loved ones are no longer . . .'*

'Don't cry, sister.'

CHAPTER 37

I Never Came to Malaysia, in Any Case

Laurent Gaffouil came back to the car and resumed his place beside the Chinese driver of the Rolls.

'She won't be long, Madame Hannah.'

The excitement of China seethed all around them. Children came up to the car, one of them stood there picking into a bowl of rice with a pair of chopsticks, which he wielded with impressive dexterity; his face was perhaps a little grubby, but he was cleanly dressed in a pair of black shorts that came down to his knees, and a beautifully ironed white shirt. In the background was a little fishing harbour with junks and sampans. The South China Sea stretched away as far as the eye could see. There was a very distinctively Chinese smell of fish and spices, blood and mire, a smell that ought to have been nauseating. Yet she had always loved it, since the first day of the first trip to China and Shanghai, ages and ages ago . . .

Laurent gesticulated and shouted, in French and English, and also in his local Ariège dialect, in the vain hope of dispersing the crowd that was gradually clinging to the doors of the Rolls.

'Leave them be,' said Hannah.

She smiled at the grubby-faced child eating soup, and asked the driver how to say, 'It tastes good' in Chinese. The driver translated for her. The child immediately forged his way through the ranks and came up and offered her with his chopsticks a piece of what was in principle – she hoped – some fish with a few grains of rice.

She closed her eyes and swallowed. She grimaced: it was horribly spicy.

'It tastes good,' she said, choking on the red chilli.

There was general hilarity. *I'm a great success here*, thought Hannah. *If I went on stage I would have a full house every night.* The other kids were now clinging to the doors. Hannah pulled one of her worst faces at them, touching the end of her nose with the tip of her tongue, and at the same time crossing her eyes. There was renewed laughter. *It has to be said, you do have a very long tongue. You could almost wipe your eyes with it when you cry!* She went on to do her Dragon act, the Golem, the Carpathian Bear, the Amorous Weasel, and all the other routines usually reserved for her great-grandchildren. And then, as it was getting late, she even sang them a dirty song, in French, that Lizzie and she had found so hilarious all those years ago, but which drove adults of the next generation to fury: 'The girls of Camaret all claim to be virgins, but when they're in my bed, they'd rather hold my wick than a candle.'

Young Hannah looked her up and down.

'He told me you would come.'

'Your father?'

'Yes.'

'He's my son. Which makes you my granddaughter, and I'm your grandmother.'

Hannah was stunningly beautiful. She must have been about twenty, at most. The smoothness of her complexion and her prettily slanting black eyes were the only traces of her semi-Asian parentage. She was almost as tall as Lizzie.

'I know very well who you are.'

'Do you speak French?' said Hannah, using the intimate form of address.

The young woman hesitated.

She does, but she doesn't want you to address her as 'tu'.

'I went to school in Hanoi, a convent school.'

The house was simple, just as Maryan had described it.

There were only three rooms, with a little kitchen and a bathroom – a shower-room, to be more precise, that had a tall earthenware jar containing water for washing. But there was a large veranda at the back, with a roof made of palm and a view over a charming creek.

'Does he sometimes come here?'

'Occasionally.'

'Has he spoken of me?'

Again she hesitated.

'No.'

'It isn't nice to tell lies, as I'm sure the nuns in Hanoi must have told you. Did he tell you how you were to behave towards me?'

Silence.

Did he tell you to throw me out, my child? You could easily manage it. Well, perhaps not, thought Hannah.

She walked around the three rooms. There were two bedrooms, one of which was the young girl's; the walls were decorated with photos of Rome, Paris, London, New York . . .

The other was undoubtedly a man's. *A man who is not often here. Does he leave this adorable child alone in Hong Kong?*

'Please go,' said Young Hannah.

'Throw me out, child. Have you ever been to Europe or America? Never, eh? Jonathan is my son, you know, the only son left to me. I had another son, Adam, but he was killed. I also have a daughter, Abigail. I'm telling you these things because I don't know how much you know. Adam had six children, Abigail has five. Which means, not counting you, that I have eleven grandchildren. They're your cousins, by the way. And I also have sixteen great-grandchildren, I wouldn't be surprised if I ended up with two dozen.'

She came back into the third room, where the young girl had remained standing.

'I was a disastrous mother. Apparently, I'm a little better at being a grandmother, though not much. As a great-grandmother I think I'm even better. If I were to live five hundred years, I would become an almost acceptable ancestor. I believe that Jonathan has spoken to you about me, quite a bit. I would have sworn that he was set to hate me for the rest of his life, but he has given you my name. I don't understand that. Unless your father hates you too?'

Young Hannah shook her head.

'For heaven's sake!' said Hannah. 'Must you be so uncommunicative?'

'I don't know what to say to you.'

'You could invite me to sit down, for instance. And offer me some tea. Preferably without sugar or poison. I don't take sugar.'

You just can't help yourself from going too far, can you? Did you have to make that stupid joke about the poison? OK, you needed to. You're damned scared of this child, aren't you, Hannah?

The light changed with startling rapidity. The sun was about to disappear behind Aguilar Peak; a turquoise mist settled over the fishing village, over the boats at their moorings and the stretched-out nets, softly muffling any sound. It was almost silent, but for the lament of the bonzes from a pagoda. *There was a lack of emotion in your mission, but this setting is doing its best to compensate . . .*

'I'm not trying to make you feel sorry for me, child. I could tell you that I'm old and about to die, and that before I die I would like to see my only surviving son, whom I haven't set eyes upon for thirty years. But that would be a lie. I don't for a minute believe I'm about to die, really I don't. I haven't made any decision of the kind. But thirty years is beginning to seem like a long time.'

And it was almost a sob that escaped her, at that moment when she no longer expected him to come and despaired of seeing him appear. She took a deep breath, terrified by her own emotion.

'I want to see my son again. There's nothing in the world I want more. I want us to make up with each other. Even if I have to humiliate myself. He's very stubborn but in that he takes after me. And I shan't leave Asia until I've seen him, is that clear?'

She turned round.

'I'm on my own, child. Would you come and have dinner with me? Please . . .'

The first salon she had opened in Hong Kong was on the island itself, on Des Voeux Road. At that time – it was in the 1930s – she had rented five adjacent Chinese shop premises, long rectangular spaces with only one narrow side opening on to the road. She had had the whole of the interior changed, and three of the St James's Park drawing rooms installed, which she had had sent over by sea, including the wall panelling and parquet flooring. So the atmosphere inside was as English as could be.

'And you would refuse to renew my lease?'

For once in her life she was talking to someone not much taller than herself. The person in question was a Chinese man of about fifty years of age, who looked like two balloons of different sizes placed one on top of the other, the smaller one being his head. His English was perfect and he had a slight Oxford accent.

'Madame, I have no idea who you might be . . .'

'Hannah,' said Hannah. 'I'm Hannah. You don't have to stand to attention but I shan't hold it against you if you do.'

She winked at Young Hannah.

'You are . . . ?' said the Chinese.

'I am.'

'Please accept my apologies.'

'What I would happily accept is a new lease. My *directrice* tells me that you won't renew it. There must have been some misunderstanding.'

'I'm afraid not,' said the Chinese man.

He explained that because of the construction fever that had seized Hong Kong, he had received an offer for the purchase of the premises which she had been renting for fifteen years. In place of the existing small buildings, a thirty-storey skyscraper was to be erected.

'And you would like to sell.'

'I'm afraid so,' said the Chinese man.

'How much?' asked Hannah.

'Five hundred thousand dollars.'

'My eye,' said Hannah.

'I beg your pardon?' said the Chineseman.

'Two hundred thousand would be too much.'

Hannah, you don't actually give a damn about these premises. What you're trying to do is to impress, and better still win over, this grandchild of yours . . .

'Three hundred thousand,' said the Chinese man.

'Ha! Ha! Ha!' said Hannah.

She gave Young Hannah a quick sideways glance, and noted with satisfaction that the young girl, at first astonished, was now beginning to enjoy herself. *You're making her laugh, that's a start; she'll soon start to like you a little. After all, she did come along with you, that's a good sign. Now you have twelve grandchildren instead of eleven. My goodness, she's pretty, a real pearl!*

'Two hundred and fifty-five,' said the Chinese man.

'What do you think, child?'

'That's still too much,' said Young Hannah.

'Tell him in Chinese, my dear.'

Young Hannah did so. Her conversation with the fellow went on and on. Eventually she said: 'He'll accept two hundred and thirty.'

'I love hearing you speak Chinese,' said Hannah. 'Come on, let's go.'

She took the young girl by the arm and led her off.

'This is fun, isn't it?'

'Yes,' said Young Hannah.

In her tight-fitting silk dress, slit up the side to the thigh, she looked like a queen. She didn't walk, she glided along, her head held high. Although slightly built, she had a wonderful body.

'You're a very pretty girl, my dear. And by the way, I had the buildings that we have just seen valued. According to the people I consulted, $260,000–$280,000 would have been a good price. Are you really wedded to that job as a sales assistant at Lane Crawford? No, don't answer that straightaway. I have some couturier friends in Paris; you'll be able to choose for yourself. Hannah? Don't lie to me; it was you who arranged our meeting, wasn't it? Your father wouldn't hear of it but you were so insistent that he finally agreed. Isn't that what happened?'

Silence.

'You dreamed of going to Europe and America and you said to yourself that your grandmother was the best-placed person in the world to help you.'

The young girl nodded, keeping her head bowed.

Hannah smiled.

'You needn't be ashamed, my dear. I've done worse. I'm delighted that you have such determination, and such a clear idea of what you want out of life. I've not been any different. I was damned determined myself. Now let's talk about your father. Where is he? Where is my son?'

'He's not in Hong Kong.'

'I'll go and see him wherever he is. You must have talked about it together, and I'm sure you must have agreed what to do, whether you would take me to him or not. Or am I mistaken, my dear?'

'I was to be the one to decide,' said Young Hannah.

'Depending on what you thought of me. I see. And have you decided?'

'Yes.'

'I've never been to Malaysia before,' she said. 'Except to Singapore.'

Their shadows fell on the sand of a little white beach, bounded by a semi-circle of leafy trees, and so disproportionate were those shadows, they looked almost grotesque. Jonathan's was almost twice the size of her own. It was barely five o'clock, it was just getting light, and the forest still lay in silence. She had arrived in Kuala Lumpur two days earlier, accompanied by her granddaughter. She had eventually found a Bentley, hired out by a kind of sultan. First they drove on a road, then along dirt tracks, and a good four hours later a sudden break in the foliage revealed the full splendour of the Malacca Straits; a luxuriant garden appeared, its regularity standing out against the wild anarchy of the jungle. Then the house came into view; it was heart-stoppingly beautiful: an elegant rectangular building, raised at least two yards in the air on stilts with a deep veranda all the way round, hung with countless bird-cages, all of them white, all with their doors open to let the birds come and go as they pleased.

Thc purr of the engine no sooner cut out than children appeared, under the supervision of a Chinese amah – the eldest was about ten years old. Then a quiet, fair-haired young woman emerged. 'My stepmother, my father's second wife,' Young Hannah had said. 'And my half-brothers and -sisters – your other grandchildren.'

'How many countries have you visited?' asked Jonathan.

'About a hundred. More than a hundred probably. I'd say a hundred and twenty or thirty.'

'And in how many do you have a beauty parlour?'

'Seventy-three.'

'You must be very rich.'

'I am.'

She turned and looked back: her footsteps and those of her son were imprinted on the sand over a distance of some six hundred and fifty yards. The house was right at the end of the bay, and only the smoke rising vertically into the still air indicated that it was inhabited, and that the Malay cook had just got her wood-burning stove lit: *You have seven or eight houses all over the world, you must be the richest woman on this planet – of those that have actually made their money for themselves – and your only son lives in a straw hut with oil lamps to provide light . . .*

'Would you have come to see me if I hadn't made the first step?'

'I don't think so.'

'Thank you for not throwing me out.'

And the moment she had said it, she regretted the irony. But the remark had escaped her – patience and even resignation had never been her strong suit. Besides, she was still reeling, not just from meeting Jonathan again but also from the nature of that meeting. She had been welcomed by her daughter-in-law, Honor, with a simplicity and naturalness that had both enchanted and exasperated her. *Anyone would think it was only yesterday that you went away!* As for the children – four of them, all blond – they had lined up to give her a kiss on the cheek and called her 'madame'. It was quite obvious that they had never heard of her, and this polite indifference almost made her want to leave.

'I haven't been back to Europe, or America, for twenty-eight years,' said Jonathan.

'Except the time when you saw Niki.'

'Except then. I had to buy a boat. But I only stayed two days in America.'

Nothing more was said about Niki. He walked beside a line of rocks that seemed to close off the beach, at the opposite end of the bay to the house. But at the last minute, a passage hewn through the rock suddenly became visible, hardly a yard wide. He entered it first, excusing himself for passing in front of her.

They emerged on to a second creek, narrower and more rocky than the other.

There were five or six straw huts here, and a little shed, and moored on the calm waters of this tiny harbour were two motorboats and a seaplane, lying among some dug-out canoes and small fishing vessels.

'Are they yours, Jonathan?'

'The seaplane and the motorboats, yes.'

'Are you rich?'

'I have two freighters and a stake in a hevea plantation. I'm quite rich enough to give my children everything they need.'

He sounded almost indifferent.

'Even when you were a baby,' she said, 'you already had my temper and an incredible pig-headedness.'

If she was hoping to make him soften a little by recalling his childhood, she might just as well have saved her breath. He did not turn a hair. He spoke in some foreign language to one of the Malays. She studied him closely. He was immensely tall and thin, but sinewy, with broad shoulders and very strong hands. At fifty-three, he had a few threads of silver in his black hair. On the rare occasions when they exchanged glances, Hannah started: their eyes were so similar that she thought she was seeing herself in a mirror. And no doubt he had the same impression as she did.

'When did you hear about Adam?'

'A few months later. I was in the Solomon Islands.'

'Did you fight against the Japanese?'

'Not in the army. I had a plantation on Bougainville

Island and the American Marines gave me a radio transmitter so that I could report shipping movements. I didn't do anything else.'

Hannah knew that there was a little more to it than that. She and her granddaughter had talked a great deal. According to Young Hannah, Jonathan was chased for months by the Japanese from one island to the other; he drove them crazy with his radio. They could hear the transmissions but they were never able to find the culprit – until the day when the Emperor's soldiers caught up with him after a relentless pursuit, and left him for dead.

'Where did you meet Honor?'

'Her father was a doctor at Port-Moresby, in New Guinea.'

'And Hannah's mother?'

'From Shanghai. She died two years after the birth of our daughter.'

Ask him now, Hannah, ask him why he gave his daughter the name of a mother he hated . . .

But instead, she said: 'Let's make it up, Jonathan.'

'We have.'

He turned to look at her again, and again she was unnerved by the reflection of herself that she saw in his eyes.

'That's obvious,' she said with immense bitterness.

'My life is here. You can come as often as you like.'

'And can she come to Paris with me?'

'Your granddaughter is old enough to decide for herself. She has always had her head firmly fixed on her shoulders.'

'And my other grandchildren?'

'Next year, Hannah will go to England with Jimmy and Clare. She'll visit you if you like.'

'That would make me very happy.'

He spoke again to the Malays. *And I'm going to have to be content with that,* she thought. *But what else could I have expected? It's only in novels that people meeting again like us end up in each other's arms. Real life isn't like that – it has a different, more ruthless logic. I haven't seen my son for thirty years or more, and before that we weren't very close. The reasons that prevented us from understanding and loving each other then, whatever they might have been, still exist.*

'I'd like to go back,' she said. 'I've never been able to stand the sun on my face.'

He nodded. Again they walked along the beach. The ethereal-looking house was visible over the delicate harmony of royal poinciana, shimmering black teak and the purple brown of the merante.

'Mother?'

She stopped dead in her tracks, thunderstruck, almost trembling.

'I didn't post the letters, but I wrote to you twice. Especially after hearing of Adam's death. He came to see me twice during the '30s, did you know that?'

'He never said anything about it to me.'

'He talked about you, but he didn't need to try and convince me. You are what you are and I have nothing to reproach you for. I have made my life here and I shall die here. I don't despise the world you live in, but it is not my own. That's all.'

'In my own way, I love you,' she said, her gaze fixed on the house which was drawing near.

'I believe that's true. But these things are very remote for me.'

'I understand.'

You don't understand at all. And it's really hurting you. You are a matter of indifference to him and that's a hundred times worse than if he hated you.

'It was Adam's idea to call her Hannah. Mother, I love my other children – Honor's children – immensely, but my daughter Hannah I adore. She is the person in the world who understands me best. I have trusted her judgement since she was very small. It was Hannah who wanted us to meet.'

'She told me.'

'And it wasn't just that she expects you to be able to help her in her career, whatever that career might be. She wanted us – you and me – to make it up. If you hadn't come, I believe she would have dragged me by the scruff of the neck all the way to Europe.'

'She's a very remarkable young girl, Jonathan.'

'I know. And I also know that she is very like my mother in many ways.'

'And yet you love her.'

'And yet I love her. I'm happy that you came, mother.'

For the first time in more than forty years, he reverted to the intimacy of the *'tu'* form of address.

The children emerged from the house, naked as the day they were born, their little bodies tanned all over.

'I'm famished,' said Hannah.

She clung to her son's arm, and pretended to have some difficulty walking on the sand.

CHAPTER 38

I've All the Time in the World . . .

In Paris, she owned two or three buildings in Rue Beethoven, the apartment in Rue de Varenne with a view over the Hôtel Matignon (the Prime Minister's residence), and another twenty apartments in the sixteenth *arrondissement*, on Avenue Maréchal-Fayolle, near the Porte Dauphine. Young Hannah opted for a view over the Bois de Boulogne. She would live in the five-room apartment with an English girl who was a friend from Hong Kong.

She moved into the apartment in the spring of 1951.

'But I want to work, grandmother.'

'I should think so too! You didn't think I was going to keep you for nothing, did you?'

In fact, she had opened a bank account in her granddaughter's name in Geneva two months earlier, with a million dollars' credit.

But even if Hannah already had her master-plan in mind, it was a good idea to suggest that her granddaughter should start by working as a model. Jacques Fath took on the young girl less than five weeks after her arrival in Paris.

'Why the devil have they changed your name?'

'They wanted something exotic.'

'Fools! Hannah's a very pretty name!'

Because she did have a master-plan. Hour upon hour of talking to her granddaughter had convinced her: the child was the stuff that great *directrices* were made of. And assuming – only assuming, just as a working hypothesis – that Hannah was going to die one day, she would have a successor. Adam's children and Abigail's just couldn't be considered as candidates, there was no point in denying it. *'I'm never wrong about these things, Lizzie. I reserve my blunders for my private life . . . But I'm making up for those now!'*

She didn't broach the subject at all with Young Hannah. The child would catch on by herself, or not at all, and if she did catch on, then she would do what was necessary.

And she did.

At first she worked two years as a model, and earned a lot of money. Then one day when she was staying with her cousins – Abigail's and Adam's children – at the Kadens' house in Beverly Hills, she was offered a part in a film. She made three films, but just when it seemed that this was to be her career, she abandoned it.

'Not in the least bit interesting. It might have been if I could have made films myself, but I am not tempted to try. You knew from the start, didn't you, that I would ask the question one day? Well, I'm asking it now: what do I have to do in order to work for you?'

She started at the bottom of the ladder, in the salon in Atlanta. Then Hannah placed her under the supervision of Eulalia Jones, the Cherokee, who had succeeded Jessie three years ago as head of the American establishments. For the next five years, she continued to study, learning German and Spanish, as well as law and business administration.

You're never wrong about these things. You knew that she would succeed you the day she bargained with that Chinese man in Hong Kong. And her name's Hannah!

Lizzie came to live with Hannah at the beginning of 1951. She couldn't stand being on her own any more, either in California or New York, and she didn't want to move in with any of her children.

'If you'll have me, of course . . .'

'I've always had a weakness for ostriches . . . But on

one condition: you're not to make any comment on the way I drive!'

In September the previous year, Hannah had in fact had dealings with the road police again. She was returning from her annual pilgrimage to Santa Barbara and was driving down to Palm Springs to meet Lizzie at a tiny bit over 120 miles an hour. The police from several counties must have joined forces to stop her. They finally put up roadblocks and six of them walked up to her Ferrari, all clinking with badges and guns and handcuffs.

'Where's the driver?'

This question annoyed her.

'I know I'm not very tall, but people can usually see me, you fools. You ought to get your eyes examined.'

Once again, she was taken before a judge, who had to lean over the bench to see her.

'And you maintain that this charming old lady was driving at over 120 miles an hour, that she hit three police cars and almost killed six people?'

'I'm not sure about being charming,' replied Hannah, 'and I'm even less sure about being a lady. But anyone who says I was driving at 120 miles an hour is a damned liar. This car is supposed to reach 150, and I had my foot right down on the floor. Or else it doesn't go as fast as the person who sold it to me said it did, and in that case I shall complain to Mr Enzo Ferrari himself. He's a friend of mine.'

Her lawyers had to intervene to save her from going to prison, and she got off with a twelve-thousand-dollar fine – which she managed to write off as a professional expense.

Lizzie and she divided their time between the Côte d'Azur (Saint-Tropez), New York, Paris (always in the Rue de Varenne) and California. Mostly. Lizzie was sometimes persuaded to go further. In 1953 they spent two months in Australia with Abigail and three of the

Kaden children, and on the way back they spent several weeks in Malaysia, with Jonathan.

The following year, with a huge group of fourteen of their grandchildren, they went up the Amazon, from Belem to Iquitos. Then Lizzie, exhausted by the humid heat, vehemently refused to go any further, but Hannah pushed on with her happy band as far as Cuzco, and celebrated her seventy-eighth birthday with a glass of champagne in Machu Picchu.

As far as grandchildren were concerned, Lizzie led by seventy-three to sixteen.

'It sounds like the score for a game of basketball,' said Hannah.

Over the last year or two, Hannah had developed a passion for sport. She read every edition of the French sports paper *L'Equipe*, the Italian *Gazetto dello Sport* and the American *Sports Illustrated*. Cricket was the only game she didn't understand at all. (But how could anyone have made head or tail of Winnie Churchill's explanations? – She was sure he had been deliberately incomprehensible.) On the other hand, she followed rugby, American football, soccer, athletics, basketball and cycling with the detailed attention she continued to bring to her business accounts. She went to Wembley to watch the Cup Final and to Helsinki for the last three days of the Olympics, where she became very enthusiastic about the long-distance runner Emil Zatopek.

As for great-grandchildren, Lizzie again had a clear advantage over Hannah, though the difference was less great: thirty-nine to thirteen. Marianne – Adam and Jacqueline's eldest child – was responsible for five of the thirteen; her brother Tadd, born in 1923, had only two; and her brother Ewan, the survivor of the *Indianapolis*, also had two (admittedly, he had only just got married, to the daughter of an industrialist from Portland, Oregon).

Plus the four that Abigail and her chemist were responsible for, which made up the total. *Lazy shirkers!*

However, Beth and Debbie, and Tim, Adam's three other children, born in 1930 and 1932, were not yet operational . . .

And then there's Young Hannah, and Jonathan and Honor's four little fair-haired kids. It would be just your luck if they didn't bring the total up to twenty.

Not for one day did Hannah relax the pressure she had always brought to bear on every one of her establishments. During the '50s, she revived the Spy Corps originally set up by Maryan; they numbered twenty-four in all, and they were nearly all women. Their mission was to visit the salons and shops as ordinary clients and take note of everything – Hannah had actually compiled a checklist that left out nothing: the presentation of the products, the way the client was advised to use them, the way the client was treated, and even the state of the lavatories and any cases of bad breath among the staff.

She had established a system that enabled a client who happened to be abroad to receive the same beauty treatment anywhere in the world, simply by presenting her personal card. It was a huge task, and she had thought of getting machines to do it. In 1946 the inventors Eckert and Manchley produced a computer with a memory. She went to see them, just as she had been to see the specialists at Radio Corporation of America who had just created the Bizmac, the first computer in the world to contain a data base; and finally she met the people at International Business Machines.

She wanted some simple answers to some simple questions: was it possible to have files on all her clients worldwide, and could these files be accessible to any one of her establishments, no matter where it was, at any time?

No, not yet. It would soon be possible, they all swore to it. In a few years' time, ten years perhaps.

'Morning or afternoon?' she asked sarcastically.

But she smiled, having come across various ways, thanks to these visits, of improving her card-index system and the monitoring of her subsidiaries, and making them more reliable.

'I'll wait. I have all the time in the world.'

She was seventy-eight, going on seventy-nine. And the only health problems she suffered were blisters on her feet – and that was only because she would sooner be chopped into little pieces than give up wearing her high-heeled Charles Jourdan shoes, which she wore even for her morning walks.

When she and Lizzie were in Europe, they preferred to be in Cannes, although they liked the villas at Saint-Jean-Cap-Ferrat and Saint-Tropez too. There was certainly no lack of space: there were thirty-four bedrooms in all and Lizzie had a kind of huge dormitory added that also served as a games room; it was in the basement and was equipped with bunks. It was here that the youngest members of the family slept when everyone met up in France during the summer.

Hannah thought of buying an aeroplane, but eventually abandoned the idea: firstly because she adored driving so much; and also because she would have liked to pilot the aircraft herself.

'I've got my pilot's licence after all. Louis Blériot himself gave it to me. Are you trying to tell me Louis Blériot couldn't fly a plane?'

It was with some regret that she gave up the idea.

'I would have liked a plane that was black with a turkey-red trim. With a pair of goggles and a leather cap, I would have been able to fly over my salons. Just the noise of my engines throbbing would have made my beauticians wet themselves out of fear . . .'

Among those who objected was Lizzie, who threatened to retire to a convent. But the decisive factor was when she found herself in front of an aircraft control panel, in November 1954, and was forced to agree that things had changed a bit since Blériot's day.

'Although I'm sure lots of these wretched buttons serve no purpose at all. They've just been put there to make it look scientific!'

The dreadful catalogue of death continued. Even Yvonne joined the list in 1953; another heartbreaking loss. The Frenchwoman had lost the use of her legs and couldn't walk any more, and for the last few months of her life was confined to her bed in her house in Bandol, near Toulon, where she was looked after by two nurses Hannah had engaged. She died peacefully in her sleep. Hannah was immediately notified and flew from Stockholm to Marseilles in a taxi-plane, in the disappointed hope of being able to embrace for the last time the woman who for half a century had been – more than a servant – a friend and almost a sister to her.

Cecily Barton too died; and Jessie from New York, and Cathy Montblanc . . . Also André Labadie, the Fournacs in Australia, Jos Wynn, most of the MacKennas in Sydney, those of her generation, at least.

These days, when she went into one of her salons, still unleashing the same panic as ever, it wasn't even the daughters of those she had first given jobs to all those years ago who worked there now, but often their granddaughters.

You're beginning to be like the ghost of Elsinore.

Lizzie died in 1962.

CHAPTER 39

As Simple as That . . .

They were surrounded by San Francisco hippies. For a while now Lizzie had been feeling tired for no particular reason. Her legs felt heavy, and sometimes she would have to stop halfway up a staircase to catch her breath. And yet she had lost weight. From eleven stone, the heaviest she had ever been, she had gone back down to nine and a half. 'I can see my toes again, between the two watermelons I have for breasts . . . Don't snigger, you little Jewess, there isn't enough to fill a sake bowl with what you have on your chest.'

They had arrived in San Francisco the previous day, in mid-November 1961. Hannah had made her annual pilgrimage to the grave, and meanwhile Lizzie had spent three weeks in Palm Springs, where her daughter Melanie and son-in-law lived. They had met up at the Hotel Fairmont, and had been to the cinema to see Sam Peckinpah's *Guns in the Afternoon*, with Randolph Scott and Joel McCrea. Hannah, who had a passion for westerns, loved it, and rated the film (which she was seeing for the third time) alongside Nicholas Ray's *Johnny Guitar* or Anthony Mann's *The Bait* . . .

'But not quite as high as Hawk's *The Big Sky*, Richard Brook's *The Last Hunt*, or of course, the best three or four films that John Ford made . . . Oh, Lizzie, the very first images of *The Searchers*! It's such a wonderful film! I've seen it seven times . . . Shall we walk back?'

Lizzie said she would rather take a taxi. ('I probably don't take enough exercise. I never left the poolside at Palm Springs.')

They agreed that for once Lizzie would accompany

Hannah on her morning walk. The itinerary was decided upon: they would go down California Street to the Wells Fargo building, then across Montgomery and Jackson Square, to Fisherman's Wharf and the Cannery, where the old Del Monte canning factory still stood.

'Then if your legs aren't worn down to the knees, we could do some real walking and continue as far as the Golden Gate – why not? It's ages since I've been there.'

'Why not Seattle and the Yukon?' was all Lizzie said, with a touch of sarcasm.

'Because of the bears. I'd frighten the poor beasts. Now stop talking and walk.'

Lizzie admitted defeat when they came within sight of Alcatraz.

'I'm all in.'

Hannah looked at her closely, suddenly anxious. A few seconds earlier she had been recalling the terrible earthquake of 1906, of which she had seen only the aftermath ('I missed it by just a few days'). Then, by an association of ideas, she had started talking about Caruso (since the celebrated singer was in the city at the time of the earthquake), who sang a Yiddish song to her one day, or rather a Polish song in Yiddish, and about the female singer Melba, whom she had met in Sydney.

'What do you mean, you're all in? I'd be surprised if we've covered two miles!'

But she examined the tall Australian-American woman's face closely. And was shocked by her sudden intuition. *Oh my God, not Lizzie, not her too!*

'Sit down, ostrich.'

She dragged Lizzie over to a bench, just by the landing stage for the pleasure boats that took tourists round San Francisco Bay. Sitting on the bench, on the back of it and all around it, was a group of long-haired bearded hippies singing about universal love.

'Scram, kids,' said Hannah. 'My friend needs to sit down.'

They made room for them, but didn't actually move away, and went on singing.

'Are you feeling any better, Lizzie?'

'Yes, much better.'

Lizzie closed her eyes. Her features were drawn.

'Have you got a pain?'

She moved her head: no.

Then: 'I just want to get my breath, Hannah.'

Hannah turned to a tall boy of about twenty-two wearing a headband, Indian style, that kept his long blond hair in place over his temples.

'Go and call an ambulance for me, please.'

'If you do that, I shan't speak to you for the next twenty years,' said Lizzie, with her eyes still closed.

'I should be so lucky,' said Hannah.

She held out some money to the boy.

'Hurry, please.'

The hippy hesitated for another half-second, then ran off.

'Tourists, dears?' asked an insipid-looking adolescent girl, with flowers stuck in her fair hair that made her look like those heads of pork garnished with parsley that you see in the windows of French delicatessens.

'Of sixty-one years' standing, you little whipper-snapper,' replied Hannah. 'We're beginning to get to know the country. Does your mother know where you are?'

There was a sickly-sweet smell of marijuana, the more acrid smell of the Pacific Ocean, and the plaintive cry of the gulls that the guitar close by tried unsuccessfully to embrace within the music. A blue mist settled over the Golden Gate; at the same time a rush of memories came flooding to mind: Mendel Visoker with them in the Panhard and Levassor, exactly sixty years ago; Mendel leaving for Alaska in a wooden sailing boat, in the days when boats still smelt good; and a different America, an incomparably brighter place and still a virgin country.

The hippies had kindly lowered their voices; they sang very softly and gathered round the two old ladies, a colourfully dressed band of well-wishers looking out to sea.

They stepped aside only when the ambulance arrived.

'How old is she?' asked the doctor at Mark Hopkins Hospital.

'Nearly seven years younger than me: seventy-nine,' replied Hannah.

She could almost see the cogs in his brain working it out: seventy-nine plus seven equals eighty-six.

'I must say, you really don't look your age.'

'I'm not the one who is ill. I expect I'm in better health than you are. What's wrong with her?'

'Has she ever told you about these lumps she's got?'

No, no, of course not! As if Lizzie had ever been the kind of woman to talk about her intimate problems! *(You've never once seen her naked . . . And she would never give you the slightest hint of what went on in bed between Maryan and her . . .)*

'What lumps?'

'The ones in her neck, which you can't really see, and those under her arms and in her groin.'

'Which are symptoms of what?'

'Chronic lymphoid leukaemia.'

'I don't even know what that is.'

'Leukaemia is a disease of the blood. Chronic lymphoid leukaemia is when there's an abnormal proliferation of lymphocytes, a type of cell believed to play a part in helping the body defend itself against germs, viruses and . . .'

'What do you mean, "believed to"? Are you saying that you're not sure, that you don't know?'

'We don't yet know, it's true. There are various theories, research done by Gesner and Ginsburg, Gowan and MacGregor, Halphern. . .'

She lost her temper.

'For God's sake, give me a simple answer! Is this leukaemia fatal?'

'Usually. Although with older people, the disease is often quite stable . . .'

'What do you mean by "often"? What are Mrs Kaden's chances?'

'There's nothing wrong with you, Lizzie. Apart from being fifty-nine years too old, perhaps.'

'Let's talk about those years. You could be my mother.'

They had returned to the Hotel Fairmont. Lizzie had spent only five hours in all at the hospital. The doctors really couldn't agree: some thought that it wasn't absolutely necessary for her to remain in hospital, others thought it was, and one of them even maintained that she should be placed in a sterile room. Lizzie refused even to hear of it, and Hannah had gone along with what she wanted.

'I think I shall go to sleep for a while,' said Lizzie, already half asleep.

She fell asleep almost immediately. Her face was still a bit pale, and she had fine bluish lines under her eyes, but she slept deeply and peacefully.

'Take your eyes off her for one second and I swear I'll have your hide,' said Hannah to Lizzie's maid, a Puerto Rican who answered to the name of Maria de Los Angeles.

As a double precaution she also placed on guard her own secretary, Marie-Claire Piani, who had taken over from Yvonne, without actually replacing her, of course.

She was Corsican, and her father was a pharmacist. Hannah had employed her six years ago, and had since had nothing but praise for her efficiency.

She returned to her hotel suite and was on the phone for the next hour. She first called Jimmy, the eldest of Lizzie's sons, who had taken over from his father in Los Angeles. She broke the news to him.

'No, I haven't yet told her, Jimmy. I'm going to get Professor Levin from New York to come and see her. He's the best specialist alive and he's a friend of mine. There's just a small chance that the doctors here in San Francisco might be mistaken. And if there's anyone you trust whom you would also like to call . . .'

She also rang Colleen, the eldest daughter, who had the same name and the same Irish diminutive as her grandmother (Colleen for Kathlyn) and whose husband, Norman Lincoln, worked in Seattle in the aeronautics industry.

And she broke the news to Melanie, with whom Lizzie had just spent three weeks.

Finally she put a call through to Sol Levin, at Mount Sinai Hospital in New York. He was on holiday in Martinique and couldn't get to San Francisco for two days, since there wasn't a plane.

'I've made the necessary arrangements,' said Hannah. 'A plane is already on its way from Miami to fetch you. Thank you, Sol.'

He arrived the following morning.

'I'm terribly sorry, Hannah. There's nothing anyone can do for her.'

For a long interminable minute she couldn't say a word. So that he eventually said: 'I've always believed in telling the patient the truth. I can do it, if you like . . .'

She shook her head.

'No, I'll do it, Sol. She would prefer it to be me.'

* * *

'Am I going to die today, Hannah?'

'Not if you don't want to. People only die when they let themselves die.'

'It's very simple, eh?'

'As simple as that.'

Five months had gone by since that day in San Francisco. All the diagnoses had been confirmed. In fact, the doctors didn't believe it possible that Lizzie would survive the last few weeks of 1961. Sol Levin himself confessed his pessimism: 'The primary effect of leukaemia is to deprive the body of its natural defences, Hannah. I shan't try and baffle you with science: the infection she's got, which is spreading, could perhaps have been overcome if her body had given us any help, which is not the case. How long have you known her? Good Lord, that's a whole lifetime . . .'

Lizzie had quietly but firmly resisted any suggestion of getting her into a clinic, despite urgent attempts by her children and grandchildren to get her to agree to it. When they implored Hannah to intervene, she stuck to her guns: it was up to Lizzie to decide, and no one else.

And when Lizzie asked to be taken to Palm Springs, Hannah didn't try to oppose her wishes: *I would take her to Australia if she expressed the desire to go there. She will die in her own time, wherever she wants to.*

The house in Palm Springs was Spanish style. It consisted of two large buildings facing each other, with linking walkways and an inside patio, a fifty-foot swimming pool and a garden. Lizzie's bedroom extended the whole length of one side of the house – it was a huge room, measuring forty feet by twenty-five, and had bay windows on two sides with views over Mount San Jacinto and Palm Canyon with its palm groves, and the desert.

'I chose this house, and of course this room. Maryan didn't like it very much, he would have preferred the San Fernando Valley, next to Clark Gable's ranch.'

Silence.

'Do you believe in an after-life, Hannah?'

'You know I don't.'

'I hope you're wrong.'

'I hope so too.'

Apart from the echo of their voices, there was also the imperceptible sound of Lizzie's drip. A nurse remained discreetly in the background, all dressed in white, not uttering a word.

The day I die, thought Hannah, *if I should make up my mind to die one day, I want to be completely alone.*

'I remember the past,' Lizzie was saying, 'with incredible clarity. Someone rang at the door of 173 Glenmore Road. Mother was in the kitchen. I went to answer it. It was September 1893 . . .'

'1892,' Hannah corrected her automatically.

'That was just a few months short of seventy years ago. I was holding a doll. I saw you and then you collapsed . . .'

'It didn't happen that quickly.'

'You hadn't eaten for a week.'

'It was only three days.'

Silence.

'I'd quite like to die, Hannah. I feel so very tired.'

'You can hold on. You can.'

Hannah had been repeating these words day after day, like an incantation. A few minutes went by. Lizzie's eyes were closed again, but the sheet rose and fell with her breathing.

'You can,' repeated Hannah. 'Don't leave me, please, Lizzie. I beg you, don't leave me.'

Lizzie responded with an affirmative squeeze of her eyelids, which were still closed. And she even managed a ghost of a smile: 'Just to please you.'

'Thank you,' Hannah managed to say.

And you can't even cry . . . Admittedly, you didn't cry either when 'he' died . . .

An hour went by.

'You're going to have to forgive me,' said Lizzie very feebly.

'Don't leave me.'

'I'm doing my best, but it's difficult . . . You're so incredibly strong, Hannah. Maryan . . .'

She broke off.

'Maryan always used to say that to me. Oh Hannah, darling, you gave me Maryan . . .'

Again she broke off. Her breathing became ragged.

Hannah felt the questioning look of the nurse and, shaken with rage, despair and sorrow, she nodded. The woman stood up, and without the slightest sound from her white canvas shoes, left the room; a minute later a subdued murmur rose through the huge house over which absolute silence had reigned.

They filed in one by one, all Lizzie and Maryan's children and grandchildren. They filled the room.

Hannah got up and moved away from Lizzie's bedside; they stepped back to let her pass. She left the room and went out on to the adjoining terrace. The Californian sun was at its height; it was nearly two o'clock on 4 April 1962.

It was about half an hour later when someone came up behind her.

Without turning round, she asked: 'Is it all over?'

'Yes.'

Someone touched her on the shoulder and tried to take her in their arms. She freed herself, on the verge of hatred. She went back inside and walked through the bedroom without once turning her head towards the bed.

In the big basement garage where some forty cars were parked, she chose the 1930s Duesenberg SSJ.

Ten minutes later she was driving along with the accelerator pedal on the floor, giving free rein to the monstrously powerful 400 horsepower engine. She headed due east. She didn't even think about it – this was the first direction that presented itself to her. She drove across the motorway and through the small town of Thousand Palms without even realizing it. Then she was in the desert, and the black and turkey-red convertible raised a cloud of dust that trailed back over more than a mile.

She stopped the car within sight of the Colorado aqueduct.

And switched off the engine.

The silence was overwhelming. She got out of the car and started walking, in her Nina Ricci dress, for the first time in her life indifferent to the sun burning her face.

She lay down on the ground and did not stir.

Around midday the next day, two Indians from the Torreo Martinez Reserve, out hunting, found her. They first of all noticed the Duesenberg, with the bonnet up. Then they followed the footprints, scarcely able to believe their eyes. It was about seven miles from there that they found her. She was stretched out on her side, her hands and face and neck burned by the sun. Her feet were bleeding and she had sand and earth under her fingernails. It was obvious that she must have crawled the last few hundred yards. After abandoning her car, she must have followed the track across the Chuckwalla Mountains in an attempt to get to Hopkins Wells.

They thought at first she was a little girl, because of her size. And they thought she was dead. But no. They had no sooner turned her over and given her something to drink than she opened her big grey eyes.

She was still alive.

CHAPTER 40

And What's This Big Pink Thing?

Patrick Fowles was the eldest of her great-grandchildren, the son of Marianne, who was herself the daughter of Adam and Jacqueline. In May 1964 he had just turned twenty-two. He was about the same height as his maternal grandfather: six foot four or five inches.

He had the utmost difficulty squeezing into the first-class seat on the Boeing 707-320 B Intercontinental.

'E9,' he announced after much deliberation.

'Sunk,' said Hannah. 'But I've still got one aircraft carrier, one cruiser and three submarines.'

By contrast, it was quite easy for her to huddle in her seat, with her knees tucked under her chin and her shoulders hunched up, in order to conceal from him where she had drawn her battleships.

She licked the end of her pencil with her little pink tongue and said: 'C6.'

'One submarine sunk,' said Patrick.

'Ha, ha, ha!' sniggered Hannah. 'You're finished, my friend. You've only got one torpedo boat left. A bit like the Swiss Navy. Unluckily for you, I learned to play this game with a certain Mr Vuille, a Swiss as it happens. And a film producer . . .'

'I'm sure that you must have cheated again.'

'Me? The very idea!'

An air hostess came by and asked them if they would like anything to drink.

'Champagne,' said Hannah. 'Dom Perignon rosé 1957. I asked for some to be put on this flight specially. If you and friends haven't already drunk them, there should be two bottles. And you can also bring me a crown of laurels and a black mourning band. The crown's for me, and the mourning band is for this young man.'

'I surrender,' said Patrick. 'On one condition: I would like to take a look at your grid. I can't help feeling suspicious.'

She immediately straightened up and crumpled her sheet of paper into a ball, and as an extra precaution she put it on her seat and sat on it.

'Why don't you tell me about the Swedish girl? The one you made love to in the lift?'

'I've already told you the whole story.'

'You didn't give many details. When the earth-shattering moment came, did she cry out, "Mother" – in Swedish of course – or did she simply go, "Yes, yes, yes"?'

'Great God in heaven!' exclaimed Patrick.

She burst out laughing in delight: *I managed to make him blush!*

They were on their way back from Sydney, where she had had a plenary meeting of all her directors for the Pacific zone. On the way out, she had stopped over in Panama, where the headquarters of several of her companies were based, and in Caracas, where Jaime Aguiló had arranged a meeting with all the Latin-American representatives. Coming back, she would have liked to go via Rio, but Patrick had to go to Boston, to submit his doctoral thesis in economics – in which he had focused on his great-grandmother's business.

Two years ago, the day after Lizzie's death, she had almost decided to end it all. Including her own life. But that little old mechanism . . .

If you had shut yourself away, and withdrawn from the world, you would have turned into a vegetable.

It just wasn't in her nature. As the days went by, while she recovered from her sunburn – from which she suffered no lasting damage – the litle mechanism inside her head had started up again. Less than three months after Lizzie had passed away, she had reappeared one morning in the great hall of the New York salon and a spine-chilling silence immediately descended on the hundreds of women present. Had she been a ghost, the reception would have been the same. More than any burst of her own vitality, it was this silence and amazed homage that had restored her to her old self. She had then begun touring her empire, the 318 beauty parlours across the world, and her 743 shops. She was seen again at the four factories, the three laboratories, in every part of her distribution network, in the offices of all the big chains of department stores and supermarkets through which her products were sold – and where beauticians and sales assistants who had graduated from her six schools now worked. There was not a single one of her establishments anywhere on the globe that had not received a visit from her during the past twenty-six months. Countless magazines all over the world had run cover stories and feature articles on her, making much of what they called her phenomenal longevity (this annoyed her considerably: *I'm not even ninety!*) or of her wealth – which was generally estimated, by *Fortune* magazine in particular, to approach two hundred million dollars – or else describing her nine homes, her fabulous collections of paintings, jewellery and cars, her no less celebrated rages, and her very famous witticisms spiced with vitriolic humour.

Jonathan died. Like Niki, of cancer. He remained true to his word: he never returned to Europe or America. And like Niki, he concealed his illness from her until the very end, refusing to undergo any treatment, which he did not in any case believe in. He died in Malaysia, in that wonderful house overlooking the Malacca Straits.

He wrote a letter to Hannah, the only one he ever sent her: *I loved you and I hated you, mother. Probably both at the same time. You made me a little too much in your own likeness. Not that I'm blaming you, especially as I believe it's only the darker side of you that I take after. I have never had your courage, your fierce love of life, your strength. And it has been very clear to me for a long time now: I fled you, just as my father did. We were both wrong, he even more so than I. I remember what you told me, that time I took you to Singapore to catch your plane. You were talking about father, and you said: 'If he had been a man and I a woman, everything would have been different . . .' It's true. It was true for him, and I realize now how much he made you suffer. And to a slightly lesser extent, it's true for me: if my father had had your personality, I would probably have had the same love-hate relationship with him. It's my fault, not yours. Adam was right in loving you blindly, as much as you deserved . . . And that's what I wanted to tell you in this letter: I'm extraordinarily proud of my mother, but my pride is far outweighed by the love I have for her, a love that I find myself able to declare only now when it's too late, when I am going to die. Forgive me.*

Three more great-grandchildren were born the following year, in 1965. And four the year after. Pablo Picasso did another portrait of her – he had done the first in 1904, the year he arrived in Paris. They had shared an almost sibling love dating back sixty years – always vying with each other as to who could tell the most saucy, if not downright dirty story.

But when she discovered what he had made of her on his canvas, she almost died laughing: there was just an eye (a blue-black eye, what's more) stuck between two ears of a size to make an elephant jealous.

'And what's that big pink thing?' she asked.

'Your tongue,' said Pablo. 'And I didn't make it as big as I'd intended to.'

There was another artist who painted a portrait of her

(actually, there had been some two dozen who had ventured to do so, starting with Klimt in Vienna, at the end of the previous century). But she became furious with this one, abusing the artist in eight or ten languages, in that thundering voice of hers that always came as such a surprise in comparison with her size. She was portrayed standing up, with her right hand on the back of an armchair, wearing a wonderful Dior dress, and everything about her – the way she held her head, the angle of her chin, and above all her eyes, which literally blazed – conveyed the most tremendous and imperious will power. She almost jumped on the canvas in anger. 'Is that woman supposed to be me?'

The worst of it was – and this made her even more enraged – that everyone seemed to think it was actually very like her . . .

'I shall end up biting someone!'

But as usual, her good humour got the better of her. At first she hung the canvas in the lavatory – 'but I can't leave it there, it makes me constipated.' In the end she hung it in one of the drawing rooms in the apartment on Fifth Avenue in New York. Except that she hung it upside down, and threatened to kill anyone who attempted to right it.

And when she had guests, she would lie on the sofa facing the painting, but with her back on the seat and her legs up in the air on the backrest, and her head hanging upside down: 'That's how I prefer it.'

The first of her great-great-grandchildren was born at the very beginning of 1968. *Now let me get this straight (you ought to draw a chart): Adam and Jacqueline, and Jonathan and his Chinese wife, and his second wife Honor, and Abie and Paul Travers are the first generation after you. Good. Adam and Jacqueline had six children, that's the second generation. The third generation are your great-grandchildren – Patrick, for instance, the son of Marianne, who is the daughter of Adam, who is . . . was your son. Good; so far, so good. Patrick has a sister called Cindy – are you with me, Hannah? – and Cindy has just laid her first egg, a girl, blazing a trail for the fourth generation – the fifth counting you – making sure it's safe to come out . . . Well, that's clear, isn't it?*

'We would like to call her Hannah,' said Cindy. 'If you agree, of course.'

'There are already seven in the family, don't you think there are beginning to be rather too many? And in any case, who is this fellow Anthony you're always talking to me about?'

'My husband,' said Cindy.

Truth to tell, without going so far as not giving a damn, Hannah had to force herself a little to take much interest in the mass births of all these children who were supposed to be descended from her. Especially as, although her memory continued to serve her admirably when it came to the names of all her directors, from Japan to Ireland, allowing her to recall without the slightest effort the balance sheets of all her establishments, she had more difficulty in remembering who was the daughter of the daughter of the daughter of whom.

She opened a notebook, as she had in the past, and applied the system of sheep which had never failed her. A blue sheep for a boy and a pink one for a girl, connected with arrows when they got married, and acquiring one leg every time they produced a child.

There were some sheep with eight legs.

Hannah was delighted: *At least I know where I am now! And they're pretty, all these sheep . . . Except that I don't much care for pink.*

In 1965 she celebrated her ninetieth birthday, with some reluctance, at a surprise party attended by all her descendants who had gathered for the occasion at Saint-Jean-Cap-Ferrat. It went quite against the grain, because she was annoyed by references to her age. But the horde of relatives came pouring off three private aeroplanes, like a tidal wave on the Japanese coastline. And after sulking a bit for the first two hours, she managed to appear very pleased to see her house invaded by 149 people.

Three years later, in 1968, she was on her way back from Japan and happened to arrive in Paris in May. *It's a long time since I had such a good laugh*, she thought, four days later, having followed the rioting in the Latin Quarter, very nearly getting herself flattened by an advancing tide of police, at the Odéon intersection. To her great disappointment, she was not arrested or thrown in prison; even though she shouted with all her might the slogans roared out by the crowd, as she stood wedged between two bearded students; and even though she carried at least four paving stones to help build a barricade.

There was a time when you would have thrown the wretched paving stones at those moronic cops. I wonder if you might not be getting a little old?

She was walking down Rue d'Antibes in Cannes. She was alone. To escape from the villa at Saint-Jean-Cap-Ferrat she had had to resort to the kind of measures a secret agent would use. Marie-Claire Piani, her personal secretary, and her two assistants, one an American girl, the other German, kept her under close watch. On the ludicrous grounds that she was ninety-five, she was not allowed to drive any more, or even to go out unaccompanied. By order of Madame Abigail . . . *I'll give you Madame Abigail! She wasn't even born when I . . . All right, it's true that I'm her mother and that she was bound not to have been born when I . . . All right . . . But I've never killed anyone at the wheel, to the best of my knowledge. I admit I shouldn't have driven into that bakery in Nice. And especially not through the window (what a mess I made of their chocolate éclairs!). But it was either that or the children coming out of school. If it hadn't been the wretched bakery, I would have killed the lot of them. My reflexes are too quick, that's the truth of it.*

She had hitch-hiked to Cannes. *And me with eighteen cars!* A very charming young man had stopped as soon as he saw her standing on the roadside, thumbing a lift. *He was very sharp-eyed, it must be said in passing; I had made the mistake of positioning myself behind a signpost which practically hid me from view.*

In any case, he was charming. Clean. With nice hands. And sensitive too: I noticed his eyes were about to fill with tears when I told him my sad story – that my daughter-in-law hated me and only kept me alive because of my pension, which she stole from me. He was already moved when I told him that she made me take the bus to visit the grave of my dear departed Alphonse, while she herself took the car to go and play tennis. But he almost broke down completely when I explained how she had poisoned my pet dog because he was eating too much, the poor creature. There are no two ways about it, I lie really well for my age . . .

She tottered down Rue d'Antibes, with her pretty Chanel boater on her head. It was a little out of fashion, but then so was she.

She had not lingered on the Croisette. *First of all, it's full of old ladies, and then the diabolical Piani has probably got people out looking for me; she's probably given the Red Alert . . .* And that was the first place they would look, since they knew she adored the Carlton bar.

He was really very charming, that young man who gave me a lift in his car. If I had been seventy-five years younger, I would have knocked him dead with a single glance. He looked a bit like Clark Gable, without the big ears – I didn't see the rest. But why on earth should he think I might want to go to the cemetery? Especially the one in Nice. It's one of the few in the world where I don't know anyone.

That's enough now, Hannah. Don't start feeling sorry for yourself. If you're still alive, it's because that's what you wanted . . .

Her feet were hurting, as usual. *Well, I can't very well wear Doc Martens, now, can I? They would look good with my Chanel boater!*

The shop caught her eye, not so much because it was beautiful; on the contrary, because of the pretty dreadful taste in which the window had been dressed. She went in.

'Could I sit down for a moment?'

The young woman was herself sitting behind her cash register, reading *Paris-Match.* With obvious reluctance she got to her feet and gave up her chair, the only one in the shop. Hannah sat down. That day the only jewellery she was wearing was the black pearl necklace that 'he' had given her, pearl by pearl, and it was hidden beneath the lace collar of her black blouse with turkey-red buttons.

The shop was maybe thirteen feet by ten. It was positively dreadful, with its ridiculous fancy goods and cheap rubbish. There were miniature Eiffel towers – *For God's sake!* – and some horrible little china dogs made in Hong Kong.

The owner of the shop must have been twenty-five. She would not have been bad-looking had it not been for her unflattering make-up, her not very clean hair, her jeans that were too tightly fitting, revealing her ample buttocks and her rather short legs.

She said that her husband was a surveyor, that they had

bought the business two years ago with some money left to them by an aunt. But the shop wasn't doing too well.

'What's a surveyor?' asked Hannah.

Someone who measures this and that in certain places for unknown purposes, on behalf of civil engineering firms, explained the young woman, whose name apparently was Marie-Pierre Gonzalo.

Yes, she had a child, a little boy aged two and a half.

'My mother looks after him for me. But as far as the shop is concerned, it's hopeless.'

She was waiting until the end of summer to close it down completely, in the hope of finding someone to buy it off her so that at least she and her surveyor husband could recover some of the money they had so stupidly invested in it with such high hopes.

'I've been promised a job on the check-out counter in a supermarket in Nice.'

'And is that what you'd really like, to be a check-out assistant?'

'I'd get social security and a pension,' said the young woman.

'You don't say!' said Hannah.

'And I'd work regular hours.'

'There's nothing like regular hours!'

'Plus paid holidays.'

'What more could anyone ask?' said Hannah.

Then she asked the young woman how the idea of going into business had occurred to her.

'Because I couldn't type and you have to be able to in order to be a secretary. What I would really like to have been is a secretary in local government . . . a public service employee. With the bonuses they get, you often earn more than in the private sector and you only do a third of the work, not to mention the fact that you can't be sacked, even if you don't do a thing. I have a friend who's a public service employee who bought herself a knitting machine. Just using it during office hours she makes pullovers that she sells to her colleagues: she doubles her monthly salary.'

For the whole of the following hour, Hannah and her young friend chatted, about everything and nothing – they certainly weren't interrupted by clients.

There came a point when Hannah said: 'As it happens, I used to run a little shop myself, once upon a time . . .'

And that's how it all began.

CHAPTER 41

Oh, My Love, My Love . . .

Hannah signed a peace treaty with the diabolical Piani – who was not in fact really all that diabolical. She was beside herself with worry, the poor thing, convinced that her mistress had been kidnapped – that's all it took to reduce her to tears and genuinely upset her. 'Madame Hannah, don't ever frighten me like that again, I beg you!'

Under the treaty, Hannah promised not to run away again, but in exchange she would be left alone every Wednesday morning when she went to Cannes. All right, all right, she agreed to be driven there by the chauffeur in the Rolls, but he was to drop her off outside the Carlton or the Majestic, or anywhere else in the centre of town, and no one was to follow her, or keep an eye on her for four whole hours.

This started in March 1970, and from that time she would go and spend four hours a week in Rue d'Antibes.

The first thing she did was to throw out the cash register, which she hated. 'Why not a guillotine while you're at it?' Then she closed the shop, concealing the interior from view with an enormous notice: *Closed for refurbishment.*

'Isn't your husband a bit of a handyman? Get him to do the notice. A surveyor should be able to draw a few straight lines, shouldn't he?'

The shop was closed for ten days: the time it took to strip the yellow wallpaper – a yellow that set your teeth on edge – and all the frippery that dated from at least the Second Empire, and which was already hideous even then.

'Just because it's old doesn't make it beautiful, child, you only have to look at me to realize that. What are we going to replace it with? White paint, nothing else. You think that looks rather bare? So what? What are you trying to sell? The walls or what will be on the shelves? When you don't have any money, you have to keep things as simple as possible. Do you have any money? No. Well, neither do I: I've only got my pension. Cheer up, there's only one more bit of wallpaper to strip, you're nearly there.'

Hannah directed operations from her chair, but she did absolutely nothing else.

'Good. Now the shop front. I see it in black. Yes, black. With just a little touch of another colour, otherwise it would look like a funeral parlour. No, not red, if you please, that's already spoken for. Not blue either, it's too cold. Yellow's all right, but it depends on the shade of yellow . . . Ah yes, orange would be even better. Very good, Marie-Pierre, you're beginning to understand.'

'And for the love of God, take off those damned awful . . . I mean, awful jeans. Wear a dress and let the men guess at what's underneath, let the fellows use their imagination. And a good shampoo twice a week. What do you mean, shampoo is expensive? Use some household soap, it works just as well, as long as you add a drop of vinegar to give your hair a shine, and an infusion of burdock to make it soft. Try it and see . . .'

'Ah, that's better! And your nails? Nail polish? Why? Your nails are very pretty, why hide them?'

'If you clean your teeth at least three times a day, brushing them the right way, that would be perfect . . . For your skin? Mix some watercress, carrots, parsley and cucumber, and drink the juice every morning – you'll find all those things in the market, and it will do you less harm than coffee, which is more expensive . . . And a burdock poultice, just one! Your skin is a little dry? Slap some cow's milk and cream on it. No, I'm not joking, I'm a respectable old lady, it's just that one of my aunts was a herbalist – if she hadn't been knocked down by a tram in Saint-Etienne at the age of 104, she would have been able to confirm all this . . . Your father's from Saint-Etienne? That's just a coincidence. And besides, my aunt was from Goondiwindi in Australia, and don't tell me that you have relatives there . . .

'Yes, of course I'm joking: do I look as if I've been to Australia?'

'You know, Marie, you're not at all bad-looking. If I'd been as pretty as you . . . If you walked more and ate less, maybe you'd get rid of some of the fat on your bottom . . . I'm not suggesting that you should have a tiny bottom, but even so . . .'

'Now, you have to decide what to sell.'

'Those things, in the corner there. They're crazy but fun . . . You remember, they were mentioned in that *Paris-Match* you were reading the first day I came into the shop. What are they called? Ah yes, gadgets . . . In London? What are you talking about? Why buy them in London when they're made in Hong Kong and Taiwan? You'll end up paying two or three times the price. No, order them directly from the Chinese. I don't speak Chinese either! But get the porter at the Palm Beach to write your letter, or someone in the Chamber of Commerce, or the British or American Consulate . . . Who should you write to? And what do you think chambers of commerce are for, you nitwit? All you have to do is address your letter to the Chamber of Commerce in Hong Kong: they'll understand, the Chinese are very intelligent. No, I haven't been to Hong Kong, any more than I've been to Australia for that matter . . . And let me give you a piece of advice: put a photocopy of your lease on the shop in the envelope, together with a postcard of the

Croisette, a photo of your shop, and one of yourself . . . No, not in the nude, not even in a bikini; in that pretty white dress that sets off your suntan with the décolleté down to your knees. By the way, does your surveyor make love to you well? Come now, we're both women . . . It's just that it's important in a marriage. Yes? No kidding? *In a hammock?* Oh, the devil! He's a smart one! But you can tell me the details another time, that's enough for now. You'll have to pay for the first consignment of goods the Chinese are going to send you. It's up to you: you can either borrow the money from a bank – personally, I'm not in favour of that – or else you can sell something, your car or your husband, whichever is less useful. What do you think? That you can make money and create something with just your imagination without taking any risks? Because that's the important thing, my child, a thousand times more important than money: to create something, to have an idea and to fight tooth and nail until it works. It's damned important. The money comes by itself, the way a medal comes to a brave soldier; and you don't make love with a medal, you put it away in a cupboard.'

She also said, later: 'I happen to have had a little experience with figures during my life. I can keep your books for you to start with, until you get yourself an accountant. You think I'm too old? Give me a four-figure number, any number, and then a five-figure number . . . 4,687 and 58,999? Why not? Do you know what you get if you multiply them? Don't bother trying to work it out, it comes to 276,528,313. You can check it if you like . . . No, I knew someone who could count four times faster than me.'

The first consignment from Hong Kong, sent by air, was paid on delivery with the money raised by selling the car and by mortgaging the business and the couple's little flat. That was on 24 May. Twenty-seven days later, Marie-Pierre Gonzalo had to cable the factory in Kowloon: she was almost out of stock.

'You've made a profit of 47,853 francs 85 centimes,' announced Hannah. 'That's after all your expenses have been deducted, including the taxes you'll have to pay next year. The tax money doesn't belong to you, pretend it doesn't exist. Except that there's nothing to stop you investing it, until you're asked to pay it; it'll earn enough interest to buy you a dress or two, at least. Advise you on how to invest it? Me? My dear child, I don't have any idea when it comes to finance . . . Ask a bank? Why not?'

At the beginning of August: 'A holiday in Saint-Tropez or the Seychelles? Both? Now listen, Marie, you have to choose: either to be successful or lie in the sun and get a tan, which in any case doesn't do your skin any good . . . And while we're on the subject of Saint-Tropez, you wouldn't by any chance have noticed, between Pampelonne and the Bailli statue, a little place where you could open another branch? Yes? Hurry over there, I'll look after the shop for you. With what money? But with the money you've just earned, my dear! If you wait, someone else will get it before you.'

And had she thought of Monte Carlo? Near the Hermitage Hotel, for instance . . .

'You don't need to buy a business, child! Not this year, anyway. Next year, perhaps, you'll see. For the moment, all you want is to come to some arrangement with a shopkeeper in a good location who's not too stupid: you do a fifty-fifty deal *à la chinoise* (that's to say, you get ninety per cent, he gets the rest) and he sells your gadgets for you . . .'

And what about Italy: What was she waiting for? If she wanted to take on a partner, go ahead, but someone from

Milan, not Naples. Unless she wanted to set up a pizzeria, and even then . . .

And after all it was time to think of branching out into other things. Gadgets were trendy, and what was once trendy soon became untrendy, as someone called Cocteau used to say . . .

In September: 'Tired, Marie? A little tiredness doesn't matter; it's like getting sweaty when you make love, it's all part of the pleasure. Your husband run a sports shop? I suggested that? I don't remember that, it must have been your idea. But it's certainly a good one, my child. Look at them all running along the Croisette in the morning, it's another craze that's here to stay, and there's a gap in the market. Another shop in Nice and one in Saint-Raphaël? Anyone would think you'd grown ambitious . . . Be careful, though, you want to keep control of your success and not be controlled by it.'

In November: 'I understand, Marie, don't apologize . . . No, no, of course, it's true I'm a little old and that these young girls you've hired are very sweet and hard-working. If they had clean hands, it would be perfect. Helped you? Me? I didn't help you, child, we just chatted together a bit, that's all. No, you simply had some wonderful ideas, and courage, and tenacity, and patience, and imagination, and enough personality not to settle for the same fate as everyone else, and yet without taking everyone else for a fool. That's all. You don't need more than that to succeed in life, it's all very simple. Goodbye, my child. No, I shan't be coming back. This is my last visit, so I won't be getting in the way any more in your shop – which has expanded quite a bit since I first came in. The last few weeks? I was visiting the grave of someone. At my age, most of one's friends are in the cemetery.'

And Hannah tottered out into Rue d'Antibes, feeling sad and at the same time rather pleased with herself.

She spent that winter in California – she was there in September and the beginning of October for her pilgrimage to Santa Barbara, and she returned again in mid-November.

Everyone had been incredibly nice to her on the plane – anyone would think they had never seen a slightly aged lady before. The crew were even kind enough to pretend to believe her when she said that she had known Wilbur and Orville Wright, and Santos-Dumont and Louis Blériot when she was young. It was true that as she told these lies she had opened her grey eyes wide with a very amused expression . . .

She spent two months in New York in the spring of 1971, and made sure she was alone on 18 April for her ninety-sixth birthday. In fact, she booked into a suite at the Hotel Pierre under a false name, and instructed Marie-Claire Piani to tell anyone who asked that she had gone to Alaska. She locked herself in, with all the curtains closed, and lay on the bed for hours and hours, unable to close her eyes for a moment.

In June she returned to France, where she spent a few days in Paris. Xan Zaval, the daughter of the former director of her salon in Chile, took her to shop at Franck Namani. Then, having tried in vain to convince the diabolical Piani that she could have taken the wheel, she was driven down to the Côte d'Azur. She was at Saint-Jean-Cap-Ferrat by the 16th. And the day after she arrived she held one of her regular conferences with her European directors from her giant bed. Furet brought something that had happened in Venice to her attention, someone else reported a relaxation of standards in Lisbon . . .

'And I happened to hear of the marriage of the daughter of Xesca Vidal, our former director in Spain, to an architect. I was not officially informed of this marriage, so I was unable to send the usual present. Why? Have you any explanation, Tomas Oliver?'

As for Margret Overtah, director for Germany, Hannah wanted to know the reason for a drop of 3.4 per cent in the sales of HH331 . . .

'And that figure is based on the past five days' sales. I'm waiting, Margret. And stop mopping your brow, it's annoying me! *It isn't hot!*'

But she was known to have been an even harder taskmaster in the past. She realized it herself. She really had to force herself to concentrate on what she was saying and on these faces from another age sitting around her. *You're like a tiny little dinosaur that has survived every glaciation* . . .

That same afternoon, the first detachments of her descendants arrived. During the days that followed, the house filled with people, from Abigail and Paul Travers, who were fifty-eight and sixty-three years old respectively, to the youngest of her great-great-grandchildren, who was just three months old. Although elsewhere in the huge house a constant hum prevailed, there was a miraculous zone of silence surrounding her private rooms. Every morning she continued to rise at about four thirty. She would go out and walk in the wonderful dawn light. She would walk down to the lighthouse and then turn right along the coast road, followed at a distance of ten yards by Marie-Claire, who had begged to be allowed to accompany her. She would walk as far as the road to Roy, turn down the Boulevard Edouard-VII, until she came to the little port and the beginning of the Saint-Hospice headland.

Then, in the full light of summer, at that point in her walk, the memories came flooding back, and she no longer did anything to stem the tide; on the contrary, she let them come, with a serene certainty that they would soon tarnish and fade along with her:

Summer came to the vast plain that stretches from the Vistula to the Ural Mountains . . . the summer was exceptionally hot and dry. Hannah's world was a tiny one: she had not so much as taken ten steps along the road to Lublin . . . nor had she dared to venture into the pine forest . . . Yasha had told her it was haunted by dybbuks and by Shibta, the she-devil who lured little children with her cakes kneaded with a magic lard and the fat of a black dog.

From the Saint-Hospice headland she came home. One day in July, she was told that Pablo Picasso had telephoned and asked if he could come to visit her. They had known each other for sixty-seven years, but he was younger than her, he was only ninety. He came, and the two of them were left alone to talk together.

At one point he said: 'Hannah, we have both had a marvellous life, I wonder if I shan't insist on an encore when the curtain comes down . . .'

'Not me. As far as I'm concerned, I think I shall just say, "Phew!"'

She continued to take her walks, more and more slowly.

Hannah went as far as the silver birches, where the path became a leafy bower. Soon she ventured beyond the trees, until the day when all the sounds of the shtetl *died away behind her and she was immersed in absolute silence, in solitude, but also in fragrance and a golden light . . .*

. . . This took place at the beginning of that scorching and bloody summer of 1882. And so it was that she met Taddeuz.

On 11 July, at the turning for the road to Roy, her legs suddenly became very heavy.

She stood absolutely still . . . And just as he had been

the last time, Taddeuz stood fifteen yards away from her . . .

Marie-Claire caught up with her, and Hannah had to hold on to her.

'I'm having a bit of trouble, Piani.'

The Rolls suddenly appeared at a mere wave from the Corsican woman.

'I hate you, Piani,' said Hannah.

'I know. Can you get in by yourself?'

'No,' said Hannah. 'No, I can't.'

And she was overcome with amazement to find herself so dependent.

'We'll finish the excursion,' she said. 'Just because my wretched legs are playing me up I'm not going to go without it.'

'It would be better . . .'

'We'll finish the excursion. I like to finish what I've begun.'

Numerous doctors came and talked their usual twaddle. She didn't listen to them, they were of no interest to her.

She was asked if she wanted to see the children.

'Why not?' she said. 'Send them in, in teams of twelve.'

They came in successive waves.

'My notebook, Piani.'

She flicked through the pages and, with the aid of a great many sheep, managed to sort out who was who.

'Piani, I want someone to buy them all a drum and trumpets for those that know how to play them. The day I decide to die, I want them to make as much of a din as possible. It will prevent me from hearing any snivelling going on. See to it. Piani?'

'I'm here.'

'That's what I suspected. I would have been surprised if you'd been in Australia. Piani, I don't hate you as much as all that.'

'I know.'

'I value you almost as much as Yvonne. Did you get your money?'

'Yes.'

'If you thank me, I shall throw you out.'

'I didn't say anything.'

'Now leave me alone.'

The next day she managed to walk as far as the lighthouse.

The day after that she reached the front gate.

And the day after that she couldn't even walk across the garden.

She was carried back to bed.

That's enough, she thought.

She was lying on her eight-foot bed with black and turkey-red silk sheets. Her eyes were open.

They walked in the sunlight, she and Taddeuz. The sun had not yet cleared the horizon. Having scrambled over the embankment, they crossed a cornfield that was on a gentle downhill slope, so that when they reached the path they were in a hardly discernible depression; ahead was an undulating landscape that shut out what lay to the east and closed in their horizons. Hand in hand, while Taddeuz talked on about Warsaw, they climbed the slight incline, now treading barley underfoot. The plaint on the ram's horn that sounded continuously grew more distant . . .

At the top of the slope they came upon the horsemen.

There were fifty of them, maybe more, and behind them marched an entire troop of men. But the troop didn't count; Hannah and Taddeuz saw only the horsemen; they were enraptured. The orangey-red sun exaggerated the already tall shadows of the mounted horsemen to unreal proportions; they rode at a gentle trot, their strength seemingly implacable, the silence punctuated at intervals by the brief snorting of a horse . . . They appeared out of nowhere, as if out of a legend. Taddeuz was transfixed, fascinated, and just from the tension with which he gripped her hand, Hannah in turn felt the same fascination . . .

She held the scarab in her free hand, the right hand.

'Oh, my love, my love, my love, my love . . .'

Abigail, her granddaughter Hannah II and Marie-Claire Piani were the first to enter the big room where the curtains gently billowed, stirred by the sea breeze in the midst of that summer.

They found her lying flat on her back, her eyes held wide open for the last time. They had to prise open the fingers of her right hand one by one to see what she was holding. It was a little piece of what appeared to be green stone, very inexpertly carved, looking not very much like a scarab, the horns of which were incredibly polished with age: the one 'he' had given to Hannah eighty-nine years earlier.